Triple Jeopardy

Triple Jeopardy

Mary Stewart

an omnibus comprising

My Brother Michael
The Moon-Spinners
This Rough Magic

BOOK CLUB ASSOCIATES
LONDON

British Library CIP Data

Stewart, Mary, date,
    Triple jeopardy.
    I. Title   II. Stewart, Mary, date,   My brother
    Michael   III. Stewart, Mary, date,   The moon-
    spinners   IV. Stewart, Mary, date,   This
    rough magic
    823'.9'1F   PR6069.T46T/

ISBN 0-340-22896-2

Triple Jeopardy Copyright © 1978 by Mary Stewart.

Contents

My Brother Michael

7

The Moon-Spinners

241

This Rough Magic

471

My Brother Michael

For
KIM
In Loving Memory

Author's Note

The quotations from Professor Gilbert Murray's translation of *The Electra* of Euripides appear by kind permission of Messrs. Allen & Unwin. I am also indebted to the Editors of the Penguin Classics for permission to use extracts from Sophocles and Euripides in translations by E. F. Watling and Philip Vellacott; to Messrs. Faber & Faber for their leave to use the lines from Dudley Fitts' translation of *The Frogs* of Aristophanes; and to the Clarendon Press, Oxford, for the lines from Ingram Bywater's translation of Aristotle *On the Art of Poetry*.

If it were possible to do so adequately, I should like here to thank my friends in Greece — especially Electra and her family — for their very great kindness to me during my visits to their country; and I must add a particular note of thanks for those people in Delphi itself who helped me to gather information for this book: Mr. George Vouzas, of the Apollon Hotel; Marios, who showed me round; "Pete" Gerousis, who patiently answered all my questions; and the caretaker of the studio, who assured me that "things like that could never happen in Delphi". I believe him. At any rate, they never did.

M.S.

If you cannot love the Greeks, you cannot love anything.

REX WARNER.

Chapter 1

Why, woman,
What are you waiting for?
SOPHOCLES: *Electra.*
(tr. E. F. Watling.)

Nothing ever happens to me.

I wrote the words slowly, looked at them for a moment with a little sigh, then put my ballpoint pen down on the café table and rummaged in my handbag for a cigarette.

As I breathed the smoke in I looked about me. It occurred to me, thinking of that last depressed sentence in my letter to Elizabeth, that enough was happening at the moment to satisfy all but the most adventure-hungry. That is the impression that Athens gives you. Everyone is moving, talking, gesticulating–but particularly talking. The sound one remembers in Athens is not the clamour of the impatiently congested traffic, or the perpetual hammer of pneumatic drills, or even the age-old sound of chisels chipping away at the Pentelic marble which is still the cheapest stone for building . . . what one remembers about Athens is the roar of talking. Up to your high hotel window, above the smell of dust and the blare of traffic it comes, surging like the sea below the temple at Sunion–the sound of Athenian voices arguing, laughing, talk-talk-talking, as once they talked the world into shape in the busy colonnades of the Agora, not so very far from where I sat.

It was a popular and crowded café. I had found a table at the back of the room near the bar. All along the outer wall big glass doors gave on the pavement, standing open to the dust and din of Omonia Square, which is, in effect, the commercial centre of

Athens. It is certainly the centre of all the noise and bustle of the city. The traffic crawled or surged past in a ceaseless confusion. Crowds—as jammed as the traffic—eddied on the wide pavements. Knots of men, most of them impeccably dressed in dark city clothes, discussed whatever men do discuss at mid-morning in Athens; their faces were lively and intent, their hands fidgeting unceasingly with the little loops of amber 'nervous beads' that the men of the Eastern Mediterranean carry. Women, some fashionably dressed, others with the wide black skirt and black head-covering of the peasant, went about their shopping. A donkey, so laden with massed flowers that it looked like a moving garden, passed slowly by, its owner shouting his wares in vain against the hurly-burly of the hot morning streets.

I pushed my coffee-cup aside, drew again at my cigarette, and picked up my letter. I began to read over what I had written.

You'll have had my other letters by now, about Mykonos and Delos, and the one I wrote a couple of days ago from Crete. It's difficult to know just how to write—I want so much to tell you what a wonderful country this is, and yet I feel I mustn't pile it on too thick or you'll find that wretched broken leg that prevented your coming even more of a tragedy than before! Well, I won't go on about that, either . . . I'm sitting in a café on Omonia Square—it's about the busiest place in this eternally busy city—and calculating what to do next. I've just come off the boat from Crete. I can't believe that there's any place on earth more beautiful than the Greek islands, and Crete's in a class by itself, magnificent and exciting and a bit grim as well — but I told you about it in my last letter. Now there's Delphi still to·come, and everyone, solo and chorus, has assured me that it'll be the crown of the trip. I hope they're right; some of the places, like Eleusis and Argos and even Corinth, are a bit disappointing . . . one leaves oneself open to the ghosts, as it were, but the myths and magic are all gone. However, I'm told that Delphi really is something. So I've left it till last. The only trouble is, I'm getting a bit worried about the cash. I suppose I'm a bit of a fool where money is concerned. Philip ran all that, and how right he was . . .

Here a passing customer, pushing his way between the tables towards the bar-counter, jogged my chair, and I looked up, jerked momentarily out of my thoughts.

A crowd of customers—all male—seemed to be gathering at the bar for what looked like a very substantial mid-morning snack. It appeared that the Athenian business man had to bridge the gap between breakfast and luncheon with something rather more sustaining than coffee. I saw one plate piled high with Russian salad and thick dressing, another full of savoury meat-balls and green beans swimming in oil, and innumerable smaller dishes heaped with fried potatoes and small onions and fish and pimentoes, and half a dozen things I didn't recognise. Behind the counter was a row of earthenware jars, and in the shadow of their narrow necks I saw olives, fresh from the cool farm-sheds in Aegina and Salamis. The wine-bottles on the shelf above bore names like Samos and Nemea and Chios and Mavrodaphne.

I smiled, and looked down again at the page.

. . . but in a way I'm finding it wonderful to be here alone. Don't misunderstand me, I don't mean you! *I wish like anything you were here, for your own sake as well as mine. But you know what I do mean, don't you? This is the first time for years I've been away on my own – I was almost going to say 'off the lead' – and I'm really enjoying myself in a way I hadn't thought possible before. You know, I don't suppose he'd ever have come here at all; I just can't see Philip prowling round Mycenae or Cnossos or Delos, can you? Or letting me prowl either? He'd have been all set to dash off to Istanbul or Beirut or even Cyprus – anywhere, in short, where things are* happening, *not centuries ago in the past, but* now – and even if they weren't happening, he'd make them.*

Fun, yes, it was always fun, but – oh, I'm not going to write about that either, Elizabeth, but I was right, absolutely right. I'm sure of it now. It wouldn't have worked, not in a million years. This trip on my own has shown me that, more clearly than ever. There's no regret, only relief that perhaps, now, I'll have time to be myself. There, now I've admitted it, and we'll drop the subject. Even if I am quite shatteringly incompetent when I am being myself, it's fun, and I muddle along somehow. But I do admit . . .

I turned the page, reaching forward absently with my left hand to tap ash from my cigarette. There was a paler circle showing still against the tan at the base of the third finger, where Philip's ring had been. In ten days of Aegean sunshine it had begun to fade . . . six long years fading now without regret, leaving behind them a store of gay memories that would fade, too, and a sneaking curiosity to know if the beggar-maid had been really happy once she was married to King Cophetua . . .

But I do admit there's another side to this Great Emancipation. Things do seem a trifle dull occasionally, after so many years spent being swept along in Philip's – you must admit – magnificent wake! I feel just a little bit high and dry. You'd have thought that something – some sniff of an adventure – would have happened to a young woman (is one still young at twenty-five?) marooned on her own in the wilds of Hellas, but no: I go tamely from temple to temple, guide-book in hand, and spend the rather long evenings writing up notes for that wonderful book I was always going to write, and persuading myself I'm enjoying the peace and quiet . . . I suppose it's the other side of the picture, and I'll adjust myself in time. And if something exciting did happen, I wonder just what sort of a showing I'd make – surely I've got some talent for living, even if it looked feeble beside his overplus? But life never does seem to deliver itself into the hands of females, does it? I'll just finish up as usual in the hotel bedroom, making notes for that book that'll never get written. Nothing ever happens to me.

I put down the cigarette and picked up my pen again. I had better finish the letter, and on a slightly different note, or Elizabeth was going to wonder if I wasn't, after all, regretting the so-called emancipation of that broken engagement.

I wrote cheerfully: *On the whole, I'm doing fine. The language wasn't a difficulty after all. Most people seem to speak a bit of French or English, and I have managed to acquire about six words of Greek – though there have been sticky moments! I haven't managed the money quite so well. I won't pretend I'm exactly broke yet, but I rather let myself go in Crete – it was worth it, ye gods, but if it means passing up Delphi I shall regret it. Not that I can miss Delphi. That's unthinkable. I must get there somehow, but I'm afraid I may have to scamp it in a one-day tour, which is all I can afford. There's a tour bus on Thursday, and I think I'll have to be content with that. If only I could afford a car! Do you suppose that if I prayed to all the gods at once . . .?*

Someone cleared his throat just above me. A shadow crept half-apologetically across the page.

I looked up.

It wasn't the waiter, trying to winkle me out of my corner table. It was a little dark man with patched and shabby dungarees, a greasy blue shirt, and a hesitant smirk behind the inevitable moustache. His trousers were held up with string, which it appeared he didn't trust, because he held on to them firmly with one grimy hand.

I must have looked at him with a chilly surprise, because the apologetic look deepened, but instead of going away he spoke in very bad French.

He said: 'It is about the car for Delphi.'

I said stupidly, looking down at the letter under my hand: 'The car for Delphi?'

'You wanted a car for Delphi, *non?*'

The sun had probed even into this corner of the café. I peered at him against it. 'Why, yes, I did. But I really don't see how–'

'I bring it.' One grimy hand—the one that wasn't holding up his trousers—waved towards the blazing doorway.

My eyes followed the gesture, bemusedly. There was indeed a car, a large shabby-looking black affair, parked at the pavement's edge.

'Look here,' I said, 'I don't understand—'

'Voilà!' With a grin, he fished what was patently a car key from his pocket, and dangled it above the table. 'This is it. It is a matter of life and death, I understand that—oh, perfectly. So I come as quick as I can—'

I said with some exasperation: 'I haven't the remotest idea what you're talking about.'

The grin vanished, to be replaced by a look of vivid anxiety. 'I am late. This I know. I am sorry. Mademoiselle will forgive me? She will be in time. The car—she does not look much, but she is good, oh, a very good car. If mademoiselle—'

'Look,' I said patiently, 'I don't want a car. I'm sorry if I misled you, but I can't hire one. You see—'

'But mademoiselle said she desired a car.'

'I know I did. I'm sorry. But the fact is—'

'And mademoiselle said it was a matter of life and death.'

'Madem—I didn't. You said that. I'm afraid I don't want your car, monsieur. I regret. But I don't want it.'

'But mademoiselle—'

I said flatly: 'I can't afford it.'

His face lighted at once with a very white-toothed and singularly attractive grin. 'Money!' The word was contemptuous. 'We do not speak of money! Besides,' he added with great simplicity, 'the deposit is already paid.'

I said blankly: 'Deposit? Paid?'

'But yes. Mademoiselle paid it earlier.'

I drew a breath that was three parts relief. It wasn't witchcraft after all, nor was it an intervention of the ironic gods of Greece. It was a simple case of mistaken identity.

I said firmly: 'I'm sorry. There has been a mistake. That is not my car. I didn't hire it at all.'

The dangling key stilled for a moment, then swung in front of me with unimpaired vigour. 'It is not the car mademoiselle saw, no, but that one was bad, bad. It had a—how do you say?—a crack in it that the water came out.'

'A leak. But—'

'A leak. That is why I am late, you see, but we get this car, oh so good, since mademoiselle say it is so urgent a matter that Monsieur Simon have the car at Delphi straight away. You leave straight away you are in Delphi in three hours–four hours . . .' his look lingered on me momentarily, summing me up . . . 'five hours maybe? And then perhaps all is well with Monsieur Simon, and the matter of–'

'Life and death,' I said. 'Yes, I know. But the fact remains, monsieur, that I don't know what you're talking about! There is some mistake, and I'm sorry. It was not I who asked for the car. I gather that this, er, Monsieur Simon's girl was to have been in this café waiting for the car . . .? Well, I can't see anybody here at present who might fill the bill . . .'

He spoke quickly, so quickly that I realised afterwards he must have followed my rapid French only sketchily, and was pouncing on a phrase that made sense–the sense he wanted to hear. The key still swung on his finger-tip as if it was hot and he wanted to drop it. He said: 'That is it. This café. A young lady sitting alone. Half past ten. But I am late. You are Simon's girl, yes?'

He looked, with that bright brown uncomprehending gaze, so like an anxious monkey that my near-exasperation vanished, and I smiled at him, shaking my head, and summoned up one of my six hard-learned words of Greek. 'Ne,' I said, as forcefully as I could. 'Ne, ne, ne.' I laughed and held out my cigarette-case. 'I'm sorry there's been a muddle. Have a cigarette.'

The cigarette seemed to be an amazing cure-all for worry. The lines vanished magically from his face. The vivid smile flashed. The key dropped with a jingle in front of me while the hand that wasn't holding up his pants reached for my cigarette-case. 'Thank you, mademoiselle. It is a good car, mademoiselle. Have a good journey.'

I was feeling in my bag for matches, and not until I raised my head did I really take in what he'd said. And by then it was too late. He had gone. I caught a glimpse of him sliding through the crowd at the café door like a whippet let off a string, then he vanished. Three of my cigarettes had gone too. But the car key lay on the table in front of me, and the black car still stood outside in the violent sunlight.

It was only then, as I sat gaping like an idiot at the key, the car, and the sunlight on the cloth where a moment ago the little man had cast a shadow, that I realised that my momentary piece of showing-off was likely to cost me pretty dear. I remembered a little sickly that, in Greek, ne means yes.

* * *

Of course I ran after him. But the crowd surged and swayed on the pavement, regardless, and there was no sign in any direction of the shabby messenger of the gods. My waiter followed me anxiously on to the pavement, ready to grab, I suppose, if I showed signs of taking off without paying him for my coffee. I ignored him and peered earnestly in all directions. But when he showed signs of retreating to bring up reinforcements to escort me personally back to my table and the bill, I judged it time to give up the search. I went back to my corner, picked up the key, threw a quick worried smile at the still-pursuing waiter, who didn't speak English, and pushed my way towards the bar-counter to seek out the proprietor, who did.

I elbowed my way through the crowd of men, with a nervously reiterated *'Parakalo'*, which, apparently, was the right word for 'Please'. At any rate the men gave way, and I leaned anxiously over the counter.

'Parakalo, kyrie –'

The proprietor threw me a harassed sweating glance over a pile of fried potatoes, and placed me unerringly. 'Miss?'

'Kyrie, I am in a difficulty. A queer thing has just happened. A man has brought that car over there – you see it, beyond the blue tables – to deliver it to someone in the café. By a mistake he appears to think I'm the person who hired it. He thinks I'm driving it up to Delphi for someone. But I know nothing about it, *kyrie;* it's all a mistake, and I don't know what to do!'

He threw a dollop of dressing over some tomatoes, pushed them towards a large man perched on a small stool at the counter, and wiped a hand over his brow. 'Do you wish me to explain to him? Where is he?'

'That's the trouble, *kyrie*. He's gone. He just left me the key – here it is – and then went. I tried to catch him, but he's vanished. I wondered if you knew who was supposed to be here to collect the car?'

'No. I know nothing.' He picked up a large ladle, stirred something under the counter, and threw another look at the car outside. 'Nothing. Who was the car for?'

'Monsieur, I told you, I don't know who –'

'You said it was to be driven somewhere – to Delphi, was it? Did this man not say who it was for?'

'Oh. Yes. A – a Mr. Simon.'

He spooned some of the mixture – it seemed to be a sort of
bouillabaisse – into a plate, handed it to a hovering waiter, and then
said, with a shrug: 'At Delphi? I have not heard of such a one. It is
possible somebody here saw the man, or knows the car. If you wait a
moment I will ask.'

He said something then in Greek to the men at the counter, and
became on the instant the centre of an animated, even passionate
discussion which lasted some four or five minutes and involved in
the end every male customer in the café, and which eventually
produced, with all the goodwill in the world, the information that
nobody had noticed the little man with the key, nobody knew the
car, nobody had ever heard of a Monsieur Simon at Delphi (this
though one of the men was a native of Chrissa, only a few kilometres
distant from Delphi), nobody thought it in the least likely that
anyone from Delphi would hire a car in Athens, and (finally)
nobody in their senses would drive it up there anyway.

'Though,' said the man from Chrissa, who was talking with his
mouth full, 'it is possible that this Simon is an English tourist
staying at Delphi. That would explain everything.' He didn't say
why, merely smiling with great kindness and charm through a
mouthful of prawns, but I got his meaning.

I said apologetically: 'I know it seems mad, *kyrie*, but I can't help
feeling one ought to do something about it. The man who brought
the key said it was –' I hesitated – 'well, a matter of life and death.'

The Greek raised his eyebrows; then he shrugged. I got the
impression that matters of life and death were everyday affairs in
Athens. He said, with another charming smile: 'Quite an adventure,
mademoiselle,' and turned back to his plate.

I looked at him thoughtfully for a moment. 'Yes,' I said slowly,
'yes.' I turned back to the proprietor, who was struggling to scoop
olives out of one of the beautiful jars. It was apparent that the
rush-hour and the heat were beginning to overset even his Athenian
good-manners and patience, so I merely smiled at him and said:
'Thank you for your goodness, *kyrie*. I'm sorry to have troubled you.
It seems to me that if the matter really is urgent, then the person
who wants the car will certainly come and get it as arranged.'

'You wish to leave the key with me? I will take it, and then you
need have no more worry. No, it will be a pleasure, I assure you.'

'I won't trouble you yet, thanks. I must confess –' I laughed – 'to a
little curiosity. I'll wait here for a bit, and if this girl comes I'll give
her the key myself.'

And, to the poor man's relief, I wriggled back out of the press and returned to my table. I sat down and ordered another coffee, then lit another cigarette, and settled down to a pretence of finishing my letter, but in reality to keep one watchful eye on the door, and the other on the shabby black car that should—surely—by now have been hurtling along the Delphi road on that matter of life and death . . .

I waited an hour. The waiter had begun to look askance again, so I pushed aside my untouched letter and gave an order, then sat playing with a plateful of beans and some small pink fish while I watched, in an expectancy that gradually gave way to uneasiness, the constant coming-and-going at the café door.

My motive in waiting hadn't been quite as straightforward as I had suggested to the proprietor of the café. It had occurred to me that, since I had become involved in the affair through no fault of my own, I might be able to turn it to advantage. When 'Simon's girl' arrived to claim the car, it might surely be possible to suggest—or even to ask outright—that I might be her passenger as far as Delphi. And the possibility of getting a lift up to Delphi was not the only one which had occurred to me . . .

So the minutes dragged by, and still no one came, and somehow, the longer I waited, the less possible it seemed to walk out of the café and leave everything to settle itself without me, and the more insidiously did that other possibility begin to present itself. Dry-mouthed, I pushed it aside, but there it was, a challenge, a gift, a dare from the gods . . .

At twelve o'clock, when nobody had appeared to claim the car, I thrust my plate aside, and set myself to consider that other possibility as coolly as I could.

It was, simply, to drive the car up to Delphi myself.

It was apparent that, for whatever reason, the girl wasn't coming. Something must have prevented her, for otherwise she would simply have telephoned the garage to cancel the order. But the car—the urgently wanted car—was still there, already an hour and a half late in starting. I, on the other hand, wanted very badly to go to Delphi, and could start straight away. I had come straight up from Piraeus off the Crete steamer, and had everything with me that I needed for a short stay in Delphi. I could go up today, deliver the car, have two days there with the money saved on the bus-fare, and come back with the tourist bus on Thursday. The thing was simple, obvious, and a direct intervention of providence.

I picked up the key with fingers that felt as if they didn't belong to me, and reached slowly for my only luggage—the big brightly-coloured hold-all of Mykonos weaving—that hung on the back of a chair.

I hesitated with my hand touching it. Then I let the hand drop, and sat, twisting the key over and over, watching with unseeing eyes the way the sun glinted on it as it turned.

It couldn't be done. It was just one of those things that couldn't be done. I must have been mad even to consider doing it. All that had happened was that Simon's girl had forgotten to cancel the order for the car and claim the deposit. It was nothing to do with me. No one would thank me for intervening in an affair that, in spite of my silly mistake, had nothing whatever to do with me. That phrase *a matter of life and death*—so glib a chorus, so persuasive an excuse to interfere—was only a phrase, after all, a phrase from which I had built up this feeling of urgency which gave me (I pretended) the excuse to act. *In any case, it had nothing to do with me.* The obvious—the only—thing to do was to leave the car standing there, hand over the key, and go away.

The decision brought with it a sense of relief so vivid, so physical almost, that it startled me. On the wave of it I stood up, picked up the car key, and swung my hold-all up to my shoulder. The unfinished letter to Elizabeth lay on the table. I reached for it, and as I folded it over to thrust it into my bag, the sentence caught my eye again. *Nothing ever happens to me.*

The paper crackled suddenly as my fingers tightened. I suppose moments of self-knowledge come at all sorts of odd times. I have often wondered if they are ever pleasant. I had one such moment now.

It didn't last long. I didn't let it. It was with a sort of resigned surprise that I found myself once more at the counter, handing a slip of paper across it to the proprietor.

'My name and address,' I said rather breathlessly, 'just in case someone does come for the car later on. Miss Camilla Haven, the Olympias Hotel, Rue Marnis . . . Tell them I—I'll take care of the car. Tell them I did it for the best.'

I was out in the street and getting into the car before it occurred to me that my last words had sounded uncommonly like an epitaph.

Chapter 2

It's a long way to Delphi.
EURIPIDES: *Ion.*
(tr. Philip Vellacott.)

EVEN IF IT wasn't Hermes himself who had brought me the key, the hand of every god in Hellas must have been over me that day, because I got out of Athens alive. More, unscathed.

There were some sticky moments. There was the shoeblack who was so urgent to clean my shoes that he followed me to the car and clung to the side and would certainly have been hurt when I started off, if only I'd remembered to put the car into gear. There was the moment when I turned–at a cautious ten miles per hour and hugging the left-hand pavement–out of Omonia Square into St. Constantine Street, and met a taxi almost head-on on what I thought was his wrong side, till the volume and fervour of his abuse shocked me back on to my own right. Then there was the encounter in the narrow alley with two furious pedestrians who stepped off the pavement without a single glance in my direction. How was I to know it was a one-way street? I was lucky with my brakes that time. I wasn't so lucky with the flower-donkey, but it was only the flowers I touched, and the driver was charming about it. He refused the note I hastily held out to him and he actually gave me the flowers I'd knocked out of the donkey's pannier.

All things considered, people were very forgiving. The only really unpleasant person was the man who spat on the bonnet as I came hesitatingly out from behind a stationary bus. There was no need for such a display of temper. I'd hardly touched him.

By the time I got to the main road that leads out of Athens along the Sacred Way I'd found out two things. One was that a few weeks spent in punting around the English country roads in Elizabeth's old Hillman (Philip, understandably, had never let me touch his car) was not really an adequate preparation for driving through Athens in a strange car with a left-hand drive. The other was that the shabby black car had an unexpectedly powerful engine. If it had been less shabby and ancient-looking–if it had been one of the sleek-winged transatlantic monsters commonly used as taxis in Athens–I should never have dared myself to drive it, but its shabby façade had reassured me. Almost it could have been the old Hillman I'd learned on. Almost. I hadn't been in it three minutes before I discovered that it had an acceleration like the kick of a jet, and by the time I'd assessed its possibilities as a lethal weapon–which were limitless–it was too late. I was out in the traffic, and it seemed safer to stay there. So I hung on grimly to the wheel, changing hands now and again as I remembered that the gear lever was on the right, and prayed to the whole Olympian hierarchy as we jerked and nudged our terrified and apologetic way out through the city suburbs, turning at length into the great double road that runs along the coast towards Eleusis and Corinth.

After the packed and flashing streets, the road seemed open and comparatively empty. This was the Sacred Way: down this wide sea-bordered road the ancient pilgrims had gone with songs and torches to celebrate the Mysteries at Eleusis. This lake now lying to the right was the holy lake of Demeter. Across that bay on the left the island of Salamis lay like a drowned dragon, and there–*there*–Themistocles had smashed the Persian fleet . . .

But I looked neither to right nor left as I drove. I had been this way before, and had got the first sharp disillusion over. There was no need, here, to leave oneself open to the ghosts; they had long since gone. Now, the Sacred Way ran straight and wide (the tar sweating a little in the sun) between the cement factories and the ironworks; the holy lake was silted up with weeds and slag; in the bay of Salamis lay the rusty hulks of tankers, and the wine-dark water reflected the aluminium towers of the refinery. At the other side of the bay belched the chimneys of Megara, and above them a trio of Vampire jets wheeled, screaming, against the ineffable Greek sky. And this was Eleusis itself, this dirty village almost hidden in the choking clouds of ochreous smoke from the cement works.

I kept my eyes on the road, my attention on the car, and drove as

fast as I dared. Soon the industrial country was behind us, and the
road, narrower now and whitening with dust under the pitiless
September sun, lifted itself away from the shore and wound up
between fields of red earth set with olives, where small box-like
houses squatted, haphazardly it seemed, among the trees. Children,
ragged and brown and thin, stood in the dust to stare as I went by. A
woman, black-clad, and veiled like a Moslem, bent to lift bread from
the white beehive oven that stood under an olive tree. Scrawny hens
scratched about, and a dog hurled itself yelling after the car.
Donkeys plodded along in the deep dust at the road's edge, half
hidden under their top-heavy loads of brushwood. A high cart
swayed along a track towards the road; it was piled with grapes,
gleaming waxily, cloudy-green. The flanks of the mule were glossy,
and bloomy as dark grapes. The air smelt of heat and dung and dust
and the lees of the grape harvest.

The sun beat down. Wherever the trees stood near the road the
shade fell like a blessing. It was not long past noon, and the heat was
terrific. The only relief was the breeze of the car's movement, and
the cloudy heads of the great olives sailing between the road and the
great brazen bowl of the sky.

There was very little traffic out in the heat of the day, and I was
determined to take full advantage of the afternoon lull, so I drove on
through the hot bright minutes, feeling confident now, and even
secure. I had got the feel of the car, and I was still steadfastly
refusing to think about what I had done. I had taken a 'dare' from the
gods, and the results would wait till I got—if I got—to Delphi.

If I got to Delphi.

My confidence in myself had been steadily growing as I drove on
through an empty landscape, through country that grew wilder and
more beautiful as the road shook itself clear of the olive groves and
climbed the hills that lie to the north of Attica. It even survived the
series of frightening hairpin bends that sink from the summit of
these hills towards the flat fields of the Boeotian plain. But it didn't
survive the bus.

This was the service bus from Athens, and I caught up with it
halfway along the dead-straight road that bisects the plain. It was
small, evil-looking, and smelly. It also seemed to be packed to the
doors with people, boxes, and various livestock, including hens and
at least one small goat. It was roaring along in a fifty-yard trail of
dust. I drew carefully out to the left, and pressed forward to pass.

The bus, which was already in the middle of the road, swung over promptly to the left and accelerated slightly. I moved back, swallowing dust. The bus went back to the crown of the road and settled back to its rackety thirty miles an hour.

I waited half a minute, and tried again. I crept cautiously up to its rear wheel and hoped the driver would see me.

He did. Accelerating madly, he surged once again into my path, got me well and truly behind him, then settled back complacently into the centre of the road. I went back once more into the choking dust-train. I was trying not to mind, to tell myself that when he had had his joke he would let me safely by, but I could feel my hands beginning to tighten on the wheel, and a nerve was jumping somewhere in my throat. If Philip had been driving . . . but then, I told myself, if Philip had been driving, it wouldn't have happened. Women drivers are fair game on the roads of Greece.

Here we passed a board which said, in Greek and English letters: THEBES 4 km., DELPHI 77 km. If I had to stay behind the bus all the way to Delphi . . .

I tried again. This time as I pulled out to approach him I sounded the horn decisively. To my surprise and gratitude he drew over promptly to the right, and slowed down. I made for the gap. There was just room, no more, between the bus and the verge, which was of deep, crumbling dry soil. Taut with nervous concentration, I pressed forward and accelerated. The bus rocked and roared alongside.

I wasn't getting past. He was travelling faster, keeping pace with me. My car had the speed of him, but the gap was narrowing and I wasn't sure enough of my judgement to force the big car past. He closed in more sharply. I don't know if he would actually have forced me off the road, but as the swaying dirty-green enamel rocked nearer, I lost my nerve, as he had known I would. I stood on the brakes. The bus roared on. I was left once more in the dust.

We were getting near the outskirts of Thebes when I realised that of course a service bus would have to stop for passengers. The thought steadied me. I dropped back out of the dust-cloud, and drove slowly in his wake, waiting.

Ahead of us I could see the first scattered houses of Thebes, the legendary city that, I knew, was gone even more irrecoverably than Eleusis. Where Antigone led the blind Oedipus out into exile, the old men of Thebes sit on the concrete pavements in the sun, beside the petrol-pumps. The game of *tric-trac* that they sit over, hour after hour, is probably the oldest thing in Thebes. There is a fountain somewhere, beloved of the nymphs. That's all. But I had no time then to mourn the passing of the legends. I wasn't thinking about Oedipus or Antigone, or even about Philip or Simon or my own miserable prelude to adventure. I just drove on towards Thebes with my eyes fixed in hatred ahead of me. There was nothing left in life at that moment but the desire to pass that filthy bus.

Presently it happened. A knot of women, waiting by the roadside, signalled him to stop, and he slowed down. I closed up behind, my eyes on the strip to the left of him, my hands slippery on the wheel, and that nerve beginning to jump again.

He stopped, right in the centre of the road. There was no possible space to pass. I stopped behind him and waited, then, as he drew away from me again, and I let in the clutch, I stalled the engine. My hand shook on the ignition. The engine wouldn't start. At the edge of my vision I caught sight of a face at the rear window of the withdrawing bus, a dark young face, split in a wide grin. As I started the car and followed I saw the youth turn as if to nudge someone on the back seat beside him. Another face turned to stare and grin. And another.

Then, close behind me – so close that it nearly sent me into the ditch with fright – I heard a horn. As I swerved automatically to the right a jeep, driven fast on its wrong side, roared up from behind, overtook me rather too wide, with the nearside wheels churning dust, and charged straight, at the same headlong pace, for the rear of the bus, with its horn still blasting like a siren. I caught a glimpse of a girl driving, a young, dark face, with lashes drooping over her eyes and a bored, sulky mouth. She was lounging back in her seat, handling the jeep with casual, almost insolent, expertise. And, woman driver or no, the bus made way for her, whipping smartly over to the right and staying there respectfully while she tore by. I didn't consciously decide to follow her; in fact I'm not sure yet whether I trod on the accelerator deliberately, or whether I was feeling for the brake, but something hit me in the small of the back, and the big black car shot forward, missed the bus by inches, and stormed past in the wake of the jeep, with two wheels on the crown of the road and the other two churning up enough dust to have guided the children of Israel straight into Thebes. Where the bus had its offside wheels I neither knew nor cared. I didn't even look in the mirror.

I swept into Thebes and dived smartly down the wrong side of the dual carriageway which is the road through to Levadia and Delphi.

*   *   *

The hand of Hermes, god of wayfarers, was over me still. There
was a horse-fair at Levadia, which, with its accompanying trappings
of *fiesta*, jammed the streets; but after that I met nothing, except
slow little caravans of country people on their way by mule
and donkey-back to the fair; and once a train of gypsies—real
Egyptians—on the move with mules and ponies covered in bright
blankets.

Soon after I had passed Levadia the country began to change. The
grim banalities of Attica, the heavy Technicolor prosperity of the
plains, sank back and were forgotten as the hills crowded in. The
road reared and twisted between great ribs of brown hill that thrust
the landscape up into folded ranges. At the foot of the steep
waterless valleys dead streams curled white along their shingle-beds,
like the sloughed skins of snakes. The sides of the valleys were dry
with the yellowish growth of burned grass, and drifts of stones and
crumbling soil.

Bigger and bigger grew the circling hills, barer the land, drawn in
with great sweeps of colour that ran from red to ochre, from ochre to
burnt umber to lion-tawny, with, above all, the burning, the
limitless, the lovely light. And beyond all, at length, a grey ghost of
a mountain-massif; not purple, not faintly blue with distance like the
mountains of a softer country, but spectre-white, magnificent, a lion
silvered. Parnassus, home of the ghosts of the old gods.

I stopped only once to rest, some way beyond Levadia. The road,
which wound high along the hillside, was in shadow, and the air, at
that height, was cool. I sat for about fifteen minutes on the parapet
that edged the road. Below me, deep in a forked valley, was a place
where three tracks met; the ghost of an ancient crossroads where
once a young man, coming from Delphi to Thebes, struck an old
man down out of his chariot, and killed him . . .

But no ghosts moved today. No sound, no breath, not even the
shadow of a hanging hawk. Only the bare lion-coloured hills, and
the illimitable, merciless light.

I got back into the car. As I started the engine I reflected that the
god of wayfarers, who had done very well by me so far, had only
some twenty miles' more duty to do, and then he could abandon me
to my fate.

In fact, he abandoned me just ten kilometres short of Delphi, in
the middle of the village of Arachova.

Chapter 3

But if I don't get out from under
pretty damned soon, there'll be a disaster in the rear.
ARISTOPHANES: *The Frogs.*
(tr. Dudley Fitts.)

ARACHOVA IS A show-place. It is not self-consciously so, but its setting is picturesque in the extreme, and the Greek style of building does the rest.

The village is perched on a precipitous hillside, and the houses are built in tiers, one up behind the other, the floor of one level with the roof of the next. The whole village looks as if it were just about to slide into the depths of the valley below. The walls are white and the roofs are rose-red, and over every wall hang flowering plants, and vines rich with grapes, and great dollops of wool dyed the colours of amber and hyacinth and blood. Along the short main street are places selling rugs which hang out in the sunlight, brilliant against the blinding white walls. The street itself has some corners, and is about eight feet wide. On one of these corners I ran into a lorry.

Not quite literally. I managed to stop with my bonnet about nine inches away from his, and there I stayed, paralysed, unable even to think. The two vehicles stood headlamp to headlamp, like a pair of cats staring one another out, one of them preserving a mysterious silence. I had, of course, stalled the engine . . .

It became apparent all too soon that it was I, and not the lorry-driver, who would have to back. The whole village—the male portion of it—turned out to tell me so, with gestures. They were charming and delightful and terribly helpful. They did everything except reverse the car for me. And they obviously couldn't understand why anyone who was in charge of such a car shouldn't be able to reverse it just like *that*.

Eventually I reversed it into somebody's shop doorway.

The whole village helped to pick up the trestle table, re-hang the rugs, and assure me that it didn't matter a scrap.

I straightened up the car and reversed again, into a donkey. The whole village assured me that the donkey wasn't hurt and that it would stop in a kilometre or so and come home.

I straightened up the car. This time I churned out a reasonably straight course for ten yards while the village held its breath. Then came a bend in the road. I stopped. I definitely was not prepared to chance reversing over the two-foot parapet into somebody's garden twenty feet down the hillside. I sat there breathing hard, smiling ferociously back at the villagers, and wishing I had never been born and that Simon hadn't either. My bolt was shot.

I had stopped in a patch of sunlight, and the glare from the white walls was blinding. The men crowded closer, grinning delightedly and making gallant and–no doubt fortunately–incomprehensible remarks. The lorry-driver, also grinning, hung out of his cab with the air of a man prepared to spend the whole afternoon enjoying the show.

In desperation, I leaned over the door of the car and addressed the most forward of my helpers, a stout, florid-looking man with small twinkling eyes, who was obviously vastly delighted with the whole business. He spoke a fluent if decidedly odd mixture of French and English.

'Monsieur,' I said, 'I do not think I can manage this. You see, it's not my car; it belongs to a Monsieur Simon, of Delphi, who requires it urgently, for business. I–I'm not very used to it yet, and since it's not mine I don't like to take risks . . . I wonder, could you or one of these gentlemen back it for me? Or perhaps the driver of the lorry would help, if you would ask him? You see, it's not my car . . .'

Some rag of pride led me to insist on this, until I saw he wasn't listening. The smile had gone from the cheerful sweating face. He said: 'Who did you say the car was for?'

'A Monsieur Simon, of Delphi. He has hired it from Athens, urgently.' I regarded him hopefully. 'Do you know him?'

'No,' he said, and shook his head. But he spoke a little too quickly, and as he spoke his eyes flickered away from mine. The man at his elbow looked at me sharply, and then asked a question in rapid Greek, where I thought I caught the word 'Simon'. My friend nodded once, with that swift flicker of a sidelong look back at me, and said something under his breath. The men near him stared, and muttered,. and I thought I saw a new kind of curiosity, furtive and perhaps even avid, replacing the naïve amusement of a moment ago.

But this was only the most fleeting of impressions. Before I could decide whether to pursue the inquiry or not, I realised that none of the men were looking at me any more. There was some more of that swift and semi-furtive muttering; the last of the cheery grins had disappeared, and the men who had been crowding most closely round the car were moving away, unobtrusively yet swiftly, bunching as sheep bunch at the approach of the dog. One and all, they were looking in the same direction.

At my elbow came the fluttering click of 'nervous beads', and the stout man's voice said softly: 'He will help you.'

I said 'Who?' before I realised he was no longer beside me.

I turned my head and looked where they all were looking.

A man was coming slowly down a steep stepped alley that led uphill between the houses on my right.

He was about thirty years old, dark-haired and tanned like all the others in the group near the car, but his clothes, no less than his air and bearing, made him look unmistakably English.

He was not tall, an inch or two under six feet, perhaps, but he was broad in the shoulder, and held himself well, with a sort of easy, well-knit movement that spoke of training and perfect physical fitness. I thought him good-looking; a thinnish sun-browned face, black brows, straight nose, and a hard mouth; but just at the moment his expression was what Jane Austen would have called repulsive—meaning that, whatever thoughts held him in that slightly frowning abstraction, it was obvious that he didn't intend them to be disturbed.

He seemed to be hardly aware of where he was, or what he was doing. A child scampered up the steps and pushed by him, apparently unnoticed. A couple of hens flapped across under his feet without making him pause. A hanging plant splashed petals in a scarlet shower over the white sleeve of his shirt, but he made no move to brush them away.

When he reached the foot of the alley-way he paused. He seemed to come abruptly out of his preoccupation, whatever it was, and stood there, hands thrust into the pockets of his flannels, surveying the scene in the street. His eyes went straight to the group of men. I saw the slight frown disappear, and the brown face became a mask, remote, cold, reflecting oddly the wariness that I had seen in the villagers. Then he looked straight at me, and it was with something of a shock that I met his eyes. They weren't dark, as I had expected. They were grey, very clear and light, and violently alive.

He came down the last step and crossed to the door of the car. The group melted away from us. He took no more notice of them than he had of the hens, or the falling geranium-petals.

He looked down at me. 'You seem to be in trouble. Is there anything I can do?'

'I'd be terribly grateful if you *could* help me,' I said. 'I–I've been trying to back the car.'

'I see.' I thought I heard amusement behind the pleasant voice, but his face still expressed nothing. I said bleakly: 'I was trying to get it to go *there*.' 'There' was a space beyond the curve of the road which, about fifty yards back, looked as remote as the moon.

'And she won't go?'

'No,' I said shortly.

'Is there something wrong with her?'

'Just,' I said bitterly, 'that I can't drive.'

'Oh.' It was amusement.

Here the lorry-driver leaned out of his cabin and shouted something in Greek, and the Englishman laughed. The laugh transformed his face. The mask of rather careful indifference broke up, and he looked all at once younger and quite approachable, even attractive. He shouted something back in what sounded to me like excellent Greek. At any rate the lorry-man understood, because he nodded and withdrew into his cab, and I heard the lorry's engine begin to roar.

The newcomer laid a hand on the door.

'If you'll allow me, perhaps I can persuade her to go.'

'I shouldn't be surprised,' I said bitterly, as I moved over. 'I was told this was a man's country. It's true. Go ahead.'

He got into the car. I found myself hoping that he would miss the gears, forget to start the engine, leave the handbrake on–do even a single one of the damned silly things I'd been doing all day, but he didn't. To my fury the car moved quietly backwards, slid into the cobbled space beyond the corner, paused about two inches away from a house wall, and waited there politely for the lorry to pass.

It approached with an appalling noise and a cloud of black smoke. As it drew level, its driver, leaning out of his cab, yelled something at my companion and sent a grinning black-eyed salutation to me

that somehow, without a word being intelligible, made me understand that, though incompetent, I was female and therefore delightful, and that was just how it should be.

The lorry roared on its way. I saw its driver glance back and lift a
hand to the men who still stood in a little group near the café door.
One or two of them responded, but most were still watching, not the
car, but my companion.

I glanced at him. I knew then that I was right. He was aware of it
too. His eyes, narrowed against the sun, showed none of that vivid
aliveness that I had suprised in them. He sent the group a look,
slow, appraising, utterly without expression. I thought he hesitated.
A hand went to the car door, as if he were going to get out, then it
dropped back on to the wheel, and he turned to me in inquiry.

I answered his look before he spoke. 'Don't give a thought to my
amour-propre, will you? Of course I should love you to drive the
beastly thing through the village for me. I haven't a rag of pride left,
and as long as I get this car to Delphi in one piece, my self-respect
can be salvaged later. Believe me, I'm terribly grateful.'

He smiled. 'You must be tired, and it's dreadfully hot. Have you
come far?'

'From Athens.'

His brows shot up, but he said nothing. The car was moving with
the minimum of noise and fuss through the narrow street. The little
group of men had disappeared, melting chin-on-shoulder into the
café as the car approached them. He didn't glance aside after them.

I said defiantly: 'Yes, all the way. And not a scratch.'

'Congratulations . . . And here we are. Clear of the houses and all
set for Delphi. You did say Delphi?'

'I did.' I regarded him thoughtfully. 'I suppose you wouldn't by
any chance be going that way yourself?'

'As it happens, yes.'

'Would you . . .?' I hesitated, then took the plunge. 'Would you
like a lift? In a manner of speaking, that is?'

'I should be delighted. And if the manner of speaking means will I
drive–with pleasure, ma'am.'

'That's wonderful.' I relaxed with a little sigh. The car purred
round the last corner and gathered speed up a long curling hill. 'I've
really quite enjoyed myself, but you know, I've missed half the
scenery.'

'Never mind. You brought some of it with you.'

'What d'you mean?'

He said coolly: 'The feathers on the bonnet. Very original they look, and quite striking.'

'The–oh!' My hand flew to my mouth. *'Feathers?* Honestly?'

'Indeed yes. Lots of them.'

I said guiltily: 'That must be the hen just outside Levadia. At least, it was a cockerel. White ones?'

'Yes.'

'Well, it was asking for it. I even hooted the horn, and if you'd heard this horn you'd know that cockerel was bent on death. I didn't kill him, though, really I didn't. I saw him come out the other side and dash away. It *is* only feathers, truly it is.'

He laughed. He, too, seemed in some indefinable way to have relaxed. It was as if he had left his preoccupations behind him in Arachova, and with them that impression he had given of a rather formidable reserve. He might have been any pleasant, casually-met stranger on holiday.

'No hen'll look at that chap till he's grown a new tail,' he said cheerfully. 'And you don't have to make excuses to me; it wasn't my cockerel.'

'No,' I said, 'but I've a feeling this is your–' I stopped.

'This is what?'

'Oh, nothing. Merciful heavens, what a view!'

We were running along a high white road that hugged the side of Parnassus. Below us to the left the steep hillside fell away to the valley of the Pleistus, the river that winds down between Parnassus' great flanks and the rounded ridges of Mount Cirphis, towards the plain of Chrissa and the sea. All along the Pleistus–at this season a dry white serpent of shingle-beds that glittered in the sun–all along its course, filling the valley-bottom with the tumbling, whispering green-silver of water, flowed the olive-woods; themselves a river, a green-and-silver flood of plumy branches as soft as sea-spray, over which the ever-present breezes slid, not as they do over corn, in flying shadows, but in whitening breaths, little gasps that lift and toss the olive-crests for all the world like breaking spray. Long pale ripples followed one another down the valley. Where, at the valley's end, Parnassus thrust a sudden buttress of gaunt rock into the flood, the sea of grey trees seemed to break round it, flowing on, flooding out to fill the flat plain beyond, still rippling, still moving with the ceaseless sheen-and-shadow of flowing water, till in the west the motion was stilled against the flanks of the distant hills, and to the south against the sudden sharp bright gleam of the sea.

I said, after a while: 'Are you staying in Delphi?'

'Yes. I've been there a few days. Have you come for long?'

I laughed. 'Till the money gives out, and I'm afraid that won't be long enough. I only hope there'll be a room for me somewhere. I came up unexpectedly and haven't booked. Someone told me the Apollon was good.'

'It's very nice. Delphi's fairly full just now, but you'll get a room somewhere, I'm sure. Perhaps we can persuade the Apollon to throw someone out for you.' A pause. 'Hadn't we better introduce ourselves? My name's Lester.'

'I'm Camilla Haven,' I said slowly, watching him, 'but I've got a sort of alias today. You might say I'm . . . "Simon's girl".'

The dark brows shot up. One of those quick, light, electrifying glances, then he was watching the road again. He said evenly: 'How very gratifying. But why? Because I rescued you in Arachova?'

I felt the blood coming into my cheeks. I hadn't thought of that one. I said quickly: 'No. I only meant I'd been deputising for her—the other girl—since Athens. With the car.'

'The car?' he said blankly.

'Yes.' I swallowed and shot a glance at him. This was going to sound even sillier than I had imagined. 'This is—oh, dear, I've begun at the wrong end but . . . well, this is your car. The one from Athens.'

I could see nothing in his glance this time except puzzlement, with possibly a dash of doubt about my sanity.

'I'm afraid I don't follow. My car? From Athens? And what "other girl"? Forgive me, but—just what are you talking about?'

'I'm sorry. I shouldn't have jumped it on you like that. I'd better begin at the beginning. I—I've done a rather silly thing, and I hope you're not going to be too angry with me, Mr. Lester. I'll explain exactly how it happened in a moment, if you'll let me, but the important thing is that this is the car you're expecting. The girl you sent to hire it didn't turn up to claim it, and I was handed the key by mistake, so—well, I brought it up here for you. I—I hope it's all right. It was the most marvellous luck to find you—'

'Just a moment. Forgive me for interrupting, but—well, I still haven't the remotest idea what you're talking about. You say someone hired this car in Athens and you were given the key, and drove it up here?'

'Yes.' This time it was my voice that sounded flat and blank. 'wasn't—it wasn't you?'

'Decidedly not. I know nothing about a car from Athens or anywhere else.'

'But back there in Arachova–' I hesitated, feeling more than ever confused and foolish.

'Yes?' The car slowed, dipped on to a little bridge set at an angle over a narrow gorge, then accelerated up the curling hill beyond. His tone was casual, but somehow I got the impression of sharp interest. 'Just what made you think I ought to know about it?'

I said quickly: 'Was I wrong? I thought . . . look, you *are* called Simon, aren't you?'

'That is my name. They told you in Arachova? Those men?'

'No. That is, yes, in a way. But . . . never mind that now. You did say you were staying in Delphi?'

'Yes.'

I said flatly, stupidly: 'Then it *must* be you! It must be!'

'I do assure you it isn't.' The quick appraising glance he gave me must have shown him the distress in my face, because he smiled then, and said gently: 'But I'm afraid I still don't quite see where the mystery comes in. Surely the garage also gave you the hirer's name and address? Have you lost it, or forgotten to write it down, or something?'

I said in a very small voice: 'That's just it. I never knew it.'

He look startled, and then, I thought, amused. 'I see. You never knew it. Except, I take it, that his name was Simon?'

'Yes. I told you I'd done something silly. It seemed all right at the time, and I thought in Arachova that it had turned out beautifully, like a story, but now . . .' My voice trailed away. I looked away from him across the blue depths of the valley, and spoke my thoughts with artless and quite unguarded emphasis: 'Oh dear, and it would have been so *wonderful* if it *had* been you!'

The words were hardly out before I realised what they sounded like. For the second time in a few minutes I felt the heat wash scarlet into my cheeks. I opened my lips to say something, anything, but before I could speak he said pleasantly: 'I wish it had. But look, don't worry so about it. It can't be as bad as you think, and perhaps, if you'll let me, I can help you. Would you care to tell me just what's happened?'

I told him. I kept to a bare recital of the facts, from the moment when the little man approached me with the key, to the fateful second of decision which had landed me–so neatly, as I had thought–at Simon Lester's feet in Arachova. Only the facts; nothing

of the miserable tangle of motive, the fear and self-questioning and uneasy bravado . . . but somehow, as I finished the story, I had a feeling that I had told him rather more than I intended. Oddly, I didn't mind. I had told him. He had said he would help. It was over to him. It was a familiar feeling, and yet not quite familiar . . .

I sat back, relaxed and at ease for the first time since eleven that morning, while below us the breeze ran with white feet over the billowing olives, and beside us, along the high hot road, the sun beat the smell of dust out of the red earth, and the rock glowed and sent the heat back like blast.

He had made no comment on the silly story as I told it. Now he merely said: 'I see. So it really only amounts to this; that you've brought up an unknown car for an unknown man who wants it for something unspecified, and you don't know where to find him.'

'That's not a very kind way of putting it, but—yes. I told you it was silly.'

'Maybe. But in your place I'd have done exactly the same.'

'*Would* you?'

He laughed. 'Of course. What right-minded person could resist a challenge like that?'

'Honestly?'

'Honestly.'

I let out a long breath. 'You've no idea how much better you've made me feel! But at least you'd have managed the adventure properly! It seems to me that it's not enough to be bold; one has to be competent as well. *You'd* never have got stuck in Arachova—and if you had, you'd have been able to back the car!'

'Ah, yes,' he said, 'Arachova.' The shutters were up once more. He added, half under his breath: 'Simon, of Delphi . . .'

I said quickly: 'It does seem odd, doesn't it? That there should be two? I told you that the man from Chrissa didn't know anyone of that name hereabouts. Delphi's small, isn't it?'

'Lord, yes.'

'Then he'd know, wouldn't he? That was why I was so sure it must be you.'

He didn't answer. There was that look again, smooth, blank; the unclimbable wall with spikes at the top. I gave him a doubtful glance he didn't see, and said, tentatively: 'Could there have been some kind of mistake? I mean, suppose it *is* you; suppose someone got a message wrong, and the whole thing is just a mix-up? Do you know anyone in Athens, perhaps, who might have . . . ?'

'No.' The syllable was definite to the point of curtness. 'It's quite impossible. I've had no communications with Athens during the last week at all, so it's hard to see how any message can have gone astray. And you say it was a girl who did the hiring. I've no idea who that could be. No, I'm afraid it's nothing whatever to do with me.' A pause, then he added in a different voice, as if he felt he had been too abrupt: 'But please don't worry about it any more. We'll soon get it straightened out, and then you can settle down and enjoy Delphi. I think you'll vote it's been worth it.'

'It'll have to be pretty good.'

'It is.' He nodded, almost idly, ahead of the car. 'You can't see the village from here, but the ruins are this side of the bluff, in the curve of the mountain under those high cliffs. There—that's Apollo's temple, below the cliffs they call the Shining Ones. You see?'

I saw. Ahead of us the mountain thrust that great buttress out into the valley, the river of olive-trees swirling round it as the water swirls round the prow of a ship, to spread out beyond into a great flat lake that filled the plain. High up, in the angle where the bluff joined the mountain, I saw it, Apollo's temple, six columns of apricot stone, glowing against the climbing darkness of the trees behind. Above them soared the sunburned cliffs; below was a tumble, as yet unrecognisable, of what must be monument and treasury and shrine. From where we were the pillars seemed hardly real; not stone that had ever felt hand or chisel, but insubstantial, the music-built columns of legend; Olympian building, left float-ing—warm from the god's hand—between sky and earth. Above, the indescribable sky of Hellas; below, the silver tide of the olives everlastingly rippling down to the sea. No house, no man, no beast. As it was in the beginning.

I realised then that Simon Lester had stopped the car. We must have stood there for some minutes, at the edge of the road in the shadow of a stone-pine. He didn't speak, and neither did I.

But I noticed that it wasn't Apollo's shining columns that held him. His gaze was on something nearer at hand, away up the side of Parnassus above the road. I followed his look, but could see nothing; only the bare rock shifting and flowing upwards with the liquid shimmer of the heat.

After a bit I said merely: 'And the village is just the other side of the bluff?'

'Yes. The road runs through those trees below the ruins and then round that shoulder into Delphi. Beyond the village it drops rather

steeply to the plain. Chrissa—where your friend in the café comes
from—is about halfway down. At the bottom the road forks for
Amphissa and Itea.'

'Itea? That's the fishing-port, isn't it? Where the pilgrims used to
land in the old days when they were making for the shrine?'

'Yes. You can just see the houses away over there at the edge of
the sea.' He turned the subject abruptly, but so smoothly that I
realised that he was following his own thoughts, and that these had
not been about the view, or the road to Itea. 'I'm still rather curious
to know how you knew my name. I understand it was from those
men in Arachova. Was . . . something said?'

'Not really. I'd been trying to explain to the men why I really
didn't dare try and reverse the car there—I'd never reversed it before,
of course, and it *is* such a length. I told them it wasn't mine, but that
it was for someone called Simon, at Delphi. I thought they looked as
if that meant something . . . Then one of them said something to the
others, and they all turned and stared at you. It was just the way
they looked, somehow. I don't know if you noticed?'

'I noticed.'

'Well, that was all. I suppose, when you arrived, they assumed
that you were the person to deal with the car. Then, when you told
me you came from Delphi, I guessed you might be Simon—my
"Simon". They . . .' I hesitated . . . 'they seemed to assume you
were the right one, too.'

There was an infinitesimal pause before his hand went to the
ignition. 'Ah well,' he said smoothly, 'the sooner we get to Delphi
and find your man the better, don't you think?'

'I do indeed.' I laughed. 'After all this, we'll probably find him
watching beside the road and dancing with impatience; that is, if the
little man was right and it really is a matter—' I stopped. Until I
repeated the words, half-automatically, I'd forgotten them myself.

'It is what?'

I said slowly, looking at him: 'A matter of life and death . . .'

*   *   *

We were moving again, quickly now. Below us the sea of olives
flowed and rippled like smoke. Above, the pitiless sun beat down on
the rock with a heat like the clang of brass.

He said: 'Is that all he told you?'

'Yes. But he repeated it.'

' "A matter of life and death"?'

'Just that. Only of course we were speaking in French. The phrase was *"il y va de la vie".*'

'And you got the impression he meant it seriously?'

I said slowly: 'Yes. I believe I did. I don't know if I took it in really urgently at the time, but you know, I think that's really why I did this silly thing with the car.'

'You took the car, and the risks with it, because of some subconscious feeling of urgency about the affair?'

I said: 'That makes it sound more definite than it was, and there were—other reasons . . . But, yes. Yes.'

The car roared up a long incline, swept round and down a curling hill. I leaned back against the hot leather, folded my hands in my lap, and said, not looking at him: 'If the little man was right, it's just as well you're not "Simon", isn't it?'

He said, quite without expression: 'Just as well. And here we are. What comes first? Simon, or the hotel?'

'Both. I imagine the hotel people are as likely to know of him as anyone, and at least I expect they speak English. My six words of Greek won't get me very far alone.'

'On the other hand,' said Simon gravely, 'they might get you a good deal further than you intended.'

Chapter 4

And thou camest to Chrissa under snow-clad Parnassus,
to its foot that faces west, and rocks overhang the spot,
and a hollow, stony, wood-clad vale stretches beneath it.

Homeric *Hymn to Apollo.*

TO MY RELIEF the hotel had a room to offer.

'But only for tonight, I'm afraid,' said the proprietor, who spoke, after all, excellent English. 'I deeply regret, but I cannot be certain about tomorrow. I have had a—what do you call it?—provisional booking. Perhaps I can take you, perhaps not. If not, there is the Kastalia further along the street, or the Tourist Pavilion at the other end of Delphi. It has a magnificent view, but,' he smiled charmingly, 'it is very expensive.'

'It couldn't have a better view than this,' I said.

This was true. The village consists only of two or three rows of flat-topped houses, washed ochre and pink and dazzling white, set in their tiers along the steep side of the hill. At the beginning of the village the road divides into a Y that makes the two main streets, and at the junction stands the Apollon Hotel, facing over the valley towards the distant gleam of the Corinthian Gulf.

Outside the hotel, on the edge of the road which was used as a terrace, two big plane trees made a deep island of shade for some wooden tables and chairs. Simon Lester had parked the car just beyond these, and was waiting there. When I had completed the formalities of booking I went out to speak to him.

'It's all right. They can take me for tonight, and just at the moment that's all I care about.' I held out my hand. 'I have to thank you very

much, Mr. Lester. I don't quite know where I'd have been without
your help. I've a feeling it might have been somewhere at the bottom
of the valley, with the eagles of Zeus picking my bones!'

'It was a pleasure.' He was looking down at me, measuringly. 'And
now what are you planning to do? Rest and have some tea first, or is
that –'a gesture indicated the car –'worrying you too much?'

I said uncertainly: 'It is rather. I think I'd better go right ahead and do
what I can.'

'Look,' he said, 'if you'll forgive me saying so, you look as if you'd
better have that rest. Won't you please leave this to me, at any rate
for the time being? Why don't you go and lie down, and have tea
brought to your room –they make excellent tea here, by the
way –while I make a few inquiries for you?'

'Why, I –you mustn't –I mean, it's absurd that you should be
landed with my difficulties,' I said, a little confusedly, and conscious
only of a strong desire that he should, in fact, be landed with them
all. I finished feebly: 'I couldn't let you.'

'Why not? It would be too cruel if you turned on me now and told me
to mind my own business.'

'I didn't mean it like that. You know I didn't. It's only –'

'That it's your affair and you want to see it through? Of course.
But I must confess I'm seething with curiosity myself by now, and
after all it's partly my affair, too, since my *alter ego* has managed to
involve me. I really would be very grateful if you'd let me help.
Besides,' he added, 'wouldn't you honestly much rather go and have
a rest and some tea now, while I do the detecting for you in my
fluent but no doubt peculiar Greek?'

'I –' I hesitated again, then said truthfully: 'I should adore to.'

'Then that's settled.' He glanced at his wrist. 'It's about twenty
past four now. Shall we say an hour? I'll report back at five thirty.
Right?'

'Right.' I looked at him a little helplessly. 'But if you do find him,
and he's angry –'

'Well?'

'I don't want you made responsible for what's happened. It
wouldn't be fair, and I'd much rather face my own music.'

'You'd be surprised,' he said cryptically, 'how responsible I feel
already. All right then. See you later.'

With a quick wave of the hand he was gone down the steps to the
lower road.

My room overlooked the valley, and had a long window with a

balcony. The shutters were closed against the sun, but even so the room seemed full of light, globed in light, incandescent with it. As the door shut behind the maid who had shown me upstairs, I went across to the window and pulled back the shutters. Like a blast the heat met me. The sun was wheeling over now towards the west, full across the valley from my window, and valley and plain were heavy with sleepy heat. The tide of olives had stilled itself, and even the illusion of coolness created by those rippling grey leaves was gone. In the distance the wedge of shining water that showed at the edge of the plain struck at the eyes like the flash from a burning-glass.

I closed my eyes against it, pulling the shutters to again. Then I slipped off my dress, and had a long, cool wash. I sat on the edge of the bed for some minutes after that, brushing my hair, till I heard the maid coming back with the tea. I had my tea – Simon Lester had been right about its excellence – propped against pillows, and with my feet up on the bed. I don't think I thought any more about Simon – either of the Simons – or about the car, or about anything except the shadowed quiet of the little white room.

Presently I put the tray off my knees on to the table by the bed, and lay back to relax. Before I knew it was even near, sleep had overtaken me . . .

I woke to a feeling of freshness and the incongruous sound of rain. But the light still drove white against the shutters, and when I opened them a crack I saw that the sun still blazed, deeper now and lower, but at full power. Half my window was in shadow now, where the plane-trees put a bough or two between it and the falling sun. The sound of rain, I realised, was the sound of their leaves, pattering and rustling in the breeze that had got up to cool the evening.

I glanced down at the terrace below the balcony. He was there, sitting under one of the plane-trees, smoking. His chair was pulled up to the railing that edged the terrace, and one arm lay along this. He sat there, relaxed, looking at nothing, completely at ease. The car was standing where he had parked it before. If – as appeared to be the case – he had not located another 'Simon' to deliver it to, the fact didn't appear to worry him unduly.

I reflected, as I looked down at him thoughtfully, that it would probably take a good deal to worry Simon Lester. That quiet manner, that air of being casually and good-temperedly on terms with life . . . with it all went something that is particularly hard to describe. To say that he knew what he wanted and took it, would be to give the wrong impression: it was rather that whatever decisions he had to make, were made, and then dismissed—this with an ease that argued an almost frightening brand of self-confidence.

I don't know how much of this I saw in him on that first day; it may be that I simply recognised straight away the presence of qualities I myself so conspicuously lacked: but I do remember the immediate and vivid impression I got of a self-sufficiency harder and more complete than anything conveyed in years of Philip's *grand-seigneur* gasconading, and at the same time quite different in quality. I didn't see yet where the difference lay. I only know that I felt obscurely grateful to Simon for not having made me feel too much of a fool, and, less obscurely, for having so calmly undertaken to help me in the matter of the 'other Simon' . . .

I wondered, as I closed the shutters again, if he had even bothered to make the gesture of looking for him.

On the whole, I imagined not.

*   *   *

In this, it seemed, I had done him less than justice.

When I went downstairs I found him, hands thrust deep in trouser pockets, in earnest contemplation of the car, together with a Greek to whose bright blue shirt was pinned the insignia of a guide.

Simon looked up and smiled at me. 'Rested?'

'Perfectly, thank you. And the tea *was* good.'

'I'm glad to hear it. Perhaps you're strong enough, then, to bear the blow?' He jerked his head towards the car.

'I thought as much. You've not found him?'

'Not a sign. I've been to the other hotels, but there's no visitor of that name. Then I went along to the museum to meet George here. He tells me that he doesn't know anyone called Simon in Delphi either.'

The Greek said: 'Only yourself, *Kyrie* Lester.'

'Only myself,' agreed Simon.

I said, rather helplessly: 'What shall we do?'

'*Kyrie* Lester,' said the Greek, watching him rather curiously, 'could it not be, perhaps, that there *is* no other Simon? And that it is not a mistake? That someone is—how do you put it?—using your name?'

'Taking my name in vain?' Simon laughed, but I knew that this had already occurred to him. It had occurred to me, too. 'It doesn't seem likely. For one thing, who would? And for another, if they

did, and it was urgent, they'd surely have appeared by now to claim
the damned thing.'

'That is probably true.'

'You can bet it's true. But I'm going to get to the bottom of this
very odd little affair – and not only for the sake of Miss Haven here,
who's worried about it. Look, George, you are sure about it? No
Simons at all, however unlikely? A grandfather with a wooden leg,
or a mule-boy aged seven-and-a-half, or one of the men working up
on the excavations?'

'About the last I do not know, of course, though assuredly you are
right and they would have come to look for it. In Delphi, nobody.
Nobody at all.'

'Then the places nearby? You're a native, aren't you? You'll know
a fair number of people all round here. Chrissa, for instance. It
might be Chrissa . . . that's only a few kilometres away. What about
that?'

George shook his head. 'No. I am sure. I would have remembered. And in Arachova . . .'

Simon ran a finger along the wing of the car, then contemplated
the tip of it for a moment. 'Yes?'

George said, regretfully: 'No, I do not remember anyone in
Arachova, either.'

Simon took out a handkerchief and wiped his finger-tip clean
again. 'In any case I can find out. I'm going back there tonight.'

The Greek gave him a quick bright glance that held, I thought,
curiosity. But he only said: 'Ah. Well, I regret, but that is all I can
tell you, except – oh, but that is not the same; it is of no use to you.'

'We'll have it, though, please. You've thought of someone?'

George said slowly: 'There is a Simonides at Itea. I do not think
this is the man, but he is the only one I know of. But perhaps, *kyrie*,
you would like to ask someone else? I do not know everybody, me.
Elias Sarantopoulos, my cousin, he is also in the Tourist Police. He
is at the office now, or perhaps he is at the café . . . if you like to
come with me I will show you the place; it is opposite the post
office.'

'I know it,' said Simon. 'Thanks, but I really doubt if your cousin
will know any more than you. This is an irritating little problem,
isn't it? It'll probably solve itself very soon, but meanwhile I suppose
we must do something. We'll try your Simonides at Itea. Who is
Simonides, what is he?'

George, of course, took him literally. 'He has a little baker's shop

near the cinema in the middle of the main street, facing the sea.
Giannakis Simonides.' He glanced at his wrist. 'The bus goes in ten
minutes. The shop is not far from the place where the bus stops.'

Simon said: 'We have a car,' then grinned as he caught my eye.
My answering smile was a rather brittle one. The car stood there like
a mockery. I hated the sight of it.

Simon nodded to George, said something in Greek, then pulled
open the car door for me.

I said doubtfully: 'Ought we to?'

'Why not? This is a quite legitimate attempt at delivery. Come
along, the sooner we get down to Itea the better. It'll be dark in an
hour. Are you tired?'

'Not now. But–you'll drive, won't you, Mr. Lester?'

'You bet I will. You haven't seen the Itea road. And please call me
Simon. It's more euphonious than "Mr. Lester", and besides . . .' his
grin, as he slid into his seat beside me, was malicious . . . 'it'll give
you an illusion of comfort.'

I didn't answer that one, except with a look, but as we drove off I
said suddenly, and almost to my own surprise: 'I'm beginning to feel
frightened.'

The glance he gave me held surprise, but, oddly enough, no
amusement. 'That's a strong word.'

'I suppose so. Perhaps it isn't, either, from me. I'm the world's
most complete coward. I–I wish I'd had the sense to let well alone.
The beastly thing should still be standing there in Omonia Square,
and–'

'And you'd still be wishing madly you were in Delphi?'

'There is that,' I acknowledged. 'But you do see, don't you?'

'Of course I do.'

The car had crept carefully through Delphi's narrow upper street,
topped the rise opposite the presbytery, and then dived down to
meet the lower road out of the village.

I said abruptly: 'Do you suppose for a moment that this
Simonides is the man we're looking for?'

'It doesn't seem very probable.' Perhaps he felt this to be a little
brusque, for he added: 'We might as well try it, all the same.'

'Something to make me feel progress is being made?' No answer
to this. I said: 'You know, it really would be carrying coincidence a
bit too far to suppose there are two Simons in Delphi.'

'It's not,' he said evenly, 'a very common name.'

I waited, but he didn't speak again. We had left the village behind, dropping in a gradual descent between dykes of red earth and stones where the road had been recently widened. The ditches and mounds showed raw as wounds in the sunburnt earth. The rich rays of the now setting sun flooded it with strong amber light, against which the dry thistles that grew everywhere stood up delicate and sharp, like intricate filigree of copper wire. Above the road the new hotel, the Tourist Pavilion, showed as raw and new and wounding as the torn ditches alongside us. The curved windows flashed as we passed beneath and wheeled into the first hairpin of the descent to the plain of olives.

I said casually: 'Are you just holidaying here in Delphi?'

I had meant it as a *non sequitur*, a conversational makeweight, the normal casual query with which you might greet anyone you met in such a place; but even as I said it I could hear how it pointed back to my last remark. I started to say something else, but he was already answering without any indication that he saw my question as other than innocent.

'In a way. I'm a schoolmaster. I have a house at Wintringham. Classics is my subject.'

Whatever I had expected it wasn't this; this seal and parchment of respectability. I said feebly: 'Then of course you're interested in the classical sites. Like me.'

'Don't tell me you're a colleague? Another beggarly usher?'

'Afraid so.'

'Classics?'

'Yes. Only in a girls' school that just means Latin, to my sorrow and shame.'

'You don't know Ancient Greek?'

'A little. A very little. Enough sometimes to catch a word and follow what's being said. Enough to know my alphabet and make a wild guess at what some of the notices mean, and to have had a queer feeling at the pit of the stomach when I went to see *Antigone* in the Herodes Atticus Theatre in Athens and heard the chorus calling on Zeus against that deep black sky that had heard the same call for three thousand years.' I added, feeling slightly ashamed of what I'd let him see: 'What a ghastly road.'

The car wheeled yet again round a hairpin and plunged on down the great shoulder of Parnassus that sticks out into the Chrissa Plain. Below us was a village, and below it again the flood of olives, flowing mile-wide now down to the sea.

Simon said cheerfully: 'The buses all have icons stuck up in front

of the driver, *and* with a little red light in front, run off the battery.
On this road the icon swings madly from side to side at the bends
and everybody crosses themselves.'

I laughed. 'Including the driver?'

'This is true. Yes, including the driver. I have a feeling that
sometimes,' said Simon, 'he also shuts his eyes.' He pulled the big
car round an even sharper bend, missed an upcoming lorry by
centimetres, and added: 'You can open yours now. This is Chrissa.'

I felt the colour come into my cheeks. 'I'm sorry. I must be losing
my nerve.'

'You're still tired, that's all. We'll have something to drink in Itea
before we seek out this Simonides.'

'No, please,' I protested, almost too quickly.

He eyed me for a moment. 'You really are scared, aren't you?'

'I—yes, I am.'

'I shouldn't worry; I really shouldn't. It can't matter, or it'd have
been settled long before this.'

'I know. I know it's nonsense. It's silly and it's trivial and it
doesn't mean a thing, but I told you I'm the world's worst coward.
It's true. I've been persuading myself for years that I'd be as
competent and self-sufficient as anyone else, given the chance, but
now I know . . . Why, I can't even bear *scenes*, so why I ever thought
I could get away with this sort of mayhem I have no idea.' I stopped.
It occurred to me with a queer little shock that I would never have
said anything like that to Philip, not in a hundred years.

Simon was saying calmly: 'Never mind. I'm here, aren't I? Whatever
we get into, I'll talk you out of it, so sit back and relax.'

'If,' I said, 'we find Simon.'

'If,' said Simon, 'we do.'

                    *   *   *

I was glad enough, when we got to Itea, to leave everything to
him.

Itea is the port which in ancient times saw the landing of the
pilgrims bound for the shrine of Apollo at Delphi. The shrine was a
religious centre for the whole ancient world for many hundreds of
years, and to us nowadays, used to modern transport, it is aston-
ishing to contemplate the distances that men travelled on foot and on
horseback or in small ships, to worship the god of light and peace
and healing, or to ask the advice of the famous Oracle enshrined

below the temple. The easy way was by Itea. The sea-journey, for all its hazards, was less exhausting and dangerous than the journey by road through the mountains, and here into the little port of Itea the pilgrims crowded, to see from the harbour the winding river valley of the Pleistus and, beyond the shoulder of Parnassus where modern Delphi stands, the bright cliffs of the Shining Ones that guard the holy spring.

Today Itea is a grubby little fishing-village, with one long street of shops and *tavernas* facing the sea, and separated from it by the road and then perhaps fifty yards of dusty boulevard where pepper-trees give shade and the men of the village gather for the usual drinks and ices and sticky honey-cakes.

Simon stopped the car under the trees and led me to a rickety iron table which seemed to have fewer attendant wasps than the others. I would have liked tea again, but felt so ashamed of this insular craving—and so doubtful of getting anything approaching what I wanted—that I asked for fresh lemonade, and got it, delicious and cold and tangy with the real fruit, and with it a *pasta* something like Shredded Wheat, but frantically oversweet with honey and chopped nuts. It was wonderful. The wasps loved it, too. When we had finished it I defiantly asked for another, and stayed to eat it while Simon went off to look for the baker's shop of Simonides.

I watched him go, thoughtfully beating off an extra large and persistent wasp.

Somehow I didn't think Giannakis Simonides was our man. 'Monsieur Simon at Delphi . . .' And there was only one Monsieur Simon at Delphi.

There was that queer reserve, too, in Simon's manner; there was Arachova; and the way he had shelved my question as to what he was doing in Delphi. The thing had ceased to be a slightly awkward puzzle. It was fast becoming a mystery, with Simon Lester at its centre. And Simon's girl . . .

I finished my cake now and got up. Simon had paid the waiter before he had left me. I could see him standing in a doorway some distance up the street. The place was apparently a restaurant, for outside it stood the big charcoal stove, and over this a whole lamb revolved slowly on the spit which was being turned by a stout woman in a blue apron. Simon appeared to be questioning her; she was nodding vigorously, and then, with a wave of her free hand, seemed to be directing him further up the street.

He looked back, saw me standing under the pepper-trees, and

raised a hand in salute. Then he made a vague gesture towards the other end of the street, and set off that way, walking fast.

Taking his gesture to mean that he had some information, but that he didn't expect me to follow him, I stayed where I was and watched him. He went perhaps a hundred yards, hesitated, then glanced up at a hoarding and plunged into the darkness of a deserted cinema. As he vanished, I turned in the opposite direction and began to walk along the boulevard. I was only too thankful to leave the inquiry to him. If he really was in the centre of the mystery, he could keep it to himself, and welcome . . .

Meanwhile I would do what I had come to Delphi for. Since chance had brought me down to Itea, the start of the ancient pilgrimage, I would try and see the shrine as the old pilgrims had seen it on their first landing from the Corinthian Gulf.

I walked quickly along the harbour's edge. On my right the sea paled towards sunset, and across the opal shimmer of the bay came a fishing-boat, turquoise and white, with her prow raked in a proud pure curve above its liquid image. Under a sail of that same scarlet had the worshippers come into harbour when the god was still at Delphi.

I left the sea's edge and walked rapidly across the street. I wanted to get behind the ugly row of houses, back into the old olive-woods, where I could look straight up towards the Pleistus valley with nothing but immemorial rock and tree and sky between me and the shrine.

Behind the main street were a few sorry alleys of concrete, with houses, as usual, scattered seemingly at random in the dust-patches between the trees. I passed the last house, skirted a building that looked like a ruined warehouse, and followed a cracked stretch of concrete which appreared to lead straight into the outskirts of the forest of olives. The concrete was criss-crossed with cracks, like crazy paving, and thistles grew in the fissures. I startled a browsing donkey, and it plunged off under the olives in a smother of dust, to be lost in the shadows. Soon the concrete came to an end, and I found myself walking through soft earth in the deeper twilight of the trees. The breeze had strengthened with the approach of evening, and overhead the olives had resumed their liquid rippling.

I hurried on towards a space ahead where stronger light promised a clearing. I was lucky. There was a slight rise in the ground, and to the north of it the great olives thinned. From the top of the little ridge, across the ruffling crests of the trees, I could see the old

Pilgrims' Way, unscarred by my own century. I stood for a few minutes, gazing up towards the shrine in the now rapidly fading light.

The temple columns were invisible behind the curve of the Chrissa bluff, but there was the black cleft of Castalia, and above it the great cliffs whose names are Flamboyant and Roseate, the Shining Ones . . . The dying sun ran up the Flamboyant cliff like fire.

This was, I thought, the way to come to Delphi . . . not straight up into the ruins in the wake of a guide, but to land from a small boat in a bay of pearl, and see it as they would have seen it, flaming in the distance like a beacon, the journey's end.

Something like a fleck of darkness went by my cheek. A bat. It was deep twilight now, the swift-falling Aegean dusk. I turned to see lights pricking out in the houses behind me. I could just see the street-lamps, faint and far between, along the sea-front. They looked a long way away. Where I stood the shadow of a huge olive brooded like a cloud. I turned to go back to the village.

Instead of returning the way I had come, I took what I judged to be the direction of the car, and, plunging down from the ridge into the depths of the olive-wood, I set off quickly through the twisted and shadowy trunks.

I had gone perhaps a hundred yards before the trees began to thin. Some way off to my left I saw the lights of the first house, an outpost of the village, and was hurrying towards it through the soft dust when a sudden flash of light quite near me, and to my right, brought me up short, startled. It was the flash of an electric torch, deep in the trees. Perhaps my adventures of the day had worked on my imagination rather too well, or perhaps it was the ancient mystery that I had been attempting to call up, but the fact remains that I felt suddenly frightened, and stood very still, with the trunk of an enormous olive between me and the torchlight.

Then I realised what it was. There was a house set by itself deep in the grove, the usual two-windowed box of a place with its woodpile and its lean-to shed and its scrawny chickens gone to roost in the vine. The flash I had seen showed me a man bending over a motor vehicle of some sort which was parked close to the side of the house. It looked like a jeep. As I watched he jerked the bonnet open, shone the light into the engine, and leaned over it. I saw his face highlighted by the queerly refracted light, a very Greek face, dark, with hair crisping down the wide cheekbones in the manner of the heroes, and a roundish head covered with close curls like a statue's.

Then somebody in the cottage must have kindled the lamp, for a soft oblong of light slanted out of one of the windows, showing the dusty clutter outside—a woodman's block with the axe still sunk in it and gleaming as the light caught it, a couple of old petrol cans, and a chipped enamel bowl for the hens' food. My causeless fear vanished and I turned quickly to go.

The man by the jeep must have seen the movement of my skirt in the darkness, because he looked up. I caught a glimpse of his face before the torch went out. He was smiling. I turned and hurried away. As I went, I thought the torch-beam flicked out to touch me momentarily, but the Greek made no move to follow.

Simon was sitting in the car, smoking. He got out when he saw me and came round to open my door. He answered my look with a shake of the head.

'No go. I've asked all the questions I could and it's a dead end.' He got into the driver's seat and started the engine. 'I really think we'll have to call it a day—go back to Delphi and have dinner and leave it to sort itself out in its own good time.'

'But will it?'

He turned the car and started back towards Delphi. 'I think so.'

Bearing in mind what I had been thinking before about the 'mystery', I didn't argue. I said simply: 'Then we'll leave it. As you wish.'

I saw him glance at me sideways, but he made no comment. The lights of the village were behind us, and we gathered speed up the narrow road between the olives. He dropped something into my lap, a leafy twig that smelt delicious when my fingers touched it.

'What is it?'

'Basil. The herb of kings.'

I brushed it to and fro across my lips. The smell was sweet and minty, pungent above the smell of dust. 'The pot of basil? Was it under this stuff that poor Isabella buried Lorenzo's head?'

'That's it.'

There was a pause. We passed a crossroads where our lights showed a sign, AMPHISSA 9. We turned right for Chrissa.

'Did you go to look for the Pilgrims' Way back there in Itea?' asked Simon.

'Yes. I got a wonderful view just before the light went. The Shining Ones were terrific.'

'You found the ridge, then?'

I must have sounded surprised. 'You know it? You've been here before?'

'I was down here yesterday.'

'In Itea?'

'Yes.' The road was climbing now. After a short silence he said, with no perceptible change of expression: 'You know, I really don't know any more about it than you do.'

The basil leaves were cool and still against my mouth. At length I said: 'I'm sorry. Did I make it so obvious? But what was I to think?'

'Probably just what you did think. The thing's slightly crazy anyway, and I doubt if it'll prove to matter at all.' I saw him smile. 'Thank you for not pretending you didn't know what I meant.'

'But I did. I'd been thinking about very little else myself.'

'I know that. But nine women out of ten would have said *'What d'you mean?'* and there we'd have been, submerged in a lovely welter of personalities and explanations.'

'There wasn't any need of either.'

Simon said: ' "O rare for Antony".'

I said involuntarily: 'What d'you mean?'

He laughed then. 'Skip it. Will you have dinner with me tonight?'

'Why, thank you, Mr. Lester–'

'Simon.'

'Simon, then, but perhaps I should–I mean–'

'That's wonderful then. At your hotel?'

'Look, I didn't say–'

'You owe it to me,' said Simon coolly.

'I owe it to you? I do not! How d'you work that out?'

'As reparation for suspecting me of–whatever you did suspect me of.' We were climbing through the twisting street of Chrissa, and as we passed a lighted shop he glanced at his wrist. 'It's nearly seven now. Could you bear to dine in half an hour's time–say at half past seven?'

I gave up. 'Whenever it suits you. But isn't that fearfully early for Greece? Are you so very hungry?'

'Reasonably. But it's not that. I–well, I've things to do and I want to get them done tonight.'

'I see. Well, it won't be too early for me. I only had a snack for lunch, and I was too frightened to enjoy that. So thank you. I'd like that. At the Apollon, you said? You're not staying there yourself?'

'No. When I got here the place was full up, so I got permission to sleep in the studio up the hill. You won't have seen it yet. It's a big, ugly square building a couple of hundred feet up behind the village.

'A studio? An artist's studio, do you mean?'

'Yes. I don't know what it was used for originally, but now it has a caretaker, and is let out to visiting artists and *bona fide* students who can't afford to pay for a hotel. I suppose I'm up there under slightly false pretences, but I wanted to be in Delphi for some days and I couldn't find a room. Now that I'm settled into the studio I find it'll do me admirably. There's only one other tenant at present, an English boy, who's a genuine artist . . . and good, too, though he won't let you say so.'

'But surely you've a perfectly good claim on the studio, too?' I said. 'After all, you count as a student. And as a classicist you've a *bona fide* claim on any concession. It's not a question of "false pretences" at all.'

He sent me a sideways look that I couldn't read in the darkness. He said rather shortly: 'I'm not here to pursue my classical studies.'

'Oh.' It sounded lame, and I hope it hadn't sounded like a question. But the syllable hung there between us like a dominant awaiting resolution.

Simon said suddenly, into the darkness straight ahead: 'My brother Michael was here during the war.'

Chrissa was below us now. Far down to our left as we climbed along the face of the bluff the lights of Itea were strung along like beads under the thin moon.

He said, still in that expressionless way: 'He was in the Peloponnese for some time, as B.L.O. –that's British Liaison Officer–between our chaps and the *andartes*, the Greek guerrillas under Zervas. Later he moved over into the Pindus region with ELAS, the main resistance group. He was in this part of the country in 1944. He stayed with some people in Arachova; a shepherd called Stephanos and his son Nikolaos. Nikolaos is dead, but Stephanos still lives in Arachova. I went over to try and see him today, but he's away in Levadia, and not expected back till this evening–so the woman of his house told me.'

'The woman of his house?'

He laughed. 'His wife. You'll find everyone has to belong, hereabouts. Every man belongs to a place, and I'm afraid that every woman belongs to a man.'

'I believe you,' I said, without rancour. 'I suppose it gives meaning to her life, poor thing?'

'But of course . . . Anyway I'm going down to Arachova again tonight to see Stephanos.'

'I see. Then this is a—a sort of pilgrimage for you? A genuine pilgrimage to Delphi?'

'You could call it that. I've come to appease his shade.'

I caught my breath. 'Oh. How stupid of me. I'm sorry. I didn't realise.'

'That he died? Yes.'

'Here?'

'Yes, in 1944. Somewhere on Parnassus.'

We had wheeled up on to the last stretch of the road before Delphi. To our left blazed the lighted windows of the luxurious Tourist Pavilion. Far down on the right the thin moon was already dying out in a welter of stars. The sea was faintly luminous beneath them, like a black satin ribbon.

Something made me say suddenly, into the dark: 'Simon.'

'Yes?'

'Why did you say "appease"?'

A little silence. Then he spoke quite lightly. 'I'll tell you about that, if I may. But not just at this moment. Here's Delphi. I'll leave you and the car at your hotel, and I'll meet you on the terrace here in half an hour. Right?'

'Right.' The car drew up where it had stood before. He came round and opened my door for me. I got out, and when I would have turned to repeat some words of thanks for his help in my afternoon's quest he shook his head, laughed, raised a hand in farewell and vanished up the steep lane beside the hotel.

With a feeling that things were moving altogether too fast for me, I turned and went indoors.

Chapter 5

*But enough of tales — I have wept for these
things once already.*

EURIPIDES: *Helen.*
(tr. Philip Vellacott.)

ANY FEARS I might have had that Simon's melancholy pilgrimage
would be allowed to cloud my first visit to Delphi were dispelled
when I came down at length to dinner, and walked out to the hotel
terrace to find a table.

Seven thirty was certainly an outrageously early hour for dining
in Greece, and only one other of the tables under the plane trees was
occupied, and that, too, by English people. Simon Lester wasn't
there yet, so I sat down under one of the trees from whose dark
boughs hung lights, which swung gently in the warm evening air. I
saw Simon then below the terrace railing, making one of an
extremely gay and noisy group of Greeks which surrounded a fair
boy in the garb of a hiker, and a very small donkey almost hidden
under its awkwardly loaded panniers.

The fair young man looked very much as if he had just completed
some arduous trek in the wilds. His face, hands, and clothes were
filthy; he had a generous stubble on his chin, and his eyes—I could
see it even from where I sat—were bloodshot with fatigue. The
donkey was in rather better case, and stood smugly beside him,
under its load of what appeared to be the paraphernalia of an
artist—boxes, roughly wrapped canvases, and a small collapsible
easel, as well as a sleeping bag and the rather unappetising end of a
large black loaf.

Half the youth of Delphi seemed to have rallied to the stranger's
welcome, like the wasps to my honey-cake. There was a great deal of

loud laughter, atrocious English, and back-slapping–the last an attention which the stranger could well have done without. He was reeling with tiredness, but a white grin split the dirty bearded face as he responded to the welcome. Simon was laughing, too, pulling the donkey's ears and exchanging what appeared to be the most uproarious of jokes with the young Greeks. Frequent cries of '*Avanti!*' puzzled me, till I realised that they coincided with the jolly slaps under which the donkey, too, was reeling. At each slap a cloud of dust rose from 'Avanti's' fur.

Eventually Simon looked up and saw me. He said something to the fair boy, exchanged some laughing password with the Greeks, and came swiftly up to the terrace.

'I'm sorry, have you been waiting long?'

'No, I've just come down. What's going on down there? A modern Stevenson?'

'Just that. He's a Dutch painter who's been making his way through the mountains with a donkey, and sleeping rough. He's done pretty well. He's just here from Jannina now, and that's a long way through rough country.'

'He certainly got a welcome,' I said, laughing. 'It looked as if all Delphi had turned out.'

'Even the tourist traffic hasn't quite spoiled the Greek *philoxenia*–the "welcome" that literally means "love of a stranger",' said Simon, 'though goodness knows Delphi ought to be getting a bit blasé by now. At least he'll get the traditional night's lodging free.'

'Up at the studio?'

'Yes. This is the end of his trek. Tomorrow, he says, he'll sell Modestine–the donkey Avanti–and get the bus for Athens.'

I said: 'I thought when I saw the easel and what-not that he must be your English painter friend from the studio.'

'Nigel? No. I doubt if a venture like that would ever occur to Nigel. He hasn't the self-confidence.'

'You said he was a good painter, though?'

'I think he's good,' said Simon, picking up the menu and absently handing it to me. It was in Greek, so I handed it back again. 'But he's convinced himself–or else some fool has told him–that his own particular style is no good any more. I admit it's not the fashion, but the boy can draw like an angel when he likes, and I should have thought that was a gift rare enough to command attention even among some of today's more strident talents.' He handed me the menu. 'He doesn't use colour much–what will you have to start with?—but the drawing's very sure and delicate, and exciting at the same time.'

I gave the menu back to him. He scutinised the scrawled columns. 'Hm. Yes. Well, some fool's told Nigel that his style's *vieux jeu*, or something. "Emasculate" was one of the words, I believe. It's got him on the raw, so he's hard at work trying to form a style that he thinks will "take", but I'm terribly afraid it won't work. Oh, he's clever, and it's arresting enough, and it may catch on and find him a market of a sort—but it's not his own, and that never works fully. Another pity is that he's been here in Delphi a bit too long and got tied up with a girl who wasn't very good for him. She's gone, but the melancholy remains.' He smiled. 'As you see, it's with me, rather. I'm all the company Nigel's had up at the studio for the last three days, and I've been playing confidant.'

'Or housemaster?'

He laughed. 'If you like. He's very young in many ways, and habit dies hard. One takes it for granted one is there to help, though I'm not just sure how much anyone can do for an artist at the best of times. And at the worst they go into a kind of wilderness of the spirit where the best-intentioned listener can't even follow them.'

'As bad as that?'

'I think so. I told you he was good. I believe the agony is in proportion to the talent . . . Look, what are you going to eat? Why don't you choose something?' He handed me the menu.

I gave it patiently back. 'I shall die of hunger in a minute,' I told him. 'Have you *looked* at this dashed menu? The only things I recognise are *patates*, *tomates*, and *melon*, and I refuse to be a vegetarian in a land which produces those heavenly little chunks of lamb on sticks with mushrooms between.'

'I'm sorry,' said Simon penitently. 'Here they are, see? *Souvlaka*. Well, so be it.' He ordered the meal, then finally cocked an eyebrow at me. 'What shall we drink? How's the palate coming on?'

'If that means can I swallow retsina yet,' I said, 'the answer is yes, though what it has to do with a palate I cannot see.' Retsina is a mild wine strongly flavoured with resin. It can be pleasant; it can also be rough enough to fur the tongue with a sort of antiseptic gooseflesh. It comes in beautiful little copper tankards, and smells like turpentine. To acquire—or to pretend to acquire—a taste for retsina is the right thing to do when in Greece. As a tourist, I'm as much of a snob as anyone. 'Retsina, certainly,' I said. 'What else, with *souvlaka*?'

I thought I saw the faintest shade of irony in Simon's eye. 'Well, if you'd rather have wine—'

I said firmly: 'They say that once you've got used to retsina it's the finest drink in the world and you won't ever take anything else. Burgundies and clarets and—well, other drinks, lose their flavour. Don't interrupt the process. The palate is faint yet pursuing, and I expect I'll like it soon. Unless, of course, *you'd* like a nice sweet Samian wine?'

'Heaven forfend,' said Simon basely, and, to the waiter, 'retsina, please.'

When it came it was good—as retsina goes—and the dinner along with it was excellent. I'm not a person whom the sight of olive oil repels, and I love Greek cooking. We had onion soup with grated cheese on top; then the *souvlaka*, which comes spiced with lemon and herbs, and flanked with chips and green beans in oil and a big dish of tomato salad. Then cheese, and *halvas*, which is a sort of loaf made of grated nuts and honey, and is delicious, And finally the wonderful grapes of Greece, bloomed over like misted agates and cooled with water from the spring above the temple of Apollo.

Simon talked entertainingly through the meal without once mentioning Michael Lester or his purpose in visiting Delphi, and I myself forgot completely the cloud that was still hanging over my day, and only recollected it when a lorry, chugging up past the terrace, slowed down to pass the car which stood parked at the edge of the narrow road.

Simon followed my look. He set down his little cup of Greek coffee, and then looked across the table at me.

'Conscience still active?'

'Not so active as it was. There's not so much room. That was a heavenly meal, and thank you very much.'

'I wondered—' said Simon thoughtfully, and then stopped.

I said just as thoughtfully: 'It's a long walk to Arachova. Is that it?'

He grinned. 'That's it. Well? It's your car.'

I said fervently: 'It's not, you know. I never want to touch it again. I—I've renounced it.'

'That's a pity, because—with your permission which I take it I have—I'm going to drive down to Arachova in a few minutes' time, and I was rather hoping you'd come, too.'

I said, in very real amazement: 'Me? But you don't want me!'

'Please,' said Simon.

For some reason I felt the colour coming hot into my cheeks. 'But you don't. It's your own – your private affair, and you can't possibly want a stranger tagging along with you. This may be Greece, but that's carrying *philoxenia* a bit too far! After all –'

'I promise not to let anything upset you.' He smiled. 'It's a long time ago, and it's not a present tragedy any more. It's just – well, you can call it curiosity, if you like.'

'I wasn't worrying about its upsetting me. I was thinking only that – well, dash it, you hardly know me, and it *is* a private matter. You said it could be called a "pilgrimage", remember?'

He said slowly: 'If I said what I really want to say you'd think I was crazy. But let me say this – and it's true – I'd be terribly grateful if you'd give me your company this evening.'

There was a little pause. The group of Greeks had long since dispersed. Both artist and donkey had vanished. The other English diners had finished and gone into the hotel. Away over the invisible sea the thin moon hung, apricot now among the white scatter of stars. Above us the breeze in the plane trees sounded like rain.

I said: 'Of course I'll come,' and got to my feet. As he stubbed out his cigarette and rose I smiled at him with a touch of malice. 'After all, you did tell me I owed you something.'

He said quickly: 'Look, I never meant –' then he caught my look and grinned. 'All right, ma'am, you win. I won't try and bully you again.' And he opened the car door for me.

* * *

'Michael was ten years older than me,' said Simon. 'There were just the two of us, and our mother died when I was fifteen. My father thought the sun rose and set in Michael – and so did I, I suppose. I remember how dead the house seemed when he was drafted off to the Med . . . and Father just sat every day with the papers and the radio, trying to learn what he could.' A little smile touched his lips. 'It wasn't easy. Michael came over here with the SAS – the Special Air Service – when Germany occupied Greece. He was doing under-cover work with the resistance in the mountains for eighteen months before he was killed, and of course news came very thinly and not always accurately. Occasionally men managed to get letters out . . . If you knew someone was going to be picked up at night and taken off you did your damnedest to get a letter to him in the hope that he in his turn would get through, and the letter might eventually be mailed home from Cairo . . . but it was chancy, and no one, in those days, carried any more papers on

him than he could help. So news was sparse and not very satisfactory. We only ever got three letters from Michael in all that time.
All he told us in the first two was that he was well, and things were
going according to plan—and all the usual formulae that you don't
believe, but that just tell you he was alive when he wrote the letter
four months before you got it.'

He paused while he negotiated a sharp bend made more hair-
raising than ever by the dark.

'We did eventually find out a certain amount about his work in
Greece from chaps who'd been with him here in Force 133, and had
been in touch with him off and on through the fighting. I told you he
was a B.L.O. attached to guerrillas. Perhaps I'd better tell you the
set-up in Greece after the German invasion—or do you know all
about it?'

'Not a great deal. Only that ELAS was the main guerrilla
organisation, and was more concerned in feathering its own Commie
nest than in fighting Germans.'

'So you do know that? You'd be surprised how many people never
grasped it, even in 1944 when the Germans got out of Greece and
ELAS turned on its own country—tried to stage a Communist *coup
d'état*—and started murdering Greeks with the arms and cash we'd
smuggled to them, and which they'd hidden safely away in the
mountains till they could use them for the Party.'

'But there were other guerrillas who did an honest job, surely?'

'Oh, yes. To begin with there were quite a few groups, and it was
Michael's job, among other things, to try and bring them together in
a more or less coherent plan of campaign. But it broke his heart as it
broke the heart of every B.L.O. in Greece. ELAS set to work and
smashed every other guerrilla organisation it could get its filthy
hands on.'

'You mean actually fought its own people *during* the German
occupation?'

'Indeed yes. Smashed some groups and assimilated others, until
eventually there was only one other important resistance group,
EDES, under a leader called Zervas, an honest man and a fine
soldier.'

'I remember. You said he was in the Peloponnese.'

'That's it. ELAS tried hard to liquidate him, too, of course. Don't
mistake me, there were some brave and good men with ELAS, too,
and they did some damned good work, but there was rather a load
of . . .' he paused fractionally, 'infamy . . . to counteract the better

things. It doesn't make good reading, the story of the resistance in Greece. Village after village, raped and burned by the Germans, was thereafter raped and burned by ELAS–their own people–for whatever pathetic supplies they could produce. And the final abomination was the famous battle of Mount Tzoumerka where Zervas with EDES was facing the Germans, and ELAS under Ares (of all the damned arrogant pseudonyms for one of the most filthy sadistic devils that ever walked)–ELAS waited till Zervas was heavily engaged, and then attacked him on the flank.'

'Attacked *Zervas*? While he was fighting the Germans?'

'Yes. Zervas fought a double-sided battle for several hours, and managed to beat off the Germans, but he still lost some of his valuable supplies to ELAS, who stored them away, no doubt, against the end of the German war and the day of the New Dawn.'

There was a silence, underlined by the humming of the engine. I could smell dust, and dead verbena. The autumn stars were milky-white and as large as asters. Against their mild radiance the young cypresses stood like spears.

'And that brings me to the reason for my visit to Delphi,' said Simon.

I said: 'Michael's third letter?'

'You're quick, aren't you? Yes, indeed, Michael's third letter.'

He changed gear, and the car slowed and turned carefully on to a narrow bridge set at right-angles to the road. He went on in his pleasant, unemotional voice: 'It came after we had had news of his death. I didn't read it then. In fact, I never knew Father had had it. I suppose he thought it would bring the thing alive again for me, when I'd just got over the worst. I was seventeen. And later, Father never talked about Michael. I didn't know of the letter's existence till six months ago, when Father died, and I, as his executor, had to go through his papers. The letter . . .'

He paused again, and I felt a curious little thrill go through me–the inevitable response (conditioned by tales told through how many centuries?) to the age-old device of fable: the dead man . . . the mysterious paper . . . the frayed and faded clue leading through the hills of a strange land . . .

'The letter didn't say much,' said Simon. 'But it was–I don't know quite how to describe it–it was excited. Even the writing. I knew Michael pretty well, for all the difference in our ages, and I tell you he was as excited as all-get-out when he wrote that letter. And I think it was something he'd found, somewhere on Parnassus.'

Again that queer little thrill. The night swooped by, full of stars. On our left the mountain loomed like the lost world of the gods. All of a sudden it didn't seem possible that I was here, and that this–this ground where our tyres whispered through the dust–was Parnassus. The name was a shiver up the spine.

I said: 'Yes?' in a very queer voice.

'You must understand,' he said, 'that when I read that letter in the end, I read it against a background of information picked up after the war. We'd found out, my father and I, just where and how Michael had been working, and we'd talked to some of the fellows he'd met here. We were told that he'd been sent up into this area in the spring of 1943, and, for over a year before he was killed, he was working with one of the ELAS bands whose leader was a man called Angelos Dragoumis. I couldn't learn very much about this Angelos–that was the name he was generally known by, and I gather that it was desperately inappropriate–only one of the other Force 133 chaps had actually met him, and the few inquiries I've made here in the last day or so have been quietly stone-walled. The Greeks aren't proud of men like Angelos. I don't mean that his group didn't do one or two brilliant things: they were with Ares and Zervas when the Gorgopotamos viaduct was destroyed in the teeth of the Germans, and there was the affair of the bridge at Lidorikion, where they–oh, well, that doesn't matter just now. The thing is that this man Angelos seems to have rather modelled himself on the ELAS Commander, Ares, and he made himself felt in the country here-abouts just as Ares did.'

'You mean he plundered his own side?'

'That and worse. The usual beastly record of burning and rape and torture and smashed houses, and people–where they weren't murdered–left to starve. The extra unpleasant touch is that Angelos came from this district himself . . . Yes, I know. It's hard to take, isn't it? He's dead, anyway . . . at least, that's the assumption. He vanished across the Yugoslav border when the Communist *putsch* failed in December 1944, and he hasn't been heard of since.'

'I imagine that in any case he'd not dare reappear in these parts,' I said.

'True enough. Well, anyway, that was the man Michael was working with, and, as I say, they did get some pretty good results in the military line–but then the Germans arrived here in force, and Angelos' band scattered and went into hiding in the hills. Michael, I gather, was on his own. He evaded capture for some weeks, hiding somewhere up here on Parnassus. Then one day a patrol spotted him. He got away, but one of their bullets hit him—not a bad wound, but enough to disable him, and with no attention it might have proved serious. One of his contacts was Stephanos, the shepherd from Arachova that we're going to see tonight. Stephanos took Michael in, and he and his wife nursed and hid him and would, I think, have got him out of the country if the Germans hadn't descended on Arachova while Michael was still here.'

Along the road the young cypresses stood like swords. They had come along this very road. I said: 'And they found him.'

'No. But they'd been told he was here, and so they took Stephanos' son Nikolaos out and shot him, because his parents wouldn't give Michael away.'

'Simon!'

He said gently: 'It was a commonplace. You don't know these people yet. They stood and let their families be murdered in front of them rather than betray an ally who'd eaten their salt.'

'The other side of the picture,' I said, thinking of ELAS and Angelos.

'As you say. And when you think harshly of ELAS, remember two things. One is that the Greek is born a fighting animal. Doesn't their magnificent and pathetic history show you that? If a Greek can't find anyone else to fight, he'll fight his neighbour. The other is the poverty of Greece, and to the very poor any creed that brings promise has a quick way to the heart.'

I said: 'I'll remember.'

'Perhaps we've forgotten,' he said, 'what poverty means. When one sees . . . ah, well, never mind now. But I think that most things can be forgiven to the poor.'

I was silent. I was remembering Philip again, and a beggar under the ramparts at Carcassonne; Philip saying 'Good God!' in a shocked voice, dropping five hundred francs into the scrofulous hand, and then forgetting it. And now here was this quiet, easy voice, talking in the dark of past infamies, expressing as a matter of course the sort of enormous and tolerant compassion that I had never met—in the flesh—before . . .

> *Poor naked wretches, wheresoe'er you are,*
> *That bide the pelting of this pitiless storm,*
> *How shall your houseless heads and unfed sides,*
> *Your looped and windowed raggedness, defend you . . .?*

It came to me with a shock like an arrow out of the dark that—mystery or no mystery—I liked Simon Lester very much indeed.

He said: 'What is it?'

'Nothing. Go on. The Germans shot Nikolaos. And Michael left?'

'Yes. Apparently he moved out again into the mountains. After this point I know very little about what happened. So far I've pieced together the bare facts from what we were told after the war by one of the other B.L.O.'s who was over here, and from the priest at Delphi, who wrote to my father some time back, when he was making his first inquiries.'

'Didn't Stephanos write?'

'Stephanos can't write,' said Simon. 'What happened next we can only guess at. Michael went off back into the hills after the tragedy of Nikolaos' death. His shoulder wasn't fully healed, but he was all right. Stephanos and his wife wanted him to stay, but Nikolaos had left a small son and a daughter, and . . . well, Michael said he wasn't risking any more lives. He went. And that's all we know. He went up there—' a gesture towards the shadow-haunted mountain—'and he was caught and killed there, somewhere on Parnassus.'

I said after a minute or two: 'And you want to talk to Stephanos and find out where he is?'

'I know where he is. He's buried at Delphi, in a little graveyard not far from the studio, above the shrine of Apollo. I've been to the grave already. No, that's not what I want from Stephanos. I want to know just where Michael died on Parnassus.'

'Stephanos knows?'

'He found the body. It was he who sent Michael's last letter off, together with the other things he found on the body. He got them smuggled somehow to this other B.L.O., and we got them eventually. We didn't know who'd sent them until later we were officially told that Michael was buried at Delphi. We wrote to the *papas*—the priest. He told us the simple facts, so of course my father wrote to Stephanos, and got a reply through the priest again, and—well, that seemed to be that.'

'Until you saw Michael's letter.'

'Until I saw Michael's letter.'

We had rounded a shadowy bluff, and there ahead, pouring down the mountain-side like a cascade, were the steep lights of Arachova.

The car drew gently in to the side of the road and stopped. Simon switched the engine off and reached into an inner pocket for a wallet. From this he took a piece of paper and handed it to me.

'Wait a moment till I get my lighter to work. Would you like a cigarette?'

'Thank you.'

After we had lighted our cigarettes he held the little flame for me while I unfolded the flimsy paper. It was a scrawl on a single sheet of cheap paper, smudged as if with rain, a bit dirty, torn here and there along the old folds, and dog-eared from being read and re-read. I opened it gently. I had the queerest feeling that I shouldn't have been touching it.

It was fairly short. *Dear Daddy*, it began . . . why should there be something so very endearing about the thought of Michael Lester, a tough twenty-seven, using the childhood's diminutive? . . . *Dear Daddy, God knows when you'll get this, as I see no chance of its getting taken off in the near future, but I've got to write. We've been having a bit of a party, but that's over now and I'm quite all right, so not to worry. I wonder, do you find this code of army-slang clichés as bloodily maddening as I do? At the best of times I suppose it has its uses, but just now – tonight – there is something I really want to say to you: to record, somehow, on paper – nothing to do with the war or my job here or anything like that, but still impossible to commit to paper and how* the hell *can I get it across to you? You know as well as I do that anything might happen before I see anyone I can send a private message by. If my memory were a little better – and if I'd paid a bit more attention to those classical studies (oh God, a world ago!) I might send you to the right bit in Callimachus. I think it's Callimachus. But I've forgotten where it comes. I'll have to leave it at that. However, I'm seeing a man I can trust tomorrow, and I'll tell him, come what may. And all being well, this'll be over some day soon, and we'll come back here together to the bright citadel, and I can show you then – and little brother Simon, too. How is he? Give him my love. Till the day – and what a day it'll be!*

> *Your loving son,*
> *Michael.*

The signature was a scrawl, running down almost off the page. I folded the paper carefully, and gave it back to Simon. He snapped the lighter out, and put the letter carefully away. He said: 'You see what I mean?'

'Well, I didn't know your brother, but I take it that wasn't his usual style.'

'Far from it. This reads very oddly to me. Queer, rapid, allusive;

almost—if I didn't know Michael so well—hysterical. A feminine type of letter.'

'I see what you mean.'

He laughed, and started the engine. 'Sorry. But it's my guess he really was under some strong emotion when he wrote that letter.'

'I think I'd agree. Of course he was in a tough spot, and—'

'He'd been in dozens before. And then all that about a private message, and "getting it across". He really had something to say.'

'Yes. I take it you've had a look through your Callimachus, whoever he may be?'

'I have. He wrote a deuce of a lot. No, there's no clue there.'

'And the "bright citadel"?'

'That's a translation of a phrase the Delphic Oracle once used to Julian the Apostate. I think that must be the one he means. It refers to Apollo's shrine at Delphi.'

'I see. That doesn't get us much further.'

We were moving again towards the lights of Arachova. I said: 'You used the word "clue". Just what are you hoping to find, Simon?'

'What Michael found.'

After a little pause I said slowly: 'Yes, I see. You mean the bit about "we'll come back here together to the bright citadel and I'll show you"?'

'Yes. He'd found something and he was excited about it and he wanted to "record" it—he uses that word, too, remember?'

'Yes. But don't you think that perhaps—?' I stopped.

'Well?'

I said, with some difficulty: 'Might you not be seeing something that isn't there? I do agree it's an odd letter, but there's another way of reading it, isn't there? A quite simple way. It's the way that I'd have taken it myself . . . except of course that I didn't know your brother Michael.'

'And that way?'

'Well, say it *was* excitement, or rather emotion, of a sort, wouldn't there be a reason for it? Might he not quite naturally have things he wanted to say to your father and to you? I mean . . .' I stopped again, embarrassed.

He said simply: 'You mean it was plain and simple affection? That Michael may have had a premonition he'd not get out of the jam he was in, and wanted to say something to my father . . . a sort of farewell? No . . . no, Camilla, not Michael. If he felt very deeply about people he kept it to himself. Nor do I think he'd dabble in "premonitions". He knew the risks, and he didn't fuss. Besides he does say he wants to "show" Father something, and me . . . here, in Greece.'

'Perhaps the country itself. Heaven knows it's exciting enough. Would your father have been interested?'

Simon laughed. 'He was a classicist too. He'd been here half a score of times before.'

'Oh. Oh, I see. Yes, that does make a difference.'

'I think so. No, I'm right. He'd found something, Camilla.' A tiny pause, and that electric thrill again, which quivered to nothing as Simon added flatly: 'I'm pretty certain I know what it was, too, but I could bear to make sure. And for a start, I'd like to know just where Michael died, and how . . .'

Another pause. He must have been thinking back to my remarks about the letter, for he said thoughtfully: 'No, all things taken together, I know I'm right. Though it does seem a little odd . . . You may be right about the "emotion"–though it wouldn't be like Mick. He was the most casual-seeming devil to talk to that you ever knew. It took quite some time before you guessed that he was probably the toughest, too, and the most self-sufficient.'

Like little brother Simon . . . The thought came so pat and so clearly that for one terrible moment I was afraid I had said it aloud. And I had an uncomfortable feeling that he knew just what I was thinking.

I said quickly and idiotically: 'Here's Arachova.'

It was one of the rather less necessary remarks. Already we were hemmed in by the crowding walls, and the coloured rugs–still hanging outside the vividly-lit shops–almost brushed the sides of the car. There were two or three donkeys, freed from rope and saddle, wandering loose in the street. I saw a goat on someone's garden wall. It gave us an evil, gleaming glance before it leaped away into shadow and vanished. There was the familiar smell of dust and dung and petrol fumes and the lees of wine.

Simon parked the car in the place where it had been that afternoon. He stopped the engine and we got out. We walked back towards the steep alley-way, where I had first seen him. Opposite the foot of it was one of the village cafés, a dozen tables in a white-washed room open to the road. Most of the tables were full. The men watched us . . . or rather, they didn't look at me. They all watched Simon.

He paused at the foot of the alley and put a hand under my elbow.

I saw that light, wary look touch the groups of dark-faced men, linger, leave them. He smiled down at me.

'Up here,' he said, 'and watch where you go. The steps are tricky and the donkeys have provided a few extra natural hazards. Stephanos, naturally, lives at the very top.'

I looked up. The alley was about four feet wide and had a gradient of one in three. The steps were just too far apart and were made of sharp chunks of Parnassus with the minimum of dressing. The donkeys—a herd of healthy donkeys—had been that way many times. There was one dim light halfway up.

For some reason it occurred to me at that moment to wonder just what I had got myself into. ELAS, Stephanos, a man called Michael dying on Parnassus and lying bleaching to earth again above Delphi . . . all this, out of nowhere, and now a steep dark little alley and the pressure of Simon's hand on my arm. I wondered sharply just what we were going to learn from Stephanos.

And suddenly, I knew that I didn't want to hear it.

'*Avanti,*' said Simon beside me, sounding amused.

I pushed the coward impulse aside, and started up the alley-way.

Chapter 6

. . . Seek
Thy brother with a tale that must be heard
Howe'er it sicken

EURIPIDES: *Electra.*
(tr. Gilbert Murray.)

STEPHANOS' HOUSE WAS a small two-storied building, set at the top of the stairway. Its bottom storey opened straight on the alley, and housed the beasts—a donkey and two goats and a gaggle of skinny hens—while stone stairs led up the outer wall of the house to the top storey where the family lived. At the head of the steps a wide concrete platform served as porch and garden in one. Its low parapet was crowded with pots full of greenery, and roofed with a trellis of rough branches which formed a pergola for the vine. I saw Simon stoop to avoid a loaded bough, and a hanging bunch of grapes brushed my cheek with a cold gentle touch. The top half of the door was open, and the light streamed out to gild the vine tendrils. There was a hot oily smell from the family's supper, mixed with goat, and donkey, and the furry musk-smell of geraniums where I had brushed a hand against one of the flower-pots.

We had been heard coming up the steps. As we crossed the platform the lower half of the door opened, and an old man stood there, large against the weak light from within.

I paused. Simon was behind me, still in shadow. I moved aside to let him pass me, and he came forward, hand outstretched, with some greeting in Greek. I saw the old man stiffen as he peered out. His mouth opened as if to make some involuntary exclamation, then he seemed to draw back a little. He said formally: 'Brother of Michael, you are welcome. The woman of the house said you would come tonight.'

Simon withdrew the hand that the old man hadn't appeared to notice, and said, with equal formality: 'My name is Simon. I'm glad to meet you, *Kyrie* Stephanos. This is *Kyria* Haven, a friend who has brought me down in her car.'

The old man's look touched me, no more. He inclined his head, saying slowly: 'You are both welcome. Be pleased to come in.'

He turned then and went into the room.

I should perhaps make it clear here that this and most of the subsequent conversation was in Greek, and that, therefore, I didn't understand it. But afterwards Simon gave me as exact a translation as he could, and at the time I was able to follow what I may perhaps call the emotional movements of the conversation. So I shall set the interview down as it occurred.

It seemed apparent to me, from the first short exchange on the balcony, that our welcome wasn't exactly a glowing one, and this surprised me. I had seen during my stay in Greece so much of the miracle of Greek hospitality, that I was both disconcerted and repelled. It didn't worry me that Stephanos hadn't spoken to me – I was only a woman, after all, and as such had pretty low social rating – but his rejection of Simon's outstretched hand had been quite deliberate, and his gesture now, as he invited us to follow him in, was heavy and (it seemed) reluctant.

I hesitated, glancing at Simon doubtfully.

He didn't appear to be in the least put out. He merely lifted an eyebrow at me, and waited for me to precede him into the house.

The single living- and sleeping-room of the house was high and square. The floor was of scrubbed boards, the walls whitewashed and hung with vivid holy pictures in appalling colours. Light came from a single naked electric bulb. In one corner stood an old-fashioned oil-stove, and above it shelves for pans and a blue curtain that no doubt concealed food and crockery. Against one wall was an immense bed, covered now with a brown blanket and obviously used during the day as a sofa. Above the bed hung a small icon of the Virgin and Child, with a red electric bulb glowing in front of it. A Victorian-looking cupboard, a scrubbed table, a couple of kitchen chairs and a bench covered with cheap American-cloth made up the rest of the furniture. A note of vivid colour was supplied by the one rug on the boarded floor. It was locally woven, in brilliant scarlet and parrot-green. The room had the air of great poverty and an almost fierce cleanliness.

There was an old woman sitting over near the stove on one of the hard chairs. I took her to be Stephanos' wife—the woman of the house. She was dressed in black, and even in the house wore the Moslem-looking headscarf, which veils mouth and chin, and which gives the field-workers of Greece such an Eastern look. It was pulled down now below her chin, and I could see her face. She looked very old, as the peasant-women of the hot countries do. Her face had lovely bones, fine and regular, but the skin had dried into a thousand wrinkles, and her teeth had decayed. She smiled at me and made a gesture of shy welcome, to which I responded with a sort of bow and an embarrassed 'Good evening' in Greek, as I took the chair she indicated. She made no further move to greet us, and I noticed that her look in reply to Simon's greeting was uneasy, almost scared. Her gnarled hands moved in her lap, and then she dropped her eyes to them and kept them there.

Simon had taken the other chair near the door, and the old man sat down on the bench. I found myself staring at him. So much a part of the land of myth was he that he might have come straight out of Homer. His face was brown, wrinkled like the woman's, and in expression patriarchal and benevolent. The white hair and beard were curled like those of the great Zeus in the Athens Museum. He was dressed in a sort of long tunic of faded blue, buttoned close down the front and reaching to his thighs; beneath it he wore what looked like white cotton jodhpurs bound at the knee with black bands. On his head was a small soft black cap. The knotted powerful hands looked as if they were uneasy without a crook to grasp.

He looked at Simon under thick white brows, ignoring me. The look was grave and—I thought—measuring. In the corner beside me the old woman sat silent. I could hear the animals moving about below us, and the quick tread of someone coming up the alley from the street.

Stephanos had just opened his mouth to speak, when there was an interruption. The quick steps outside mounted the stone stairs at a run. A youth came across the balcony with a rush and paused in the doorway, one hand on the jamb of the door, the other thrust into his waistband. It was a very dramatic pose, and he was a very dramatic young man. He was about eighteen, lean and brown and beautiful, with thick black curls and a vivid, excited face. He wore ancient striped flannels, and the loudest and most awful Teddy-boy shirt I have ever seen.

He said: 'Grandfather? He's come?'

Then he saw Simon. He didn't appear to notice me at all, but I was getting used to that, and merely sat quiet, like the woman of the house. The boy flashed a delighted smile at Simon, and a flood of rapid Greek, which was interrupted by his grandfather's saying repressively: 'Who told you to come, Niko?'

Niko whirled back to him. All his movements were swift like those of a graceful but restless young cat. 'They told me at Lefteris' that he had come again. I wanted to see him.'

'And now you see him. Sit down and be silent, Niko. We have much to say.'

I saw Niko throw a quick appraising glance at Simon. 'Have you told him?'

'I have told him nothing. Sit down and be silent.'

Niko turned to obey, but his look lingered on Simon. The dark eyes glinted with something that could have been excitement mixed with amusement—or even malice. Simon met it with that masked indifferent look that I was beginning to know. He had taken out his cigarette case and now he glanced at me. I shook my head. 'Niko?' The boy put out a hand, then stopped, drew it back, and sent Simon another of his vivid smiles. 'No, thank you, *kyrie.*' A glance at his grandfather, then he crossed to the big bed and threw himself on it. Simon found his lighter, lit a cigarette with a certain deliberation, then put the lighter carefully back in his pocket before he turned to Stephanos.

The latter was sitting motionless. He still didn't speak. The silence came back, heavy, charged, and the boy stirred restlessly on the bed. His eyes never left Simon's face. Beside me the woman hadn't moved, but as I glanced at her I saw her eyes slide sideways to meet mine, only to drop swiftly to the hands in her lap as if in an ecstasy of shyness. I realised then that she had been covertly studying my frock, and the knowledge came to me suddenly, warmingly, that Stephanos, too, was shy.

Perhaps Simon had divined this, too, for he didn't wait for Stephanos, but spoke easily, bridging the moment.

'*Kyrie* Stephanos, I'm glad to meet you at last, and the woman of your house. My father and I wrote to you to thank you for what you did for my brother, but—well, letters can't say it all. My father is dead now, but I'm speaking for him, too, when I say thank you again. You'll understand it isn't always possible to put into words all that one feels—all one would like to say—but I think you will understand what I feel, and what my father felt.' He turned his head to smile at the woman. She didn't smile back. I thought she made a little sound as if of pain, and she moved in her chair. Her narrow lips worked in and out, and her fingers gripped each other painfully.

Stephanos said, almost roughly: 'There is nothing for you to say, *kyrie*. We did no more than we should.'

'It was a very great deal,' said Simon gently. 'You couldn't have done more if he, too, had been your son.' A quick glance at the old woman. 'I shan't say much about that, *kyria*, because there are memories that you won't want to revive; and I shall try not to ask any questions that might distress you. But I had to come and thank you, for my father, and for myself . . . and to see the house where my brother Michael found friends in the last days of his life.'

He paused, and looked round him slowly. There was silence again. Below us the animals shuffled and one of them sneezed. There was nothing in Simon's face to read, but I saw the boy's glinting glance on him again before it turned as if in impatience to his grandfather. But Stephanos said nothing.

At length Simon said: 'So it was here.'

'It was here, *kyrie*. Below, behind the manger, there is a gap in the wall. He hid there. The dirty Germans did not think to look behind the sacks of straw, and the dung. Would you like me to show you?'

Simon shook his head. 'No. I told you I don't want to remind you of that day. And I don't think I need ask you anything much about it, as you told us most of it in the letter that the *papas* wrote for you. You told me how Michael had been wounded in the shoulder and had come here for shelter, and how, after . . . later on, he went back into the mountains.'

'It was just before dawn,' said the old man, 'on the second of October. We begged him to stay with us, because he was not yet well, and the wet weather comes early in the mountains. But he would not. He helped us to bury my son Nikolaos, and then he went.' He nodded towards the intent youth on the bed. 'There was that one, you understand, and his sister Maria, who is since married to Georgios who has a shop in the village. When the Germans came the children were out in the fields with their mother, or who knows? They, too, might have been killed. *Kyrios* Michael'—he pronounced it as a trisyllable, Mi-ha-eel—'would not stay, because of them. He went up into the mountain.'

'Yes. A few days later he was killed. You found his body somewhere over between here and Delphi, and you took it down to be buried.'

'That is so. What I found on his body I gave after three weeks to

Perikles Grivas, and he took it to an Englishman who was going by night from Galaxidion. But this you know.'

'This I know. I want you to show me where he was killed, Stephanos.'

There was a short silence. The boy Niko watched Simon unwinkingly. I noticed that he had taken out a cigarette of his own and was smoking it.

The old man said heavily: 'I will do that, of course. Tomorrow?'

'If it's convenient.'

'For you, it is convenient.'

'You're very good.'

'You are the brother of Michael.'

Simon said gently: 'He was here a long time, wasn't he?'

Beside me the woman moved suddenly and said in a clear soft voice: 'He was my son.' I saw with a wrench of discomfort that there were tears on her cheeks. 'He should have stayed,' she said, and then repeated it almost desperately: 'He should have stayed.'

Simon said: 'But he had to go. How could he stay and put you and your family in that danger again? When the Germans came back –'

'They didn't come back.' It was Niko who spoke, clearly, from the bed.

'No.' Simon turned his head. 'Because they caught Michael in the mountains. But if they hadn't caught him – if he had still been hiding here – they might have come back to the village, and then –'

'They did not catch him,' said the old man.

Simon turned back sharply. Stephanos was sitting still on the bench, knees apart, hands clasped between them, his heavy body bent slightly forward. His eyes looked fathoms dark under the white brows. The two men stared at one another. I found myself stirring on my hard chair. It was as if the scene were taking place in slow-motion, silent and incomprehensible, yet powered with emotions that plucked uncomfortably at the nerves.

Simon said slowly: 'What are you trying to tell me?'

'Only,' said Stephanos, 'that Michael was not killed by the Germans. He was killed by a Greek.'

'By a Greek?' Simon echoed it almost blankly.

The old man made a gesture that might have come straight from *Oedipus Rex*. To me, still not understanding anything except that the men's talk had an overtone of tragedy, it conveyed a curiously powerful impression of resignation and shame.

'By a man from Arachova,' he said.

It was at this moment that the light chose to go out.

*   *   *

The Greeks were obviously accustomed to the whims of the electric system. With scarcely a moment's delay the old woman had found and lit an oil-lamp, and placed it on the table in the middle of the room. It was a frightful-looking lamp of some cheap bright metal, but it burned with a soft apricot light and the sweet smell of olive-oil. With the heavy shadows cast on his face, Stephanos looked more than ever like a tragic actor. Niko had rolled over on his stomach and was watching the two other men bright-eyed, as if it were indeed a play. I supposed that for him his father's death was so remote that this talk of it was no more than a breath from an exciting past.

Simon was saying: 'I . . . see. That makes a lot of things a lot plainer. And of course you don't know who it was.'

'Indeed we do.'

Simon's brows shot up. The old man smiled sourly. 'You are wondering why we have not killed him, *kyrie*, when we called Michael our son?'

From the bed Niko said in a smooth voice that was certainly malicious: 'That is not the way the English work, Grandfather.'

Simon flicked him a look but said, mildly, to Stephanos: 'Not exactly. I was wondering what had happened to him. I gather he's alive.'

'I'll explain. I should tell you first of all that the man's name was Dragoumis. Angelos Dragoumis.'

'*Angelos?*'

The old man nodded. 'Yes. You know of him, of course, I told you in the letter the *papas* wrote for me that Michael had worked with him. But I should never have told you this of Angelos, if you had not come. Now that you are here, these things cannot be hidden. It is your right to know.'

Simon was carefully extinguishing his cigarette in the lid of a match-box. His face was still and shuttered, his eyes hidden. I saw the boy Niko roll over again on the bed and grin to himself.

'You know that Angelos was the leader of the ELAS troop that Michael was working with,' said Stephanos. 'When Michael left here he went up, I think, with the intention of rejoining them. They had scattered when the big German search operation started in the hills, and most of them had moved north, Angelos with them. What brought Angelos back in this direction I don't know, but certain it is that he fetched up against Michael over on Parnassus and murdered him there.'

'Why?'

'I do not know. Except that such murders were not rare in those days. It may be that Michael and Angelos had had some quarrel over the action of Angelos' troops. Perhaps Michael was putting too much pressure on him; we know now that Angelos was anxious to save his men and his supplies for a different battle later—after the Germans had gone.'

I saw Simon look up sharply, those light-grey eyes vividly intent. 'Angelos was one of them? Are you sure?'

'Certain. He played for high stakes, did Angelos Dragoumis. He was in Athens soon after the Germans had left Greece, and we knew he was active in the massacre at Kalamai. Oh yes, you may be sure that he was betraying the Allies all the time.'

He smiled thinly. 'I do not think that Michael can have known. No, this was some other quarrel. It may simply have been that two such men could never come together, and agree. Angelos was bad, bad from the heart, and Michael . . . he did not like having to work with such a one. They had quarrelled before. He told me so. Angelos was an arrogant man, and a bully, and Michael—well, Michael could not be driven either.'

'True enough.' Simon was selecting another cigarette. 'But you said he was "murdered". If two men quarrel and there's a fight, that isn't murder, Stephanos.'

'It was murder. It was a fight, but not a fair one. Michael had been wounded, remember.'

'Even so—'

'He was struck from behind first, with a stone or with the butt of a gun. There was a great mark there, and the skin was broken. It is a miracle that the blow didn't kill him, or stun him at least. But he must have heard Angelos behind him, and turned, because in spite of the traitor's blow from behind, and Michael's wounded shoulder, there was a fight. Michael was—a good deal marked.'

'I see.' Simon was lighting his cigarette. 'How did Angelos kill him? I take it he wasn't using a gun. A knife?'

'His neck was broken.'

The lighter paused, an inch from Simon's cigarette. The grey eyes lifted to the old man's. I couldn't see their expression from where I sat, but I saw Stephanos nod, once, as Zeus might have nodded. Niko's eyes narrowed suddenly and glinted between their long lashes. The lighter made contact. 'It must have been quite a scrap,' said Simon.

'He wouldn't be easy to kill,' said the old man. 'But with the wounded shoulder, and the blow on the head . . .'

His voice trailed off. He wasn't looking at Simon now; he seemed to be seeing something beyond the lamplit walls of the room, something remote in place and time.

There was a pause. Then Simon blew out a long cloud of tobacco-smoke. 'Yes,' he said. 'Well. And the man Angelos . . . what happened to him?'

'That I can't tell you. He has not been back to Arachova, naturally. It was said that he went with many of his kind into Yugoslavia, when their bid for power failed. In fourteen years nobody has heard of him, and it is probable that he is dead. He had only one relative, a cousin Dimitrios Dragoumis, who has had no news of him.'

'A cousin? Here?'

'Dragoumis lives now at Itea. He also fought in Angelos' troop, but he was not a leader, and—well, some things are best forgotten.' The old man's voice roughened. 'But the things that Angelos did to his own people, these are not forgotten. He was at Kalamai; it is said he was also at Pyrgos, where many hundred Greeks died, and among them my own cousin Panos, an old man.' The gnarled hands moved convulsively on his knees. 'No matter of that . . . But I do not speak merely of his politics, *Kyrie* Simon, or even of what such as he do in war. He was evil, *kyrie*, he was a man who delighted in evil. He liked the sight of pain. He liked best to hurt children and old women, and he boasted like Ares of how many he himself had killed. He would put a man's eyes out—or a woman's—and smile while he did it. Always that smile. He was an evil man, and he betrayed Michael and murdered him.'

'And if he has not been seen here since my brother died, how can you be sure he murdered him?'

'I saw him,' said the old man simply.

'*You saw him?*'

'Yes. It was he beyond doubt. When I came on them he turned and ran. But I couldn't follow him.' He paused again, one of those heavy terrible little pauses. 'You see, Michael was still alive.'

I saw Simon's eyes jerk up again to meet his. The old man nodded. 'Yes. He lived only a minute or so. But it was enough to hold me there beside him and let Angelos get away.'

'Angelos made no attempt to attack you?'

'None. He, too, had been badly mauled.' There was satisfaction in the old shepherd's eyes. 'Michael died hard, even with that traitor's bash on the back of the head. Angelos might have shot at me, but later I found his revolver lying under a boulder, as if it had been flung there in the struggle. The countryside was full of Germans, you see, and he must have counted on killing Michael quietly, after he'd stunned him, but he wasn't quick or clever enough, and Michael managed to turn on him. When I came to the head of the cliff and saw them below me, Angelos was just getting to his feet. He turned to look for his gun then, but my dog attacked him, and it was all he could do to get clear away. Without his gun, he could have done nothing.' He wiped his mouth with the back of a knotted brown hand. 'I took Michael down to Delphi. It was the nearest. That's all.'

'He didn't speak?'

Stephanos hesitated, and Simon's glance sharpened. Stephanos shook his head. 'It was nothing, *kyrie*. If there had been anything I would have put it in the letter.'

'But he did speak?'

'Two words. He said: *"the Charioteer"*.'

The words were *'o eniochos'*, and they were classical, not modern, Greek. They were also familiar to me, as to many visitors to Delphi, because they refer to the famous bronze statue that stands in the Delphi Museum. It is the statue of a youth, the Charioteer, robed in a stiffly pleated robe, still holding in his hands the reins of his vanished horses. I glanced at Simon, wondering where, in an exchange bristling with the names *Angelos*, and *Michael*, the Charioteer could have a place.

Simon was looking as puzzled as I. ' "The Charioteer"? Are you sure?'

'I am not quite sure. I had run hard down the path to the foot of the cliff, and I was out of breath and much distressed. He lived only a matter of seconds after I got to him. But he knew me, and I thought that was what he said. It is a classical word, but of course it is familiar because it is used of the statue in the Delphi Museum. But why Michael should have tried to tell me about that I do not know. If indeed that was what he whispered.' He straightened his back a little. 'I repeat, I would have told you if I had been sure, or if it had meant anything.'

'Why did you not tell us about Angelos?'

'It was over then, and he had gone, and it was better to let Michael's father think he had died in battle and not at the hand of a traitor. Besides,' said Stephanos simply, 'we were ashamed.'

'It was so much over,' said Simon, 'that when Michael's brother comes to Arachova to find out just how his brother died, the men in Arachova avoid him, and his host won't shake his hand.'

The old man smiled. 'Very well then. It is not over. The shame remains.'

'The shame isn't yours.'

'It is that of Greece.'

'My country's done a thing or two lately to balance it, Stephanos.'

'Politics!' The old man made a gesture highly expressive of what he would wish to see done to all politicians, and Simon laughed. As if at a signal, the old woman got to her feet, pulled back the blue curtain, and brought out a big stone jar. She put glasses on the table and began to pour out the dark sweet wine. Stephanos said: 'You will drink with us, then?'

'With the greatest of pleasure,' said Simon. The old woman handed him a glass, then Stephanos, Niko, and finally me. She didn't take one herself, but remained standing, watching me with a sort of shy pleasure. I sipped the wine. It was as dark as mavrodaphne and tasted of cherries. I smiled at her over the glass and said tentatively, in Greek: 'It's very good.'

Her face split into a wide smile. She bobbed her head and repeated delightedly: 'Very good, very good,' and Niko turned over on the bed and said in American-accented English: 'You speak Greek, miss?'

'No. Only a few words.'

He turned to Simon. 'How come you speak such good Greek, eh?'

'My brother Michael taught me when I was younger than you. I went on learning and reading it afterwards. I knew I would come here one day.'

'Why you not come before?'

'It costs too much, Niko.'

'And now you are rich, eh?'

'I get by.'

'Oriste?'

'I mean, I have enough.'

'I see.' The dark eyes widened in a limpid look. 'And now you have come. You know about Angelos and your brother. What would you say if I told you something else, *kyrie*?'

'What?'

'That Angelos is still alive?'

Simon said slowly. 'Are you telling me that, Niko?'

'He has been seen near Delphi, on the mountain.'

'What? Recently?' said Simon sharply.

'Oh, yes.' Niko flashed that beautiful malicious smile up at him. 'But perhaps it is only a ghost. There are ghosts on Parnassus, *kyrie*, lights that move and voices that carry across the rocks. There are those who see these things. Myself, no. Is it the old gods, not?'

'Possibly,' said Simon. 'Is this the truth, Niko? That Angelos was seen?'

Niko shrugged. 'How can I tell? It was Janis who saw him, and Janis is–' He made a significant gesture towards his forehead. 'Angelos killed his mother when the *andartes* burned his father's farm, and ever since then Janis has been queer in the head, and has "seen" Angelos–oh, many times. If ghosts are true, then he still walks on Parnassus. But Dimitrios Dragoumis–that is true enough. He has asked many questions about your coming. All the men here in Arachova know that you are coming, and they talk about it and wonder–but Dragoumis, he has been to Delphi and to Arachova and has asked questions–oh, many questions.'

'What is he like?'

'He is a little like his cousin. Not in the face, but in the–what do you say?–the build. But not in the spirit either.' His look was innocent. 'It may be that you will meet Dragoumis. But do not be afraid of him. And do not worry yourself about Angelos, *Kyrie* Simon.'

Simon grinned. 'Do I look as if I was worrying?'

'No,' said Niko frankly, 'but then, he is dead.'

'And if Janis is right, and he is not dead?'

'I think,' said Niko almost insolently, 'that you are only an Englishman, *Kyrie* Simon. Not?'

'So what?'

Niko gave a charming little crack of laughter and rolled over on the bed. Stephanos said suddenly and angrily, in Greek: 'Niko, behave yourself. What does he say, *Kyrie* Simon?'

'He thinks I couldn't deal with Angelos,' said Simon idly. 'Here, Niko, catch.' He threw the boy a cigarette. Niko fielded it with a

graceful clawed gesture. He was still laughing. Simon turned to
Stephanos: 'Do you think it's true that Angelos has been seen
hereabouts?'

The old shepherd slanted a fierce look at his grandson under his
white brows. 'So he has told you that tale, has he? Some rumour
started by an idiot who has seen Angelos at least a dozen times since
the end of the war. Aye, and Germans, too, a score of times. Don't
pay any attention to *that* moonshine.'

Simon laughed. 'Or to the lights and voices on Parnassus?'

Stephanos said: 'If a man goes up into Parnassus after sunset, why
should he not see strange things? The gods still walk there, and a
man who would not go carefully in the country of the gods is a fool.'
Another of those glowering looks at his grandson. 'You, Niko, have
learned a lot of folly in Athens. And that is a terrible shirt.'

Niko sat up straight. 'It is not!' he protested, stung. 'It is
American!'

Stephanos snorted and Simon grinned. 'Aid to Greece?'

The old man gave a gruff bark of laughter. 'He is not a bad boy,
kyrie, even if Athens has spoiled him. But now he comes home to
work, and I will make a man of him. Give *Kyrios* Simon some more
wine.' This to his wife, who hurried to refill Simon's glass.

'Thank you.' Simon added, in a different tone: 'Is it true that this
man Dragoumis had been asking questions about me?'

'Quite true. After it was known that you were coming, he asked
many questions—when you came, for how long, what you meant to do,
and all that.' He smiled sourly. 'I don't speak much to that one, me.'

'But why? Why should he be interested? Do you suppose he had
anything to do with Michael's death?'

'He had nothing to do with it. That much we found out after the
war, before he came back here. Otherwise he would not,' said
Stephanos simply, 'have dared come back. No, he knew nothing
about it. Once before, a year—more—eighteen months ago—he spoke
to me and asked me what had happened, and where it was that
Michael was killed. He showed a decent shame and he spoke well of
Michael; but I do not talk of my sons to every man. I refused to
speak of it. And no one else knew the whole truth except the priest at
Delphi who is since dead, and my own brother Alkis who was killed
in the war.'

'And now me.'

'And now you. I will take you there tomorrow and show you the
place. It is your right.'

He looked up under the white brows at Simon for another considering moment. Then he said slowly, irrelevantly: 'I think, *Kyrie* Simon, that you are very like Michael. And Niko – Niko is even more of a fool than I had thought . . .'

Chapter 7

The oracles are dumb,
No voice or hideous hum
Runs through the arched roof in words deceiving.
Apollo *from his shrine*
Can no more divine . . .

MILTON: *Nativity Hymn.*

SIMON DIDN'T SPEAK on the way back to Delphi, so I sat quietly beside him, wondering what had been said in that sombre and somehow very foreign-seeming interview. Nothing that Stephanos—exotically Homeric—had said could have been ordinary, while about Niko's racy intelligent beauty there was something essentially Greek—a quicksilver quality that is as evident today under the cheaply Americanised trappings of his kind as it was in the black and red of the classical vase-paintings.

When at length, as we neared Delphi, trees crowded in above the road blocking out the starlight, Simon slowed the car, drove into a wide bay, and stopped. He switched the engine off. Immediately the sound of running water filled the air. He turned out the lights, and the dark trees crowded closer. I could smell the pines, cool and pungent. They loomed thick in the starlight, rank on rank of scented stone-pines crowding up towards the cleft where the water sprang. Beyond the trees reared the immense darkness of rock, the Shining Ones no longer shining, but pinnacles and towers of imminent blackness.

Simon took out cigarettes and offered one to me. 'How much of that did you understand?'

'Nothing whatever, except that you were talking about Michael and the ELAS leader Angelos.' I smiled. 'I see now why you didn't mind my sitting in on your private affairs.'

He said abruptly: 'They've taken a very queer turn.'
I waited.
'I'd like to tell you, if I may.'
'Of course.'
So we sat there in the car and smoked, while he told me, fully and accurately, what had passed in the shepherd's cottage. So vivid were my own visual impressions of the recent scene that I was able without difficulty to impose my picture, so to speak, over his, and see where movement and gesture had fitted in with the words.

When he had finished I didn't speak, for the sufficient reason that I could find nothing to say. The instinct that had halted me at the foot of the alley steps had been a true one: these waters were too deep for me. If I had felt myself inadequate before—I, who had been afraid of a mild skirmish over a hired car—what was I to feel now? Who was I to offer comfort or even comment on a brother's murder? The murder might be fourteen years old, but there's a kind of shock in the very word, let alone the knowledge of the deed, however many years lie between it and the discovery. I didn't know Simon well enough to say the right thing, so I said nothing.

He himself made no comment, beyond telling me the story of the interview in that give-nothing-away voice of his that I was beginning to know. I did wonder fleetingly if he would say anything more about Michael's letter, or about the 'find' which he, Simon, had said he knew of . . . But he said nothing. He threw his finished cigarette over the side of the car into the dust, and it appeared that he threw the story with it, because he said, with a complete change of tone and subject:

'Shall we walk up through the ruins? You haven't seen them yet, and starlight's not a bad start. Unless of course you'd rather wait and see them for the first time alone—'
'No. I'd like to go.'
We went up the steep path through the pines. Now that my eyes were used to the darkness it was just possible to see the way. We crossed the narrow rush of water and were on a track soft with pine-needles.

After a while we came out from under the trees into an open space where fallen blocks made treacherous walking, and dimly in the starlight I could see the shape of ruined walls.

'The Roman market-place,' said Simon. 'Those were shops and so on over there. By Delphi's standards this is modern stuff, so we by-pass it quickly . . . Here we are. This is the gate of the temple precinct. The step's steep, but there's a wide smooth way up through the building to the temple itself. Can you see?'

'Fairly well. It's rather . . . stupendous by starlight, isn't it?'

Dimly I could make out the paved road that zigzagged up between the ruined walls of treasuries and shrines. The precinct seemed in this light enormous. Everywhere ahead of us, along the hillside, below among the pines that edged the road, above as far as the eye could reach in the starlight, loomed the broken walls, the spectral pillars, the steps and pedestals and altars of the ancient sanctuary. We walked slowly up the Sacred Way. I could make out the little Doric building that once housed the Athenian treasure, the grim stone where the Sybil sat to foretell the Trojan War, the slender pillars of the Portico of the Athenians, the shape of a great altar . . . then we had reached the temple itself, a naked and broken floor, half up the mountain-side, held there in space by its massive retaining-walls, and bordered with the six great columns that even in the darkness stood emphatic against the star-crowded sky.

I took a little breath.

Beside me, Simon quoted softly: ' "The gods still walk there, and a man who would not go carefully in the country of the gods is a fool." '

'They *are* still here,' I said. 'Is it silly of me? But they are.'

'Three thousand years,' he said. 'Wars, treachery, earthquake, slavery, oblivion. And men still recognise them here. No, it's not silly of you. It happens to everyone with intelligence and imagination. This is Delphi . . . and, well, we're not the first to hear the chariot-wheels. Not by a long way.'

'It's the only place in Greece I've really heard them. I've tried to imagine things—oh, you know how one does. But no, nothing, really, even on Delos. There are ghosts at Mycenae, but it's not the same . . .'

'Poor human ghosts,' he said. 'But here . . . I suppose that if a place was, like Delphi, a centre of worship for—how many?—about two thousand years, something remains. Something inheres in stone, I'll swear, and here it's in the very air. The effect's helped by the landscape: I suppose it must be one of the most magnificent in the world. And of course this is just the setting for the holy place. Come up into the temple.'

A ramp led up to the temple floor, which was paved with great stone blocks, some broken and dangerous. We picked our way carefully across this until we stood at the edge of the floor, between the columns. Below us was the sheer drop of the retaining-wall; below that the steep mountain-side and the ghosts of the scattered shrines. The far valley was an immensity of darkness, filled with the small movements of the night wind, and the sound of pine and olive.

Simon's cigarette beside me glowed and faded. I saw that he had turned his back on the spaces of the starlit valley. He was leaning against a column, gazing up the hill behind the temple. I could see nothing there, but the thick shadows of trees, and against them more pale shapes of stone.

'What's up there?'

'That's where they found the Charioteer.'

The word brought me back to the present with the tingle of a small electric shock. I had forgotten, in the over-powering discovery of Delphi, that Simon would have other preoccupations.

I hesitated; it was he, after all, who had sheered away from the story on to the neutral ground of Delphi. I said a little awkwardly: 'Do you suppose Stephanos was right? Does it make any kind of sense to you?'

'None at all,' he said cheerfully. His shoulder came away from the pillar. 'Why don't you come up to the studio now, and meet Nigel, and have some coffee or a drink?'

'I'd like to, of course, but isn't it awfully late?'

'Not for this country. As far as I can make out nobody goes to bed at all, except in the afternoons. When in Greece, you know . . . Are you tired?'

'Not a bit. I keep feeling I ought to be, but I'm not.'

He laughed. 'It's the air, or the light, or the simple intoxication of being alive in Hellas. It lasts, too. Then you will come?'

'I should love to.'

As I picked my way across the temple floor with his hand under my arm I had time to feel surprise at myself, and a sort of resignation. Here I went again, I reflected . . . Just in this way I had drifted along at Philip's bidding, in Philip's wake. But this was different. Just what the difference was I didn't stop to analyse.

I said: 'Aren't we going down to the road? Why this way?'

'We don't need to go down. The studio's away up above the temple, just over the mountain's shoulder towards Delphi. It's easier to go up through the rest of the shrine.'

'But the car?'

'I'll go and get it later when I've seen you down to your hotel. It's no distance from there by the road. This way, and watch your step.

It's easier here . . . These steps lead up towards the little theatre.
That thing on the right was put up by Alexander the Great after a
narrow escape in a lion-hunt . . . Here's the theatre. It's tiny
compared with Athens or Epidaurus, but isn't it a gem?'

In the starlight the broken floor looked smooth. The semi-circular
tiers of seats rose, seemingly new and unbroken, towards their
back-drop of holly-oak and cypress; it lay, a little broken marble cup
of a theatre, silent except for the tiny scuffling of a dry twig that the
breeze was patting idly along the empty flags.

I said on an impulse: 'I suppose you wouldn't—no, I'm sorry. Of
course not.'

'What do you suppose I wouldn't do?'

'Nothing. It was silly, under the circumstances.'

'The circumstances? Oh, that. Don't let that worry you. I suppose
you want to hear something recited here in Greek, even if it's only
thalassa! thalassa! Is that it? . . . What's the matter?'

'Nothing. Only that if you go on reading my thoughts like that
you're going to be a very uncomfortable companion.'

'You ought to practise too.'

'I haven't the talent.'

'Perhaps that's just as well.'

'What d'you mean?'

He laughed. 'Never mind. Was I right?'

'Yes. And not just *thalassa*, please. Some lines of verse, if you can
think of anything. I heard someone reciting in the theatre at Epidaurus
and it was like a miracle. Even a whisper carried right up to the topmost
tier.'

'It does the same here,' he said, 'only it's not so stupendous. All
right, if you'd like it.' He was feeling in his pockets as he spoke. 'Half
a minute; I'll have to find my lighter . . . If you want to get your
voice properly carried you have to locate the centre of the stage . . .
it's marked by a cross on the flagstones . . .'

As he pulled the lighter from his pocket I heard the small musical
chink of metal on stone. I stooped quickly after the sound. 'Something fell; some money, I think. Here . . . not far away, anyway.
Shine the light down, will you?'

The lighter flicked into flame, and he bent with it near the
ground. Almost immediately I saw the sharp gleam of a coin. I
picked it up and held it towards him. The orange-coloured flame slid
alive and sparkling across the little disc in my palm. I said: 'That's
surely—*gold*?'

'Yes. Thank you.' He took it and dropped it into his pocket. He might have been discussing a lost halfpenny, or at most a threepenny stamp. 'That was one of the souvenirs that Stephanos sent us. I told you he sent what was on Michael's body when he died. There were three of these gold sovereigns.' He moved away from me, holding the lighter low over the flags, searching for the central mark. You'd have thought there was nothing in his mind except the pleasant task of showing a girl over the Delphic ruins.

'Simon . . .'

'Here it is.' He straightened up, the lighter still burning in his hand. He must have seen my look, because he smiled at me, that sudden, very attractive smile. 'You know, I did tell you it was no longer a present tragedy, didn't I? I told you not to worry. Now, come here to the centre, and hear how your voice is picked up and carried high over those tiers of seats.'

I moved forward to the spot. 'I know you did. But when you told me that, you didn't know that your brother Michael had been murdered. Doesn't that make a difference?'

'Perhaps. There, do you hear the echo?'

'Glory, yes. It's weird, isn't it? As if the sound was coming back at you from those crags up there, and swirling all round you. It's like something tangible; like—yes, like sound made solid . . . Are you really going to recite something, or would you rather not?'

I thought he misunderstood me deliberately. 'With this lack of audience, I think I might. What'll you have?'

'You're the classicist. I leave it to you. But wait a moment. I'm going up into the back stalls.'

I climbed the narrow aisle and found a seat two-thirds of the way up the amphitheatre. The shaped marble of the seat was surprisingly comfortable, and the stone was still warm from the day's sun. The circular stage looked small below me. I could just make out its shape. Simon was nothing but a bodiless shadow. Then his voice came up out of the well of darkness, and the great rolling Greek lines rose and broke and echoed, rounding like a wind among the high crags. A phrase, a name, swam up from the flood of sound, giving directions to the music, like flights to an arrow. *Hades, Persephone, Hermes* . . . I shut my eyes and listened.

He stopped. There was a pause. The echo went up the cliff, hung like the murmur of a gong, and died. Then his voice came clearly and softly, speaking in English; music translating music:

> '. . . *Hades, Persephone,*
> *Hermes, steward of death,*
> *Eternal Wrath and Furies,*
> *Children of gods,*
> *Who see all murderers*
> *And all adulterous thieves, come soon!*
> *Be near me, and avenge*
> *My father's death, and bring*
> *My brother home!'*

He had stopped speaking again. The words died into silence high above me, and in the wake of the echo, it seemed, the night wind moved. I heard the hollies rustle behind me, and then, further up the hill, a scatter of dust and pebbles under the foot of some wandering beast, a goat, perhaps, or a donkey; I thought I heard the clink of metal. Then the night was still again. I got up and started down the steep aisle.

Simon's voice came, pitched quietly and perfectly clear. 'That do?'

'Beautifully.' I reached the bottom and crossed the stage. 'Thank you very much: but—I thought you said the tragedy was over?'

For the first time since I had known him (some seven hours? Could it possibly be only half a day?) he sounded disconcerted. 'What d'you mean?' He left the centre of the stage and came to meet me.

'That speech was a bit—immediate, wasn't it?'

'You recognised it?'

'Yes. It's from Sophocles' *Electra*, isn't it?'

'Yes.' There was a pause. He had a hand in his pocket, and now as he withdrew it I heard the chink of coins. He jingled them absently up and down. Then he said: 'I was wrong, then. It's not over . . . at least not until Stephanos shows us the place tomorrow, and—'

He stopped. I reflected that Simon Lester seemed to have a remarkably royal habit of using the first person plural. I should have liked to say ' "Shows *us*?" ' but didn't. I said merely: 'And?'

He said abruptly: 'And I find what Michael found—what he was killed for. The gold.'

'*The gold?*'

'Yes. I told you I'd an idea what it was that Michael might have found. I thought that, as soon as I read his letters, and remembered the sovereigns he was carrying. And after what Stephanos told us

I'm sure. It was gold he found. Angelos' little hoard of British gold, stored away against the day of the Red Dawn.'

'Yes, but Simon . . .' I began, then stopped. He knew Michael better than I did, after all.

The sovereigns clinked together as he thrust them back into his pocket. He turned away towards the side of the amphitheatre. 'This is the way up to the path. I'd better go first, perhaps; the steps are badly broken in places.'

He reached a hand back to me, and together we mounted the steep flight. At the top he paused and seemed to reach up into the darkness. I heard the rustle of leaves. He turned back to me and put something round and polished and cool into my hand. 'There you are. It's a pomegranate. There's a little tree growing behind the topmosts seats, and I've been longing for an excuse to pick one. Eat it soon, Persephone; then you'll have to stay in Delphi.'

The path led us out at last above the trees, where we could see our way more clearly. It was wide enough now to walk side by side. Simon went on, speaking softly: 'I think I'm right, Camilla; I think that's what Michael found. I'd suspected it before, but now I know he was murdered by this man Angelos. I'd bet on it for a certainty.'

I said rather stupidly, still following my own thoughts: 'But Stephanos said he was killed in a quarrel. Angelos and he—'

'If Michael had been quarrelling with a type like that he wouldn't be very likely to turn his back on him,' said Simon. 'I'm surprised Stephanos didn't think that one out for himself.'

'But if it was an old quarrel, and Michael thought it was forgotten, but Angelos—'

'The same applies. I just don't see Michael trustfully turning his back on a man who'd once had—or thought he had—the sort of grudge that leads to murder.'

'I suppose not.'

'But take all the bits of the picture and put them together,' said Simon, 'and what d'you get? I told you that we—the British—were flying in arms and gold during the Occupation, for the use of the *andartes*. Angelos, as we now learn from Stephanos, was working for the Communist *putsch* at the end of the German Occupation of Greece, therefore we can assume that he had an interest in holding back arms and supplies for later use. That's an assumption; but what facts have we? Angelos, when his men scatter northwards to avoid the Germans, comes south—alone. He meets Michael and kills him. He is interrupted before he can search the body, and on Michael are found gold sovereigns, and a hastily scribbled letter indicating that he has found something.'

'Yes,' I said, 'but –'

'If Angelos had such a cache of guns and gold, and Michael, the B.L.O., had found it, would it not be the complete motive for Michael's murder?'

'Yes, of course it would. You mean that Michael, when he met him, tackled him about it and – oh, no, that won't do, will it? There's the same objection – that Angelos wouldn't have had the chance to hit him over the head.'

'I can't help thinking,' said Simon softly, 'that Angelos saw something that told him Michael had found the cache. It's probably in some cave or other – Parnassus is honeycombed with them – and supposing that Michael, after he left Stephanos' house, had taken shelter in the one where the stuff was hidden? He'd stay there a few days till the Germans left the area, and then Angelos, doubling back to his treasure-chest, would see the British officer coming out of the cave, his cave . . . It could be, you know. And if Michael didn't see Angelos, as seems obvious, the Greek waited and took his chance and tried to wipe him off then and there. Which means –'

'Which means that, if you're right, the cache was very near the place where Michael was murdered,' I said.

'Exactly. Well, we shall see.'

'If there was anything it'll have been taken long since.'

'Probably.'

'Angelos would come back and take it. If not immediately, then later.'

'If he lived to come back. Three months after Mick's death he was out of the country for good.'

I said, as casually as I could: 'Was he? And what if Niko was possibly – just possibly – right? If he *were* still alive? Now, I mean?'

Simon laughed. 'It's in the lap of the gods, isn't it?' One of the coins spun in his hand as he tossed and caught it. 'What do you say? Shall we offer gold to Apollo if he'll bring Angelos back to Delphi now?'

'Aegisthus to Orestes' knife?' I tried to speak equally lightly, but in spite of myself the words sounded harsh and hollow.

'Why not?' The coin dropped into his hand again and his fingers closed on it. He was a shadow in the starlight, watching me. 'You know, I told you the truth when I said the tragedy was over. I don't

feel chewed up or dramatic about Mick's death, even after what I've
learned tonight. But, damn it all, he was murdered, in a filthy way,
and–if I'm right–for the filthiest of motives. And the murderer got
away with it, and possibly with a fortune into the bargain. I've no
particular desire to find the fortune, but I want to know, Camilla.
That's all.'

'Yes, I see.'

'I came here to talk to Stephanos and see Michael's grave, and to
leave it at that. But I can't leave it now, not till it's really over, and I
know why it happened. I don't suppose there'll be anything left to
tell me, after all this time, but I have to look. And as for Orestes–' I
heard the smile in his voice–'I've no particular ambition for revenge,
either, but if I did meet the murderer . . . Don't you see that I'd
quite like a word with him?' He laughed again. 'Or do you share
Niko's opinion of my abilities?'

'No. No, of course not. But this man Angelos . . . well, he's–' I
floundered and stopped.

'Dangerous? So you don't think that–if I do meet him–I ought to
have it out with him?'

'An eye for an eye?' I said. 'I thought we didn't believe in that
any more.'

'Don't you believe it. We do. But in England there's a fine,
impersonal, and expensive machinery to get your eye for you, and
no personal guilt except your signature on a cheque to the Inland
Revenue. Here, it's different. Nobody's going to do the dirty work
for you. You do it yourself and nobody knows but the vultures. And
Apollo.'

'Simon, it's immoral.'

'So is all natural law. Morals are social phenomena. Didn't you
know?'

'I don't agree.'

'No? You stick to that, Camilla. This is the loveliest country in
the world, and the hardest. Much of it, and you're apt to find
yourself thinking in its terms instead of your own. There are times,
I'd say, when you have to . . . But you stand by your guns.' He
laughed down at me. 'And for a start, don't believe a word I say. I'm
a normal law-abiding citizen, and a most upright and solemn
schoolmaster . . . Now, enough of this Oresteian tragedy. Michael's
dead these fourteen years, and Delphi's been here three thousand, so
we'll let Delphi bury its dead. It does it just here, incidentally; that's

the graveyard just beside the path, under the trees. And now, if you're to get any sleep at all tonight, what about chasing up that drink? That's the studio there.'

Without another glance in the direction of the graveyard, he led the way at a quickened pace over level ground towards the lights of the studio.

Chapter 8

THE STUDIO WAS a big rectangular building situated on top of the bluff behind the village of Delphi. Later in daylight I was to see it as a big ugly box of a place, set down on a flat plateau quarried out of the living rock, so that, while its front windows commanded a magnificent view of the valley, its back looked out on to a wall of rock as high as its second storey. On this, the north side, were the big 'front' doors, impressive affairs of plate-glass which were never used. The tenants got in and out by a small door in the east end, which gave on the corridor running the length of the ground floor.

Inside, the place was as bare and functional as possible. Corridors and stairs were of marble, and spotlessly clean. On the lower floor, and to the left of the corridor, were the artists' bedrooms, facing south over the valley. These were simple in the extreme, each bedroom holding nothing but an iron bedstead with blankets and pillows, a wash-basin with h. and c., both perpetually c., a small and inevitably unsteady table, and hooks for hanging clothes. Opening off each bedroom was a marble-floored shower-cupboard – also, presumably, c. Opposite the bedrooms were other doors which I never saw opened, but which I imagined might be some sort of kitchen premises, or rooms for the caretaker. The resident artists worked on the upper floor where the light was better; here a row of rooms on the north side of the corridor served as studios and storerooms for their work.

But all this I was to discover later. Tonight the building was merely an ugly oblong box of a place planted down in a small quarry, with the light from a bare electric bulb showing us the door.

We hardly got into the echoing corridor when a door a short way along it opened, and a young man came out like a bullet from a gun. He caught at the jamb of the door as he catapulted out and hung on, almost as if he felt the need of the door's support. He said in a high excited voice: 'Oh, Simon, I was just–' Then he saw me and stopped, disconcerted, still theatrically posed in the stream of light that came from the door.

There was something about his method of appearance that was very like Niko's, but there the resemblance ended. The young man–who I supposed was Nigel–had none of Niko's beauty or promise of strength, and very little, in consequence, of Niko's assurance. There was no conscious drama in his actions, and indeed now he was looking miserably embarrassed, almost as if he would have liked to retreat into his room and lock the door. He was tallish, thin and fair. His skin had taken the sun badly, and his eyes, which were that puckered blue that you see in sailors and airmen and men who habitually gaze into the distances, looked as if they had had too much sun. He had a straggling little beard that made him look young and rather vulnerable, and his hair was bleached to the colour and texture of dry hay. He had a weakly sensual mouth and the strong ugly hands of the artist.

Simon said: 'Hullo, Nigel. This is Camilla Haven, who's staying at the Apollon. I've brought her up for a drink, and she wants to see your drawings. Do you mind?'

'Oh. No. Not at all. Delighted,' said Nigel, stammering a little. 'C-come into my room, then. We'll have a drink here.' As he stood aside for me to pass him, slightly more flushed than before, I found myself wondering if he had been drinking alone in his room. There was that queer look about his eyes, a sort of sense that he was clutching at himself as really, as physically, as he had clutched at the door-jamb, and in the same effort of control.

His room, basically as bare as the rest of the building, was frantically but rather pleasantly untidy. It was as if the artist's personality, far richer than it appeared from the look of him, had spilled over without his knowing it into the monastic-looking little cell. At the foot of the bed a rucksack stood on the floor, its contents bursting out in confusion. I saw two shirts, as brightly but rather more respectably coloured than Niko's, a tangle of rope, some dirty handkerchiefs which had obviously been pressed into use as paint-rags, three oranges, and a copy of the *Collected Poems of Dylan Thomas*. The towel which was flung over the edge of the wash-basin was as brightly yellow as a dandelion. Nigel's pyjamas, in a huddle on the bed, were striped in wine and turquoise. And everywhere on the cracked white walls there were sketches, drawing-pinned haphazardly; they were in a variety of styles, so that, looking from the bold to the delicate, from the pencil-sketches to the water-colours curling up at the edges as they dried, I remembered what Simon had told me.

But I had no time to do more than glance, because our host had dived past me, and was dragging forward the room's best chair, a canvas affair of grubby orange.

'W-won't you sit down, Miss Er? It's the best there is. It's quite clean really.'

I thanked him and sat down. Simon had wandered over to the window and hitched himself up on to the wide sill, where he sat with one leg swinging. Nigel, still with that air of disconcerted fussiness, had dived into the shower-cupboard and was rummaging rather wildly among bottles on the floor. In a moment he emerged clutching two tumblers and a large bottle of ouzo.

'Do you like this stuff?' he asked me anxiously. 'It's all there is.'

There was something about Nigel that disarmed me into a deliberate lie. 'I love it,' I said, and waited resignedly while he poured a generous dollop into one of the tumblers and handed it to me.

'Would you like water with it?'

Now, ouzo is the Greek absinthe. It is made from aniseed, and tastes fairly mild and (to my mind) incredibly unpleasant. I find it quite undrinkable neat. On the other hand if you add sufficient water to make it swallowable, there is a lot more to swallow.

I said bravely: 'Yes, please.'

Nigel grabbed a carafe from above the wash-basin. Again it struck me sharply that his movements were a parody of Niko's. They were swift and abrupt and angular, but where Niko's had the grace of a striking cat, Nigel's were clumsy and almost unco-ordinated. It was odd for an artist to be clumsy, I thought; then as I watched Nigel pour water into my glass, I saw that his hand was shaking. That was still odder.

The liquid misted, clouded, and went entirely beastly like quinine. I said: 'When. Thanks,' and smiled at Nigel, who was watching me with an anxious-puppy expression that made him look

younger than ever. He was, I judged, about twenty-three, but the
beard made him look nineteen. I smiled bravely and lifted the glass.

'*Gia sou*, *Kyrie* Nigel,' I said. 'I'm sorry, but I don't know your
other name.

'Make it Nigel,' he said unhelpfully, but with apparent pleasure.

As I drank carefully I caught Simon's eye, to see that he knew
quite well what I felt about ouzo. I scowled at him and took another
drink, reflecting yet again that *Kyrios* Simon Lester saw a damned
sight too much. I controlled the shudder that shook me as the liquor
went down, and then watched fascinated as Nigel filled Simon's
tumbler two-thirds full, grabbed a toothglass for himself and filled
that, and then raised it to his lips, said '*Gia sou*' quickly, and drank
half of it at one fell gulp, neat.

'Cheers, comrade,' said Simon. 'Have you had a good day?'

Nigel, flushing and choking a little over the liquor, managed to
say: 'Yes. Oh yes, thanks. Very.'

'Where did you go?'

The young man waved a vague hand, which almost knocked the
ouzo bottle off the table, but unfortunately didn't quite. 'Up there.'

'You mean up in the precinct?'

'No. Up the hill.'

'On to Parnassus again? Did you go up over the old track to hunt
up some shepherds after all?' He turned to me. 'Nigel's got a
contract for a series of drawings of "Hellenic types"–heads of
peasants and old women and shepherd boys and so forth. He's done
some quite striking ones in a sort of heavy ink line-and-wash.'

Nigel said suddenly: 'It's exciting. You can't know how exciting.
You see a grubby little boy watching the goats, and when you really
start to draw him you realise you've seen him a dozen times already
in the museums. And I found a girl last week in Amphissa who was
pure Minoan, crimped hair and all. It makes it difficult, too, of
course, because try as you will it looks as if you're copying the
original Grecian Urn.'

I laughed. 'I know. I've met one Zeus and one rather wicked Eros
and a couple of dozen assorted satyrs today already.'

'Stephanos and Niko?' said Simon.

I nodded. 'Nigel ought to meet them.'

Nigel said: 'Who are they?'

'Stephanos is a shepherd from Arachova and he's straight out of
Homer. Niko's his grandson and he's–well, simply a beauty in
American teenager rig. But if it's only the head you want, you could

hardly do better.' I reflected, as I spoke, that Simon had apparently told Nigel nothing about Michael or his mission that evening.

Nor did he tell him now. He said: 'You may meet them yet. Stephanos is usually some way up between Delphi and Arachova—near that track I took you over yesterday. Is that the way you went again today? How far?'

'Quite a long way.' Nigel looked round him vaguely, as if embarrassment had descended on him again, and added quickly: 'I was sick of sitting about in the precinct and the valley. I wanted a walk. I got up above the Shining Ones and on to the track and then—well, I just went on walking. It was hot, but up there there was a breeze.'

'No work today?'

Simon's question was no more than idle, but a flush had crept up under Nigel's raw sunburn. It made him look cagey, but I guessed it was only shyness. He said: 'No,' very shortly, and buried his nose in his glass.

I said: 'No shepherds playing Pan-pipes to their flocks? On Parnassus? You shake me, Nigel.'

He grinned at that. 'No, more's the pity.'

'And no gods?' I said, thinking of the starlit temple.

But his shyness asserted itself here completely. He buried his face in his glass and said, almost snappily: 'No! I tell you I did hardly anything! I was just walking. Anyway those heads are a bore. They're only bread and butter. You wouldn't like them.'

'I'd love to see some of your work, though, if you could be bothered to show it. Simon's been telling me how awfully good your drawings are—'

He interrupted in a voice so quick and hoarse that it gave the effect of a small outburst of temper: 'Good? Simon's talking bilge. They're not good. They please me, but that's all.'

'Some of them are, very good,' said Simon quietly.

Nigel sneered at him. 'The niminy-piminy ones. The sweet little Ruskin-and-water ones. Can't you just hear the Sunday-paper critics turned loose over them? They're useless and you know it.'

'They're first-class and *you* know it. If you could—'

'Oh God, if, if, if,' said Nigel rudely. He set his glass down on the table with a sharp click. 'You know damn well they're useless.'

'But they're what you want to do, and they show the way you want to go, and that's the point, isn't it? They are "Nigel Barlow", and what's more, they're uncommon.'

'They're useless.' The repetition was emphatic.

'If you mean they're not easy to make a living out of here and now, I agree. But I still think—'

' "To thine own self be true"?' said Nigel, on a high edged note that might have been excitement but sounded like bitterness. 'Oh God, don't be a prosy old bore! And anyway it doesn't matter a damn. Not a damn, do you hear me?'

Simon smiled at him. I think it was then that I first really saw what lay behind that good-tempered and apparently unruffled self-command of Simon's; what made it so very different from the more flamboyant self-confidence I had envied. Simon cared. He really did care what happened to this casually-met, troubled, and not very attractive boy who was being so wretchedly rude. And that was why he had come back after fourteen years to find out what had happened to Michael. It was not a present tragedy, and he was not, after all, an Orestes. But he cared—for his father's sake, for Stephanos', for the woman's. *Any man's death diminishes me, because I am involved in mankind.* That was it. He was involved in mankind, and, just at this moment, that meant Nigel. *'One takes it for granted,'* he had said, *'that one is there to help.'* I suppose one gets to know men quickest by the things they take for granted.

He had set his glass down and now laced his fingers round one knee. 'All right. Exit Polonius. Well, d'you want us to find you a selling line, Nigel?'

Nigel said, not rudely now, but still with a touch of that hot and slightly sulky impatience: 'You mean a gimmick to make people come and look at them? A bloody little quick-sales-trick to crowd a one-man-show somewhere in the wilds of Sheffield or something? Two pretty drawings sold and my name in the local press? Is that what you mean?'

Simon said mildly: 'One has to start somewhere. Couldn't you count it as part of the fight? And at least it might mean you hadn't to fall back on the ultimate degradation.'

'What's that?' I asked.

He grinned. 'Teaching.'

'Oh. Well, I do see what you mean,' I said.

'I thought you would.'

Nigel said sulkily: 'It's all very well to laugh, but I wouldn't be any good at it and I should loathe it, and that would be dreadful.'

'The final hell,' agreed Simon cheerfully. 'Well, we must find you a gimmick, Nigel. Make them come to mock and remain to pay. You must make your pictures out of sequins, or do all your painting under water, or get yourself into the popular press as the man who 'Always Paints to the Strains of Mozart.'

Nigel gave him a reluctant and slightly shame-faced grin. 'Count Basie, more likely. All right, what shall it be? *Art trouvé*, or bits of rusty iron twisted any old way and called *Woman in Love*, or *Dog eat Dog*, or something?'

'You could always,' I said, 'travel through Greece with a donkey, and then write a book, illustrated.'

Nigel turned to me at that, but with the look of someone who has hardly been listening. I wondered again if he had been drinking too much. 'What? A donkey?'

'Yes. There was a Dutch boy in Delphi this evening who'd just got in from Jannina. He'd been walking over the hills like Stevenson, with a donkey, and painting by the way. I gathered that he'd done a lot of sketching in the villages and more or less paid his way with them.'

'Oh, that chap. Yes, I've met him. He's here now.'

'Of course, I forgot. Simon told me he'd come up here to sleep tonight. Did you see his work?'

'No. He was too tired to bother. He went to bed at about nine, and I think it'd take an atom bomb to wake him.' His look lingered on me as if he were with difficulty bringing me into focus and himself back into the conversation. He said slowly: 'Being true to oneself . . . knowing that one can do a thing if only the world will give one the chance . . . but having to fight for it every step of the way . . .' The blurred blue gaze sharpened and fixed itself on Simon. 'Simon . . .'

'Yes?'

'You say a gimmick would be "part of the fight", because, in the first place, it would make people stop and look? If my stuff's not really good, no gimmick will get it anywhere beyond the first hurdle. You know that. But if it *is* good, then once people have stopped and paid attention, the *work itself* is what'll count? That's true, isn't it?'

'It could be. In your case I imagine a lot might depend on the gimmick.' Simon smiled. 'I have a feeling that quite a few good artists have been driven along a path they never intended in the first place as anything but an odd deviation—a wallop in the public's eye. Naming no names, but you know who.'

Nigel didn't smile. He seemed still hardly to be listening, but very

busy following his own thoughts. He hesitated, then said suddenly:
'Well, and that's being true to oneself, isn't it? And don't you think
that means, come what may, one should take what one wants and
needs? Go straight ahead the way you know you have to go, and the
devil take the hindmost? Artists—great artists—work that way, don't
they? And doesn't the end justify them?' As Simon seemed to
hesitate, he whipped round on me. 'What do *you* think?'

I said: 'I don't know specially about great artists, but I've always
imagined that the secret of personality (I won't say "success") was
one-track-mindedness. Great men *do* know where they're going, and
they never turn aside. Socrates and the "beautiful and good".
Alexander and the Hellenising of the world. On a different level—if I
may—Christ.'

Nigel looked at Simon. 'Well?' His voice was sharp, like a
challenge. *'Well?'*

I thought: there *is* something going on here that I don't understand. And I don't think Simon understands it either, and it worries
him.

Simon said slowly, those cool eyes vividly alive now, watching
the younger man: 'You're partly right. The great men know where
they're going; yes, and they get there, but surely it's a case of driving
themselves without pause, rather than juggernauting over all the
opposition? And I thought Polonius was a prosy old bore? You
brought him in, not me. I don't agree with him, but do him the
justice of looking at the end of the quotation. *"To thine own self be true
. . . thou canst not then be false to any man."* If being true to oneself
means ignoring the claims of other people then it simply doesn't
work, does it? No, your really great man—your Socrates—doesn't
drive along a straight path of his own cutting. He knows what the
end is, yes, and he doesn't turn aside from it, but all the way there
he's reckoning with whatever—and whoever—else is in his way. He
sees the whole thing as a pattern, and his own place in it.'

I quoted, thinking back: ' *"I am involved in mankind"?'*

'Exactly.'

'What's that?' said Nigel.

'A quotation from John Donne, a poet who became Dean of St.
Paul's. This comes in one of his Devotions . . . *"No man is an island,
entire of itself."* He's right. In the end it's our place in the pattern that
matters.'

'Yes, but the artist?' said Nigel almost fiercely. 'He's different,
you know he is. He's driven by some compulsion: if he can't do what

he knows he *has* to do with life he might as well be dead. He's got to break through the world's indifference, or else break himself against it. He can't help it. Wouldn't he be justified in doing almost anything to fulfil himself, if his art were worth it in the end?'

'The end justifying the means? As a working principle, never,' said Simon. 'Never, never, never.'

Nigel sat forward in his chair, his voice rising again with excitement: 'Look, I don't mean anything dreadful like –like murder or crime or something! But if there was no other way –'

I said: 'What are you planning to do, for goodness' sake? Steal the donkey?'

He swung round on me so sharply that I thought he was going to fall off his chair. Then he gave a sudden laugh that sounded very much to me like the edge of hysteria. 'Me? Walk to Jannina and write a book about it? Me? Never! I'd be scared of the wolves!'

'There aren't any wolves,' Simon's voice was light, but he was watching Nigel rather closely, and I saw the shadow of trouble in his face.

'The tortoises then!' He grabbed the bottle again and turned back to me. 'Have some more ouzo? No? Simon? Here, hold your glass. Did you know, Miss Camilla I've-forgotten-your-other-name, that there were tortoises running about on the hills here? Wild ones? Imagine meeting one of those when you were all alone and miles from anywhere.'

'I'd run a mile,' I said.

'What *is* it, Nigel?' asked Simon from the window-sill.

For a moment I wondered just what was going to happen. Nigel stopped in mid-movement, with the bottle in one hand. He was rigid. His face went redder, then white under the peeling sunburn. His ugly spatulate fingers clenched round the bottle as if he were going to throw it. His eyes looked suffused. Then they fell away from Simon's, and he turned to set the bottle down. He said in a curiously muffled voice: 'I'm sorry. I'm behaving badly. I was a bit high before you came in, that's all.'

Then he turned back to me with one of his quick angular movements that were like those of an awkward small boy. 'I don't know what you must think of me. You must think I'm a pretty good heel, but things were getting me down a bit. I–I'm temperamental, that's what it is. Great artists are.' He grinned shamefacedly at me, and I smiled back.

'It's all right,' I said. 'And all great artists have had a horrid struggle for recognition. As long as it doesn't come after you're dead, it's all the sweeter when you get it, and I'm sure you will.'

He was down on his knees, lugging a battered portfolio from under the bed. I noticed still that febrile air about him, and his hands were unsteady. 'Here,' he said, 'I'll show you my drawings. You can tell me if you think they're worth anything. You can tell me.' He was dragging a sheaf of papers out of the portfolio.

I said feebly: 'But my opinion's no use. I really don't know anything about it.'

'Here.' He thrust a drawing into my hand. 'That's one of the ones Simon talks about. And this.' He sat back on his heels on the floor, and sent Simon a look that might almost have been hatred. 'I'll be true to myself, Polonius. You can be bloody sure I will. Even if it means being true to nobody else. I'm not involved with mankind, as your parson friend puts it. I'm myself. Nigel Barlow. And some day you'll know it, you and all the rest. Do you hear?'

'I hear,' said Simon peaceably. 'Let's see what you've done, shall we?'

Nigel pushed a drawing towards him, and then a handful at me. 'This. And this. And this and this and this. They may never set the Thames on fire, but given a push and a bit of luck they're good enough to make me . . . Aren't they?'

As I looked down at the drawings on my knee I was conscious of Nigel's fixed stare. For all the wild and whirling words the vulnerable look was there again, and on that final question the over-emphatic voice had broken into naïve and anxious query. I found myself hoping with ridiculous fervour that the drawings might be good.

They were. His touch was sure and strong, yet delicate. Each line was clean and definite and almost frighteningly effective; he had managed to suggest not only shape, but bulk and texture, by pure drawing with the minimum of fuss. Somehow the technique suggested the faded elegance of a French flower-print combined with the sharp, delicate, and yet virile impact of a Dürer drawing. Some were mere sketches, but over others he had taken greater pains. There were rapid studies of the ruined buildings – part of a broken arch with the sharp exclamatory cypresses behind it; Apollo's columns standing very clear and clean; a delightful drawing of three pomegranates on a twig with shiny drooping leaves. There were several of olive-trees, lovely twisted shapes with heads of blown silver cloud. In the plant- and flower-studies he used colour, in faint washes of an almost Chinese subtlety.

I looked up to see him watching me with that anxious-puppy stare from which all trace of belligerence had gone. 'But, Nigel, they're wonderful! I told you I didn't know much about it, but I haven't seen anything I liked as much in years!'

I got up from my chair and sat down on the bed, spreading the drawings round me, studying them. I picked one of them up; it was the drawing of a clump of cyclamen springing from a small cleft in a bare rock. The textural differences of petal, leaf and stone were beautifully indicated. Below the flower, in the same cleft, grew the remains of some rock-plant that I remembered to have seen everywhere in Greece; it was dead and dry-dusty, crumbling away against the rock. Above it the cyclamen's winged flowers looked pure and delicate and strong.

Over my shoulder Simon said: 'Nigel, that's terrific. I haven't seen it before.'

'Of course you haven't. I only did it today,' said Nigel rudely, making a quick movement as if to snatch it back. Then he appeared to remember, as I had, that he'd told Simon he had done no work that day, for he flushed that raw red again, and sat back on his heels looking uncomfortable.

As usual, Simon took no notice. He lifted the drawing and studied it. 'Did you mean to use colour in it? What made you change your mind?'

'Simply that there wasn't any water handy.' And Nigel took the paper from him and put it back in the portfolio on the floor.

I said, rather quickly: 'May I see the portraits?'

'Of course. Here they are—my bread and butter drawings.' There was a curious note in his voice, and I saw Simon glance again at him sharply.

There was a whole sheaf of portraits, done in an entirely different style. This was effective in its way, the beautiful economy of his drawing telling even in the thick, dramatic, and over-emphatic line. His brilliance of execution had here become a slickness, the clever blending of a few stock statements into a formula. In a way, too, the originals of the portraits might have come from stock. What Nigel had been doing was, of course, to find 'types' and to set these down, but, while some of these were discernibly living people, others could have been abstractions of well-known 'Hellenic types' taken from statues or vase-paintings or even from the imagination. There was one fine-looking head that might have been Stephanos, but it had a formal and over-typed air like an illustration to a set of Greek myths. A girl's face, all eyes, and deep shadows thrown by a veil, could have been captioned: *Greece: the Gate to the East.* Another portrait—more familiar in type to me and so possibly more alive—was that of a young woman with the Juliette Gréco face, large lost eyes and a sulky mouth. Beneath it was the drawing of a man's head that, again, seemed purely formal, but was oddly arresting. The head was round, set on a powerful neck, and covered with close curls that grew low on the brow, like a bull's. The hair grew down thickly past the ears, almost to the jawline, as one sees it in the heroic vase-paintings, and these sidepieces were drawn in formally, like the hard curls on a sculptured cheek. The upper lip was short, the lips thick, and drawn tightly up at the corners in the fixed half-moon smile that shows always on the statues of the archaic gods of Greece.

I said: 'Simon, look at that. That's the real "archaic smile". When you see it on crumbly old statues of Hermes and Apollo you think it's unreal and crude. But I've actually seen it on men's faces here and there in Greece.'

'Is that new too?' asked Simon.

'Which? Oh, that. Yes.' Nigel gave him a quick upward glance, hesitated, then appeared to abandon his pretences, whatever they were. 'I did it today.' He took the drawing from me and studied it for a moment. 'Perhaps you're right; it's too formal. I did it half from memory, and it's gone a bit too much like a vase-painting. However.'

'It's the Phormis head to the life,' said Simon.

Nigel looked up quickly. 'Yes, so it is! That's it. I wondered what he reminded me of. I suppose I drew it in. Still, it makes a "type" for the collection, and as Camilla says, it does exist. She's seen that queer fixed grin here and there, and so've I. Interesting, I thought.'

'What's the Phormis head?' I asked.

Simon said: 'It's a head found, as far as I remember, at Olympia, and is supposed to be that of Phormis, who was a playwright. That head is bearded, and this isn't, but it's got the same heavy wide cheeks and tight curls, and that typical smile.'

I laughed. 'Oh dear, and it's still walking these mountains. It makes me feel raw and new and very, very Western. That face, now—'

My hand was hovering over the Juliette Gréco girl.

Simon laughed. 'That's real enough, and very Western indeed,' he said. 'That's our one and only Danielle, isn't it, Nigel? You're surely not going to put her in among the "Hellenic types"?'

'Danielle?' I said. 'Oh, she *is* French, then? Somehow I thought she looked it.'

Nigel had taken the drawing from Simon, and was stuffing that, too, away. He said in a muffled voice: 'She was here as secretary to a chap attached to the French School.'

'French School?'

'Of Archaeology,' said Simon. 'It's the French School which has the "right" or whatever they call it to excavate here at Delphi. They've been working here again recently on the site—there was some talk of a hunt for a lost treasury fairly high up on the hill. You'll see a lot of exploratory pits dug on both sides of the road, too, but all they found there was Roman.'

'Ah, yes. Modern stuff.'

He grinned. 'That's it. Well, they've had to pack up, because I believe funds gave out. Some of their workmen are still here tidying up—there are trucks and tools and what-have-you to be removed. But the archaeologists have gone, more's the pity.'

I saw Nigel throw him a sidelong glance, and remembered suddenly something that Simon had said to me earlier. '*He's been here in Delphi too long, and got tied up with a girl who wasn't good for him.*'

I said: 'Yes. I'd rather have liked to watch them at it. And think of the excitement if anything did turn up!'

He laughed. '*That* sort of excitement, I believe, is the rarest kind! Most of the long years are spent shifting tons of earth a couple of yards, and then putting them back again. But I agree. It would be terrific. And what a country! Did you see that glorious thing of the negro and the horse that the workmen dug up when they were mending the drains in Omonia Square a few years ago? Imagine wondering what you might find every time you set out to dig your garden or put a plough to the hillside! After all, even the Charioteer—' He stopped, and turned his cigarette over in his fingers as if he was admiring the twist of blue smoke that curled and frothed from it.

Nigel looked up. 'The Charioteer?' His voice still sounded cagey and queer. He was still kneeling on the floor, shuffling the drawings in the folder into some sort of order. 'The Charioteer?' he repeated mechanically, as if his mind was on something else.

Simon drew on the cigarette. 'Uh-uh. He wasn't dug up till 1896, long after the main shrines and treasuries had been excavated. Not long ago I read Murray's *History of Greek Sculpture*, and wondered why the author was so sketchy about Delphi, till I realised that, when he wrote his book in 1890, the half was not told him. Who knows what else is still up there in the odd corners under the trees?'

Nigel had sat back on his heels, his hands moving vaguely and clumsily among the drawings. If they were indeed his bread and butter he was, it occurred to me, remarkably careless of them.

He looked up now, the drawings spilling again from his hands.

'Simon.' It was that strung-up voice again.

'Well?'

'I think I –' Then he stopped abruptly and turned his head. The studio's outer door had opened and shut with a bang. Rapid footsteps approached along the corridor.

To my surprise Nigel went as white as a sheet. He swung round towards me, swept the rest of the drawings off the bed into an unceremonious heap, then hastily gathered them all together to shove back into the folder on the floor.

As unceremoniously, the door burst open.

A girl stood there, surveying the untidy and crowded little room with an expression of weary distaste. It was the girl of the portrait, Gréco-look and all. She drawled, without removing the cigarette from the corner of her mouth: 'Hullo, Simon, my love. Hullo, Nigel. On your knees praying over my picture? Well, the prayer's answered. I've come back.'

Chapter 9

A girl —
No virgin either, I should guess — a baggage
Thrust on me like a cargo on a ship
To wreck my peace of mind!
                    SOPHOCLES: *Women of Trachis.*
                        (tr. E. F. Watling.)

DANIELLE WAS SLIGHTLY built, of medium height, and had made the most (or the worst, according to the point of view) of her figure by encasing it in drainpipe jeans and a very tight sweater of thin wool, which left nothing to wonder at except how in the world did she get her breasts that shape and into that position. They were very high and very pointed and the first thing that one noticed about her. The second was her expression, which was very much the weary waif-look of Nigel's picture. Her face was oval, and palely sallow. Her eyes were very big and very black, carefully shadowed with a blend of brown and green that made them look huge and tired. She had long curling lashes that caught the smoke wisping up blue from the cigarette that appeared fixed to her lower lip. She wore pale lipstick, which looked odd and striking with the sallow face and huge dark eyes. Her hair was black and straight and deliberately untidy, cut in that madly smart way that looks as if it had been hacked off in the dark with a pair of curved nail-scissors. Her expression was one of world-weary disdain. Her age might have been anything from seventeen to twenty-five. She looked as if she hoped you would put it at something over thirty.

I should perhaps say here that her eyelashes were very long, quite real, and quite beautiful. This is in case it should be thought that my

description of Danielle smacks of prejudice. The only reason that I
had then for prejudice was the expression on Nigel's face, stuck
there on his knees on the floor with his ungainly hands full of the
delicate drawings, turning to face the door, and saying *'Danielle!'* in a
cracked young voice that gave him away immediately and very
cruelly.

He shoved the drawings clumsily into the folder and got to his
feet.

After that first greeting she had ignored him. Nor, after one cool
glance, had she looked at me. Her eyes were all over Simon.

She said again: 'Hullo.' I don't quite know how she made the
simple disyllable sound sexy, but she did.

'Hullo,' said Simon, not sounding sexy at all. He was looking ever
so slightly amused, and also wary, which annoyed me. Why it
should, I'm not prepared to say, and didn't try at the time.

Nigel said hoarsely: 'What are you doing here? I thought you'd
left Delphi.'

'I had. But I came back. Aren't you going to ask me in, Nigel
dear?'

'Of course. Come in. It's wonderful—I mean I didn't expect you
back. Come in. Sit down.' He darted forward and dragged out the
best chair—the one I had vacated—for her. But she walked past it
towards Simon, who was standing by the window. She went very
close to him. 'I'm sleeping in the studio, Simon. I got tired of the
Tourist Hotel, and anyway I can't afford it now. You don't mind me
coming here, do you . . . Simon?'

'Not in the very least.' He looked across her at me. 'You'd better
be introduced. Camilla, this, as you'll have guessed, is Danielle.
Camilla Haven: Danielle Lascaux. I told you that Danielle was here
for some time with the French School. She was Hervé Clément's
secretary. You probably know the name. He wrote *Later Discoveries
at Delphi.*'

'I read it not long before I came here. How d'you do?' I said to
Danielle.

She gave me a brief stare, and a barely civil nod. Then she turned,
and with what looked like very conscious grace, sat down at the
opposite end of the bed from me, curled her slim legs up under her,
and leaned back against the bed-head. She tilted her head and sent
Simon a long look between narrowed lids.

'So you've been talking about me?'

Nigel said eagerly: 'It was your portrait—the one I did of you.'

With one of his ungraceful gestures he indicated the untidily stuffed portfolio lying on the bed beside me.

'Oh, that.'

'It's very good, don't you think?' I said. 'I recognised you as soon as you came in.'

'Uh-huh. Nigel's quite a clever boy, we know that.' She sent him a smile that was a shadow of the one she'd given Simon, then reached out an idle hand and pulled two or three sheets out of the folder. I saw Nigel make a small sharp movement, as if of involuntary protest, then he sat down in the orange canvas chair, his hands dangling between his bony knees.

'Yes, I suppose it's a good enough portrait. Are my eyes really as big as that, Nigel?' She was leafing through the drawings: her own portrait; the one we had called the 'Phormis head', with the close curls and tight smile; the cyclamen; and a drawing I hadn't yet seen, of a man's head and shoulders. 'Flowers?' said Danielle. 'Are they *paying* you to do things like that, Nigel? . . . *Who's this?*'

Her voice had changed on the query, so abruptly that I was startled. I saw Simon turn his head, and Nigel almost jumped. 'Who? Oh, that. That's a chap I saw today on Parnassus. We were just saying before you came in that he was rather like an archaic –'

'No, no!' She had been holding the Phormis head, and another drawing. She dropped the former abruptly, and thrust the other forward. 'Not that one. This.'

Something in her voice suggested an effort for self-command, and to my surprise her hand was unsteady. But when I said 'May I?' and leaned forward to take the drawing gently from her, she let it go without protest. I looked at it with interest, and then more sharply. It showed the head and bared throat of a young man. The face was beautiful, but not with Niko's vital and very Greek beauty; this was remote, stern, perhaps a little sad. He was not, I thought, a 'Hellenic type' at all, though something about him was oddly familiar. But it appeared that he was not intended to form part of Nigel's gallery. This was the only portrait I had seen where Nigel had used what I might call his 'flower technique'. It was in his own style; the work was delicate, sure and arrestingly beautiful.

'Why, *Nigel* . . .' I said. 'Simon, look at this!' Danielle let the others fall to the coverlet. She appeared abruptly to have lost interest, only asking: 'Did you do those today?'

'Yes.' And Nigel, before Simon had time to do more than glance at the drawing, had finally and this time effectively swept every drawing back into the folder and shoved it under the bed. He looked flustered, and every bit as resentful as he had done earlier. But Danielle didn't pursue the subject. She leaned back again and said in her usual slightly bored tone: 'For God's sake, Nigel, *are* you going to offer me a drink?'

'Of course.' Nigel dived for the bottle of ouzo, put it down again so that it rocked and nearly spilt, then dashed to rinse a tumbler out in the basin.

I put my own glass down and made as if to get to my feet. But at that moment I caught Simon's eye, and I thought he shook his head very slightly. I sat back.

He looked down at the girl. 'I thought you'd gone, Danielle? Hasn't the "dig" packed up?'

'Oh, that. Yes. We got to Athens last night, and really I thought it would be rather a *thing* to be back in civilisation again, but I had the most dreary scene with Hervé, and then I thought to myself I really might as well be back in Delphi with . . .' she smiled suddenly, showing very white teeth . . . 'back in Delphi. So here I am.'

Nigel said: 'You mean you've got the sack?'

'You could call it that.' She watched him for a moment through the cigarette-smoke, then she turned to me. 'Simon told you the polite fiction,' she said. 'Actually, of course, I was Hervé Clément's mistress.'

'*Danielle!*'

'For God's sake, Nigel!' She hunched an impatient shoulder. 'Don't pretend you didn't know.' Then to me: 'But he was getting to be a bit of a bore.'

'Really?' I said politely.

I thought her look was calculating under the long lashes. 'Yes, really. They all do, sooner or later, don't you think? Do you find men bore you, Camilla Haven?'

'Occasionally,' I said. 'But then so—occasionally—do women.'

That one went straight past her. 'I hate women anyway,' she said simply. 'But Hervé, he was honestly getting to be the utter *end*. Even if he hadn't quit the "dig" here and gone back to Athens, I'd have had to leave him.' She blew out a long cloud of smoke, and turned her head to look up at Simon. 'So back I came. But I'll have to sleep here, at the studio. I'm on my own now, so I haven't got the cash for the Tourist Pavilion, or anywhere else for that matter . . .' She smiled slowly, still looking at Simon. 'So I'll have to sleep rough.'

What it was in her intonation I do not know, but somehow she managed to say the last simple sentence as if it meant sharing a bed with a sadist, and that meant Simon. I felt another spasm of intense irritation. I knew I should have wanted to feel sorry for Danielle, or even amused, but somehow it wasn't possible. I was beginning to suspect that she was not trying to ape a pathetic maturity; the *weltschmerz* wasn't a pose, it was real, and rather dreadful. So was the weariness in the big lost eyes. But the pity I should have owed her I felt for Nigel, now feverishly drying the tumbler and saying rapidly:

'It's wonderful to have you back. You know that. And of course you must stay in the studio. We'd love to have you, and you'll be quite all right here. There's only me and Simon and a Dutch painter–'

'A Dutch painter?'

Simon said smoothly: 'A boy of about twenty who has walked from Jannina and is very, very tired.'

She shot him a look up under the fabulous lashes. 'Oh.' She threw the half-smoked cigarette into the wash-basin where it lay smouldering. 'Give me another cigarette, Simon.'

He obeyed. 'Camilla?'

'Thank you,' I said.

Nigel pushed past me with a tumbler three parts full of neat ouzo. 'Here's your drink, Danielle.' His face was anxious, concentrated. He might have been carrying the Holy Grail. She took it from him and gave him a brilliant smile. I saw him blink, and the flush on the burnt cheek-bones deepened. 'Nigel, darling. I'm glad I came back.'

'Danielle–' He made a clumsy movement towards her but she evaded it without seeming to see it, and lifted the glass towards him as she sat back against the bed-head.

'*Gia sou*, Nigel darling. . . but you're not drinking with me.'

It should have been corny, but it wasn't. The expression on the boy's face was naked. He turned and grabbed the bottle and poured an inch or two of liquor into his empty glass. But even as he turned back, the girl yawned, stretched, tilted her head back on its long neck, and put out a hand towards Simon. Her finger-nails were very long and very red. Her fingers ran caressingly down his sleeve. 'Actually,' she said, still in that bored, velvet voice, 'actually, you know, I'm Simon's girl. Aren't I, Simon?'

I must have jumped about a foot. Simon looked down through the smoke of his cigarette, and said lazily: 'Are you? Delighted, of course. But perhaps in that case you'll tell me why you hired a car for me in Athens this morning?'

The hand froze, then withdrew quickly. The thin body twisted on the bed in the first movement she had made unconsciously since she came in. It wasn't sexy in the least. It was plain startled.

'What are you talking about?'

'The car you hired in my name this morning. The car you were to have picked up at the Alexandros restaurant.'

The black eyes held his for a moment, then dropped. 'Oh, that.' Her voice was calm and husky as usual. 'How did you find out?'

'My dear Danielle, you hired it for me, didn't you? And you failed to pick it up. Naturally the people at the Alexandros got in touch with me.'

'But that's impossible! How did they know?' She was scowling up at him now.

'Never mind how. Tell me why.'

She shrugged and drank ouzo. 'I wanted to come back to Delphi. I told you that I hired a car. They never take any notice in Greece of a woman, so I gave your name.'

'And said it was a matter of life and death?'

'What? Don't be silly. Of course I never said that.' She laughed. 'You're very dramatic, Simon.'

'Perhaps. A dramatic place, this. It gets into the blood. But you did hire the car.'

'Yes.'

'And came without it.'

'Yes.'

'Why?'

I thought unhappily, because a fool of a girl called Camilla Haven had already taken it. Why couldn't Simon let well alone? Somehow I didn't particularly want to tangle with Danielle Lascaux. And she had every right to be mad with me if she had hired the beastly car—in whatever name—and had then had to come up to Delphi by bus. She didn't look tired and bad-tempered, but it seemed she had arrived very late, and that was presumably my fault.

'Why?' said Simon.

She said sulkily: 'Because I got the offer of the jeep from Hervé. It was more convenient.'

I said, before I thought: 'I knew I'd seen you before! You were the girl in the jeep that overtook me just before Thebes. I remember you particularly. You were driving on the wrong side of the road.'

She yawned, showing her tongue between her teeth. She didn't even look at me. 'Probably. I find it more exciting that way.'

Simon said: 'Then you got up here well before Camilla did. Where've you been?'

She said, almost bad-temperedly: 'What's it matter? Around.'

I said. 'In Itea?'

Danielle shot upright on the bed. Some ouzo spilled. 'What are you talking about?' I saw a look of surprise touch Simon's face, then the familiar expressionless mask shut down. With the faintest quickening of the blood, I thought: *He's interested. This means something.*

I said: 'I saw the jeep in Itea this evening. It was parked beside a house that stands right away from the village in the olive-woods. I hadn't realised till this minute that it was the same one, but now I remember. It had a little tinsel doll hanging in the wind-screen—where they usually have the icons. I remember noticing that when you passed me near Thebes.'

She wasn't drinking. The smoke from that eternal cigarette crept up in a veil, hiding the expression of her eyes. 'This evening? How can you be so sure? Wasn't it dark?'

'Oh, yes. But there was a man with a torch tinkering with the engine, and the light caught the tinsel. Then the lights went on in the house.'

'Oh.' She drank a gulp of neat ouzo. It didn't appear to affect her. 'Well, I expect it was the same jeep. I was down there, with . . . someone I know.' Again that intonation, that glance up towards Simon. Nigel was watching her like a lost dog. I thought it was some—surprising—impulse of mercy that made her add: 'I always go down to Itea in the afternoons. I've done it for weeks. I go to swim. Nigel knows that.'

Nigel responded instantly, almost as if the last sentence had been a plea of proof. 'Of course I know. But—did you really go there today before you even came up here?'

'Uh-huh.' She gave him a narrow, glinting smile. 'You were out, weren't you?'

'Yes.'

'I thought you might be. And I'd brought Elena a present from Athens, so—'

'Elena?' said Nigel quickly.

'My friend in Itea. She often bathes from the same place as me, so I went back to her house with her.'

'Oh!' said Nigel.

I thought she watched him for a second before she turned back to me. 'And you, Camilla Haven? *You* went down to Itea first, before you came up here?'

'I only came up here an hour ago. I'm only visiting. I'm staying at the Apollon.'

'But you went straight to Itea.' The words were sharp, almost, and sounded so much like an accusation that I said quickly: 'I called at the hotel first.' Then I added: 'I went down to Itea to find the hirer of the car.'

There was a little silence. 'The . . . hirer of the car?' repeated Danielle.

'Yes. I—it was I who brought the car up from the Alexandros in Omonia Square. I—I was looking for the "Monsieur Simon" who was alleged to be wanting it.'

She blew out a small cloud of smoke and leaned back against the head of the bed, regarding me through it. 'I . . . see. You brought my car up here? You?'

'Yes,' I said unhappily. 'I was in the Alexandros restaurant when the man from the garage came, and he mistook me for you. He gave me the keys and told me it was urgent, and that "Monsieur Simon" wanted the car at Delphi as soon as possible. I—we got in a muddle of cross-purposes, and he vanished, leaving me with the key, and no idea of the address of the garage. I didn't know what to do, but I wanted to come here myself, and—well, he'd been so insistent that it was a "matter of life and death" that—'

'That stuff again,' said Danielle.

'That stuff again.' I added: 'I'm glad I don't seem to have inconvenienced you after all. You must have got here well before me. I told you you passed me before Thebes.'

She said quite sharply: 'And why did you have to go to Itea to find Simon?'

'Oh, I didn't. I—well, he found me quite easily. But of course as he didn't know anything about the car, that didn't help. We went to look for another "Simon", actually a Simonides who keeps a baker's shop near the cinema.'

'That's not,' said Danielle, 'in the olive-woods.'

'No. I went to see the Pilgrims' Way.'

'The Pilgrims' Way?' she said blankly.

Simon said: 'Yes. You ought to know all about that, Danielle.'

She said quickly: 'Why?'

'My dear girl. Because you've worked here as an archaeologist's secretary.'

'Mistress,' said Danielle automatically.

Nigel said suddenly from behind me: 'I wish you wouldn't talk like that.'

She opened her mouth as if to say something blistering, but shut it again, and gave him one of the slow smiles. I didn't look at him. I said quickly: 'Look, Danielle, I really am terribly sorry about this car. I suppose I—yes, I did think I might be doing the right thing, but it seems I was a bit hasty. I do hope it isn't going to cause any inconvenience *now*, because—'

'You brought it up here.' She turned her head to give me a narrow look through the curling smoke. 'You keep it.'

I looked at her for a moment. Then I said slowly: 'I suppose that is fair enough.'

'You weren't asked to bring it here. I don't want it. You're stuck with it, and I hope you can afford to pay for it.' She turned away to flick ash towards the wash-basin. It missed and fell to the floor.

There was a short silence. I said carefully: 'Whom do I pay?'

Her head came quickly back to me. 'What d'you mean?'

'What I said.'

'Well, me, of course. Didn't they tell you the deposit had been paid?'

'Oh, yes, they told me that.'

'So what?' said Danielle.

I stood up and picked up my handbag. 'Only that it surprises me a bit that you didn't call in on the garage after you'd got the jeep, and cancel the car. If you're as short of money as you've been telling us, I'd have imagined the deposit would have come in very handy. In fact, I can't see why you should have hired a car at all. The bus is cheaper. Perhaps you'll let me have the receipt, with the address of the garage?'

She sounded sulky. 'Tomorrow. I have it somewhere.'

'Very well.' I turned to smile at Nigel. 'I really must go, Nigel, or it'll be dawn before I get to bed. Thank you very much for the drink, and for letting me see the drawings. I think they're wonderful—I honestly do; and that last one is . . . well, a masterpiece. That isn't trite; it's true. Good night.'

Simon was on his feet. As I turned to go he made as if to move forward, but Danielle came off the bed in one quick wriggle, like a snake. It brought her very close to him.

'Simon –' the claws were on his arm again – 'my room's the one at the end, and the shower's stuck, or something. The damned thing drips and I'll never get to sleep. D'you suppose you could fix it for me?'

'I doubt if I'd be much good with it. In any case I'm seeing Camilla home now, and then I –'

I said stiffly: 'There's not the slightest need to see me home. I can find my way quite easily.'

'– and then I've got to go back and pick the car up. We left it below the shrine.'

Nigel had opened the door for me. I looked back at Simon, with Danielle clinging to his arm. 'You really needn't trouble. The car is my responsibility . . . as Danielle has pointed out.'

His eyes, amused, met mine. I bit my lip, and said: 'All right. I – it's very kind of you.'

'Not at all. After all, if the car was hired in my name I've a sort of responsibility myself, wouldn't you say, Danielle?'

She flashed me one look of pure venom, under her lashes, then lifted them again to him. Her voice was all honey. 'Not really. But if that's how you feel . . . You'll come and fix that shower later, won't you? It really is a bore.'

'Not tonight,' said Simon. 'Good night. Good night, Nigel, and thanks a lot. See you later.'

On the way down to the hotel, which took about twelve minutes and was very steep and rough, we concentrated on not breaking our ankles and on not talking about Danielle. For me, the first was the easier task of the two.

At the hotel Simon said: 'Camilla.'

'Yes?'

'Come off it.'

I laughed. 'Very well.'

'I grant you every right to the highest horse, or deepest dudgeon, or whatever it is, in Christendom. All right?'

'Perfectly.'

'Don't worry about the damned car. I didn't pursue it in front of – well, back there, but I'll be very glad of it myself now that it's here, so don't give it another thought.'

'I will not,' I said clearly, 'allow you to pay for my – my folly.'

'We will not,' said Simon calmly, 'argue about it now. You should be in bed. You've had a long day, and tomorrow will probably be longer.'

'I shall probably have to go tomorrow.'

'Tomorrow? My God, the dudgeon isn't as deep as that, is it?'

'Dudgeons are high. No, it's not that. But there may not be a room at the hotel.'

'Oh, I forgot. Well, look here, why not come up to the studio? You've seen it. It's plain, but clean, and very convenient. And now it seems—' the grey eyes crinkled at the corners—'that you'll be chaperoned.'

'I'll think about it,' I said, without much enthusiasm.

He hesitated, then said: 'I hope you will. I—please don't go tomorrow. I was hoping you'd come with me.'

I stared at him. 'But—I thought you were going up Parnassus with Stephanos?'

'I am. I want you to come. Will you?'

'But Simon—'

'Will you?'

I said huskily: 'This is absurd.'

'I know. But there it is.'

'It's your own very private business. Just because I—I bulldozed you into my affairs it doesn't mean you have to ask me to tag along in yours.'

The amusement was there again. 'No. Will you?'

'Yes. Of course.'

'It'll be a long trek. An all-day job. If the hotel say they can't keep you you'll let me ring up Athens for you and get you into the studio?'

'Ring up Athens?'

'It's the property of the University Fine Arts Department, and you're not an accredited artist any more than I am. You'll have to come in as a student.'

'Oh, of course. And Danielle?'

He grinned. 'Maybe archaeologists count. If she gives my name to hire a car, she may give Hervé's when she wants a room in the studio.'

'I suppose so. Well, please ring up Athens for me and I'll move in tomorrow night. What time do we start?'

'I'll call for you at half past eight.' He gave me his sudden smile.

'Good night, Camilla. And thank you.'
  'Good night.'
  As he turned to go I said, before I could prevent myself: 'Don't forget to go and fix the taps, will you?'
  'Taps,' said Simon gently, 'bore me. Good night.'

Chapter 10

What a personage says or does reveals a certain moral purpose; and a good element of character, if the purpose so revealed is good. Such goodness is possible in every type of personage, even in a woman.
ARISTOTLE: *The Art of Poetry.*
(tr. Ingham Bywater.)

NEXT MORNING I awoke early, so early that, when I found I couldn't easily go to sleep again, I decided to get up and see the ruins on my own before the day's adventures started. The thought made me, with a wry little smile, remember that I hadn't yet posted my letter to Elizabeth. When I was ready to leave my room I fished it out of my bag, opened it, and added a hasty postscript:

Did I say nothing ever happened to me? It's started as from yesterday. If I live I'll write and let you know what you're missing.
Love, Camilla.

The sun was already hot and bright, though it was only just a little past seven o'clock. I walked along the village street to post my letter, then turned into the steep way that climbs between terraced streets to the mountain-side above.

This was a flight of wide steps, bounded by whitewashed walls from which the sun beat back. The already blinding white was muted everywhere by greenery; from every wall and roof spilled vines and hanging ferns, the vivid pinks and scarlets of geraniums, and brilliant cascades of marigolds and black-eyed Susans. At my feet hens pecked and scratched about. Now and then I stood aside as a donkey or a mule picked its dainty accurate way down the steps, while a black-veiled peasant woman, following it, smiled and gave me a soft 'Good morning'.

The steps took me eventually clear of the village, on to the hillside where piles of rubble and kerbstones indicated that a new road was being built. I made my way carefully along this, watched by the friendly and curious stares of the workmen, and, before I was aware that I had come so far, found myself clear of the last house, and out on the open hillside above the studio.

The climb had been steep, and the sun was hot. The path led along the foot of a low cliff-wall, which cast, at this early hour, a narrow shade. I found a flat rock in a recess of shadow, and sat down to recover from the climb.

The path that I was on seemed to be a continuation of the one that Simon and I had taken last night. It passed above the studio, then slanted down into the knot of pines that I remembered, and vanished thence more steeply towards the ruined temple precincts. Not far from where I sat, below me now and to the right of the path, I could see the studio, dumped down raw and square and ugly in its quarried plateau. Beyond it the valley of the olives swam and shimmered in the immense liquid distance of light, and beyond that again mountain after mountain, and the sea.

Then my attention was taken by a movement near the studio.

Someone was as early abroad as I. I heard the scuffle of footsteps mounting the rough path that led up from the plateau. Then I saw him, a thin, fair-haired figure carrying a rucksack, and clambering at a fair speed but with very little noise, towards the path where I sat in the shadow. He hadn't looked in my direction; he was making for the knot of pines above the shrine, and moving away from me rapidly.

He reached the path. He was about seventy yards away from me, near the fence that marked the graveyard. He stopped, and turned, as if to pause for breath and survey the view.

I was just about to get to my feet and hail him, when something about the way he was acting caught my attention, and I stayed still. He had taken a couple of quick steps back and sideways, into the shadow of a pine-tree. The dappled shade netted and hid him, maculate, invisible. He stayed there, stock-still, and he wasn't looking at any view; his head was bent as if he studied the ground at his feet, but I knew, suddenly, that he was listening. He didn't move. There was no sound in the lovely bright morning but the chime of a goat-bell from the other side of the valley, and the crowing of a cock down in the village. No sound from the studio; no movement.

Nigel lifted his head, and was looking about him, still with those wary, abruptly stealthy movements. It was quite obvious that, wherever he was going, he didn't want to be followed, and remembering Danielle, I thought I saw his point. And I wouldn't interrupt his getaway either. Smiling to myself, I stayed where I was. I didn't think he would see me unless I moved, and nor he did. He turned suddenly, and, leaving the path, plunged uphill through the pines towards the higher levels where the ancient stadium stood, and, beyond it, the track that led above the Shining Ones and away into the upper reaches of Parnassus.

I gave him a minute or two, and then I got up and went on. Soon I, too, was under the shadow of the pines, and to my right was the tumbledown fence, and the thicket of dried weeds that edged the graveyard.

I don't quite know what made me do it, except that somehow, already, Michael Lester's affair was my own. I pushed open the creaking gate and went in among the stones. When I found it I had to spell it out very slowly to be sure it was the one.

ΜΙΧΑΕΛ ΛΕΣΤΗΡ

This alien cross, an alien epitaph . . . and in my ear Simon's voice, claiming him still: '*My brother Michael.*' And behind that again I could hear the ghosts of other voices, other claims: '*The woman of my house, the cousin of Angelos, the brother of Michael*' . . . ' "*No man is an island, entire of itself*".'

I stood there in the hot early-morning silence and thought about Simon. Today, I was committed to Simon's quest. I, too, had answered a claim. He was going to see the place where Michael had died, and he had wanted me to go, too.

And I? Why had I said that I would go? I had said last night that it was absurd, and so it was . . . But I had a queer feeling that, quite apart from Simon's need of me, I had a need of my own. I, too, had something to find.

A bird, small and bright as a blown leaf, flew across the hot stillness. I turned away and made my way between the dusty mounds towards the gate.

I was thinking now, not of Simon, but of myself. Not of the self, the identity I had felt it so necessary to assert when I had sent back

Phil's ring, but of the identity I had assumed so lightly yesterday
and which, it seemed, I could not yet put off. Not Camilla Haven,
but just 'Simon's girl'.

I let myself quickly through the gate, and hurried down the path
till it brought me out above the ruins of the great shrine.

*　　*　　*

I've already written enough of Delphi, and indeed it's not easy to
write about. The place takes the heart and the senses and wrings
them dry. Eyes and ears and the instinct of worship are all that is
needed there.

I walked slowly downhill in the sunlight. Here was the little
pomegranate tree, clinging to a cleft in the marble of the theatre. Its
leaves hung now without a rustle, dark green and still. The fruit was
flame-coloured and as glossy as witchballs. Here were the breakneck
steps . . . and here the stage of the theatre, where Simon had spoken
last night; I could see the mark at the centre, where one's voice was
taken and flung high up the mountainside. And now the steps to the
precinct . . . that must be the monument of Alexander . . . and this
the temple floor of Apollo.

The six great columns stood up like fire against the immense
depths of the valley.

No one was about. I crossed the temple floor and sat down at the
edge with my back to one of the columns. The stone was hot. Above
my head the crumbling capitals were alive with the wings of
martins. Far below me the olives shimmered along the valley. In the
distance Helicon was blue, was silver, was grey as Aphrodite's
doves. Everywhere were the voices of songbirds, because Delphi is
sanctuary. Somewhere in the morning distance sheepbells were
ringing . . .

It was still only eight o'clock when I left my seat and walked down
the Sacred Way from the temple to the edge of the precinct, where a
thick rank of pines keeps it from the road below. I went along the
path under the pines, then down to the museum which sits in a
curve of the road. I already seemed to have been up and about for so
long that it was a surprise to find the doors still shut. There was a
man in guide's uniform sitting under the trees on the other side of
the road, so I crossed over to speak to him.

'The museum?' he said in answer to my query. 'I am afraid it doesn't open till half past nine. But would you like a guide now for the ruins, no?'

'Not this morning, thank you,' I said. 'I've just been up there. But possibly tomorrow, if I'm still in Delphi. . . Will you be about here?'

'Always, at this time.' He had a dark square face, and, surprisingly, blue eyes. His look was sophisticated, and he spoke very good English.

I said: 'I wanted to see the Charioteer.'

'Of course.' He grinned, showing very white teeth. 'But there are other things too, here in Delphi.'

'Oh, yes, I know, but isn't he the first thing everyone looks for in the museum?'

'Of course,' he said again. 'If you come with me tomorrow I will take you also round the museum myself.'

'I should like that very much.' I hesitated. 'Do you—I wonder if you know the young English artist who is staying up at the studio? Thin and fair, with a little beard?'

'Yes. I know him. He has been here in Delphi for quite a time, no?'

'I believe so. Does he—has he been to the museum much?'

'Indeed, yes. He comes very often to draw. Have you seen any of his drawings, *kyria*? They are very good, very good indeed.'

'He showed me some of them last night, but not, I think, any of the statues and antiquities. I imagine he would do those well. Did he do any of the Charioteer?'

'Of course. Did you not say yourself that he is the first thing one looks for? And certainly in our small museum he is the *pièce de résistance*.'

'Was he—did you notice if the artist was here yesterday?'

The guide didn't seem to be at all surprised at the odd catechism. His experience of tourists must have bred in him a vast tolerance. He shook his head. 'I do not think so. I was here all day, but he may have been down here while I was up in the ruins. The tour takes nearly an hour. If you wish to see him, he sleeps up at the studio above the site, where they are building the new road.'

'Perhaps I'll see him later.' I judged it time to drop that particular catechism. 'What new road are they making away up there above the village? Where can it possibly go?'

'To the stadium. Have you seen that yet?'

'Not yet.'

'It is high above the shrine. Many tourists who come to Delphi never see it at all, because the climb is too steep. It is very

beautiful—just the old oval race-track with the tiers of seats, exactly
as it was in ancient times, and with the view . . . always that view of
the olives and the valley and the sea. So now they make a road to let
the cars and buses take the tourists up.'

I stifled a pang at the thought of yet another wild and lovely
sanctuary invaded by cars and buses, and said: 'Ah, yes. I suppose
anything that will bring money into Greece is a good thing. You are
a native of Delphi, *kyrie*?'

'No. I am a man of Tinos.'

'Oh. Then . . . I suppose you weren't here during the war?'

He smiled. 'No. I was busy—very busy—on my island.'

My island. There it was again. *A man of Tinos*.

Then he would not remember Michael Lester. It was possible that
he had never heard of him. In any case—I caught at myself—I must
not let myself go beyond even Simon's claim on my interest. I said
merely: 'Of course.'

He was rolling a cigarette with neat, quick movements.

'There was certainly no need *then* for guides in Delphi, *kyria*. No
one was troubling then about the shrine and the sanctuary and the
Charioteer! We may say, if you like, that it is a pity—if men had had
the time to come, as they came here in the days of the Oracle, when
Delphi was the centre of the world, no doubt they would have found
their quarrels healed.' That quick sophisticated look, and the sudden
grin again. 'That, you understand, is what I always say when I show
my tourists round. It is a very effective bit of patter. The Amphictionic League of Delphi. The League of Nations. U.N.O. Very
effective.'

'I'm sure it is. Do you add the bits about the fights between
Delphi and her neighbours, and the laying waste of Chrissa, and the
monuments for Athenian victories over the Spartans, and Spartan
victories over the Athenians, and the Argive monument stuck down
just where it would annoy the Spartans most, and—'

'Sometimes.' He was laughing. 'I shall have to—what do you
say?—watch my step when I show you round tomorrow, shall I not?'

'Not really. I read an awful lot up specially before I came. It
makes it more exciting to *know* what happened here. I looked at a lot
of photographs, too.' I hesitated again. 'The Charioteer . . .' I said
slowly. 'What of him?'

I was carrying a guide-book in my hand; *A Concise Guide of Delphi*,
it was called, and on the cover there was a photographic rep-
roduction of the head of the famous statue. I held it out. 'This. I've

heard so much about him, but I can't help wondering if I'll really
like him. Those eyes; they're inlaid with onyx and white enamel,
aren't they? And there are long metal eyelashes? They do look alive,
I admit, but–look, you see what I mean?' I indicated the print.
'That narrow forehead and the heavy jaw; it's not strictly a beautiful
face, is it? And yet everyone says he's so wonderful.'

'And so will you. No picture gives the true impression. It's the
same with the great Hermes at Olympia. In photographs he is
effeminate, the marble too smooth, and shining like soap. But the
statue itself takes away the breath.'

'I know. I've seen it.'

'Then prepare yourself to see the Charioteer. It is one of the great
statues of Greece. Do you know the thing that comes to me first
whenever I see him again–which is every day?'

'What?'

'He is so very young. All that gravity, that grace, and so young
with it. It used to be thought that he was the owner of the team–the
winner of the race–but now they say that he was probably the
driver for some lord who owned the chariot.'

I said hesitantly: 'There's a bit in Pausanias' account of Delphi,
isn't there, about a chariot of bronze with a naked "lord of the car"
who might have had a driver, a youth of good family?'

'I believe there is, yes. But it could hardly apply to our Charioteer, *kyria*; the evidence is that he was probably buried in a great
landslip during an earthquake in 373 B.C., and, without being
uncovered again, was built into the–what do you call it?–the
supporting wall (the "earth-holder" is the Greek word), that was
erected to stop the rocks and earth from engulfing the temple again.'

'Retaining-wall,' I said.

'Ah, thank you. The retaining-wall. Well, you see, our Charioteer
had vanished a few centuries before Pausanias came to Delphi.'

'I see. I didn't know that.'

He had finished rolling the cigarette. He put it between his lips
and lit it with a spluttering of loose tobacco.

He said: 'They say now that the Charioteer was part of a
victory-group erected by one Gelon, the winner of a chariot-race,
but anything may be true. So much was lost or destroyed or stolen
over the centuries that the truth about our discoveries is only
guesswork. And Delphi suffered much, because she was so rich. I
think it is reckoned that there were six thousand monuments
here–at any rate that is the number of inscriptions that have been

uncovered.' He smiled, showing very white teeth. 'The landslide that broke and hid the Charioteer was an act of the gods, because it kept him out of the hands of the robbers. The Phocians laid the sanctuary waste barely twenty years after he was buried, and of course in later times countless treasures were destroyed or stolen.'

'I know. Sulla and Nero and the rest. How many bronzes do they reckon Nero took to Rome?'

'Five hundred.' He laughed again. 'I *shall* have to watch my patter tomorrow, I can see!'

'I told you I only read it up just before I came. And there's so much –'

A sudden clatter and a volley of shouts from somewhere behind the museum startled me, and I stopped and glanced over my shoulder. 'What on earth's that?'

'Nothing. A little disagreement among the workmen.'

'A little disagreement? It sounds like a major war!'

'We are always a fighting race, I am afraid. There is trouble today among the workmen. There are still men here from the "dig" of the French archaeologists – the "dig" is finished, but workmen have remained to clear up, and to remove the rails that the trucks ran on, and things of that kind. A mule strayed during the night, and now they have discovered that some tools are missing, and they are accusing the men who work on the stadium road of theft, and so – well, you hear that there is a little disagreement.'

'Some tools and a mule?' I listened to the uproar for a moment or two. It sounded like the battle of El Alamein in stereophonic sound. I said drily: 'Perhaps they haven't heard of the Amphictionic League and the peace of Delphi.'

He smiled. 'Perhaps not.'

'And now I really must go. I'll let you know if I can come with you tomorrow. You say you'll be here at this time?'

'Always.'

I had a sharp inner vision of a life where one would be – always – serenely on the Delphi road in the early morning sun. 'I'll try and be here by eight if I'm coming. If I can't –'

'It does not matter. If you come, I will take you with the greatest of pleasure. If not, it does not matter. Are you staying at the Apollon?'

'Yes.'

'It is very nice, yes?'

'Delightful.' I lingered for a moment, looking at the closed door of the museum. He was watching me through the smoke of his cigarette with that shrewd, incurious blue gaze. I said: 'Kyrie . . . you weren't here during the war, of course, but you'll know what happened to the statues and things from the museum? The Charioteer, for instance? Where was he? Hidden?'

'Only in a manner of speaking. He was in Athens.'

'Oh. Yes. I see.'

Behind me a shabby black car slid to a halt. Simon grinned at me over the door and said: 'Good morning.'

'Oh, Simon! Am I late? Have you had to hunt for me?'

'The answer to both those is no. I was early and they told me you'd come down here. Have you had breakfast?'

'Hours ago.'

'Why people should adopt that disgustingly self-righteous tone whenever they manage to achieve breakfast before eight o'clock I do not know,' said Simon. He leaned across the car and opened the door for me. 'Come along, then, let's go. Unless of course you'd like to drive?'

I didn't bother to answer that one, but slipped quickly into the passenger's seat beside him.

As the car turned the corner and gathered speed along the straight stretch below the temple I said, without preliminary: 'The Charioteer was in Athens during the war. Presumably in hiding.'

He gave me a quick glance. 'Oh. Yes, it would be, wouldn't it?' I saw him smile.

I said, almost defensively: 'Well, you did get me into it, after all.'

'I did, didn't I?' A little pause. 'Did you come down through the temple this morning?'

'Yes.'

'I thought you might do that. I've been up there myself most mornings by about six.'

'Not today?'

He smiled. 'No. I thought you'd like it to yourself.'

'You're very –' I began, and stopped. He didn't ask me what I'd been going to say. I said, not quite irrelevantly: 'Do you ever lose your temper, Simon?'

'What in the world makes you ask that?'

'Oh, come, I thought you were a thought-reader!'

'Oh. Well, let me see . . . Last night?'

'That didn't take much guessing. Yes, of course. Nigel was abominably rude to you. Didn't you mind?'

'Mind? No.'

'Why not?'

'I don't think I'd have minded from Nigel anyway, because he's not very happy. Life isn't easy for him, and on top of everything he has to fall for that girl, and she's led him the hell of a dance. But last night–' He paused, and I saw again that pucker of worry round his eyes. 'Last night there was something wrong. Really wrong, I mean; not just Nigel's too-usual brand of nerves and temperament and frustrated talent, and that little witch playing him on a very barbed hook. There was something more.'

'Are you sure he wasn't just a bit drunk? He said he was.'

'Possibly. But that's part of the trouble; he doesn't drink much as a rule, and last night he was fairly putting it away, though he's like you–he doesn't like ouzo. No, there was definitely something very wrong, and I'd give quite a lot to know what it was.'

'I take it he didn't tell you anything after you got back to the studio? I got the impression he was going to come out with something just as Danielle interrupted.'

'Yes, so did I. But I didn't see him again. His room was empty when I went back. I waited a bit, but eventually went to bed. I didn't hear him come in.'

'Perhaps,' I said a little drily, 'he was fixing the taps.'

'That did occur to me. But no. Danielle's door was standing open. She wasn't there either. I think they'd gone for a walk, or down to the village for another drink, or something. And Nigel had gone when I got up this morning.'

I said: 'He went up the mountain. I saw him.'

'You saw him?'

'Yes, at about seven o'clock. He went up past the graveyard through those pines, as if he was going further up the hill.'

'Alone?'

'Yes. In fact he looked rather as if he wanted to be left very much alone. I didn't speak to him, and I don't think he saw me.'

Simon said: 'Well, let's hope he does some work today, and draws it out of himself, whatever it is. I expect I'll see him tonight.' He glanced at me, smiling. 'Did you make any more discoveries this morning?'

'Only one,' I said, before I thought.

'And that?'

I found myself telling him, quite simply. 'It was just my own discovery. We talked about it last night, with Nigel. It's something

we're taught from childhood, but I'd never really had it brought
home to me till now.'

'What is it?'

'That saying of "your parson friend", as Nigel called him.'

'Ah, yes, that.' He was silent for a moment, then he quoted it
softly, as if half to himself: ' *"No man is an island, entire of itself; every
man is a piece of the Continent, a part of the main; if a clod be washed away
by the sea, Europe is the less, as well as if a promontory were, as well as if a
Manor of thy friends' or of thine own were. Any man's death diminishes me,
because I am involved in mankind; and therefore never send to know for
whom the bell tolls; it tolls for thee"* . . . Terrific piece of writing, isn't
it? One should remember it more often.'

The car slowed down and drew out to pass a little group of three
donkeys pattering along in the dust at the edge of the road. On the
foremost an old woman sat sideways; she had a distaff in her left
hand, the spindle in her right, and as she rode she spun the white
wool ceaselessly, without looking at it. She ducked a smiling salute
to us as we went by.

Simon said: 'What brought that home to you this morning?'

I hesitated, then said flatly: 'Michael's grave.'

'I see.' And I thought he did.

I said: 'It's this confounded country. It does things to one—
mentally and physically and I suppose morally. The past is so living
and the present so intense and the future so blooming imminent. The
light seems to burn life into you twice as intensely as anywhere else
I've known. I suppose that's why the Greeks did what they did so
miraculously, and why they could stay themselves through twenty
generations of slavery that would have crushed any other race on
earth. You come here thinking you're going to look at a lot of
myth-haunted ruins and picturesque peasants and you find that . . .'
I stopped.

'That what?'

'No. I'm talking piffle.'

'It's good piffle. Go on. What do you find?'

'You find that the grave of Michael Lester is as moving and as
important as the tomb of Agamemnon at Mycenae, or Byron or
Venizelos or Alexander. He, and the men like him, are a part of the
same picture.' I stopped, and then said helplessly: 'Greece. Damn it,
what is it that it does to one?'

He was silent a moment, then he said: 'I think the secret is that it
belongs to all of us—to us of the West. We've learned to think in its

terms, and to live in its laws. It's given us almost everything that our world has that is worth while. Truth, straight thinking, freedom, beauty. It's our second language, our second line of thought, our second country. We all have our own country – and Greece.'

We sailed round a bend of the road and ahead of us the deep valley opened to show a great rounded beauty of a mountain, silver-green, blue-veined, cloud-grey.

'Why, damn it all,' said Simon. 'That hill in front of us. That's Helicon. *Helicon.* And then you wonder why this country gets you in the wind?'

'Not any more,' I said.

And we didn't speak again till we came to Arachova and found Stephanos and Niko waiting for us in the café on the corner.

*　　*　　*

'Do you like my socks?' asked Niko.

'They're wonderful,' I said truthfully. They were indeed, in that landscape, something to be wondered at. They were luminous, and of a startling shade of shocking pink. They shone among the bleached hot stones of the mountain track like neon signs against a clear sky.

'They light up,' explained Niko.

'I can see that. Where did you get them?'

'In Athens. They are the latest thing from New York.'

'Do you go to Athens often?'

'No. I went to work there when I was fourteen. I was a page boy at the Acropole Palace Hotel.'

'I see. Is that where you learned your English?'

'Some of it. I also learn it here in the school. Is good, huh?'

'Very good. Why didn't you stay in Athens?'

'Is better here.' Niko looked back along the track we were climbing. Away below us Arachova had dwindled to a toy waterfall of coloured roofs. Niko turned back to me almost as if he were puzzled. 'Here there is nothing. Is no money. But is better here. Arachova is my village.' Again that look. 'You think I am crazy? *You* come from London where there is plenty money. All Greeks are a little crazy, huh? But you think I am stupid to leave Athens?'

'There is a sort of divine madness about all the Greeks I've met,' I said, laughing. 'But you're not crazy, Niko. It's better here, certainly, money or no money. Don't ever live in a town unless you have to! And I don't live in London. I live miles away from it, in a country village, just like you.'

'Like Arachova?' He was vastly surprised. I had long since discovered that to all Greeks England meant London and nothing else. London, the huge, the golden-pavemented, the jacinth-gated.

'Not quite like Arachova.'

'And that is your village, as Arachova is mine.'

I said: 'Not quite, Niko. We've lost that way of feeling, I'm afraid. How far is this place that we're making for?'

'Making? *Oriste?*'

'Going to. The place where Michael died.' I said it softly, with my eyes on Simon's back where he walked with Stephanos a few yards ahead of us.

'About an hour from here. More, perhaps. It is nearer to Delphi than Arachova. It is in a . . . I do not know the word, a hollow place, a –' He stopped and made a scooping gesture.

'A corrie? Like this?'

'Yes. That is it. A corrie, where the rocks have fallen near the foot of a cliff. My grandfather know the way. He tell me it looks to the north-west – that is, away from Delphi and Arachova, towards Amphissa. This track goes along the face of the mountains, and then we leave it and climb up towards these cliffs where the corrie is. I think that many, many years ago there was a road for beasts, but not now. I do not know how far. I have never been, me. My grandfather he know the way. You are tired?'

'No. It's rather hot, but I'm not tired.'

'In Greece,' said Niko reflectively, eyeing me, 'the women are very strong.'

I thought of the village cafés, with their day-long complement of cheerfully idle men. 'I imagine they have to be,' I said.

'Oh, yes.' Niko misunderstood me, probably deliberately. 'In Greece the men are tough. Oh, very tough.'

Somehow, at that moment, Niko's racy beauty managed to look very tough indeed. His swagger, and the look he gave me, were the plainest possible invitation to the kind of suggestive verbal sparring that the Mediterranean men seem to love. But two could play at the game of misunderstanding. I said cheerfully: 'Then if we do meet the shade of Angelos on the hill, I shall feel quite, quite safe with you, Niko.'

'How?' He was momentarily thrown off his stride. 'Oh, yes! But of course you will be safe with me! I should kill him, you understand. He helped to kill my great-grandfather's brother's son Panos, so of course I should kill him. And—' the swagger gave away again to Niko's own brand of youthful and artless high spirits—'it would be easy, because he is old and I am young.'

'I suppose he's all of forty,' I agreed. 'And just how old are you, Niko?'

'I am seventeen.'

I said mendaciously: 'Really? I'd have thought you were much older than that.'

He flashed me his delighted smile. 'Would you? Would you really? And how old are you, beautiful miss?'

'Niko! Don't you know the rules better than that? I'm twenty-five.'

'So old? But you do not look like twenty-five,' he said generously. 'It is a good age to be, not? See, this bit is rough. Take my hand, miss.'

I laughed. 'I'm not as old as all that, Niko. And I'm truly not a bit tired. Just hot.'

It was indeed very hot. As we climbed steadily north-west the sun beat down on the right, throwing shadows sharp and hard as graphite along the white rock. The track where we walked was only by courtesy a track. It was not steep, cutting at a slant along the great flank of the mountain, but it was very rough, and some of the stones were sharp. We had long since left any trees behind, and the mountain-side, unpunctuated now by pine or cypress, stretched one great wing of burning white from the high hard blue sky down to the dry watercourse deep on our left. Beyond the tortured path of this dead stream, the rock rose again, this time violently blocked in with cobalt shadow. High above, so that to glance at them hurt the eyes, three birds hung, circling slowly and with moveless wings, like some mobile toy on invisible threads. I thought I could hear their faint, sweet mewing. Nothing else broke the silence except the scrape and clink of our feet, and the sound of our breathing.

The track ran straight up to what looked like a wall of fallen rocks and rubble, and there stopped, obliterated. Stephanos, in front, had halted, and turned to speak to Simon, who was just behind him. He said something, gesturing towards the barricade of rock.

It looked like a landslip, a great torrent of red and ochreous earth frozen even as it poured down the steep wing of the mountain. It was spiked with broken rock and great white slabs of fallen limestone. Further down the mountain-side it fanned out like the delta of a red river. Enormous blocks of stone had hurtled down with it, flung carelessly, as by the hand of an angry god, to dam the narrow gash of the watercourse.

Stephanos had turned aside to climb rather painfully up the steep hill-face beside the landslide.

'Is this where we leave the track?' I asked.

Simon turned. 'No. That's still with us. This stuff's just lying across it. If we follow Stephanos up a little there's a place where it's safer to cross.'

'It must have been quite a storm,' I said, surveying the torrent of rocks in front, and the gigantic flung boulders far below us.

'Not storm. Earthquake,' said Simon, then laughed at my expression. 'Yes, one forgets, doesn't one? I told you this was a savage country. And this, I believe, is a baddish area. They've had quite a history of tremors hereabouts. The miracle is that any of the old shrines and temples have a single pillar left standing. Can you manage?'

'Yes, thanks. Don't help me, Simon. I've got to keep my end up with Niko.'

'Of course—and mine, too, I think . . . That's it. We cross here. It seems stable enough, but watch yourself.'

We made our way slowly across the detritus of the earthquake. From higher up I could see where a whole slice of the mountain-cliff above us had been torn away and thrown down. It had splintered into great white spearheads, against which the smaller fragments were piled in the drift of dark red earth. We scrambled down this uncomfortable ramp towards the path which had shaken itself clear of the debris.

'I suppose the Earth-Shaker turned over in his sleep,' I said, 'and not so very long ago, either, by the look of it. The cracks look fairly fresh, don't they?'

Stephanos must have understood the drift of what I was saying. He had turned to wait for us on the track, and now spoke to Simon. 'What does he say?' I asked.

'He says that there were two or three small shocks—this, by the way, is a small shock—about twelve years ago. A little further on the mountain has been shifted about much more drastically. He says that only someone who was out on this part of Parnassus almost daily would still know his way about, once he had left the track. He also says that the place we are making for is almost completely changed since he found Michael there. It was just an open space at the foot of a low cliff, and now it's closed in by fallen rock into a kind of corrie, or hollow.'

Stephanos nodded as he finished. He gave me a look from under his magnificent white brows. He asked Simon a question.

'Are you tired?' asked Simon.

'No, thanks.'

Simon smiled. 'Don't exhaust yourself keeping Britain's end up, will you?'

'I'm not. It's only the heat.'

There was a flash of shocking pink socks beside me as Niko dropped off the rubble to land as neatly as a goat. He dragged a water-bottle out of a large pocket and unscrewed the top. 'Have a drink, miss.'

I drank thankfully. The bottle smelt ammoniac, like a nice donkey, but the water was good and still reasonably cool.

'Greek peasant women,' said Niko, watching me with that limpid look of his, 'can go for hours over the roughest country without food or drink.'

'So,' I said, stoppering the bottle and handing it back to him, 'can camels. Thank you, Niko, that was wonderful.'

'It was a pleasure, beautiful miss.' Niko turned to Simon and held out the bottle. His look and gesture expressed, somehow, the most tender solicitude.

Simon, smiling, shook his head.

'Good,' said Stephanos, and turned to go on. He and Simon forged ahead once more, and Niko and I took up our positions in the rear.

It must have been getting on for noon when we neared the corrie.

We left the track some way beyond the fall of rock and turned, in Stephanos' unfaltering wake, up into a markless desert of rock and dry earth. Sometimes we trudged upwards through sienna-coloured dust strewn cruelly with small boulders, and sometimes we walked more easily across great serrated flanges of the white and living rock. The sun was at its height and the heat was intense. The air wavered with it till the whole vast sweep of rock seemed to pulsate. If it hadn't been for the cool breeze that blew steadily at that height, it would have been insupportable.

By the time we were two-thirds of the way to the corrie, and had done most of the climbing, I had got my second wind, and was walking fairly easily. I was, I felt, upholding British Womanhood not too badly.

'The Greek peasant women,' said Niko, beside me, 'used to carry great loads of wood and grapes and things across here. Regularly.'

'If you tell me one more thing about Greek peasant women,' I said, 'I shall scream and lie down and refuse to move another step. Besides, I don't believe you.'

He grinned. 'It is not true,' he conceded. 'I think that you are very wonderful.'

'Why, Niko, that's nice of you!'

'And very beautiful, too,' said Niko. 'Would you like an apple?'

And he fished an apple out of his pocket and handed it to me with very much the air of a Paris presenting the prize to Aphrodite. His look of intense and dazzled admiration was, one felt, one that had been tried before and found to work.

It still worked. My morale soared. I laughed and took the apple and thanked him, and then a diversion was created because neither he nor Stephanos would allow me to eat it without peeling it, and Niko wanted to peel it for me and Stephanos had the knife, so, being Greeks, they plunged into a passionate discussion about this while Simon peeled the apple and then handed it to me.

'For the fairest,' he said.

'There's not,' I said, 'a lot of competition. But thank you all the same.'

Soon after that we reached our destination.

Chapter 11

That ground will take no footprint. All of it
Is bitter stone . . .
                    EURIPIDES: *Electra.*
                    (tr. Gilbert Murray.)

THE CORRIE DID not lie at any great height. Arachova itself is
almost three thousand feet above sea level, and we had climbed no
more than eight or nine hundred feet in all since we had left the
village. We were still only in the foothills of the vast highland of
Parnassus, but we might have been lost, a million miles from
anywhere. Since the village had dwindled out of sight we had seen
no living creature except the lizards, and the vultures that circled
and cried so sweetly, high in the dazzling air.

The place wasn't, properly speaking, a corrie. It was a hollow
scooped out of a line of low cliffs that topped a steep, mile-long ridge
like the crest along a horse's neck. From a distance the cliff looked
fairly uniform, but on approach it could be seen that it had been split
and torn into ragged bays and promontories where half a hundred
winter torrents had gouged their headlong way down the
mountain-side.

Here and there lay evidence of a swifter and more wholesale
violence. Earthquakes had wrested great chunks from the crag,
quarrying back into the limestone face, throwing the enormous
debris down, so that for hundreds of feet below the jagged cliffs, a
loose and sometimes dangerous scree valanced the sloping hillside.

As we neared the edge of this Stephanos turned aside, into a short
steep detour that took us out above the level of the clifftop, and we
approached the line of crags at a long slant that brought us
eventually to the edge.

The old man stopped then, leaning on his crook, and waited for us to come up with him.

Simon stood beside him, looking down.

'This is the place?'

'This is the place.'

It could have been a quarry hacked out of the cliff-face during countless patient years. It had probably taken five seconds of earthquake for the Earth-Shaker to tear that semi-circular scar back into the cliff and fling the wreckage down before it in still formidable walls of jagged rock. The result of the earthquake's action was to make a roughly circular hollow, a sort of irregular crater some seventy yards across, which was walled to the north by the living cliff on which we stood, and shut in almost completely for the rest of its diameter by the vast sections of tumbled rock.

The centre of the crater floor was clear, but the encircling walls were piled in the now familiar way with red dust and rock-debris. In spring, I thought, it would probably be beautiful, for it was sheltered, and I could see the dead remains of some scrubby plants and bushes where the melting snows and then the rain must have fed some alpine vegetation. Below us clung the lovely green of a little juniper, and just beside my feet the rock held two thick bushes that looked like holly, but which bore, incongruously, acorns with enormous cups as prickly as sea-urchins.

To the right, on the west side of the corrie, was what appeared to be the only way out. This was a break in the wall of rock, towards which the smooth crater floor lifted in a rocky ramp. From the height where we stood I thought I could see, beyond and below this 'gate', the ghost of an old track, leading westwards to vanish round a spur of the mountain.

Stephanos caught the direction of my glance. 'That is the way he went.'

He spoke in Greek, of course, and Simon translated for me, at the time in snatches, and more fully later; but once again I shall put the old man's words down directly, as they came.

'That is the way he went, down the old track towards Amphissa. It comes out above a disused quarry near the Amphissa road, behind the olive-groves.' He fell silent for a moment or two, looking down at the hollow beneath our feet. No one spoke. The sun beat on the backs of our necks, and I felt, suddenly, very tired.

Then the old man spoke again, slowly, reminiscently. 'I came to the head of the cliff just at this point. It was different then, you

understand . . . here, where we stand, there was a pinnacle of rock,
like a cat's tooth. It disappeared in the earthquake, but then it was a
landmark that even an Athenian could not have missed. And below
the cliff, then, there was no hollow, as you see it now, walled and
gated like a fortress. There was only the cliff, and below us some big
rocks lying, and a space of clean stone. It was there that I saw them,
Michael and Angelos. And the place is not covered. I marked it, and
I know. It was there.' The crook pointed. Almost in the centre of the
dazzling floor of smooth stone, a little pile of stones, a cairn, threw a
small triangular shadow. 'I put those there later,' said Stephanos,
'after the earthquake had moved the cliff, and the place was altered
beyond recognition.' There was another pause of silence, then he
glanced sideways at me. 'We will go down now . . . Will you tell the
lady to be very careful, *Kyrie* Simon? The path is steep, and made
only for goats, but it is the quickest way.'

As Simon transmitted the warning, I saw that there was indeed a
path down into the corrie. It left the cliff-top just beside us, between
the two bushes of holly-oak, and wound steeply down past more
mats of holly and the dusty ghosts of thistles, into the bottom of the
hollow. It was down this way that the dog must have raced to attack
Angelos, and then Stephanos himself, to run to Michael's side as he
lay dying in the sun . . .

The sun was so high that almost the whole of the corrie bottom
was shadowless. But where the cliff-path debouched on to the level,
a wing of rock cast a comforting angle of blue shade. I stopped there,
and sat down with my back against the warm stone. Stephanos
moved forward without pausing, and Simon followed him. Niko
flung himself down beside me on the dusty ground. I hoped he
wouldn't speak, and he didn't. He broke off a piece of a dead thistle
and began scratching patterns in the dust. He wasn't paying much
attention to his drawing; his intent gaze never left the other men.

Stephanos led Simon across the floor of the corrie, and stopped
beside the little cairn. He was pointing down at it and talking,
rapidly now. His hand moved and gestured, then came back to the
same spot. Almost I could see the dying man lying there in the
baking sun, the shepherd coming to the cliff-top where a fang of rock
stuck up like a cat's tooth, the dog dashing down that snaking path,
the murderer turning to bolt out of the 'gate' and down the track
towards Amphissa and the sea . . .

Then Stephanos turned heavily and trudged back to where we
sat. He lowered himself down beside me with a sigh, then said

something short to Niko, who got out a battered packet of cigarettes and handed him one. He gave his grandfather a light, then turned, with his brilliant smile, to offer a cigarette to me. We lit up in silence.

Simon was still standing in the centre of the corrie, but he wasn't looking down at the cairn where his brother had died. He had turned, and that cool appraising stare of his was slowly raking the sides of the corrie . . . the tumbled wall of rock that hemmed us in . . . the great sections that had fallen outward from the crag, and now made the two sidewings of the corrie, piled high in vast slabs and wedges against the old solid rock of the cliff . . . the hollow curve of a shallow cave exposed in the scooped segment of broken crag, a cave that had been deep before the front of the cliff had fallen away and left its recesses naked to the air . . .

My cigarette was mild and loosely packed and tasted slightly of goat; there was something about the beautiful Niko, I reflected, that harked back fairly consistently to the lower animals. I had half smoked it, and Niko's was gone entirely, when Simon's shadow fell beside us.

'What about lunch?' he asked.

The slight tension—of Stephanos' making, not Simon's—was broken, and we chatted over lunch as if it had been a normal picnic. My tiredness was rapidly dissolving, with the rest in the pleasant shade, and the solid excellence of the food we had bought in Arachova. We had rolls—a little dry after their progress in Niko's rucksack—with generous pieces of cold lamb sandwiched in; cheese in thick juicy slices; a paper full of olives that felt as if they were warm from the tree but were really warm from Niko; a hard-boiled egg; a very solid and very sweet chunk of some sort of cake made with fresh cherries; and a large handful of grapes, also warm and slightly tired-looking, but tasting ambrosially of the sun.

I noticed that Simon, as he ate, still looked about him, his eyes returning time after time, thoughtfully, to the recently-torn cliff behind us: 'This was done in the earthquake you spoke of, soon after the war?'

Stephanos said, through a mouthful of cake: 'That is so. There were three or four shocks that year. It was 1946. The villages were not affected, but a lot of rock was moved up here.' He jerked his head towards the cliff. 'This is not the only place of its kind. All along this ridge there are places where the tremors, and then the weather, have taken bites out of the hill. What the earthquake starts, the ice and snow don't take many winters to finish. There are three, four, five hollows, much like this one, where very little trace of the original cliff-face remains. Only the goat-track that we came down on . . . see? There the cliff itself has not been moved, but you see the rocks piled against it as high as a ruined church. Oh yes, I told you, *Kyrie* Simon, that a man who was not always out on the hill would soon miss his landmarks.'

'The pinnacle, for instance, that used to stand above the cliff?'

'I told you about that? Yes, I did, I remember. It was not so very high, but it served as a landmark for kilometres around. It was what guided me to Michael on that day. He knew of a cave here, he said, near the Cat's Tooth, and he meant to lie up in it until the German drive was over. I came up, bringing him food, and to try and make him come back to Arachova where his wound might be cared for. But this I have spoken of already.'

Simon's eyes were on the shallow apse of the exposed cave. They were narrowed slightly, as if against the sun, and his face gave nothing away. 'A cave? That one? It would be deep enough before half of it fell in.'

Stephanos lifted his heavy shoulders. 'I do not know if that was the one or not. Possibly. But you must understand that the cliff is full of caves . . . some parts of Parnassus are a honeycomb of such places where an army could hide in safety.'

Simon had taken out cigarettes. 'Camilla? I think I'd like to take a quick look around, all the same. Cigarette? Catch, Niko . . .' He got slowly to his feet, and stood looking down at the old man sitting heavily in the shade. 'And you carried Michael from here to Delphi?'

Stephanos smiled 'It was fourteen years ago, and I was younger. And the way to Delphi is much shorter than the way we came . . . but steep, you understand, because Arachova lies nearly four hundred metres higher than Delphi. That is a big start on a climb like this, so we came by Arachova today.'

'I still think it was . . . well, quite a feat. And now I'm going to poke around for a bit. I want a good look at that cave. It looks as if there's another small opening at the back of it. Will you come, or are you resting?'

'I will come.'

'Niko?'

One swift graceful wriggle, and Niko was on his feet and brushing dust from his trousers. 'I come. I have very good eyesight, me. If there is anything to be seen, I will see it. I can see in the dark as well as any cat, so if there is an inner cave I shall guide you, *Kyrie* Simon.'

'We'll follow your socks,' said Simon drily, and Niko grinned. The socks flashed across the corrie at a run, and were dimmed in the shadow of the cave's recess. Stephanos was getting slowly to his feet. Simon looked down at me and raised his eyebrows.

I shook my head, so he and Stephanos left me, and went more slowly in the wake of the luminous socks. A buttress of shadow swallowed them.

I finished the cigarette and stubbed it out, then sat relaxed and still, enjoying the shade and the silence and the bright dazzle of heat beyond my shadowed corner. The men were out of sight, either in the cave or somewhere beyond the piles of massive debris that buttressed the far side of the corrie. I couldn't hear them now. The silence was intense, thick as the heat. I was part of it, sitting as still as a lizard on my stone.

Some movement, real or imagined, at the head of the cliff-path, caught my eye, and I turned to look, wondering half-idly if Niko had found some way back to the cliff's head while I had been sitting there half-asleep. But there was nothing there, only the sun hammering on the white rock. The shadows, purple and anthracite and red, seemed themselves to flicker with movement. Against the violent patterns of light and shade, the green of the holly-oaks and the cool curve of the juniper arching out from the face of the cliff were as refreshing as the sound of a spring. I remembered, suddenly, that as I had clambered down past them there had been other green things below us, hardly noticed in the hazards of that steep exhausted scramble down the cliff.

Where there was green there must certainly, in September, be water . . . cold water, not Niko's tepid bottle that smelled of goat. The thought brought me eagerly to my feet. A shadow at the cliff-top flickered again, but I hardly noticed. My eyes were on the corner below the slim bow of the juniper, where, like a mirage, showed a glimpse of vivid emerald . . .

I got up, skirting the corrie's edge, picking my way between the enormous fallen blocks. I slid between two rough rocks that caught at my clothes, bent my head to pass under a wing of limestone that shored up the cliff like a flying buttress—and there was the grass. The colour was so startling, and so beautiful after the dazzling changes rung by sun and stone that I must have stood quite still, gazing at it, for a full minute. It flowed in a deep and vivid ribbon of green between two boulders streaked liberally with the red of water-borne iron. But there was no water now. There might be some spring, I thought, that was dependent on intermittent showers high on the peaks; perhaps, like snow on the desert's face, the grass sprang up in the wake of a shower and faded with the next day's sunset . . . It lay there, itself like a small pool of cool water, a green thought in a green shade, moist to the touch, and lending the corner of the corrie a freshness that the shadowed rock had not had.

I sat gratefully down, with my hands spread on the ground and the soft grass springing up between my fingers. Among the green were tiny flowers, bells of pale blue, like pigmy harebells. Some of these grew on the face of the cliff itself, and their seeds had, in the last decade, flown and rooted everywhere in the fallen debris of earthquake. Only here in this moist corner were they still in flower, but I could see fading clumps of seeding stems on all sides among the boulders. Other alpines had grown here, too; there was something with a pale furry leaf and a thin dry flower-stem left sticking out like a humming-bird's tongue; a tuft of tendrils dried into hexagonal shapes till they looked like bunches of brown chicken-wire; a tiny plant of the acorned holly, rooting purposefully in a thin crack. Then with another shock of pleasure I saw one more flower that had not yet died of drought. In a cleft just above eye level there was a plant of cyclamen. The leaves, blue-green and veined palely, were held out in stiff formal curves on their red stems. The flowers were soft rose-pink, a dozen of them, and clung like a flight of moths to the dry cliff. Below the flowers, in the same cleft, grew the remains of another rock-plant, dead, fraying away to dust in the drought. Above it the cyclamen's flowers looked pure and delicate and strong . . .

Something was fretting at the edge of my mind. I stared at the cyclamen, and found I was thinking of the Dutch painter and his donkey surrounded by the laughing village lads, and I wondered, without knowing why, what Nigel was doing now.

*   *   *

We went back by the shorter route.

It appeared that the search of the cave had yielded nothing, and apparently Simon didn't want to delay Stephanos and Niko by making a more prolonged investigation. We left the corrie by the gap in the west side, and scrambled down the steep slope below the scree.

We had nearly reached the bottom of the dry valley that lay below the ridge, when we came on the barely-visible track that I had glimpsed from the top of the crags. Even this was appallingly rough going. We made our careful way along it for some hundred yards or so, and then it forked. The right branch fell steeply away, curling out of sight almost at once round a spur of cliff. The left-hand branch turned downhill for Delphi. We took this, and in just over half the time the outward journey had taken we saw ahead of us the edge of the high land and, beyond it, the gap where the Pleistus valley cuts its way down to the sea.

Stephanos paused and spoke to Simon. The latter turned to me.

'Stephanos has come back this way because he thinks you may be tired. This path will lead you straight down to Delphi. It comes out above the temple, and you can get down behind the Shining Ones, and then through the stadium. The drop down to the cliff-top is steep, but there's no danger if you take care. I'll come down with you if you like, but you can't possibly miss the way.'

I must have looked slightly surprised, because he added: 'The car's at Arachova–remember? I thought I'd go back along the top with Stephanos now, and collect it. But there's no need to drag you the whole way.'

I said gratefully: 'Oh, Simon–that car! I'd forgotten all about it. I don't really see why you should have to shoulder all the responsibility for my bit of nonsense, but I must confess I'll be awfully glad if you will! Don't tell Niko, but I really am beginning to feel I'd like to be home.'

'Well, it won't take you long from here, and it's all downhill. No–look, dash it, I'll come with you.'

'I wouldn't dream of letting you, if it means your trailing back later on to Arachova for the car. I can't possibly get lost between here and Delphi, and I promise to be careful on the cliff-path.' I turned to hold out a hand to Stephanos and thank him, then did the same to Niko. It was like Stephanos, I thought, virtually to ignore me all the time, and yet to lead the whole party some hour or so out of its way to show me the quick way home. The old man nodded gravely over my hand and turned away. Niko took it with a melting look from those beautiful eyes and said: 'I will see you again, miss? You come to Arachova often?'

'I hope so.'

'And you will come to see the rugs in my sister's shop? Is very good rugs, all colours. Local. Is also brooches and pots of the very best Greek style. For you they are cheap. I tell my sister you are my friend, yes?'

I laughed. 'If I buy any rugs and pots I'll come to your sister's shop, Niko. That's a promise. And now goodbye, and thank you.'

'Goodbye, miss. Thank *you*, beautiful miss.'

The luminous socks plunged away along the path after Stephanos.

Simon grinned. 'His grandfather'd have the hide off him if he could understand half he says. Is there such a thing as innocent depravity? Niko's it if there is. A little of Athens superimposed on Arachova. It's a fascinating mixture, isn't it?'

'When it's as beautiful as Niko, yes . . . Simon, was it true that you didn't find anything in the cave? Or was there something that you didn't want to talk about in front of the others? You didn't see anything at all?'

'Nothing. There was a small inner cave, but it was as blank as a scoured pot . . . I'll tell you about it later on; I'd better be off after them now. I'll be in to the Apollon for dinner and I'll see you then. Afterwards we'll get you installed at the studio. You'll dine with me, of course?'

'Why, thank you, I–'

'Take care of yourself, then. See you at dinner.' And with a lift of the hand he was gone in the wake of the shocking pink socks.

I stared after him for a few seconds, but he didn't look back.

It occurred to me, with a slight sense of surprise, that this time yesterday I hadn't even met him.

I turned and began to make my careful way down towards Delphi.

Chapter 12

Seize her! Throw her from Parnassus,
send her bounding down the cliff-ledges,
let the crags comb our her dainty hair!
EURIPIDES: *Ion.*
(tr. Philip Vellacott.)

IT WAS LATE afternoon, and the sun was straight ahead of me when at length I came out on top of one of the great cliffs that stand above the shrine at Delphi. Far below me and to the right lay the temple precinct, its monuments and porticos and its Sacred Way looking small and very clean-cut in the sun, like the plaster models that you see in museums. The pillars of Apollo were foreshortened, and tiny as toys. Directly beneath me was the cleft of the Castalian Spring. The tangle of trees filled it like a dark waterfall. Already, beyond the tree-filled cleft, the Flamboyant cliff was taking the late afternoon sun like flame.

I moved back a few feet from the edge, and sat down on a stone. To one side of me grew a thicket of tallish juniper. Beyond and all around this was the usual dusty expanse of hot stone. The path to the stadium led off to the right past the bushes, but I was tired, and here at the cliff-top a cool breeze from the sea allayed the still-hot blaze of afternoon.

I sat quietly, chin on hand, looking down at the dreaming marbles of the shrine below, at the blue-and-silver depths of the valley where hawks circled below eye-level, at the great cliff beside me burning in the sun . . . No, I thought, I could not leave Delphi yet. Even if it meant sleeping in the studio near the intolerable Danielle, in order to save what I must owe on the car, I couldn't leave. There must be tomorrow—and the day after, and the day after . . . how long a succession of days would it take before I had begun to learn and see and taste what Delphi had to show? I must stay. And my decision (I told myself quickly) had nothing to do with Simon Lester and his affairs. Nothing. Nothing *whatever*. On the thought I found myself wondering just what Simon would have decided that we should do tomorrow . . .

'What are you doing up here?'

The question came from close behind me. I turned sharply. Danielle had come out from behind the thicket of juniper. Today she had on a wide bell of scarlet skirt and a turquoise-coloured blouse that was open at the neck. Very open. The inevitable cigarette clung to her bottom lip. Her mouth was rouged a pale pink against her sallow skin. Today her finger-nails were pale pink, too. On the thin brown hands it looked odd and slightly improper.

'Why, hullo,' I said pleasantly. If I was to be the girl's neighbour tonight in the studio, it didn't do to let last night's irritation with her bad manners reappear.

But Danielle had no such scruples. It was quite obvious that manners, bad or good, had no place in her scheme of things. She simply was, and if others didn't like it, they had to endure it. She repeated in that sharp voice that sounded as if she really wanted to know: 'What are you doing up here?'

I said, letting a note of mild surprise creep in: 'Sitting looking at the view. And you?'

She came towards me. She moved like a model, hips thrown forward and knees close. She stood between me and the edge of the cliff in one of the attitudes you see in fashion drawings—one hip out, toes at twenty past seven, one thin hand gesturing with the cigarette. Any minute now she would open her mouth and let the tip of her tongue appear.

She said: 'It's a long climb from the spring on a hot afternoon.'

'Isn't it? Has it tired you very much, or did you just come round the top from the studio?'

She gave me a glittering glance. I couldn't see for the life of me why she should care what I was doing up here, but she obviously did. And I certainly wasn't going to tell her where we had been. That was Simon's pilgrimage, and no one else's. If he chose to take me along, well, that was his affair. But I wasn't going to tell Danielle.

She said: 'Where's Simon?'

'I don't know,' I said truthfully. 'Were you looking for him?'

'Oh, not really.' To my surprise she came forward and sat down not two yards from my feet. She swore once, viciously, in French, as her hip met a thistle, then she settled herself gracefully on the dusty ground and smiled at me. 'A cigarette?'

'Why, thanks very much,' I said, before I thought.

She regarded me for a while in silence, while I smoked and tried not to feel annoyed that now I could hardly get up and leave her, which I very much wanted to do. Really, I reflected, when faced with this sort of person why do we hold madly on to our own tabus; why could my careful manners not allow me to get up—as Danielle certainly would have done in my place—say: 'I'm bored and you are a mannerless little trollop and I don't like you,' and then walk away down the hill? But there I sat and looked pleasantly non-committal and smoked her cigarette. I must admit that it was a good one, and—after Niko's—nectar and ambrosia. I wondered why she had offered the olive-branch, and eyed her warily. *I fear the Greeks when they bring gifts* . . .

'You weren't in to lunch at the Apollon.'

'No,' I agreed. 'Were you?'

'Where did you have lunch?'

'I had a picnic. Out.'

'With Simon?'

I raised my eyebrows, and tried to register cold surprise at the inquisition. It had no effect whatever. 'With Simon?' she repeated.

'Yes.'

'I saw him go out in the car.'

'Did you?'

'He picked you up somewhere?'

'Yes.'

'Where did you go?'

'South.'

This set her back for half a minute. Then she said: 'Why don't you want to tell me where you went and what you've been doing?'

I looked at her rather helplessly: 'Why should I?'

'Why shouldn't you?'

'Because,' I said, 'I don't like being catechised.'

She digested this. 'Oh?' She turned those big tired eyes up to me, and asked: 'Why? Have you and Simon been up to something?'

Said by Danielle, the harmless question could only mean one

thing. I said explosively: 'My God!' Then I began to laugh. I said: 'No, Danielle. We have not. We took the car down to Arachova and left it there, then we walked back over the hill towards Delphi. We had a picnic at a place where there is a lovely view of Parnassus. Then I came on towards home and Simon went back for the car. If you sit here long enough you'll see him drive past below you. In case you don't know it by sight, the car you hired is a big black one. I don't know the make. I know very little about cars. Will that do? And thank you for the cigarette. I must be going.' And I stubbed out the two-thirds-smoked cigarette and got to my feet.

She made a little movement without getting up, a sinuous little wriggle in the dust, like a snake. She smiled up at me. The cigarette had dropped from her lip and was smouldering on the ground beside her. She made no attempt to retrieve it. She was smiling and showing pretty white teeth with her tongue between them. The tongue was pale like her lips and nails. 'You're annoyed with me,' she said.

I felt suddenly very old with all the adult weight of my twenty-five years. 'My dear girl,' I said, 'what could possibly lead you to imagine that?'

'You see, it's only,' said Danielle from the dust, 'that I'm jealous about Simon.'

I wanted passionately to turn and run, but this gambit hardly provided me with a good exit line. I merely shed most of those adult years at one go and said feebly and childishly: 'Oh?'

'Men,' said the voice of the dust-snake, 'are all the same, mostly. But there really is something about Simon. I expect even you feel it, don't you? On the whole my lovers bore me, but I want Simon. I genuinely do.'

'Really.'

'Yes. Really.' The flat little voice held no inflection. 'And I can tell you just what it is about Simon. It's –'

I said sharply: 'No, really, Danielle!'

She shot me a look. 'You're in love with him yourself, aren't you?'

'Don't be absurd!' To my horror I sounded almost too emphatic. 'I hardly know him! And besides, this is not the –'

'What difference does that make? It takes me two seconds to know whether I want a man or not.'

I turned away. 'Look,' I said, 'I must go. I expect I'll be seeing you later. Goodbye.'

'Are you seeing him again tomorrow?'

The question was said idly, in the same flat voice; but it was not quite idle. Something made me pause and turn back to her. I said: 'I–I'm not sure.'

'What's he doing tomorrow?'

Definitely not quite idle. I said: 'How do I know?' as coldly as I could, before it occurred to me that I did know, quite well. He would certainly go straight back to the corrie, to look for Michael's hypothetical cave. And he just as certainly wouldn't want Danielle tagging after him. The whole of this embarrassing interview seemed to indicate that she was prepared to do just that.

I said, in a tone of one conceding a point to a stubborn adversary: 'All right. I'll tell you. I am seeing him. We're going to Levadia for the day. There's a horse-fair, and gipsies, and he wants to take photographs.'

'Oh.' She was looking away over the valley with eyes narrowed against the sun. Then she sent another of those glinting looks up at me. 'But what a bloody waste,' she said.

Though I was used to her by now, I didn't quite manage to control the little flicker of anger that ran through me. I said: 'So he didn't come to repair the taps last night?'

The beautiful eyelashes fluttered, and her eyes narrowed over a look of the most intense venom. 'You're very outspoken, aren't you?' said Danielle.

'My bad manners,' I said. 'I'm sorry. And now I must go if I'm to get a bath before dinner. See you later. Did you know I was to come and stay at the studio from tonight?'

Her eyes opened wide. The dislike was still there, and now annoyance, and then both were suddenly, curiously, overlaid by what looked like calculation. 'That'll be convenient, won't it?' said Danielle, meaning what only Danielle could mean. Then I saw her look change again. It slid over my shoulder and I saw surprise in her face, and something else.

I turned quickly.

A man had come out from behind the clump of juniper. He was obviously a Greek, dark, broad-cheekboned, with crisp curled hair that showed a hint of grey, and a smudge of a moustache over a mouth at once thin-lipped and sensual. He was of medium height, and stockily built. I guessed his age to be around forty. He was dressed in a grey striped suit, rather shabby, and a dark crimson shirt with a vermilion tie that would have clashed if the colours had not been harmlessly faded.

He spoke in French. 'Why, hullo, Danielle.'

It was as if he had told her quite plainly: *'It's all right.'* I could see the look of surprise fade. She relaxed. 'Hullo. How did you know I was here?'

I thought: because you've just been together behind the juniper-bushes and I interrupted you. Then I shook the thought away with the wry reflection that this was what contact with Danielle did. Five minutes with her, and a full half-pound of civet would hardly sweeten the imagination.

Danielle said idly—too idly—from the dust: 'This is Camilla Haven. She's been out with Simon this afternoon and she's sleeping at the studio tonight.'

The man bowed and sent me a smile. *'Enchanté.'*

'Dimitrios,' said Danielle to me, 'is—'

'A guide,' said Dimitrios. 'Mademoiselle has been to see the shrine this afternoon?'

As if you hadn't heard from behind your juniper-bush, I thought. I said: 'No. I went this morning early.'

'Ah. And now you come up to the top of the Shining Ones to see the last of the sun.'

I said: 'It'll be some time still till dark, surely?'

'Perhaps not so long,' said Dimitrios. I saw Danielle turn her head to look at him. Her head was on a level with my thigh, and I couldn't see her eyes for the curtaining lashes. Something crept along my spine like a cold-footed insect. The man, no less than the girl, gave me the creeps.

I gave myself another of those hearty mental shakes. 'I must be going. If I'm to have a bath before dinner and arrange about—'

'These rocks,' said Dimitrios, 'are called the Phaedriades, the Shining Ones. Always I tell my tourists the story of the Shining Ones. Between them flows the Castalian Spring, whose water is the best in Greece. Have you tried the water of the spring, mademoiselle?'

'No, not yet. I—'

He came a step nearer. I was between him and the edge of the cliff. 'They stand over the shrine like guardians, do they not? Because that is what they are. They were not only the protectors of the holy place, but they were themselves the place of execution. There were people executed on these cliffs—for sacrilege, mademoiselle. Did you know that?'

'No. But—'

Another step. He was smiling, a smile of great charm. He had a pleasant voice. Beside me in the dust I saw Danielle lift her head. I saw that her eyes now watched me, not the man. She was smiling at me with the utmost friendliness, her eyes for once bright, not tired at all. I moved back from him a step or two. It brought me within four feet of the edge.

Dimitrios said suddenly: 'Be careful.' I jumped and his hand came out to my arm. It was gentle on the flesh. 'You are not here for execution as a traitor to the god, mademoiselle.' He laughed, and Danielle smiled, and I thought suddenly, wildly, why the hell can't I just pull my arm away and run? I hate the pair of them and they frighten me, and here I stand because it isn't polite to go while the damned man's talking.

'I always tell my tourists,' he was saying, 'one particular story. There was a certain traitor who was brought up here for execution. Two of them came with him to the edge . . . just there . . . to throw him over. He looked over . . . yes, mademoiselle, it is a long way down, is it not? . . . and then he said to them, please will you not send me over face first, please will you let me fall with my back to the drop? One understands how he felt, mademoiselle, does one not?'

His hand was still on my arm. I pulled back against it. It slid gently up the flesh to the inside of my elbow. I noticed that his nails were bitten to the quick and that his thumb was badly cut and crusted with dried blood. I started to turn from him and to pull my arm away, but his fingers tightened. His voice quickened a little in my ear: 'So they threw him over, mademoiselle, and as he fell, he –'

I said breathlessly: 'Let me go. I don't like heights. Let me go, please.'

He smiled, 'Why, mademoiselle –'

Danielle's voice said, dry and thin: 'Are these your tourists, Dimitrios?'

He gave an exclamation under his breath. His hand dropped from my arm. He turned sharply.

Three people, a man and two women, were coming slowly along the path from the direction of Arachova. The women were plain, dumpy, middle-aged; the man was stoutish, and wore khaki shorts and had an enormous camera slung over one perspiring shoulder. They looked at us with incurious red faces as they plodded past like beef cattle in a row, like angels of heaven.

I shot away from the brink of the cliff the way a cork leaves the very best champagne. I didn't bother to say anything polite to Dimitrios, and I didn't even fling a goodbye at Danielle.

I hurried down the path in the wake of the three tourists. Neither the Greek nor the girl made any move to follow me, and after a while I slackened my pace and walked more slowly, trying to control my thoughts. If Danielle and her damned lover – for that the Greek was her lover I had no doubt at all – had tried for some silly reason to frighten me, they had succeeded. I had felt both frightened and a fool, and it was a beastly mixture. But there had surely been nothing more than that . . . a spiteful trick and a distorted sense of humour? It was absurd to imagine anything more. I had only done so because I had spent an exacting and physically tiring day. I disliked Danielle and I had shown it, and she had wanted to frighten and humiliate me because I had interrupted her sordid meeting with the Greek behind the junipers. And even, perhaps, because of Simon . . .

I had reached the stadium. The flat race-track lay empty and silent in the sun, cupped in its tiers of marble seats. I almost ran across the bare dust, hurried between the columns of the starting-gate, and down into the path that led to the shrine. I found that my heart was still hammering in my breast, and my throat was tight. The path dipped, dropped, twisted past a well where water trickled, and came precipitously down on to the smooth track above the theatre. There were my three tourists, still comfortably trudging along, talking something incomprehensible that might have been Dutch. There were people, too, in the theatre just below me, people on the steps, people everywhere on the floor of Apollo's temple. It was quite safe to stand here under the trees and wait for my heart to slow down. Quite safe . . .

The slanting sun was golden on the quiet stones, was apricot, was amber, was a lovely liquid wash of light and peace. A bee went past my cheek.

Beside me was the pomegranate tree. The fruit glowed in the rich light. I remembered the cool feel of it in my hand last night, and Simon's voice saying: '*Eat it soon, Persephone; then you'll have to stay in Delphi* . . .'

Well, I was going to stay. I was still going to stay.

Someone said, very clearly, just beside me: 'If you'll just walk up there, it'll give me the touch of colour I need.'

I jumped and looked about me. There had been no sign of anyone on the path a moment since. There was still no one here. Then I saw, small below me, a grey-haired man with a ciné-camera, standing in the centre of the amphitheatre. He had the camera to his eye, and he was photographing a section of the tiered seating. A young woman, perhaps his daughter, walked slowly up the steep steps, turned rather self-consciously, and sat down to face the camera. As clearly as if it were beside me, I could hear the whirr of the mechanism as he took the picture. It was he who had spoken, and the wonderful acoustics had done the rest. If anyone had stood here above the theatre last night, they might well have been startled to hear, rising out of the dark well of silence, the great cry of vengeance from *Electra* . . .

My breathing was back to normal. Apollo the healer had done his work.

I went composedly down the steps, across the sunbaked circle of the theatre, down through the scented pines that rim the shrine, and along the main road to the hotel.

Even when, washing for dinner, I saw on my bare arm a streak of dried blood–Dimitrios' blood from that cut thumb–I felt only a brief moment of disgust. I had been stupid and imaginative and had had a fright; that was all.

But I felt a curious reluctance to go down to dinner before Simon appeared, and I wished with a quite startling fervour that I was not committed to sleeping in the studio that night.

Chapter 13

. . . With hollow shriek the steep of Delphos *leaving.*
MILTON: *Nativity Hymn.*

IT MUST HAVE been close on three o'clock in the morning when something woke me. My room was second from the end of the long corridor, next to Danielle's, and at the opposite end from the outer door, near which were the rooms of the two men. The Dutch painter had gone that day, so we four were the only occupants of the studio.

For some time I lay in that heavy state between sleep and waking where it is hard to disentangle reality from the trailing clouds of dream. Something had woken me, but whether I had heard a noise, or whether it was the dream itself that had startled me awake, I couldn't tell. There was no sound outside. The quiet air of Delphi wrapped us round. I moved my cheek against the hard pillow –pillows in Greece are always made like bricks – and prepared to drift back into sleep again.

From the next room came the sound of a movement, and then the creak of the bed–two sounds so completely normal and expected that they should never have roused me further. But with them came a third sound that brought my eyes wide open in the dark and my cheek up off the pillow, and made nonsense of the normality of the night. Someone was talking, very softly: a man.

My first thought was embarrassment at having heard, my next irritation, succeeded by disgust. If Danielle had to have her lover in her room I didn't want to be pilloried, sleepless, on the other side of a too-thin partition. I turned over with as much fuss of bedclothes and creak of bed-springs as I could, to let them know how thin the wall was, then I pulled the sheet–it was too hot for blankets–over my head, and tried to stop my ears to the sounds that succeeded the whispering.

Sleep had gone for good. I lay rigid under the sheet with my eyes wide open in the darkness and my hands as hard as I could bear to hold them over my ears. It wasn't that I'm particularly a prude; but being forced to listen in on anyone's more private moments isn't pleasant, and I didn't want any part or parcel or hint of the more private moments of Danielle. Her public moments were quite embarrassing enough.

I wondered how the unpleasant Dimitrios had got into the place. Even though he was only here to visit Danielle, I didn't one bit like the idea of his being free to come and go. I supposed that he might have climbed in by her window, and if so, sooner or later he would go out the same way. I would no doubt hear him scramble out and drop the twelve feet or so to the floor of the rocky platform where the studio was built. I waited, furious with Danielle for subjecting me to this, furious with myself for minding, furious with Dimitrios for pandering to her monstrous egotism. It was a beastly experience.

How long it was before there was quiet from the next room I don't know. It seemed an age. But after a while all was silent, except for the whispering again, and then I heard someone moving furtively across the floor. I waited for the sounds of the window, and the cat-foot drop to the ground outside. But they didn't come. I heard the door to the corridor open, and steps went stealthily past my door.

That brought me upright in bed with a quick nervous jerk of the heart. If Danielle wanted to let a man in and out of her room, very well. But she had no damned right to let a man like Dimitrios loose inside the place. Had she–*had she?*–given him a key?

Then, out of the dark, came another thought that kicked through those nerves again.

Perhaps it wasn't Dimitrios at all.

Perhaps it was Nigel.

I was out of bed and had thrust my feet into my slippers, and was shrugging my way into the light summer coat that also served me for a dressing-gown, before I quite realised myself what I was going to do. Then I had fled across the little room and had, very softly, opened my door and was peering out into the corridor.

I suppose this bit isn't pretty. It wasn't any business of mine if Nigel had gone to Danielle's room and got what had been so patently his heart's desire. But when I had thought of him I had had a

memory, sudden and bright and clean, of the young eagerness of
Nigel's face; the vulnerable eyes and the weak mouth and the silly
boy's beard. And I had seen his drawings, the visions of tree and
flower and stone that he had translated with such impeccable and
yet impassioned skill. If this, too, was Nigel . . . I had to know. Call
it sheer, vulgar, woman's curiosity if you like, but I had to know if
the impossible Danielle could really annex him like that–if she was
really prepared to make Nigel, whom she despised, squander
himself in worship at her shoddy little shrine.

I believe I was thinking, incoherently, that something must be
done to stop her ruining Nigel, and then, even more incoherently, of
Simon. Simon must be told tomorrow. Simon would know what to
do . . .

I slipped softly out of my room. The outer door at the end of the
corridor had its upper half of glass, and outside it the dark was
slackening off into dawn. The pane was grey. Against it I saw him.

He was almost at the end of the corridor, standing outside a
door–Nigel's door–as if he had paused there waiting for something.
I shrank against the wall, but even if he had looked back he could not
have seen me against the darkness at my end of the passage. I stayed
still, pressed against the cold marble, and felt humiliated and angry
and ashamed all at once, wishing I hadn't known, wishing I was still
fathoms deep in sleep, wishing I could remember Nigel by his work
and not, as now, through the smudgy little whispers of Danielle . . .
'Men are all the same anyway . . . it bores me . . . I want Simon. I
genuinely do . . .'

The silhouette at the corridor's end moved at last. He took a step
forward and put his hand to the knob of the door. Then he paused
again, momentarily, with his head bent, as if listening.

I thought I must have made some sound and that he had heard
me, because I could see, now, that it wasn't the Greek: it was too
tall. It wasn't Nigel either. It was Simon.

*   *   *

If I had been in a condition to think, the swift and complete
rebellion of every nerve and muscle in my body, and of every drop
of blood in my brain, would have told me finally about myself and
Simon. But I had hardly realised what I had seen when the night
broke open rather more really, and very much more noisily.

Simon pushed open Nigel's door. I saw him reach up as if for the light-swtich, but even as he moved the beam of a powerful torch speared out of the darkness of the room to catch him full on the face and chest. I saw his fractional check and recoil, as if the light were a physical blow in the eyes, but the pause was less than momentary, no more than the tensing before the spring. Before he had even blinked once he had launched himself forward along the beam of light, with the speed of a bullet. I heard an impact, a curse, the swift stamp and flurry of feet on the stone floor, and then all hell seemed to break loose inside the room.

I ran down the corridor and paused in the doorway. The little room seemed to be a pandemonium of violently struggling bodies. In the weaving, flashing beam of the torch the two men looked enormous, and their shadows towered and waved grotesquely over ceiling and walls. Simon was the taller, and seemed to have a momentary advantage. He had the other's wrist in one hand and seemed to be struggling to twist the man's arm so that the torch would light his features. The beam swung wildly, erratically, as the other fought to resist him, the light sweeping in violent, broken arcs through the darkness. It caught me, standing in the doorway, and raked a brilliant curve across my feet and the skirt of the nightdress below my coat. Someone snarled something incomprehensible in Greek, and then the man had wrenched his arm free from Simon's grip and, with a grunt of effort, brought the heavy torch down in a vicious blow aimed for Simon's head. Even as the blow whistled down, Simon jerked aside, so that the torch came down with a sickening sound on the side of his neck. It must have struck a muscle, for his grip seemed to loosen, and the Greek tore free.

It must, after all, have been Dimitrios. I saw the stocky body and broad shoulders in the erratic light before Simon was on him again, and the torch flew wide, to strike the wall beside me and fall to roll somewhere near the foot of the bed. Darkness stamped down. I had no time to wonder about Dimitrios; why he had come to Nigel's room, why Simon had followed him, or even—strangest of all—why Nigel himself didn't appear to be here, when the two men, at grips again, hurtled past me to come violently up against the door of the shower-cupboard. There was a crack as a wooden panel gave way; somewhere on the floor was the sharp explosion of breaking glass; one of the flimsy chairs went over with a splintering sound; then the bed-springs crashed and whined as the two bodies went down on the bed together.

I flung myself to my knees not two feet from the heaving bed,

groping wildly for the torch. Somewhere here I had heard it roll . . .
not far, surely? . . . these things rolled in semi-circles . . . ah! there
it was. I clutched it, groping at the metal to find the catch,
wondering if the fall had broken the bulb . . .

It was a heavy torch and the catch was stiff. The bed, rocking like
a ship in a storm, shot away a foot from the wall on screaming
castors, hurtled back again with a crash that should have brought the
plaster off the walls. The springs creaked, strained, gave again with
an appalling noise as the men slithered to the edge and then fell to
the floor.

A moment of gasping stillness, and then they were on their feet
again. A pause, filled with the sound of heavy breathing. I jumped
to my feet, still wrestling with the torch, and suddenly the thing
flashed on in my hand. For the second time that night it caught
Simon full in the eyes. And this time the Greek, seizing the
advantage like lightning, charged down the beam, out of the blinding
light. Simon went down with a crash that shook the room. I saw him
catch the edge of the bed with his shoulder as he fell. The blow must
have momentarily crippled him, but, surprisingly, the Greek didn't
follow it up. Nor did he turn to deal with me. He had his back to
me, and the light waveringly pinned for a moment the heavy
bull-like shoulders, the dark curled hair . . . He didn't even look
round. I heard a gasping snarl in French: '*Put the bloody thing out, will
you?*'

I hit him as hard as I could over the head.

I missed him. Just as the blow fell, something warned him. He
didn't turn into the light. He lashed backwards with a crooked
elbow that caught the torch, knocking it flying, then swept on to
strike me full across the breast in a heavy blow that sent me
staggering to fall at the foot of the bed. The torch hurtled wide a
second time and went out for good. As I went down I saw, in one
swift flash of the flying light, the Greek turn and leap for the
doorway, with Simon after him in a lunge. And in the doorway
stood Danielle, fully-dressed, with wide brilliant eyes and parted
lips.

She whipped back to let the man pass. Then, with a languid-
seeming movement that was nevertheless as swift as a snake's, she
stepped into the path of Simon's rush. I heard the other man
running up the corridor towards her room and the open window, as
Simon came violently up against her body. I heard her gasp as his
weight jammed her hard against the doorpost. He stopped short.

I couldn't see more than the dim outlines of movement against the grey light of the corridor, but she must have been clinging to him, for he said, harsh and breathless, *'Let me go!'* and she laughed in her throat. Along the corridor a door slammed. Simon moved sharply and I heard him say, very softly: 'Do you hear me? Take your hands away, or you'll get hurt.'

I hadn't heard him even sound ruffled before; now I realised with something like a sharp little shock that he was angry. Danielle must not have set much store by it, for I heard her murmur, with the breath hurrying through the husky voice: 'Go on doing that. I like it . . .'

There was a second of frozen silence, then in the near-darkness the group by the door exploded into movement. The girl was flung aside against the other door-jamb with a violence that sent the breath out of her in a sharp cry that held more surprise than anything else. Before she could recover herself Simon was back in the room, hurling himself across it towards the window, tearing at the catch.

The casement was rusty, and it must have been stiff. As it screeched wider I heard, like an echo at the other end of the building, the shriek of rusty hinges, and the thud as a heavy body dropped to the ground. Steps clattered and slithered away into the darkness.

Simon was up on the sill, a dark bulk against the greying sky. But before he could swing himself out and after the quarry Danielle flew after him like an arrow and clung to his arm.

'Simon . . . Simon, let him go. Simon dear, what a fuss . . .' In spite of his recent violence she clung to him still, pleading in that voice which under its overtones of sexiness might have held a touch of fear. 'Simon, no! He was with me. Don't you understand? *With me.'*

I saw his hand fall from the window-catch. He turned. 'What? What d'you mean?'

'What I say. He was in my room. He only came to see me.'

I said from the floor beside the bed where I was still sitting: 'It's true. I heard them.'

I heard her laugh again, but the sound didn't hold its usual assurance. Simon shook her off as if she didn't exist and dropped lightly back into the room. 'I—see. He's gone, anyway . . . Camilla? Are you all right?'

'Perfectly. Is there any light?'

'I think the bulb's out. Half a minute.' He seemed to be feeling in his pockets. 'What are you doing down there? Did that brute hit you?'

'Yes, but I'm all right. I was just—I was keeping out of the way.' I got up a bit unsteadily and sat on the bed, just as Simon found matches and struck one. He surveyed me by its light. I smiled rather waveringly up at him. I saw then that he was dressed only in a pair of grey flannels. In the light of the match I could see the gleam of sweat on his chest and a shining dark trickle of blood from a cut at the base of the neck, where a deep vee of sunburn showed. He was breathing a little faster than usual—not much, but perceptibly a bit faster—and his eyes for once didn't look cool and amused at all. But the match burned steadily in a tremorless hand. I asked anxiously: 'What about you?'

'Don't give it a thought. Honours were about even . . . more's the pity.'

Danielle said petulantly: 'What did you have to fight for?'

He said crisply: 'My dear girl, he attacked me. What would you expect me to do?' He had lit another match and was looking round the room for the light-bulb.

I said: 'That was Dimitrios, wasn't it?'

Simon gave me a fleeting look of surprise as he picked the light-bulb up from the wash-basin. Danielle turned her head as if startled, then smiled that cat-and-cream smile of hers. 'You recognised him? Of course.'

Simon had dragged one of the wooden chairs forward, and now mounted it to fit the light-bulb into its socket. The light flashed on, harsh on the disorder of the bare little room. He got off the chair, looking at me.

'Are you sure you're all right?'

'Quite. But Simon—where's Nigel?'

'I've no idea. He hasn't been to bed; that much is apparent.' In spite of the tossed state of the bed, the sheet still lay tucked flatly in. No one had slept there. Simon hesitated, then turned to Danielle. She was standing near the door, leaning against the wall in a pose of lazy grace. Her eyes looked long and sleepy again under the thick lashes. She had taken a cigarette out of a pocket and was lighting it. She dropped the burnt-out match on the floor. All through the operation the narrow glinting gaze had been on Simon . . . all over him.

He said flatly: 'You say that man was with you? How did he get in?'

'I let him in.'

'By the door?'

'No. By my window.'

'Come off it, Danielle. Your window's twelve feet from the ground. Don't tell me you plaited sheets or let down your hair for him. Did you unlock the door for him, or has he got a key?'

She said sulkily, under the coldness of his voice: 'I don't see what the hell it's got to do with you, but yes, I did unlock it.'

'It's got everything to do with me that your visitor was apparently prowling round where he's no damned right to be. And there's the little detail that he went for me with apparent intent to do damage, if not worse. What was he doing in Nigel's room?'

'How do I know?'

'He jumped out of your window in the end. He could have gone that way in the first place. Why didn't he?'

'It was easier to get out through the door, and quieter. The key's in the lock.'

'Then why did he come in here?'

She shrugged. 'He must have heard you moving and dodged in so that you wouldn't see him. I don't know.'

'He wasn't to know there was no one in the room.'

'I'd told him they were nearly all empty. I expect he took a chance. And now I'm tired of this, and tired of the inquisition, and I'm going to bed.' She straightened, yawning deliberately and daintily, like a cat, showing all her pretty teeth and that pale pink tongue. Then she turned her head and let the big sleepy eyes move insolently over me. Simon had found the end of a battered carton of cigarettes in his trouser pocket and had given me one. He bent over me to light it. His breathing was quite even again now. If it hadn't been for the cut where the torch had hit him, and that thin glaze of sweat drying on his skin, you would never have guessed that a few minutes ago he had been fighting for his life in the dark.

Danielle said, sounding suddenly waspish: 'What are you doing here anyway, Camilla?'

'I heard a noise and I came along.'

She smiled. 'And got knocked down. Did he hurt you?'

'I hope not as much as I hurt him.'

She looked momentarily startled, and this gave me a quite absurd prick of satisfaction. 'You hurt him? How?'

'I hit him over the back of the neck with the torch. Hard.'

She stared at me for a moment longer, a very queer look.

'You hit him?' Her voice sounded quite shaken. 'I can't see—you have no business . . . He is my lover, and if I wish to let him come here—'

I said sharply: 'He was doing his best to kill Simon. And besides, I owed him something.'

She looked at me almost stupidly. 'You—owed him something?'

'Yes. And don't play the innocent, Danielle. You didn't look so innocent on the Shining Ones this afternoon.'

'I . . . see.'

She let out a breath. Simon said sharply: 'What are you talking about? What happened?'

'Nothing. It was Camilla's imagination. She thinks Dimitrios—oh, it's so silly that I won't speak of it. It was a joke. And now I'm sick of this. I'm going.' She dropped the half-smoked cigarette on the floor and turned quickly. I got to my feet.

'Just a minute,' said Simon pleasantly. 'No, please don't go yet, Camilla. We're forgetting Nigel. Danielle, have you any idea where he might be? Did he say anything last night to—?'

She said viciously: 'Why should I know where the fool went? I don't know and I don't care. He could be dead as far as I'm concerned.'

I said: 'I think I know where he went.'

Simon was dabbing at his cut neck with a handkerchief. I saw his brows shoot up. 'You seem to know an awful lot tonight.'

'Doesn't she?' Danielle had stopped in the doorway, and turned her head sharply. Her voice was not, like his, amused. 'All right, you tell us.'

I said: 'It's only a guess. But . . . well, Simon, d'you remember our talk in here the other night, about Nigel and his work, and needing a gimmick, and the Dutch boy walking from Jannina and all that?'

'Yes. You're not suggesting that Nigel has taken a leaf out of that boy's book, are you?'

I said: 'There's been a mule stolen from the excavations above the shrine. I know because the guide told me this morning . . . yesterday morning, I suppose I should say. And you know I saw Nigel early the same morning, and he was trying not to be seen—'

'Where?' asked Danielle.

'Just outside the studio here.'

'Which way was he going?'

'I didn't see. He seemed to be making further up Parnassus – towards the stadium.'

'Ah well,' said Simon, 'you may be right. I suppose what Nigel does is very much his own affair, and he was certainly feeling thoroughly unsettled. He may easily have cut loose for a few days.' He turned to rinse his bloodstained handkerchief out under the tap. 'I think we'd better just tidy his room up and get out of it. There's blood on the wash-basin here, and I'm afraid the floor isn't all it should be. We'd better have a look at the damage and do what we can.'

I said: 'Leave that. I'll clean the basin up. But let me have a look at that cut, will you? Danielle, perhaps you'll be good enough to clear the floor and pick up that broken glass?'

She sent me one of those looks of glittering dislike, which was, this time, quite justified. 'It won't take you long. I'm tired. You forget, I haven't been to sleep yet tonight, and oh, how I need that sleep . . .' She yawned, sent another narrow-eyed look at me, and went out rather quickly, shutting the door behind her. My eyes met Simon's in the mirror. I said: 'You wanted to get rid of her, didn't you?'

'You're coming on, aren't you, thought-reader? Yes.'

'Why?'

The smile vanished. He turned and looked down at me. His eyes were grave, sombre even. 'Because I don't like the feel of this thing, Camilla.'

'The feel of it?'

'Yes. Too much is happening. Some of it may be irrelevant, or it may matter the hell of a lot. Danielle and this man, for instance . . . and Danielle and Nigel. I've begun to wonder.'

'Then I was right. Turn round towards the light and let me have a look at that cut . . . you didn't want me to go on talking about Nigel in front of her?'

'No.'

'It's not deep, but you're going to have a bruise and a stiff shoulder, I think. Have you any antiseptic in your room? You don't think he's gone off with a Modestine into the mountains?'

'Yes. No, I mean. No, I don't believe he's off on a trip, but yes, I have some antiseptic.'

'Then don't forget to put it on. The wound's quite clean and it's stopped bleeding.' I stood back and looked at him inquiringly. 'Then what have Danielle and Nigel and this Greek of hers got to do with us–with you, I mean?'

He said slowly: 'This Greek–this lover of Danielle's . . . you said his name was Dimitrios.'

'Yes. I met him yesterday on the way back from the corrie. He was with her above the Shining Ones.'

'Ah, yes. The Shining Ones. What happened there, incidentally? What did you "owe" Dimitrios?'

'Oh, it was nothing, really. He was unpleasant in a greasy sort of way, and talked a lot about people being thrown off the cliff and so on. We were awfully near the edge and he could see I didn't like it, and it amused him . . . and Danielle, too. It was just a nasty little trick to make me look a fool–which I did, I may say. I bolted.'

There was a frown between his eyes. 'I see. Camilla, has nothing occurred to you about this–Dimitrios?'

'Occurred to me? What sort of thing? I don't like him, and I think–' I stopped short. I said, on a long breath: *'Dimitrios!'*

'Exactly. You remember? Angelos had a cousin called Dimitrios Dragoumis, who had gone to live at Itea. At Itea, mark you.'

'And I saw the jeep down at Itea . . . Danielle had driven it straight down there when she got in from Athens! If it's the same Dimitrios . . . then Dimitrios Dragoumis is Danielle's lover, and that was his house I saw. She wasn't visiting any friend called "Elena", she was visiting him, and I'll bet, if the jeep's anything to go by, that she was there when I passed the house!'

'You're certain it was the same jeep?'

'Quite. I told you I recognised the doll hanging in the windscreen. There was someone tinkering with the engine, and that wasn't Dimitrios, but all the same, I've a feeling we're right. It's the same Dimitrios. That would explain why Danielle's so darned interested in you.' I added: 'Or partly.'

He passed that one.

'Well, then, say we're right, and let's look at what we have . . . Dimitrios Dragoumis is Danielle's lover. Whether there actually is anyone called Elena or not, it's quite true that Danielle has been in the habit of spending her afternoons down near Itea, swimming. She told me once she'd found a secluded little cove where the water was clean (it's filthy in Itea itself) but she wouldn't tell me where it was. My guess is that she met, not "Elena", but Dimitrios, on these swimming expeditions, and took up with him. He may have been there to fish–he's a fisherman, did I tell you, and owns a caique?'

'He told me he was a guide.'

'There's no guide in Delphi of that name, that I do know. And if he took the trouble to lie . . .' He didn't finish the sentence. He was frowning down at his cigarette. 'Well, let's go on. Dimitrios, the cousin of Angelos, sends Danielle into Athens to hire him a car—on a matter of life and death. In other words, in a hell of a hurry.'

'Well?'

His eyes lifted. 'An expensive need. And he's a sailor. Why would he want a car?'

I sat down again on the bed. 'I don't know. Go on.'

Absently, he flicked a gout of ash into the wash-basin.

'Danielle hired a car for him, but then got the better offer of a jeep from her French friend Hervé Clément, and came up in that. She didn't revisit the garage to let them know . . . and she hadn't given them Dragoumis' name—hence all the nonsense about "Monsieur Simon", and the interfering but well-meant efforts of Miss Camilla Haven. But Danielle's actions do spell something, don't they?'

'Urgency,' I said slowly, 'yes. And secrecy?'

'Exactly. And I could bear to know what's urgent and secret about Danielle, and Dimitrios the cousin of Angelos,' said Simon.

Chapter 14

Courage is a thing
All men admire. Think what it will mean
For your good name and mine, if you do this.
SOPHOCLES: *Ajax.*
(tr. E. F. Watling.)

A PAUSE. A beetle blundered in through the open casement, hit the wall with a crack like a pistol-shot, and zoomed out again into the dark.

'But—the car?' I said, seizing on what was still my own piece of the mystery. 'Why the car? You said Dimitrios Dragoumis was a fisherman. What would he need a car for, from Athens, with all that hush-hush nonsense about it?'

'That's just it,' said Simon. 'He is a fisherman, and he owns a boat. And now he has a jeep . . . got from Athens and kept very quiet locally. To me, that adds up to one thing. Transport.'

I said, in a voice that sounded queer: 'Urgent, secret transport. . . .' Then, sitting up briskly: 'But—*no*, Simon. It's absurd.'

'Why?'

'I can see what you're getting at . . . the reason why Angelos' cousin might need this urgent and secret transport. You mean that you think Dimitrios has found Angelos' cache—whatever it was that Michael found on Parnassus? And the jeep and the caique are to carry—oh!'

'Well?'

'*The mule!* Simon—the mule!'

He nodded. 'You can't take a jeep up Parnassus, can you? The mule was stolen the night I saw Stephanos. Danielle brought the jeep up the same day. I'll bet you anything you like that Dimitrios'

caique will shortly be lying carefully invisible in one of the tiny
inlets beyond Amphissa.'

I said: 'Look, hold on, Simon. You're only guessing. It *could* have
been Nigel who took the mule. He's gone off somewhere, and we
were talking about the Dutch boy to him, and—'

'And it would have been very much simpler for Nigel to have
bought the donkey—which went dirt cheap—off the Dutch boy,' said
Simon, 'than to have stolen a mule from the excavations. He wasn't
all that hard up, and there really wasn't all that need of secrecy for
him. In fact, if he was off on a trek of that sort, you'd even have
thought publicity was necessary.'

'Yes, I suppose so. All the same, he looked pretty secretive when I
saw him sloping off yesterday morning.'

'Oh? But I still don't think he took the mule. It vanished on
Monday night, and that night Nigel was up here. Of course he did
go out later for a walk with Danielle, but I hardly think—'

I said tautly: 'You're right. It wasn't Nigel. I've just remembered
something. When we were in the theatre, and you were reciting, I
was up near the top row of seats, and I heard something moving up
the hillside above me. You know how you hear something without
really taking it in consciously, until, later, something reminds you?
Well, it was like that. I thought nothing of it—if I heard it at all, I
thought it was just the breeze, or a stray goat or donkey or
something. But I remember now that I heard metal—a small
chinking of metal, like a shod hoof, or the nails of a boot.'

Simon smiled slightly. 'The beasts here aren't shod. Hadn't you
noticed? And the locals wear rope-soled espadrilles on the hill. If
you heard movement and the chink of metal, Camilla, then you
heard a beast's bridle. It sounds to me as if you really might have
heard the mule being stolen. Friend Dimitrios, taking the mule off
up the hill. Well, well.'

There was a little silence. Then I said: 'But Simon, you can't be
right. It really is absurd. Maybe Dimitrios *is* up to no good, and
maybe Danielle *is* in it, and maybe they *did* steal the mule and hire
the car to transport something, but it can't, it just can't, be Michael's
"treasure"!'

'Why not?'

'Because it's too much to swallow that Dimitrios should have
spent fourteen years or so looking for the stuff, and just have found
it now. Oh, I grant you he could have searched a thousand years and
never found it, especially if he didn't have precise information from

Angelos – and he probably didn't, because you can be sure Angelos meant to come back when things had simmered down enough for him to leave Yugoslavia and come home. He may not have told Dimitrios at all. Dimitrios may merely have guessed that Angelos had hidden something, and not have known where to start looking. But what I can't swallow is the assumption that he should have found Angelos' cache *now*, this week, the very week you're in Delphi. That's too much of a coincidence, and I don't believe it.'

'But is it?'

'How d'you mean?'

He said slowly: 'You've got it the wrong way round. Supposing those two things *have* happened at the same time: I am here in Delphi, and Dimitrios finds Angelos' cache on Parnassus. You call it coincidence. I call it cause and effect.'

'You mean –?'

'That the two incidents are certainly related, but not by chance. Dimitrios found the hiding-place, not just while I happen to be here – but simply *because* I'm here.'

I stared up at him. I passed my tongue over my lips. 'You mean – that he followed us up to the corrie yesterday?'

'Precisely that. He could have found out when we were going and he could have come to spy.'

I said hoarsely: 'He did. When I was sitting there in the corrie and you were in the cave with the other two men, I thought I saw something move at the top of the cliff. It could have been someone watching.'

His gaze sharpened. 'Are you sure of that?'

'Not really. But I thought there was movement, and looked up, but couldn't see anything. The sun was in my eyes.'

'I see. Well, it might have been Dimitrios. And then he followed us down, intending to meet Danielle on top of the Shining Ones. Could be.'

I said: 'I did her an injustice. I thought they'd been together, and I'd interrupted them.'

'He'd hardly have had time to get down there before you. Most of the way it's pretty open, and we might have seen him.' He thought for a few moments. 'Well, let's look at the sequence of events, shall we? Dimitrios, you'll remember, did try to find out from Stephanos – the only man who knew anything definite about the place where Michael died – anything he could about Michael's death. He didn't get anything out of Stephanos. Perhaps he did try to find the place himself. Perhaps he did gather a slender clue or two from his cousin before he left the country. But even with definite instructions from Angelos he still could have been raking the mountain all this time and found nothing. All the marks, like the Cat's Tooth pinnacle, have gone, and anything could lie buried under that earthquake rubble for fourteen years—or fourteen hundred—undiscovered. Angelos himself, if he were still alive, and if he came back to look, would be in exactly the same case.'

I said, rather breathlessly: 'Niko said there were ghosts on the hill . . . lights . . . d'you remember?'

'Niko talked a lot of rubbish, but he may well have told the truth there. Dimitrios may have been seen searching. But, to go on with the story—supposing he *had* searched all that time, and had had no luck in locating the cache, then, after years, he heard that I, Michael Lester's brother, was coming to Delphi. This might prove to be his chance. What is more likely than that Stephanos would show me, Michael's brother, the place? When I arrived Stephanos was away in Levadia, but Dimitrios could easily find out when he was coming back. It's quite some time since I planned this visit; Dimitrios could have known, and taken time over his preparations. Supposing we were right, and he had noticed Danielle driving down almost daily to Itea with the jeep to bathe? Here was transport of the kind he would need. He wouldn't dare buy or hire transport locally; he's well known, and people would ask questions. But it would be easy enough to scrape acquaintance with Danielle, and buy her silence —and her help—with a promise to cut her in on the final haul. It would only remain to collect a mule or a donkey, and there again Danielle was the answer. I'll bet you she took the mule; she'd worked with the archaeologists for weeks, and she knew just where everything was kept and how to get at it . . . What is it?'

'I've just remembered. It wasn't only a mule. I remember. The guide said *"some tools and a mule"*.'

'*Did* he?' His voice was still quiet, but the light-grey eyes blazed in his brown face. 'Well, well, well . . . Does it make sense, or not? Or am I jumping ahead too fast?'

'Pretty fast. They're rather scrappy bricks, and made with awfully little straw, but they could be solid. Go on.'

'Where was I? Yes: Dimitrios has everything lined up for the day when Simon Lester should arrive and lead him straight to the spot where Michael died. But then he—Dimitrios—has a stroke of bad luck.'

'Danielle's boss leaves Delphi, and she has to go too—with the jeep?'

'Exactly. She went on Sunday, perforce. She must have gone straight to the garage in Athens and arranged to pick up a car next day, as soon as she could get free of Monsieur Clément.' He grinned. 'We know what happened next. Her error. But luck came in again, as she persuaded Hervé to let her have the jeep. And she came back. She took the jeep down to Itea. Whether she brought Dimitrios up that night with her we can't know, but she probably did. She—or he—took the mule and a crowbar or so from the workmen's sheds above the shrine, *et voilà.*'

I said: 'And then all Dimitrios had to do was to wait and follow us. Too easy.'

'Much too easy. I should have thought of it after what Stephanos told me, but I admit it never seriously occurred to me (till I saw the earthquake damage up there) that anything that Mick found might still be hidden. However, there it is. You can bet your boots he was up there yesterday, and now all he has to do is to hunt that fairly small stretch of cliff, and then he and Danielle are made for life.' He smiled down at me. 'I admit it *is* a lot of bricks to make with very little straw, but where else is the straw to go? We have certain facts, and we must fit them in somewhere with the knowledge that friend Dimitrios is up to no sort of good.'

'And he is the cousin of Angelos . . . Yes, I see what you mean. But why did he come here tonight? Just to see Danielle again?'

He said soberly: 'Ah, that . . . That's what I meant when I said I didn't like the feel of this affair. What we've discovered—or guessed, if you like—so far, is straightforward enough, but Nigel . . .' He paused, then turned to pitch the stub of his cigarette out of the open window. 'Nigel. He's in this somewhere and I want to know where.'

'You mean that Dimitrios came to see *him*?'

'No. Dimitrios came here looking for something. And I could bear to know what.' He glanced round the room. 'And I could also bear to know where Nigel is.'

I said: 'The drawings have gone.'

'What? Oh, the ones on the wall. So they have. Well, the sooner we find out what else is gone the better . . .' He began to move round the bare untidy little room as he spoke. 'We'll soon see if he intended—no, don't you bother, Camilla. Sit still. There's not much searching to be done in a place this size, even if a couple of gorillas have turned everything upside down first . . .'

'Dimitrios didn't take anything with him, anyway,' I said.

'No, he didn't, did he? One might say he hardly had time. That's one satisfactory thing about tonight's affair.'

'Perhaps Danielle was telling the truth. Perhaps he did only come in here to hide from you when he heard you move.'

'Not on your life.' He had opened the shower-cupboard and was rummaging inside. 'He didn't have time, after he'd heard me move, to take that light-bulb out. He did that as soon as he got into the room, and to me that means he had some business in here that was going to take a minute or two, and he didn't want to risk being surprised and recognised. I must have heard him almost straight away—I'd been lying awake wondering where the blazes Nigel was, and as soon as I heard the movements I got up. It didn't take me long to roll off the bed and grab my flannels and get into them, and then to get to the door. He hadn't quite shut the door—for quietness' sake, I suppose—and when I saw torchlight moving beyond it I knew it wasn't Nigel, and I went carefully. As I shoved the door open, I saw the light swinging round the room as if it was looking for something. That was all, because of course he turned on me.'

I laughed. 'Yes, and you told Danielle he attacked you—which, sir, was a lie. I was watching, and you went bald-headed for the poor chap before he even had time to say "good evening"!'

He grinned. 'And for a very good reason. He whipped round when he heard me at the door, and he pulled a knife. I thought it best not to give him time to think about using it.'

I drew a long breath. 'I—see. You were right about the feel of this thing, weren't you? All I can say is, that for a member of our staid and slightly stuffy profession, your reactions are—well, fairly rapid—not to say decisive.'

He was still smiling. 'Two strenuous years' conscription in the tough end of the Artists' Rifles . . . besides what Michael taught me all unofficial-like. It bears fruit—besides, I'm rather afraid I enjoyed it. I like a good and dirty fight . . . I say, Camilla.'

'Yes?'

'His things *are* all gone.'

'Everything? Not just his painting things?'

'Everything, I think. The rucksack—see, he used to hang it on this peg. I suppose he didn't carry a razor, but the towel's gone, too, and the soap, and what clothes he had. And unlike me he was conventional even in this climate and wore pyjamas. Are they tucked down there under the sheet?'

'I don't think so. No, they're not.'

He said, sounding at once puzzled and relieved: 'Then he meant to go anyway. Damn the boy, he might have told me, and saved me a couple of sleepless hours. Well, at least he isn't sitting up on Parnassus somewhere with a sprained ankle, whatever else he's got himself into. I'll just make sure there's nothing down here . . . ah, there's the Greek's knife. I thought I heard it fly under the bed. And that hellish clanging noise we made was Nigel's apology for a waste-paper basket . . . Lord, what a mess! Orange peel and pencil shavings and all the dud drawings he's thrown away. I really think we'll have to bribe our way out of this Camilla, my girl.'

'For goodness' sake let me help.' I slipped from the bed to the floor and gathered up a handful of papers. I dropped them into the biscuit-tin that served Nigel for a waste-basket. 'I'll clear this stuff up. You see if that chair'll mend, and straighten the table. There's no damage except the broken glass, and we'd better leave that till morning and see if we can find a brush and—*Simon!*'

He was busy straightening the furniture. He swung round. 'What is it?'

'These papers . . . They're not "dud drawings" at all. They're —they're the finished things, his Hellenic types!' I shuffled them through my hands. 'Yes, look, here they are! There's that head that's a bit like Stephanos, and the smiling one that looked like a statue, and that must be the Minoan girl he told us about—and here's a shepherd boy. And more . . . look.' I began to leaf through them rapidly. My hand wasn't quite steady. I said: 'I know he was doing them under protest, and he *was* feeling at odds with life, but surely, Simon, he can't afford to throw them away? What in the world—?' I stopped short.

Simon said sharply from above me: 'What is it?'

I said shakily: 'This one. This is the head, that lovely, lovely head. The young man with the strange face. And look, he's torn it up. Not the others, but this. It's torn right across.' I looked down at the fragments on my lap and said sadly: 'He needn't have torn it up. It was beautiful.'

He stooped to take the pieces from me, and studied them for a few moments in silence.

At length he said: 'What else is there? Not the flower-studies, surely?'

'No. No. They're all the "types", except that lovely head.'

I heard him take a breath, as if of relief, and when he spoke I knew

he had had the same fleeting stab of fear as I myself. 'Then
–whatever made him go–I don't think we need worry over-
much. That fit of the blues hasn't made him plan anything foolish
after all; he's taken the good stuff with him. Except this . . .' He
opened his fingers, and let the fragments drift down on to my lap.
The action was like a shrug; a sigh. 'Ah, well, we can't guess what's
biting the boy. But I'll be thankful when I know–'

I said abruptly: 'The cyclamen.'

He said, suddenly sounding very weary: 'Is that there as well,
after all?'

'No. It's not here. That's not what I meant. But I've remembered
something, Simon, and I think it's important. Yesterday, when we
were up in the corrie–Michael's corrie–I saw a plant of cyclamen
growing in the rock. I didn't realise it at the time–at least I think I
must have done subconsciously, because I know I was thinking
about Nigel as I looked at it–but it was the same plant that was in
the drawing. I tell you, I didn't connect it then; but now, when we
were talking about his drawings, I somehow saw it again. And it was
the same. I'm sure of it. And that means that Nigel's been up in that
corrie, too!' I drew a deep breath. 'And perhaps, if *Nigel* had found
Angelos' cave, that would explain some of the things he said on
Monday night! Simon, Nigel was in that corrie, and if you ask me,
Nigel found the cave! And Angelos' hoard was still there!'

Simon said, hard and sharp: 'Then if Nigel found anything in that
corrie, he found it on Monday. He did that drawing on Monday.'

'Yes, and he told you he'd done no work, till we found that he'd
slipped up over the Phormis head and the cyclamen!'

He said slowly: 'It could be. I went up some of the way over the
track with him on Sunday. He might have gone back on his own and
stumbled on the place. One of those weird freaks of chance, but they
do happen. Oh, my God, suppose he did?'

We stared at each other. I said: 'And yesterday morning I saw him
setting off again . . . and looking secretive about it. Simon, perhaps
it was *Nigel* who took the mule. Perhaps we're wrong about
Danielle. Perhaps Nigel's trying to move the stuff, whatever it is,
himself.'

Simon said, in a harsh voice that was anything but casual: 'And if
he is? If he's got across that damned Greek in the process? Don't
forget he's somewhere in this too.'

'Perhaps he's working with that damned Greek,' I said.

'Perhaps.'

I said: 'Simon, don't worry so. One thing's obvious; he did mean to go. He's cleared up here, and he's scrapped the stuff he didn't want. Whatever he's up to, and even if his affairs *have* tangled with Dimitrios', he's gone deliberately. He may have got himself into something illegal, or at most immoral, but he meant to, and—well, you can't really be his keeper to that extent, can you?'

He hesitated, then suddenly smiled. 'I suppose not. At least, not till it's daylight.'

I said, making a statement of it: 'You're going up there, of course.'

'Of course. I intended to anyway, and now it seems I shall have to.'

'When do we start?'

He looked down at me for a moment. That unreadable mask had shut down again over his face. I don't know what I expected him to say. I know what nine men out of ten would have said—and Philip would have said it twice.

Simon didn't say it at all. He said merely: 'I'll come and call you. And now you'd better go and sleep. We'll have to make an early start.'

I got to my feet. 'Will you take Stephanos and Niko?'

'No. For one thing it would take too long, and for another, if there's anything to be found that Nigel and/or Dimitrios haven't already found and moved, I don't want witnesses till I know where Nigel comes in, and whose property it is. If it is arms and gold, the ownership might be a rather delicate political question under present circumstances.'

'Heavens, yes. I hadn't thought of that.'

'And now let me see you back to your room . . . By the way, I haven't thanked you yet for bashing friend Dimitrios over the head for me.'

'I'd never have got near him,' I said truthfully, 'if he hadn't thought I was Danielle. And I missed him anyway.'

'All the same it was a stout effort.'

He opened the door, and I went past him into the chilly corridor.

'They taught us a lot,' I said sedately, 'in the tough end of St. Trinian's.'

Chapter 15

Tell the Emperor that the bright citadel is fallen to the ground.
Apollo hath no longer any shelter, or oracular laurel-tree, or
speaking fountain. Even the vocal stream has ceased to flow.
The Delphic Oracle to the Emperor Julian.

IT CAN'T HAVE been much after six when Simon woke me. I had
sleepily answered 'come in' to his knock before I remembered that I
was no longer in the hotel, and this was not likely to be a
chambermaid with a cup of tea. As I turned my head, looking, still
sleepy-eyed, towards the door, it opened. Simon didn't come in, but
I heard his voice.

'Camilla.'

'Mmm? Oh—Simon. Yes?'

'Could you bear to get up now, d'you suppose? I think we ought
to move. I've got coffee on a Primus if you'd like to come along and
get it when you're dressed.'

'All right.'

'Good.' The door shut. I shot, fully awake now, out of bed, and
began to dress quickly. From my window I could see the morning
sunlight sliding like apricot-bloom over the rounded top of Mount
Cirphis.

In my room it was still cool, for which I was grateful. I wasn't so
grateful about the icy gush of water from the taps—both taps—but in
any case washing at Delphi is a penance; the water is as hard as
pumice-stone, and just about as good for the skin . . . but it woke me
up fully and finally, and it was with a tingling sense of new
adventure that at length I went quickly along to Simon's door and
tapped.

'Come in.'

I noticed that he was making no attempt to keep his voice low this morning, and he must have seen a query in my face as I entered, because he looked up from the Primus he was tending and said briefly: 'Danielle checked out an hour ago.'

'Oh?'

'I followed her down as far as the upper road. I didn't see where she went in the village, but I did see a jeep drive off north.'

'That means she's either making for Itea or further along towards Amphissa?'

'Yes. Coffee?'

'Lovely. Simon, this smells like heaven. Rolls too? You're very efficient.'

'I went along to the baker's after I'd seen Danielle off the premises. Here's the sugar.'

'Thank you. Where do you think she's gone?'

'God knows, and there's not much point in guessing. Probably to pick Dimitrios up in Itea—though if the jeep was in Delphi it seems odd he didn't take it last night when he got out of the studio. How d'you feel today?'

'I'm fine, thanks. And you? How's the shoulder? You're sure that was all the damage?'

'Certain. And it's really hardly stiff at all. I feel ready for anything.'

He was sitting on the edge of his bed, a cup of coffee in one hand and a roll in the other, looking, as ever, completely relaxed and at ease. 'And you?' he said. 'Ready for your adventure?'

I laughed. 'I can hardly believe that two days ago I was writing to my friend that nothing ever happened to me. Is it Goethe who says somewhere that we ought to beware what we ask the gods for, because they might grant it? I asked for adventure, and it seems I got it.'

He didn't smile. He appeared to consider what I'd been saying for a minute or two, then he said, quite seriously: 'I ought not to let you come, you know.'

I didn't ask why. I drank coffee and watched the sunlight wheel a fraction to touch the edge of the window-frame. A butterfly hovered, then winnowed down to cling to the strip of sunlit stone. Its wings fanned gently, black velvet shot with gold.

Simon said: 'Don't mistake me. I don't think we—you, are in any danger; but it'll be a hard day, especially following after yesterday and last night. The only possible danger is running unexpectedly into Dimitrios, who'll certainly be up there, but if we're reasonably careful that can be avoided. I don't think he'll be expecting us. He probably thinks that now I've seen the place, that closes the account for me.'

'In any case I told Danielle we were going to the fair at Levadia.'

'*Did* you? Good for you. Was she showing interest, then?'

I smiled. 'Yes, she showed interest. She asked me flat out where you were going today. I—well, I'm afraid I just mistrusted her on principle, and told her a lie.' I set down my coffee-cup. 'It seems it's just as well. Dimitrios certainly won't be looking out for us.'

'Excellent,' said Simon. 'Of course, there's no reason anyway why he should have expected me to go up there again, is there? He doesn't know I know of the existence of any "treasure". If Michael had sent any information home, Dimitrios might well imagine I'd have come long ago. Cigarette?'

'Thank you.'

He leaned forward to hold his lighter for me. 'No,' he said, 'I think Dimitrios will see it as a pilgrimage for me; and that's over. All the better. But we'll be very careful, just the same. With any luck we'll see what's going on, and where Nigel comes in—and then we can think about possible reinforcements.' He sent me a grin as he got up off the bed and reached for his haversack. 'In any case, not to worry. All things being equal, I can deal with friend Dimitrios. And I refuse to be afraid of Nigel. Even if he has got himself mixed up in anything for the sake of the cash, he'd never in a million years do violence for gain. Or so I think.'

'I agree.'

'Apart from those two there's Danielle.' That swift grin again. 'Well, I wouldn't like to swear that I could precisely "deal with" Danielle, but let's say I'm not afraid of her.'

'We might be wrong about them,' I said. 'There may be nobody up there at all, except Nigel.'

'It's possible—' he was packing the haversack as he talked: more of the fresh rolls, some fruit, chocolate, water; Spartan fare, but none the less appropriate for that—'it's quite possible that we are wrong about Dimitrios and Danielle, but in any case I'm not concerned at the moment with Michael's "find" except as it touches Nigel.' A look. 'You're convinced about those flowers in the drawing, aren't you?'

'Absolutely.'

'Well, that's one thing we're sure of in a maze of guess work. We don't really know a damned thing about Dimitrios and Danielle, but we do know Nigel has been in that corrie, and we do know he was wildly excited about something that same night. And Dimitrios came here, for some purpose, to visit Nigel's room. We'll freeze on to those facts, and let the rest develop as it will . . . Are you ready to start?'

'Yes.'

'Then let's go.'

Already the morning sun was warm overhead, but the rocks were still cool from the night. The path past the graveyard was wide enough for us to walk side by side.

Simon said: 'All I'm hoping today is that—if you're right—we run across Nigel and see what he's up to, and knock some sense into his silly young head before he gets himself involved in something he can't get out of. And incidentally—this is the path off to the stadium—and incidentally, find the cave.'

He had stopped where the narrow path left our track, and waited for me to precede him. I paused, and looked at him straightly. 'Tell me one thing. Why *are* you letting me come?'

For the second time since I had known him he seemed oddly at a loss. He hesitated, as if looking for the right words.

I said: 'Granted that you don't want Stephanos and Niko along. But you'd get along much faster and do much better alone, *Kyrie* Lester, and you know it. You also know quite well that if we *do* run into Dimitrios it might develop into quite a sticky party. Why don't you leave me at home to get on with my knitting?'

A pine-branch cast a bar of shade across his face, but I thought I saw a smile behind the light-grey eyes. 'You know the reasons quite well.'

'Reasons?'

'Yes.'

'Well, I know the first. I wished a little too hard for an adventure, so I can darned well take what comes, and four eyes are better than two if we want to find Nigel and the cave?'

'Not quite. I had the idea that you were looking rather hard for something on your own account.'

I turned abruptly and led the way up the narrow path between the pines. I said, after a bit: 'Perhaps I was.' Then, later still: 'You—do see rather a lot, don't you?'

'And you know the second reason.'

It was shady under the pines, but my cheeks felt hot. I said: 'Oh?' and then felt furious with myself because the syllable seemed to be inviting an answer. I added hastily: 'I can show you where the cyclamen is, of course.'

'Of course,' said Simon agreeably.

We had reached the stadium. We crossed the slanting shadows of the starting-gate and left the trees. Behind us in the holly-oaks and cypresses the birds flashed and sang. The singing echoed and rang up the limestone cliffs.

We crossed the stadium floor in silence and took the steep path that led to the rocky reaches of Parnassus.

* * *

We saw no one on our way to the corrie.

Most of the way from Delphi the track was easy to follow, and, apart from one open stretch soon after we had left the top of the Shining Ones, it wound along rocky valleys which would have offered plenty of cover in case of alarm. But the hot desert of broken rocks seemed as empty as yesterday. We travelled in short bursts, going fairly fast, but with frequent pauses in the shade to get our breath and to scan the surrounding country for signs of movement.

At length, as we made our way up a steep dry watercourse, I looked upwards to the right and saw the line of cliffs that held the corrie. Simon, who was ahead of me, stopped and turned.

'We'll wait here, I think, and eat. Look, here's a good place, in the shade between these two boulders. We can't be seen, and we can keep an eye on the valley and on those cliffs. I'd like to be quite sure no one else is about before we make our way up.'

I sat down thankfully in the place he indicated, and he produced food from the haversack. The rolls didn't taste quite as good as they had done in the cool of the morning, but as I ate I began to feel better. The tepid water was a benison, and the fruit was ambrosia itself . . .

I let Simon do the watching. After I had eaten I relaxed against the rock with eyes half-shut against the light, and he lit a cigarette for me. He showed no sign of hurry or impatience, or even curiosity. We smoked in silence, and I saw his eyes move almost idly across the landscape, up to the corrie, along the cliff, down the scree, back to the corrie.

At the very edge of my vision there was a movement.

I turned my head sharply, eyes fully open now. I could see nothing. But there had been a movement; of that I was sure. I was just about to touch Simon's arm when I saw it again; it was as if one of the rocks of the scree had moved . . . a goat. It was only a goat. As it walked forward, taking shape against the void of tumbled rocks, I saw others with it, two, three of them, moving purposefully along some age-old track of their own. I was wondering half-idly if there was a goat-herd with them, and if, perhaps, they had strayed from the troop, when I thought I heard, far away over the cliff-top, the sound of a pipe. Even as I heard it and strained my ears to catch the notes, it faded, and I dismissed it as fancy. The thin, broken stave had been purely pastoral, something from a myth of Arcady, nymphs and shepherds and Pan-pipes and green valleys. But this was Parnassus, home of more terrible gods.

I relaxed again and watched the smoke from my cigarette wind up in the sunlight. I remember that I didn't think at all about the business of the day. I thought about Parnassus, and the gods who lived there, and Simon . . .

I stole a look at him. He was looking almost dreamily up towards the cliffs. He looked about as tense and vigilant as in the fifth hour of the House Cricket Match. He caught my look and smiled, and moved his hand lazily to knock ash from his cigarette. I said: 'A penny for them?'

'I was wondering if there was anyone with those goats. I don't think so.'

'I thought I heard a pipe being played, away over there,' I said, 'but I expect I imagined it. Did you hear anything?'

'No. But it's possible. I don't think those three would be up here on their own. You must have very good hearing. I never heard a sound.'

He crushed out his cigarette and got up, reaching a hand down to me. 'Shall we go up now? I think we're unobserved, but I don't want to cross that big open stretch towards the corrie "gateway". If we skirt it, and go up that gully there, I think we can get round without the risk of being seen, and it'll bring us out above the cliff where we were yesterday. It'll be a bit of a stiff pull, I'm afraid. Are you tired?'

'Not a bit.'

He laughed. 'One up to British womanhood. Come along. And keep down. This is where the real stalk starts.'

*   *   *

Simon lay flat at the corrie's lip, looking downwards. I crouched behind him, a little way back from the cliff edge. I waited, watching him for a signal.

It seemed an age before he moved. Then he turned his head and lifted a hand, with a slow cautious movement that carried its own warning.

In spite of myself, I could feel tension pull my nerves taut, like cold wires touching my skin. I inched forward until I lay beside Simon. I was screened by one of the low holly-oaks. I lifted my head slowly till my eyes were above the level of the edge. I looked down into the corrie. There was no one there.

As I looked at him, with surprise in my face and a question, he put his lips to my ear. 'Dimitrios is here.'

Again that coward jerk of the heart. Every vein in my body was contracting, little thrilling wires tightening till my muscles wouldn't obey me. I found I had ducked my head down again behind the holly-oak, and my cheek was on my hand in the hot dust. The hand was cold.

Simon breathed, just beside my ear: 'He's just vanished some-where underneath us. I saw him duck under that piece in the corner.' He jerked his head slightly towards it. 'Is that where you went exploring yesterday?'

I nodded. I swallowed, and managed to say quite evenly: 'What was he doing?'

'I don't know. He just seemed to be hanging about. Waiting for someone or something. Nigel, perhaps, or –'

He broke off and seemed to go lower into the ground. I shrank down beside him. The holly-oak hid me, and I peered down.

Then I saw Dimitrios. He came out from somewhere below us, ducking his head as he passed under the flying buttress that seemed to shore up the cliff. He was smoking, and his eyes were frowning and narrowed against the high blaze of the sun. He walked carefully over the rocky floor of the corrie towards the northern gap in the wall. Every now and again he stopped, and slanted his head as if to listen.

He reached the corrie entrance, and stopped there, looking down towards Amphissa. Once he turned his head and looked the other way, the way we had come, from Delphi. Then he came back into the corrie. He flung down the butt of his cigarette and lit another. I noticed sweat on his dark face and dust yellowish-white on his clothes. He wasn't in the dark suit today; he was wearing dungarees in dull faded blue, and a khaki shirt with a red kerchief knotted at the neck.

The cigarette was lit now. He dropped the match, then looked round him for a few moments as if undecided. He took a few steps into the corrie, and I thought he was going back towards the corner where the cyclamen was, but he stopped suddenly, as if impatient of waiting, turned sharply on his heel, and walked, rapidly now, as if his mind was at last made up, out of the corrie.

Simon said in my ear: 'Gone to meet Nigel, or Danielle, do you suppose? Give him a minute or two.'

We gave him five. They seemed very long minutes. There was no other sound in the hot morning but our own breathing. The sun beat down on us as we lay on the bare earth. I was thankful when Simon moved at last.

We got quickly to our feet, and went down the twisting little path like a couple of mountain goats. We almost ran across the corrie floor and ducked under the fallen rock into the corner.

There it was, the patch of brilliant green, and the drifts of tiny blue bells, the lovely traces of the mountain rain. But today it was different.

Simon had checked. 'Is this the place?'

'Yes, but–' I caught my breath and pushed past him, to stand staring at the cliff.

The cyclamen had gone. Where it had clung to its crack in the rock there was now a black fissure. The crack had widened, split, and gaped open, as pressure had been exerted on the weather-rotted rock. I could see the raw white marks where the crowbars had gained their leverage.

A slab, similarly marked, lay at our feet, newly fallen, and crushing the fresh grass. Yesterday it had been leaning against the rock-face, masking what lay behind from my casual glance. Today there was a split in the face of the rock, some seven feet high by a foot and a half wide–a narrow fissure which angled sharply up to a point at the top. It opened on to darkness. The cave. Michael's cave.

My mouth was dry. I said hoarsely: 'Yesterday that slab was leaning up against the cliff, at an angle. There was a crack behind it, very narrow. I remember now. It didn't look like an entrance to anything, but that must have been it.'

He nodded, but he wasn't looking at me, or at the mouth of the cave. He looked past me, up at the cliff-top, the corrie-walls, all round us.

No movement: no sound.

There was a pile of mule-droppings on the grass, that hadn't been there yesterday. I pointed to them silently, and Simon nodded. He said softly: 'We were right, then . . . We'll go in. You wait here a moment. And keep those ears of yours open. I won't be long.'

He disappeared into the darkness of the cleft. I waited. Once again, far away, I thought I heard that little thread of music, the ghostly echo of the Pan-pipes. Heard now, in this hot cruel corrie, the sound spoke no longer of Arcadia, and the kindly god of flocks and herds. It was a panic prickle along the flesh.

It had gone. I had imagined it again. I stood with my hands tightly clasped together in front of me, and made myself wait without moving.

Simon showed in the darkness of the cleft, like a beckoning ghost. I almost ran towards him into the cool darkness of the cave.

After the glare of day the place was dead-dark. It was like running against a black velvet curtain. I stopped, blinded. I felt Simon's arm come round me, guiding me in out of the light, then he switched on a torch. The light seemed feeble and probing after the blaze of day, but we could see.

We were in a widish passage which sloped gently downwards for some five or six yards and then turned abruptly to the left. The original entrance must have been wide, but it had been blocked by successive falls of stone to leave only the narrow cleft through which we had come. The passage itself was clear enough, and smelt fresh and cool.

Simon said: 'The slope gets steeper. There's another twist down to the right, and then the cave itself . . . Here. Quite a place, isn't it?'

It was indeed. The main cave was huge, a great natural cavern the size of a young cathedral, with a high curved ceiling that vanished into darkness, and clefts and recesses that swallowed the feebly-probing torchlight. Stalactites and stalagmites made strangely-shaped, enormous pillars. Fallen rock lay here as well. In some of the dimly-seen apses there were boulders and masses of rough stone showing, in the elusive light, like the massive tombs that lie between the columns of a cathedral. Somewhere I could hear the faint drip of water. The place was impressive, magnificent even, but it was a ruin. Dust and rubble lay everywhere, some of it recent-looking, some of it apparently undisturbed for centuries.

The torchlight moved, swept, checked . . .

Simon said: 'There.'

He said it softly, almost idly, but I knew him now. My heart gave that painful little jerk of excitement. The light was holding something in its dim circle, a circle which seemed to have brightened, sharpened, focused . . . There was a pile of rubble by a column to the left of the cavern-mouth. It looked at first like any of the other heaps of fallen debris, then I saw that among the shapes of the broken rock, more regular shapes showed . . . a cubed corner . . . the dusty outline of a box . . . And beside them in the rubble the dull gleam of metal: a crowbar and a shovel.

The torchlight swept further. 'See that? They've shifted some of it already. See where it's been dragged through the dust?' He sent the light skating quickly round the rest of the great cavern. Nothing. Another time I would have exclaimed over the ghostly icicles of rock, the arches, the chambered darknesses that the corners held, but now my whole interest, like the torchlight, was centred on that pile of rock-debris and what it contained.

Simon paused for a moment, cocking his head. No sound except the drip of water somewhere, very faintly. He moved forward with me beside him, and bent over the exposed corner of the box.

He didn't disturb it. The torch worked for him. 'There's the Government stamp. This isn't gold, Camilla. It's guns.'

'Guns?'

'Uh-huh. Small and useful Sten guns.' He straightened up and switched the light out for a moment. In the thick darkness his voice was soft and grim. 'There's an excellent market for this sort of thing at several points in the Med. just now. Well, well.'

I said: 'I don't believe that Nigel would do that.'

The torch flashed on again. 'Come to think of it, neither do I I wonder . . .' He moved off round the pile, exploring deeper into the darkness behind the big stalagmite.

'Simon,' I said, 'd'you mean these were flown in here during the war?'

'Yes. I told you. Gold and arms galore.'

'But that was 1942, wasn't it? They wouldn't keep, surely?'

I heard him laugh. 'You talk as if they were fish. Of course they'll "keep". They're packed in grease. They'll come out as good as new . . . Ah . . .'

'What is it?' In spite of myself my voice sharpened.

'Ammo. Stacks of it. My God, this'd take a couple of days to shift, this stuff. No wonder . . .' His voice trailed away.

'Simon? What is it?'

He said without a trace of inflection: 'The gold.'

I moved forward so fast that I tripped over a root of the stalagmite and almost fell. '*Where?*'

'Steady there. So this is what treasure trove does to you? Here.' The torchlight was steady on the pile of broken rock. Among the dust and splintered fragments the corners of two small boxes showed. They were of metal, but the corner of one had been smashed open, and under the dusty gaping metal was the living gleam of gold.

Simon was saying: 'That's Michael's little find, Camilla. That's why Mick was murdered. But I still don't quite see . . .' He paused, and I saw his brows draw together, but after a while he went on in his even voice: 'Well, we were right, as far as it went. Two boxes at least, and there may be more under the rubble.'

'They're very small, aren't they?'

'One of them would be one man's work, all the same. Did you know that gold was almost twice as heavy as lead? They'll have quite a job shifting what they've got here.'

I said: 'They?'

He answered my look. 'I'm afraid you were right about Nigel. I think he *was* on his way up here yesterday morning, and it's Nigel who's been working here while Dimitrios was in Delphi.'

I said apprehensively: 'But we still don't know they're working together. If Dimitrios came up last night, or early today, and found Nigel here, and set about him the way he did with you –'

He shook his head. 'No. Think it out. There must be two of them in it. Look at this stuff again; look how it's buried. Angelos probably did throw a bit of rubble and small stones over it to hide it, but he never put this pile of rock over it. This has come down in an earth tremor – probably the one that shut the cave and broke the cliff above us. Shifting this kind of thing is sheer hard work, and Dimitrios just hasn't had time to do everything alone.'

'You mean –?'

'Work it out. There must be two men on the job, Camilla. If Nigel found the cave, it still hadn't been opened up yesterday, enough to let those boxes be carried out. Whether Nigel showed it to Dimitrios, or whether Dimitrios found it himself as soon as we left the corrie yesterday, the man simply hasn't had time single-handed to do all this. Remember he followed us almost straight down to Delphi; he wouldn't have had time to get his tools from where they were hidden and shift that slab. And even if he came back to do that later, he was down in Delphi again in the middle of the night.'

'What about Danielle?'

'She couldn't have got up here and then back again between the time you saw her on the Shining Ones, and the time she went to bed last night. What's more, she couldn't, physically, do this sort of job.'

He paused for a moment, as if listening, and then went on: 'And look at the situation just now. We know Danielle went north with the jeep. She won't have had time to get up here from the Amphissa road. Dimitrios is waiting for someone, but it's not Danielle. The mule's been here, hasn't it, and gone? At a guess, Dimitrios is waiting for whoever has taken the mule over, loaded, to meet the jeep. Nigel.'

The torch flashed again, momentarily, over the gold. He said: 'You remember Stephanos saying that the old track leads to a disused quarry near the Amphissa road? It sounds the sort of place where they might park the jeep out of sight while they ferry the stuff across the hill with the mule. They seem to have made a start on the guns. I imagine they'll stack the loot somewhere down near the road, till they can get it all away together; and if they've any sense they'll leave the gold safely here till the last minute . . . Did you hear anything?'

We stood very still with the light out. 'No,' I said. Then, slowly: 'You know, I–I don't trust Dimitrios.'

I heard the ghost of a laugh in the dark. 'Today's great thought, Camilla my darling? You surprise me.'

He had surprised me, too, but I hoped my voice didn't show it. I said: 'I was thinking of Nigel. Even if they are working together now, it's only because Nigel found the stuff first, and Dimitrios wants help to shift it. Once the work's done–' I stopped, and licked dry lips.

'I know.' No trace of amusement now. 'Well, we're here now, so that should be taken care of.'

'Yes. But Simon–' even to me the whisper sounded thin and miserably uncertain–'Simon, what are we going to do?'

'Wait. What else can we do? We don't know the score yet, but no doubt we soon will.'

He switched on again, and the light flicked round the cavern. 'There's plenty of cover here, and we'll hear them in good time–or at least you will. If Nigel comes up alone, all the better, but if it should be Dimitrios coming back . . .'

He grinned down at me, but some quality in the grin brought the reverse of comfort. I said suddenly, accusingly: 'You *want* him to come back.'

'And if I do?' The smile deepened at the expression on my face. 'By God, Camilla, don't you see? I pray he does come back. There's your score to settle as well as mine, and now there's that idiotic boy to straighten out . . . It would be better if Dimitrios came. Don't you see?'

'Oh yes, I see.'

His hand came out, momentarily, to touch my cheek, a moth-light touch. 'Don't be scared, my dear. I'm not going to get myself killed and leave you alone with the wolves.' He gave a little laugh. 'I've not the slightest intention of fighting fair . . . and two can play at the game of attacking down a torch-beam.'

I said, I hoped steadily: 'He may be armed.'

'I'm pretty sure he's not. There wasn't room for a gun in those dungarees.'

'He's probably got himself another knife.'

'Probably. And I've got his. Two can play at that game, too.'

'*Simon!*'

I heard him laugh again as he moved away. 'Poor Camilla . . . Now, half a minute. Stay where you are. I'll be back.'

He slid, with wary flashes of the torch, out of the cave, and the small light dwindled and vanished into the curve of the passageway. He was gone perhaps two minutes. I stayed just where I was, with the gold at my feet, and one hand nervously fingering the bulk of the Greek's torch in my pocket. Then the will-o'-the-wisp light danced back along the passage wall, and Simon was beside me.

'Not a sign of either of them, so we'll have a closer look at this stuff, I think.'

'Do you want any help?'

'No, thanks. Scout around and find a bolt-hole to make for when he comes.' He was already busy, crouching beside the pile of rubble, his hands moving gently over the dusty surfaces.

I left him to his task, his hands moving among the dust just as Michael's hands must have moved fourteen years ago when he made the same discovery. I flashed my torch back momentarily as I moved away. It showed his crouching body, the quiet intent face, the hands . . . Michael Lester finding evidence of treachery to the Allies. For some reason I gave a little shiver. They said ghosts walked, didn't they? And the ghost of Angelos, who smiled as he killed? '*If ghosts are true,'* Niko had said, *'then he still walks on Parnassus . . .'*

The cave was even bigger than I had thought. I passed between pillars of stalagmites as massive as Apollo's columns at Delphi, and into an anteroom as deep as a private chapel. There was ample cover. Simon and I could lie hidden almost anywhere, when Dimitrios came . . .

The light was uncertain in my hand. Its beam touched the walls, the fallen masses that blocked the antechamber, and diffused itself into nothingness among the dark recesses. But even as I turned back, the edge of the light shimmered momentarily with a sliding, liquid gleam. I paused. There was the drip of water again, more clearly now. I went forward, the torch exploring ahead of me. The floor lifted a little, and there was a streak of damp on it that caught the light. I could feel the freshness in the air, above the dead dust-smells of the cave, and there was the drip of water, closer now and clearer; there must be some spring in the cave—perhaps the same spring whose overflow fed the grass and flowers outside. I went forward quickly now, the light flicking over the rock in eager search. There was the now-familiar pile of broken rock against the rear wall of the cave; there was the wall itself, streaked with damp and seamed with black fissures; there a wrecked stalagmite leaning drunkenly against a slab that lay at an angle to the wall . . .

There was something very familiar about the slab. It only took me a couple of seconds to realise why. It was the same shape, and leaned in the same way, as the slab that yesterday had barred the cave-mouth, and today lay tumbled in the grass outside.

I approached it slowly, knowing what I could find. As I paused beside it I could hear the drip of water plainly. Then I felt the skin prickle cold again along my arms and back.

With the drip of water came another sound, a sound that I had heard already twice that day and disbelieved, as I disbelieved it now. The sound of a pipe. Pan's pipe . . . It played a delicate little fall of notes; another; again. Silence, and the drip of water.

And the sound had come from behind the leaning slab.

With the hair lifting along my arms I bent to peer behind it. I was right. There was a gap, narrow, perhaps eight inches wide, but still a gap. And it didn't, like the other cave-mouth, give on to darkness. Beyond it, the darkness slackened.

I think I had forgotten Dimitrios. I said softly, and even to me the echoes of my voice sounded queer: 'There's a way through here. I'm going to see.'

I don't know if Simon answered. I was squeezing through the narrow gap. The rock scraped me, caught at my clothes, then let me through. I was in a widish passage which led upwards in a gentle curve. The floor was smooth. Round me the darkness slackened further, and more clearly through the torchlight the walls of the gallery took shape. Ahead of me it curved more sharply to the right, and beyond the curve I could see that the light grew clearer. The drip of the water was clear and loud.

Then it came again, the sound I had been listening for above the trickle of water; a little stave of music, hauntingly off-key . . .

I rounded the corner. Ahead was the light, the arch of the gallery framing a blaze muted by moving green. I caught a glimpse of grass, and the hanging boughs of some slender tree dappling the sunlight at the mouth of the tunnel.

I almost ran the rest of the way. I ducked under the arch and came suddenly, blindingly, into a little dell.

It wasn't a way out. It was a small enclosure, like a light-well. Centuries ago this had been a circular cave into which the gallery had run, but the roof had fallen in and let in the sun and the seeds of grass and wild vines, and the spring had fed them, so that now, in the heart of the mountain, was this little well of vivid light roofed with the moving green of some delicate tree.

The music had stopped. The only sound was the drip of the spring and the rustle of leaves.

But I had no thought to spare for Pan and his music. Apollo himself was here. He was standing not ten feet from me as I came out of the tunnel. He was naked, and in his hand was a bow. He stood looking over my head as he had stood for two thousand years.

I heard Simon coming along the tunnel behind me. I moved aside. He came quickly out of the dark archway into the dappled light. He was saying: 'Camilla, I –' then he stopped as if he'd been struck in the throat. I heard him say: 'Oh, God,' under his breath. He stopped just behind me.

Some draught moved the curtain of leaves. Light flickered and burned from the gold of the bow, and shifted along the bronze of the throat and face. A broken arrow lay in the grass at the statue's feet.

After a lifetime or so I heard myself saying shakily: 'This . . . *this* is what Nigel found. He was here. Look.'

I stooped and picked up the little water-pot from where it lay in the damp moss at my feet.

Chapter 16

Apollo shows himself not to everyone, but only to him who is good. He who sees him is great; he who sees him is not a small man. We will see thee, O far-striker, and we will never become small!

CALLIMACHUS: 2.9.

'YES.' SIMON TURNED the pot over in his hand. 'That's Nigel's. He may have heard the water when he was drawing the cyclamen outside, and that led him into the cave and then through here . . . to this.' His eyes, like mine, were fixed on the statue. The face was god-like; remote, wise, serene, but young, with a kind of eagerness behind the level brows.

I said breathlessly: 'It's the face in the drawing, isn't it?—the lovely drawing he tore up . . . I said it looked like a statue. D'you remember how he snatched it back from us?'

Simon said slowly: 'That was when Danielle was there. But before that—d'you remember my saying that he seemed to be on the verge of telling me something, and then when Danielle came in he stopped short and shut up?'

'Of course. Then she *can't* have recognised it, can she? He'd only found the cave that day, and it's obvious he wasn't going to tell her about it!'

'And by God he was right,' said Simon. 'Guns and gold is one thing; in a way that kind of treasure trove is legitimate prey for greasy thugs like Dimitrios, and if the boy thought he could get something out of a spot of gun-running, well, that's his affair. But *this* . . .' he went down on one knee in the grass. Very gently he lifted the golden arrow. Where it had lain the whitened grass-roots showed a clear print. He put it down again. 'As I thought. Nothing's been touched. You can't tell me friend Dimitrios could have kept his paws off a bit of loose gold.' He got to his feet with a breath of relief. 'No, the boy's kept his mouth shut, and there's quite enough in the outer cave to fix Dimitrios' interest there. Thank God for the artist's conscience. But I think the sooner I get hold of Nigel the better.'

'You—you don't think Dimitrios'll come exploring, like I did, and find it?'

He laughed under his breath. 'I'd bet on it that he won't. He's far too busy for one thing, and for another, now that I come to think of it, even if he was dying of thirst he'd never squeeze through the gap.'

'I suppose not. But how in the world did *he* get in here? And why?' I put a hand to my head. 'I—I can't seem to think straight about anything just at the moment. I feel knocked kind of sideways.'

'I'm not surprised. No wonder Nigel was "high" that night. He must have been half out of his mind with excitement. And no wonder Mick—well, never mind that now. I doubt if we'll ever know just how and why the Apollo got here, but we can make a pretty good guess, I think. You know that the sanctuary at Delphi, after it ceased to be able to protect itself and its vast wealth, was plundered again and again. We don't know where a fraction of the stolen statues went. It was the metal ones that were taken; gold went first, of course; and then bronze, to be melted down for weapons . . . From the look of this one, it would be one of the most precious, and certainly one of the most beautiful. Why shouldn't some priest, or some small band of devotees, have decided to save it; cart it out of Delphi and find sanctuary for it till the troubled times were over?'

'But—why here? And *how*?'

'There used to be a track this way—the natives refer to it as "the old track", and, in these parts, God knows how old it might be. We came along it part of the way. Even so, it must have been quite a trek. Myself, I'd have brought the thing up in a mule-litter. I suppose the plan was to retrieve the statue later when things were safe, or even, if this happened at a very desperate time, to set up a sort of small secret sanctuary high on the mountain. If they'd just wanted to hide the statue, after all, they could have buried it, but they've *placed* it, haven't they? And with the Greek instinct for drama, they've put it at the end of a dark tunnel, in the blazing light, and all its trappings round it . . . Did anything strike you about the cave, Camilla?'

'You mean it was a bit like a cathedral—or a temple?'

He nodded. 'It's a common enough quality in big vaulted places

with stalactites and so on, but none the less impressive. The priests
who were so fanatical to save this statue must have known of the
cave for long enough. Not only that . . . there was this inner shrine,
full of light, the perfect "bright citadel" for the god—so here he is.
Look at that vine, Camilla, and that tree.'

I looked at him stupidly. 'The vine? It's a wild vine, isn't it? And
the tree—is that a sort of laurel?'

'A bay. Apollo's laurel,' said Simon softly.

'But Simon, after two thousand years—'

'Trees live a long time, and when they die they leave seedlings.
And vines run wild. Those were planted, Camilla. You notice how
the Apollo is just under the lip of the overhang, and the vines and
that spindly tree make a screen? I don't know if you *can* get to the top
of this light-well and look down, but you'd see nothing . . . And
there is the spring. Yes, I think this was a sacred cave, with a sacred
spring, and what more natural than that the priest who was so eager
to save his god should house him here? And I'll bet that if we look
closely we'll find that the entrances to both inner and outer caves
were artificially blocked up—'

'They were. I noticed that. The slab that Dimitrios had moved
was the same as the one that was across this inner tunnel.'

'And then, after God knows how many years, the earthquakes
opened the doors again . . . for Angelos. And Michael.'

'*Michael!*' I looked at him almost guiltily. I had forgotten Michael.
'Of course. The letter. The bright citadel. Oh, Simon.'

He gave a little smile, and quoted it softly: ' *"Tell the Emperor that
the bright citadel is fallen to the ground. Apollo hath no longer any shelter, or
oracular laurel tree, or speaking fountain. Even the vocal stream has ceased
to flow."* Yes, Mick proved the Delphic Oracle wrong. That's what
the letter meant.'

I said: 'You know, I didn't say anything, but I thought your
brother wouldn't have written quite the way he did about a cache of
arms, or even gold. All he'd have had to do, surely, was to divert
them back to their proper uses?'

'I know. That's what got me, too. But I never thought of anything
like *this*.' His voice didn't change, but suddenly I got the sharp
impression of intense excitement. 'My God,' said Simon, 'who could
have imagined this?'

We stood side by side staring at the statue. I think it was the
loveliest thing I have ever seen. The shadows played over the
bloomed bronze of the body; the eyes dwelt on some remote distance

beyond and above our heads, as the eyes of lions do. They were curiously alive, carefully inlaid with enamel and some black stone, so that the dark pupils seemed to flicker and glow with the movement of light and shade. I only knew of one other statue that had eyes like that.

Simon echoed my thoughts, softly: 'The Charioteer.'

I said: 'You think so? You think he's by the same hand?'

'I don't know a darned thing about it, but that's what he makes me think of.'

'That's what he made Michael think of,' I said.

He nodded. 'And Nigel, too, if you remember . . . It was when we were talking about the Charioteer that Nigel seemed suddenly to make up his mind to tell me about this. It may only have been because we were talking in general about discovering statues, but I don't think so. I seem to recollect some tension when the Charioteer was mentioned.'

'It's not only the eyes,' I said, 'but the whole impression of strength going along with grace . . . a sort of liquid quality—no, that's the wrong word, it sounds too weak, whereas this is—well, terrific. Simon, why shouldn't he be not only by the same hand, but part of the same group? It's only so much guesswork, isn't it, that the Charioteer was part of a victory statue for some potentate or other? Heavens above, if there were six thousand statues there, you'd think there might have been a chariot-statue of Apollo somewhere in Apollo's own sanctuary? And why shouldn't the Charioteer be the driver, and this—the god himself—the Lord of the Car?'

'Why not indeed?' said Simon.

'What are you smiling at? I can't help getting excited, can I? And why shouldn't I have a theory? It seems to me—'

'No reason at all. And it seems to *me* that one theory's as good as another. Yours at any rate is the most exciting one that comes to hand . . . No, I was smiling at something quite different. Dimitrios.'

'Oh!' It was like being jerked out of the sunlight into cold water. 'I—I'd forgotten all about him.'

'I should like to . . . now,' said Simon. He had never taken his eyes off the statue. 'But I'm afraid we must deal with that little matter before we come back to this.'

'What do we do about it?' I asked, rather blankly.

He gave it one long look before he turned away. 'We leave it here

in its bright citadel, and we get back to the land of shadows, my
dear. We know now what Michael found, and we also know what
Michael was murdered for. That chapter's closed, I think, with the
death of Angelos. But the one that's still open is what we've got to
deal with now. Nigel found the bright citadel, too, and I admit to
feeling rather strongly that Dimitrios and Danielle shouldn't really
be let in on . . . this.'

I said almost violently: 'They'll not touch it if I can stop them.'

'Then we'd better get back into the cave and play watch-dog.
Camilla . . .'

'Yes?'

He stood for a moment looking down at me. The guarded look
was there again, with some expression behind the cool eyes that
made me wonder what was coming. But he only said, rather lamely:
'I shouldn't have let you come.'

I didn't answer.

He said: 'You're frightened, aren't you?'

Still I said nothing. I wasn't looking at him. I wondered fleetingly
why I didn't mind his knowing. All at once he was very close to me,
and his hand came under my chin, gently lifting my face to meet his
gaze. 'You know why I brought you, don't you?'

'Yes.'

'And I was right.'

'Yes. I know.'

'You underrate yourself so shockingly, Camilla. You're not to
play second fiddle any more. Understand?'

'Yes.'

He hesitated, and then said, rather abruptly: 'You made a
discovery yesterday; remember? "*No man is an island.*" It's true in
more ways than one. Don't go on hating yourself because there are
some things you can't do and can't face on you own. None of us can.
You seem to think you ought to be able to deal with anything that
comes along, much as I might, or someone like me. That's absurd;
and it's time you stopped despising yourself for not being something
you were never meant to be. You'll do as you are, Camilla; believe
me, you will.'

I didn't quite trust myself to answer. After a second or so I said
lightly: 'All I ask the gods is that one day I'll see you, too, shaken
right out of that—that more-than-sufficient calmness of yours, on to
the plane of mortals like me! The day that happens, I'll sacrifice to
Apollo myself!'

He grinned. 'I might have to hold you to that. But meanwhile you can be sure that it won't be friend Dimitrios that'll do it. I'm going back now to see if he's around – or Nigel. Would you rather stay through here?'

'No. I'll come with you. I – I'd like to know what's going on.'

His hand touched my cheek as it had once before, a moth's touch. 'Then don't be scared, please. I'll not let Dimitrios get near you.'

'All right. What do I do?'

'Nothing yet. Just keep out of sight, and do as you're told before you're told to do it.'

'What could be simpler? Very well.'

'And now we'll go back.'

The Apollo looked serenely over our heads as we turned and left the sunlight.

*   *   *

The cave was still empty. We waited in the shelter of the cleft, listening, and then Simon squeezed his way through without using the torch. After a minute or two I heard his voice softly in the dark. 'It's all right. You can come through.'

I slid through the narrow opening. The beam of Simon's torch lit the way for me, and then played over the tilted slab. 'See? Those are chisel-marks. You were right. The slab was hacked to fit across the opening. And that crack above . . . that'll be where the rock shifted in the tremor that opened up the cave again for you and me . . . and Michael.'

I ran a slightly unsteady finger along one of the marks. 'Two thousand years . . . Oh Simon, I wish we could know –' I stopped abruptly.

'Mmm?' The torch was still moving over the old tool-marks. He seemed absorbed.

I managed to whisper calmly enough: 'He's coming back. I can hear him.'

The torch snapped out. A moment's unbreathing silence. 'Yes. You get back through the cleft and wait till we see what he's up to. I hope to God it's Nigel.'

As the breathed sentence ended I felt his hand on my arm. I obeyed him, slipping back through the narrow opening to wait, heart beating jerkily again, against the rock on the other side of the slab. I felt him beside me, pressed close to the edge of the cleft.

The steps came closer, hesitated at the door of the cave, and then came in. The sounds were at once dulled by the dust and made hollower by the cave's echoes. They were succeeded by other sounds: the dull thud of a spade hacking at the pile of rubble; the chink as it struck stone, and then metal; the sounds of breathing and effort; a soft expletive in Greek and then the splintering of wood and a thud; a dragging sound . . . He had uncovered a box and was dragging it nearer the mouth of the cave in readiness for transportation.

I felt Simon's body, close to mine, tense like a runner's at the starting-tape. His arm was across me, holding me still against him. It was like a steel bar. I wondered if he would attack Dimitrios now, out of the dark . . .

But he didn't move, except to shift his shoulders and head slightly so that I thought he could see round the edge of the slab. He stayed like that for what seemed an age, rock-still. I could feel the pulse beating in the hollow of his elbow; it was unhurried. Mine, under it, was tumbling along anyhow like a faulty engine.

The arm relaxed. I felt him turn his head, and his breath was on my temple. I heard the barest thread of a whisper: 'He's gone out again. Did you hear a mule?'

'I don't think so.'

'Stay here. I'll come back.'

A swift, compelling pressure of the arm round me, then it lifted. A movement beside me, the scrape of cloth on stone, and he was gone. The cleft felt cold and damp. I shifted my shoulders with the sudden chill and hunched my arms close to my sides and waited, listening. The echo of my coward pulses seemed to fill the cave . . .

I heard his steps in the dust just before he reached the cleft again and slid through. It was warmer with him there. He bent his head and said softly: 'He's left the box just inside the entrance and gone out again. He seems uneasy; I think he's wondering if anything's happened to whoever's coming with the mule. I think I'd better go after him.'

He wasn't touching me, so he didn't feel the jerk of my heart. He just heard me say: 'Yes?' quite calmly.

'It's just on the cards something has happened to delay Nigel, and I'd like to know what. And I want to know the way they're taking. That track peters out very soon. I'll follow Dimitrios down till I see where he's bound, and then if a chance occurs I'll . . . well, deal with him.'

'You mean you'll *kill* him?'

'Good God, no. But I'd like him put safely out of action while we get time to work this thing out our own way . . . And now I must go, or I'll lose the blighter.'

I hadn't realised that my hand had gone up to the breast of his shirt. His came up to cover it, warm and steadying. I said, and I couldn't quite keep the shake out of my voice: 'Simon, take care.'

'Be sure of that. Now, don't worry, my–don't worry. I'll be all right, and so will you. Stay here, under cover. You'll be as safe as a house in this part of the cave, and anyway I promise you I won't let Dimitrios out of my sight. Right?'

'R-right.'

His other arm came round my shoulders, and momentarily he pulled me against him. It was a gesture of comfort and reassurance, no more . . . But I thought his lips brushed my hair.

For the second time the arm dropped from my shoulders and he turned away as swiftly and lightly as a ghost. This time he switched on his torch, and I saw his shadow leap back, gigantic, along the wall of the cleft as he slipped through. I pressed forward till I could see into the cave. The little circle of light danced away through the faintly echoing spaces of darkness; the pillars and buttresses and masses of rock sent towering shadows reeling up the walls to stretch and lose themselves into the blackness of the vaulted roof. Simon, moving swiftly, himself like a shadow, dwindled across the empty darkness and was gone like a wraith into the outer tunnel. A shadow flickered back momentarily over the rock, then darkness swallowed it.

My hands were spread flat against the inner side of the slab. My eyes ached with the darkness. It was cold again. I had to exert all my self-control to stop myself running out and across the cave after him into the blessed sunlight.

At length I turned and made my way rather drearily back to the bright solitude of Apollo's sanctuary.

*   *   *

How long I waited there I don't know. At first I sat quietly enough in a corner where the sun fell unmasked by leaves, gazing at the statue of the god and trying to empty my mind of all worry about what was going on outside.

But after a while the very beauty and stillness of the place began to oppress me. I found I could sit still no longer, and, getting to my feet, I picked up Nigel's water-pot and carried it over to the spring. Under the thin trickle I rinsed it carefully, and drank. I rummaged in Simon's haversack and found what remained of our food, half of which I ate. After that I got myself another drink. Then I fidgeted about the little glade, examining the statue more closely, look-ing – but without touching them – at the broken pieces of gold in the grass, fingering the leaves and ferns . . .

When I found myself stooping for a third time to drink at the spring, I realised that fear had given place to a sort of impatient irritation. Sunlight and peace had done their work too well; I was now thoroughly on the fidget. I found myself glancing almost second by second at the watch on my wrist – an automatic act which irritated my nerves still further, as I hadn't the remotest idea what time it had been when Simon left me. I hovered near the mouth of the tunnel, fingering my torch . . .

After all, I told myself, I was perfectly safe. Simon was with Dimitrios, and I wasn't in the least afraid of Nigel. I wanted something to do; I wanted to know what was going on; I wanted Simon's presence . . .

I went cautiously along the tunnel, back into darkness, hesitated in the shelter of the slab, then let myself through into the main cave.

I, too, used my torch this time. A last absurd jump of the nerves made me send the light skating once round the vaulted darkness, almost as if I expected to find that, after all, Dimitrios had not gone. But the place was empty. There really was nothing to be afraid of; if he came back I would hear him, and would have ample time to take sanctuary again. Moreover, Simon was on his tail, and if Dimitrios returned I could depend on Simon to come with him.

The torch-beam was steady now. I went softly across to the arch of the other tunnel, and then turned off the light. I felt my way carefully along the wall of the curving passage, until, as I rounded the first bend, the darkness slackened, and I could see my way.

There was no box standing beside the entrance. Dimitrios must have set off carrying it. So much the better, I thought vaguely. It meant he did intend to go right down to the jeep; and it would slow him down and make it easier for Simon to follow him.

I edged forward until I could see out into the corrie.

Here, too, that faint sense of surprise assailed me to see it unchanged; dazzlingly-hot, still, deserted . . .

The glare hit at the eyes. I could smell the dust and the

mule-dung, and some dried aromatic plant that crumbled to powder under the hand I put up to the rock beside me. There was no sound at all. Nothing moved; even the hot air hung still.

I hesitated. The temptation to get out of the cave was strong, to climb the cliff-path above me, and take refuge somewhere higher up the mountain where I could at once be free and yet hidden, and, more important, see any movement that there might chance to be near the corrie. But Simon must know where to find me, and he had told me to stay here. I must stay.

I went back into the cave.

I remember that I stood there for some minutes, looking round me almost idly. I was trying to picture the place before the earthquake that had first shaken down some of the stuff that blocked the aisles and recesses between the pillars. It was very possible that this had been a sacred cave. Here the Apollo had been carried by hasty, reverent hands; here, perhaps, sacrifices and other acts of worship had been made before the holy place had been finally sealed and hidden and left to its two thousand years of silence.

The beam of my torch suddenly dimmed, then brightened again. But the warning spurred me into movement. With only one brief glance back at the entrance, and a couple of seconds' pause to listen for sounds of Dimitrios' approach, I set myself to a careful exploration of the cave.

I don't quite know what I was looking for. I certainly wasn't consciously hoping to find further 'treasure'–either of the kind in Angelos' hoard, or relics of Apollo's worship. But it wasn't very long before I did in fact come on evidence of another cache. In a deep bay between two pillars, at the edge of the cave not far from the stack of boxes, a pile of rubble–a shallow barrow of the stuff heaped away in a bay of rock–looked as if it had been recently disturbed.

I approached it and bent over, sending the now perceptibly dimming beam probing among the broken fragments.

I could see nothing that suggested boxes or articles concealed there, but, quite clear in the dust at my feet, there was the print of a rope-soled shoe, and the marks beside it as of something being dragged.

I went closer and stooped to peer. The beam slid over the pile, caught on something, and halted. It jerked in my hand once, then fixed, still, and far too bright now, on what lay behind the pile of rock and dirt.

The murderer hadn't bothered to bury Nigel. His body had been dragged and then flung into this meagre hiding, and now lay, stiff and horrible and indescribably grotesque, between the heaped rubble and the wall of the cave.

In the paralysed moment before I dropped the torch from a numbed hand, and let the merciful darkness loose again, I saw what had happened to Nigel. You can see an awful lot in a split second's acute terror and shock: the picture your brain registers then is complete, the stuff of a million lingering nightmares still to come. Nothing is missed: every bestial detail is there for the mind to come back to, turn over, re-picture without ceasing.

He had been tied. The rope had gone now – no doubt the murderer had need of it – but the boy's wrists were scored raw where he had struggled. He had been tied, and tortured. In that one glance I had seen the shabby green shirt ripped down off one thin shoulder, and, on the upper arm, shocking against the peeling skin, a series of marks whose sickening regularity could mean only one thing. He had been burned four or five times, deliberately. Other things I saw that, at the time, meant nothing, but which, in nightmare recap-itulations of that second's horror, I have since seen and recognised a score of times. I don't intend to describe them. Let it remain that Nigel had died, in pain. His eyes were open. I remember how they gleamed in the light of the torch. And his teeth clenched, grinning, on some fragment that might have been skin . . . Dimitrios' bitten thumb . . . the filthy murderous hand that had slid down my arm yesterday at the Roseate cliff.

It was on that flash of realisation that the torch dropped and the dark stamped down. I don't know what happened then. I remember, one moment, the picture in the torchlight, vivid, terrible, complete, then the next moment it was dark, and the rock was cold; it was crushing me, tearing my clothes, tripping my running footsteps; it was soft to my falling, whimpering body . . .

I was lying at Apollo's feet on the damp moss. My hair was wet, and my hands, and the breast of my frock. Something was hurting my right hand where it pressed deeply into the grass. It was the broken end of the gold arrow. I sat looking at it for a very long time before I even saw it.

Dimitrios, I was thinking stupidly, confusedly; Dimitrios . . . He had murdered Nigel yesterday. While we had been here in the corrie, in the bright sunlight, Nigel had been in the cave with his murderer, tied and hurt and – no, that wouldn't do; he hadn't been gagged, and we'd have heard him. He was dead before we got up here, and then Dimitrios had come down to Delphi to search his room . . .

I stared down at the beautifully-worked fragment of gold in my hand, and tried to think . . . But all that would come to me was that Nigel, poor muddled, eager young Nigel, who was a good artist, had been murdered by Dimitrios . . .

Dimitrios! This time the thought came anything but confusedly: it whipped into my brain with a point as sharp as the one that pricked my palm. I was on my feet, and the gold arrow spun, glittering, forgotten, to the grass. Dimitrios, whom Simon and I had casually dismissed as someone who could easily be 'dealt with'–Dimitrios was out there on the hillside, and Simon was tailing him, waiting for a chance to attack him, unconscious of the fact that the Greek was a murderer as vile and ruthless as ever his cousin Angelos had been . . .

Momentarily I had forgotten poor Nigel. I ran back into the tunnel with never a thought of what lay there in the cave.

The darkness came up against me like a tangling net. As I rounded the first bend in the tunnel I had to stop short, then feel my way forward slowly, my hands shaking and slipping on the cool rock.

I reached the slab. I pressed my body into the narrow cleft, craning to peer forward into the cave. But I couldn't see at all; the darkness boiled still against my wide-open eyes with shapes and spangles of a million fizzing colours. Without my torch, and blinded like this with my swift dive back out of the light. I would be helpless to cross the cave. I shut my eyes and waited there for the swarming dark to clear. The slab felt cold and damp under my flat-spread hands.

Then I heard him.

I thought at first it was the surge of the knocking pulses that nailed me to the rock, but then I knew it was the soft tread of rope-soled shoes in the dust.

I stayed where I was, frozen to the rock, and opened my eyes.

I could see now. Light was moving in the cave, a powerful light. Not Simon–Simon's torch, like mine, had begun to fail . . . and, in any case, the steps had not been Simon's. But at least where Dimitrios was, Simon would be. And from the way the Greek came forward into the cave with unhurried confidence, he still didn't know of Simon's presence.

Even as the thought came, I heard a tiny sound outside the cave. My eyes flew in apprehension to the Greek. He was behind the light

and I couldn't see him, but the moving beam never faltered. He
hadn't heard. The sound came again, and now I knew it for what it
was; the chink of metal as a bit jangled. Dimitrios had brought the
mule.

The Greek passed out of my small range of vision. I waited till I
heard the familiar scrape and shift of a box and the clatter of settling
stones, and the grunts and short breathing of effort. Then I inched
my way nearer the edge of the slab and peered round it, a centimetre
at a time.

He had put the torch down in a little niche above him, so that the
beam was directed on to the rock-pile. His thick powerful body was
stooping over this. His back was towards me; he had laid his jacket
down beside him, and under the blue shirt I could see the bulge and
play of his muscles as he heaved at one of the half-buried boxes.
Then he dragged it out into his arms, and straightened up holding it.
I hadn't realised before how immensely strong he must be. He
carried the box slowly over to the cave-mouth, and went out of sight
with it up into the tunnel. I heard him dump it there. I heard him
coming back. Still with that unhurried soft tread he came out of the
tunnel-mouth, into the steady beam that illuminated the cave.

For the second time in those few minutes, I felt the kick of shock
over the heart.

It wasn't Dimitrios. It wasn't anyone I had seen before.

But, hard on the moment of shock and confusion, I knew that I
was wrong. I had seen him before, and more than once. Now, faced
in the queerly-lit darkness with that heavy head, the thick dark curls
tight like a bull's and crisping down the swarthy cheekbones towards
the smiling thick-lipped mouth, I knew him. This was the Phormis
head of Nigel's drawing: this was the face like an archaic statue's,
with the wide fleshy cheekbones and the up-cornered, tight-lipped
smile. More–this was the face I had seen, unnoticing and unre-
membering, bending over the engine of the jeep outside Dimitrios'
cottage. And it must after all have been *this* face, not the Apollo
(which it was certain she had never seen), that Danielle had
recognised among Nigel's drawings . . .

But before I could follow this further, two other memories
flashed, sparks into the dry tinder of fear . . . Nigel saying to
Danielle: 'That's a chap I saw today on Parnassus . . .' and Simon's
voice in the dark, translating for me something Stephanos had told
him: 'He'd kill, and smile while he did it. Always that smile . . .'

Angelos. Angelos himself. And Dimitrios was God knew where. And Simon was with him.

Angelos turned back to the pile of rubble. The torchlight slid over the thick skin shiny with sweat. The smile never altered. No doubt he had smiled as he and Dimitrios killed Nigel between them. No doubt he would smile when Simon, having disposed of Dimitrios, came openly up to the cave to find me . . .

Angelos straightened his thick body and stood still, as if listening. He turned his head. There were sounds outside, not metal-shod this time, but the sounds of someone hurrying towards the cave.

I remember thinking, with a kind of numbed calmness, that if I screamed it would warn Simon – but it would warn Angelos, too. He was expecting Dimitrios, and he could have no idea that Simon and I were here. He had made no move to douse the torch. But, on the other hand, if Simon had dealt with Dimitrios, Simon, too, would be off his guard . . .

The steps came closer; were in the tunnel. Angelos' hand went to his pocket. I took in my breath.

With a stumbling rush and a flurry of breathing, Danielle hurried into the cave.

Chapter 17

As there is Justice in heaven,
And fire in the hand of God,
The reckoning must be made in the end.
SOPHOCLES: *Electra.*
(tr. E. F. Watling.)

THE MAN RELAXED, but his voice, pitched low, was angry. 'What the hell are you doing here?'

She had stopped at the edge of the torchlight. She looked at once younger and much prettier than I had seen her. She had on the turquoise blouse and scarlet cotton skirt, and her haste had flushed her face and hurried her breathing, making her seem more normal and less cynically in control of herself. She hadn't looked at Angelos. Her eyes were riveted on what remained of the cache of boxes.

'So that's it?' Like him, she spoke in French.

'That's it.' He regarded her sourly. 'I told you last night we'd located it, didn't I? So why the devil didn't you do as you were told and stay out of sight till I came for you?'

She walked forward slowly while he was speaking, her eyes still on the stuff at his feet. Now she looked up under her lashes with that provocative *gamine* grin. 'I wanted to see for myself what was going on. Don't be angry . . . nobody saw me come.'

'Did you see Dimitrios on your way up?'

She shook her head. She was stooping over the pile, prodding with a toe at the broken box that showed the gleam of gold. I saw her breast rise and fall quickly as if with excitement. He said sharply: 'No sign of him?'

'No.'

He swore and struck the spade almost savagely into the stones. 'Then where the hell is he? I came by the high way—it's shorter if you know your road . . . and if you didn't see him either—'

'I came by the high way, too.' Again that smiling look up through the lovely lashes. 'How did you think I found my way here? I waited where I thought you'd come, and then I followed you.'

He grunted. 'Clever, eh? Then that means he's gone down the other way to look for me. Blast the man; he's as jumpy as a bean on a griddle, and about as much use. And you—you should have stayed away till I came for you. I told you I didn't want you up here.'

She laughed. 'Maybe I didn't trust you, Angelos. Maybe you wouldn't have come for me.'

He gave a short laugh. 'Maybe.'

'Well, I wanted to see *this*,' she said, almost childishly, 'and besides, I didn't want to hang about down there all day. That damned jeep's dynamite anyway.'

'Why? The stuff's not in it.'

'No, but—'

'Did you park it where I told you?'

'Of course I did. Angelos, why d'you have to do this in daylight? You're crazy.'

'I know what I'm doing. There's next to no moon just now, and this country's murder with a mule on a black night, and I daren't use a light. There'll be nobody about between here and the place where I'm stacking the stuff, and we can ferry the whole lot from there to the jeep in a couple of hours after dusk.' He added, with a sort of heavy irony: 'Always providing, of course, that you do as you're told, and that my cool-headed cousin gets back in time to give me a bit of help with the hard work!'

She laughed. She had recovered her breath now, and with it her own particular brand of throaty charm. She straightened up and gave him one of her long-lidded glinting looks. 'Well, I can help instead, can't I? You won't send me back now? Don't you think, *Angelo mou*, that you might pretend to be a little bit pleased to see me?'

She moved up close to him as she spoke, and he pulled her to him and kissed her in a way that managed to be perfunctory and yet lustful. I saw her press her thin body against him, and her hands crept up to move among the thick curls on the back of his head.

I drew back a little in my crevice, shutting my eyes momentarily as if against this new discovery. *Angelos* her lover. *Angelos*. Through the whirl of fear and confusion the facts twisted and readjusted themselves into a different pattern.

It had been Angelos, not Dimitrios, who had scraped acquaintance with Danielle on those long afternoons at Itea; this deliberately, not only to while away the boredom of inaction, but because she had the use of the jeep, whereas to buy or hire other transport would involve inquiries later, and provoke the very gossip the cousins had to avoid.

And by the same token it had been Angelos, not Dimitrios, who had broken into the studio last night. I remembered now, quite clearly, that the hand which had reached back for the torch had not had a torn thumb. And I remembered Danielle's little smile when I had so swiftly identified her lover as Dimitrios . . .

Angelos pushed her away, not too gently. 'You know damned well you should have stayed away. There's no room in the games I play for anyone with baby-nerves.'

She was lighting a cigarette and said, almost snappishly: 'It wasn't nerves; it was curiosity, and I've a right to know what's going on. Baby-nerves, indeed, after what I've done for you! You'd never have got the jeep but for me, and I got you the tools and the mule on Monday night, didn't I? And I've played spy on the Englishman and that wretched girl he's taken in tow—and all you do is walk in last night out of the blue, stay with me half an hour, and tell me damn all except that today's the day, and I'm to get the jeep to the quarry, and you expect that to be that! You might have landed me in the hell of a jam last night, but you never said a word to me!'

'What d'you mean?' He was working again, levering at a solid lump of rock that was wedging down a couple of boxes. The dislodged dirt and small stones hissed down to the floor. He seemed hardly to be listening to her.

She said sharply: 'You know quite well what I mean. When you came to my room last night, you said you hadn't seen Nigel, and—'

'Nigel?'

'The English artist. I told you. He was throwing out hints on Monday night about getting rich and famous, and he was drunk. After the others had left I gave him another couple of ouzos and took him for a walk . . . Did I tell you that?' She was watching the man through the wisping smoke of her cigarette, and her tone was provocative. He neither looked up nor took the slightest notice.

She tapped ash off with a sharply pettish movement. 'Well? It was obvious he'd found something up here on the hill. You said you were going to wait for him yesterday and find out what it was, and where –'

'So what? We didn't need to, did we? Your English friends came and showed us the way.'

'They showed you the cave, too?'

He laughed shortly. 'Hardly. If they'd found the cave yesterday we'd not have been able to get near it now for troops three deep round the door!'

She moved impatiently. 'I didn't mean that way. Of course they didn't find it, or they wouldn't be trailing harmlessly off to Levadia today. But you *did* find it pretty quickly, didn't you? Dimitrios told me at the Shining Ones that you'd found the place, and that you were working on it then while he came down to do some final clearing-up.'

He had laid aside the crowbar, and was using the spade to shift some of the smaller debris. The thud of digging echoed dully. He didn't look up. He said: 'When Stephanos showed them the spot where I broke Michael's neck I knew where the cave lay. Everything was changed, but I knew the crack must open on the cave. I couldn't get through it the way it was, but after I'd sent Dimitrios down I got to work and opened it up.'

'I know. You told me this last night.' She wasn't, as usual, letting the cigarette hang from her lips as she talked. She was smoking in jerky movements that spoke of tightly-strung nerves. She said, making it sound like an accusation: *'But you never mentioned Nigel.'*

He straightened up from his work, eyeing her, his head thrust forward like a bull's, his look at once formidable and wary. The fixed half-moon smile on the thick mouth was in its own way terrifying. He said roughly: 'Come on. What is all this? Why the hell should I mention Nigel?'

She blew a long plume of smoke, then said flatly: 'When you left me last night you went to Nigel's room. Why?'

'That's simple enough, isn't it? You'd told me he'd done a drawing of me as like as a photograph. I wanted to destroy it.'

'But he'd cleared out – packed up and gone. You knew that. I'd told you that. I'd been in myself that evening to try and find the drawing, and all his stuff was gone. He'd taken it with him.'

'Oh no,' said Angelos, 'he hadn't.'

'What d'you mean? You never saw him. How d'you know what he had on him?'

She stopped. I saw her eyes widen as they met his look. Her lips parted so that the cigarette fell to the ground and lay there smouldering. She ignored it. She was staring at him. He was standing very still, leaning on the spade, watching her. I could see sweat on the heavy face and on his hairy forearms.

He said again, softly: 'Well?'

Her voice was shaken clear of any of its carefully affected overtones. It came clear and thin, like a little girl's. 'You did see him? Yesterday? He *did* tell you where the cave was?'

'Yes, we saw him. But he didn't tell us anything. I told you the truth about that.'

'Then—then—why did you lie about seeing him?'

The smile deepened as the thick lips parted. 'You know why. Don't you?'

There was a long pause. I saw the pink tongue come out to lick once, quick as a lizard's, across her rouged lips. 'You—killed him? Nigel?'

No reply. He didn't stir. I saw her throat muscles move as she swallowed. There was no horror or regret or fear in her face; it was blank of expression, with parted lips, and wide eyes fixed on the man. But her breathing hurried. 'I . . . see. You didn't tell me.'

His voice was soft, almost amused. 'No, I didn't tell you. I didn't want to scare you away.'

'But—I still don't understand. Didn't he know about the cave? Wasn't I right?'

'He knew; you can be sure of that. But he didn't tell us. We tried, but he wouldn't come through with anything that made sense.'

She swallowed again. She hadn't taken her eyes off him. She might have been a waxwork but for the eyes, and the convulsive muscles of the throat. 'Did you—have to kill him?'

He shrugged his heavy shoulders. 'We didn't, in a manner of speaking. The bloody little pansy died on us. A pity.' His head sank lower. The smile seemed to thicken. 'Well? Scared? Going to scream and run?'

She moved then. She came close to him again, and her hands came up to the breast of his shirt. 'Do I look as if I wanted to run, *Angelo mou*? Would I be the sort you'd want along with you if I was that kind of baby-nerve?' The hands slid up his shoulders and over them to the back of his neck. She pressed closer. 'I know all about you, Angelos Dragoumis . . . Don't think that I don't. They still tell quite a few stories about you, here in Delphi . . .'

A laugh shook him. 'You surprise me.'

She pulled his head down, and said, against his mouth: 'Do I? Does it surprise you to know that that's why I'm here? That that's why I like you?'

He kissed her, lingeringly this time, then thrust her away from him with his free hand. 'No. Why should it? I've met women like you before.' He still held the spade in his other hand, and now he turned back to his task. Danielle said, eyeing the broad back a little sulkily: 'Where is he?'

'Near enough.'

I saw her eyes show white for a moment as she gave a quick over-the-shoulder look into the shadowed corners. Then she shrugged and reached in her pocket for another cigarette. 'You may as well tell me what happened.'

'All right. Only stand back out of the way. That's better. Well . . . We waited beside the Delphi track for the boy, but he didn't come that way. He must have started early and gone some other way round, because the first we saw of him was when he was away beyond us and almost up to these cliffs. We got up as close as we could without his seeing us, but when we'd worked our way up that gully that lies east of here, he'd vanished. We got up above the line of cliff, and separated; then waited. After a bit we saw him, just appearing walking out of the corrie here, as cool as you please. So we came down the cliff and got hold of him.'

'Why did you have to do that? The English couple were coming. Once you saw the place where Michael died –'

'A bird in the hand,' said Angelos, and I saw the thick grin deepen again. 'For all I knew, Stephanos wouldn't remember the exact spot, and it was certain that your artist friend had just come out of some hiding-place. Besides, he'd done that drawing of me. He'd seen me.'

She was lighting another cigarette. The flame of the match wasn't quite steady. Her eyes looked wide and brilliant above it. 'What did you do?'

He sounded indifferent. 'We tried to scare him into talking at first, but he wouldn't come through. To tell you the truth I began to think you were wrong and he hadn't found a thing, only then he began to babble something about a cave and "something beyond price" and he was damned if he'd let us touch it. Then we really got going . . .' He straightened up and got out a cigarette. He thrust it between his lips, and leaned forward to get a light from hers.

I thought, I shall see that smile in my dreams . . .

'But he still wouldn't say anything that made sense,' said Angelos.

'Babbled about water, and some flowers . . .' The contempt in the thick French made the words sound obscene. 'My English is fair enough, but I couldn't get all the words. In the end there was something about gold, I'm pretty sure, but just as we were getting to that he died on us. God knows we'd hardly started. It looked to me as if he had a groggy heart.'

'What happened then?'

'We'd hardly finished with him when we saw Stephanos and the boy from Arachova bringing the English couple along. We threw the body behind some rocks and waited and watched till the old man took them to the corrie and showed them the place. It's altered completely; I might have looked for a thousand years, let alone the last two. As soon as they'd gone, I got down into the corrie and started looking around. It was dead easy. Your Nigel helped us after all with his crazy blathering; there was only one place where grass grew, and flowers, and it was much where I expected the cave to lie, if Stephanos had been accurate. We soon saw where the entrance was. Getting into it was another matter, but, of course, with the boy dead on our hands we had to be sure there'd by no inquiries until we'd got clear off and no traces left. So I got on with the job alone while I sent Dimitrios down to see you as arranged. I told him not to tell you about Nigel, but to get quietly into the studio and clear the stuff out of his room as if he'd packed up and gone. He did that. You'll find all the boy's stuff in the back of the jeep under the sacking. Dimitrios brought a big folder of drawings, but like a fool he was in too much of a hurry to check them, and he never saw that the picture of me wasn't there . . . It mightn't have mattered, but that's the sort of detail that can sometimes matter the hell of a lot. I thought it worth attending to, anyway. I'm officially dead, and by God I'm staying that way, and no rumours!'

'Did you find it?'

'No. I didn't have time. There was a lot of paper with the rubbish in a tin on the floor in his room. That fool Dimitrios hadn't thought it worth bothering about. But in fact if that's where the drawings are, nobody's going to take any notice of them. They'll just think he's tidied up and left.'

'They do. The English couple think he's gone on a trek over the hills—with the mule.'

'Do they?' He sounded amused. 'Then that's that, isn't it?'

He had cleared the boxes now of their covering of stones. He stooped to work one of them clear of the pile. She watched the play

of the great muscles for a few moments in silence. Then she said
again: 'Where is he?'

'Who?'

'My God, Nigel, of course! Did you just leave him out there for
the vultures?'

'Not likely. They'd have given us away more quickly than
anything else. He's here.'

For the first time I saw some strong feeling move her. It was like a
spring tensing. *'Here?'*

He jerked his head sideways. 'Over there.' He wrenched the box
free at last, straightened up, and carried it out of the cave. The torch
still shone strongly enough from its niche on the pillar. Danielle
stood still for a moment, staring towards the dark corner where
Nigel's body lay, then, as if with an effort, she walked forward, took
the torch down from its niche, and went over to the pile of rubble
that hid the pathetic body. The light shone down on what lay,
mercifully, beyond my range of vision.

It was at that moment that I remembered my own torch, dropped
near Nigel's body. If she saw it . . . if the light from her torch picked
up its glint in the dust . . .

Angelos was coming back. He said irritably: 'Still no sign. He
seems to have taken one of the small boxes down himself by the
lower track. We'd have seen him else.' Then he looked across and
saw where she was. She still had her back to him. The heavy face
watching her didn't change its expression, but something in the look
of the eyes made my blood thicken. 'Well?'

She turned abruptly: 'Are you going to leave him here?'

'Where else? Take him in the jeep to the bay at Galaxidion?'

She ignored the irony. 'Aren't you going to bury him?'

'My God, girl, there's no time. I've got enough to do shovelling
half Parnassus off this stuff. You can throw some dirt down over
him if you like, but it hardly matters. Something for you to do while
I load up.'

She came quickly back into the middle of the cave. 'I'm not
staying here.'

He laughed. 'As you wish. I thought you weren't squeamish, *ma
poule?'*

'I'm not,' she said pettishly, 'but can't you see it won't do to leave
him here, even if we do cover him? It's obvious already there's been
someone at work here, and if anyone does come up they're bound to
see –'

'Why should anyone come?'

She hesitated, eyeing him. 'The Englishman, Simon—'

'What of him? You told me yourself he'd gone off to Levadia.'

'I know, but—well, I was still thinking about what happened in the theatre, on Monday night.'

In the theatre, on Monday night . . . I leaned back against the rock, trying, through the mists of tension and fear, to remember . . . The sounds I had heard as I sat there: the tiny jingling . . . it had after all been Danielle, taking the stolen mule off to meet the men. And Simon and I had talked, down there in the theatre . . . It wasn't only the speech from the *Electra* that those wonderful acoustics would have sent up to Danielle, above us in the dark. And Danielle understood English . . . What had we said? *What, in heaven's name, had we said?*

It appeared that, whatever it was, she had reported it to him before. He laughed. 'Oh, that. It's no news. Of course he knows Michael was murdered. D'you think Stephanos wouldn't tell him that? What difference does it make? Nobody knows *why*.'

'But if he suspected you were still alive—'

'Him?' The thick voice held nothing but amused contempt. 'In any case, how should he? Nigel's dead, and no one's going to recognise that picture now.'

'There was the gold,' said Danielle.

The dark was boiling round me. As clearly as if he were just beside me, I heard Simon's voice again: *'It's not over* . . . *till I find what Michael found* . . . *the gold.'*

'Gold, gold, gold—you see it everywhere, don't you, *ma poule?*' He laughed again. For some reason his spirits seemed to be rising. 'You didn't *see* it was gold, now, did you? She picked something up and you saw it glitter, and your imagination did the rest.'

'I tell you it was gold. I saw her staring at it.'

The dark slowly cleared. Against it I saw a picture—not the one they were speaking of, but later; Simon, coming away from the centre mark just before he spoke . . . She hadn't heard. By the mercy of the gods of the place, she hadn't heard.

Angelos had turned away and was lugging another box clear of the pile. 'There. That's as much as the poor bloody mule can take on one trip . . . Now, forget that nonsense for five minutes, and you can give me a hand loading up. He found no gold yesterday, and that's a fact. He's got no reason to come back here. He's been, and seen all he can. Why should he come again? To bring a posy for Michael?'

He laughed again, unpleasantly. 'By God, I almost wish he would! . . . I owe him something, after all.'

She said, with a sort of spite: 'And her. She hit you.'

'She did, didn't she?' he said cheerfully. 'I think we'll wait till Dimitrios comes. He can't be much longer.' He paused, looking round the cave. 'It's queer to be back . . . and it looks just the same. Just the same. These pillars, and that bit of rock like a lion's head, and the drip of water somewhere. I never found the spring . . . Can you hear it?'

She said impatiently: 'But Nigel. You must do something about the body. Can't you see–?'

'You may be right.' His voice was almost absent. It was clear that Nigel had long since ceased to matter at all. 'In fact he may do us a better turn dead than he did alive . . . *He* can go over the cliff with the jeep. Yes, there's the water. I thought so. It's over here somewhere . . .'

Danielle's voice stopped him as he moved. There was a note in it that I hadn't heard before. 'The jeep? Over the cliff? I didn't know you planned to do that.'

'You don't know all I plan to do, my fair lady,' he said. He turned back to her as he spoke, and I couldn't see his face. I saw hers. It looked suddenly thinner, and sharp, like a frightened urchin's. He said: 'What is it now? We've got to get rid of the jeep somehow, haven't we? If the boy's found in the sea with it that accounts for him as well.'

She said, almost in a whisper: 'It's mine. Everybody knows I brought it up from Athens.'

'So what? Everybody'll assume you were in it, too, and that will be that.'

Still she didn't move, but stared up at him. She looked very childish in the turquoise top, and scarlet bell of skirt. He went towards her till she had to tilt back her head to look him in the eyes. He said on a note of impatience, and something else: 'What is it now? Scared?'

'No. No. But I was wondering–'

'What?'

She spoke still in that hurried whisper. 'What you were going to do with the jeep if you . . . if you hadn't had Nigel's body to send over the cliffs with it?'

He said slowly: 'The same, of course. They'd have thought you were in it and had been–'

He stopped abruptly. Then I heard him laugh. His big hand went slowly out and ran down her bare arm. It looked very dark against her pale olive flesh. There were black hairs on the back of it. 'Well, well, well . . . My poor little pretty, did you really think I'd do a thing like that to you?'

She didn't move. The thin arm hung slack by her side. Her head was tilted back, the big eyes searching his face. She said in that flat little voice: 'You said "*He* can go over the cliff in the jeep . . ." as if you'd planned it for someone else. As if –'

He had an arm round her now, and had pulled her close to him. She went to him unresisting. His voice thickened. 'And you thought I meant you? *You?* My little Danielle . . .'

'Then who?'

He didn't answer, but I saw her eyes narrow and then flare wide again. She whispered: '*Dimitrios?*'

His hand came quickly over her mouth and his body shook as if with a laugh. 'Quietly, little fool, quietly! In Greece, the mountains have ears.'

'But, *Angelo mou –*'

'Well? I thought you said you knew me, my girl? Don't you see? I had to have his help, and his boat, but when did *he* earn the half share of a fortune? The stuff's mine, and I've waited fourteen years for it, and now I've got it. D'you think I'm going to share it – with anyone?'

'And – what about me?'

He pulled her unresisting body closer to him. He laughed again, deep in his throat. 'That's not sharing. You and I, *ma poule*, we count as one . . .' His free hand slid up her throat, under her chin, and then forced her head up so that her mouth met his. 'And I still need *you*. Do I still have to convince you of that?' His mouth closed on hers then, avidly, and I saw her stiffen for just a moment as if she was going to resist, then she relaxed against him and her arms went up to his neck. I heard him laugh against her lips, and then he said hoarsely: 'Over there. Hurry.'

I shut my eyes. I turned my head away so that my cheek, like my hands, pressed against the cool rock. It smelt fresh, like rain. I remember that under my left hand there was a little knob of stone the shape of a limpet shell . . .

I don't want to write about what happened next, but in justice to myself I think I must. As I shut my eyes the man was kissing her, and I saw his hand beginning to fumble with her clothes. She was clinging to him, her body melting towards his, her hands pulling his head down fiercely to meet her kisses. Then when I couldn't see any more I heard him talking, little breathless sentences I couldn't catch—didn't try to catch—in a mixture of Greek and his thick fluent French. I heard him kick a stone out of the way as he pulled her down on to the dusty floor of the cave near the rubble-pile . . . near Nigel's body . . .

I only heard one sound from her, and it was a little half-sigh, half-whimper of pleasure. I'll swear it was of pleasure.

I was shaking, and covered with sweat, and hot as though the chilly cleft were an oven. Under the fingers of my left hand the stone limpet had broken away. I was holding a fragment of it in my curled fingers, and it was embedded in the flesh, hurting me.

I don't know how long it was before I realised that the cave was quiet, except for the heavy breathing.

Then I heard him getting to his feet. His breathing was heavy and even. He didn't say anything, and I didn't hear him move away. There was no sound from Danielle.

I opened my eyes again, and the dimming torchlight met them. He was standing beside the pile of rubble, smiling down at Danielle. She lay there, still, looking up at him. I could see the glint of her eyes. The sweat on his face made the wide fleshy cheeks gleam like soapstone. He stood quite still, smiling down at the girl who lay at his feet staring back at him, her bright skirt all tossed-looking in the dust.

I thought, with crazy inconsequence: how uncomfortable she looks. Then, suddenly: she looks dead.

Presently Angelos stooped, took her body by the shoulders, and dragged it across the cave to pitch it down in the rubble beside Nigel.

And that is how Danielle Lascaux was murdered within twenty yards of me, and I never lifted a finger to help her.

Chapter 18

—*Go while the going's good,*
Is my advice . . .
SOPHOCLES: *Philoctetes.*
(tr. E. F. Watling.)

BY THE MERCY of providence I didn't faint, or I'd have pitched straight out into the torchlight. But the narrow cleft held my body up, and my mind (numbed, I suppose, by the repetition of shock) seemed only very slowly to take in what had happened.

It was as if some sort of mental censor had dropped a curtain gauze between me and the scene in the cave, so that it took on a kind of long-distance quality, the murderer moving about his dreadful business at a far remove from me, as a creature of fiction moves on a lighted stage. I was invisible, inaudible, powerless, the dreamer of the dream. With light would come sanity, and the nightmare vanish.

I watched him, still in that queer dead trance of calm. I think if he had turned in my direction I would hardly have had the wit to draw back, but he didn't. He dropped Danielle's body down in the dust beside Nigel's, and stood for a moment looking down at them, lightly dusting his hands together. I wondered for a moment if he was after all going to shovel the dirt over the bodies, then it occurred to me that Danielle's useless spark of instinct had been right; his plan for disposing of Nigel in the jeep had come a little too pat. It was Danielle who had brought the jeep; it was Danielle who was to be found with the wreck of it . . . That had been his plan all along. I saw it now clearly. I didn't believe for a moment that he intended to kill his cousin Dimitrios—but, even if that were true, he had certainly never intended to share anything with Danielle. What she had to offer was only too easily found elsewhere. What was equally certain was that he hadn't wanted to kill her here. He must have intended to save himself the transport of her body by killing her when the job was over, but her half-frightened queries had aimed just a little too near the mark for comfort. Better kill her now, and risk the extra load to be ferried down after dusk.

He had turned back now to the pillar where the torch was lodged. I watched him, still as if he were an actor in a play—a bad actor; there was no expression on his face, no horror, or anxiety, or even interest. He reached up a hand, picked up the torch, and switched it off. The darkness came down like a lid on a stifling box. He seemed to be listening. I could hear his untroubled breathing, and the tiny rustle of settling dust under the girl's body. There was no sound from outside.

He switched on the light again and went out of the cave. A bridle jingled as the mule moved, but it appeared that he hadn't untied it. I heard him move off, his soft footsteps unaccompanied by the sharper ones of the beast. He must have decided to reconnoitre the corrie before daring to lead out the mule . . .

The footsteps dwindled steadily. I couldn't hear them any more. I waited, straining my ears. Nothing but the soft movement of dust in the cave, and the restless shifting of the mule's hoofs in its corner. He must have left the corrie—perhaps to look for Dimitrios' approach.

One thing was certain: Angelos had no idea that Simon had any reason for further curiosity about the corrie. He felt as safe from discovery in this remote stretch of Parnassus as he would on the mountains of the moon.

And Simon? Simon, too . . .

I was out of the cleft and flying across the dark cave. There was no light, but I don't remember that I needed it. My body was acting of itself, like a sleepwalker's, and like a sleepwalker's it must have dodged every obstacle by instinct. My brain, too . . . I had no conscious plan, not even any coherent thought, but at some queer submerged level I knew I had to get out of that cave, to Simon . . . There was something about Dimitrios coming back, and Simon . . . something about warning Simon that here was not one shifty little crook to deal with, but two men who were murderers . . . something important to tell Simon . . . And more important than anything, I had to get out of the darkness, out of that stifling cage of rock, into the blessed light . . .

The sun struck down at me like a bright axe. I put a hand to my eyes, flinching as if at an actual blow. I was blinded, swimming in a sea of light. My other hand, groping out before me, touched something warm and soft, that moved. I jerked away with a little gasp of terror, and in the same moment realised that it was the mule, tethered in the narrow corner outside the cave. Its muzzle was deep in the grass, and it hardly paused to roll a white eye back at me before it resumed its eager cropping. The warm ammoniac smell of its coat brought a momentary, comfortless memory of Niko. I thrust past it, ducked heedlessly under the buttress, and ran out into the corrie.

There was no sign of Angelos. I turned and ran for the foot of the cliff-path.

The heat in the bottom of the corrie was palpable. I felt the sweat start out on my body as soon a I left the shade. The air weighed on me as I ran. My lungs laboured to drag it in, and dust was burning and rough in my throat. The corrie was a well of heat in which nothing moved except me, and I thrust through it blindly, with the whip of panic on me . . .

I reached the foot of the cliff. I believe I realised that if Angelos had gone to meet his cousin, he would have gone by the gateway, and not up the cliff. But this again was not a conscious thought. I only knew that I had to get up, out of the hot enclosing walls of rock, out on the high open stretches above the cliff.

The afternoon sun shone full on the cliff where the path lay. The brightness of the white limestone splintered against the eyes. As I plunged up the steep, twisting little goat-track I felt the rock burn the soles of my shoes like hot metal. When I put a hand to the face of the cliff it seemed to scorch the flesh.

I climbed as fast as I dared, trying to make no sound. The dust hissed like sand under my feet. A pebble rolled and fell to the foot of the cliff with a crack like a pistol-shot. My breathing was as loud in the still air as sobbing.

I was a little less than halfway up when I heard him coming back.

I stopped dead, pilloried against the naked rock, clamped to it, like a lizard on the bare stone. The rock burned through my thin dress. As soon as he got to the gateway he would see me. I couldn't possibly get to the top in time. If there were somewhere to hide . . .

There was nowhere to hide. A bare zigzag of goat-track; a couple of steep steps of natural rock open to the sun; a ledge holding a low tangle of brown scrub . . .

Regardless now of noise I scrambled anyhow over the rocky steps, pulled myself off the path on to the ledge, and flung myself down behind the meagre shelter of the dead bushes.

There was one small holly-oak, shining green, among a mass of foot-high tufted stuff like a tangle of rusty wire-netting. This was prickly to the touch, but as I dragged myself nearer its shelter, pressing against it, it crumbled under my desperate hands. I remember that it seemed quite a natural part of the nightmare, that the barrier between me and murder should crumble as I touched it.

I drew back from the dead bushes and pressed myself deep into the dust of the ledge, as if like a mole I could dig myself into the ground for safety. I put my cheek to the hot dust and lay still. Above me an overhang dealt a narrow shade, but where I lay the ledge was exposed to the sun. I could feel its cruel weight on my back and hand, but I hardly heeded it. Through the wiry scrub I was watching the corrie below me.

Angelos came up into the gateway and then walked quickly down the ramp and across the corrie. He didn't look up, but made straight for the cave, disappearing from my view in the corner.

I waited, pressed down in the burning dust. He didn't appear, and I couldn't hear anything. I wondered if he would load the mule now, or if I would have time to reach the top of the cliff, and shelter, before he came once more into view.

I was just getting ready to move, when I saw him again. He came out into the sunlight, moving very quietly now, and looking about him. He had brought his jacket out of the cave, and held it carefully over one arm. In the other hand he held something that shone in the sunlight. It was the torch I had dropped by Nigel's body. Angelos' own torch.

The black arched brows were drawn frowning over his eyes. The smile pulled the thick lips. He stopped in the centre of the corrie, turning the torch over in his hand.

I lay still. Invisible, the mule moved restlessly, and metal clinked.

Angelos raised his head and sent one long look round the corrie. It raked the cliff, touched me, passed me by. Then the massive shoulders lifted in a tiny shrug, and he thrust the torch into a pocket of the jacket. I saw him slide his hand into the other pocket and bring out a gun. He weighed this for a moment in his hand, thoughtfully, and then turned back towards the cave.

My hands braced themselves in the dust. He would have recognised the torch, no doubt of that. He was going back into the cave

to search for whoever had dropped it. And this time I didn't propose
to linger till he came out again. I wasn't going to wait here, to be
brushed off the cliff by that gun like a lizard off a wall.

I felt my muscles tighten up like vibrating wires. He was moving
deliberately across the corrie floor. Soon he would be out of sight.

Something fell on to my hand with a sharp little rap of pain that
nearly made me cry out. A pebble. Then a shower of dust and small
stones, dislodged from somewhere above me, rattled down the cliff
like a charge of small shot.

Angelos stopped dead, turned, and stared upwards straight at me.

I didn't move. I didn't think he could see me at that angle. But my
mind stampeded with another, and worse panic, as I heard the
sounds approaching the top of the cliff. Dimitrios, as yet scatheless,
with Simon behind him? Or Simon, coming cheerfully to tell me
that justice had been done on 'last night's marauder'? Any hope I
had had that Dimitrios might have been forced into telling Simon
himself about Angelos, vanished now as I listened to that incautious
approach.

I saw Angelos stiffen, then he whipped out of sight behind a jut of
rock.

The sound came nearer. I turned my head till, by twisting my
eyes in their sockets, I could see the cliff-top. If it was Simon I must
shout . . . my mouth opened ready for the cry, and I licked the dust
off my dry lips. Then something moved suddenly against the sky at
the brim of the cliff, and I saw what it was.

A goat. Another. Three big black goats, yellow-eyed, flop-eared,
peacefully intent on the dry scrub at the cliff's head . . . They
turned aside at the brink of the cliff and moved slowly across above
me, outlined against the deep blue of that translucent sky. As they
went I thought I heard again the sweet faraway stave of the
goat-herd's pipe. The coolly pastoral sound fell through the heat like
the trickle of Apollo's spring.

The relief was dizzying. The rock swam in the dazzling light. I
shut my eyes and put my head down beside the dusty scrub.
Something smelt sweet and aromatic—some memory, wisping out
of the dust, of potpourri and English gardens and bees among the
thyme . . .

I don't know how long it was before I realised that the afternoon
held no sound at all.

When I looked again Angelos had come out of concealment, and

was standing where he had been before, in the centre of the corrie
floor. He was standing very still, staring up, not at me, but at the
edge of the cliff above me where the goats had been. Slowly I
followed his gaze. I could feel the breath of the hot stone on my
cheek.

The goats were still there. They, too, were standing stock-still,
side by side, at the brink of the cliff. They were looking down, with
ears forward and eyes intent and curious . . . six yellow satyrs' eyes,
staring fixedly down at me, some forty feet below them.

Angelos dropped his coat on to a boulder beside him, and started
for the foot of the cliff.

At his movement I heard the flurry of dust and pebbles as the
goats fled. It echoed the quick jump and kick of my own heart. But I
didn't move. Whether some instinct kept me clamped still like a
hiding animal, or whether the flood of fear that washed and ebbed
through my blood actually drained the power of movement from
me, I can't tell. At any rate I lay flat for the few decisive moments
during which the Greek crossed the corrie and plunged up the
goat-path towards me. And then it seemed that he was almost on
me, and it was too late to escape. I remembered the gun and lay
there, unbreathing, pressed flat to the hot earth.

I had a shelter of a sort from below, and from above the overhang
might partly hide me. The path sloped sharply past the end of the
ledge where I lay. It was possible—it was surely possible?—that he
might hurry past it and never look back to see me lying there behind
the crumbling scrub? My dress was of pale-coloured cotton, now
sufficiently streaked with dust. Against the glaring rock and the red
pebble-strewn dust he might miss me. He might yet—surely?—miss
me.

He was just below me now. He stopped. His head was a few feet
below the level of my ledge. I couldn't—daren't—look, but I heard
the climbing steps stilled, and then his breathing close beneath me.
He was looking up. My own breath hardly stirred the dust under
my mouth.

The next angle of the track would bring him upwards and past the
end of the ledge where I lay. He paused where he was for a few seconds,
and then I heard the soft steps moving on. But they didn't come on up
the track. They moved carefully away to the left, below my ledge.

Through the pathetic barrier of dead plants I could just see the top
of his head. It was turned away now, and I knew that he must have

left the track. I could hear loose pebbles slither and spatter down the rock, and the rustle of the dry plants he trod over. He went very carefully, with pauses almost between each step.

I had to know what he was doing. I moved my head slightly, and saw him better.

There was a ledge below mine, with a few sparse plants and a tumble of loose fragments of stone. I had noticed it in that second's wild glance round for shelter. It wouldn't have hidden anyone larger than a child. But he searched it, gun in hand, quartering it methodically, like a dog.

Then he left it, and came back carefully on to the track. He paused there briefly once again, so that for a silly moment I wondered if he were satisfied, and would go down again into the corrie, thinking perhaps that the goats had been watching a snake . . . But he turned without further hesitation and started up the steep section that would bring him up to me.

I don't even think I was frightened; not now. It was as if fear had been raised to such a pitch that it killed itself, like a light that goes vividly bright just before it goes out. I was back in that dim-lit, remote theatre of unreality. This wasn't happening to me.

I suppose that nobody, in their heart of hearts, ever believes that they themselves will die. Volumes of philosophies have been written out of this belief alone. And I'm sure that nobody ever believes that a foul thing like murder can overtake them. Something will stop it. It can't happen. To others, but not to them. Not to *me*.

I lay, almost relaxed, abandoned to fate and chance, in the hot dust, and Angelos swiftly climbed the path towards me. In a moment now he would reach the end of my ledge. He might see me straight away, or he might turn aside and beat the scrub till he flushed me, scared and filthy with dust, from my hiding-place. He was there now. He couldn't miss me . . .

I have read somewhere that when a man is hunted for his life, one of the chief dangers he undergoes is the desperate urge to give himself up, and have done. I had never believed it. I had thought that fear would drive him till he dropped, like a hunted hare. But it's true. It may have been that something forbade me to let the man find me crouching, dirty and frightened, at his feet; it may simply have been the terrible blind instinct of the hunted. But the impulsion came and I didn't attempt to resist it.

I stood up and began to brush the dirt off my frock.

I didn't look at him. He had stopped dead when I moved. He was standing just where my ledge left the track. To get off it I would have to pass him.

I walked forward through the scrub and stones as if I were walking in my sleep. I didn't meet his eyes, but watched my feet on the rough going. He moved a little to one side and I passed him. I went slowly down the path again to the bottom of the corrie. He came just behind me.

When I got to the level ground I stumbled and nearly fell. His hand took hold of my arm from behind, and my flesh seemed to wince and shrink from the touch. I stopped.

The hand tightened, then with a jerk he pulled me round to face him. I think if he had gone on touching me I would have screamed then and there, but he let me go, so I kept silent. I knew that if I tried to scream I would be killed out of hand. But I backed away from him a step or so till a boulder touched the back of my legs. Without meaning to, I sat down; I couldn't have stood. I put both hands flat on the hot surface of the stone as if I could draw strength from it, and looked at Angelos.

He was standing perhaps five feet from me, his legs a little apart, one hand thrust negligently into the belt of his trousers, the other arm hanging loose at his side with the gun dangling. His head was forward slightly, like a bull's when it is deciding to charge. The heavy face was terrifying with the tight curved smile, the perfect arch of the black brows and the cruel eyes that seemed to be solid, opaque black, without pupils, and without light from within. The thick nostrils were flared and he was breathing fast. The bulls'-curls along his forehead were damp and tight with sweat.

He had recognised me, of course. I saw that as his slow stare raked me. He must have seen me distinctly last night in the light of the torch.

He said: 'So it's my little friend of the studio, is it?' He was speaking in the quick guttural French he had used with Danielle.

I tried to say something, but no sound came. As I cleared my throat I saw the smile deepen. My voice came back. 'I hope I hurt you,' I said.

'That score,' said Angelos, very pleasantly, 'will soon be quite even.' My hands pressed hard on the warm stone. I said nothing. He said abruptly: 'Where's the Englishman?'

'I don't know.'

He made a small movement towards me and I shrank back against the boulder. His expression didn't change but his voice did.

'Don't be a fool. You didn't come up here alone. Where is he?'

I said hoarsely: 'I—we were sitting up there on the cliff and we saw a man hanging about . . . that chap Dimitrios. He's a guide . . . I don't know if you know him. Simon . . . my friend . . . went off to speak to him. He—he thought it was him last night at the studio and I think—I think he wanted to find out what he'd been after.'

It was so near the truth that I hoped he might be satisfied as far as Simon was concerned. But it wouldn't help me. Nothing would.

'And you've been up on the cliff all this time?'

'I—why, no. I went over the hill a little way, and then I thought Simon might have come back, so I—'

'And you haven't been in the cave?'

'Cave?' I said.

'That's what I said. The cave.'

The sun was cold. The rock was cold. I suppose even till this I had been hoping against silly hope, but now I knew for certain. Of course I was going to die. Whatever I had seen or not seen—the mule, the cave, the treasure, Nigel, Danielle—it wouldn't help me in the least to play the innocent. None of these things mattered beside the one fact that now I had seen Angelos.

He had taken two paces away to where his coat lay over a boulder. He slipped a hand in the pocket and brought out the torch. 'You left this, didn't you?'

'Yes.'

A gleam of surprise in the black eyes showed that he had expected me to deny it. I said flatly: 'I dropped it when I saw Nigel's body. And I was in the cave just now when you killed Danielle.'

The metal of the torch flashed as he made a sudden little movement. At least I had startled him into interest. If I could keep him talking . . . if I could keep alive for just a few more minutes . . . perhaps the miracle would happen, and I wouldn't die. Murderers were conceited, weren't they? They talked about their murders? But then Angelos took murder so for granted that it had hardly seemed to interest him to commit, let alone to discuss . . . But he was a sadist, too; perhaps he would enjoy talking to frighten me before he killed me . . .

I said hoarsely, gripping the stone: 'Why did you torture Nigel? Did you really mean to kill Danielle?'

It wasn't going to work. He dropped the torch back on top of the coat, and gave a quick glance round the encircling cliffs. Then he put the gun down gently beside the torch, and turned to me.

I did manage to move then, but the thrust of my hands that took me off the warm stone sent me a pace towards him. As I whirled to run he caught me from behind and pulled me back as easily as if I had been a rag doll. I suppose I fought him; I don't remember anything except the blind panic and the feel of his hands and the acrid smell of his sweat, and the appalling iron strength that held me as effortlessly as a man's hand holds a caught moth. One hand came hard over my mouth, crushing my lips against my teeth, but the palm was slimy with sweat; it slipped, and I wrenched my head away and managed at the same moment to kick him hard on the shin-bone. I paid dearly for the moment of advantage, for as I twisted my body in a vain attempt to break away, he half-lunged forward to drag me close again and silence me, trod on a loose stone that rolled under his foot, and we fell together.

If I had fallen undermost I should probably have been badly hurt, if not stunned, for he was a heavy man; but he went down on to his side in a stumbling fall, dragging me with him. Even then the brutal grip never loosened, and as we hit the ground he moved like lightning, flinging himself over my body with a quick heave, and holding me down on the ground underneath him.

Then his grip shifted. I was on my back, my left arm twisted up under me, so that our double weight held it there, almost breaking. My right wrist was in his grip, clamped down against the rock beside me. His free hand flashed up to my throat. The heavy body held me down; I couldn't move, but frantic now with terror I screamed and twisted uselessly under him and jerked my head from side to side, trying to avoid the hand that slipped and groped on my throat for the hold he wanted. I screamed again. He cursed in Greek and hit me hard across the mouth and then as my head went back against the rock the hand gripped my throat at last, moved a little, tightened . . .

*   *   *

I was still alive. It was years later and the boiling agonised black had cleared, and I was still alive. I was still lying on my back in the hot dust, and above me the sky arched in a great flashing, pulsating dome of blue. Angelos' weight was still on me. I could feel the heave of his heavy breathing; the smell of his sweat was rank; his hand was wet and sour and foul across my mouth: the other hand was still on my throat, but it lay loosely there, and now it lifted.

He didn't move away. He lay there quite still, with rigid muscles, looking up and away from me towards the entrance to the corrie. Then his hand slid from my face and went down on to the dusty rock beside my head, ready to thrust him to his feet. I remember that the hand was on my spread hair, and the tug as he put his weight on it hurt me. The tiny pain was like a spur. It pricked me back to consciousness. I stopped blinking up into the vibrating blue of the sky, and managed to move my head a fraction, to look where Angelos was looking.

He was staring straight into the sun. At first I could see nothing in the dazzle at the mouth of the corrie. Then I saw him.

I knew who it was straight away, though he was only a shadow against the glare. But even so I felt the sharp cold thrill run up the marrow of my spine as I felt Angelos' heart jerk, once, in his body, and heard him say, thickly: 'Michael?'

Chapter 19

I am come,
Fresh from the cleansing of Apollo . . .
. . . To pay the bloody twain their debt
Of blood.

EURIPIDES: *Electra.*
(tr. Gilbert Murray.)

REALISATION, SHOCK, RECOGNITION – it must only have taken a
few seconds, but it seemed an age.

One moment Simon was silhouetted in fractional pause against
the glare of the gateway, the next Angelos had swung himself off my
body and on to his feet as lightly as a dancer. He must have
forgotten that his gun had been laid aside, for I remember that his
hand flashed as if automatically to his hip just as Simon, coming
down the ramp with the speed of a ski-jumper, brought up not five
yards from him in a flurry of dust and shale.

Angelos was standing right over me, hand still at hip, watching
him.

Simon had stopped dead where he was. I couldn't see his
expression, but I could see Angelos', and fear seeped back into my
blood as agonisingly as warmth after frostbite. I stirred in the dust
and tried to say something, to tell Simon who and what he was, but
my throat was swollen and sore, and the brilliant light swam round
me sickeningly as I moved, and I couldn't make a sound. Angelos
must have felt me move at his feet, but he took no notice. Simon
hadn't glanced at me either. The two men watched one another, as
wary and slow as two dogs circling before a fight.

I waited for Simon to rush him as he had done last night. I didn't
notice then how hard he was breathing, fighting to get heart and

lungs under control after his rush up the steep track towards my terrified screaming. Nor did I realise that he still thought the Greek might be armed . . . and I was lying where knife or gun could reach me, seconds before Simon could make contact . . . None of this was I in any state to realise. I only knew that Simon didn't move, and I remember wondering, with a sick cold little feeling, if he was afraid. Then he took two paces forward, very slowly, and now that he was no longer between me and the sun, I saw his face. The cold feeling went, and I wasn't afraid any more. With the fear, the tenseness went out of my body, and I felt myself relax and begin to tremble. The bruises the Greek had inflicted began to hurt. I turned on my side and tried to pull myself a little further away from him. I couldn't have got up, but I dragged myself a foot or so away to crouch, shaking and still gasping for breath, against the base of the boulder where I had sat before.

He took no notice of me. He had dealt with me, and thrown me aside, and now he was going to deal with Simon. I could be finished after that.

Simon said pleasantly: 'I take it you are Angelos?' His breathing was still over-fast, but his voice was level.

'The same. And you are Michael's little brother.'

'The same.'

The Greek said, on a note between satisfaction and contempt: 'You are welcome.'

Simon's lips thinned. 'I doubt that. I believe, Angelos, that you and I have met before.'

'Last night.'

'Yes.' Simon looked at him for a few seconds in silence. His voice went flat and uninflected. Knowing him now, I felt my heart tighten and begin to race. He added: 'I wish I had known – last night.'

I turned my head painfully and managed to say: 'He killed Nigel . . . and Danielle.' It was some seconds before I realised that I had made no sound at all.

'You murdered my brother Michael.' Simon hadn't even glanced at me. He was breathing evenly now, his face wiped clean of all expression but that light, watchful look. I recognised it for what it was. Just so must Michael have looked when he faced Angelos here all those years ago. Just so must this blazing sky have looked down, those indifferent rocks throwing back its blinding heat. Time had run back. Angelos faced Michael again, and this time the odds were on Michael.

It seemed that Angelos didn't think so. He laughed. 'Yes, I killed Michael. And I shall kill you, little brother. In your country they do not teach men to be men. It is different here.'

Simon was moving now, very slowly, forward a pace; another.

'How did you kill my brother, Angelos?'

'I broke his neck.' I noticed with surprise that the Greek was giving ground. He had lowered his head in that characteristic way he had. I could see the contraction of the flat black eyes against the light. I saw him blink rapidly once or twice, and he moved his head as a bull does whose horns pain him. Then he took a slow step backwards, sidling a little . . .

I thought for a moment that he was trying to get Simon out of line with him and the sun, and wondered fleetingly at the same time why he should have let the other play for time like this, when suddenly, like a flash out of a black night, I knew what he was doing. I remembered the gun, lying hidden from Simon in the tumble of Angelos' dropped coat.

Somehow I moved. It was like lifting a mattress stuffed with clay to lift my body from the scuffled dust, but I rolled over, kicked myself along the ground with one convulsive jack-knifing motion, like a fish, and grabbed at the dangling sleeve of the coat just as Angelos took a sudden, swift step aside, and stooped for the gun.

I had the sleeve. I yanked at it with all my strength. It caught at a bit of the rock, tore, and came with a jerk. The torch flashed over like a rocket and crashed on a stone by my head. The gun flew high and wide, hit a pile of stones three yards away, and slithered out of sight. It actually struck the Greek's hand as he reached to grab it. He whirled with a curse and kicked me and then went down sickeningly across the boulder as Simon hit him like a steam-hammer.

Simon came in with the blow. The Greek's forearm, even as he went down over the rock, just managed to block the side-handed chop at the throat that followed it, and counter in the same movement with a wicked elbow-punch that took Simon in the lower part of the stomach. I saw pain explode through him like a bursting shell, and as he recoiled the Greek, using the rock as a springboard, came away from it in a lunge with all his weight behind it. Simon's mouth disappeared in a smear of blood. His head snapped back in front of another blow that looked as if it had broken his neck, and he went down, but as he went he hooked one leg round Angelos' knee and, using the man's own momentum, brought him crashing down over him. Before the Greek hit the ground Simon had rolled aside and was above him. I saw the Greek lash out with a foot, miss, and aim a short chopping blow with the edge of a hand at Simon's neck; Simon hit him in the throat and then the two were locked, heaving and rolling in the dust that mushroomed up round them.

I couldn't see . . . couldn't make out . . . Angelos was on his back, and Simon seemed to be across him, trying to fix the man's arm in a lock, to drag it under him as Angelos had dragged mine; the Greek smashed again and again at his face; the shortened punches hadn't much force behind them but the blood was running from Simon's mouth. Then suddenly the flailing fist opened, clawed, came down on to Simon's cheekbone and slithered across it, the big spatulate thumb digging, digging, for his eye . . .

I had dragged myself to my feet, holding on to the boulder beside me. He couldn't do it after all; he couldn't be expected to do it . . . he was younger, and he knew how to fight, but Angelos had the weight, and all those desperate years behind him . . . If I could help . . . if I could only help . . .

I stooped giddily, and reached for a lump of rough rock, lifting it in hands that shook like leaves. I could hit him as I had last night . . . if I could have found a weapon – perhaps the torch – *the gun*.

I dropped the knot of rock and flung myself, with sobbing little breaths, at the pile of stones where the gun had gone. Here, surely, it had struck and slid out of sight? No sign. Then here? No. Here . . . oh, dear God, *here* . . .

There, white on the limestone, a scratch had marked its passage . . . I drove a shaking hand down between the jammed rocks. They scraped the skin and it hurt me, but I hardly noticed. I thrust my arm down as far as I could. My fingers, stretching, touched something cold and smooth . . . metal. I couldn't reach it; the tips of my fingers slipped over it, no more. I could feel my lips trembling as the tears spilt salt on to them. I lay down hard against the stones and thrust my arm further into the narrowing crack. The cruel stone rasped at the skin and I felt blood running down my wrist. My fingers slid further, curled, gripped. I had the gun. I tried to withdraw it. But with my hand now curved round the butt I couldn't pull it back between the stones. I dragged at it, hopelessly, stupidly, and my hand hurt till I cried out with the pain, but I couldn't drag the gun out . . .

Simon had twisted back from that gouging thumb. The Greek lunged violently to one side as the other's hold slackened, and then somehow, was free. With a movement incredibly quick for a man of his build he had rolled aside and was bunching to jump to his feet. As he went I saw his hand close, like mine, on a cruelly jagged chunk of rock. But Simon was as quick. The same movement that threw him back and away from the clawing hand had brought him to his feet. He saw the Greek clutch the rock. Even as the fist closed on it and the arm-muscles tightened Simon jumped. His foot stamped down on the man's hand. The rock was undermost, and I heard the man make a dreadful sound as his hand was smashed down on to it. But he whipped over and brought his foot up with what looked like appalling force into Simon's groin. Simon saw it coming, and tried to sidestep. The foot grazed the inside of his thigh. Simon's hand came up under the lashing ankle: I saw a heave and a twist, and the Greek crashed back on to his side like a felled ox, and Simon plummeted down on to him again in the smother of dust. Another blow, a sick sound of flesh and bone smacking together, and then Angelos was uppermost, his fist smashing down like a hammer . . .

I opened my hand and let the gun go. I dropped to the base of the pile of stones, and began to claw at them with those useless, shaking fingers, trying to pull the heavy stuff aside. From behind me came the thud and slither of their bodies on the ground, the torn dreadful breathing, and, again, the sudden sharp sound of pain. I thought it came from Simon.

The stone under my hands gave way, and I threw it down and tore at the next. And the next. And then a pile of dry earth and small jagged pebbles.

Then I saw the blue-dark gleam of the gun.

I thrust the last lump of rock aside and pushed my hand through. The muzzle was towards me. I grabbed it and dragged the thing out. I didn't even think once of the danger of holding it like that. I just dragged it out between the rough stones and turned, holding it in my aspen hands. I remember thinking with surprise how heavy it was . . .

I'd never touched a gun before in my life. But of course it was quite easy. You simply pointed it and pressed the trigger; I knew that. Provided I got close enough . . . and if the men would only break apart for a moment and let me see through that stifling dust . . . One simply pointed the thing and pulled the trigger, and Angelos would be dead, blasted out of life in a fraction of time. It didn't occur to me that this was in any way a wrong or a momentous thing to do. I took a couple of faltering steps in the direction of the struggling bodies on the ground . . .

It was funny, but it was difficult to walk. The ground was
unsteady and the dust dragged at my feet and the gun was too heavy
and the sky was far too bright but still I couldn't see properly . . .

The locked bodies on the ground moved as the man underneath
made a seemingly titanic effort. Both men were covered with dust; I
couldn't see who it was lying prone with one arm twisted into that
cruel lock behind his back . . . or who it was who lay astride him,
shifting his grip now, straining in some final agonising effort. If
only they would break apart . . . if only I could see which was
Angelos . . .

The man uppermost lay clamped over the other, one hand hard
round the wrist of the locked arm, his own free arm flung round the
prone man's neck in a tight embrace. As I watched, the embrace
tightened still further . . .

The prostrate man's head came painfully back. The red dust was
thick in the black curls. The broad cruel face was smeared red with
it, too, an archaic mask carved grimacing in red sandstone. It was
Angelos who lay there in the dust, breath sobbing through the
grinning lips, trying with weaker and weaker movements to throw
Simon off his body.

I stood there, the gun drooping in my hand, the driving purpose
snapped in me, staring like someone in a dream at the two bodies
that heaved, breathing as one, on the ground at my feet.

A muscle bunched in Simon's shoulder. The Greek's head moved
back another fraction. The grin was a rictus, fixed, horrible. His
body gave one last desperate heave to rid itself of its killer, threshing
sideways across the dusty rock. But Simon's grip didn't shift. Even
as the two bodies, still locked, slithered a yard or so across the dusty
rock to fetch up hard against the cairn where Michael had been
murdered, I saw Simon's arm tense, and jerk tightly back, and heard
Angelos' breath tear out of his throat in a sort of whistling gasp that
broke off short . . .

I knew then that Simon didn't need me or the gun. I turned aside
and sat down on the boulder. I leaned back very wearily against the
hot rock and shut my eyes.

After a while there was silence.

*   *   *

Angelos lay still, sprawled face downward against the little cairn.
Simon got very slowly to his feet. He stood for a moment looking

down. His face was filthy with dust and blood, and lined with fatigue. I could see how his muscles slumped with weariness as he stood there. He put up the back of his hand to wipe the blood from his face. His hands were bloody too.

Then he turned away and for the first time looked at me. He made as if to speak, and then I saw his tongue come out to wet the dust-caked lips. I answered his look quickly.

'I'm quite all right, Simon. He—he didn't hurt me.' My voice had come back, hoarse and not too steady. But there was nothing to say. I whispered: 'There's a rope on the mule. It's down by the cave.'

'Rope?' His voice wasn't his own either. He was coming slowly towards me. 'What for?'

'Him, of course. If he came round—'

'My dear Camilla,' said Simon. And then, as he saw the look in my face, in a kind of anger: 'What else did you expect me to do?'

'I don't know. Of course you had to kill him. It's just—of course you did.'

His mouth twisted. It wasn't quite a smile, but nothing about him seemed, just at the moment, to be like himself. It was a stranger who stood in front of me in the blazing sunlight, with a stranger's voice, and something gone from his face that I remembered there. He stood there in silence, looking down at his hands. I still remember the blood on them.

The nausea had gone, and the world steadied. I said quickly, almost desperately, out of a rush of shame: 'Simon. Forgive me. I—I guess I can't think straight yet. Of course you had to. It was only . . . coming so close to it. But you were right. There comes a time when one has to . . . accept . . . things like this. It was damnable of me.'

He did smile then, a trace of genuine amusement showing through the weariness. 'Not really. But—just exactly what were you planning to do with that?'

'With what?' Following his look, I stared stupidly down at the gun in my hand.

He leaned forward and took it from me gently. The blood-stained fingers avoided mine. They were shaking a little. He laid the gun carefully to one side. 'I think perhaps it's safer there.'

Silence. He stood over me, looking down still with that stranger's look.

'Camilla.'

I met it then.

'If you hadn't got rid of that thing,' he said, 'I should be dead.'

'And so should I. But you came.'

'My dear, of course. But if he'd got to that gun . . .' A tiny pause, so slight it didn't seem that what he said could be important. 'Would you have shot him, Camilla?'

Quite suddenly, I was shaking uncontrollably. I said, with a sort of violence: 'Yes. Yes, I would. I was just going to, but then you . . . you killed him yourself . . .'

I began to cry then, helplessly. I reached out blindly with both hands, and took his between them, blood and all.

*   *   *

He was sitting beside me on the boulder, with his arm round me. I don't remember what he said: I think part of the time he was swearing under his breath, and this seemed so unlike him that I had to fight harder to control the little spurts of laughter that shook me through the sobbing.

I managed to say: 'I'm sorry. I'm all right. I'm not hysterical. It's—it's reaction or something.'

He said with violence, the more shocking because it was the first time I had heard it from him: 'I'll not forgive myself in a hurry for dragging you into this, by God! If I'd had any idea—'

'You didn't drag me in. I asked to be in, so I had to take what came, didn't I? It wasn't your fault it turned out like this, and since you *did* feel like that about Michael after all, you did it. That's all.'

'About Michael?'

'Yes. You said the tragedy was over, but of course once you knew Angelos was still alive—'

'My dear girl,' said Simon, 'you didn't imagine that I really killed him for Mick, did you?'

I looked up at him rather numbly. 'No? But you told Angelos—'

'I was talking the language he'd understand. This is still Orestes' country, after all.' He looked down at the scuffled dust between his feet. 'Oh, I admit it was partly Mick—once I found myself here, and facing him. I felt murderous enough about him when I knew he was still alive, even before Dimitrios told me the rest.'

'Dimitrios? Of course. He told you?'

'He was persuaded to, quite quickly. Niko turned up and helped me.' A pause. 'He told me what the two of them had done to Nigel.'

'Then you know . . .' The breath I drew was three parts relief. I remembered that look in Simon's eyes, and the smooth single-mindedness with which he had killed Angelos. I shivered a little. 'I see.'

'And then,' he said, 'there was you.'

I said nothing. My eyes were on two—no, three specks in the bright air, circling slowly, high above the corrie. Simon sat beside me without moving, looking at the trampled dust. He looked all at once unutterably weary. If it hadn't been for the evidence sprawled across the stones one might almost have thought that he, not Angelos, had been beaten. *Any man's death diminishes me . . .* I thought of Nigel, tumbled grotesquely behind the pile of dirt, and understood.

The silence drew out. Away somewhere on the mountain I thought I heard something, the clatter of stones, a breathless call. Simon didn't move. I said: 'Tell me about Angelos. How did he get into it? Why did he wait till now to come back?'

'He's been before. We were right in our guesses about the search for the gold—the lights and voices, and Dimitrios' questions—but we were wrong about the name of the seeker. It wasn't Dimitrios himself. He knew nothing about the cache originally. When Angelos left Greece for Yugoslavia at the end of 1944, he intended to come back as soon as he could. But he committed murder—political murder this time—in his adopted country, and was put away for "life". He was released two years ago, and came back secretly to look up his cousin. He let him into the secret, since he had to have somewhere to hide, and an agent to help him. They looked for the stuff—just as we guessed—but failed to find it. Dimitrios did his best to pump Stephanos, and the two of them must have searched desperately over the earthquake area at intervals through the spring and summer, then they gave up for the time being, and Angelos went back to live in Italy. I imagine he intended to come back again in the spring of this year, as soon as the snows had melted, but by then I had written to Stephanos, and the rumours were going about that I was coming to Delphi. He decided to wait and let us show him the place. That's all.'

He glanced down at me. 'And now what happened to you? Why on earth did you come out of the cave? Surely he never found you in there, in sanctuary?'

'No.' I told him then all that had happened since he had left me to follow Dimitrios. I found that I could tell it all quite calmly now, with that queer detachment I had felt in the cave, as if it were a play; as if these things had happened, not to me, but in some story I had read. But I remember being glad of the feel of Simon's arm round my shoulders, and of the heat of the sun.

He listened in silence, and when I had finished he still didn't speak for some minutes. Then he said: 'I seem to have rather more to forgive myself for than just bringing you in on—that.' For the first time his eyes went back to the cairn where the body lay. They were as I first remembered them, vivid and hard and cool. 'Quite a score,' he said. 'Mick, Nigel, poor silly little Danielle. And then, of course, you . . . It would almost take an Orestes, wouldn't it?' He took in his breath. 'No, I doubt if the Furies, the Kindly Ones, will haunt me for this day's work, Camilla.'

'No, I don't think they will.'

There was a shout from the gateway behind us. With a clatter of stones, Niko hurled himself into the corrie and raced down towards us.

'Beautiful miss!' he yelled. '*Kyrie* Simon! It's all right! I'm here!'

*   *   *

He slithered to a halt in front of us. His startled gaze took us both in—my torn and filthy dress, the bruises, my scraped wrists and hands, and Simon covered with blood and dust and the marks of battle. 'Mother of God, then he *was* here? Angelos was here? He got away? He—'

He stopped abruptly as he caught sight of the body lying against the cairn. He gulped, and flashed a look at Simon. He looked at me as if he were going to speak, but he just shut his mouth again, tightly, and then went—it seemed reluctantly—across to where Angelos lay. There was the sound of slower footsteps from the gateway of the corrie, and Stephanos came into sight. He paused there for a moment, just as Simon had done, then came deliberately down the ramp towards us. Simon got stiffly to his feet. The old man stopped at my elbow. His eyes, too, were on Angelos. Then he looked at Simon. He didn't speak, but he nodded, slowly. Then he smiled. I think he would have spoken to me then, but Niko had straightened up and now came running back. A flood of Greek was poured out at Simon, who answered, and presently seemed to be telling his story. I caught the name *Michael* several times, and then *the Englishman*, and *the French girl*, and the word '*speleos*', which I took to mean 'a cave'. But I was suddenly too tired to pay any attention. I leaned back into a bar of shadow and waited, while the three of them talked across me. Presently, with a word from Simon, he and Stephanos left me and went towards the cave.

Niko lingered for a moment. 'You are not well, beautiful miss?' he asked anxiously. 'That one – that Bulgar – he hurt you?'

To call anyone a Bulgarian is the worst term of abuse a Greek can think up; and they have quite a range. 'Not really, Niko,' I said. 'I'm a bit shaken, that's all.' I smiled at him. 'You should have been here.'

'I wish I had been!' Niko's sidelong glance at the cairn was perhaps not as enthusiastic as his voice, but apparently it took more than murder really to dim his lights. He turned his look of dazzled admiration on me. 'I should have dealt with him, me, and not on account of my grandfather's cousin Panos, but for *you*, beautiful miss. Though *Kyrios* Simon,' he added generously, 'did very well, not?'

'For an Englishman,' I said deprecatingly.

'Indeed, for an Englishman.' He caught my look and grinned, unabashed. 'Of course,' he added, 'I help him with Dimitrios Dragoumis. I, Niko.'

'He told me so. What did you do with him?'

The black eyes opened wide. He looked shocked. 'I could not tell you *that*. You are a lady, and – oh, I *see*.' The devastating smile flashed out. 'Afterwards, you mean? I take him down to the road, but not to Delphi, because I want to get back and help *Kyrios* Simon, you understand. There is a lorry, and I explain to the men, and they take him to Delphi to the police. The police will come. I shall go presently to meet them and guide them here. And so.'

'And so.' I said it very wearily. It seemed as good a period to the day as anything.

Beyond my bar of shadow the sun seemed white-hot. Niko had on a shirt of vivid electric blue, patterned with scarlet lozenges. The effect was blinding. He seemed to shimmer at the edges.

I heard him say cheerfully: 'You are tired. You do not want to talk. And the other men will be needing me, not? I go.'

As I shut my eyes and leaned back, I heard him crossing the corrie at his usual impetuous gallop.

It seemed a long time before the three of them came out of the cave again into the sunlight.

Niko came first, leading the mule. He seemed subdued now, and a little pale. He didn't come over to me again, but swung himself on

to the mule's back, kicked it into reluctant motion, and, with a wave
to me, clattered out of the corrie.

Stephanos and Simon stood talking for a few minutes longer.
Stephanos looked sombre. I saw him nod to something Simon said,
then he gestured upwards towards the blazing arch of sky where
those black specks still hung and circled. Then he turned and
trudged slowly across to a patch of shade near the body. He sat
down there, and settled himself, as if to wait, leaning forward with
his head against the hands clasped on his staff. He shut his eyes. He
looked suddenly very old—with that Homeric head and the shut
eyes as old as time itself.

It was a picture I was never to forget, that quiet tailpiece to
tragedy. There was the blue arch of the brilliant sky; there the body
that the Kindly Ones had hunted down and killed on the very spot
where he himself had shed blood; there the old man, bearded like
Zeus himself, nodding in the shade. At the head of the cliffs stood
the black goats, staring.

From somewhere, not too far distant now, came the little stave of
music; the goat-herd's pipe whose sound, drifting down through the
light-well, had led me to the Apollo of the holy spring. At the sound
the goats lifted their heads, and turning, moved off, black against the
sky, an Attic frieze in slow procession.

Simon's shadow fell across me.

'Niko's gone to guide the police here. He wanted to escort you to
Delphi, but I told him you wouldn't be fit for the trek quite yet. You
and I have something still to do, haven't we?'

I hardly heard the question. I said, apprehensively: 'The police?'

'Don't worry. There'll be no trouble for me. Apart from everything else, and God knows he's done plenty, he was trying to kill
you.' He smiled. 'And now, are you coming? Stephanos is asleep,
by the looks of it, so he won't wonder where we've gone.'

'You didn't tell him and Niko about the shrine?'

'No. The question of what to do about the guns and gold is out of
our hands now, thank heaven, but the other question's our own to
answer. Do you know the answer?'

I looked at him inquiringly; perhaps a little doubtfully.

Then he nodded, and I said, slowly: 'I suppose so.'

He smiled and put down a hand to me.

We went into the cave in silence. Simon's torch was almost dead,
but it showed the way. It was not strong enough to probe too far into
the shadows. He paused just inside the entrance, and I saw him step

aside and stoop over something that lay near the pile of rubble where the boxes had been. He straightened up with one of Angelos' crowbars in his hand. I didn't look further, but followed the mercifully dimming light through the pillared vaults until the slab barred the way.

The light paused on the old marks of tooling in the stone. 'There,' said Simon softly. 'It should slide back easily enough. Even another three or four inches should block the entrance . . . I'll leave this here for the moment.'

He laid the crowbar down and we went through the cleft for the last time, and up the curving tunnel that led to the bright citadel.

*   *   *

He had stood there without move or change for more than two thousand years: now, it seemed a miracle that in the last hour he had remained untouched, unaltered. The sun had slid further towards the west, and the light fell more slantingly through the leaves; that was all.

We knelt at his feet and drank. I cupped my hands under the spring and splashed the water over my face and neck, then held my wrists under the icy runnel. It stung on the bruises and the scraped flesh of my wrists, a sharp remedial stinging that seemed to signal my body's return from whatever numb borderlands of shock I had been straying in. I sat back, flicking the cool drops off my hands.

I noticed then that the mark had gone from the third finger of my left hand. There was no sign at all of the pale circle where Philip's ring had been.

I sat looking at my hands.

Simon was leaning forward, putting something on the stone plinth at the statue's feet. There was the gleam of gold.

He caught my look and smiled, a little wryly. 'Gold for Apollo. I asked him to bring Angelos back, and he did it, even though it was done in that damned two-edged Delphic way that one always forgets to bargain for. However, there it is. It was a vow. Remember?'

'I remember.'

'It comes to me that you made a vow, too, in this very shrine.'

'So I did. I'll have to share your coin, Simon. I've nothing here to give.'

'Then we'll share,' he said. That was all; in that casual easy voice with no change in it; but I turned quickly to look up at him. The vivid grey eyes held mine for a moment, then I turned from him almost at random and picked up Nigel's little water-pot. 'We'll leave this here too, shall we?'

Something glinted, deep in the grass down beside the edge of the stone plinth. I smoothed the long stems aside and picked it up. It was another gold coin.

'Simon, look at this!'

'What is it? A talent? Don't tell me Apollo's provided a ram in the thicket for –' He stopped short as I held my hand out towards him.

I said: 'It's a sovereign. That means Nigel did find the gold as well as the statue. He must have left this here.'

'Must he?'

'Well, who else –?' Then I saw his face and stopped.

He nodded. 'Yes. Of course. Michael made an offering, too.'

He took it from me gently and laid it beside the water-pot, at the feet of the god.

The Moon-Spinners

For
KITTY and GERALD
RAINBOW

The author is indebted to Mr. A. E. Gunther
for permission to quote from his father's
edition of *The Greek Herbal of Dioscorides*.

Chapter 1

Lightly this little herald flew aloft . . .
Onward it flies . . .
Until it reach'd a splashing fountain's side
That, near a cavern's mouth, for ever pour'd
Unto the temperate air . . .

KEATS: *Endymion*

IT WAS THE egret, flying out of the lemon-grove, that started it. I won't pretend I saw it straight away as the conventional herald of adventure, the white stag of the fairy-tale, which, bounding from the enchanted thicket, entices the prince away from his followers, and loses him in the forest where danger threatens with the dusk. But, when the big white bird flew suddenly up among the glossy leaves and the lemon-flowers, and wheeled into the mountain, I followed it. What else is there to do when such a thing happens on a brilliant April noonday at the foot of the White Mountains of Crete; when the road is hot and dusty, but the gorge is green, and full of the sound of water, and the white wings, flying ahead, flicker in and out of deep shadow, and the air is full of the scent of lemon-blossom?

The car from Heraklion had set me down where the track for Agios Georgios leaves the road. I got out, adjusted on my shoulder the big bag of embroidered canvas that did duty as a haversack, then turned to thank the American couple for the lift.

'It was a pleasure, honey.' Mrs. Studebaker peered, rather anxiously, out of the car window. 'But are you sure you're all right? I don't like putting you down like this, in the middle of nowhere. You're sure this is the right place? What does that sign-post say?'

The sign-post, when consulted, said, helpfully, *ΑΓ ΓΕΩΡ-ΓΙΟΣ.* 'Well, what do you know?' said Mrs. Studebaker. 'Now, look, honey –'

'It's all right,' I said, laughing. 'That *is* "Agios Georgios", and, according to your driver–and the map–the village is about three-quarters of a mile away, down this track. Once round that bit of cliff down there, I'll probably be able to see it.'

'I surely hope so.' Mr. Studebaker had got out of the car when I did, and was now supervising the driver as he lifted my one small case from the boot, and set it beside me at the edge of the road. Mr. Studebaker was large and pink and sweet-tempered, and wore an orange shirt outside his pearl-grey drill trousers, and a wide, floppy linen hat. He thought Mrs. Studebaker the cleverest and most beautiful woman in the world, and said so; in consequence she, too, was sweet-tempered, besides being extremely smart. They were both lavish with that warm, extroverted, and slightly naïve kindliness which seems a specifically American virtue. I had made their acquaintance at my hotel only the evening before, and, as soon as they heard that I was making for the southern coast of Crete, nothing would content them but that I should join them for part of their hired tour of the island. Now, it seemed, nothing would please them better than for me to abandon my foolish project of visiting this village in the middle of nowhere, and go with them for the rest of their trip.

'I don't like it.' Mr. Studebaker was anxiously regarding the stony little track which wound gently downhill from the road, between rocky slopes studded with scrub and dwarf juniper. 'I don't like leaving you here alone. Why–' he turned earnest, kindly blue eyes on me– 'I read a book about Crete, just before Mother and I came over, and believe me, Miss Ferris, they have some customs here, still, that you just wouldn't credit. In some ways, according to this book, Greece is still a very, very primitive country.'

I laughed. 'Maybe. But one of the primitive customs is that the stranger's sacred. Even in Crete, nobody's going to murder a visitor! Don't worry about me, really. It's sweet of you, but I'll be quite all right. I told you, I've lived in Greece for more than a year now, and I get along quite well in Greek–and I've been to Crete before. So you can leave me quite safely. This is certainly the right place, and I'll be down in the village in twenty minutes. The hotel's not expecting me till tomorrow, but I know they've nobody else there, so I'll get a bed.'

'And this cousin of yours that should have come with you? You're sure she'll show up?'

'Of course.' He was looking so anxious that I explained again. 'She was delayed, and missed the flight, but she told me not to wait for her, and I left a message. Even if she misses tomorrow's bus, she'll get a car or something. She's very capable.' I smiled. 'She was anxious for me not to waste any of my holiday hanging around waiting for her, so she'll be as grateful to you as I am, for giving me an extra day.'

'Well, if you're sure . . .'

'I'm quite sure. Now, don't let me keep you any more. It was wonderful to get a lift this far. If I'd waited for the bus tomorrow, it would have taken the whole day to get here.' I smiled, and held out my hand. 'And still I'd have been dumped right here! So you see, you *have* given me a whole extra day's holiday, besides the run, which was marvellous. Thank you again.'

Eventually, reassured, they drove off. The car gathered way slowly up the cement-hard mud of the hill road, bumping and swaying over the ruts which marked the course of winter's overspills of mountain rain. It churned its way up round a steep bend, and bore away inland. The dust of its wake hung thickly, till the breeze slowly dispersed it.

I stood there beside my suitcase, and looked about me.

The White Mountains are a range of great peaks, the backbone of the westerly end of the mountainous island of Crete. To the south-west of the island, the foothills of the range run right down to the shore, which, here, is wild and craggy. Here and there along the coast, where some mountain stream, running down to the sea, has cut a fresh-water inlet in the ramparts of the cliff, are villages, little handfuls of houses each clinging to its crescent of shingle and its runnel of fresh water, backed by the wild mountains where the sheep and goats scratch a precarious living. Some of these villages are approached only by steep tracks through the maze of foothills, or by caique from the sea. It was in one of them, Agios Georgios, the village of St. George, that I had elected to spend the week of my Easter holiday.

As I had told the Studebakers, I had been in Athens since January of the previous year, working in a very junior capacity as a secretary at the British Embassy. I had counted myself lucky, at twenty-one, to land even a fairly humble job in a country which, as far back as I could remember, I had longed to visit. I had settled happily in Athens, worked hard at the language (being rewarded with a fair fluency), and I had used my holidays and week-ends in exploration of all the famous places within reach.

A month before this Easter holiday was due, I had been delighted
to hear from my cousin, Frances Scorby, that she planned to visit
Greece on a cruise she was making with friends that spring. Frances
is a good deal older than I am, being my parents' contemporary
rather than my own. When my mother's death, three years before,
had orphaned me (I had never known my father, who was killed in
the war), I went to live with Frances in Berkshire, where she is
part-owner of a rather famous rock-plant nursery. She also writes
and lectures on plants, and takes beautiful colour-photographs
which illustrate her books and talks. My ecstatic letters to her about
the Greek wildflowers had borne fruit. It seemed that friends of hers
were taking a small hired yacht from Brindisi to Piraeus, where they
intended to stay for a few days while they explored Athens and its
environs, after which they planned a leisurely sail through the
islands. Their arrival in Piraeus was to coincide with my own Easter
holiday, but (as I had written at some length to Frances) not even for
her would I spend my precious few days' holiday among the Easter
crowds, and the milling throng of tourists who had been pouring
into the city for weeks. I had suggested that she abandon her party
for a few days, and join me in Crete, where she could see the
countryside—and the legendary flowers of the White Mountains—in peace. We could join the yacht together, when it called at
Heraklion the following week, on its way to Rhodes and the
Sporades; then later, on the way home, she could stay off in Athens
with me, and see the 'sights' unencumbered by the Easter crowds.

Frances was enthusiastic, her hosts were agreeable, and it was left
to me to discover, if possible, some quiet place in south-west Crete
which combined the simple peace and beauty of 'the real Greece'
with some of the standards of comfort and cleanliness which the new
tourist age is forcing on it. An almost impossible mixture of
virtues—but I believed I had found it. A café-acquaintance in
Athens—a Danish writer of travel-books, who had spent some weeks
exploring the less frequented parts of the Greek archipelago—had
told me of a small, isolated village on the southern coast of Crete at
the foot of the White Mountains.

'If it's the real thing you want, an unspoiled village without even a
road leading to it—just a couple of dozen houses, a tiny church, and
the sea—Agios Georgios is your place,' he said. 'You'll want to swim,
I suppose? Well, I found a perfect place for that, rocks to dive off,
sandy bottom, the lot. And if you want the flowers, and the
views—well, you can walk in any direction you please, it's all

glorious, and as wild as anyone could wish. Oh, and Nicola, if you're interested, there's a tiny, deserted church about five miles eastward along the coast; the weeds are right up to the door, but you can still see the ghost of a rather quaint Byzantine mosaic on the ceiling, and I'll swear one of the door-jambs is a genuine Doric column.'

'Too good to be true,' I had said. 'All right, I'll buy it, what are the snags? Where do we have to sleep? Over the taverna, with the genuine Doric bugs?'

But no. This, it appeared, was the whole point. All the other attractions of Agios Georgios could be found in a score of similar villages, in Crete or elsewhere. But Agios Georgios had a hotel.

This had, in fact, been the village *kafenéion*, or coffee-shop, with a couple of rooms over the bar. But this, with the adjoining cottage, had been recently bought by a new owner, who was making them the nucleus of what promised to be a comfortable little hotel.

'He's only just started; in fact, I was their first guest,' said my informant. 'I understand that the authorities are planning to build a road down to the village some time soon, and meanwhile Alexiakis, the chap who bought the taverna, is going ahead with his plans. The accommodation's very simple, but it's perfectly clean, and – wait for it – the food is excellent.'

I looked at him in some awe. Outside the better hotels and the more expensive restaurants, food in Greece – even the voice of love has to confess it – is seldom excellent. It tends to a certain monotony, and it knows no variation of hot and cold; all is lukewarm. Yet here was a Dane, a well-rounded, well-found Dane (and the Danes have possibly the best food in Europe), recommending the food in a Greek village taverna.

He laughed at my look, and explained the mystery. 'It's quite simple. The man's a Soho Greek, originally a native of Agios Georgios, who emigrated to London twenty years ago, made his pile as a restaurateur, and has now come back, as these folk do, and wants to settle at home. But he's determined to put Agios Georgios on the map, so he's started by buying up the taverna, and he's imported a friend of his from his London restaurant to help him. They've not seriously started up yet, beyond tidying up the two existing bedrooms, turning a third into a bathroom, and cooking for their own satisfaction. But they'll take you, Nicola, I'm sure of that. Why not try? They've even got a telephone.'

I had telephoned next day. The proprietor had been surprised, but pleased. The hotel was not yet officially opened, he told me; they were still building and painting, I must understand, and there were no other guests there; it was very simple and quiet . . . But, once assured that this was exactly what we wanted, he had seemed pleased to welcome us.

Our plans, however, had not worked out quite smoothly. Frances and I were to have taken Monday evening's flight to Crete, stayed the night in Heraklion, and gone to Agios Georgios next day, by the bi-weekly bus. But on Sunday she had telephoned from Patras, where her friends' boat had been delayed, and had begged me not to waste any of my precious week's holiday waiting for her, but to set off myself for Crete, leaving her to find her own way there as soon as possible. Since Frances was more than capable of finding her way anywhere, with the least possible help from me, I had agreed, swallowed my disappointment, and managed to get straight on to Sunday evening's flight, intending to have an extra day in Heraklion, and take Tuesday's bus as planned. But chance, in the shape of the Studebakers, had offered me a lift on Monday morning, straight to the south-west corner of Crete. So here I was, with a day in hand, set down in the middle of a landscape as savage and deserted as the most determined solitary could have wished for.

Behind me, inland, the land rose sharply, the rocky foothills soaring silver-green, silver-tawny, silver-violet, gashed by ravines, and moving with the scudding shadows of high cirrus which seemed to smoke down from the ghostly ridges beyond. Below the road, towards the sea, the land was greener. The track to Agios Georgios wound its way between high banks of maquis, the scented maquis of Greece. I could smell verbena, and lavender, and a kind of sage. Over the hot white rock and the deep green of the maquis, the judas-trees lifted their clouds of scented flowers the colour of purple daphne, their branches reaching landwards, away from the African winds. In a distant cleft of the land, seemingly far below me, I saw the quick, bright gleam that meant the sea.

Silence. No sound of bird; no bell of sheep. Only the drone of a bee over the blue sage at the road-side. No sign of man's hand anywhere in the world, except the road where I stood, the track before me, and a white vapour-trail, high in the brilliant sky.

I picked my case up from among the dusty salvias, and started down the track.

A breeze was blowing off the sea, and the track led downhill, so I went at a fair speed; nevertheless it was fully fifteen minutes before I reached the bluff which hid the lower part of the track from the road, and saw, a couple of hundred yards further on, the first evidence of man's presence here.

This was a bridge, a small affair with a rough stone parapet, which led the track over a narrow river—the water-supply, I supposed, on which Agios Georgios lived. From here the village was still invisible, though I guessed it could not be far, as the sides of the valley had opened out to show a wide segment of sea, which flashed and glittered beyond the next curve of the track.

I paused on the bridge, set down my case and shoulder-bag, then sat down on the parapet in the shade of a sycamore tree, swinging my legs, and staring thoughtfully down the track towards the village. The sea was—as far as I could judge—still about half a mile away. Below the bridge the river ran smoothly down, pool to pool dropping through glittering shallows, between shrubby banks lit by the judas-trees. Apart from these the valley was treeless, its rocky slopes seeming to trap the heat of the day.

Midday. Not a leaf stirring. No sound, except the cool noise of the water, and the sudden *plop* of a frog diving in the pool under the bridge.

I looked the other way, up-stream, where a path wound along the water-side under willows. Then I slid to my feet, carried my case down below the bridge, and pushed it carefully out of sight, into a thicket of brambles and rock-roses. My canvas bag, containing my lunch, fruit, and a flask of coffee, I swung back on to my shoulder. The hotel was not expecting me; very well, there was no reason why I should not, in fact, take the whole day 'out'; I could find a cool place by the water, eat my meal, and have my fill of the mountain silence and solitude before going down later to the village.

I started up the shady path along the river.

The path soon began to rise, gently at first, and then fairly steeply, with the river beside it rockier, and full of rapids which grew louder as the valley narrowed into a small gorge, and the path to a roughly-trodden way above a green rush of water, where no sun came. Trees closed in overhead; ferns dripped; my steps echoed on the rock. But, for all its apparent seclusion, the little gorge must be a highway for men and beasts: the path was beaten flat with footprints, and there was ample evidence that mules, donkeys, and sheep came this way daily.

In a few moments I saw why. I came up a steepish ramp through thinning pines, and emerged at once from the shade of the gorge, on to an open plateau perhaps half a mile in width, and two or three hundred yards deep, like a wide ledge on the mountain-side.

Here were the fields belonging to the people of Agios Georgios. The plateau was sheltered on three sides by the trees: southwards, towards the sea, the land fell away in shelving rock, and slopes of huge, tumbled boulders. Behind the fertile ground, to the north, soared the mountain-side, silver-tawny in the brilliant light, clouded here and there with olives, and gashed by ravines where trees grew. From the biggest of these ravines flowed the river, to push its way forward across the plateau in a wide meander. Not an inch of the flat land but was dug, hoed and harrowed. Between the vegetable fields were rows of fruit trees: I saw locust-trees, and apricots, as well as the ubiquitous olives, and the lemon-trees. The fields were separated from one another by narrow ditches, or by shallow, stony banks where, haphazard, grew poppies, fennel, parsley, and a hundred herbs which would all be gathered, I knew, for use. Here and there, at the outlying edges of the plateau, the gay little Cretan windmills whirled their white canvas sails, spilling the water into the ditches that threaded the dry soil.

There was nobody about. I passed the last windmill, climbed through the vine-rows that terraced the rising ground, and paused in the shade of a lemon-tree.

Here I hesitated, half inclined to stop. There was a cool breeze from the sea, the lemon-blossom smelt wonderful, the view was glorious—but at my feet flies buzzed over mule-droppings in the dust, and a scarlet cigarette-packet, soggy and disintegrating, lay caught in weeds at the water's edge. Even the fact that the legend on it was *EΘNOΣ*, and not the homely *Woodbine* or *Player's Weights*, didn't make it anything but a nasty piece of wreckage capable of spoiling a square mile of countryside.

I looked the other way, towards the mountains.

The White Mountains of Crete really are white. Even when, in high summer, the snow is gone, their upper ridges are still silver—bare, grey rock, glinting in the sun, showing paler, less substantial, than the deep-blue sky behind them; so that one can well believe that among those remote and floating peaks the king of the gods was born. For Zeus, they said, was born in Dicte, a cave of the White Mountains. They showed you the very place . . .

At that moment, on the thought, the big white bird flew, with slow, unstartled beat of wings, out of the glossy leaves beside me, and sailed over my head. It was a bird I had never seen before, like a small heron, milk-white, with a long black bill. It flew as a heron does, neck tucked back and legs trailing, with a down-curved, powerful wing-beat. An egret? I shaded my eyes to watch it. It soared up into the sun, then turned and flew back over the lemon-grove, and on up the ravine, to be lost to view among the trees.

I am still not quite sure what happened at that moment.

For some reason that I cannot analyse, the sight of the big white bird, strange to me; the smell of the lemon-flowers, the clicking of the mill-sails and the sound of spilling water; the sunlight dappling through the leaves on the white anemones with their lamp-black centres; and, above all, my first real sight of the legendary White Mountains . . . all this seemed to rush together into a point of powerful magic, happiness striking like an arrow, with one of those sudden shocks of joy that are so physical, so precisely marked, that one knows the exact moment at which the world changed. I remembered what I had said to the Americans, that they, by bringing me here, had given me a day. Now I saw that, literally, they had. And it seemed no longer to be chance. Inevitably, here I was, alone under the lemon-trees, with a path ahead of me, food in my bag, a day dropped out of time for me, and a white bird flying ahead.

I gave a last look behind me at the wedge of shimmering sea, then turned my face to the north-east, and walked rapidly through the trees, towards the ravine that twisted up into the flank of the mountain.

Chapter 2

When as she *gazed into the watery glass*
And through her *brown hair's curly tangles scanned*
Her *own wan face, a shadow seemed to pass*
Across the mirror . . .

WILDE: *Charmides*

IT WAS HUNGER, in the end, that stopped me. Whatever the impulse that had compelled me to this lonely walk, it had driven me up the track at a fair speed, and I had gone some distance before, once again, I began to think about a meal.

The way grew steeper as the gorge widened, the trees thinned, and sunlight came in. Now the path was a ribbon along the face of a cliff, with the water below. The other side of the ravine lay back from it, a slope of rock and scrub studded here and there with trees, but open to the sun. The path was climbing steeply, now, towards the lip of the cliff. It did not seem to be much used; here and there bushes hung across it, and once I stopped to gather a trail of lilac orchids which lay, unbruised, right at my feet. But on the whole I managed to resist the flowers, which grew in every cranny of the rock. I was hungry, and I wanted nothing more than to find a level place in the sun, beside water, where I could stop and eat my belated meal.

Ahead of me, now, from the rocks on the right, I could hear water, a rush of it, nearer and louder than the river below. It sounded like a side-stream tumbling from the upper rocks, to join the main water-course beneath.

I came to a corner, and saw it. Here the wall of the gorge was broken, as a small stream came in from above. It fell in an arrowy rush right across the path, where it swirled round the single stepping-stone, to tumble once again, headlong, towards the river. I didn't cross it. I left the path, and clambered, not without difficulty, up the boulders that edged the tributary stream, towards the sunlight of the open ground at the edge of the ravine.

In a few minutes I had found what I was looking for. I climbed a tumble of white stones where poppies grew, and came out on a small, stony alp, a level field of asphodel, all but surrounded by towering rocks. Southwards, it was open, with a dizzying view down towards the now distant sea.

For the rest, I saw only the asphodel, the green of ferns by the water, a tree or so near the cliffs, and, in a cleft of a tall rock, the spring itself, where water splashed out among the green, to lie in a quiet pool open to the sun, before pouring away through the poppies at the lip of the gorge.

I swung the bag off my shoulder, and dropped it among the flowers. I knelt at the edge of the pool, and put my hands and wrists into the water. The sun was hot on my back. The moment of joy had slackened, blurred, and spread itself into a vast physical contentment.

I stooped to drink. The water was ice-cold, pure and hard; the wine of Greece, so precious that, time out of mind, each spring has been guarded by its own deity, the naiad of the stream. No doubt she watched it still, from behind the hanging ferns . . . The odd thing was—I found myself giving a half-glance over my shoulder at these same ferns—that one actually did feel as if one were being watched. Numinous country indeed, where, stooping over a pool, one could feel the eyes on one's back . . .

I smiled at the myth-bred fancies, and bent to drink again.

Deep in the pool, deeper than my own reflection, something pale wavered among the green. A face.

It was so much a part of my thoughts that, for one dreaming moment, I took no notice. Then, with that classic afterthought that is known as the 'double-take', reality caught up with the myth; I stiffened, and looked again.

I had been right. Behind my mirrored shoulder a face swam, watching me from the green depths. But it wasn't the guardian of the spring. It was human, and male, and it was the reflection of someone's head, watching me from above. Someone, a man, was peering down at me from the edge of the rocks high above the spring.

After the first startled moment, I wasn't particularly alarmed. The solitary stranger has, in Greece, no need to fear the chance-met prowler. This was some shepherd-lad, doubtless, curious at the sight of what must obviously be a foreigner. He would probably, unless he was shy, come down to talk to me.

I drank again, then rinsed my hands and wrists. As I dried them on a handkerchief, I saw the face there still, quivering in the disturbed water.

I turned and looked up. Nothing. The head had vanished.

I waited, amused, watching the top of the rock. The head appeared again, stealthily . . . so stealthily that, in spite of my common sense, in spite of what I knew about Greece and the Greeks, a tiny tingle of uneasiness crept up my spine. This was more than shyness: there was something furtive about the way the head inched up from behind the rock. And something more than furtive in the way, when he saw that I was watching, the man ducked back again.

For it was a man, no shepherd boy. A Greek, certainly; it was a dark face, mahogany-tanned, square and tough-looking, with dark eyes, and that black pelt of hair, thick and close as a ram's fleece, which is one of the chief beauties of the Greek men.

Only a glimpse I had, then he was gone. I stared at the place where the head had vanished, troubled now. Then, as if he could still be watching me, which was unlikely, I got to my feet with somewhat elaborate unconcern, picked up my bag, and turned to go. I no longer wanted to settle here, to be spied on, and perhaps approached, by this dubious stranger.

Then I saw the shepherds' hut.

There was a path which I hadn't noticed before, a narrow sheep-trod which had beaten a way through the asphodel towards a corner under the rocks, where a hut stood, backed against the cliff.

It was a small, un-windowed penthouse, of the kind that is commonly built in Greece, in remote places, to house the boys and men whose job it is to herd the goats and sheep on the bare hillsides. Sometimes they are used as milking-places for the sheep, and cheeses are made there on the spot. Sometimes, in stormy weather, they serve to house the beasts themselves.

The hut was small and low, roughly built of unshaped stones, the spaces packed with clay. It was roofed with brushwood and dried scrub, and would hardly be seen at all from any sort of distance, among the stones and scrub that surrounded it.

This, then, was the explanation of the watcher of the spring. The man would be a shepherd, his flock, doubtless, feeding on some

other mountain-meadow above the rocks where he lay. He had
heard me, and had come down to see who it was.

My momentary uneasiness subsided. Feeling a fool, I paused
there among the asphodel, half minded, after all, to stay.

It was well after noon now, and the sun was turning over to the
south-west, full on the little alp. The first warning I had was when a
shadow dropped across the flowers, as sudden as a black cloth falling
to stifle me.

I looked up, with a gasp of fright. From the rocks beside the
spring came a rattle of pebbles, the scrape of a foot, and the Greek
dropped neatly into my path.

There was one startled moment in which everything seemed very
clear and still. I thought, but not believing it: the impossible really
has happened; this is danger. I saw his dark eyes, angry and wary at
the same time. His hand—more incredible still—grasped a naked
knife.

Impossible to remember my Greek, to cry, 'Who are you? What
do you want?' Impossible to run from him, down the break-neck
mountain. Impossible to summon help from the vast, empty silence.

But of course, I tried it. I screamed, and turned to run.

It was probably the silliest thing I could have done. He jumped at
me. He caught me, pulled me against him, and held me. His free
hand covered my mouth. He was saying something half under his
breath, curses or threats that, in my panic, I didn't understand. I
struggled and fought, as if in a nightmare. I believe I kicked him,
and my nails drew blood on his wrists. There was a clatter of kicked
stones, and a jingling as he dropped the knife. I got my mouth free
for a moment, and screamed again. It was little more than a shrill
gasp this time, barely audible. But in any case, there was nobody to
help.

Impossibly, help came.

From behind me, from the empty mountain-side, a man's voice
called out, sharply, in Greek. I didn't hear what he said, but the
effect on my attacker was immediate. He froze where he stood. But
he still held me, and his hand clamped tightly again over my mouth.

He turned his head and called, in a low, urgent voice: 'It's a girl, a
foreigner. Spying around. I think she is English.'

I could hear no movement behind me of anyone approaching. I
strained round against the Greek's hand to see who had saved me,
but he held me tightly, with a low, 'Keep still, and hold your noise!'

The voice came again, apparently from some way off. 'A girl?

English?' A curious pause. 'For pity's sake, leave her alone, and bring her here. Are you mad?'

The Greek hesitated, then said sullenly to me, in strongly accented but reasonably good English: 'Come with me. And do not squeak again. If you make one other sound, I will kill you. Be sure of that. I do not like women, me.'

I managed to nod. He took his hand from my mouth then, and relaxed his hold. But he didn't let go. He merely shifted his grip, keeping hold of my wrist.

He stooped to pick up his knife, and motioned towards the rocks behind us. I turned. There was no one to be seen.

'Inside,' said the Greek, and jerked his head towards the shepherds' hut.

* * *

The hut was filthy. As the Greek pushed me in front of him across the trodden dust, the flies rose, buzzing, round our feet. The doorway gaped black and uninviting.

At first I could see nothing. By contrast with the bright light at my back, the interior of the hut seemed quite dark, but then the Greek pushed me further in, and in the flood of light from the doorway, I could see quite clearly even into the furthest corners of the hut.

A man was lying in the far corner, away from the door. He lay on a rough bed of some vegetation, that could have been ferns or dried shrubs. Apart from this, the hut was empty; there was no furniture at all, except some crude-looking lengths of wood in another corner that may have been parts of a primitive cheese-press. The floor was of beaten earth, so thin in places that the rock showed through. What dung the sheep had left was dried, and inoffensive enough, but the place smelt of sickness.

As the Greek pushed me inside, the man on the bed raised his head, his eyes narrowed against the light.

The movement, slight as it was, seemed an effort. He was ill; very ill; it didn't need the roughly swathed cloths, stiff with dried blood, on his left arm and shoulder, to tell me that. His face, under the two-days' growth of beard, was pale, and hollowed under the cheekbones, while the skin round his eyes, with their suspiciously bright glitter, looked bruised with pain and fever. There was a nasty-looking mark on his forehead, where the skin had been scraped raw, and had bled. The hair above it was still matted with the blood, and filthy with dust from the stuff he was lying on.

For the rest, he was young, dark-haired and blue-eyed like a great many Cretans, and would, when washed, shaved, and healthy, be a reasonably personable man, with an aggressive-looking nose and mouth, square, capable hands, and (as I guessed), a fair amount of physical strength. He had on dark-grey trousers, and a shirt that had once been white, both garments now filthy and torn. The only bed-covering was an equally battered windcheater jacket, and an ancient khaki affair which, presumably, belonged to the man who had attacked me. This, the sick man clutched to him as though he was cold.

He narrowed those bright eyes at me, and seemed, with some sort of an effort, to collect his wits.

'I hope Lambis didn't hurt you? You . . . screamed?'

I realized then why he had seemed to be speaking from some distance away. His voice, though steady enough, was held so by a palpable effort, and it was weak. He gave the impression of holding on, precariously, to every ounce of strength he had, and, in so doing, spending it. He spoke in English, and such was my own shaken condition that I thought at first, merely, what good English he speaks; and only afterwards, with a kind of shock, he *is* English.

Of course that was the first thing I said. I was still only just taking in the details of his appearance; the bloody evidence of a wound, the sunken cheeks, the filthy bed. 'You're—you're English!' I said stupidly, staring. I was hardly conscious that the Greek, Lambis, had dropped his hand from my arm. Automatically, I began to rub the place where he had gripped me. Later, there would be a bruise.

I faltered: 'But you're hurt! Has there been an accident? What happened?'

Lambis pushed past me, to stand over the bed, rather like a dog defending a bone. He still had that wary look; no longer dangerous, perhaps, but he was fingering the knife. Before the sick man could speak, he said, quickly and defensively: 'It is nothing. An accident in climbing. When he has rested I shall help him down to the village. There is no need—'

'Shut up, will you?' The sick man snapped it, in Greek. 'And put the knife away. You've scared her silly as it is, poor kid. Can't you see she's nothing to do with this business? You should have kept out of sight, and let her go past.'

'She'd seen me. And she was coming this way. She'd have come in here, as likely as not, and seen you . . . She'll blab all over the village.'

'Well, you've made sure of that, haven't you? Now keep quiet, and leave this to me.'

Lambis shot him a look, half defiant, half shamefaced. He dropped his hand from the knife, but he stayed beside the bed.

The exchange between the two men, which had been in Greek, had the effect of reassuring me completely, even if the discovery of the sick man's nationality hadn't already (absurdly enough) begun to do so. But I didn't show it. At some purely instinctive level, it seemed, I had made a decision for my own protection—which was that there was no positive need for me to betray my own knowledge of Greek . . . Whatever I had stumbled into, I would prefer to stumble out of again as quickly as possible, and it seemed that the less I knew about 'this business', whatever it was, the more likely they were to let me go peaceably on my way.

'I'm sorry.' The Englishman's eyes turned back to me. 'Lambis shouldn't have frightened you like that. I—we've had an accident, as he told you, and he's a bit shaken up. Your arm . . . did he hurt you?'

'Not really, it's all right . . . But what about you? Are you badly hurt?' It would be a very odd sort of accident, I thought, that would lead a man to attack a stranger as Lambis had attacked me, but it seemed only natural to show some sort of curiosity and concern. 'What happened?'

'I was caught by a fall of stone. Lambis thought it was someone further up the hill who set it away, in carelessness. He swore he heard women's voices. We shouted, but nobody came.'

'I see.' I had also seen Lambis' quick glance of surprise, before the sullen brown eyes went back to the ground. It wasn't a bad lie on the spur of the moment, from a man who plainly wasn't as clear in the head as he would have liked to be. 'Well,' I said, 'it wasn't me. I've only just arrived at Agios Georgios today, and I haven't—'

'Agios Georgios?' The glitter this time wasn't only put there by fever. 'You've walked up from there?'

'From the bridge, yes.'

'Is there a track all the way?'

'Not really, I suppose. I followed it up the ravine, but left it where this spring comes in. I—'

'The track comes straight here? To the hut?' This was Lambis, his voice sharp.

'No,' I said. 'I told you I left the path. But in any case the place is seamed with paths—sheep-tracks. Once you get some way up the ravine, they branch all over the place. I stayed by the water.'

'Then it is not the only way down to the village?'

'I don't know; I'd say almost certainly not. Though it may be the easiest, if you're thinking of going down. I wasn't taking much notice.' I opened my hand, where I still held some crushed shreds of the lilac orchids. 'I was looking at the flowers.'

'Did you . . . ?' It was the Englishman this time. He stopped, and waited a moment. I saw he was shivering; he waited with clenched teeth for the fit to pass. He was clutching the khaki jacket to him as if he was cold, but I saw sweat on his face. 'Did you meet anyone, on your . . . walk?'

'No.'

'No one at all?'

'Not a soul.'

A pause. He shut his eyes, but almost immediately opened them again. 'Is it far?'

'To the village? Quite a long way, I suppose. It's hard to tell how far, when you're climbing. Which way did you come yourself?'

'Not that way.' The phrase was a full stop. But even through his fever he seemed to feel its rudeness, for he added: 'We came from the road. Further east.'

'But—' I began, then paused. This was perhaps not the moment to tell them that I was quite well aware that there was no road from the east. The only road came in from the west, and then turned northwards over a pass which led it back inland. This spur of the White Mountains was served only by its tracks.

I saw the Greek watching me, and added, quickly: 'I started at about midday, but it wouldn't take so long going back, of course, downhill.'

The man on the bed shifted irritably, as if his arm hurt him. 'The village . . . Where are you staying?'

'The hotel. There's only one; the village is very small. But I haven't been there yet. I only arrived at noon; I got a lift out from Heraklion, and I'm not expected, so I—I came up here for a walk, just on impulse. It was so lovely—'

I stopped. He had shut his eyes. The gesture excluded me, but it

wasn't this that stopped me in mid-sentence. It was the sharp
impression that he had not so much shut me out, as shut himself in,
with something that went intolerably far beyond whatever pain he
was feeling.

I got my second impulse of the day. Frances had often told me
that one day my impulses would land me in serious trouble. Well,
people like to be proved right sometimes.

I turned sharply, threw the crushed and wilted orchids into the
sunlight, and went across to the bed. Lambis moved as swiftly,
thrusting out an arm to stop me, but when I pushed it aside he gave
way. I dropped on one knee beside the wounded man.

'Look –' I spoke crisply –'you've been hurt, and you're ill. That's
plain enough. Now, I've no desire to push my way into what doesn't
concern me; it's obvious you don't want questions asked, and you
needn't tell me a single thing; I don't want to know. But you're sick,
and if you ask me, Lambis is making a rotten job of looking after
you, and if you don't watch your step, you're going to be very
seriously ill indeed, if not downright dead. For one thing, that
bandage is dirty, and for another –'

'It's all right.' He was speaking, still with closed eyes, to the wall.
'Don't worry about me. I've just got a touch of fever . . . be all right
soon. You just . . . keep out of it, that's all. Lambis should never
have . . . oh well, never mind. But don't worry about me. Get down
now to your hotel and forget this . . . please.' He turned then, and
peered at me as if painfully, against the light. 'For your own sake. I
mean it.' His good hand moved, and I put mine down to meet it. His
fingers closed over mine: the skin felt dry and hot, and curiously
dead. 'But if you do see anyone on your way down . . . or in the
village, who –'

Lambis said roughly, in Greek: 'She says she has not been to the
village yet; she has seen no one. What's the use of asking? Let her go,
and pray she does keep quiet. Women all have tongues like magpies.
Say no more.'

The Englishman hardly seemed to hear him. I thought that the
Greek words hadn't penetrated. His eyes never left me, but his
mouth had slackened, and he breathed as if he were all at once
exhausted beyond control. But the hot fingers held on to mine.
'They may have gone towards the village –' the thick mutter was still
in English –'and if you're going that way –'

'Mark!' Lambis moved forward, crowding me aside. 'You're
losing your mind! Hold your tongue and tell her to go! You want

sleep.' He added in Greek: 'I'll go and look for him myself, as soon as I can, I promise you. He's probably back at the caique; you torture yourself for nothing.' Then to me, angrily: 'Can't you see he's fainting?'

'All right,' I said. 'But don't shout at me like that. I'm not the one that's killing him.' I tucked the now unresponsive hand back under the coat, and stood up to face the Greek. 'I told you I'm asking no questions, but I am not going away from here and leaving him like this. When did this happen?'

'The day before last,' sullenly.

'He's been here two nights?' I said, horrified.

'Not in here. The first night, he was out on the mountain.' He added, as if defying me to go further: 'Before I find him and bring him here.'

'I see. And you've not tried to get help? All right, don't look like that, I've managed to gather that you're in some sort of trouble. Well, I'll keep quiet about it, I promise you. Do you think I *want* to get mixed up in whatever skulduggery you're up to?'

'*Oriste?*'

'Whatever trouble you're in,' I translated impatiently. 'It's nothing to me. But I told you. I don't intend to walk away and leave him like that. Unless you do something about him—what was his name? Mark?'

'Yes.'

'Well, unless something's done about your Mark, here and now, he will die, and that will be something more to worry about. Have you any food?'

'A little. I had bread, and some cheese—'

'And fine stuff it looks, too.' There was a polythene mug lying in the dirt beside the bed. It had held wine, and there were flies on the rim. I picked it up.

'Go and wash this. Bring my bag, and my cardigan. They're where I dropped them when you jumped on me with your beastly knife. There's food there. It's not sickroom stuff, but there's plenty of it, and it's clean. Oh, look, wait a moment, there's a cooking-pot of a sort over there—I suppose the shepherds use it. We ought to have hot water. If you fill it, I can get some wood and stuff together, and we'll get a fire going—'

'No!' Both men spoke together. Mark's eyes had flown open on the word, and I saw a look flash between them which was, for all Mark's weakness, as electric as a spark jumping across points.

I looked from one to the other in silence. 'As bad as that?' I said at length, 'Skulduggery was the word, then. Fallen stones, what nonsense.' I turned to Lambis. 'What was it, a knife?'

'A bullet,' he said, not without a certain relish.

'A *bullet*?'

'Yes.'

'Oh.'

'So you see,' said Lambis, his surliness giving way to a purely human satisfaction, 'you should have kept away. And when you go, you will say nothing. There is danger, great danger. Where there has been one bullet, there can be another. And if you speak a word in the village of what you have seen today, I shall kill you myself.'

'Yes, all right.' I spoke impatiently; I was scarcely listening. The look in Mark's face was frightening me to death. 'But get my bag first, will you? And here, wash this, *and* make sure it's clean.'

I thrust the mug at him, and he took it, like a man in a dream.

'And hurry up!' I added. He looked from me to the mug, to Mark, to the mug again, then left the hut without a word.

'Greek,' said Mark faintly from his corner, 'meets Greek.' There was the faintest definable gleam of amusement in his face, under the pain and exhaustion. 'You're quite a girl, aren't you? What's your name?'

'Nicola Ferris. I thought you'd fainted again.'

'No. I'm pretty tough, you don't have to worry. Have you really got some food?'

'Yes. Look, is the bullet out? Because if it's not—'

'It is. It's only a flesh wound. And clean. Really.'

'If you're sure—' I said doubtfully. 'Not that I'd know a darned thing about bullet-wounds, so if we can't have hot water, I'd better take your word for it, and leave it alone. But you've a temperature, any fool could see that.'

'Out all night, that's why. Lost a bit of blood . . . and it rained. Be all right soon . . . in a day or two.' Suddenly he moved his head, a movement of the most violent and helpless impatience. I saw the muscles of his face twist, but not—I thought—with pain.

I said feebly: 'Try not to worry, whatever it is. If you can eat something now, you'll be out of here all the sooner, and believe it or not, I've got a flask of hot coffee. Here's Lambis coming now.'

Lambis had brought all my things, and the newly rinsed mug. I took the cardigan from him, and knelt by the bed again.

'Put this round you.' Mark made no protest when I took the rough jacket away, and tucked the warm, soft folds of wool round his shoulders. I spread the jacket over his legs. 'Lambis, there's a flask in the bag. Pour him some coffee, will you? Thanks. Now, can you lift up a bit? Drink this down.'

His teeth chattered against the edge of the mug, and I had to watch to make sure he didn't scald his mouth, so eagerly did he gulp at the hot stuff. I could almost imagine I felt it running, warming and vital, into his body. When he had drunk half of it he stopped, gasping a little, and the shivering seemed to be less.

'Now, try to eat. That's too thick, Lambis; can you shred the meat up a bit? Break the crust off. Come on, now, can you manage this. . .?'

Bit by bit he got the food down. He seemed at once ravenously hungry, and reluctant to make the effort to eat. From the former fact I deduced thankfully that he was not yet seriously ill, but that, if he could be got to care and help, he would recover fairly quickly. Lambis stood over us, as if to make sure I didn't slip poison into the coffee.

When Mark had eaten all that could be forced into him, and drunk two mugs of coffee, I helped him lower himself back into the bedding, and tucked the inadequate covers round him once more.

'Now, go to sleep. Try to relax. If you could sleep, you'd be better in no time.'

He seemed drowsy, but I could see him summoning the effort to speak. 'Nicola.'

'What is it?'

'Lambis told the truth. It's dangerous. I can't explain. But keep out of it . . . don't want you thinking there's anything you can do. Sweet of you, but . . . there's nothing. Nothing at all. You're not to get mixed up with us . . . Can't allow it.'

'If I only understood –'

'I don't understand myself. But . . . my affair. Don't add to it. Please.'

'All right. I'll keep out. If there's really nothing I can do –'

'Nothing. You've done plenty.' An attempt at a smile. 'That coffee saved my life, I'm sure of that. Now go down to the village, and forget us, will you? Not a word to anyone. I mean that. It's vital. I have to trust you.'

'You can.'

'Good girl.' Suddenly I realized what his dishevelment and sickness had disguised before; he was very young, not much older, I thought, than myself. Twenty-two? Twenty-three? The drawn look and painfully tightened mouth had hidden the fact of his youth. It was, oddly enough, as he tried to speak with crisp authority that his youth showed through, like flesh through a gap in armour.

He lay back. 'You'd . . . better be on your way. Thanks again. I'm sorry you got such a fright . . . Lambis, see her down the hill . . . as far as you can . . .'

As far as you dare . . . Nobody had said it, but he might just as well have shouted it aloud. Suddenly, out of nowhere, fear jumped at me again, like a shadow dropping across the flowers. I said breathlessly: 'I don't need a guide. I'll follow the water. Good-bye.'

'Lambis will see you down.' The edged whisper was still surprisingly authoritative, and Lambis picked up my bag and moved towards me, saying flatly: 'I will go with you. We go now.'

Mark said 'Good-bye,' in a voice whose dying fall made it utterly final. I looked back from the doorway, to see that he had shut his eyes and turned away, pulling my cardigan close with a small nestling movement. Either he had forgotten about it, or he valued its comfort too highly to have any intention of returning it.

Something about the movement, about the way he turned his cheek into the white softness, caught at me. He seemed all at once younger even than his years; younger by far than I.

I turned abruptly and left the hut, with Lambis close behind me.

Chapter 3

*When the sun sets, shadows, that showed at noon
But small, appear most long and terrible.*
NATHANIEL LEE: *Oedipus*

'I WILL GO first,' said Lambis.

He shouldered past me without ceremony, then led the way through the flowers towards the spring. I noticed how his head turned from side to side as he walked; he went warily, like a nocturnal beast forced to move in daylight. It was not a comforting impression.

Here was the naiad's pool, and, not far from it, the trail of orchids I had dropped. A few steps further, and we were out of sight of the hut.

'Lambis,' I said, 'one moment.'

He turned, reluctantly.

'I want to talk to you.' I spoke softly, though we could certainly not be heard from the hut. 'Also –' this hurriedly, at his movement of protest – 'I'm hungry, and if I don't eat *something* before I set off for Agios Georgios, I shall die in my tracks. You could probably do with a sandwich yourself, if it comes to that?'

'I am okay.'

'Well, I'm not.' I said firmly. 'Let me see that bag. There's tons of stuff here, he's eaten very little. I left the coffee for him, and you'd better keep the oranges and the chocolate, and some of the meat. There: we'll leave those. Surely you can help me eat the rest?'

I thought he hesitated, eyeing the food. I added: 'I'm going to, anyway. You really needn't see me any further, you know. I'll be quite all right on my own.'

He jerked his head sideways. 'We cannot stay here, it is too open. There is a place above, where we can see, and not be seen. You can see the hut from there, and the way up to it. This way.'

He slung my bag over his shoulder, turned aside from the pool, and began to clamber up through the rocks, towards the place where I had first caught sight of him. I saw him pause once, glancing about him with that tense, wary look, and his free hand crept, in the gesture I was beginning to know, towards the hilt of his knife. He was coatless, and the wooden hilt, worn smooth with much handling, stuck piratically up from the leather sheath in his trouser-belt.

He jerked his head again. 'Come.'

I hesitated, then looked determinedly away from that polished knife-hilt, and followed him up the dizzy goat-track that led past the spring.

The place he chose was a wide ledge, some way above the little alp where the hut stood. As a hiding-place and watchtower combined, it could hardly have been bettered. The ledge was about ten feet wide, sloping a little upwards, out from the cliff face, so that from below we were invisible. An overhang hid us from above, and gave shelter from the weather. Behind, in the cliff, a vertical cleft offered deeper shelter, and a possible hiding-place. A juniper grew half across this cleft, and the ledge itself was deep with the sweet aromatic shrubs that clothed the hillside. The way up to it was concealed by a tangling bank of honeysuckle, and the spread silver boughs of a wild fig-tree.

I found myself a place at the back of the ledge, and sat down. Lambis stretched himself full-length near the edge, his eyes watchful on the rocky stretches below us. From this height I could see a wide reach of the sea. Its bright leagues of water hurt the eyes. It seemed a long way off.

We shared what food there was. Lambis abandoned all pretence, and ate ravenously. He didn't look at me, but lay, propped on one elbow, never taking his eyes off the mountain-side below us. I kept silent, watching him, and when at length I saw him give a sigh, and reach into a pocket for a cigarette, I spoke, gently.

'Lambis. Who shot Mark?'

He jumped, and turned his head sharply. The ready scowl came down.

'Not that I care,' I added, mildly, 'but you've made it obvious that you expect them, whoever they are, to have another bash at him so you're both in hiding. That's all very well, but you can't stay that way indefinitely . . . I mean, for ever. And you ought to have the sense to see it.'

'Do you think I do not know this?'

'Well, when do you plan to go—if not for help, then for supplies?'

'Is it not obvious that I cannot leave him—?'

'It's obvious he can't be moved, and he ought not to be left, but the way things look now, if someone doesn't get help very soon, he'll get worse. Let's face it, he may even die. If not of the wound, then of exposure. You told me he'd had a night in the open. People die of that—shock, pneumonia, goodness knows what, didn't you know?'

No answer. He was lighting his cigarette, and he didn't look at me, but at least he was making no move to leave me, or hurry me on my way.

I said abruptly: 'You came here by boat, didn't you? Was it your own?'

His head jerked up at that, and the match went fizzing down among the dry juniper-needles. Absently, he put the heel of his hand down on the tiny gyre of blue smoke to crush it out. If it burnt him, he gave no sign. His eyes were on me, unwinking.

'By—boat?'

'Yes, by boat. I heard you say something about "the caique", to Mark.' I smiled. 'Good heavens, everybody knows that much Greek. And then, Mark lied about how you got here. There's no road from the east; in fact, there's only one road through this corner of Crete, and if you'd come by that you'd not have needed to ask me all those questions about the route down to the village. If Mark hadn't been feverish, he'd have known I'd see through such a silly lie. Well? You can't have come by the supply-boat from Chania, because that'd tie up in Agios Georgios, and—again—you'd know the way. *Was* it your own boat?'

A pause. 'Yes, it is mine.'

'And where is it now?'

A longer pause. Then a reluctant gesture towards a part of the coast out of our sight, some way to the east. 'Down there.'

'Ah. Then I assume you'll have supplies on board—food, blankets, medical things?'

'And if I have?'

'Then they'll have to be fetched,' I said calmly.

'How?' He said it angrily; but at least, I thought, he was listening. His initial mistrust gone, he might even be half-way to accepting me as a possible ally. 'You might not find the boat. The way is not easy. Besides, it is not safe.'

So he had accepted me. I waited for a moment, then said, slowly: 'You know, Lambis, I think you had better tell me about this—affair. No, listen to me. I know you don't really trust me, why should you? But you've had to trust me this far, and you'll have to again, when I finally do go down to the village. So why not trust me a bit further? Why not take advantage of the fact that I came along? There may not be much I can do, but there may be something, and I promise to be very careful. I won't interfere where I'm not needed, but obviously I'm less likely to make mistakes, if I know what's involved.'

The dark eyes were fixed on my face. They were quite unreadable, but the stony sullenness had gone from his mouth. He seemed to be hesitating.

I said: 'I have understood one thing, I think. It was a man from Agios Georgios who shot Mark?'

'We do not know. We do not know who did it.'

I said sharply: 'If you don't intend to tell me the truth even now—'

'This is the truth. Can you not see? If we knew from where the danger comes, or why, then we would know what to do. But we do not know. This is why I am afraid to go into the village, or to ask there for help from anyone—even the headman. I do not know if this is some affair of family, or who may be concerned in it. You are from England: perhaps you have stayed in Athens, or even in the *Peloponnisos*—' I nodded—'but still you do not know what it is like in these mountain villages of Crete. It is a wild country, still, and the law does not always reach here. Here, in Crete, they still kill sometimes for affairs of family, you understand? They still have the—I do not know the word, family killings and revenge—'

'Vendettas. Blood-feuds.'

'Yes, "vendetta" I know; killing for blood. Blood will always have blood.'

He pronounced this involuntarily Shakespearian line in a matter-of-fact voice that chilled me. I stared. 'Are you trying to tell me that Mark has injured someone—by mistake, I presume? And was shot at in revenge, or something, by someone he doesn't know? Why, it's absurd! I suppose it *could* have happened, in a country like Crete, but surely they must realize by now—'

'He injured nobody. That was not his mistake. His mistake was that he saw a murder done.'

I heard my breath go out between my teeth. 'I—see. And the *murderer's* mistake was that Mark is still alive to talk about it?'

'That is so. And we do not know even who the people were . . . the murderers, and the man they killed; and so we do not know in what direction we can go for help. We only know that they still search for Mark, to kill him.' He nodded at my look. 'Yes, these are wild parts, *thespoints*—miss. If a man is injured, his whole family, perhaps his whole village, will support him, even in the case of murder and death. Not always, of course, but sometimes, in some places. Often here, in these mountains.'

'Yes, I'd read it, but somehow one doesn't—' I paused, and drew in my breath. 'Are you a Cretan, Lambis?'

'I was born in Crete, yes. But my mother was from Aegina, and when my father was killed, in the war, she returned to her mother's house. I lived in Agia Marina, in Aegina.'

'I know it. Then you don't belong to this part of the world? It couldn't have been anything to do with you, this horrible affair?'

'No, I was not even here. I found him next morning. I told you.'

'Oh yes, so you did. But I still can't think that it literally isn't safe to go down for supplies, and even to see the headman in Agios Georgios. Why, he'd be—'

'No!' He spoke sharply, as if in sudden fear. 'You do not know it all. It is not so simple.'

I said gently: 'Then supposing you tell me.'

'I will do that.' But he waited for a moment, letting his eyes move slowly over the empty reaches of the mountain-side below us. When he was satisfied that there was no movement anywhere, he settled himself more comfortably on his elbow, and took a deep drag at his cigarette.

'I told you I have a caique. I live now in Piraeus. Mark hired me there, to take a voyage to some of the islands. We have been to different places, during two weeks, but no matter of that, two days ago we come round to the south of Crete. We mean to come in to Agios Georgios, perhaps, later that night. I speak of Saturday. Well, Mark he know of an old church, in a hollow of the mountains, not far from the coast, to the east of Agios Georgios. This church is very ancient—' he pronounced it 'auncient' '—perhaps classical, who knows, and I think it is in the old books.'

'I've heard of it. There was a classical shrine, I think, then later a church was built on the site. Byzantine.'

'So? Well, in the auncient times there was a harbour near by.

Still, in calm weather, you can see the old wall under the water, and a small caique can get right in where the old landing-place was. Mark, he tells me to stop there. We had been sailing for two days, and now they were wanting to go on land, to walk –'

'They?'

'Mark and his brother.'

'Oh!' I stared at him, with the beginnings of frightened comprehension. I was remembering the look of agonized helplessness on Mark's face, and something Lambis had said, to quiet him: *'I'll go and look for him myself, as soon as I can.'*

'I begin to see,' I said, rather hoarsely. 'Go on.'

'Well, Mark and Colin leave the caique, and go up through the hills. This is Saturday, did I say? They are to be gone all the day. They have food and wine with them. I stay with the caique. There is a small thing wrong with the engine, so I am to go along to Agios Georgios for what I need, then return in the evening to meet Mark and Colin. But I find the engine goes right quite easily, so I just stay and fish, and sleep, and swim, until it is evening, and they have not come. I wait and wait, but not knowing when they will come, or if perhaps I should go and look . . . you know how this is –'

'I know.'

'Then it is night, and they are not coming, and now I am very anxious. These are wild hills. I do not think they can be lost, but I think of accidents. At last, when I can wait no more, I lock the cabin on the caique, and put the key where they will know to find it, then I take a torch, and go up to find the little church. But you will understand that, even with the torch, it is not possible to find a way.'

'I can well believe that.'

'I shout, of course, and I go as far as I can, but I do not even find the church. I do not wish myself to be lost, so I go back where I can hear the sea, and I wait for the moon.'

'It's rising late, isn't it?'

He nodded. He was talking easily now. 'It was a long time to wait. When it rose, it was not a big moon, but I could see the way well enough. I go slowly, very slowly. I find the church, but they are not there. I do not know where to go from there, but then there is cloud, and sharp rain, and it is dark again, very dark. I have to take shelter till first light. I shout, but there is nothing. I do not think they have passed me, back to the boat, so when it is light, I go on. I am lucky. I find a path – not just a goat-path, but a wide one, of stones worn flat, as if men went that way. Perhaps in the old days it was the road from Agios Georgios to the church and the auncient harbour, I do not know. But it was a path. I go along it. Then, on it, I see blood.'

The bare simplicity of Lambis' style, together with the matter-of-fact tone he used, had an absurdly sensational impact. As he paused, with totally unconscious effect, to grind his cigarette out on a stone, I found myself watching him so tensely that when a shadow scudded across the ledge between us, I flinched from it as if it had been a flying knife. It was only a kestrel, sailing in to feed its young in a nest on the rock above us. The air shrilled with the ecstatic hissing with which they greeted the food.

Lambis never even glanced up, his nerves being that much better than mine. 'Now,' he said, 'I am sure there is an accident. This has happened before the rain, because the rain has washed most of it away, but I see blood between the stones. I am afraid. I call, but there is no answer.' He hesitated, and glanced up at me. 'Then – I cannot explain you why – but I do not call any more.'

'You don't have to explain. I understand.'

I did understand, very well. I could picture it as he had told it me: the man alone on the mountain-side; the blood on the stones; the eerie silence, and the echoing rocks; the creeping fear. I had been to Aegina, the idyllic little island in the Saronic Gulf where Lambis had been brought up. There, one solitary hill, sea-girdled, is crowned with a temple which stands among its sunlit pines. From between the pillars, on every side, you can see woods and fields, edged with the calm, blue sea. The road winds through gentle valleys, past slopes where little Christian shrines perch, it seems, every fifty yards or so, among the ferns and wild blue iris . . . But here, in Crete, it is a different world. These cloud-bound crags, with their eagles and ibexes and wheeling vultures, have, time out of mind – it is said – been the haunt of outlawed and violent men. So, Lambis had hunted in silence. And, finally, he had found Mark.

Mark was lying some three hundred yards further on, full in the path. 'He had crawled that way, from where the blood was spilt. How, I do not know. I think at first that he is dead. I see then that he is fainting, and that he has been shot. I do what I can, quickly, then I look for the boy.'

'The boy? You mean that the brother – Colin – is *younger*?'

'He is fifteen.'

'Oh, God. Go on.'

'I do not find him. But now it is light, and I am afraid
they—whoever it is who has done this—will come back to look for
Mark. I cannot take him back to the boat, it is too far. I carry him
away, off the path, up through the rocks and along under the ridge,
and then I find this place. It is easy to see that there has been nobody
here for many weeks. I look after Mark, and make him warm, then I
go back to the place where I find him, to cover the marks with dust,
so that they will think he recovered and went away. I will tell you of
that later. Now I will tell you what Mark told me, when he could
speak.'

'Just a minute. You've not found Colin yet?'

'No. There was no sign.'

'Then—he's probably alive?'

'We do not know.'

The whistling in the cliff had stopped. The kestrel flew out again,
rocked in a lovely curve below eye level, then tore away to the right,
and vanished.

'What did Mark tell you?'

Lambis had taken out another cigarette. He had rolled over on his
stomach, and gazed out over the hot hillside as he talked. Still
briefly, unemotionally, he told me Mark's story.

Mark and Colin had walked to the little church (he said), and had
their meal there. After they had explored it, they had walked on, up
into the hills, intending to spend the whole day out before returning
to the caique. Though the day had been fine, clouds had begun to
pile up during the latter part of the afternoon, so that twilight came
early. The two brothers had gone perhaps a little further than they
had intended, and when at length they regained the path with the
'worn stones' that led down towards the church, the dusk was
already gathering. They were walking fast, not talking, their
rope-soled shoes making very little sound on the path, when suddenly,
just ahead of them round a bend in the track, they heard voices
speaking Greek, raised as if in some sort of quarrel. Thinking
nothing of this, they held on their way, but, just as they came round
the bluff of rock that masked the speakers from them, they heard
shouts, a scream from a woman, and then a shot. They stopped
short by the corner, with a very eloquent little tableau laid out just
ahead of them at the edge of a wooded gully.

Three men and a woman stood there. The fourth man lay on his
face at the gully's edge, and it didn't need a closer look to know that
he was dead. Of the three living men, one stood back, aloof from the

rest of the group, smoking–apparently unmoved. He seemed, by
the very calmness of his gestures, no less than by his position, to be
demonstrating his detachment from what was going on. The other
two men both had rifles. It was obvious which one had fired the
recent shot; this was a dark man in Cretan costume, whose weapon
was still levelled. The woman was clinging to his arm, and
screaming something. He shook her off roughly, cursing her for a
fool, and struck her aside with his fist. At this the second man
shouted at him, and started forward, threatening him with his
clubbed rifle. Apart from the woman, whose distress was obvious,
none of them seemed very concerned with the fate of the dead man.

As for Mark, his first concern was Colin. Whatever the rights and
wrongs of what had happened, this was not a moment to interfere.
He dropped an arm across the boy's shoulders to pull him back out
of sight, with a muttered, 'Let's get out of this.'

But the third man–he of the unconcerned cigarette–turned, at
that unlucky moment, and saw them. He said something, and the
faces of the group turned, staring, pale in the dusk. In the moment
of startled stillness before any of them moved, Mark thrust Colin
behind him. He had opened his mouth to shout–he was never
afterwards quite sure what he had been going to say–when the man
in Cretan costume threw his rifle to his shoulder, and fired again.

Mark, as the man moved, had flinched back, half-turning to dodge
out of sight. It was this movement that had saved him. He was near
the gully-edge, and, as he fell, the momentum of his turn, helped by
the swing of the haversack on his shoulder, pitched him over it.

The next few minutes were a confusion of pain and distorted
memory. Dimly, he knew that he was falling, bumping and
sprawling down among the rocks and bushes, to lodge in a thicket of
scrub (as he found later) some way below the path.

He heard, as from a long way off, the woman screaming again,
and a man's voice cursing her, and then Colin's voice, reckless with
terror: 'You've killed him, you stupid swine! Mark! Let me get down
to him! Mark! Let me go, damn you! *Mark!*'

Then the sound of a brief, fierce scuffle at the gully's edge, a cry
from Colin, bitten off short, and after that, no further sound from
him. Only the woman sobbing, and calling in thick Greek upon her
gods; and the voices of the two Cretans, furiously arguing about
something; and then, incongruously–so incongruously that Mark,
swimming away now on seas of black pain, could not even be sure it
was not a dream–a man's voice saying, in precise and unconcerned

English: 'At least take time to think it over, won't you? Three corpses is a lot to get rid of, even here . . .'

And that, said Lambis, was all that Mark remembered. When he awoke to consciousness, it was almost daylight. The thought of Colin got him, somehow, up out of the gully and on to the path. There he lay awhile, exhausted and bleeding, before he could summon the strength to look about him. The dead man had gone, and there was no sign of Colin. Mark had retained the dim impression that the murderers had gone inland, so he started to crawl along the path after them. He fainted several times in his passage of three hundred yards. Twice the rain revived him. The last time, Lambis found him lying there.

Lambis' voice had stopped. I sat for a few minutes—for ages it seemed—in silence, with my hands pressed to my cheeks, staring, without seeing it, at the bright, far-off sea. I had imagined nothing like this. No wonder Lambis had been afraid. No wonder Mark had tried to keep me out of it . . .

I said hoarsely: 'I suppose they'd left Mark for dead?'

'Yes. It was dark, you see, and they may not have wanted to go down the gully after him. It was a very steep place. If he was not then dead, he would be dead by morning.'

'Then—when the Englishman told them to "think it over", he must have been meaning Colin? The other two "corpses" being Mark and the dead man?'

'It seems so.'

'So Colin *must* have been alive?'

'The last Mark heard of it, yes,' said Lambis.

A pause. I said, uncertainly: 'They would come back, by daylight, for Mark.'

'Yes.' A glance from those dark eyes. 'This I guessed, even before I heard his story. When I went back to cover our tracks, I brushed the dust over them, and went down for the haversack, then I hid above, among the rocks, and waited. One came.'

Again the breathless impact of that sparse style. 'You saw him?'

'Yes. It was a man of perhaps forty, in Cretan dress. You have seen this dress?'

'Oh, yes.'

'He had a blue jacket, and dark-blue breeches, the loose kind. The jacket had some—what is the word for little balls of colour along the edge?'

'What? Oh—I suppose I'd call them bobbles, if you mean that

fancy braided trimming with sort of tufts on, like a Victorian fringed table-cloth.'

'Bobbles.' Lambis, I could see, had filed my thoughtless definition away for future reference. I hadn't the heart to dissuade him. 'He had red bobbles, and a soft black cap with a red scarf tied round, and hanging, the way the Cretans wear it. He was very dark of face, with a moustache, like most Cretans; but I shall know him again.'

'Do you think it was the murderer?'

'Yes. It was very nearly dark when the shooting happened, and Mark did not see faces, but he is certain that the man who did the shooting was in Cretan dress. Not the others.'

'What did he do when you saw him?'

'He looked about him, and went down into the gully, looking for Mark. He took a long time, as if he could not believe that he had gone. When he could find no body, he looked puzzled, and then anxious, and searched further, to see if perhaps Mark had crawled away, and died. He searched all the time below, in the gully, you understand. He did not think that Mark could have climbed up to the path. But when he looked for a long time without finding, then he came back to the path. He was very worried, I could see. He searched the path, then, but I think he saw nothing. After a time he went off, but not towards Agios Georgios. He went up there—' a gesture vaguely north '—where is another village, high up. So we still do not know from where the murderers come.'

'No. I suppose you couldn't—?' I hesitated, picking my words. 'I mean, if he was alone . . .?'

For the first time, Lambis smiled, a sour enough smile. 'You think I should have attacked him? Of course. I do not have to tell you that I wait for the chance to force him to tell me the truth, and what they have done to Colin. But there is no chance. He is too far from me, and between us is the slope of open hillside. And he has his rifle, which he carries, so.' A gesture, indicating a gun held at the ready. 'He is too quick with his gun, that one. I have to let him go. If I take a risk, me, then Mark dies also.'

'Of course.'

'And because of Mark, who looks to be dying, I cannot follow this Cretan, to see where he goes . . .' Suddenly he sat up, turning briskly towards me. 'So now you understand? You see why I speak of danger, and why I do not dare to leave Mark, even to find where Colin is? Mark wishes me to go, but he is too ill, and when he has the fever, he tries to leave the hut, to look himself for his brother.'

'Oh, yes, I can see that all right. Thank you for telling me all this. And now, surely, you'll let me help?'

'What can you do? You cannot go down now to the village, and buy food or blankets, and then come back here. The whole village would know of it within the hour, and there would be a straight path back there, to Mark. And you cannot go to the boat; it will be dark soon, and I have told you, you could not find the way.'

'No, but you could.'

He stared.

I said: 'Well, it's obvious, isn't it? You go, and I'll stay with him.'

You would have thought I had offered to jump straight off the side of the White Mountains. '*You?*'

'What else is there to do? Someone has to stay with him. Someone has to get supplies. I can't get supplies, therefore I stay with him. It's as simple as that.'

'But—I shall be gone a long time, perhaps many hours.'

I smiled. 'That's where the luck comes in. The hotel doesn't expect me until tomorrow. Nobody in Agios Georgios knows I've arrived. Whatever time I get there, nobody's going to ask questions.'

He scooped up a handful of the dry juniper needles, and let them run softly through his fingers. He watched them, not looking at me as he spoke. 'If they come back, these murderers, to look for Mark, you will be alone here.'

I swallowed, and said with what I hoped sounded like resolute calm: 'Well, you'll wait till it gets dusk, won't you, before you go? If they haven't been back and found the hut before dark, they're not likely to find it afterwards.'

'That is true.'

'You know,' I said, 'this isn't silly heroics, or anything. I don't *want* to stay here, believe me. But I simply don't see what else there is to do.'

'You could do what Mark told you, and go down to your hotel and forget us. You will have a comfortable bed, and a safe one.'

'And how well do you think I should sleep?'

He lifted his shoulders, with a little twist of the lips. Then he gave a quick glance at the western sky. 'Very well. At first dark, I shall go.' A look at me. 'We shall not tell Mark, until I have gone.'

'Better not. He'd only worry about me, wouldn't he?'

He smiled. 'He does not like to be helpless, that one. He is the kind that tries to carry the world.'

'He must be half out of his mind about Colin. If he could only sleep, then you might even be able to go, and get back again, without his knowing.'

'That would be best of all.' He got to his feet. 'You will stay up here, then, until I give you a signal? I shall see to him before I leave him. There will be nothing for you to do except see that he does not wake with fever, and try to crawl out of the hut, to look for his brother.'

'I can manage that,' I said.

He stood looking down at me with that unreadable, almost surly expression. 'I think,' he said slowly, 'that you would manage anything.' Then suddenly, he smiled, a genuine smile of friendliness and amusement. 'Even Mark,' he added.

Chapter 4

*Mark how she wreaths each horn with mist, yon late
and labouring moon.*

WILDE: *Panthea*

LAMBIS LEFT AT dusk. Soon after the sun had vanished below the
sea, darkness fell. I had been watching from the ledge, and, in the
two long hours before sunset, I had seen no sign of movement on the
mountain-side, except for Lambis' short trips from the hut to get
water from the pool.

Now, as the edges of sea and landscape became dim, I saw him
again, small below me, appearing at the door of the hut. This time
he came out a short way, then stopped, looked up in my direction,
and lifted a hand.

I stood up and raised an arm in reply, then made my way
carefully down to meet him.

He said, low-voiced: 'He is asleep. I gave him the rest of the
coffee, and I have bathed his arm. It looks better, I think; he has
been a little feverish, talking stupid things, but no longer fighting to
be out. He will be okay with you. I have filled the flask now with
water; you will not need to come out again.'

'Very well.'

'I will go now. You are not afraid?'

'I am a little, but then that's only natural. It doesn't change
anything. You'll take great care?'

'Of course.' He hesitated, then there came again this familiar
gesture of hand to hip. 'You would like this?'

'This' was his knife. It lay across his palm.

I shook my head. 'Keep it. If one of us is going to need it, I hope it'll be you! In any case, it would be wasted on me – I wouldn't quite know how to start using it. Oh, and Lambis –'

'Yes.'

'I've been thinking, sitting up there. Isn't it just possible that Colin may have got away? Or even that they've actually let him go? They know Mark's got away, and may be still alive, so they must know it'd only be running into worse trouble if they kill Colin. I mean, the first murder may be a local affair that they think they can get away with, but it'd be a different matter to involve two British nationals.'

'I have thought this myself.'

'And if he were free – Colin, I mean – he'd go first of all to look for Mark's body, then, when he didn't find it, he'd go straight to the caique, wouldn't he?'

'I have thought this also. I have been hoping I shall find him there.'

I said doubtfully: 'As long as *they've* not found the caique . . . I suppose, if they have, they'd be bound to connect it with Mark? Does the path, the "ancient path", lead straight to the old harbour? Would they assume that was where Mark and Colin were making for? If so, you'd think they'd have followed it up.'

He shook his head. 'The path goes on right over the hills, past the church, then it divides towards the hill village to the north, Anoghia, where the Cretan went, and to another village further along the coast to the east. There, there is a road to Phestos, where the antiquities are, and the tourists go. It is certain that the murderers would think that Mark was going that way. Why should they think of a boat? Mark and Colin had a haversack, and it would seem, perhaps, that they were walking, and sleeping out – going, perhaps, to sleep that night in the old church. People do these strange things, especially the English.'

'Well, let's hope you're right. Let's hope they never think about a boat. Can it be seen easily, from the shore above?'

'No, but I shall hide it better. There was a cave . . . not quite a cave, but a deep place between rocks, which could not be seen from the shore paths. I shall put her in there; she will be safe enough; there will be no wind tonight.'

'But if Colin came back to where you had left her before –'

'He will still find her. If he does go down to the place, and she is not there, you know what he will do, what anyone does. He will think, first, that this is not the same place, and he will search; there

are many rocks and little bays, he will search them all, near by. And
so he will see her.'

'Yes, of course. It's what one does. If you expect to see something
in a certain place, you simply don't believe it can't be there.' I looked
at Lambis with a new respect. 'And you? Do you really expect to
find him there?'

He gave a quick glance at the door of the hut, as if he were afraid
that Mark might hear him. 'I know no more than you, *thespoinís*. It
may be that they are now afraid because they have shot at Mark, and
that they try only to persuade Colin to be silent – and that Colin is
even now searching for his brother. I do not know. It may be that
there is no danger at all.'

'But you don't believe that.'

In the pause before he answered, I heard, high overhead in the
darkening sky, the call of some late-going gulls. The sound was
muted by distance, and very lonely.

'No,' he said at length, 'I do not believe it. There is danger here.
The man I saw, he was dangerous, as a wild beast is dangerous. And
the men Mark spoke of . . . yes, there is danger, I can feel it. It is in
the air of these mountains.'

I smiled, I hope cheerfully. 'Perhaps that's only because you're
not used to them. You've become a city-bird, like me. High
mountains frighten me now.'

He said seriously: 'The city, the hills, they are all the same, where
there are wicked men. When I was a child, in my village, it was the
same. We were afraid in our houses, in our own beds . . . only then, for
a young boy, the war was also exciting. But this . . . no, not now.'

There was a sound from inside the hut, the rustle of dried leaves
and a sighing breath, then silence again.

Lambis lowered his voice. 'I must go. I will bring everything I can
carry. Be careful, *thespoinís*.'

'Nicola.'

'Nicola, then.'

'Good-bye, and good luck.' I swallowed. 'You be careful, too.
We'll see you soon. And for pity's sake don't fall and break your leg
in the dark . . . How long do you think it will take?'

'I shall wait for daylight. Perhaps three hours after that.'

'Right,' I said, as steadily as I could. 'And if you're not back by
noon, I'll come and look for *you*.'

'Okay.'

He was soon invisible down the darkening hillside. His steps faded. I heard the crack of a twig, then, more faintly, the rattle of a displaced stone, and then silence.

The sea-birds had gone. To the east, beyond the high towers of rock, the sky looked clouded, but from here to the sea it seemed clear, deepening rapidly towards night. The early stars, king-stars, burned there already, bright and steadfast. I remembered that last night there had been a moon of a kind, a pale quarter, waning, like silver that is polished so thin that it has begun to wear away . . .

Beside me, the entrance to the hut gaped black, like a cave-mouth. The hut itself crouched back against the rock as if huddling there for protection, as indeed it was. I glanced from it again up at the sky. For Lambis' sake, I hoped there would be a moon, any sort of a moon, rising clear of the clouds, and dealing even a little light. But for my own, and Mark's, no night could be dark enough.

I shook the thought away. It did not do to think about the possibility of our being found. We would not be found. And if we were, the whole thing was a mistake, and there was no danger at all. None.

On this reflection—or bit of mental bluster—I turned and groped my way into the darkness of the hut.

'Lambis?'

So he was awake. I went quietly across towards the voice, and sat down at the edge of the brushwood bed.

'Lambis has gone down to the boat, to get supplies, and to see if Colin's there.'

'*You?*'

'Yes. Now don't worry, please. Someone had to go down. We couldn't either of us get stuff in the village, and I didn't know the way to the boat. He'll be back by morning. Are you hungry?'

'What? No. A bit thirsty. But look, this is nonsense. I thought you'd have been safe in your hotel by this time. You ought to go, they'll ask questions.'

'No, I told you, I'm not expected till tomorrow. My cousin Frances was delayed, and she can't arrive before tomorrow, either, so no one'll be worrying about me, honestly. Now stop thinking about it; I'll get you a drink, there's water in the flask . . . if I can just see to pour it out . . . Here.'

As his hand met mine, gropingly, on the cup, I could feel him searching for words. But he must have been weary, and still fogged with fever, for he accepted my presence without further argument, merely fetching a long sigh when he had drunk, and going back to the first thing I had said. 'He's gone to the boat?'

'Yes.'

'He's told you all about it? About Colin?'

'Yes. We think it's possible Colin may already have made his way to the boat.'

He said nothing. I heard the bedding rustle as he lay back. A dry, sharp scent came from it, not quite strong enough to counteract the smell of dirt and sickness. 'How do you feel now?' I asked.

'Fine.'

I found his pulse. It was light and fast. 'I wish to goodness I dared heat some water. How's the arm?'

'It's sore, but it's not throbbing quite so much.' He answered patiently, like an obedient child. 'It'll be better by morning.'

'If we can keep you warm enough,' I said, 'and you get some sleep. *Are* you warm?'

'Lord, yes, boiled.'

I bit my lip. The night, mercifully, was far from cold, and, as yet, the rock surfaces of the mountain breathed warmth. But there were hours to go, and the chill of dawn to come, and the possibility, at that time of year, of low cloud, or rain.

Under my fingers the light pulse raced. He lay, slack and silent, in his corner.

He said, suddenly: 'I've forgotten your name.'

'Nicola.'

'Oh, yes. I'm sorry.'

'It doesn't matter. You're Mark—Mark what?'

'Langley. When will he get back?'

'He didn't say,' I lied. 'He's going to move the boat out of sight of the coast paths. He'll need daylight for that.'

'But if Colin goes back to the boat—'

'He'll find it. He'll hunt. It'll be quite near, only closer under the cliff. Now stop thinking about it. We can't do anything till daylight, so if you can empty your mind, and rest and sleep, then you might be well enough tomorrow to move down towards the boat.'

'I'll try.' But he moved restlessly, as if the arm hurt him. 'But you? You should have gone. I'd have been all right alone. You really will go tomorrow? You'll get out of this—whatever it is?'

'Yes,' I said soothingly, 'when Lambis comes back, I'll go. We'll talk about it in the morning. You must be quiet now, and try to sleep.'

'Did Lambis say there was an orange somewhere?'

'Of course. Wait a moment till I peel it.'

He was silent while I dealt with the orange, and took the piece I handed to him, almost greedily, but when I passed him another, he suddenly seemed to lose all interest, pushed my hand aside, and began to shiver.

'Lie down,' I said. 'Come on, pull this up round you.'

'You're cold yourself. You've got no coat.' He sat up, seeming to come to himself. 'Heavens, girl, I've got your woolly thing here. Put it on.'

'No. I'm fine. *No*, Mark, damn it, you've got a temperature. Don't make me fight you every inch of the way.'

'Do as you're told.'

'I'm the nurse, you're only the patient. Put the beastly thing on and shut up and lie down.'

'I'm dashed if I do. With you sitting there with nothing on but that cotton thing–'

'I'm all right.'

'Maybe. But you can't sit there all night.'

'Look,' I said, in some alarm, for his teeth were beginning to chatter, 'lie down, for pity's sake. We'll share the wretched thing. I'm coming in with you, then we'll both be warm. *Lie down*.'

He shivered his way down into the bedding, and I slid down beside him, at his uninjured side. I slipped an arm under his head, and, quite simply, he half turned away from me and curled his back into the curve of my body. Avoiding the bandaged shoulder, I put my arms round him, and held him closely. We lay like this for some time. I felt him slowly begin to relax into warmth.

'There are probably fleas,' he said drowsily.

'Almost certainly, I should think.'

'And the bed smells. I wouldn't be surprised if I smelt a bit myself.'

'I shall wash you tomorrow, cold water or not.'

'You certainly won't.'

'You try stopping me. That Greek of yours'll kill you with his notions of super-hygiene. I'd like to see what you look like, anyway.'

He gave what might even have been called a chuckle. 'It's not worth it. My sisters tell me I'm nice, but plain.'

'Sisters?'

'Charlotte, Ann, and Julia.'

'Good heavens, three?'

'Yes, indeed. And Colin.'

A little pause. 'You're the eldest?'

'Yes.'

'I suppose that's why you're not used to doing as you're told?'

'My father's away a lot, and I suppose I've got into the habit of looking after things. At present he's in Brazil—he's Resident Engineer on Harbour Construction at Manaos, on the Amazon, and he'll be there two years, off and on. Before that he was in Cuba. It's lucky, really, that I've been able to be at home most of the time . . . though of course they're all away now, mostly—Charlotte's at RADA, and Ann's in her first year at Oxford. Julia and Colin are still at school.'

'And you?'

'Oh, I followed in Father's footsteps—I'm a civil engineer . . . just. I did a couple of years in a drawing-office straight after school, then took a degree at Oxford. Passed last year. This trip's a reward, in a way . . . Father stood us three weeks in the Islands, and of course we waited till now, for the best weather . . .'

He talked on, half drowsily, and I let him, hoping that he would talk himself to sleep before he thought again, too closely, about Colin . . .

'What's the time?' He sounded thoroughly drowsy now.

'I can't see. You're lying on it. There.'

My arm was under his head. I turned my wrist, and felt him peering at it. The luminous dial was worn, but distinct enough. ' 'Bout midnight.'

'Is that all? Are you sleepy now?'

'Mm. Nice and warm. You?'

'Yes,' I lied. 'Shoulder comfortable?'

'Marv'llous. Nicola, you're marv'llous girl. Feel quite at home. Feel as if I'd been sleeping with you for years. Nice.' I felt him hear what he had said, then his voice came, sharply, shaken into wakefulness. 'I'm awfully sorry. I can't think what made me say that. I must have been dreaming.'

I laughed. 'Think nothing of it. I feel the same. Shockingly at home, just as if it was a habit. *Go to sleep*.'

'U-huh. Is there a moon?'

'A sort of a one, just up. Waning quarter, all fuzzy at the edges, like wool. There must be a bit of cloud still, but there's enough light; just enough to help Lambis, without floodlighting everything he does.'

He was silent after that, for so long that I hoped he had gone to sleep, but then he moved his head restlessly, stirring up the dust in the bedding.

'If Colin *isn't* at the boat –'

'You can bet your boots he is. He'll come up with Lambis in a few hours' time. Now stop that, it gets us nowhere. Stop thinking, and go to sleep. Did you ever hear the legend of the moon-spinners?'

'The what?'

'Moon-spinners. They're naiads – you know, water-nymphs. Sometimes, when you're deep in the countryside, you meet three girls, walking along the hill tracks in the dusk, spinning. They each have a spindle, and on to these they are spinning their wool, milk-white, like the moonlight. In fact, it *is* the moonlight, the moon itself, which is why they don't carry a distaff. They're not Fates, or anything terrible; they don't affect the lives of men; all they have to do is to see that the world gets its hours of darkness, and they do this by spinning the moon down out of the sky. Night after night, you can see the moon getting less and less, the ball of light waning, while it grows on the spindles of the maidens. Then, at length, the moon is gone, and the world has darkness, and rest, and the creatures of the hillsides are safe from the hunter, and the tides are still . . .'

Mark's body had slackened against me, and his breathing came more deeply. I made my voice as soft and monotonous as I could.

'Then, on the darkest night, the maidens take their spindles down to the sea, to wash their wool. And the wool slips from the spindles, into the water, and unravels in long ripples of light from the shore to the horizon, and there is the moon again, rising from the sea, just a thin curved thread, re-appearing in the sky. Only when all the wool is washed, and wound again into a white ball in the sky, can the moon-spinners start their work once more, to make the night safe for hunted things . . .'

Beyond the entrance of the hut, the moonlight was faint, a mere greyness, a lifting of the dark. Enough to save Lambis a fall or a sprain; enough to steer his boat into hiding without waiting for daylight; but not enough for prying eyes to see the place where Mark and I lay, close together, in the dark little hut. The moon-spinners were there, out on the track, walking the mountains of Crete, making the night safe, spinning the light away.

He was asleep. I turned my cheek on the tickling shrubs. It met his hair, rough, and dusty, but smelling sweetly of the dried verbena in our bed.

'Mark?' It was barely a breath.

No answer. I slipped a hand down under the khaki jacket, and found his wrist. It was clammy, and warm. The pulse was still fast, but regular, and stronger. I tucked the coat round him again.

For no reason, except that it seemed the thing to do, I kissed his hair, very lightly, and settled myself down to sleep.

Chapter 5

There bathed his honourable wounds, and dressed
His manly members in the immortal vest.
                                    POPE: *The Iliad of Homer*

I GOT SOME sleep—enough—though I was stiff when I finally woke.
Mark was still sound asleep, curled back against me. His breathing
sounded easy and normal, and his skin, where I cautiously felt it,
was cool. The fever had gone.

It was still early. The light which came through the doorway was
pearled, but without sun. My wrist was somewhere under Mark's
cheek, and I dared not move it again to try to see my watch. I
wondered whether the cool light were only that of early morning, or
if, today, those cirrus clouds were lying lower, across the sun. In
some ways, it would be better for us if they were; but they would be
cold and damp; and, until we had blankets . . .

The thought brought me fully awake. Lambis. Surely Lambis
should have been back by now?

I raised my head cautiously, and tried to turn my wrist where it
lay under Mark's head. He stirred, gave a little grunting snore, and
woke. He put a hand up to rub his eyes, and then stretched. The
movement pushed him against me, and the discovery brought him
round with a jerk that must have hurt his arm.

'Why, hullo! Good heavens, I'd forgotten you were there! I must
have been half-seas-under last night.'

'That's the sweetest thing a man's ever said to me after a long
night together,' I said. I sat up, and began to extricate myself from
the bedding, brushing it off me. 'If I could have got out without
waking you, I'd have done it, but you were so touchingly curled
up—'

He grinned, and I realised it was the first time I had really seen
him smile. Even with the two-days' beard and the strained pallor of
his face, the effect was to make him look very young. 'Bless you,' he
said, as if he meant it. 'I got a good sleep and I feel wonderful. I even
feel as if I might be able to make a move today. Heaven knows, I'd
better. But you—did you get any sleep at all?'

'Some,' I said, truthfully. 'Enough, anyway. I feel wide awake.'

'What's the time?'

'Just after five.'

I saw the creases of worry settle back between his brows. He
shifted the arm as if it had suddenly begun to hurt. 'Lambis isn't
back?'

'No.'

'I hope to heaven nothing's happened to him. If I've got *him* into
this mess as well—'

'Look,' I said, 'don't for pity's sake take Lambis on to your
shoulders, too. He wouldn't thank you, and it's my guess he can
look after himself.' I got up, still brushing bits off. 'Now, I've been
thinking, while you lay snoring. I think we should get you out of
this hut. And the sooner the better.'

He rubbed a hand over his face, as if chasing the last mists of
sleep. His eyes still looked blurred with the clogging weariness and
worry of the night. 'Yes?'

'If anyone does come looking for you again, and gets up here—and
mind you, if they've any sense they'll go hunting where the water
is—they're bound to look in the hut first thing. Lambis was right to
bring you here in the first place, for shelter. But now that you're a bit
better, I think you should find a place in the open, in the warmth and
air, a shady place, where we can see around us. You're much better to
be hidden out on the mountain-side, than in the only obvious shelter on
the hill.'

'That's true. And I can't say I'll be sorry to get out of this . . . For
a start, could you help me outside now?'

'Sure.'

He was heavier than he looked, and also a good deal less able to
help himself than he had hoped. It took quite a time before he was at
last upright, half-propped against the wall of the hut, half-leaning on
me. I saw now that he was not tall, but compactly and toughly built,
with broad shoulders and a strong-looking neck.

'Okay.' He was panting as if he had run a race, and there was
sweat on his face. 'Keep near the wall. I can make it.'

Slowly, we made it. As we reached the doorway, the sun came up, brilliance streaming from the left between the tall asphodels. Long shadows from the flowers ran along the turf. The corner where the hut stood was still in shadow, and the air was chilly.

I left Mark sitting on the trunk of a fallen olive-tree, and went across to the spring.

The pool, too, was still in shadow, and the water was icy. When I had washed, I went back to the hut for the metal pot that I had noticed there. This was a sort of kettle, or small cauldron, which must have been used by the shepherds. Though the outside of the pot was smoked black, the inside was clean enough, with no speck of rust. I scoured it out as best I could, with coarse sand from the stream, then filled it, and went back to Mark.

He was sitting on the ground now, beside the fallen tree-trunk, slumped back against it, looking exhausted, and so ill, in the cold daylight, that I had to control an exclamation of panic. If only Lambis would come; Lambis, blankets, hot soup . . .

I scooped a mugful of the icy water out of the pot.

'Here's a drink. And if you want a wash of a sort, I've a clean hankie . . . No, on second thoughts, I think you'd better let me. Keep still.'

He made no objection this time, but allowed me to wash his face for him, and then his hands. I let it go at that. Cleanliness might be next to godliness, but the water was ice-cold. He looked like a rather badly-off tramp. I had a feeling that I probably looked a pretty suitable mate for him. Today, I hadn't had the hardihood to look into the naiad's pool.

Breakfast was rather horrible. The bread was as hard as pumice, and had to be soaked in the icy water before he could eat it. The chocolate was better, but was cloying and unsatisfying. The orange had gone soft, like limp suède, and tasted of nothing in particular.

The effort of will with which he chewed and choked down the unappetising stuff was palpable. I watched him with anxiety, and a dawning respect. Stubborn and autocratic he might be, but here was a kind of courage as definite as any gun-blazing heroics, this grim private battle with his own weakness, this forcing himself to remain a lay-figure for long enough to gather effective strength, when every nerve must have been screaming the necessity of action. To me, it was a new slant on courage.

When the beastly little meal was finished, I looked at him uncertainly. 'There was a place where Lambis took me yesterday;

it's a sort of ledge, and there's plenty of cover, and you can see for miles. The only thing is, it's a bit higher up. Round that bluff and then up, quite a clamber. There, do you see? If you can't manage it, I can scout round now, and find something else.'

'I'll manage it.'

How he did, I shall never quite know. It took us the best part of an hour. By the time he was lying, white-faced and sweating, on the ledge, I felt as if I had run from Marathon to Athens myself, and with bad news to tell at the end of it.

After a while I sat up, and looked down at him. His eyes were shut, and he looked terrible, but the sun was on the ledge, and he was lying with his face turned almost greedily towards its growing warmth.

I got to my knees. 'I'm going back for the haversack now, and to cover our tracks at the hut. And when I get back, I don't care what you say, I'm going to light a fire.'

His eyelids flickered. 'Don't be silly.'

'I'm not. But first things first, and the essential thing for you is warmth. You must have something hot to drink, and if I'm to do your arm, I must have hot water.' I nodded towards the cleft-like cave behind us. 'If I lit a small one, deep in there, with very dry stuff that didn't make much smoke, we could get something heated. Better to do it now, before anyone's likely to be about.'

He had shut his eyes again. 'As you like,' indifferently.

It didn't take long to cover our traces in the hut. Any shepherd might have left the bedding, and, while it might still look suspicious, I felt reluctant to remove it, in case Mark should need it again that night. I merely ruffled it over, until it showed no signs of having been recently lain on, then, with a broom of twigs, scattered dust over our recent foot-prints.

A quick look round, and then I was climbing back to the ledge, a fresh potful of water held carefully in my hands, and the bag and haversack over my shoulder, filled with as much dry kindling as they would hold.

Mark lay exactly where I had left him, eyes shut. I carried my load quietly into the cleft. As I had hoped, this ran back fairly deeply into the cliff, and, some way in, under a smoothed-off overhang for all the world like a chimney-breast, I built the fire. When it was ready, I made a swift but cautious survey from the ledge. Nothing, nobody, no movement, except of the kestrel hunting along the edge of the ravine. I went back and set a match to the fire.

I am not much good at making fires, but with the dry cones and the verbena scrub I had collected, anyone could have done it. The single match caught hold, fingered the strands of dead stuff with bright threads, then went streaming up in a lovely blaze of ribbon flames. The sudden heat was wonderful, living and intense. The pot crackled as it heated, tilting dangerously as a twig charred and broke under it, and the water hissed at the edges against the burning metal.

I glanced upwards anxiously. What smoke there was, was almost invisible, a transparent sheet of vapour no thicker than pale-grey nylon, sliding up the curved cliff-face, to vanish, before it reached the upper air, in a mere quivering of heat-vapour. Ten minutes of this could do no harm.

The pot hissed and bubbled. I broke the last of the chocolate into the mug, poured boiling water over it, and stirred it with a bone-white twig which was as clean as the weather could scour it. The fire was dying rapidly down in a glow of red ash. I replaced the pot in its still hot bed, then carried the steaming mug out to Mark.

'Can you drink this?'

He turned his head reluctantly, and opened his eyes. 'What is it?' His voice sounded blurred, and I wondered, with a pang of real fear, if I had done wrongly in allowing the dreadful effort of the climb. 'Good lord, it's hot! How did you do it?'

'I told you. I lit a fire.'

I saw the sudden flicker of alarm in his eyes, and realised that he had been too exhausted to take in what had been said earlier. I smiled quickly, and knelt beside him.

'Don't worry, the fire's out. Drink this now, all of it. I've saved some hot water, and I'm going to do your arm when you've had this.'

He took the mug, and sipped at the scalding liquid. 'What is it?'

'My own recipe; healing herbs gathered under a waning moon in the White Mountains.'

'It tastes to me like weak cocoa. Where in the world did you get it?' His head jerked up as a thought struck him, and some cocoa spilled. 'Have they – has Lambis come?'

'No, not yet. It's only the chocolate, melted up.'

'There wasn't much left, I saw it. Have you had yours?'

'Not yet. There's only one mug. I'll have mine if you'll get that drunk up. Hurry up.'

He obeyed me, then lay back. 'That was marvellous. I feel better already. You're a good cook, Nicolette.'

'Nicola.'

'I'm sorry.'

'So you should be. Now grit your teeth, hero, I'm going to take a look at your arm.'

I went back to my fire, which had died down to white ash. I drank a mugful of hot water—which tasted surprisingly good—then went back to Mark, with the steaming pot, and my courage, held carefully in both hands.

I am not sure which of us showed the more resolution during the ensuing process, Mark or myself. I knew very little about wounds and nursing—how should I?—and I had a strong feeling that the sight of anything unpleasant or bloody would upset me shamefully. Besides, I might have to hurt him, and the idea was horrifying. But it had to be done. I tightened my stomach muscles, steadied my hands, and—with what I hoped was an air of calm but sympathetic efficiency—set myself to undo the distinctly nasty wrappings that Lambis had last night put back on Mark's arm.

'Don't look so scared,' said the patient comfortingly. 'It stopped bleeding hours ago.'

'Scared? Me? For pity's sake, where did Lambis *get* this stuff?'

'Part of his shirt, I think.'

'Good heavens. Yes, it looks like it. And what in the world's this? It looks like *leaves*!'

'Oh, it is. More of your healing herbs gathered under a waning moon. It's something Lambis found. I can't remember what he called it, but he swore his grandmother used it for practically everything, from abortions to snake-bite, so you'd think—' He stopped on a sharp intake of breath.

'I'm sorry, but it's stuck a bit. Hang on, this will hurt.'

Mark didn't answer, but lay there with his head turned away, examining the rock above the ledge with apparent interest. I gave him a doubtful look, bit my lips together, and started to sponge the stuff loose from the wound. Eventually, it came.

The first sight of the exposed wound shocked me inexpressibly. It was the first time I had seen any such thing, and the long, jagged scoring where the bullet had ploughed through the flesh looked sickening. Mark had been lucky, of course, several times lucky. Not only had the murderer, aiming at his heart, scored a near miss, hitting nothing that would matter, but the bullet had gone clean through, ploughing its way upwards for about four inches through the flesh of the upper arm. To me, on that first shrinking glance, it looked awful enough. The edges were not lying cleanly together, and the jagged scar looked inexpressibly raw and painful.

I blinked hard, braced myself, and looked again. This time, to my surprise, I was able to see the wound without that slight lurching of the stomach. I put the dirty wrappings aside, out of sight, and concentrated.

Find out if the wound was clean; that was the main thing, surely? These dried smears and crusts of blood would have to be washed away, so that I could see . . .

I started gingerly to do this. Once, Mark moved, uncontrollably, and I faltered, cloth in hand, but he said nothing. His eyes seemed to be following the flight of the kestrel as it swept up to the nest above us. I went doggedly on with the job.

The wound was washed at last, and I thought it was clean. The flesh surrounding it looked a normal enough colour, and there was no sign of swelling anywhere. I pressed gentle fingers here and there, watching Mark's face. But there was no reaction, except that almost fierce concentration on the kestrel's nest over our heads. I hesitated, then, with a hazy memory of some adventure novel I had read, bent down and sniffed at the wound. It smelt faintly of Mark's skin, and the sweat of his recent climb. I straightened up, to see him smiling.

'What, no gangrene?'

'Well,' I said cautiously, 'hope on, hope ever, it takes some days to set in . . . Oh, Mark, I don't know a darned thing about it, but it honestly does look clean to me, and I *suppose* it's healing.'

He twisted his head to look down at it. 'It looks all right. Keep it dry now, and it'll do.'

'All *right*! It looks just *awful*! Does it hurt terribly?'

'That's not the thing to say at all, didn't you know? You should be bright and bracing. "Well, my lad, this looks wonderful. On your feet now, and use it all you can." No, really, it does look fair enough, and it is clean, though heaven knows how. Maybe those herbs did do the trick; queerer things have happened. Though if I'd been in a fit state to know that it was Lambis' old shirt, that he'd worn at least since we left Piraeus –'

'These tough types. It just shows what you can do when you leave it all to Nature. Who'd want silly little modern things like antiseptics? Lie still, will you? I'm going to tie it up again.'

'What with? What's that?'

'Nicola's old petticoat, that she's been wearing ever since Athens.'

'But look here –'

'Lie *still*. Don't worry. I washed it this morning. It's been drying like a flag of truce over that bush just inside the cleft.'

'I didn't mean that, don't be silly. But you can't shed any more clothes, my goodness. I've got your jersey, and now your petticoat –'

'Don't worry. I won't give you anything else. If it comes to that, I've nothing else to spare. There, that looks better, and it'll keep dry. How does it feel?'

'Wonderful. No, honestly, it does feel better. No more throbbing, just beastly sore, and hurts like blazes if I jar it.'

'Well, there's no need for you to move any more. You stay where you are, and keep a look-out on the hill. I'm going to bury these rags, and then I'll bring up a fresh supply of water, so that we can stay up here if we have to.'

By the time I had got back with the water and fresh kindling, and relaid my fire in readiness, it was a few minutes short of eight o'clock. I lay down beside Mark, and propped my chin on my hands.

'I'll watch now. Lie down.'

Without a word, he did as he was told, closing his eyes with that same air of fierce and concentrated patience.

I looked down the long, bare wings of the mountain. Nothing. Eight o'clock of a fine, bright morning.

It was going to be a long day.

Chapter 6

Push off . . .
TENNYSON: *Ulysses*

IT WAS, IN fact, barely twenty minutes before the man appeared.

I saw the movement, far down the hillside, south-east of where we lay. My first thought was, naturally, that this might be Lambis returning, but then, as the tiny figure toiled nearer, it struck me that he was making remarkably little effort to conceal himself.

I narrowed my eyes against the sun. At that distance I could make out very little, except that the man was wearing something dark, which could have been Lambis' brown trousers and navy-blue jersey; but he did not seem to be carrying anything except a stick, and not only did he walk openly across the barest stretches of the hillside, but he seemed to be in no hurry, pausing frequently, and turning to stare about him, with his hand up to his eyes as if to shield them from the glare of the sun.

When he had stopped for the fourth time in as many minutes, I had decided – still more in curiosity than apprehension – that it could not be Lambis. Then, as his hand lifted, I caught the flash of the sun on something he held to his eyes. Binoculars. And then, as he moved on, another gleam, this time on the 'stick' that he carried under one arm. A rifle.

I lay flattened against the juniper-needles that strewed the ledge, watching him, now, as I would have watched a rattlesnake. My heart, after the first painful kick of fear, settled down to an erratic, frightened pumping. I took deep breaths, to help control myself, and glanced down at Mark beside me.

He lay motionless, with shut eyes, and that awful look of exhaustion still on his face. I put a hand out, tentatively, then drew it back. Time enough to disturb him when the murderer came closer.

That it was the murderer, there could be no possible doubt. As the small figure, dwarfed by distance, moved nearer across an open stretch of the mountain-side, I caught a glimpse of red—the red head-band of which Lambis had spoken—and the impression of the baggy outline of Cretan dress. Besides, the man was patently hunting for something. Every minute or so he paused to rake some part of the hillside with his glasses, and once, when he turned aside to beat through a stand of young cypresses, he did so with his rifle at the ready . . .

He came out from the shadow of the grove, and paused again. Now the glasses were directed upwards . . . they were swinging towards the ledge . . . the shepherds' hut . . . the way Lambis would come . . .

The glasses moved past us, back eastwards, without a pause, and were directed for a long look at the tree-thicketed rocks above the cypress-grove where he stood. Finally he lowered them, gave a hitch to his rifle, and began to make his way slowly uphill, until a jutting crag hid him from view.

I touched Mark gently. 'Are you awake?'

His eyes opened immediately at the whisper, and their expression, as he turned his head, showed that the significance of my stealthy movement and dropped voice hadn't escaped him. 'What is it?'

'There's someone out there, some way below us, and I think he may be your man. He seems to be looking for something, and he's got a gun.'

'In sight of the ledge now?'

'Not at the moment.'

Mark turned awkwardly on to his stomach, and cautiously peered down through the junipers. I put my mouth to his ear. 'Do you see those cypresses away down there? The grove beyond the stunted tree with a dead branch like a stag's horn? He's been making his way uphill from there. You can't see from here, but there are trees above there, away beyond that cliff, and the top of a gorge like this one, only smaller. I think I saw a little waterfall running down to it.' I swallowed, painfully. 'I—I said he'd hunt where the water was.'

Mark was craning his neck to study the rocks above and below our own ledge. 'I wasn't fit to notice, when we were on our way up here. This place really can't be seen from below?'

'No, at least no one would think there was a ledge. All you can see is these shrubs, and they look as if they were in a crack in the face of the cliff.'

'And the way up?'

'That's hidden, too, among those bushes at the bottom, by the fig-tree.'

'Mm. Well, we'll have to chance it. Can you crawl back into that cave without showing yourself or making a single sound?'

'I—I think so.'

'Then get back in there, now, while he's out of sight.'

'But if he comes up here at all, he'll look in there, and there's nowhere we can hide. It's quite bare.' I shifted my shoulders. 'Anyway, I—I'd rather stay out here. If there was a fight, we'd stand a better chance out here—'

'A fight!' Mark's breath was sucked in with sudden, furious exasperation. 'What sort of a fight do you think we could put up against a rifle? Penknives at thirty yards?'

'Yes, I know, but I could surely—'

'Look, there isn't time to argue, just get in there out of sight, for pity's sake! I can't make you do as I say, but will you please, for once, *just do as you're told*?'

I have never seen anyone's jaw drop, but I'm sure mine did then. I felt it. I just sat there gaping at him.

'He's looking for me,' said Mark, with a kind of angry patience. *'For me.* Only. He doesn't even know you exist—or Lambis either, for that matter. You'll be quite safe in the cave. Now, have you got that, dimwit?'

'But . . . he'll kill you,' I stammered, stupidly.

'And just how,' said Mark savagely, 'do you propose to stop him? Get killed yourself as well, and add that to my account? Now get in there and shut up. I haven't the strength to argue.'

I turned, without a word.

But it was too late. Even as I began to slither backwards from my hide between the junipers, Mark's good hand shot out, and gripped and held me still.

For a moment I couldn't see why; then, just a glimpse, nearer through the green, I saw the red head-dress. Immediately afterwards—so close was he now—I heard plainly the grate of his boot-soles in the dust, and the flick of a kicked pebble.

Mark lay like an image. He looked, despite the bandaged arm and the shocking pallor, surprisingly dangerous. Surprisingly, when you saw that all the weapon he had was a clasp-knife, and a pile of stones.

The Cretan came on steadily, along the path by which Lambis had gone. It would lead him past the little field of asphodel, below the shepherds' hut, past the spring which marked the beginning of the climb to our ledge . . .

I could see him clearly now. He was a strongly-built man, not tall, but tough-looking, with mahogany-dark skin. While I could not at that distance make out his features, I could see the squared cheekbones, and full lips under a thick moustache. The sleeves of his dark-blue shirt were pushed up, showing brown knotty forearms. I could even see the scarlet trimming of the sleeveless jacket, and the swathed sash with the knife stuck into it, that completed the Cretan 'heroic' dress.

He lifted the field-glasses again. We lay as still as stones. A long, heart-shaking minute passed. The sun poured on to the rock; the scents of verbena and thyme and sage winnowed up around us in the heat. Encouraged by our stillness, a small brown snake crept out from the rock a few feet away, lay for a moment watching us, his little eyes catching the light like dewdrops; then he poured himself away down a hole. I hardly noticed; there was room for no more fear; this was hardly the moment to worry about a small brown snake, while a murderer stood down there at the edge of the alpine meadow, with his glasses to his eyes . . .

The swing of the glasses checked. The man froze like a pointer. He had seen the shepherds' hut.

If he was a local man, he must already have known of its existence, but it was obvious, I thought, that until this moment he had forgotten it. He dropped the glasses on their cord round his neck, and shifted his rifle forward once more; then, with his eyes fixed unwaveringly on the door of the hut, he moved forward, warily, through the asphodel.

I turned my head, to meet a question in Mark's eyes. I knew what it was. Was I certain I had removed all traces? Feverishly, I cast my mind back: the bedding; the floor; my bag, and its contents; Mark's haversack; the traces of our meal; the dressings from Mark's shoulder; the orange-peel. Yes, I was certain. I gave Mark a jerky little nod of reassurance.

He sketched the ghost of a thumbs-up sign, which meant congratulation, then gestured with his head towards the cleft behind us. This time there was a smile in his eyes. I returned it, after a fashion, then obediently slithered back, rather in the style of the small brown snake, into the shadow of the narrow cave.

The cleft ran back at an angle to the ledge, so that from where I settled myself, well towards the back, I could see only a crack of daylight, with a narrow section of the ledge, and one of Mark's legs, from the knee down.

For all its illusion of shelter, the cave was worse than the ledge, for there, at least, I had been able to see. I sat close, listening to my own heart-beats.

Presently, I heard him. He was walking carefully, but in the tranced stillness of the morning his steps sounded loud. They came nearer, moved from grass to stone, from stone to dust, were lost behind a barrier of rock where the trickle of the spring drowned them . . .

Silence. So long a silence that I could have sworn, watching that narrow section of light, that the sun wheeled, and the shadows moved . . .

Then suddenly, he was here, just below the ledge. The soft steps trod through the stony dust. The bushes by the fig-tree rustled as he parted them. I saw the muscles of Mark's leg tense themselves.

The rustling stopped. The footsteps felt their way through dust again, moved away a little, paused . . .

In my mind's eye I could see him standing, as before, with the glasses to his eyes, raking the crannies and clefts above him for a possible hiding-place. Perhaps even now he was discovering the cave where I crouched, and wondering how to get up to it . . .

A shadow swept across the sector of light. The kestrel. I heard, in that deadly stillness, the small sound it made as it met the edge of the nest: I could swear, to this day, that I heard the whiffling of air in its feathers as it braked, flaps down, for the final approach. The hissing, mewing delight of the young ones shrilled as piercingly in the stillness as a double-sized pipe band on the dead air of a Scottish Sunday.

The flake of shadow swept out again. The young ones fell abruptly silent. A twig cracked under the fig-tree.

Then all at once, it seemed, the watcher had moved away. It was possible that the fearless approach of the bird had convinced him that there was nothing on that section of the cliff; whatever the case, he had certainly gone. The sounds retreated, faded, ceased. As my pulses slowly steadied, I found that I had shut my eyes, the better to hear that reassuring diminuendo.

Once more, at last, silence. I opened my eyes on the wedge of light at the mouth of the cleft, to see that Mark's leg had vanished.

If I had been in a fit state to think at all, I suppose I would have assumed that he had merely inched further along the ledge, the better to watch the Cretan out of sight. But as it was, I stared at the empty gap of light with horror, for two eternal minutes, with my common sense in fragments, and my imagination racing madly through a series of nightmare pictures that would have done credit to a triple-X film . . . Perhaps, after all, the murderer hadn't gone; perhaps, even now, Mark was lying, throat cut, staring at the sky, while the murderer waited for me at the mouth of the cleft, with dripping knife . . .

But here, at last, some sort of courage and common sense asserted itself. For one thing, the man had had a rifle, and for another, disabled though Mark was, the Cretan could hardly have shot, stabbed, or clubbed him to death in perfect silence . . .

I craned forward to see. Nothing but a tuft of salvia, purple-blue, with scented grey leaves, flattened where Mark had lain. Nothing to be heard, either, but a faint rustling . . .

The snake. That was it. He had been bitten by the snake. With hideous promptitude, the new picture presented itself: Mark, dead in (silent) agony, lying with blackened face, staring at the sky . . .

If I didn't stare at the sky pretty soon myself, I should go mad. I crawled forward to the mouth of the cleft, lay flat, then peered out.

Mark wasn't lying dead, and his face wasn't black. It was, on the contrary, very white indeed, and he was on his feet, looking as if he had every intention of climbing down from the ledge in pursuit of the murderer. Of the latter there was no sign. Mark was pulling aside the trails of honeysuckle that masked the entrance to the ledge.

'Mark!'

He turned, as sharply as if I had thrown something.

I was across the ledge like an arrow, and had hold of his sound arm. I said furiously: 'And just where do you think you're going?'

He answered with a sort of desperation: 'He's gone back along the hillside. I want to see where he goes. If I could follow, he might lead me to Colin.'

I had just been very badly frightened, and was still ashamed of my reactions to that fear. It made it difficult, for the moment, to think straight. 'Do you mean to tell me that you were just *going*, and leaving me *alone in there*?'

He looked bewildered, as if the question were irrelevant; as I suppose it was. 'You'd have been quite safe.'

'And you think *that's* all that matters? You think I don't even care whether you–?' I stopped short. Things were coming straight now, rather too straight for speech. In any case, he wasn't listening. I said, still angrily, because I was annoyed with myself: 'And just how far do you think you'd get? Have a grain of common sense, will you? You wouldn't get a hundred yards!'

'I've got to try.'

'You can't!' I swallowed, conscious of the greatest reluctance to say anything more at all. I never wanted to leave the shelter of that ledge as long as I lived. But one must save a rag of pride to dress in. 'I'll go,' I said huskily. 'I can keep out of sight–'

'Are you mad?' It was his turn to be furious; more, I could see, with his own helplessness than with me. That the conversation was conducted in hissed whispers did nothing to detract from its forcefulness. We glared at one another. 'You don't even begin to–' he began, then stopped, and I saw his face change. The relief that swept into it was so vivid that for the moment all exhaustion and worry seemed wiped away, and his smile was almost gay. I swung round, to look where he was looking.

A man had dropped lightly from the tumble of rocks above the little alp, and was making a cautious way between the clumps of asphodel. Brown trousers, dark-blue jersey, bare head: Lambis. Lambis, watching the watcher, following him down to Colin . . .

In a few moments more he, too, skirted the base of the cliff, and vanished.

*   *   *

'He got away,' said Lambis, breathlessly, in Greek. 'There's another gorge further along the hill, where a stream runs down. It's full of trees–plenty of cover. I lost him there.'

It was perhaps an hour later. Mark and I had waited, watching the hillside, until we saw Lambis returning. He approached slowly and wearily, pausing at length at the edge of the flowery plateau to look up towards the rocks where we lay. It was obvious from his bearing that he was alone, so Mark had waved some sort of signal to show him where we were, while I had made a hurried way down, to meet him on the narrow path above the spring. He was empty-handed still. I guessed that he had cached whatever he had been carrying, in order to follow the Cretan.

'Was he heading downhill–down the gorge?' I asked quickly.

'That's probably another way down to Agios Georgios; in fact, I don't see where else it can go. Did you see?'

The Greek shook his head, then rubbed the back of his hand over his forehead. He looked tired, and was sweating profusely. He had spoken in his own language as if too exhausted to attempt English, and I had answered in the same tongue, but he gave no sign that he had noticed this. 'No. I couldn't get too close to him, you understand, so it was not easy to follow him. I lost him among the rocks and bushes. He could have climbed out of the gorge and gone further east, or he may have been making for the village. Look, I must tell Mark. He got up there?'

'Yes. I helped him up. He's much better. What about Colin?'

'Eh? No. Nothing. He wasn't there. He had not been to the boat.' He spoke, I thought, as if his mind was not quite on what he was saying. He had hardly looked at me, but kept his eyes on the upper rocks where Mark lay. He rubbed a hand again across his damp face, and made as if to push past me without further speech.

I caught at his sleeve in a sudden flash of apprehension. 'Lambis! Are you telling me the truth?'

He paused and turned. It seemed to take two or three seconds before his eyes focused on me. 'The truth?'

'About Colin. Have you got bad news for Mark?'

'No, of course I haven't! Of course I'm telling you the truth, why not? I went to the boat last night; he was not there. There was no sign, no sign of him at all. Why should I lie to you?'

'I—it's all right. I just thought . . . Sorry.'

'It is because I have nothing to tell him that I am angry now. If I had found out something from this man—' a quick exasperated shrug—'but I did not. I have failed, and this is what I have to tell Mark. Now let me go, he will be wondering what's happened.'

'Wait just a moment, he knows you haven't got Colin, we were watching you from the ledge. But the food—did you get the food and stuff?'

'Oh. Yes, of course I did. I brought all I could carry. I should have been here a long time ago, but I had to stop and hide, because of that one.' He jerked his head downhill, a curiously dismissive gesture. 'When I saw him come this way, I hid the things, and came, quickly. It was a good thing you'd left the hut.'

'He saw it, did you know?'

'Yes. I guessed that he had. When I came here, he was just coming along under this ledge, and I knew he must have seen the hut. But he was still hunting . . . and I had heard no shot . . . so I knew that you had gone. I guessed you would be here.'

'Where did you put the food? We ought—never mind, Mark'll want to hear your news first. Come along, then, let's hurry.'

This time it was Lambis who hung back. 'Listen, why don't you go for the food straight away, yourself? Just the food, leave the other things; I can carry them later.'

'Well, all right. If you think I can find the place.'

'It's near the top of the gorge where I lost him. Follow round where you saw me go—see? There's a goat-track of a kind; it takes you along the foot of the ridge to where the stream runs down into the gorge. It's rocky at the top, but there are trees lower down. You can see their tops.'

'Yes.'

'At the head of the gorge, where the spring leaves the rocks, there is an olive-tree. It is in shelter, and has grown big, and very old, with a hollow body. You must see it, there are no others near. I left the things inside it. I shall come when I have seen Mark.'

Almost before he had finished speaking, he had turned away. I got the sharp impression of preoccupation, almost as if I had been dismissed, and with relief. But the nagging little thought that this brought to me didn't last long. Even if Lambis (having presumably fed on board the caique) could so lightly dismiss the thought of food and drink, I could not. The very thought of what the hollow tree contained drove me towards it at the speed with which a pin approaches a magnet.

I found it easily enough. It was the only olive-tree in sight, but even without that, I felt sure that I should have flown straight to the food by instinct, like a vulture to its kill, even had that been buried in the very middle of Minos' labyrinth.

I rummaged eagerly in the hollow trunk. There were two blankets, wrapped round what appeared to be a sizeable collection of stuff. I untied the blankets, and foraged for what he had brought.

There were medical supplies, bandages, antiseptic, soap, a razor . . . But for the moment I pushed these aside, to concentrate on the food.

The thermos flask, full. Some tins, among them one of Nescafé, and some sweetened milk. Tins of corned beef. Biscuits. A small bottle of whisky. And, final miracle, a tin-opener.

I threw these happily into one blanket, tied the corners up into a bundle, and set off back again.

Lambis met me half-way. He didn't speak, just nodded at me, as he made way for me on the path. I was glad of this, as it is not easy to speak politely with one's mouth full of Abernethy biscuit, and to speak Greek—which contains gutturals—would have been less elegant still.

All the same, I would have been the happier for something to lighten the look he gave me. It wasn't that the distrust had come back; it was something far less positive than that, and slightly more disconcerting. Say, rather, that confidence had been withdrawn. I was back on the outside.

I wondered what he and Mark had been saying.

*   *   *

I found Mark sitting at the back of the ledge, leaning against the rock, staring out over the open hillside. He turned with a start when I spoke.

'Here's the thermos,' I said. 'Lambis says there's soup in it. There, have the mug, I'll use the top of the thermos. Get yours straight away, will you? I'm going to light the fire again, for coffee.'

I waited for his protest, but it didn't come. He took the flask from me without speaking. I added, hesitatingly: 'I—I'm sorry Lambis didn't have better news.'

The thermos top seemed to have stuck. He gave it a wrench with his hand, and it came. 'Well, it's what I expected.' He glanced up then, but I had the impression that I wasn't fully in focus. 'Don't worry any more, Nicola.' A smile, that looked like something taken out to wear, that one wasn't used to. 'Sufficient unto the day. Let's eat first, shall we?'

I left him carefully pouring soup, and hurried into the cleft to get the fire going.

It was a wonderful meal. We had the soup first, then corned beef, sandwiched between the thick Abernethy biscuits; some cake stiff with fruit; chocolate; and then the coffee, scalding hot, and sweetened with the tinned milk. I ate ravenously; Lambis, who had fed himself on the boat, took very little; Mark, making after the first few mouthfuls an obvious effort, did very well. When at last he sat cradling his half-empty cup of coffee between his hands, as if treasuring the last of its warmth, I thought he looked very much better.

When I said so, he seemed to come with a jerk out of his thoughts. 'Well, yes, I'm fine now, thanks to you and Lambis. And now, it's time we thought about what happens next.'

Lambis said nothing: I waited.

Mark blew a cloud of smoke, and watched it feather to nothing in the bright air. 'Lambis says this man was almost certainly making for Agios Georgios, and—since it's the nearest—it does seem only reasonable to suppose that, whoever these blighters are, they come from there. That makes it at once easier, and more complicated. I mean, we know where to start looking, but it's certain, now, that we can't go down there for official help.' He shot a quick glance at me, as if prepared for a protest, but I said nothing. He went on: 'All the same, obviously, the first step is to get down there—somehow—and find out about my brother. I'm not such a fool as to think—' this with a touch of weary hopelessness—'that I could do very much myself yet, but even if I can't make it, Lambis will go.'

Lambis made no reply; indeed, he hardly seemed to be listening. I realized, suddenly, that between the two men, everything that had to be said had already been said. The council of war had been held already—while I had been sent to get the food—and is first conclusions reached. I thought I knew what they were.

'And so,' Mark was saying smoothly, without looking at me, like someone trying out a delicate tape-recorder set somewhere in the middle distance, 'will Nicola, of course.'

I had been right. First order in council: *Women and camp-followers, out of the way; the campaign's about to start.*

He was addressing me directly now. 'Your cousin's coming today, isn't she? You'll have to be there, or there'll be questions asked. You could be down at the hotel, and checked in . . .' a glance at his wrist . . . 'good heavens, by lunch-time, probably. Then you can—well, forget all this, and get on with that holiday of yours, that Lambis interrupted.'

I regarded him. Here we were again; I thought: the smile, friendly, but worn as a vizard to anxiety; the obstinate mouth; the general wariness of manner which meant 'thank you very much, and now, please go away—and stay away.'

'Of course,' I said. I pulled my canvas bag towards me over the juniper needles, and began putting my things into it, rather at random. He was perfectly right, I knew that; and anyway, there was nothing more I could do. With Frances coming today, I would have to get out, and keep out. Moreover—I was rather sharply honest with myself here—I wasn't exactly eager to run into any more situations such as I had met last night and today, with their tensions, discomforts, and moments of extreme fear. Nor was I prepared to be regarded – as Mark, once on his feet, would obviously regard me – as a responsibility, even a liability.

So I smiled rather tightly at him, and pushed things into my bag.

'Bless you.' The smile he gave me now was one of swift and genuine relief. 'You've been wonderful, I don't have to tell you how wonderful, and I don't want to seem filthily ungrateful now, after all you've done, but – well, you've seen something of what's going on, and it's obvious that if I can keep you out of it, I must.'

'It's all right, you don't have to bother. I'm the world's crawlingest coward anyway, and I've had enough excitement to last me a lifetime. I shan't cramp your style. You won't see me for dust once I get within sight of the hotel.'

'I hope to heaven your luggage is still where you left it. If it's not, you'll have to be thinking up some story to account for it. Let me see . . .'

'I'll dream up something, something they can't disprove till I've left. Good heavens, you don't have to start worrying about that! That's *my* affair.'

If he noticed that one, he let it pass. He was crushing out his cigarette, frowning down at it, withdrawing into those dark thoughts again.

'There's one thing, and it's desperately important, Nicola. If you do see Lambis – or even me – around in the village, or anywhere else for that matter, you don't know us.'

'Well, of course not.'

'I had to mention it.'

'That's okay,' I hesitated. 'But you will let me know some-how – sometime – what happens, won't you? I'll be back in Athens soon. I work at the British Embassy there.'

'Of course.'

'The British Embassy?' Lambis had looked up sharply.

'Yes.' Mark's eyes met his, in that now-familiar, excluding look. Then, to me, 'I can get you there?'

'Yes.'

'I'll write to you. Another thing . . .'

'What?'

He wasn't looking at me, he was fingering the stones beside him. 'You'll have to promise me something, for the sake of my peace of mind.'

'What is it?'

'You won't go near the police.'

'If I'm getting out of your affairs, I'm not likely to complicate them by doing that. But I still can't see why you don't go at least to the headman in Agios Georgios. Personally, I'm all for doing the simplest thing, and going straight to the authorities, wherever I am. But it's your affair.' I looked from one man to the other. They sat in uncompromising silence. I went on, slowly, feeling more than ever an intruder: 'Mark, you know, you haven't done anything wrong. Surely, now they realize you're just an English tourist –'

'That won't hold water.' He spoke dryly. 'If they didn't realize on Saturday night, they did on Sunday, and this morning. And still our friend's looking for me with a gun.'

Lambis said: 'You're forgetting Colin. He is the reason for this.' His gesture took in the ledge, the scraps of food, all the evidence of our rough-and-ready camp. 'Until we know where Colin is, how can we do anything? If he is still alive, he is their – I do not know the word – ό όμερος.'

'Hostage,' said Mark.

'Yes, of course. I – I'm sorry. Well . . .' My voice faded feebly, as I looked from one to the other; Mark wooden, Lambis sullen and withdrawn once more. Suddenly I was conscious of nothing but a longing to escape, to be away down the mountain-side, back to yesterday – the lemon-grove in the sunshine, the egret, the point where I came in . . .

I got up, and Lambis rose with me.

I said: 'Are you coming too?'

'I will see you part of the way.'

I didn't demur this time; didn't want to. Besides, I supposed he would want to make his own way into the village, once he had seen me, so to speak, off his pitch. I turned to Mark. 'Don't get up, don't be silly.' I smiled, and put down a hand, which he took. 'Well, I'll say good-bye. And good luck, of course.'

'You got your cardigan?'

'Yes.'

'I'm sorry I couldn't return your petticoat.'

'That's all right. I hope your arm will soon be better. And of course I hope . . . well, that things will turn out right.' I lifted my bag and slung it over my shoulder. 'I'll be going. I expect in a couple of days' time I'll think all this has been a dream.'

He smiled. 'Pretend it has.'

'All right.' But I still hesitated. 'You can trust me not to do anything silly; for one thing, I'd be too scared. But you can't expect

me to shut my eyes and ears. You see, if Agios Georgios *is* the guilty
village, then I'm bound to see that man with the rifle, and find out
who he is, and all about him. And I'm bound to find out who speaks
English. I certainly won't bother you, unless I hear something terribly
important. But if I do, I–I think I ought to know where to find you.
Where's the boat?'

Lambis looked swiftly at Mark. Mark hesitated, then said, across
me, in Greek: 'We'd better tell her. It can do no harm. She knows
nothing, and–'

'She understands Greek,' said Lambis sharply.

'Eh?' Mark threw a startled, incredulous look at me.

'She speaks it almost as well as you do.'

'*Does* she?' I saw his eyes flicker, as he did a bit of rapid
back-thinking, and, for the first time, a trace of colour came up
under his skin.

'It's all right,' I said blandly, in Greek. 'You haven't given much
away.'

'Oh well,' said Mark, 'it serves me right for being rude. I'm sorry.'

'That's all right. Are you going to tell me about the boat? After
all, you never know, *I* might need help. I'd feel better if I knew
where to find you.'

'Well,' said Mark, 'of course,' and he began to give me instructions
as to how to reach the caique from the ruined Byzantine church.
'And you could ask anyone the way over to the church itself, that
would be quite a normal trip for an English visitor to want to make. I
think that's clear enough? Yes? But I hope it won't be necessary for
you to come.'

'That,' I said, 'has been made awfully clear. Well, good-bye again.
All the best.'

Lambis went first. My last glimpse of Mark was of him sitting
stiffly, as if braced against the warm rock, with the empty mug
beside him, and that grey look of worry still draining the youth from
his face.

Chapter 7

Oh mistress, by the gods, do nothing rash!
MATTHEW ARNOLD: *Merope*

LAMBIS SPOKE VERY little on the way down through the ravine. He
kept a short way ahead of me, reconnoitring with some caution at
the corners, but most of the time we walked as fast as the roughness
of the path would allow. We met nobody, and came in good time
through the tangle of young oaks above the lemon-groves. Already,
through the boughs, I could see the white flanks of a windmill, and
the gleam of sunlight on the open water of the stream.

Lambis stopped in a patch of sunlight, and waited for me to catch
up with him.

Beside the path where he stood was a little wayside shrine. This
was merely a wooden box, wedged somehow back among a pile of
rocks, with primitive little oil-lamps burning in front of a brightly
coloured plaque of the Panaghia, the Virgin who is at once Mother
of God, and the Mother herself, the ancient Goddess of the earth. A
beer-bottle, standing to one side, held oil for the lamps. Verbena
grew near, and violets.

Lambis gestured towards the lit lamps, and the small bunch of
flowers that stood there in a rusty tin.

'I will leave you here. People come this way, and I must not be
seen.'

I said good-bye, wished him luck again, and, leaving him there,
went down through the lemon-groves towards the open sunlight
with, it must be confessed, a definite lightening of the spirits.

It was about noon, and the heat of the day. The breeze had
dropped, and even the silky poppy-heads, and the quaker-grass that

bordered the path, hung motionless. The white sails of the
windmills rested still and slack. A donkey browsed beside a
tumbledown wall, in the shade of an ilex. Flies buzzed over the dust.

There was nobody about. People would be at home for the
midday meal, or eating it in the fields, somewhere in the shade. I
could see no one except a boy, sprawled sleepily in the sun while his
goats cropped the vetches, and one man, working a field away,
beyond a thick barrier of sugar-cane. Neither looked up as I passed.

I stopped for a moment, gratefully, as I reached the spare shade of
the pines at the edge of the lower valley. I looked back.

There it all lay, the hot fields, the lemon-trees, the wooded gorge
leading up into the silver wilderness of rock.

From here, there could be seen no sign of life in that empty
landscape. Lambis had long since disappeared; the lemon-trees hung
without a quiver; above them the mountain-side was dead, empty
of all motion. But this time yesterday . . .

There was the movement of wings over the gorge. For a split
second I stared, incredulous. But this time the wings weren't white:
what had caught my eye was the slow wheel of enormous brown
feathers climbing the sky. An eagle? More likely a vulture, I
thought; perhaps the lammergeier itself. At any other time I would
have watched with excitement. Now, because the big bird had
reminded me of the white egret, and of yesterday, I felt tears rising
in my throat.

I turned my back on it, and made my way down to the bridge.

*　　*　　*

When I reached it, I thought for a moment that my luck had
deserted me. Two children were leaning over the parapet, spitting
orange-pips into the water; a boy and a girl, thin and dark and
burned brown, with huge dark eyes and black hair, and the shy
manners of the country children. They were spitting very close to
my suitcase.

'How do you do?' I said formally.

They stared in silence, backing a little, like calves. I regarded
them. I knew quite well that now they would never let me out of
their sight until I reached the hotel, and probably not even then. I,
the stranger, was their capture. I was news. Whatever I said or did,
as from now, would be all over the village within the hour.

I crooked a finger at the boy. 'What's your name?'

He began to grin, probably at the humour of my speaking Greek. 'Georgi.'

It always was. 'And yours?' I asked the little girl.

'Ariadne.' I could hardly hear the whisper.

'Hullo, then, Georgi and Ariadne. I'm a foreigner, English. I've come from Chania this morning, to stay at the hotel in Agios Georgios.'

Silence. There was no answer to this, so they didn't make one. They stood and stared, the boy with the beginnings of that urchin grin, the girl Ariadne taking in every detail of my frock, sandals, bag, wrist-watch, hair-do . . . Even from a child of eight it was not a comfortable scrutiny: I had done my best, with comb and lipstick, before I finally left the ledge, but I would hardly, I thought, look as if I had just recently left the portals of Chania's best hotel.

'Georgi,' I said, 'do you think you could carry a case down to the hotel for me?'

He nodded, looking round him, then reached for my canvas bag. 'This?'

'No, no, a proper case. It's in the bushes, hidden.' I added, carefully: 'I came with a car from Chania, and carried my case down from the road. I left it here, because I wanted to eat my – have my coffee, that is, in the shade further up the river. So I hid my case and left it here. Can you see it? Down there, under the bridge?'

The little girl ran to the parapet and peered over. The boy went more slowly after her. 'You can't see it? I hid it very well,' I said, laughing.

A shriek from Ariadne. 'There, there, Georgi! See!'

Georgi scrambled over the parapet, hung by his hands, and dropped some ten feet into the bushes. He could easily have gone round by the bank, but, being a boy, and a Cretan at that, he no doubt felt obliged to do it the hard way. His sister and I watched him with suitable expressions of admiration, while he dusted his hands on his seat, dived intrepidly (and quite unnecessarily) through some brambles, and finally dragged my case from its hiding-place. He carried it up to the road – this time by the orthodox route – and the three of us set off for the village.

Ariadne, her shyness gone, skipped along beside me, chattering all the time, in a dialect that was too fast and in places too thick for me to follow. Georgi trudged along more slowly, concerned, I could see, to carry my case with apparent ease. Both children answered my questions readily, supplying a lively commentary of their own which I made no attempt to check.

. . . Yes, the hotel was just at this end of the village. Yes, it faced the sea; the back of it, you understand, looked right on the bay. There was a garden, a beautiful garden, right on the shore, with tables and chairs, where you could eat wonderful food, 'real English food', promised Ariadne, wide-eyed, while Georgi hurried to explain this magnificence. It was due to the new owner – I had heard of Stratos Alexiakis, of course, since I came from England, and so did he? He was very rich, and he came from London, which was in England, and he spoke English so that you could not tell he was a Cretan. Indeed, he –

'How can you tell?' I asked, laughing.

'Tony says so.'

'Tony? Who's he?'

'The bar-man,' said Georgi.

'No, the cook,' amended Ariadne, '*and* he waits at table, and sits at the desk, and – oh, he does everything! Mr. Alexiakis is not always there, you see.'

'A sort of manager?' I said. I remembered what my Danish informant had told me about the new owner's 'friend from London'. 'This Tony –' I hesitated. Somehow I didn't really want to ask the next question. 'Did he come from England, too?'

'He is English,' said Georgi.

A short silence. '*Is* he?' I said.

'Yes, oh yes!' This was Ariadne. 'Mr. Alexiakis had a taverna there, a *huge* taverna, very splendid, and so –'

'Are there any other English people in Agios Georgios just now?' It would have been a natural question to ask, anyway; and the context made it doubly so. I hoped my voice sounded normal.

'No.' Georgi's replies were getting shorter. His face had reddened, and there were beads of sweat on it, but I knew better than to offer to relieve him of the case. His pride as a *pallikári* – a man's man – was involved. 'No,' he said, shifting the case from one hand to the other, 'only Tony, and the English ladies. That is you.' He looked doubtfully at me, and finished on a question. 'They said there would be two ladies?'

'My cousin's coming later today.' I didn't feel like attempting to explain further, and luckily, being children, they took the statement for granted, as they had taken my apparent eccentricity over the suitcase. I was thinking furiously, and not very pleasantly. I had told Mark – had known quite well – that if the *dramatis personae* of his murder-play were in fact from Agios Georgios, I would be bound, in such a tiny place, to come across traces of them almost straight away. But to do so as soon as this, and in the hotel itself . . .

I wetted my lips. I might be wrong. After all, people could come and go. I tried again. 'Do you get many visitors here?'

'You are the first at the new hotel. The first this year.' This was Ariadne, still intent on offering me what honour she could.

'No,' Georgi contradicted her, stolidly. 'There was another, a foreigner.'

'English?' I asked.

'I don't know. I don't think so.'

'He *was* English!' cried Ariadne.

'The fat one who went all the way to see the old church on the mountain? And took the picture that was in the *Athens News*? I'm sure he wasn't!'

'Oh, *that* one! No, I don't know what he was. I wasn't counting him, he wasn't a proper visitor.' By 'visitor', I gathered that Ariadne meant 'tourist'. I had already recognized my Danish friend. 'No, I meant the one who came here the other day. Don't you remember? Tony met him at the harbour, and we heard them talking as they went to the hotel, and you said it was English they spoke.'

'He wasn't a proper visitor either,' said Georgi obstinately. 'He came by caique one afternoon, and stayed only one night, and went away again next morning early. I think he must have gone by the road. There was no boat.'

I said: 'When did he come?'

'Three days ago,' said Ariadne.

'Saturday, it was,' said Georgi.

'What do you come here for, to Agios Georgios?' asked Ariadne.

I must have gazed at her blankly for a moment, before, with an effort as great as any Georgi was making, I heaved myself back out of deep waters into the safe shallows of small-talk.

'Oh, just for a holiday. It's – it's so very pretty here.' I gestured, rather lamely, towards the flower-strewn rocks, and the glittering sea. The children looked at me blankly. It had not occurred to them that scenery could be pretty. I tried another harmless lead. 'The vines are good this year?'

'Yes, they are good. They are the best vines in Crete.'

Stock response; of course they were. 'Really? We don't have vines in England. Or olives, either.'

They looked at me, shocked. 'Then what do you eat?'

'Bread, meat, fish.' I realized too late that bread and meat were a rich man's diet, but the admiration in their eyes showed no trace of envy. If there is one thing a Greek respects above intelligence, it is riches. 'And drink?' asked Ariadne.

'Tea, mostly.'

This time the look in their faces made me laugh. 'Yes, but not Greek tea. It's made differently, and it's *nice*. We make our coffee differently, too.'

This didn't interest them. 'No vines!' said Ariadne. 'Tony at the hotel says that in England everybody has electricity and a wireless and you can have it on all day and all night as loud as you like. But also, he says, it is very cold and full of fog, and the people are silent, and London is not a healthy place to live in. He says it is better here.'

'Does he? Well, you do get the sun, don't you? We do see it sometimes in England, but not like this. That's why we come here for holidays, to sit in the sun, and swim, and walk in your hills, and look at the flowers.'

'The flowers? You like flowers?' Ariadne, darting like a humming-bird, was already pulling up the anemones in handfuls. I had to restrain myself. To me, they were exotics as gorgeous as any I had seen at Kew: to the child, weeds. But I ate meat every day. Riches? Perhaps.

Georgi wasn't interested in flowers. The case changed hands again, as he stumped heroically forward. 'You like swimming?'

'Very much. Do you?'

'Of course. No one bathes here yet; it's still too cold, but later it's very good.'

I laughed. 'It's quite warm enough for me. Where's the best place to swim?'

'Oh, that way is best.' He waved his free hand vaguely towards the west. 'There are bays, with rocks, where you can dive.'

'Oh, yes, I remember, a friend told me that was the best way. Does one have to go far?'

'To the Dolphins' Bay? No, not very.'

'It's miles and *miles*!' cried Ariadne.

'You are only small,' said her brother contemptuously, 'and your legs are short. For me, or for the *thespoinis*, it is not far.'

'My legs are not much shorter than yours!' Ariadne bristled, with every intention, I saw, of doing instant battle. I intervened hastily, wondering, with some pity, at what age the Cretan girls are actually taught their place in the masculine scheme of things: 'Why do you call it Dolphins' Bay? Do you really see dolphins there?'

'Oh, yes,' said Georgi.

'Sometimes they come amongst the swimmers!' cried Ariadne, happily diverted. 'There was a boy once, who used to ride on them!'

'Was there?' What ancient story was this, still surviving here among the children? Pliny's boy from Baiae? Arion on the dolphin's back? Telemachus, the son of Odysseus? I smiled down at her. 'Well, I've never even seen a dolphin. Do you suppose they'd come and play with me?'

Truth struggled in her face with the Greek's desire to please the stranger at all costs. 'Perhaps . . . but it is a long time since they did this . . . I am eight years old, but it was before I was born, *thespoinís*. People tell stories . . .'

'But you'll *see* them,' promised Georgi, confidently, 'if the weather stays warm. It's best if you go out in a caique, into deeper water. Sometimes, when I have been out fishing, we have seen them, swimming near the boat, sometimes with their young ones . . .'

And, my earlier questions forgotten, he embarked happily on the Cretan version of the fisherman's yarn, until he was interrupted by his sister, who pushed into my arms an enormous bunch of slim, purple-red gladioli, the sort that are called 'Byzantine' in our seedsmen's catalogues, where the corms retail at about fivepence each. In Crete, they grow wild in the corn. The bundle was shaggy with lilac anemones, dragged up anyhow, and scarlet tulips with pointed petals—a variety that rates at least sevenpence apiece in Frances' nurseries.

'For you, *thespoinís*!'

My delighted thanks took us round the last bend in the track, and there was the hotel.

*   *   *

This was, at first sight, hardly deserving of the name.

Originally, there had been two houses, square-built and two storeyed, joined to make one long, lowish building. The one on the right had been an ordinary dwelling-house—large, as village standards went—of perhaps five rooms in all. The other had been the village *kafenéion* or coffee-shop: its big ground-floor room, with shutters pulled back, was open to the street, and played, now, the dual role of village *kafenéion* and hotel dining-room. Across one corner of this room was a curved counter, stacked with crockery and glasses, and with shelves of bottles behind it. Between the coffee-making apparatus and the stove for *loukoumáthes*, were some sophisticated-looking pyramids of fruit. A door at the back of the room led, presumably, to the kitchen premises. The restaurant still had the scrubbed board floor and white-washed walls of the village coffee-shop, but the white cloths on the tables were of starched linen, and on some of them were flowers.

At the end of the building, against the outer wall of the restaurant, was an outside stairway, built of stone, leading to the rooms above. This was still in use, it appeared; each worn step was whitened at the edge; and on every one stood a flowering plant, blue convolvulus with long belled strands looping down the wall below; scarlet geraniums; and carnations of every shade from deep flame to the mother-of-pearl flush of a Pacific shell. The walls of the building were newly whitewashed, and the paintwork blue.

The effect was simple, fresh, and—with the flowers, and the tamarisk trees at the back, and the glimpse of the sea beyond—delightful.

Georgi dumped my case with a flourish that effectively hid his relief, and was persuaded, without much difficulty, to accept five drachmae. His *pallikarás* dignity concealing his delight, he went staidly off, with Ariadne scampering beside him. But just before he was out of sight past the first cottage wall, I saw him break into a run. The news was on the wing already.

Georgi had abandoned me at the edge of a covered terrace which had been built right along the front of the hotel. In the shade of its trellised roof were set a few little metal tables, where the elders of the village sat. This morning three of them were there, two playing backgammon, the third watching in motionless appraisal. A youth sat on a table near them, swinging his legs and smoking; he looked up, and watched me with some interest, but the old men never even gave me a glance.

As I turned towards the main door—it had been that of the house on the right—the youth turned his head, and called something, and a man who had been busying himself somewhere at the back of the dining-room came hurrying out past the backgammon players.

'You must be Miss Ferris?'

The voice was unmistakably English. This, then, was 'Tony'. I looked at him with sharp interest.

He was young, somewhere under thirty, it was difficult to guess where; of middle height, slightly-built, but moving with the kind of tough grace that one associates with ballet. His hair was fairish, fine and straight, rather too long, but impeccably brushed. His face was narrow-featured, and clever, with light-blue eyes. He wore close-fitting and very well-tailored jeans, and a spotlessly white shirt. He was smiling, a rather charming smile; his teeth were small and even, like milk-teeth.

'Yes,' I said. 'How do you do? You're expecting me for tonight, aren't you? I know I'm a little early, but I was hoping for lunch.'

'Early?' He laughed. 'We were just going to put the police on your trail. You've no idea. Miss Scorby thought–'

'*Police?*' I must have sounded startled beyond all reason, and I thought I saw the flicker of surprise in his eyes. My heart jumped painfully, then ground jaggedly into top gear. 'Miss Scorby? What are you talking about? Is my cousin here already?'

'No, no. She rang up last night. She said the boat was still held up in Patras, but that she'd gone by train to Athens, and managed to catch a flight after all.'

'Oh, good for her! Then she'll get today's bus? She'll be here for dinner?'

'For tea. She said she wasn't going to wait for the bus; she thought the vegetable caique might be more fun, and would get her here sooner.' The small teeth showed. 'An enterprising lady. She should be here at any time now. The boat's overdue as it is.'

I laughed. 'I might have known Frances would make it! And *before* she was due, at that! That's marvellous!'

'Yes, she did think she'd been rather clever. She thought she'd be catching you up in Heraklion–you were both to have got the bus today, weren't you?–but you'd gone. They told her you'd left yesterday, with a message saying you were coming straight here.'

He finished on a note of perfectly normal inquiry. I managed to say, I hoped naturally: 'I did. I did leave Heraklion yesterday, and I fully intended to come on here, if I could. But I was offered a lift by some sweet Americans, and they decided to stay overnight in Chania, to look at the Turkish quarter. They'd offered to bring me on here today, and there was no hurry, as I didn't think you were expecting me.'

'Ah, well, that explains it. We weren't really worried, you know, dear, we thought you'd have let us know if you were coming sooner, and, to tell you the truth, I doubt if we could have taken you before today.'

'Full up?'

'No, no, nothing like that. But busy, you know, busy. We're still only half in order here. Did you walk down from the road?'

'Yes. I had some coffee near the bridge, and then Georgi carried my case the rest of the way.'

'Well, come and sign the Golden Book, then I'll show you your room.'

The lobby was merely a wide passage running straight through the house. Half-way along it stood an old-fashioned table with a chair behind it, and a rack holding four keys. This was the reception desk. A door beside it was marked 'Private'.

'Not just the Ritz, you know,' remarked Tony cheerfully, 'but all in good time, we're expanding like mad. We've got four whole bedrooms now. Not bad, for Agios Georgios.'

'It's delightful. But how do you come to be here—you're English, aren't you?' The visitors' book was brand new, its blank pages as informative as a shut eye.

'Yes, indeed. My name's Gamble, but you can call me Tony, everybody does. Gamble by name, and gamble by nature, to coin a phrase. There's money to be made over here, you know, with this tourist boom, and hotels going up everywhere like mushrooms; not so much just yet, perhaps, but when they build the road this way—real money. We want to be ready for that. And the climate's nice, too, for someone like me, with a chest.' He paused, perhaps feeling that he had been a shade over-eager with his explanations. Then he smiled, and an eyelid flickered. '*La dame aux camélias*, and all that, you know. That's really what persuaded me to settle so far from the dear old Vicarage.'

'Oh?' I said. 'Bad luck. Ariadne did tell me that you'd found London unhealthy. That must have been what she meant. Well, this seems a lovely place, so I wish you luck. Is this where I write, at the top?'

'Yes, just there.' A beautifully-kept finger indicated the first line of the virgin page. 'Our very first guest, dear, did you know? One thing, you can be certain the sheets are clean.'

'I wouldn't have dreamed of doubting them. But what about my Danish friend, the man who sent me here? You should have collected his signature—it's famous, in a mild way.' I gave his name.

'Oh, yes, but he doesn't count. We weren't officially "open", and Stratos only put him up for the publicity, and because there was nowhere else. We were still painting.'

I wrote my name with what I hoped was a casual flourish. 'And the Englishman?'

'Englishman?' His stare was blank.

'Yes,' I picked up the blotting-paper and smoothed it over my signature. 'I thought those children said you'd had an Englishman here last week?'

'Oh, him.' There was the tiniest pause. 'I know who they mean.' He smiled. 'He wasn't English; he was a Greek, a friend of Stratos'. I suppose those brats heard him talking to me?'

'Probably, I hardly remember. There,' I pushed the book across to him.

He picked it up, ' "Nicola Ferris". A very pretty start to the page. Thanks. No, dear, he didn't count either; he didn't even stay here, just called on business, and left the same night. Well, come and see your room.' He flicked a key off its hook, picked up my case, and led the way back towards the front door.

'You said the boat was due now?'

'Any minute, but you know how it is. She'll certainly be here by tea-time.' He grinned over his shoulder. 'And that's one of your worries away, let me tell you. I make the tea myself.'

'Oh? Good. She loves her tea. Not me; I've had time to get acclimatised.'

'Acclimatised? You mean you've been here for a bit?' He sounded genuinely interested.

'Over a year. I work at the British Embassy in Athens.'

I thought his glance was appraising. He swung my case as if it weighed no more than an ounce. 'Then you'll talk the lingo, I suppose? This way, dear. We go up the outside steps; rather primitive, I'm afraid, but it's all part of our simple, unstudied charm.'

I followed him up the flower-bordered steps. The smell of carnations was thick as smoke in the sun.

'I've picked up a bit of Greek.' I had had to decide on this admission when I met the children, and he would certainly find out—in fact, I had already implied—that I had talked to them. I added, apologetically: 'But it's terribly difficult, and of course there's the alphabet. I can ask simple questions, and so on, but as for *talking*—' I laughed. 'In my job we tend to mix, most of the time, with our own people, and I room with an English girl. But one day I really mean to get down to learning the language. What about you?'

'Oh my dear, a little, only a little, and ghastly Greek at that, I do assure you. I mean, one gathers it *works*, but I never speak it unless I have to. Luckily, Stratos' English is quite shatteringly good . . . Here we are. Primitive, but rather nice, don't you think? The décor was my own idea.'

Originally, the room had been plain and square, with roughly plastered walls, a scrubbed wooden floor, and a small window cut in the thick wall facing the sea. Now the rough walls were washed blue-white, some fresh straw matting covered the floor, and the bed, which looked comfortable, was covered with a dazzling white counterpane. The sun, reaching round towards afternoon, already poured a slanting shaft through the window embrasure; the shutters were open, and there were no curtains, but outside there was a vine sifting the sunlight so that the walls of the room were patterned most beautifully with the moving shadows of leaf and tendril.

'A shame to shut it out, don't you think?' said Tony.

'It's lovely. Is *this* your "décor"? I thought you meant you'd designed it.'

'Oh well, you could say I did in a way. I stopped them spoiling it. Stratos was all for Venetian blinds, and two colours of wallpaper, just like home sweet home.'

'Oh? Well, I'm sure you were right. Is, er, "Stratos" your name for Mr. Alexiakis?'

'Yes, he's the owner, you knew that? Did your Danish friend tell you about him? Quite the romantic local-boy-makes-good story, isn't it? That's what all the emigrants from these poverty-stricken rabbit-hutches dream of doing—coming home after twenty years, buying up the place, and showering money on the family.'

'Oh, he has a family?'

'Well, there's only a sister, Sofia, and between you and me, dear, there's a little bit of difficulty about showering money on her.' Tony dumped my case on a chair, and turned confidingly, with very much the air of one who has been missing the pleasures of a nice, cosy gossip. 'It would mean showering it on her husband, too, and dear Stratos doesn't but *doesn't* get on with his brother-in-law. But then, who does? I can't say I just fell madly for him myself, and I'm fearfully easy to please, far too easy-going, really. I remember—'

'What's wrong with him?'

'Josef? Oh, first of all, he's a Turk. Not that I mind *that*, but some of these village types think it's just the *last* thing, next to a Bulgarian or a German. And the poor girl was left well off, respected papa and all that, just the job for a nice local Cretan boy, but she had to go and marry this Turkish foreigner from Chania, who's frittered and drunk most of it away—won't lift a finger, *and* rather pushes her around. Oh, the usual, you know, *such* a dreary tale. What's more, he won't let her go to church, and *that*, of course, is the last straw. Quaint, isn't it?'

'Can't the priest help?'

'We haven't one, dear, he only visits.'

'Oh. Poor Sofia.'

'Yes, well, things have looked up for her since brother Stratos got home.'

'He must have done well for himself; he had a restaurant, didn't he? Where was it, Soho somewhere?'

'Oh, you wouldn't know it, it wasn't big—though of course the locals think it was the Dorchester, no less, and give Stratos an income to match. Far be it from him to disillusion them. It was a nice little place, though; I was there myself for six years. That's where I picked up my bit of Greek; most of the boys were Greeks, made Stratos feel at home, he said. Ah well,' he twitched the peach-coloured table-cloth straight, 'it's quite amusing here, tarting the place up a bit, though I don't know that little Tony'd just want to settle here for life. We're going to build, you know, on to the other end. Get a nice long, low block, facing the sea. Take a look at that view.'

'It's wonderful.'

The window faced south-west, over one end of the land-locked bay. To the left, I caught a glimpse of the edge of a roof; that was all; the rest of the village was out of sight. Directly below me, through the masking vine, I could see a flat space of gravel where a few tables and chairs were set—this, no doubt, would be Ariadne's 'beautiful garden'. What flowers there were grew in pots, enormous earthenware *ptthoi*, like the old wine-jars from the Cretan palaces. A clump of tamarisk trees stood where the gravel gave way to the flat rock of the foreshore; this, smoothed and fissured by water, burned white in the sun. In every cranny of rock blazed brilliant pink and crimson sunbursts of ice-daisies, and, just beside them, the sea moved lazily, silky and dark, its faint bars of light and shadow gently lifting and falling against the hot rock. Beyond the stretch of sea, at the outer curve of the bay, tall cliffs towered jaggedly, their feet in the calm summer water, and along their bases curled the narrow golden line of shingle that rings the islands of the tideless Aegean. Even this, if the wind stiffened from the south, would be covered. A small boat, painted orange and cobalt, rocked, empty, at anchor a little way out from the shore.

'Next stop, Africa,' said Tony, behind me.

'It's lovely, oh, it's lovely! I'm glad I came before you've built your new wing, you know.'

'Well, I do see what you mean, not that I think we'll exactly put Billy Butlin out of business,' said Tony cheerfully. 'If it's peace and quiet you want, dear, we've bags of that.'

I laughed, 'Well, that's what we came for. Is it warm enough to swim yet? I asked Georgi, but he has a different sort of built-in thermostat from me, and I don't know if I can take his word for it.'

'Well, heavens, don't take mine, I've not tried it, and I don't suppose I ever shall, not being just a child of Nature. I wouldn't risk the harbour, it's dirty, but there are bound to be plenty places where it's safe. You'd better ask Stratos; he'll know if there are currents and things. Your cousin'll go with you, I suppose?'

'Oh, she'll probably sit on the shore and watch—though it wasn't safety I was thinking about; there won't be any currents here that could matter. No, Frances isn't a swimmer, she's mainly interested in flowers. She's a rock garden expert, and works in a big nursery, and she always takes a busman's holiday somewhere where she can see the plants in their natural homes. She's tired of Switzerland and the Tyrol, so, when I told her what I'd seen last spring over here, she just had to come.' I turned away from the window, adding casually: 'Once she sees the place, I probably shan't be allowed time off for swimming. I'll have to spend the whole time tramping the mountainside with her, hunting for flowers to photograph.'

'Flowers?' said Tony, almost as if it were a foreign word he had never heard before. 'Ah, well, I'm sure there are plenty of nice ones around. Now, I'll have to be getting down to the kitchen. Your cousin's room is next door—that one, there. There's only the two in this end of the place, so you'll be lovely and private. That's a bathroom there, no less, and that door goes through to the other side of the house. Now, if there's anything you want, just ask. We don't rise to bells yet, but you don't need to come down; just hang out of the door and yell. I'm never far away. I hear most that goes on.'

'Thanks,' I said, a little hollowly.

'Cheerio for now,' said Tony amiably. His slight figure skated gracefully away down the stairway.

I shut my door, and sat down on the bed. The shadows of the vine moved and curtseyed on the wall. As if they were my own confused and drifting thoughts, I found that I had pressed my hands to my eyes, to shut them out.

Already, from the fragments I had gleaned, one thing showed whole and clear. If the murder which Mark had witnessed had had any connection with Agios Georgios, and if his impression of the Englishness of the fourth man had been correct, then either Tony or the mysterious 'Englishman' from the sea—whom Tony had denied—must have been present. There were no other candidates. And, in either case, Tony was involved. The thing could be, in fact, centred on this hotel.

I found a wry humour in wondering just what Mark would have said, had he known that he was packing me off, with prudent haste, from the perimeter of the affair into its very centre. He had wanted me safely out of it, and he had made this abundantly clear, even to the point of rudeness; and I—who had taken my own responsibilities for long enough—had resented bitterly a rejection that had seemed to imply a sexual superiority. If I had been a man, would Mark have acted in the same way? I thought not.

But at least emotion no longer clouded my judgement. Sitting here quietly, now, seeing things from the outside, I could appreciate his point of view. He wanted to see me safe—and he wanted his own feet clear. Well, fair enough. In the last few minutes, I had realised (even at the risk of conceding him a little of that sexual superiority) that I wanted both those things, quite fervently, myself.

I took my hands from my eyes, and there were the patterned shadows again, quiet now, beautiful, fixed.

Well, it was possible. It was perfectly possible to do as Mark had wished; clear out, forget, pretend it had never happened. It was obvious that no suspicion of any sort could attach itself to me. I had arrived as expected, having successfully dropped the dangerous twenty-four hours out of my life. All I had to do was forget such information as came my way, ask no more questions, and—how had it gone?—'get on with that holiday of yours, that Lambis interrupted'.

And meanwhile, Colin Langley, aged fifteen?

I bit my lip, and snapped back the lid of the suitcase.

Chapter 8

She shall guess, and ask in vain . . .
THOMAS LOVELL BEDDOES: *Song of the Stygian Naiades*

THERE WAS A woman in the bathroom, just finishing with a cloth and pail. When I appeared, towel on arm, she seemed flustered, and began picking up her tools with nervous haste.

'It's all right,' I said, 'I'm not in a hurry. I can wait till you've finished.'

But she had already risen, stiffly, to her feet. I saw then that she was not old, as her movements had led me to imagine. She was of medium height, a little shorter than I, and should have been broadly built, but she was shockingly thin, and her body seemed flattened and angular under the thick, concealing peasant clothing. Her face, too, was meant to be full and round, but you could see the skull under the skin—the temporal bone jutting above deep eye-sockets, the sharp cheekbones, and the squared corners of the jaw. She was shabbily dressed, in the inevitable black, with her dress kilted up over her hips to show the black underskirt below, and she wore a black head-covering, wrapped round to hide neck and shoulders. Under this her hair seemed thick, but the few wisps which had escaped the covering were grey. Her hands were square, and must have been stronger than they looked; they seemed to be mere bones held together by sinews and thick, blue veins.

'You speak Greek?' Her voice was soft, but full and rich, and still young. And her eyes were beautiful, with straight black lashes as thick as thatch-eaves. The lids were reddened, as if with recent weeping, but the dark eyes lit straight away with the pleased interest that every Greek takes in a stranger. 'You are the English lady?'

'One of them. My cousin will arrive later. This is a lovely place, *kyria.*'

She smiled. Her mouth was thinned almost to liplessness, but not unpleasantly. In repose it did not seem set, but merely showed a kind of interminable and painful patience, a striving for mindlessness. 'As for that, it is a small village, and a poor one; but my brother says that you know this, and that many people will come, only to be tranquil.'

'Your brother?'

'He is the patron.' She said this with a kind of pride. 'Stratos Alexiakis is my brother. He was in England, in London, for many years, but last November he came home, and bought the hotel.'

'Yes, I heard about it from Tony. It's certainly very nice, and I hope he does well.'

I hoped the conventional words had concealed my surprise. So this was Sofia. She had the appearance of the poorest peasant in a poor country—but then, I thought, if she was helping her brother start up his hotel, no doubt she would wear her oldest clothes for the rough work. It occurred to me that if she had fallen heir to Tony's cooking it hadn't—as yet—done her much good.

'Do you live in the hotel?' I asked.

'Oh, no,' hastily, 'I have a house, down the road a little, on the other side of the street. The first one.'

'The one with the fig-tree? I saw it. And the oven outside.' I smiled. 'Your garden was so lovely; you must be very proud of it. Your husband's a fisherman, is he?'

'No. He—we have a little land up the river. We have vines and lemons and tomatoes. It is hard work.'

I remembered the cottage, spotlessly clean, with its ranked flowers beside the fig-tree. I thought of the hotel floors, which she had been scrubbing. Then of the fields, which no doubt she would till. No wonder she moved as if her body hurt her. 'Have you many children?'

Her face seemed to shut. 'No. Alas, no. God has not seen fit.' A gesture to her breast, where a tiny silver ornament—a Greek cross, I thought—had swung loose on its chain while she was scrubbing. Encountering this, her hand closed over it quickly, an oddly protective movement, with something of fear in it. She thrust the cross quickly back into the breast of her frock, and began to gather her things together.

'I must go. My husband will be home soon, and there is a meal to get.'

My own meal was a good one; lamb, which the Cretans call *amnos*—many of the classical terms still survive in the dialect—and green beans, and potatoes.

'*Sautées*, my dear, in olive oil,' said Tony, who served me. 'Butter's too scarce here, but I do assure you I made them go steady on the oil. Like them?'

'Fine. But I like olive oil. And here, where it's so to speak fresh from the cow, it's terrific. You were right about the wine, *King Minos*, *sec*. I must remember that. It's dryish for a Greek wine, isn't it?—and the name is wonderfully Cretan!'

'Bottled in Athens, dear, see?'

'Oh, no, you shouldn't have showed me that!' I glanced up. 'I met Mr. Alexiakis' sister upstairs.'

'Sofia? Oh yes. She helps around,' he said vaguely. 'Now, will you have fruit for afters, or *fromage*, or what my dear friend Stratos calls "compost"?'

'It depends rather on what that is.'

'Between you and me, tinned fruit salad, dear. But don't worry, we'll really let ourselves go at dinner. The caique gets in today—oh, of course you know all about that.'

'I'm not worrying, why should I? That was excellent. No, *not* an orange, thank you. May I have cheese?'

'Sure. Here. The white one's goat and the yellow one with holes is sheep, so take your pick . . . Excuse me one moment. Speak of angels.'

He twitched the coffee-percolator aside from its flame, and went out of the dining-room, across the terrace into the sunlight of the street. A woman was waiting there, not beckoning to him, or making any sign, just waiting, with the patience of the poor. I recognized her; it was Stratos' sister, Sofia.

If only one could stop doing those uncomfortable little addition-sums in one's head . . . If only there was some way to switch off the mechanism . . . But the computer ticked on, unwanted, adding it all up, fraction by fraction. Tony and the 'Englishman'. And now, Tony and Sofia. There had been a woman there, Mark had said. Sofia and her brother . . .

I ate my cheese doggedly, trying to ignore the unwanted answers that the computer kept shoving in front of me. Much better concentrate on the cheese, and there was some wine left, and the coffee, which was to follow, smelt delicious; *café français*, no doubt Tony would call it . . . Here, the computer ticked up a fleeting memory of Mark, dirty, unshaven, hag-ridden, swallowing indifferent thermos coffee, and choking down dry biscuits. I stamped fiercely on the switch, expunged the memory, and turned my attention back to Tony, graceful and immaculate, standing easily in the sun, listening to Sofia.

She had put one of those flattened claws on his arm, almost as if in pleading. Her coif was drawn up now, shadowing half her face, and at that distance I could not see her expression, but her attitude was one of urgency and distress. Tony seemed to be reassuring her, and he patted the hand on his arm before he withdrew it. Then he said something cheerfully dismissive, and turned away.

As he turned, I dropped my gaze to the table, pushing my cheese-plate aside. I had seen the look on Sofia's face as Tony turned and left her. It was distress, and she was weeping; but there was also, unmistakably, fear.

'*Café français*, dear?' said Tony.

* * *

Not even the computer—aided by two cups of coffee—could have kept me awake after lunch. I carried my second cup out to the garden, and there, alone with the drowsy sound of bees, and the tranquil lapping of the sea, I slept.

It was no more than a cat-nap, a doze of half an hour or so, but it must have been deep and relaxing, for, on waking, I found that I had none of the hangover feeling that one sometimes gets from sleeping in the afternoon. I felt fresh and wide-awake, and full of a sense of pleasant anticipation which resolved itself into the knowledge that Frances would soon be here. Frances, who would know just what to do . . .

I didn't pursue this thought; didn't even acknowledge it. I sat up, drank the glassful of water—tepid by now—that had been served with my coffee, and dutifully set about writing a postcard to Jane, my Athens room-mate. That Jane would be very surprised to get it was another of the things I didn't acknowledge; I merely told myself that I wanted a walk, and that the card would be a good excuse for a quiet little stroll down as far as the village post office. I certainly did not stop to consider why I should need the excuse, or why, indeed, I should want a walk, after the amount of exercise I had already had that day. Jane (I said to myself, writing busily) would be delighted to hear from me.

The message that was to arouse all this astonished delight ran as follows: '*Arrived here today; lovely and peaceful. Frances due here this afternoon. She'll be thrilled when she sees the flowers, and will spend pounds on film. Hotel seems good. Am hoping it will be warm enough to swim. Love, Nicola.*'

I wrote this artless missive very clearly, then took it into the lobby. Tony was there, sitting behind the table, with his feet up, reading *Lady Chatterley's Lover*.

'Don't get up.' I said hastily. 'I just wondered if you had stamps. Just one, for a local postcard; one drach.'

He swung his feet down, and fished below the table to pull open a cluttered drawer.

'Sure. One at one drach, did you say?' The long fingers leafed through three or four sad-looking sheets of postage stamps. 'Here we are. Only two left, you're lucky.'

'Thanks. Oh, are there any at five? I might as well get them now, for air mail to England.'

'I'll see. Five . . . How nice that one's very first tourist knows all the ropes. I can never remember that sort of thing–I'd make the lousiest information-clerk ever. Railway time-tables simply *panic* me, you've no idea.'

'Then you've come to the right place. D'you mean,' I asked innocently, 'that you've never written home once, since you came to Greece?'

'My dear, I couldn't shake the dust of the dear old Vicarage off my feet fast enough. No, I'm sorry, we've no fives, only twos and fours. Are you in a hurry, because I can easily get some for you?'

'Don't trouble, thanks, I'd like to go out anyway, to explore. Oh look, I'm sorry, I can't even pay you for this one now, I've left my purse upstairs. I'll be down in a minute.'

'Don't worry about that. We'll put it on the bill. Double for the trouble, and don't mention it.'

'No, I'll need it anyway, to get the stamps in the village. And I must get my dark specs.'

I left the postcard lying on the desk, and went upstairs to my room. When I got back, I could swear the card had not been moved, not even by a millimetre.

I smiled at Tony.

'I suppose this town does have a post office?'

'It does indeed, but I won't insult you by directing you, dear. Agios Georgios isn't exactly complicated. Once down the main street and straight into the sea. Have a lovely walk.' And he subsided into *Lady Chatterley's Lover*.

I picked up my postcard and went out into the street.

'Street,' of course, is a misleading word for the dusty gap between Agios Georgios' straggling houses. Outside the hotel was a wide space of trodden, stony dust where hens scratched, and small, brown, half-naked children played under a pistachio-tree. The two cottages nearest the hotel were pretty in their fresh whitewash, each with a vine for shade, and with a low white wall fencing the tiny yard where the vine grew. Sofia's house stood by itself at the other side of the street. This was a little bigger than the others, and meticulously kept. A fig-tree—that most shapely of trees—grew near the door, its shadow throwing a vivid pattern against the brilliant white wall. The little garden was crammed with flowers; snapdragons, lilies, carnations, mallows—all the spired and scented profusion of the English summer, growing here, as rank as wildflowers, in the Cretan April. Against the outer wall of the house was a primitive fireplace whose blackened pots stood on trivets of a design so old that it was as familiar as the skin of one's hands. A vine-covered wall at the back did its best to hide a cluttered yard where I saw the beehive shape of a baking oven.

I walked slowly downhill. All seemed innocent and quiet in the afternoon heat. Here was the church, very small, snow-white, with a Reckitt's-blue dome, perched on a little knoll with its back to the cliffs. In front of it some loving hand had made a pavement of sea-pebbles, blue and terracotta and slate-grey, hammered down in patterns into the iron ground. Beyond it, the street sloped more steeply towards the sea, and here, though every house had a pot or two of flowers outside, the place looked barer, and there had been very little use of paint or whitewash. It was as if the richness of the flowery hills had faded and died, dwindling down to starve in the sea-bare poverty of the harbour.

And here was the post office. It was, also, the only shop the village boasted; a dark cave of a place, with double doors open to the street, beaten earth floor, and sacks of produce standing everywhere—beans, maize, and pasta, along with huge square tins swimming with oily-looking pilchards. On the counter were earthenware bowls of black olives, a stack of cheeses, and a big, old-fashioned pair of scales. Shelves, crowded with jars and tins, sported (it seemed incongruously) the familiar labels of everyday advertising. Beside the door, casually supporting a stack of brushes, was the letter-box, painted the dark post-office blue. And, on the wall opposite the doorway, the telephone, in the very middle of the shop. You threaded your way between the sacks to get to it.

The shop was, obviously, the meeting-place of the village women. Four of them were there now, talking over the weighing of some flour. As I entered, a little hesitantly, conversation stopped abruptly, and they stared; then good manners reasserted themselves, and they looked away, talking more quietly, but not, I noticed, about the foreigner; their conversation–about some sick child–was taken up where it had ceased. But all made way for me, and the shop-keeper put down the flour-scoop and said inquiringly: 'Miss?'

'These ladies–' I said, with a gesture meaning that I could not take their turn.

But I had to in the end, defeated by their inflexible courtesy: 'I only came for some stamps, please. Six at five drachs, if you will be so good.'

Behind me I heard the stir and whisper: 'She speaks Greek! Listen, did you hear? English, and she speaks Greek . . . Hush, you ill-mannered one! Silence!'

I smiled at them, and made some remark about their village, and was, on the instant, the centre of a delighted group. Why did I come to such a place? It was so small, so poor, why did I not stay in Heraklion, where there were big hotels, like Athens or London? Did I live in London? Was I married? Ah, but there was a man? No? Ah, well, one could not always be fortunate, but soon, soon, if God willed . . .

I laughed, and answered as best I could, and asked, in my turn, as many questions as I dared. Did they not get many strangers, then, in Agios Georgios? Many English? Oh, yes, Tony, of course, but I meant visitors like myself, foreigners . . . The Danish gentleman, yes, I had heard of him, but nobody else? No? Ah, well, now that the hotel was getting under way, and so efficiently, no doubt there would soon be many visitors, Americans too, and Agios Georgios would prosper. Mr. Alexiakis was making a good job of it, wasn't he? And his sister was helping him? Yes, Sofia, I had met her; I believed she lived in the pretty house at the top of the village, opposite the hotel. . .?

But on Sofia, we stuck. Beyond swiftly-exchanged glances

–kindly enough, I thought–and murmurs of 'Ah, yes, poor Sofia, it was lucky for her that such a brother had come home to look after her,' the women said nothing more, and the conversation died, to be ignited again by one of them, young and pretty, with a child clinging to her hand, and an air of assurance, inviting me to her house. The others, who seemed only to have waited for her lead, pressed eagerly forward with similar invitations. How long was I to be in Agios Georgios? I would come and see them, yes, and bring my cousin, too. Which house? The one by the harbour wall–the one above the bakery–behind the church . . . it was no matter, (this with laughter), I had only to walk in, there was no house in Agios Georgios where I would not be welcome, so young and pretty, and speaking such good Greek . . .

Laughingly promising, but temporarily parrying all the charming invitations, I finally escaped, not much the wiser about Georgi's phantom Englishman, but having learned what I had come for, and more as well.

First, the telephone was out. Even without my promise to Mark, there was no chance, whatever happened, of getting in touch with authority, either the Embassy, or even Heraklion, by telephone. The one in the hotel, impossible. The one in the post office, open to the day in what amounted to the Ladies' Clubroom–in English or in Greek, it couldn't even be tried. We were on our own.

I found that, without conscious direction, I had reached the tiny harbour. A sea-wall, and a little curved pier, held the water clear and still as a tear in a flower-cup. Someone had scrawled CYPRUS FOR GREECE along the harbour wall, and someone else had tried to scratch it out. A man was beating an octopus; some family would eat well tonight. Two boats lay at anchor, one white, with vermilion canvas furled along her beautiful spars, the other blue, with the name *Eros* along her bows. On *Eros* a youth was working, coiling down a rope. He was wiry and quick-moving, and wore a green sweat-shirt and blue denim trousers tucked into short gum-boots. It was the lad who had been watching the backgammon players. He eyed me curiously, but did not interrupt his work.

I stood there a moment or two longer, conscious of eyes watching me from the dark doorway of every house, where the women sat. I thought: if only Lambis' boat would come in now, sailing quietly in from the east, with them all on board; Lambis at the engine, and Mark steering, and Colin in the bows, with a fishing line, laughing . . .

I turned sharply away from the shining stretch of the empty sea, and, the terms of my self-deceit forgotten, brought my mind back with a jerk to my problem, the other thing I had discovered in the village shop—that there was, in fact, no house in Agios Georgios which could have anything to hide. Colin Langley was not here. Nothing could be served by my prying further in a village where every woman must know all her neighbours' affairs. Any answer to the mystery was only to be found at the hotel.

Or—and here I started to walk slowly back up the street, conscious of the eyes that watched me from the dark doorways—or at Sofia's cottage.

There might, in fact, be one house in Agios Georgios at which I was not welcome.

Well, there was nothing like trying. And if the husband was still at home, over his meal, then I should be quite interested to meet him, too.

I wondered if he favoured Cretan dress.

Chapter 9

She seem'd an ancient maid, well-skill'd to cull
The snowy fleece, and wind the twisted wool
POPE: *The Iliad of Homer*

SHE WAS SITTING just inside the door of her cottage, spinning. In all my months in Greece, I had never quite got used to the pleasure of watching the peasant women at this primitive task. The soft, furry mass of white wool on the distaff, the brown fingers pulling it out like candy-floss to loop across the front of the black dress, the whirling ball of woollen thread on the spindle – these made a pattern that it would have been hard not to appreciate.

She had not looked up at my approach; the trunk of the fig-tree must have hidden the movement from her. I paused for a moment, just beyond its shade, to watch her. In the deep shadow where she sat, the lines of trouble could no longer be seen: her face showed the smooth planes of youth, while even the ugly hands, caught in the fluid movements of her task, had taken on a kind of beauty.

I thought, then, of the legend I had told Mark, the story of the moon-spinners that had been intended to send him to sleep, and to bring me comfort. I looked again at Sofia, a black-clad Cretan woman, spinning in the hot afternoon. An alien, a suspect, an incomprehensible native of this hard, hot country, whose rules I didn't know. Somebody to be questioned.

I walked forward and put my hand on the gate, and she looked up and saw me.

The first reaction was pleasure, of that I was sure. Her face split into a smile, and the dark eyes lighted. Then, though she did not move her head, I got the impression that she had cast a quick glance into the cottage behind her.

I pushed open the gate. 'May I come in and talk to you?' I knew that such a direct query, though perhaps not good manners, could not, by the rules of island hospitality, be refused.

'Of course.' But I thought she looked uneasy.

'Your husband has gone?'

She watched me with what could have been nervousness, though the deft, accustomed movements helped her to an appearance of ease, as a cigarette will sometimes help in a more sophisticated situation. Her glance went to the small fire of twigs outside, where a pot still simmered. 'He did not come.' Then, making as if to rise: 'Be pleased to sit down.'

'Thank you – oh, please don't stop your spinning, I love to watch it.' I entered the tiny yard, and, obedient to her gesture, sat on the bench near the door, under the fig-tree. I began to praise her spinning, admiring the smoothness of the wool, and fingering the piece of woven cloth she showed me, until soon she had forgotten her shyness, and put down her work to fetch more of her weaving and embroidery to show me. Without being asked, I left my seat, and followed her indoors.

The cottage had two rooms, with no door between them, merely an oblong gap in the wall. The living-room, opening straight off the yard, was scrupulously neat, and very poor. The floor was of earth, beaten as hard as a stone, with a drab, balding rug covering half of it. There was a small fireplace in one corner, unused at this time of year, and across the back of the room ran a wide ledge, three feet from the floor, which served apparently as a bed-place, and was covered with a single blanket patterned in red and green. The walls had not yet been freshly whitewashed, and were still grimed with winter's smoke. Here and there, high up in the plastered walls, were niches which held ornaments, cheap and bright, and faded photographs. There was one in a place of honour, a child – a boy – of perhaps six; behind this was a fuzzy print, much enlarged, of a young man in what looked like irregular battle-dress. He was handsome in a rather glossy and assured way. The boy was very like him, but stood shyly. The husband, I supposed, and a lost child? I looked for the family ikon, but could see none, and remembered what Tony had told me.

'My little boy,' said Sofia, behind me. She had come out of the

inner room with an armful of cloths. She betrayed neither resentment nor surprise that I should have followed her into the house.
She was looking sadly at the picture, with–you would have
sworn–no other thought in mind. 'He died, *thespoinís*, at seven years
old. One day he was well, and at school, and playing. The
next–pff–dead. And it was the will of God that there should be no
more.'

'I'm sorry. And this is your husband?'

'Yes, that is my husband. See, this cushion that I have made last
year . . .'

She began to lay the things out in the sunlight near the door. I
bent over them, but turning, so that I could see into the inner room.

This was darkened, with shutters drawn against the sun. It was
merely a small oblong box of a room, with a double bed, a wooden
chair, and a table by the window covered with a pink cloth with
bobbles on. Every corner of the house seemed open to the view . . .

She was putting up her work again.

'And now, if you will sit in here, where it is cool, I will get you a
glass of the peppermint drink which I make myself.'

I hesitated, feeling ashamed. I had not wanted to take her meagre
hospitality, but, since I had asked myself into her house, I had
forced her to offer it. There was nothing to do but thank her, and sit
down.

She reached to a shelf near the door where, behind a faded curtain
of that same red and green, stood a stock (how pitifully scanty a
stock) of food. She took down a small bottle and glass.

'Sofia?'

It was a man's voice calling outside. I had heard–but without
attending–the footsteps coming rapidly down the track from the
bridge. They had paused at the gate.

Sofia, near the door, turned quickly, glass in hand. The man was
still beyond my range of vision, and he could not have seen me.

'All is well,' he said shortly. 'And as for Josef–what is the matter?'

This, as Sofia made some little hushing gesture, indicating that
she was not alone. 'Someone is with you?' he asked sharply.

'It is the English lady from the hotel, and–'

'*The English lady?*' The swiftly-spoken Greek was almost explo-
sive. 'Have you no more sense than to invite her in to show off your
work, when at any moment Josef–'

'It is all right to speak Greek in front of her,' said Sofia. 'She
understands it perfectly.'

I heard his breath go in, as if he had shut his mouth hard on whatever he had been going to say. The latch clicked.

I stepped forward. The newcomer had swung open the gate and we met in the sunlit doorway.

He was a powerful-looking man in the late forties, broadly built and swarthy, with the gloss of good living on his skin. His face was square, going to fat a little, with high cheekbones and the inevitable moustache; a typical Greek face, which could have been the one I had last seen under the red head-dress, but I didn't think it was. In any case, he was not wearing Cretan dress. He had obviously been working, and wore shabby grey trousers covered with dust, and a khaki shirt, with a scarlet kerchief knotted at the neck. A brown linen jacket hung from his shoulders. This last garment looked expensive, and bore, almost visibly, the label of a Knightsbridge 'sports' department. My interest focused and sharpened. This must be my host, Stratos Alexiakis.

'This is my brother,' said Sofia.

I was already giving him my nicest smile, and my hand. 'How do you do? I'm sorry, I know I shouldn't have taken Kyria Sofia's time, when her husband is expected home for his meal. But I was walking through the village, and your sister was the only person I knew, so I invited myself in. I'll go now.'

'No, no, indeed!' He had retained my hand, and now led me, almost forcibly, to the seat under the fig-tree. 'I am sorry, I would never have spoken so, if I had realized you understood me! But my sister's husband is not a man for company, and I thought if he came home to find her gossiping–' a grin and a shrug–'well, you know how it is if a man is hungry, and a meal not ready. No, no, please sit down! What would my sister think of me if I drive her guest away? You must taste her peppermint drink; it is the best in the village.'

Sofia, her face expressionless, handed me the glass. There was nothing to show that either of them was relieved at the way I had interpreted his remarks. I tasted the drink, and praised it lavishly, while Stratos leaned one powerful shoulder against the door-jamb, and watched me benignly. Sofia, standing stiffly in the doorway, watched him.

'He is late,' she said. The statement sounded tentative, like a question, as if Stratos might have known the reason why.

He shrugged, and grinned. 'Perhaps, for once, he is working.'

'He did not–help you in the field?'

'No.'

He turned back to me, speaking in English.

'You're comfortable at my hotel?' His English was excellent, but still, after twenty years, hadn't lost the accent.

'Very, thank you, and I love my room. You've got a good place here, Mr. Alexiakis.'

'It is very quiet. But you told me on the telephone that this is what you want.'

'Oh, yes. I live in Athens, you see, and it gets a bit crowded and noisy towards summer. I was longing to get away somewhere, where the tourist crowds didn't go . . .'

I talked easily on, explaining yet again about my own and Frances' reasons for choosing Agios Georgios. I didn't even try to conceal from myself, now, that I wanted to establish a very good reason for the time I intended to spend exploring the mountain and shore round about. A movie camera, I thought, as I talked on and on about film (of which I know nothing), is an excellent excuse for a lot of unholy curiosity . . .

'And the boat,' I finished, 'will pick us up on Monday, if all goes well. The party's going on to Rhodes from here, and I'll join them for a couple of days, then I must go back to Athens. They'll go on to the Dodecanese, then my cousin'll come to stay with me in Athens, on her way home.'

'It sounds very nice.' I could see him chalking up the score; a party, a boat, a private tour; money. 'So you work in Athens? That accounts for your excellent Greek. You make mistakes, of course, but you are very fluent, and it is easy to understand what you mean. Do you find that you follow all you hear, as well?'

'Oh, no, not really.' I wondered, as I spoke, how often tact and truth go hand in hand. 'I mean, I couldn't translate word for word, though I get the gist of speech pretty well, except when people talk fast, or with too much of a regional accent. Oh, thank you,' to Sofia, who had taken my empty glass. 'No, no more. It was lovely.'

Stratos was smiling. 'You've done very well, all the same. You'd be surprised how many English people stay over here for quite some time, and never trouble to learn more than a word or two. What is your work in Athens?'

'I'm a rather unimportant junior secretary at the British Embassy.'

This was chalked up, too, and with a shock: I saw it.

'What does she say?' This, almost in a whisper, from Sofia.

He turned his head, translating carelessly: 'She works at the British Embassy.'

'Oh!' It was a tiny exclamation as the glass slipped to the ground, and broke.

'Oh, dear!' I exclaimed. 'What a shame! Let me help!'

I knelt down, in spite of her protests, and began to pick up the fragments. Luckily the glass was thick and coarse, and the pieces were large.

Stratos said, without stirring: 'Don't worry, Sofia, I'll give you another.' Then, with a touch of impatience: 'No, no, throw the pieces away, girl, it'll never mend. I'll send Tony across with a new glass for you, a better one than this rubbish.'

I handed Sofia the pieces I had collected, and stood up. 'Well, I've enjoyed myself very much, but, in case your husband does come home soon, *kyria*, and doesn't appreciate a crowd, I think I'll go. In any case, my cousin should be arriving any minute now.'

I repeated my thanks for the drink, and Sofia smiled and nodded and bobbed, while giving the impression that she hardly heard what I was saying; then I went out of the gate, with Stratos beside me.

He walked with his hands dug deep into his pockets, and his shoulders hunched under the expensive jacket. He was scowling at the ground so ferociously that I began to wonder uneasily what he might say. His first words showed, disarmingly enough, that he was deeply chagrined that I had seen the threadbare poverty of his sister's home.

'She won't let me help her.' He spoke abruptly, as if I should have known what he was talking about. 'I've come home with money, enough to buy all she needs, but all she will take is a little payment for work in the hotel. Scrubbing work. My sister!'

'People are proud sometimes.'

'Proud! Yes, I suppose it's that. It's all she has had for twenty years, after all, her pride. Would you believe it, when we were children, my father had his own caique, and when his uncle died, we inherited land, the land up at the head of the plateau, where it is sheltered, the best in Agios Georgios! Then my mother died, and my father had ill-health, and the land was all there was for my sister's dowry. I went to England, and I worked. Oh, yes, I worked!' His teeth showed. 'But I have something to show for those years, while she—every drachma she has, she makes herself. Why, even the fields—'

He broke off, and straightened his shoulders. 'Forgive me, I should not throw my family troubles at you like that! Perhaps I needed a European ear to pour them into—did you know that a great many Greeks regard themselves as living east of Europe?'

'That's absurd, when you think what Europe owes them.'

'I dare say.' He laughed. 'Perhaps I should have said an urban and civilized ear. We're a long way from London, are we not–even from Athens? Here, life is simple, and hard, especially for women. I had forgotten, in the time I have been away. One forgets that these women accept it . . . And if one of them is fool enough to marry a Mussulman, who uses his religion as an excuse for . . .' His shoulders lifted, and he laughed again. 'Well, Miss Ferris, and so you're going to hunt flowers and take movies while you're here?'

'Frances will, and I dare say I'll tag along. Does the *Eros* belong to you, Mr. Alexiakis?'

'The *Eros*? Yes, did you see her, then? How did you guess?'

'There was a boy working on her, that I'd seen up at the hotel. Not that that meant anything, but I just wondered. I rather wanted to ask . . .' I hesitated.

'You would like to go out, is that it?'

'I'd love it. I'd always wanted to see this coast from the sea. Some children told me there was a good chance of seeing dolphins; there's a bay a short distance to the west, they said, with rocks running out deep, and sometimes dolphins even come in among the swimmers.'

His laugh was hearty, even a little too hearty. 'I know the place. So that old legend still goes on! There hasn't been a dolphin seen there since the time of Pliny! I ought to know, I fish that way quite often. Not that I go out much with the caique, that's Alkis' job; I'm not used to hard work of that kind any more. But the caique was going cheap, so I bought her; I like a lot of irons in the fire, and some day, when business gets keen, I shall make money with visitors. Meanwhile, I get my fish cheap, and soon, I think, we shall be able to bring our own supplies from Chania.'

We were in front of the hotel now. He stopped.

'But of course you may go out with Alkis, any time. You must go eastwards, the coast is better, and some way along there is a ruin of an old harbour, and if you walk a little way, there is an old church, if these things interest you?'

'Oh, yes. Yes, of course they do.'

'Tomorrow, then?'

'I–well, no, that is, perhaps my cousin'll have some ideas . . . I mean, she's just been cruising, after all, and I expect she'll want a day or so ashore. Later, I–I'd love it. You . . . don't use the caique yourself, you said?'

'Not often. I have little time at present. I only fish for sport, and for that I have a small boat.'

'Oh, yes, that little boat beside the hotel? The orange one? You mean that you go light-fishing, with those huge lamps?'

'That's right, with a spear.' Again that grin, friendly, slightly deprecating, claiming—but not offensively—a common bond of knowledge unshared by the villagers. 'Nice and primitive, eh? But terrific sport—like all primitive pastimes. I used to be very good at it when I was a young man, but one gets a little out of practice in twenty years.'

'I watched the light-fishers once, in the bay at Paros. It was fascinating, but one couldn't see much from the shore. Just the lights bobbing, and the man lying with the glass, peering down, and sometimes you could see the one with the spear, striking.'

'Do you want to come out with me?'

'I'd love to!' The words were out, genuinely, thoughtlessly, before it came back to me, with a kick of recollection, that—until I knew a great deal more about him—I quite definitely was not prepared to spend a night with Stratos Alexiakis in a small boat, or anywhere else.

'Well,' he was beginning, while my mind spun uselessly, like a gramophone with a broken spring, when Tony came running down the steps to meet us, as lightly as something out of the chorus of *The Sleeping Beauty*.

'*There* you are, my dears, you've met. Stratos, that wretched get, from Chania wants twelve drachs each for the wine, he says he won't send it else. Dire, isn't it? He's on the blower now, could you cope? Did you have a nice walk, dear? Find the post office? Marvellous, isn't it? But you must be *flaked*. Let me bring you a lemon *pressé*, eh? Guaranteed straight off our very own tree. Oh, look, isn't that the caique, just come in? And someone coming up from the harbour as ever was, with Georgi carrying her case. How that child always manages to be in the way of making a couple of drachs . . . Just like our Stratos here, madly lucky. It is your cousin? Now, isn't that just ducky? By the time Miss Scorby's unpacked it'll be just nice time for tea.'

Chapter 10

And, swiftly as a bright Phoebean dart
Strike for the Cretan isle: and here thou art!
KEATS: *Lamia*

'WELL,' SAID FRANCES, 'it's very nice to be here. And the tea is excellent. I suppose Little Lord Fauntleroy makes it himself?'

'Hush, for goodness' sake, he'll hear you! He says if you want him, you only have to yell, he's always around. What's more, he's rather sweet. I've fallen for him.'

'I never yet met the male you didn't fall for,' said Frances. 'I'd begin to think you were ill, if you weren't somewhere along the course of a love-affair. I've even learned to know the stages. Well, well, this is really very pleasant, isn't it?'

We were sitting in the hotel 'garden', in the shade of the vine. There was nobody about. Behind us, an open door gave on the empty lobby. Tony was back in the bar: faintly, round the end of the house, came the sound of talk from café tables on the street.

The sun was slanting rapidly westward. There was a little ripple now, running across the pale silk of the sea, and the breeze stirred the sleepy scent from the carnations in the wine-jars. In full sunlight, at the edge of the gravel, stood a big pot of lilies.

Frances stretched her long legs in front of her, and reached for a cigarette. 'Yes, this was a ve-ery good idea of yours. Athens at Easter could be a bit much. I can see that. I'd forgotten, till you wrote, that the Greek Easter would be later than ours. We had it last week-end when we were in Rome. I imagine the Greek country

Easter'll be a bit of a contrast, and I must say I'm looking forward to
it. Oh, thanks, I'd love another cup. Now, how long since I saw
you? Good heavens, nearly eighteen months! Tell me all about
yourself.'

I regarded her with affection.

Frances, though a first cousin, is very much older than I. She was
at this time something over forty, and though I know it is a sign of
immaturity to think of this as being a vast age, I know that it seemed
so to me. From the earliest days I remember, Frances has been
there. When I was very small I called her 'Aunt Frances', but she put
a stop to that three years ago – at the time when, after my mother's
death, I went to live with her. Some people, I know, find her
formidable; she is tall, dark, rather angular, with a decisive sort of
voice and manner, and a charm which she despises, and rarely
troubles to use. Her outdoor job has given her the kind of
complexion which is called 'healthy'; she is as strong as a horse, and
an excellent business woman. She dresses well, if severely. But her
formidable exterior is deceiving, for she is the most genuinely
tolerant person I know, and sometimes carries 'live and let live' to
alarming lengths. The only things she cannot stand are cruelty and
pretentiousness. I adore her.

Which is why, on her command to 'tell her all about myself', I did
just that – at least, I plunged into a haphazard and pretty truthful
account of my job, and my Athens friends. I didn't trouble to edit,
though I knew that some of the latter would have fitted a bit oddly
into Frances' staid Berkshire home.

She heard me out in amused silence, drinking her third cup of tea,
and tapping ash into the nearest *píthos*.

'Well, you seem to be getting a lot of fun out of life, and after all
that's what you came for. How's John? You don't mention him.'

'John?'

'Or was it David? I forget their names, though heaven knows why
I should, as your letters are spotted with them like a currant-cake,
while the fit's on. Wasn't it John, the reporter from the *Athens News*?'

'Oh, him. That was ages ago. Christmas, anyway.'

'So it was. Come to think of it, your last two letters were
remarkably blank. Heart-whole and fancy-free?'

'Entirely.' I pulled a pink carnation near to me on its swaying
stalk, and sniffed it.

'Well, it makes a change,' said Frances mildly. 'Of course, it's all
very well having a heart like warm putty, but one of these days your

impulses are going to land you in something you won't easily get out of. Now what are you laughing at?'

'Nothing. Is the *Paolo* calling for us on Monday?'

'Yes, all being well. You are coming with us to Rhodes, then? Good. Though just at the moment I feel I never want to move again. This is what the travel guides call "simple", but it's nice, and terribly restful . . . Listen.'

A bee in the lilies, the soft murmur of the sea on the shingle, the subdued Greek voices . . .

'I told Tony I wished they could keep it like this,' I said. 'It's heaven just as it is.'

'Mmm. And you were right, my love. The flowers I've seen so far, even just along the roadside, are enough to drive a woman to drink.'

'But you came by boat!'

'Oh, yes, but when we were stuck that Sunday night, in Patras, three of us hired a car and went exploring. We didn't have time to go far before dark, but I made the driver stop so often, while I rushed off into the fields, that he thought I was mad—or else that my bladder was permanently diseased. But as soon as he gathered that it was just the flowers I was looking at, do you know what he did?'

I laughed. 'Picked some for you?'

'Yes! I came back to the car, and there he was, six foot two of what *you* would recognize as magnificent Hellenic manhood, waiting for me with a bunch of orchids and anemones, and a kind of violet that sent my temperature up by several degrees. Aren't they sweet?'

'Well, I don't know which violet—'

'Not the violets, ass, the Greeks.' She stretched again, luxuriously. 'My goodness, I'm glad I came! I'm going to enjoy every minute, I can see that. Why, oh *why* do we live in England, when we could live here? And incidentally, why does Tony? Live here, I mean, when he could live in England?'

'He said there was money to be made here when they put up the new wing, which is a polite way of saying when they build a hotel that *is* a hotel. I wondered if he had money in it himself. He *says* he's got a weak chest.'

'Hm. He looks a pretty urban type to settle here, even for a short spell . . . unless the *beaux yeux* of the owner have got something to do with it. He came with him from London, didn't he? What's *he* like?'

'Stratos Alexiakis? How did you—oh, of course, I told you the set-up in my letter, I forgot. He seems very nice. I say, Frances.'

'Mmm?'

'Would you care for a walk along the shore? It gets dark here fairly soon. I—I'd quite like a stroll, myself.'

This was not true, but what I had to say could hardly be said under the listening windows.

'All right,' she said amiably, 'when I've finished this cup of tea. What did you do with yourself in Chania, if that's how you pronounce it?'

'You don't say the "ch" like ours; it's a *chi*, a sort of breathed "k", like in "loch" . . . Chania.'

'Well, what was it like?'

'Oh, it—it was very interesting. There are Turkish mosques.'

Another thing I should have mentioned about Frances: you can't fool her. At least, I can't. She's had too much practice, I suppose, in detecting the little off-white lies of my childhood. She glanced at me, as she shook another cigarette loose from the pack. 'Was it, now? Where did you stay?'

'Oh, it's the biggish hotel in the middle of the town, I forget the name. You're chain-smoking, you'll get cancer.'

'No doubt.' Her voice came muffled through the lighting of the cigarette. She looked at me across the flame, then she got to her feet.

'Come along, then. Why the shore?'

'Because it's lonely.'

She made no comment. We picked our way through the vivid clumps of ice-daisies, to find that a rough path of a sort led along the low, dry rocks that backed the shingle. Further along there was a ridge of hard sand, where we could walk side by side.

I said: 'I've got something I want to talk to you about.'

'Last night's stay in Chania?'

'Clever, aren't you? Yes, more or less.'

'Is that why you laughed when I said that your impulses'd land you in trouble one day?' As I was silent, she glanced at me sideways, quizzically. 'Not that I'm any judge, but Chania seems an odd place to choose to misbehave in.'

'I wasn't even *in* Chania last night! And I haven't—!' I broke off, and suddenly giggled. 'As a matter of fact, I *did* spend the night with a man, now that I come to think about it. I'd forgotten that.'

'He seems,' said Frances tranquilly, 'to have made a great impression. Well, go on.'

'Oh, Frances, darling, I do love you! No, it's not some foully embarrassing love-tangle—when did I ever? It's—I've run into trouble – not my trouble, someone else's, and I wanted to tell you about it, and ask you if there's anything in the world I can do.'

'If it's not your trouble, do you have to do anything?'

'Yes.'

'A heart like warm putty,' said Frances resignedly, 'and sense to match. All right, what's his name?'

'How d'you know it's a he?'

'It always is. Besides, I assume it's the one you spent the night with.'

'Oh. Yes.'

'Who is he?'

'He's a civil engineer. His name is Mark Langley.'

'Ah.'

'It isn't "ah" at all! As a matter of fact,' I said, very clearly, 'I rather detest him.'

'Oh, God,' said Frances, 'I knew this would happen one day. No, don't glare at me, I'm only teasing. Well, go on. You've spent the night with a detestable engineer called Mark. It makes a rousing start. Tell all.'

*   *   *

Her advice, when I had at length told all, was concise and to the point.

'He told you to get out and stay out, and he's got this man Lambis to look after him. They sound a pretty capable pair, and your Mark's probably fairly well all right by now. The two of them will be back on their boat, you may be sure, with everything under control. I should stay out.'

'Y-yes, I suppose so.'

'Besides, what could you do?'

'Well, obviously, I could tell him what I've found out. I mean, I'm absolutely certain it must be Tony and Stratos Alexiakis and Sofia.'

'Quite probably. Granted that your Mark remembers accurately what he saw and heard, and that there was an Englishman there on the scene of the murder, along with a man in Cretan dress and another Greek, and a woman . . .' She paused a moment. 'Yes, once you've accepted Tony's involvement, the others follow as the night the day. It's a little closed circle, Tony, Stratos, Sofia, Josef – and the stranger, whether English or Greek, whom Tony certainly knew and talked to.'

I stopped in my tracks, staring at her. 'Him? But how? He wasn't there. There was only the Greek, and the Cretan, and–'

'My dear,' she said gently, 'you've got yourself so involved with Mark's side of this that you've forgotten how it started.'

'How it started?'

'There was a murdered man,' she said.

Silence, broken only by the crisping of the shingle at the sea's edge. I stooped, picked up a flat pebble, and skimmed it at the surface of the water. It sank immediately. I straightened up, dusting my hands.

'I've been awfully stupid,' I said humbly.

'You've been right in the thick of it, honey, and you've been frightened, It's easy for me, walking calmly in at half-time. I can see things more clearly. Besides, I'm not emotionally involved.'

'Who said I was?'

'Aren't you?'

I was still watching the place where my pebble had struck. 'Frances, Colin Langley's only fifteen.'

She said gently: 'Darling, that's the point. That's why I'm telling you to keep away from it unless you actually do find out what's happened to him. Otherwise you might only do harm. Look, don't you think we'd better go back now? The sun's nearly gone, and the going's getting beastly rough.'

This was true. As I had told my story, we had been making our way round the bay, and had reached the foot of the big cliffs at the far side. What had looked from the distance like a line of shingle round their feet, proved to be a narrow storm-beach of big boulders piled there by the south wind and the sea. Above this, between the topmost boulders and the living cliff, ran a narrow path, steep and awkward. It skirted the headland, then dived steeply down towards the crescent beach of a small, sandy bay.

'It looks nice along there,' said Frances. 'I wonder if that's your Bay of Dolphins?'

'I think that's further along, the water's too shallow here at the edge, and Georgi said you could get right out along the rocks above deep water, and even dive. Look, that must be it, beyond the next headland, I think you can see the rock-stacks running out. With the sun going down behind them, they look just like shadows.'

We stood for a few minutes in silence, shading our eyes against the glitter of the brilliant sea. Then Frances turned away.

'Come along, you're tired. And you could do with a good stiff drink before dinner, by the look of you.'

'It's an idea.' But my voice sounded dreary, even to myself. I turned to follow her back the way we had come.

'Don't think I don't know how you feel.' Her tone was matter-of-fact and curiously soothing. 'It isn't just to keep you out of trouble that I'm telling you to keep away from Mark. I can give you good reasons. If you went trailing up there looking for him, you might be seen, followed, anything: you might lead them to him. Or, if you made them suspicious, you might—and this is more important—frighten them into killing Colin . . . if, that is, Colin is still alive.'

'Oh, God, I suppose you're right. I—I've not been thinking very straight.' I put a hand to my head. 'If you'd seen Sofia. That's what really frightened me . . . when Josef didn't come home. You should have seen her face.'

Incoherent as I was, she understood me. 'You mean that she's not worrying in case he's broken his neck out there on the mountain-side, but because she's afraid of what he may be doing?'

'Yes. And there are only two things I can think of that he might be doing.'

She was blunt. 'Meaning that if Josef is your Cretan murderer—and I'd risk a bet on it myself—he's either still out hunting for Mark, to kill him, or he's mounting guard over Colin somewhere?'

'And she's terrified.' I swallowed. 'If he's with Colin, and she knows it, and she's afraid of what he may be doing . . . Well, there it is.'

My voice trailed off, miserably. She didn't answer, and we trudged along for some minutes in silence. The sun had gone now, dipping swiftly into the sea, and the shadow of the cliffs had reached after us. The breeze had dropped. At the other side of the bay there was a light in the hotel. It seemed a long way away.

I said at length: 'You're right, of course. Mark told me to keep out, and he meant it. Unless I actually found Colin—'

'That's it, you see. That's why he wouldn't go to the authorities, he told you that. If any question were asked, or if Mark and Lambis came here openly, or if anyone shoved the affair to the point where accusations were made—I wouldn't give you twopence for the boy's chances of surviving to tell his part of the story. He's the hostage.'

'I see that. Mark told me himself, after all. All right, I—I'll stay put, Frances, don't worry. But all the same—'

'Well?'

'There's nothing to stop me *looking* for him, is there? If I'm terribly careful? I–I can't just put him out of my head, can I?'

'No, love. You go ahead. I don't see how you could stop looking, even if you wanted to. It isn't just a thing one forgets overnight, like losing a pencil. All you can do, for the sake of your own peace of mind, is to assume he's still alive, and keep your eyes open. One thing, for a start; if he's alive, he's got to be fed.'

'Of course! And not too far away, at that. If one kept a tight eye on Sofia–I'll bet it's she who feeds him . . . though it could be Tony, I suppose.'

She smiled. 'My bet's on Sofia. Whoever does it probably has to get up at crack of dawn to avoid being seen, and I don't just see Little Lord Fauntleroy frisking around in the dew.'

'Well, I shall, and tomorrow as ever was. I'll go for an early-morning swim near the hotel, and keep my eyes skinned.'

'You do that,' said Frances. 'Look, there's someone out there now. That's the little boat putting out, isn't it? The man in it–is that Stratos Alexiakis?'

A man, a dim figure in the fast-falling dusk, had been stooping over the small boat, which was now moored beside the rocks by the hotel. He climbed in, and cast her off. He busied himself over something in the stern, and presently we heard the splutter of an engine. The boat started towards us, keeping well inshore.

'I think so,' I said. 'He must have taken an out-board motor down . . . I wonder where he's going?'

We had both stopped to watch him. He was standing well forward, and, as we drew nearer, we could see that the rudder had a long lever attached, to enable him to steer while peering over the shoulders of the boat into the lighted water. The huge lamps were in their places in the bows, but were as yet unlit.

She was drawing level with us, and he had seen us. It was Stratos. He grinned and waved, then he moved aft for a minute, and the engine slowed to a soft *put-put*, so that the boat seemed to be just drifting by. I could make out the white letters on her bows: ΨΥΧΗ.

His voice came cheerfully over the water. 'Hullo there! Would you like to come?'

'Another time!' We both grinned and waved in what we hoped was a cordial refusal. 'Thanks all the same! Good fishing!'

He raised a hand, stooped again to the engine, and *Psyche* veered away in a long, lovely curve for the tip of the headland. Her wash lapped the shore beside us, and the small shingle hissed and grated.

'Hm,' said Frances, 'very matey.'

'I asked him about light-fishing before.'

'Well, there's something for us, anyway. Detection without tears. Colin's not along that way, or Stratos would hardly welcome visitors.' She turned to go, then said quickly: 'What's the matter?'

I was standing still, like a dummy, with the back of my hand to my mouth.

'Frances! The *Eros*!'

'The what?'

'He's got a boat, a big one, lying in the harbour! *That's* where he'll be!'

She said nothing for a moment, regarding me with a frowning look I couldn't quite read. Then she nodded. 'Yes, that's something we could try. If we're allowed near the *Eros*, we may be sure she's innocent; if not, then I think you can certainly go straight up to look for Mark tomorrow. It would be the easiest thing in the world for those two to bring their caique in after dark, and board the *Eros*, and search her. They could be clear away in no time. We could do something about keeping Stratos and Co. away from the har-bour – burn down the hotel, or something like that.'

I laughed, then looked curiously at her. 'Do you know, I believe you meant that?'

'If it was the only thing that would do the trick,' said Frances crisply, 'why not? There's a boy being frightened and hurt by a bunch of thugs, and what's more, he probably believes, all this time, that his brother's dead. Oh, yes, if a little arson would help, I don't mind in the least burning Mr. Alexiakis' hotel, with him inside it. Meanwhile, we can certainly take a look at the *Eros*. We'll go straight down tonight, if only to put your mind at rest.'

'We?'

'Why not? It'd look more natural. Look, is that Tony on the terrace, waiting for us?'

'Yes.'

'Then for heaven's sake let's start looking natural straight away. I'm supposed to be a botanist, and you seem to have given me a build-up that would have flattered Linnaeus. Now, would you like to pause one moment, and peer passionately at this plant here – no, *here*, you owl, the one in the rock!'

'Is it rare?'

'Darling, it grows in every wall in the South of England. It's pellitory-of-the-wall, but you can bet your boots Tony won't know that! Go on, pick a bit, or one of those mesembryanthemums or something. Show willing.'

'The ice-daisies?' I stooped obediently. Tony was waiting under the tamarisks, not fifty yards away. 'Look,' I said, holding it out to her, 'they've shut. Don't they look like tiny plastic parasols?'

'Dear heaven,' said Frances devoutly, 'and to think I once hoped to make a naturalist of you! And another thing, that egret you mentioned; according to the books, there are no egrets in Greece.'

'I know that.' Without looking his way, I knew that Tony had come out from under the tamarisks, and was standing at the edge of the gravel. My voice must be carrying clearly to him. 'Just as there aren't any golden orioles, either—officially. But I've seen them at Epidaurus, and honestly, Frances, I saw a pair today between Chania and Kastelli, and I couldn't be wrong about a golden oriole; what else could they have been? I admit I might be wrong about the egret, but I can't think what else that was, either!'

'A squacco heron? They look white in flight. Oh, no, you said black legs and yellow feet . . . Why, hullo, Tony, something smells good.'

I said cheerfully: 'I hope it's not the octopus I saw down at the harbour today?'

'No, my dears, it's a *fricassée*, my very own *fricassée* of veal . . . done with wine, and mushrooms, and tiny, tiny peas. I call it *veau à jouer*.'

'Why on earth?'

'Well, veal by Gamble,' explained Tony. 'Now, ladies, dinner's almost ready, I'll have your drinks waiting for you when you come down. What's it to be?'

Chapter 11

What bird so sings, yet so does wail?
O 'tis the ravish'd nightingale.
Jug, jug, jug, jug, tereu, she cries,
And still her woes at midnight rise.
                                LYLY: *Campaspe*

THE CAIQUE WAS still where she had been, lying without movement in the still waters of the harbour. There was a riding-light on the mast; its reflection glimmered, stilly, feet below the level of her keel. Another light, bigger, glowed in its iron tripod at the end of the pier. Apart from these, all was darkness, and the dank, salt smell of the harbour water.

The youth, Alkis, must have left the caique for the night, for the dinghy no longer nuzzled her sides. It lay alongside the pier, at our feet.

We regarded it in silence.

Then a voice spoke suddenly from somewhere beside my elbow, nearly startling me straight into the harbour.

'You want to row out?' asked Georgi. 'I'll take you!'

I glanced at the caique again, lying so quietly in the darkness. Stratos was away fishing, Tony was in the bar, Alkis had presumably gone home. On the face of it, it looked like the sort of chance that shouldn't be missed . . . But—with Georgi? If Alkis had made the offer, well and good. That would have been proof enough, and we could have refused him, with another possibility safely eliminated. But to row across now, and, perhaps, actually find Colin there . . . in the village . . . at this time of night . . .

'What's he saying?' asked Frances.

I told her of Georgi's offer, and my own conclusions.

'I'm afraid you're right. We'll have to wait till morning to find out. If we did find him on board –' a little laugh – 'the only solution would be to up anchor, and sail full speed away, *Eros* and all, to meet the other caique. No doubt that's exactly what your capable friend would do, but let's face it, this is one of the occasions where being a woman has its limitations. I suppose you *can't* drive one of those things, can you?'

'Well, no.'

'That's that, then.'

'There is the rowing-boat.' I offered the suggestion with a marked lack of conviction, and she made a derisive sound.

'I can just see us rowing along the coast of Southern Crete in the pitch darkness, looking for a caique that's been hidden in a creek somewhere. I'm sorry, but we'll have to accept our female limitations and wait till morning.'

'As usual, you're so right.' I sighed. 'Well, I'll tell Georgi that we'll ask Stratos properly, in the morning.' I looked down at the boy, who had been following this incomprehensible exchange wide-eyed. 'Thanks a lot, Georgi, but not tonight. We'll ask Mr. Alexiakis tomorrow.'

'We can ask him now,' said Frances dryly. 'Here he comes . . . and how nice it would have been, wouldn't it, if we'd both been on the *Eros*, struggling madly with the gears and the starting-handle? I think, Nicola, my pet, that you and I must definitely keep to the less strenuous paths of crime.'

The soft *put-put* of the light-boat's engine sounded clearly now, as she rounded the pier.

'Here he is!' announced Georgi buoyantly, skipping to the extreme edge of the concrete, where he stood on tiptoe. 'He's been spear-fishing! *Now* you will see the big fish, the sea-bass! He must have got one, or he wouldn't have come back so soon!'

I found myself watching the boat's approach with, ironically, relief: at least now there was no question of heroics. Moreover, they were unnecessary. We could find what we wanted to find, the easy way. We didn't have to wait till morning.

We didn't even have to ask: Georgi did it for us. The boat, with its engine cut, glided alongside, and Stratos threw Georgi a rope, sending us a cheerful greeting.

'What did you get?' demanded Georgi.

'I wasn't spear-fishing. I've been to the pots. Well, ladies, out for another walk? It's Miss Scorby, is it not? How do you do? I see you

lose no time in exploring our big city. It's a pity you didn't take the
trip with me, it's a lovely night.'

'The ladies were wanting to go to the *Eros*,' said Georgi. 'Shall I
carry those up for you?'

'No, I'm taking the boat round again to the hotel. I came to put
some gear on the *Eros*.' He stood easily in the rocking boat, looking
up at us. 'Do you really want to have a look at her? She's not much
of a boat, but if you're interested –' A gesture of invitation completed the sentence.

I laughed. 'As a matter of fact, it was Georgi's idea, he wanted to
row us out. I would like to see her, of course, but let's wait till
daylight, when we take that trip. What have you caught?'

'*Scháros*. You'll have it tomorrow; it's very good.'

'I've heard of it, but I've never had it. Is that it? How do you catch
them?'

'You set pots rather like lobster-pots, and bait them with green-
stuff. I assure you, they're better than lobster, and handsome too,
aren't they? Here, Georgi, you can take this to your mother . . .
How that boy guessed I'd be coming in this way . . .!' This with a
grin and a grimace, as Georgi ran happily off, clutching the fish.

'Was that what he was waiting for?'

'Sure. He knows everything, that child; he'd be a godsend at
Scotland Yard. You ladies don't want a lift back to the hotel, then?'

'Oh, no, thank you, we're doing a tour of the town.'

Stratos laughed. ' "Agios Georgios by Night?" Well, you'll hardly
need a guide, or a bodyguard, or I'd offer to come with you. Good
night.'

He thrust with an oar against the pier, and the boat drifted away
towards the silent bulk of the *Eros*.

We walked back towards the houses.

'Well, I suppose that's something,' I said at length. 'The caique's
innocent, and our tour of the village doesn't worry him, either. *Or*
the fact that our nosy little Georgi's sculling around the place night
and day, and nattering Greek to me nineteen to the dozen. In fact,
I'd have said Stratos hadn't a care in the world. Wherever Colin is,
Stratos isn't worrying about his being found.'

'No,' was all Frances said, but not quite guardedly enough. We
were passing a lighted doorway, and I saw her expression. My heart
seemed to go small, painfully, as flesh shrinks from the touch of ice.

I said at last. 'You've been sure all along that Colin's dead, haven't
you?'

'Well, my dear,' said Frances, 'what possible reason can they have for keeping him alive?'

*   *   *

The night was very dark. Though it would soon be midnight, the moon was not yet up, and the stars were veiled by cloud. I had borrowed Frances' dark-blue poplin coat, and, hugging this round me, waited at the head of the stone steps outside my room.

There was still a light in Sofia's cottage. Though I had forced myself to admit that Frances might be right about Colin, I wasn't prepared to accept it without an effort, and I was ready to ride herd on Sofia all night if need be, and, if she left the cottage, to follow her. But midnight came, and the next slow half-hour, and still the lamplight burned, though every other house in the village was darkened.

It was twelve-thirty before a move was made, and then it was a harmless one; the crack of light round the cottage door vanished, and a small light flowered behind the thick curtains of the bedroom window. She had sat up late, perhaps to wait for Josef, and now she was going to bed. But I stayed where I was: if Sofia had not stirred from her cottage and the yard behind it, it might be for a good reason. I would give her a few minutes longer, and then, Frances or no Frances, I was going to take a look at that yard myself.

I went like a ghost down the steps, and skirted the open ground like a stealthy cat, hugging the shelter of the pistachio-trees. The dust underfoot made silent walking, and I slipped soundlessly past Sofia's garden wall, and round the end of her house into the narrow lane that twisted up from the end of the village towards the meagre vineyards under the cliff.

Here was the yard gate, in the wall behind the cottage. Beyond it, visible only as dimly-looming shapes, were the huge cone of the baking-oven, the great spiky pile of wood in a corner, and the shed backed against the rough wall that edged the lane.

I wondered if the gate would creak, and put a cautious hand down to it, but the hand met nothing. The gate stood wide already.

I paused for a moment, listening. The night was very still. I could hear no sound from the cottage, and no window faced this way. My heart was beating light and fast, and my mouth felt dry.

Something moved beside my feet, almost startling me into a cry, until I realized it was only a cat, on some errand as secret as my own, but apparently quite ready to welcome a partner in crime. It purred softly, and began to strop itself on my ankles, but when I stooped it slid away from my touch, and vanished.

It seemed I was on my own. I took a long breath to steady those heart-beats, then went in through the gate.

The door of the shed must lie to the right. I felt my way towards it, treading cautiously among the debris underfoot.

Somewhere beyond the cottage, across the square, a door opened suddenly, spilling light, and throwing the squat shape of the cottage into relief. As I shrank back towards the shadow of the wood-pile, the light was lopped off again as the door shut, and I heard rapid steps cross a strip of board flooring, then tread quickly across the square through the dust, coming this way.

Stratos, coming over from the hotel to see his sister. If Colin were here – if Stratos came into the yard . . .

He didn't. He pushed open the garden gate and went quietly to the cottage door. It wasn't locked. I heard the latch click, then the soft sound of voices, question and answer. Sofia must have brought the lamp out of the bedroom again, to meet him at the door, for again I could see the faint glow of light from beyond the dark bulk of the cottage.

His visit was certainly not secret, and his purpose, therefore, not likely to be sinister, but while through my confusion I realized this, I wasn't taking any chance of being found by him in Sofia's yard at nearly one in the morning. If I had to be found, much better be found in the lane . . .

From what I had seen of this in daylight, it was a dirty and unrewarding little cul-de-sac that led up between clumps of cypress, to peter out in a small vineyard under the cliff. What excuse I could give for being there I didn't know, but since Stratos had no earthly reason for suspecting me, no doubt I could get away with the age-old excuse of sleeplessness, and a walk in the night air. And anything was better than being caught lurking here. I melted quickly out of the gate and into the lane.

There I hesitated. One glance towards the hotel was enough to tell me I couldn't get that way without being seen; the light from the cottage door fell clear to the garden wall, and I could even see the moving edge of Stratos' shadow. It would have to be the lane.

I trod softly, hurrying away from the gateway, and almost immediately stepped on a loose stone that nearly brought me down. Before I had recovered, I heard the cottage door shut, and Stratos' quick steps to the gate.

I stood still, face turned away. I could only hope that, coming fresh from the lamplight, his eyes would not yet be adjusted to the dark. Otherwise, if he looked this way as he passed the corner of the wall, he would be bound to see me.

My fists were pressed down hard into the pockets of Frances' blue coat, while my mind spiralled like a feather in a current of air. What could I say to him? What plausible reason could I give for a midnight stroll up this unappetizing dead-end of a lane?

The answer came, piercingly sweet and loud, from a clump of cypresses beyond the wall; a nightingale's song, pouring into the silence from the crowded spires of the grove, and straight away it seemed as if the whole of that still night had been waiting, just for this. I know I held my breath. The trills and whistles and long, haunting clarinet-notes poured and bubbled from the black cypress. The bird must have sung for two full minutes while I stood there, blessing it, and waiting, with one ear still tuned for Stratos' retreating steps.

The nightingale stopped singing. Clearly, ten yards away, I heard the rattle of loose change in a pocket, then the scrape of a match. Stratos had stopped at the corner, and was leisurely lighting a cigarette.

The flaring match seemed unnaturally bright. If he looked up now . . .

He was lifting his head to inhale the first breath of smoke. My hand, thrust down in the pocket of Frances' coat, met the shape of a packet of cigarettes.

I turned. 'Mr. Alexiakis?'

His head jerked round, and the match dropped into the dust, and fizzled out. I moved towards him, with one of Frances' cigarettes in my hand. 'Do you mind? Have you a light, please? I came out without one.'

'Why, Miss Ferris! Of course.' He came to meet me, and struck and held a match for me. 'You're out very late, aren't you? Still exploring?'

I laughed. ' "Agios Georgios by Night?" Not really. I did go up to bed, but then I heard a nightingale, and I had to come out to track it down.'

'Ah, yes, Tony told me you were keen on birds.' He sounded unworried to the point of indifference. He leaned a shoulder back against the wall behind him, gesturing with his cigarette in the direction of the cypresses. 'Up there, was it? They always sing there, ever since I was a boy I remember them. I don't notice them now. Was there one tonight? It's a little early for them.'

'Just one, and he seems to have stopped.' I smothered a yawn. 'I think I'll go to bed now. It's been such a long day, but such a lovely one. Perhaps tomorrow—'

I stopped short, because he moved with a sharp, shushing gesture, as if some sound had startled him. I had heard it, too, but it had not registered with me as quickly as it had with Stratos; for all that relaxed, indifferent air, the man must be as alert as a fox.

We had been standing close against the wall of the shed that I had come to search. This was built of big, rough stones, crudely plastered, and with many gaps between. The sound had come apparently through some gap just beside us—a small, scraping sound, then a soft rustle as of spilled dust. Something moving, inside Sofia's shed.

Stratos had stiffened, head cocked. I could see the sideways gleam of his eyes in the tiny glow of his cigarette.

I said quickly: 'What is it?'

'I thought I heard something. Wait.'

Colin, I thought wildly, *it's Colin* . . . but then I saw that fear was making me stupid. If it were indeed Colin, then Stratos would know it, and would certainly not have informed me of the boy's presence in the shed. But if there was someone in the shed, I knew who it would be . . . I didn't even think of Lambis, who might very well have hung around till dusk to start a close search of the village; my mind jumped straight to Mark. There was no reason why I should have been so sure, but, as clearly as if I had heard him speak, I knew he was there, just on the other side of the wall, waiting and listening, and trying, after that one betraying movement, not even to breathe . . .

I moved away quickly, scraping my feet carelessly among the stones. 'I didn't hear a thing. Are you going back now? It may just have been—'

But he was already moving, and, close to him as I was, I could see that his hand had dropped, quite casually, to his hip. As he went through the yard gate I was on his heels.

I had to stop him somehow, somehow give warning. I cried out, 'Good heavens, is that a gun?' and put a detaining hand on his arm, holding him back, trying to sound merely nervous and feminine, and, with the genuine tremor in my voice, probably succeeding. 'For goodness' sake!' I quavered. 'You don't need that! It'll be a dog

or something, and you really can't just shoot it! Please, Mr.
Alexiakis—'

'If it is a dog, Miss Ferris, I shall not shoot it. Now, please, you
must let me—ah!'

From the shed had come a whole series of sounds, now quite unmistakable. A scrape and a clatter, a curious clucking noise, and the
thud of a small, soft body landing from a height. Then from the
half-open door shot a vague, slim shape which slid mewing between
our feet, and was gone into the shadowed lane.

Stratos stopped, and his hand dropped from his hip. He laughed.
'A cat! This is the criminal on my sister's property! You may calm
yourself, Miss Ferris, I shall certainly not shoot *that*!'

'I'm sorry,' I said shamefacedly. 'That was silly of me, but guns
and things do panic me. Besides, you might have got hurt or
something. Well, thank goodness that's all it was! I was talking to
that cat in the lane a while ago; he must have been ratting.'

'Nothing so useful,' said Stratos cheerfully. 'My brother-in-law
keeps a decoy quail in there. The cats can't get at it, but they keep
trying. Well, we'll shut the door, shall we?'

He pulled it shut, and turned out of the yard. We walked back to
the hotel together.

*　　*　　*

Sofia's yard seemed darker than ever. The shed door was still
shut. The cat had gone, and the nightingale was silent in the
cypresses. A cracked bell from somewhere near the harbour tolled
three.

The door opened with only the slightest creak. I slipped through
it into the shed, and pulled it shut behind me.

'Mark?' It was only a breath.

No reply. I stood still, listening for his breathing, and hearing
only my own. There was brushwood stacked somewhere; I could
smell rosemary, and dried verbena, and all the sweet sharp scents of
the bed he and I had shared last night.

'Mark?' I began to feel my way cautiously over to the wall that
skirted the lane. A small sound behind me brought me round
sharply, with eyes straining wide against the dark, but it was only
the scrabbling of claws, and a small rustling movement from a
corner where the quail's cage must be. No other sound.

I groped my way over to the wall. As my hands met the stone the nightingale, outside in the grove, began to sing again. The sound filled the darkness, full and near. I felt along the wall. Stone, rough stone, cold stone. Nothing else; and no sound but the rich music from the cypress-grove. I had been wrong; Mark hadn't been here after all; the strong sense I had had of his presence had only been something evoked by the verbena-scents of the piled brushwood. It had been the cat, and only the cat, that we had heard.

My hand met something that wasn't stone, something smooth and sticky, and still faintly warm, that made the hair rise up the back of my neck, and my stomach muscles tighten sharply. I pulled the hand away and stood there, holding it stiffly before me, fingers splayed.

So instinct had been right, after all. Mark had been there, leaning against the wall within inches of Stratos and me, perhaps betrayed by exhaustion into some revealing movement, while his shoulder bled against the stone. In sudden fear I stooped to feel if he had fallen there, at the foot of the wall. Nothing. The shed was empty. There was only his blood.

Outside, the nightingale still sang in the cypresses.

I don't remember getting back to the hotel. I know I took no care. But I met no one, and no one saw me running back across the square, with one hand closed tightly over its smeared palm.

Chapter 12

. . . One clear day when brighter sea-wind blew
And louder sea-shine lightened, for the waves
Were full of god-head and the light that saves . . .
SWINBURNE: *Thalassius*

THE WATER WAS smooth and gentle, but with an early-morning sting to it, and a small breeze blew the salt foam splashing against my lips. The headland glowed in the early sunlight, golden above the dark-blue sea that creamed against the storm-beach at its feet.

Here, where I swam, the water was emerald over a shallow bar, the sunlight striking right down through it to illumine the rock below. It threw the shadow of the boat fully two fathoms down through the clear, green water.

Psyche rocked softly at her old moorings, orange and blue. I swam up to her, and threw an arm over the side. She tilted and swung, but held solid, squatly-built and fat-bellied, heavier than she looked. I waited a moment to get my breath, then gripped and swung myself in.

The boat rocked madly, bucked round on her rope, then accepted me. I thudded down on the bottom-boards, and sat there, dripping and panting, and rubbing the salt drops from my eyes.

I had had no reason for coming out to Stratos' boat, except that a boat anchored in a bay is a natural challenge to an idle swimmer. I sat on the broad stern-seat, resting in the sun, and reflecting that this was as good a place as any from which to watch the hotel.

If I had had any doubts about the innocence of Stratos' fishing-trip last night, one look at the boat would have dispelled them. There was no hiding-place for anything larger than a puppy, and nothing to be seen except the small-boat clutter that one might expect; oars, carefully laid along the sides, a baling-tin, a rope basket for fish, a kind of lobster-pot—the *scháros*-pot, I supposed—made of cane, a coil of rope, some hollow gourds for use as floats, and a folded tarpaulin. The only things strange to me were the fish-spear—a wicked double trident, with five or six barbed prongs set in a circle—and the glass. This was a sort of sea-telescope, a long metal tube with a glass the size of a dinner-plate set in the end. The fisherman lies in the bows, pushing this thing under water as far as it will go, and watches the depths.

I fingered it curiously, then lifted it, and lay down on the flat boarding behind the big brackets that held the lights. I carefully lowered the glass into the sea, and peered down through it.

You might, in a simpler world, have said it was magic. There was the illuminated rock of the sea-bed, every pebble clear, a living surface shifting with shadows as the ripples of the upper sea passed over it. Sea-weeds, scarlet and green and cinnamon, moved and swayed in drowsy patterns so beautiful that they drugged the eye. A school of small fish, torpedo-shaped, and barred like zebras, hung motionless, then turned as one, and flashed out of sight. Another, rose-coloured, and whiskered like a cat, came nosing out of a bed of grey coralline weed. There were shells everywhere.

I lay and gazed, with the sun on my back, and the hot boards rocking gently under me. I had forgotten what I had come out for; this was all there was in the world; the sea, the sun hot on my skin, the taste of salt, and the south wind . . .

Two shadows fled across the glimmering underworld. I looked up, startled.

Only two birds, shearwaters, flying low, their wings skimming the tops of the ripples; but they had brought me back to the surface. Reluctantly, I put the glass back where it had been, and turned to look at the hotel.

People were beginning to move now. A shutter was thrown back, and presently a wisp of smoke curled from the chimney. In the village a black-clad woman carried a jar to the well, and a couple of men were making for the harbour.

I sat there for a little longer, prolonging the moment, basking in the sheer physical joy brought by the salt water and the sun. Then I slid over the boat's side, and swam back to the hotel.

I picked up my towel from under the tamarisks, and padded up the steps to my room. Sofia's cottage door was open, and I caught a glimpse of her moving inside. She was sweeping. Below me, in the restaurant, Tony was singing '*Love me tender*' in a passionate counter-tenor. Stratos, in his shirt-sleeves, was outside in the square, talking to a couple of half-naked workmen with buckets and trowels. In the other cottages, people were moving about.

I went in to dress.

*　　*　　*

'Not a move out of place,' I reported to Frances. 'Everything as innocent as the day. I'm beginning to think the whole thing was a mirage.' I stretched, still feeling the luxurious physical pleasure of the salt water, and the mood it had inspired. 'And, oh my goodness, how I wish it was! I wish we had nothing in the world to think about except tramping off into the hills and looking at the flowers!'

'Well,' said Frances, reasonably, setting down her coffee-cup—she was finishing her breakfast in bed, while I sat on the edge of the table, swinging my legs—'what else *is* there? We can hardly plan anything. We've done all that lies ready to hand, and it does look now as if Lambis and your Mark have given the village a good going-over between them.'

'That's at least the fourth time you've called him my Mark.'

'Well, isn't he?'

'No.'

Frances grinned. 'I'll try to remember. As I was saying, all we can do now is behave as we normally would, and keep our eyes open. In other words, we go out for the day, and take the camera.'

I remember that I felt a kind of shame-faced relief. 'Okay. Where d'you want to go?'

'Well, since we've seen the shore and the village, the mountain seems the obvious choice, so we can extend our search there quite nicely. Anyway, nothing will keep me away from those irises you told me about last night.'

'So thick on the ground that you had to tread on them,' I said cheerfully, 'and cyclamens, all over the rock. And wild gladioli and tulips. And three colours of anemone. A yellow oxalis as big as a penny. Rock-roses the size of breakfast-cups and the colour of Devonshire cream. And, of course, if you go really high, those purple orchids that I told you about—'

Frances gave a moan, and pushed her tray aside. 'Get out of this, you little beast, and let me get up. Yes, yes, yes, we'll go as high as you like, and I only hope my aged limbs will stand it. You're not pulling my leg about the orchids?'

'No, honestly. Lady's-slippers, or something, as big as fieldmice, and trailing things, like the ones in shops that you can never afford.'

'I'll be with you in half an hour. Get Ceddie to have some lunch put together. We may as well take the whole day.'

'Ceddie?'

'Little Lord Fauntleroy. I forgot, your generation never reads,' said Frances, getting out of bed. 'A thumping good lunch, tell him, *and* some wine.'

The on-shore breeze had found its way well inland, and it was deliciously cool by the river-bridge. We went along the river, up the path that I had taken yesterday.

Our progress was slow. Frances, as I had known she would be, was enraptured by everything she saw. The sugar-canes, standing deep along the ditches, rustling. A pair of turtle doves, flying up out of a patch of melon-flowers. A jay, vivid and chattering. A nest of rock-nuthatches that I found on a broken wall. And the flowers . . . Soon she stopped exclaiming, and in a short while managed to overcome the feeling that one ought not to touch—let alone pick—the pale lilac anemones with indigo hearts, the miniature marigolds, the daisies purple, yellow, and white. Between her delight, and my own delight at her pleasure (for Greece was, I liked to think, my country, and I was showing her round it), we reached the upper plateau with its fields and windmills before I even had time to remember my preoccupations of yesterday.

There were a few people at work among the fields. We saw a man and his wife working with primitive long-handled hoes, one on either side of a furrow of beans. In another field a donkey stood patiently beside the ditch, waiting for its owner. Further on, a child sat on a bank beside a patch of crude pasture where vetches and camomile grew, watching over his little flock of four goats, two pigs, and a ewe with her lamb.

We left the main track and picked our way along the narrow beaten paths between the fields, pausing frequently for Frances to use her camera. Everything made a picture—the child, the beasts, the men bent over their work; even the long views of the plateau and the upper mountain were brought alive by the whirling sails of the windmills. These were everywhere on the plateau, dozens of them, skeleton structures of iron like small pylons, ugly in themselves, but now, with their white canvas sails spread and spinning in the morning's breeze, they looked enchantingly pretty, like enormous daisies spinning in the wind, filling the hot morning with the sigh of cool air and the sound of spilling water.

Then Frances found the irises.

These were the same as I had seen further up the hill-side, tiny irises three inches high, lilac and bronze and gold, springing out of ground baked as hard and—you would have sworn—as barren as fireclay. They grew on the stony banks, on the trodden pathway, in the dry verges of the bean-field, and swarmed as thick as butterflies right up to the walls of a windmill.

This, as luck would have it, was no ugly iron pylon, but a real mill, one of the two corn-mills that served the plateau. It was a solidly-built, conical structure, much like the windmills we know, with a thatched roof, and ten canvas sails. The sails, unlike those of the water-mills, were furled along their spokes, but this idle mill, with its arched doorway and dazzling whitewash, was beautiful. The irises—in places crushed and trodden—were thick around it, and just beside the doorstep stood a clump of scarlet gladioli. Behind the white mill crowded the lemon-groves that edged the plateau, and beyond these rose the silver slopes of Dicte.

Muttering strange oaths, Frances reached for her camera yet again. 'My God, I wish I'd brought five miles of film, instead of five hundred miserable feet! Why didn't you tell me that the very *dust* of this country was so damned photogenic? If only there was some movement! Why aren't the sails going?'

'It's a corn-mill. The owners only run it when somebody hires them to grind the corn. Each settlement has two or three, to serve everyone.'

'Oh, I see. Well, look, would *you* go into the picture, and—ah, that's lucky, there's a peasant woman . . . just what it needs, the very job . . .'

The door of the mill had been standing half open. Now it gaped wider, and a Greek woman, clothed in the inevitable black, and carrying a cheap rexine shopping-bag, came out. She turned, as if to pull the door shut, then she saw us, and stopped short in the act, with her hand still out to the big old-fashioned key that jutted from the lock.

Frances' camera whirred on, unconcernedly; but my heart had started to beat in erratic, painful thuds, and the palms of my hands were wet.

I thought: If I tell Frances that's Sofia, that'll be two of us acting our heads off, instead of only one. Frances, at least, must be left to behave naturally . . .

The camera stopped. Frances lowered it, and waved and smiled at

Sofia, who stood like stone, staring at us, with her hand still out to the door.

'Nicola, go and tell her it's a movie, will you? There's no need to pose, I want her moving. Ask her if she minds. And get in the picture yourself, please; I want that turquoise frock beside the gladioli. Just walk up to her and say something. Anything.'

Just walk up to her and say something. Dead easy, that was. *Have you got Colin Langley hidden in the mill, Sofia?* The sixty-four-thousand-dollar question.

I swallowed. I was scrubbing my hands surreptitiously on my handkerchief. 'I'll ask her,' I said, steadily enough, 'to show me into the mill. You'll get a good picture as we go into that dark archway.'

I walked across the irises to greet Sofia.

Frances still has the film. It is the only one, of many which she has of me, in which I walk and behave as if quite oblivious of the camera. As a rule, in front of a camera, I am stiff and shy. But on this occasion I wasn't thinking about Frances and her film; only about the woman who stood unmoving in the bright sunlight, with that half-shut door beside her, and her hand on the big key. It is a very effective piece of film, but I have never liked watching it. This was not a day that I care, now, to remember.

I trod through the irises, and smiled.

'Good morning, *kyria*. I hope you don't mind being photographed? This is my cousin, who's very keen, and she'd like a picture of you and the mill. This is your mill?'

'Yes,' said Sofia. I saw her tongue wet her lips. She bobbed her half-curtsey at Frances, who made some gesture of greeting, and called out 'How do you do?' I hoped that both would assume that an introduction had been made.

'It's a moving picture.' My voice sounded strained, and I cleared my throat. 'She just wants us to stand and talk here for a moment . . . there, you can hear the camera going again . . . and then, perhaps, walk into the mill.'

'Walk — into the mill?'

'Why, yes, if you don't mind? It makes a bit of action, you see, for the film. May we?'

For one long, heart-stopping minute I thought she was going to refuse, then she put a hand flat against the door, and pushed it wide. With an inclination of the head, and a gesture, she invited me in. It was a movement of great dignity, and I heard Frances give a little grunt of satisfaction as the camera got it.

I mounted the single step, and went into the mill.

*   *   *

Just inside the door a stone stairway, built against the wall, spiralled upwards. Within its curve, on the ground, stood sacks of grain, and a pile of brushwood for repairing the thatch. Against the wall was a stack of tools; a rough hoe, a spade, something that was probably a harrow, and a coil of light rope. A sieve hung from a nail.

I couldn't hear if the camera was still going. Sofia was just behind me. I looked up the curling stairway.

'May I go up?' Already, while I was speaking, I had mounted two steps, and my foot was on a third before I paused to glance back at her. 'I've always wanted to see inside a mill, but the only other one I've been to was derelict. That was on Paros . . .'

Sofia had her back to the light, and I couldn't see her face. Again I sensed that hesitation, and again my pulses thudded, while I gripped the narrow handrail. But she could hardly, without a boorishness comparable to my own, have refused.

'Please do.' Her voice was colourless. She put her bag down on the floor, and followed me closely up the stairs.

The chamber on the first floor was where the flour was weighed. Here were the old-fashioned scales, a contraption of chains and bar and burnished bowls, which would be slung from a hook on the massive wooden beam. All about the floor stood the big square tins which caught the milled flour as it came down the chute from the grindstones. Some of the tins were full of a coarse, meal-coloured flour. Here, too, were sacks of grain.

But no Colin Langley. And no place to hide him.

So much I took in while I was still climbing out of the stairwell. The place was as innocent as Stratos' boat had been. There was no hiding-place for anything much bigger than a mouse. As I stepped out on to the boarded floor, a mouse did indeed whisk out of the way between two tins, carrying some titbit in its mouth.

But there was another stairway, and another floor . . .

Beside me Sofia said, still in that colourless voice that was so unlike her: 'Since you are interested, *thespoints* . . . That is the chute down which the flour comes. You see? These are the scales for weighing it. You hang them up, so . . .'

I watched her in the light from the single window. Was it imagination, or was she more waxen-pale than ever in the bright glare of morning? Certainly she was acting with a reserve which might have been construed as uneasiness, or even anxiety, but her stolid peasant dignity had come to her aid, and I could see nothing in her face that I could put a name to; except that, today, my intrusion and interest in her doings were less than welcome.

She had finished whatever she was explaining to me, and began to dismantle the scales with an air of finality.

'And now, if the *thespoinís* will excuse me –'

'Oh, don't put them away yet!' I cried. 'I know my cousin'll want to see this – it's terribly interesting! Frances!'

I ran to the stairs and called down, adding warmly, as poor Sofia hesitated, scales in hand: 'It's awfully good of you; I'm afraid we're being a lot of trouble, but it really is marvellous to see all this, and I know my cousin will love it all! Here she comes. Now I must just go up *quickly*, and see the rest –'

'*Thespoinís* –' Something had touched that colourless voice at last. It was sharp. '*Thespoinís*, there is nothing up there except the millstones, nothing at all! Do not go up; the floor is rotten!'

This was true. From below I had seen the holes in the boards.

I said cheerfully, not even pausing: 'It's all right, I'm not afraid. After all, I suppose it holds you when you have to come up here to work, doesn't it? I'll be careful. Heavens, are these the grindstones? It's a marvel there's ever wind enough to move them at all!'

I hadn't yet paused to think what I would do if Colin were there, but the small, circular room was empty – if one could apply that word to a space almost filled by the giant millstones, and crowded with primitive machinery.

The ceiling was conical, and was the actual roof of the mill. From the apex of this wigwam-like thatch down the centre of the chamber, like a tent-pole, ran the huge axle on which the millstones turned. These, some eight to ten feet across, looked as if no power short of a steam-turbine could ever move them. Jutting out from the wall was a metal lever by which the whole roof could be swung round on its central pivot, to catch any wind that blew; and a vast, pegged wheel, set at right angles to the millstones, no doubt transferred the drive to them from the sails. This driving-wheel was of wood, hand-hewn and worm-eaten, like the floor. But everything was clean, and the room was fresh and very light, for there were two windows cut in the thick walls, one on either side, at floor-level. One of these was shuttered, and fastened with a wooden peg; and, beside it, pushed back into a rough pile against the wall, was a jumble of brushwood left over – as was apparent – from a recent job of thatching.

I stepped over the hole in the aged flooring, and looked thoughtfully down at the brushwood. A clay jar hung from a nail near by,
and a short-handled broom stood underneath it. The brushwood
looked as if it had just been bundled back against the wall, and the
floor had been newly swept . . .

I wondered how recently the jar had been used, and whether, if I
tilted it, I would find a few drops of water still in the bottom . . .

I had no chance to try, for now Sofia was at the head of the stairs,
and I could hear Frances coming up.

I turned quickly. 'Frances! This is wonderful, it's like the Bible or
Homer or something. Bring the camera up, there's plenty of light!'
Then, brightly, to Sofia: 'I'm so glad we've seen this! We have
nothing like this, you know, in England—at least, I believe there still
are some windmills, but I've never seen inside one. May my cousin
take a picture? Would it be all right to open the other window?'

I chattered on at her, as disarmingly as I could. After all, she
could only be annoyed: I had shown myself yesterday to be a
busybody without manners, and if an extension of this character
today would get me what I wanted, then my reputation was gone in
a good cause.

Frances came quickly up, exclaiming with pleasure. Sofia,
unbending perhaps at her palpably innocent interest, moved wil-
lingly enough to unlatch the window, and began to explain the
action of the millstones. I translated what she said, asking a few
more harmless questions, and then, when Frances had started work
with the camera, and was persuading Sofia to mime some of the
movements with lever and grain-chute, I left them casually—oh, so
casually!—and started down the stairs again.

I had seen what I was looking for. Of that I was sure. Sofia had
cleaned up efficiently, but not quite efficiently enough. After all, I
myself had just done the self-same job in the shepherds' hut, and my
eye was fresh to the signs. Nobody who was not looking for it would
have guessed that, until recently, a prisoner had been kept in the
mill. But I had known what to look for.

I was sure I was right. The brushwood on the top floor had been
ruffled up again, and pushed back, but someone had lain there, And
Sofia had swept the floor, but had overlooked the fact of the rotten
boards beside the bedding. Some of her sweepings must have fallen
through on to the floor below . . .

I ran lightly down the steps, and paused on the landing.

Yes: again I had been right. On the boards beneath the hole were a few fragments of broken brushwood and dusty fronds. This, in itself, would have meant nothing, but among them there were crumbs. It had been a crumb of bread that I had seen the mouse carrying. And here were more, as yet unsalvaged, tiny traces of food which, without the mouse, and the sharpened eyes of suspicion, I would never have seen.

I never thought I should live to be grateful for the time that one has to wait about while Frances takes her films. I could hear her now, conversing with Sofia with–presumably–some success, and much laughter. Sofia, no doubt feeling herself safe, appeared to be relaxing. The whirr of the camera sounded loud in the confined space. I ran on down the stairs.

I had remembered the coil of rope that lay beside the grain-sacks. If you had a prisoner, presumably you tied him. I wanted to see that rope.

I reached the ground floor, and paused for a moment, throwing a swift glance round me. I could hear them still busy with the camera, and, even if they came down, I should have plenty of warning: they could not see me until they were half-way down the stairs. I bent over the rope.

The first thing I saw was the blood.

It sounds simple when I write it like that, and I suppose I had even been expecting it. But what one expects with the reasoning mind, and one's reactions to it as a fact, are two very different things. I think it was the driving need for haste, and secrecy, that saved me. Somehow, I managed to stay cool enough, and, after the first moment or so, to look more closely.

There was very little blood; only (I told myself) the sort of stain one might get from bound wrists scraped raw with struggling. The slight staining came at intervals along one of the ropes, as it might if this were coiled round someone's wrists.

Somehow, I fumbled among the coils to find the end of the rope. They were unfrayed, still bound.

As I let them fall back where they had lain, Sofia's shopping-bag caught my eye, standing near. Without a second's compunction I pulled the mouth wide, and looked inside.

There wasn't much; a bundle of the faded, red-and-green patterned cloth that I had seen in her house, a crumpled newspaper stained with grease, and another strip of the cloth, much creased, and stained as if with damp.

I opened the bundle of cloth; there was nothing it it but a few crumbs. The newspaper too; the marks on it could have been made by fat, or butter. She must have brought the boy's food wrapped in paper, then bundled up in a cloth. Then there was the other cloth, the creased strip, that looked as if it had been chewed . . .

Just that, of course. The boy could hardly have been left here, lying bound. They would have had to gag him.

I dropped it back into the bag, with hands that shook, then pushed the other things back after it, and straightened up.

It was true, then. Colin had been here: and Colin had gone. The unfrayed rope told its own tale; there had been no escape, no bonds sawn through. The rope had been untied, then neatly coiled away, presumably by Sofia when she had cleared away the gag, the bedding, and the traces of food.

But if Colin was still alive—my brain was missing like a faulty engine, but it hammered on, painfully—if they still had Colin, alive, then surely he would still be bound? If the rope was here, discarded, then might it not mean that Colin had been set free deliberately, and that he might now, in his turn, be looking for Mark?

I had been standing, staring blindly down at the clutter of stuff beside the wall. Now my eyes registered, with a jerk that was almost physically painful, the thing at which they had been staring, unseeingly; the thing that stood there beside the rope, gleaming in its obviousness.

The spade. Once I had seen it, I could see nothing else.

It was an old spade, with a well-worn handle, but the blade shone, with recent use, as if it were new. There was still earth clinging to it. Some of this had dried and crumbled, and lay in little piles on the floor. The spade had been used very recently, and for deep digging: not just the dry, dusty topsoil, but the deep, damp earth that would cling . . .

I shut my eyes on it then, trying to push aside the image that was forming. Someone had been digging; all right, that was what a spade was for, wasn't it? The fields had to be tilled, hadn't they? It needn't mean a thing. Anybody could have been using it, for a variety of reasons. Sofia could have been digging vegetables, or Josef, or Stratos . . .

And now the picture, unimportant, unremembered until this moment, showed complete—yesterday's picture of these tranquil fields: the sleeping boy; the man, alone, digging behind that patch of sugar-cane, beyond the mill. He had been a broad-shouldered man, with a red kerchief round his neck. He had not noticed me, nor

I him. But now, in my mind's eye, I could see him again, clearly.

As I had seen him later, when he had finished his work and had come down to Sofia's cottage to tell her what he had done, and that she could come up to the mill to clear away.

Somehow, I got outside. The sun was brilliant on the irises, and a sulphur butterfly quested among the purple petals.

The back of my hand was pressed so hard to my mouth that my teeth hurt it.

'I'll have to tell Mark,' I said, against the bitten flesh. 'Dear God, I'll have to tell Mark.'

Chapter 13

Ah! if you see the purple shoon,
The hazel crook, the lad's brown hair,
The goat-skin wrapped about his arm,
Tell him that I am waiting . . .
WILDE: Endymion

'NICOLA–NICKY, HONEY–what is it?'

'It's all right. Give me a minute, that's all.'

'I knew there was something. Look, we can sit down here. Take your time.'

We had reached the wayside shrine above the lemon-grove. The fields were out of sight; the windmill no more than a gleam of white through the trees. I could not remember getting here: somehow, I must have taken a civil leave of Sofia; somehow waited, while she and Frances exchanged farewell compliments; somehow steered a blind way up through the trees, to stop by the shrine, staring wordlessly at Frances.

'Here,' she said, 'have a cigarette.'

The sharp smell of the match mingled, too evocatively, with the scents of verbena and lavender that grew beside the stones where we sat. I ran my fingers up a purple spike of flowers, shredding them brutally from the stem, then let the bruised heads fall; but the scent of lavender was still stronger on the flesh of my hand. I rubbed it down my skirt, and spoke to the ground.

'They've killed Colin. You were right. And they've buried him down there . . . just near the mill.'

There was a silence. I was watching some ants scurrying to examine the fallen flower-heads.

'But–' her voice was blank–'how do you know? Do you mean you saw something?'

I nodded.

'I see. The mill. Yes, why not? Well, tell me.'

When I had finished, she sat a little longer in silence, smoking rather hard. Then I saw her shake her head sharply, like someone ridding themselves of a stinging insect. 'That nice woman? I can't believe it. The thing's fantastic.'

'You didn't see Mark, lying up there in the dirt, with a bullet-hole in him. It's true enough, he's dead. And now I'll have to tell Mark. We can get the police on it, now that it's too late.' I swung round on her, anxiously. 'You said you guessed something was wrong. You mean I showed it? Would Sofia guess I knew something?'

'I'm sure she wouldn't. I wasn't sure myself, and I know you pretty well. What could she have guessed, anyway? She's not to know you knew anything about it; and there was nothing to see, not unless someone was deliberately looking for traces.'

'It was the mouse. If I hadn't seen the mouse with that bit of bread, I'd never have found anything. I'd have wondered about the brushwood, but it would never have entered my head to hunt for crumbs, or to look at that rope.'

'Well, she didn't see the mouse, so it wouldn't occur to her, either. I should stop worrying about that side of it. She'll have gone off quite satisfied with the result of her tidying-up, and you and I are still well in the clear.'

The ants were scurrying about aimlessly among the lavender-flowers.

'Frances, I'll have to tell Mark.'

'Yes, I know.'

'You agree I should, now?'

'I'm afraid you'll have to, darling.'

'Then–you think I'm right? You think that's what's happened?'

'That Colin's dead? I'm afraid it looks like it. In any case, Mark ought to hear the evidence. It's got well beyond the stage at which he can deal with things himself. Are you going now?'

'The sooner I get it over, the better. What about you?'

'You'll be better on your own, and in any case, I ought to be here to cover up for you if you're late back. I'll stay around taking film and so on, and then go back for tea, as arranged. I'll tell them that you've gone farther than I cared to, but that you'll keep to the paths, and be back by dark.' She gave me an anxious smile. 'So take care of yourself, and see that you are. I'm not at all sure that I could be convincing if you chose to spend another night up there!'

'You needn't worry about that, I'll be even less welcome than I was last time.' I hadn't meant to speak quite so bitterly. I got quickly to my feet, adding prosaically: 'Well, the sooner the better. How about dividing the lunch-packet?'

*   *   *

My plan, if it could be called a plan, was relatively simple.

It was possible that Mark and Lambis, after last night's foray, had gone back for the rest of the night to the shepherds' hut, sooner than undertake the long trek over to their caique. But, if the blood in Sofia's shed was evidence, Mark might not have been able to face the stiff climb to the hut. He and Lambis could have holed up till morning somewhere nearer the village, and it might even be that Mark (if his wound had broken open badly) would have to stay hidden there today.

Whatever the case, it seemed to me that my best plan was to find the track which led across to the ruined church—the track on which the first murder had been committed—and follow that along the lower reaches of the mountain-side. It was a reasonable way for a tourist to go, it would lead me in the same general direction that Mark and Lambis would have to take, and it was, as I knew, visible for long stretches, not only from the alp and the ledge, but from a wide range of rocks above.

I remembered how clearly the Cretan had stood out, yesterday, against the stand of cypresses beside the track. If I stopped there, and if Mark and Lambis were anywhere above me, they would surely see me, and I could in some way make it apparent that I had news for them. No doubt—since I had promised that I would only interfere again if I had vital news—they would show some sign, to let me know where they were, and after that I could make my way up to them as cautiously as I could. If no signal showed from above, then I would have to decide whether to go up and look at the ledge and the hut, or whether to push on along the track, and try to find the caique. It was all very vague and unsatisfactory, but for want of more exact knowledge, it was the best I could do.

As for the murderer, whom I was determined, now, to identify with Josef, I had coldly considered him, and was confident that there I ran very little risk. If I should meet him on the track, I had every excuse (including Stratos' own advice to visit the Byzantine church) for being there. It was only after I had exchanged signals with Mark that I should need caution, and then no doubt Mark and Lambis would make it their business to protect me. It was odd that this idea didn't irk me, as it would have done yesterday. Today, I could think of nothing beyond the moment when I should have discharged my dreadful burden of news, and with it the respon-sibility for future action.

From the shrine, where I had left Frances, a narrow path led up through the last of the lemon-trees, on to the open ground above the plateau. Like the track from the bridge, it looked as if it was much used by the village flocks, so it occurred to me that it might eventually join the old mountain road which led towards the church and the 'ancient harbour'.

This proved to be the case. Very soon my narrow path took me upwards over bare, fissured rock where someone had tried to build a dry wall, to join a broader, but by no means smoother, track along the mountain-side.

It was already hot. On this stretch of the hill there were no trees, other than an occasional thin poplar with bone-white boughs. Thistles grew in the cracks of the rock, and everywhere over the dry dust danced tiny yellow flowers, on thread-like stalks that let them flicker in the breeze two inches above the ground. They were lovely little things, a million motes of gold dancing in a dusty beam, but I trudged over them almost without seeing them. The joy had gone: there was nothing in my world now but the stony track, and the job it was taking me to do. I plodded on in the heat, weary already. There is no one so leaden-footed as the reluctant bringer of bad news.

The track did not bear steadily uphill. Sometimes it would twist suddenly upwards, so that I had to clamber up what was little more than a dry water-course. Then, out of this, I would emerge on to a stretch of bare, hot rock that led with flat and comparative ease along some reach of the mountain's flank. At other times I was led—with an infuriating lack of logic—steeply downhill, through drifts of dust and small stones where thistles grew, and wild fig-trees flattened by the south wind. Now and again, as the way crossed an open ridge, or skirted the top of a thorn-thicket, it lay in full view of the high rocks that hid the shepherds' hut: but whether I could have seen Mark's ledge, or whether he, if he was still there, could have seen me, I did not know. I kept my eyes on the nearer landscape, and plodded steadily on. It would be time enough to expose myself to the gaze of the mountain-side when I had reached the grove of cypresses.

It was with curiously conflicting feelings of relief and dread that, following the track round a jutting shoulder, I saw at length, dark against the long open wing of the mountain, the block of cypresses.

They were still a fair distance off. About half-way to them I could see the jagged scar, fringed with the green of tree-tops, which was the narrow gully running roughly parallel to the big ravine up which I had first adventured. It was at the head of this gully, in the hollow olive-tree, that Lambis had hidden the provisions yesterday.

It was downhill all the way to the gully. I paused at the edge at last, where the track took a sudden sharp run down to the water. At this point the stream widened into a shallow pool, where someone had placed stepping-stones. Downstream from this, the stream-bed broadened soon into a shallow trough where the water tumbled from pool to pool among the bushy scrub, but upstream, the way I might have to go, was a deep, twisting gorge crowded with the trees whose tops I had glimpsed from the distance. It was the thickest cover I had seen since I had left Frances in the lemon-grove, and now, though reason told me that I had no need of cover, instinct sent me scrambling thankfully down towards the shady pool with the thought that, if I must rest anywhere, I would do so here.

Where the track met the pool it widened, on both banks, into a flattened area of dried mud, beaten down by the feet of the flocks which, year in and year out, probably since the time of Minos, had crowded down here to drink, on their journey to the high pastures. There had been a flock this way recently. On the far side the bank, sloping gently up from the water, was still muddy where the sheep had crowded across, splashing the water up over the flattened clay. Superimposed on the swarming slots in the mud I could see the blurred print of the shepherd's sandal. He had slipped in the clay, so that the print was blurred at the toe and heel, but the convoluted pattern of the rope sole was as clear as a photograph.

A rope sole. I was balanced on the last stepping-stone, looking for a dry place to step on, when the significance of this struck me, and—after a horrible moment of teetering there on one leg like a bad imitation of Eros in Piccadilly—I stepped straight into the water. But I was too startled even to care. I merely squelched out of the stream, carefully avoiding that beautiful police-court print, and stood there shaking my soaking foot, and thinking hard.

It was very possible that, as I had first thought, this was the print of the shepherd's foot. But if that was so, he had the same kind of shoes as Mark.

This, again, was possible, but seemed unlikely. Most of the Greek country-folk appeared to wear either canvas slippers with rubber soles, or else a kind of cheap laced plimsoll; and many of the men (and some of the women) wore boots, as in summer the dry fields were full of snakes. But rope soles were rare; I knew this, because I like them, and had been trying both in Athens and Heraklion to buy some for this very holiday, but with no success.

So, though it was possible that a Cretan shepherd was wearing these rope soles, it was far more likely that Mark had been this way.

The thought brought me up all standing, trying to revise my plans.

The print was this morning's, that much was obvious. Whatever had happened last night, this meant that Mark was fit enough to be on his feet, and heading away from the village—not for the hut, but back towards the caique.

I bit my lip, considering. Could he—*could* he have already found out what I was on my way to tell him? Had he somehow found his way into the mill, before Sofia had been able to remove traces of its occupant?

But there I checked myself. I couldn't get out of it that way. I still had to try to find him . . . But it did look as if the job might be simplified, for there were other prints . . . A second much more lightly-defined than the first, showed clearly enough; then another, dusty and blurred; and another . . . then I had lost him on the dry, stony earth of the bank.

I paused there, at fault, staring round me at the baked earth and baking stone, where even the myriad prints of the tiny, cloven hoofs were lost in the churned dust. The heat, unalloyed in the gorge by any breeze, drove down from the fierce sky as from a burning-glass.

I realized, suddenly, how hot and thirsty I was. I turned back into the shade, set down my bag, and stooped to drink . . .

The fourth print was a beauty, set slap down in a damp patch under a bush, right under my eyes.

But not on the track. He had left it here, and headed away from it, up the gully-bottom, through the tangle of trees beside the water. He wasn't making for the caique. He was heading—under cover—up in the direction of the shepherds' hut.

I gave a heave to the bag over my shoulder, and stooped to push after him under a swag of old-man's-beard.

If it had been shelter I wanted, there was certainly plenty of it here. The cat-walk of trodden ground that twisted up under the trees could hardly have been called a path; nothing larger than rats seemed to have used it, except for the occasional blurred prints of those rope-soled feet. The trees were spindly, thin-stemmed and light-leaved; aspens, and white poplars, and something unknown to me, with round, thin leaves like wafers, that let the sun through in a dapple of flickering green. Between the stems was a riot of bushes, but luckily these were mostly of light varieties like honeysuckle and wild clematis. Where I had to push my way through, I was gratified to notice various signs that Mark had pushed his way through, too. Old Argus-Eyes, I thought, momentarily triumphant. Girl Crusoe in person. Not such a slouch at this sort of thing after all. Mark would have to admit . . . And there the mood faded, abruptly, back to its dreary grey. I plodded doggedly on.

The stream grew steeper, the way more tangled. There were no more signs now, and if there were footmarks I never saw them. The air in the bottom of the gully was still, and the shade was light, letting a good deal of sunshine through. I stopped, at length, to have another drink, then, instead of drinking, turned from the water with sudden resolution, sat down on a dry piece of fallen tree-trunk in the shade, and opened my bag.

I was hot, tired, and exhausted by depression. It was going to help no one if I foundered here. If the news I was bearing (I thought crudely to myself) had knocked the guts out of me, better have a shot at putting them back in working order.

I uncorked the bottle of *King Minos*, *sec*, and, with a silent blessing on Frances, who had insisted on my taking it, took a swig that would have done credit to Mrs. Gamp and her tea-pot. After that I felt so much better that—in homage to the gods of the place—I poured a few drops on the ground for a libation, then tackled lunch with something like an appetite.

Frances had also given me at least two-thirds of Tony's generous lunch-packet. With a little more help from King Minos, I ate a couple of the fresh rolls crammed with roast mutton, some olives from a poke of grease-proof paper, and then a rather tasteless apple. The orange I would not face, but dropped it back into the bag.

A little stir of the breeze lifted the tree-tops above me, so that the sun-motes spilled dazzlingly through on to the water, and shadows slid over the stones. A couple of butterflies, which had been drinking at the water's edge, floated off like blown leaves, and a goldfinch, with a flash of brilliant wings, flirted its way up past me into some high bushes in an overhanging piece of cliff.

I watched it, idly. Another slight movement caught my eye, a stir of light colour among some piled boulders below the overhang, as if a stone had moved. Then I saw that there was a lamb, or a ewe, lying up there, under a tangle of honeysuckle. The breeze must have lifted the fleece, so that the ruffling wool had shown momentarily above the boulders.

I watched, attentive now. There it was again, the stroking finger of the breeze running along the wool, and lifting it, so that the light caught its edge and it shone softly for a moment, like bloom along the stone.

I had been wrong, then. The foot-print had not been Mark's. The sheep were somewhere near by, and with them, no doubt, would be the shepherd.

I began quickly to pack the remnants of lunch away, thinking, more confusedly than ever, that now I had better revert to my first haphazard plan, and make for the cypress grove.

I got to my feet warily, then stood, listening.

No sound except the chatter of the water, and the faint hushing of the wind in the leaves, and the high liquid twittering of the goldfinches somewhere out of sight . . .

I had turned back downstream, to find a place where I could clamber more easily out of the gully, when it occurred to me that the sheep had been oddly still and quiet, all through the time that I had been eating. I glanced back. It lay on the other side of the stream, some way above me, half under the overhang. It could have slipped from above, I thought, unnoticed by the shepherd, and it might well be dead; but if it was merely trapped on its back, or held down by thorns, it would only take me a few moments to free it. I must, at least, take time to look.

I stepped across the stream, and clambered up towards the boulders.

The sheep was certainly dead; had been dead some time. Its fleece was being worn as a cloak by the boy who lay curled under a bush, in the shelter of the boulders, fast asleep. He wore torn blue jeans and a dirty blue shirt, and the sheepskin was pulled over one shoulder, as the Greek shepherds wear it, and tied into place with a length of frayed string. This, not Mark, was the quarry I had been stalking. The mud on his rope-soled shoes was hardly dry.

The noise of my approach had not disturbed him. He slept with a sort of concentration, deep in sleep, lost in it. A fly landed on his cheek, and crawled across his eye; he never stirred. His breathing was deep and even. It would have been quite easy to creep quietly away, and never rouse him.

But I made no such attempt. I stood there, with my heart beating in my throat till I thought it would nearly choke me. I had seen that kind of sleep before, and recently – that almost fierce concentration of rest. I thought I had seen those eyelashes before, too; I remembered the way they lay on the brown cheeks in sleep. And the way the dark hair grew.

The thick lashes lifted, and he looked straight at me. His eyes were blue. There was the quick flash of alarm shown by any sleeper who is startled awake to find himself being stood over by a stranger; then a second look, half-relieved, half-wary, as he registered my harmlessness.

I cleared my throat, and managed a hoarse '*Cháirete*'. It is the country greeting, and means, literally, 'Rejoice'.

He stared for a moment, blinking, then gave me the conventional 'Good day.'

'*Kalí méra.*' His voice sounded stupid and slurred. Then he thrust his knuckles into his eyes, and pushed himself into a sitting posture. He moved, I thought, a little stiffly.

I wetted my lips, and hesitated. 'You're from Agios Georgios?' I still spoke in Greek.

He was eyeing me warily, like a shy animal. '*Óchi.*' The denial was hardly audible, a thick mutter as he got quickly to one knee, and turned to grope under the bush, where he had put down his shepherd's stick.

This was the genuine article, gnarled fig-wood, polished by years of use. Shaken by a momentary doubt, I said sharply: 'Please – don't go. I'd like to talk to you . . . please . . .'

I saw his body go tense, just for a second; then he had dragged the stick out from where it lay, and was getting to his feet. He turned on me that look of complete and baffling stupidity that one sometimes sees in peasants – usually when one is arguing the price of some commodity for which they are over-charging by about a hundred per cent. '*Thén katalavéno* (I don't understand),' he said, '*adío*,' and jumped past me, down the bank towards the stream. Round the wrist of the hand that held the stick was tied a rough bandage of cloth in a pattern of red and green.

'Colin –' I said, shakily.

He stopped as if I had struck him. Then, slowly, as if to face a blow, he turned back to me. His face frightened me. It still looked stupid, and I saw now that this was real; it was the blank look of someone who is beyond feeling punishment, and who has long since stopped even asking the reason for it.

I went straight to the root of the matter, in English. 'Mark's alive, you know. It was only a flesh wound, and he was quite all right, last time I saw him. That was yesterday. I'm on my way to find him now, I—I'm a friend of his, and I think I know where he'll be, if you'd care to come along?'

He didn't even need to speak. His face told me all I wanted to know. I sat down abruptly on a boulder, looked away, and groped for a handkerchief to blow my nose.

Chapter 14

'Wonder of time,' quoth she, 'this is my spite,
That, thou being dead, the day should yet be light.'
SHAKESPEARE: *Venus and Adonis*

'DO YOU FEEL better now?' I asked.

It was a little time later. I had made him sit down then and there, by the stream, and drink some of the wine, and eat the rest of the food I had brought. I hadn't asked him any questions yet, but while he ate and drank I told him all I could about Mark's end of the story, and my own.

He said very little, but ate like a young wolf. They had fed him, I gathered, but he 'hadn't been able to eat much'. This was all he had said so far about his experiences, but the change in him—since the news about Mark—was remarkable. Already he looked quite different; the bruised look was gone from his eyes, and, by the time the *Minos Sec* was half down in the bottle, there was even a sparkle in them, and a flush in his cheeks.

'Now,' I said, as he gave the neck of the bottle a final wipe, corked it, and set it down among the wreck of papers that was all he had left of my lunch, 'you can tell me all your side of it. Just let me get all this rubbish stowed away, and you can tell me as we go. *Were* you in the windmill?'

'I'll say I was, tied up like a chicken and dumped on a bundle of rubbish,' said Colin warmly. 'Mind you, I hadn't a clue where I was, when they first took me there; it was dark. In fact, I didn't know till today, when I left, except that I'd got the impression I was in a sort of round tower. They kept the shutters up all the time—in case I saw them, I suppose. What are you doing?'

'Leaving the crumbs for the mice.'

'Crumbs for the *mice*?'

I laughed. 'You'd be surprised how much the mice have done for us today. Never mind, skip it. How did you get away? No, wait, let's get on our way. You can tell me while we go; and start at the very beginning, when Mark was shot at, and the gang jumped on you.'

'Okay.' He got to his feet eagerly. He was very like his brother to look at; slighter, of course, and with a frame at once softer and more angular, but promising the same kind of compact strength. The hair and eyes, and the slant of the brows were Mark's, and so—I was to discover—were one or two other things.

'Which way are we going?' he asked briskly.

'For the moment, back down the gully a bit. There's a place quite near, a clump of cypresses, which you can see from anywhere higher up. I'm going over to that. If he and Lambis are somewhere about, they'll be keeping a lookout, and they'll surely show some sort of signal, then we can go straight up to them, via the gully. If not, then we'll aim for the caique.'

'If it's still there.'

This thought had been worrying me, too, but I wasn't going to admit it. 'It will be. They knew, if you were free, that you'd make straight for it; where else could you go? Even if they've moved it again, you can bet your life they're keeping a good lookout for you.'

'I suppose so. If you're going up into the open to signal them, had I better stay down here?'

'Oh, yes. And whichever way we go, we'll stay in cover. Thank goodness, anyway, one of the problems is gone—you'll know the way from the old church to the caique. Come on.'

'How did you find me, anyway?' asked Colin, scrambling after me across the stream, and down the narrow gully-path.

'Followed your tracks.'

'*What?*'

'You heard. That's one of the things we'll have to put right before we go. You left some smashing prints down by the stepping-stones. You can sweep them out while I go up to the cypress-grove.'

'Well, but how did you know they were mine?'

'Oh, I didn't; I thought they were Mark's. You've the same sort of shoes.'

'Have a heart, Nicola, he takes nines!'

'Well, I wasn't really thinking. Anyway, you'd slipped in the mud, and the toe and heel were blurred, so the prints looked longer. If it hadn't been for recognizing Mark's shoes, I'd never have noticed them. He was—a bit on my mind, at the time. All the same, you'd better wipe them out.'

'Gosh—' Colin sounded thoroughly put out at this evidence of his inefficiency—'I never thought of prints. I suppose, with its being dark, and then I was pretty well bushed—'

'You had other things to think about. Here we are. There, see them? Now, I'll go up, and if there's no one to be seen, then I'll give the all-clear, and you can come out and deal with the evidence, while I show myself up yonder and wait for the green light.' I paused, and looked at him uncertainly. In the shadow of the trees he looked disconcertingly like his brother. 'You—you will still be here, won't you, when I come back?'

'You bet your sweet life I will,' said Colin. 'But look here—'

'What?'

He was looking uneasy. 'Look, I don't like you going out there, it mightn't be safe. Can't we think of some other way?'

'I'm quite safe, even if I bump head-on into Josef, as long as *you* keep out of sight,' I said firmly. 'You're very like your brother, aren't you?'

'For my sins,' said Colin, and grinned.

He waited there in the dappled shade while I climbed to the rim of the gully. I looked about me. The landscape was as bare of life as on the first four days of Creation. I gave Colin a thumbs-up sign, then set off briskly for the cypress-grove.

The track was smooth, the sun brilliant, the sky a glorious, shining blue. The tiny yellow flowers danced underfoot, like jewels in the dust. The goldfinches flashed and twittered over the lavender-bushes, and the freckled snake slipping across the path was as beautiful as they . . .

Everything, in fact, was exactly the same as it had been an hour before, except that now I was happy. My feet were as light as my heart, as I almost ran across the rocks towards the dark, standing shadow of the grove.

I had been wondering how to attract the men's attention quickly. It now occurred to me, for the first time, that there was no reason why I should not simply make a noise. I felt like singing. Well, why not sing?

I sang. The sound echoed cheerfully round the rocks, and then was caught and deadened by the cypresses. Remembering how

sound had carried on this same hillside yesterday, I was certain that
I would be heard clearly by anyone in the reaches immediately
above.

I took my stance, deliberately, in front of the thickest backdrop of
cypress, then paused, as if to look at the view. At last I was able to
tilt my head, shade my eyes, and stare towards the head of the main
ravine.

Even knowing the place as well as I did, it took some time to get
my bearings. I had to start from the ravine, and let my eye travel to
the rock where the naiad's spring was . . . yes, there was a
recess—looking absurdly small—where the flower-covered alp must
lie. The shepherds' hut would be back in that corner, out of sight.
And the ledge . . .

The ledge defeated me. It might have been in any one of half a
dozen places; but I had the general direction right, and I watched
patiently and carefully, for something like six minutes.

Nothing stirred. No movement, no flicker of white, no sudden
flash of glass or metal. Nothing.

The test was far from satisfactory, but it would have to do. I gave
it another minute or two, then turned to hurry back. Overriding
even my desire to find Mark quickly was the fear—irrational,
perhaps, but nevertheless strong—that Colin, in some mysterious
manner, would vanish again while I was away from him. But no, he
was there, sitting under a bush. He rose to greet me, his face eager.

I shook my head. 'Not a sign. I honestly didn't expect it. They'll
have gone to the caique. So we'll go after them, and we'd better
hurry, because I've got to get back.'

'Look, you don't have to fag yourself going all that way. I can
manage on my own,' said Mark's brother.

'I dare say, but I'm coming with you. For one thing, I've got a lot
that Mark ought to know; for another, even Josef might think twice
before shooting you in front of me.'

'Well,' said Colin, 'let me go in front. I can clear the way a bit with
this stick. And give me that bag; I oughtn't to be letting you carry it.'

'Thank you.' I surrendered the bag meekly, and followed him up
the path through the trees.

He went at a fair speed. Every moment he seemed more himself
again, and obviously all he wanted now was to find his brother with
the least possible delay, and shake the Cretan dust off his rope soles.
I didn't blame him.

'What did you sing that for?' he asked, over his shoulder.

'Sing what? I can't even remember what I *was* singing.'
'*Love me tender.*'
'Was it? Oh, yes, I believe it was.'
'No wonder Mark didn't come out!' he said, laughing.

It was a crudity I wouldn't have expected of him, young as he was. I felt the blood sting my cheeks. 'What *do* you mean?'

'He's so square he's practically a cube. Nothing more tuneful than *Wozzeck* will do for Mark, or somebody-or-other's concerto for three beer-glasses and a bassoon. Charlie's the same, but with her it's show-off; too too RADA for words, Charlie is. Charlie's my sister Charlotte. Julia and I like pop—she's the next youngest to me. Anne's tone-deaf.'

'Oh, I see.'

'You're a bit out of date, though, aren't you?'

'I suppose so. But look, I'm dying to hear what happened to you. Suppose you tell me, and we might be able to get some sort of a story pieced together before we find Mark.'

So he told me, in snatches, breathlessly, as we toiled up the gully.

When Mark had fallen, wounded, from the track, Colin had run to him, only to be dragged back by Stratos and Josef. In the resulting struggle Colin had been knocked on the temple, and had fainted, but only for a few minutes. When he came to, they had secured him with some sort of rough bonds, stuffed a rag in his mouth, and were carrying him downhill, he could not tell in which direction. He kept as limp and still as he could, in the hazy hope that they might leave him for dead, or even relax sufficiently to give him a chance to get away.

It was a long way, and rough, and by now it was fairly dark, so his captors used most of their energy for the trek, and a good deal of their talk was in Greek, but he gathered that they were disagreeing violently about something.

'I can't be absolutely sure I remember properly,' he said, 'because of course I was muzzy in the head, and scared because I thought they'd murder me any minute—and besides, I was half crackers about Mark . . . I thought he was either dead, or lying bleeding to death somewhere. But some of the argument was in English—when the ones that called themselves Stratos and Tony got going—and I do remember quite a bit of what was said.'

'Try, anyway. It could be important.'

'Oh, I've tried. I had nothing else to do for three days except think what it was all in aid of; but it's more *impressions* than actual *memory*,

if you see what I mean. I do know that Tony was blazing mad at
them for shooting Mark and taking me along. We'd never have
traced them, he said, we hadn't seen them properly; and in any case
they could give each other alibis, "but taking the boy like this—it's
stupid!" '

'Well,' I said, 'so it was. I still don't know why they did it.'

'Sofia,' said Colin, simply. 'I'd had this cut on the head, and I was
bleeding like a pig. She thought if they left me, I'd bleed to death,
and she made such a fuss and she was so cut up about the whole
thing, I gathered, that they gave in, and just hustled me away. It
was partly Tony, too. In the end he said that they might get away
with Mark's shooting, as an accident, but if we were both found
dead, or badly hurt, there'd be a fuss that might take in the whole
district, and uncover "Alexandros' murder", and that would get
back to them, and "the London affair".'

' "The London affair"?' I asked sharply.

'I think that's what he said. I can't be sure.'

'It could be. And the man who was murdered was "Alexandros",
was he? It certainly sounds as if he might be someone catching up on
Stratos and Tony from their London life, doesn't it? I wonder if he
was Greek or English? He talked English to Tony, but then Tony's
Greek isn't good.'

'He'd be Greek, surely, if his name was—oh, I see, you mean they
may just have been, what's the word? giving his name the Greek
form?'

'Hellenizing, yes. But it doesn't matter; if you heard right, then
he was killed for something that happened in London. I remember
now, Tony did say something about London "not being healthy"
—not to me, he was only joking, to some children, but it struck
me at the time. Well, to get back to Saturday night, what on earth
did they intend to do with you?'

'Quite honestly, I think they were in such a general flap about
what had happened, that they were just getting away from it as
quickly as they could. I gathered that Stratos and Tony were livid
with Josef for losing his head and shooting Mark, and that Josef was
all for cutting their losses and killing me as well, then and there, but
Stratos was swithering a bit, and Tony and Sofia were dead against
it. In the end they sort of gave up, and bundled me off—clear out
first and think later; you know. In fact, Tony was all for bolting—really bolting, I mean, getting right away. He wanted to get
straight out. I remember all that bit clearly, because I was praying

he wouldn't go; with him being English, I thought I might stand a better chance talking to him than the others. And he *hadn't* a part in it, really.'

'You mean Tony wanted to clear out on his own?'

'Yes. I remember exactly what he said. "Well, once you shot that tourist, you landed yourselves, whatever you do with the boy. I had nothing to do with it, or with Alex, and you know that's true. I'm getting out. I'll take my cut here and now, and don't pretend you'll not be glad to see the last of me, Stratos, dear." That was the way he talked, in a kind of silly voice; I can't quite describe it.'

'Don't bother, I've heard it. What did Stratos say?'

'He said, "They're no use to you, they're still hot. You can't get rid of them yet." Tony said. "I know that. You can trust me to be careful," and Stratos gave a beastly sort of laugh and said, "I'd as soon trust you as I'd"—' Colin stopped abruptly.

'Yes?'

'Oh, just an expression,' said Colin. 'A—a slang expression, I can't quite remember what. Meaning that he wouldn't trust him, you know.'

'Oh, yes. Well, go on.'

The gorge had widened out as we climbed higher. There was room now to walk two abreast.

'Then Stratos said where could he go, he had no money, and Tony said, "For a start, you can give me some," and Stratos said, "Blackmail?" and Tony said, "Well, I could talk quite a lot, couldn't I? And *I've* done nothing that matters. There's such a thing as Queen's Evidence." '

'He's got a nerve,' I said, half-admiringly. 'Fancy coming out with that one, to old Stratos, with two dead men behind you, and a bleeding boy on your hands. I—er, I meant that literally.'

Colin grinned. 'I was, too, buckets of it, and it wasn't much of a cut, when all came to all. Well, I thought Stratos would blow his lid at that, but he must have known Tony didn't mean it, because he didn't answer, and then Tony laughed in that silly way and said, "Dear boy, we were going to split anyway, so come through with the stuff now, and we'll call it a day. Where is it?" Stratos said, "When I think it's time to come through, I'll tell you. And not so much of the holier-than-thou stuff, either. What about Alex?" Tony said, "You mean the other time? I only helped afterwards; it was nothing to do with me," and Stratos gave that laugh again and said, "Nothing ever is. You'd like to stand by looking like the Queen of

Hearts and keeping your lily hands clean, wouldn't you? Well, you'll get them dirty soon enough. We've got to get the pair of them buried yet. So save your breath." '

'And that was all?'

'Tony just laughed and said, "You poor sweets, I'll have some coffee and sandwiches ready for you when you get back from the graveyard." Then,' said Colin, 'we got to the mill. I just knew it was a building of some sort, because I heard a door creak open, and then they humped me up the stairs. It was foully bumpy.'

'It can't be exactly easy to carry a body up a narrow spiral staircase.'

'It's beastly for the body,' said Colin cheerfully. 'They got a rope from somewhere, and one of them tied me up properly. By that time, Tony had gone. I heard him say, "I said you could count me out. I had nothing to do with it, and I'll have nothing to do with this, either. If you touch him, you're bigger fools than I thought you were." And he went.'

'The Levite,' I said.

'What? Oh, passing by on the other side, you mean? I suppose so, but he may have been some use, because after he'd gone there was another really terrific argument, and the woman started sort of screaming at the men, till it sounded to me as if someone had put a hand over her mouth. It was dark, of course; they used their torch in flashes, and kept well back where I couldn't see them. When Sofia insisted on doing my head, she had her veil pulled right up so's I could only see her eyes. She cleaned my face and put something over the cut. It had stopped bleeding. Then she took that horrible gag out of my mouth and gave me a drink, and made them put a more comfortable one on. She was crying all the time, and I think she was trying to be kind. The men were arguing in whispers, in Greek. In the end Stratos said to me, in English, "You will be left here, and we will not hurt you. You cannot escape, even if you get the ropes off. The door will be watched, and you will be shot." I had a feeling that it might be bluff, but I wasn't wild keen to call it, not just then, anyway. And later, when I did try to get free, I couldn't.' He paused. 'That was all. In the end they went.'

'If I'd only known. I passed your mill twice when you were in it.'

'Did you? I suppose,' said Colin wisely, 'that if there'd been only the one, you'd have thought of it straight away, but with those dozens, all with their sails going, and so conspicuous, you wouldn't even notice them. If you see what I mean.'

'Oh, yes. *The Purloined Letter.*'

'The what?'

'A story by Poe. A classic about how to hide something. Go on. What happened next day?'

'Sofia came very early and gave me food. She had to loose my hands and take the gag off for that, so I tried to ask her about Mark, and begged her to let me go. Of course she would know I'd be asking about Mark, but all she would do was shake her head and dab her eyes on her veil, and point up the mountain. In the end, I latched on to it somehow that the men had gone up to look for him by daylight.'

'Josef had, anyway.'

'Yes, and found him gone. But I wasn't to know that, more's the pity. Mind you, I'd a pretty good idea that once they'd made sure Mark was dead, I'd be for the high jump myself, but I couldn't get any more out of Sofia, when she came again. That night, when she brought me food, she wouldn't talk at all. Her eyes just looked scared, and sort of dumb. Then yesterday morning I knew they'd decided to kill me. I'm sure they had. That's what made me sure Mark was dead.'

He might have been discussing the weather. Already the past had slipped away from him in the moment of happiness and present hope. In spite of that tough independence he was, I thought, still very much a child.

He went on: 'I didn't think it all out at the time, but, looking back, I think I can see what happened. They'd been worrying themselves sick about where Mark had got to; Josef must have spent the whole two days out raking the countryside, and found no trace. You said he'd been up to the hill-villages too, and he'd have drawn blank there; and of course nothing had happened in Agios Georgios. So they'd reckoned they could count Mark dead. I don't think Josef would ever have thought twice about murdering me, but I expect Sofia made trouble with Stratos, and Tony may have been against it, too—if he ever bothered to mention it again, that is. He may just have shut his eyes and let them get on with it.'

'Perhaps. I think you're right, though; I don't see how they could ever have let you go—I know Frances just assumed they'd have murdered you. What happened?'

'It was Josef, not Sofia, who brought the food yesterday. I'd heard a man's boots coming up the stairs and I managed to roll over and peek down through those holes in the floor. He was in that Cretan rig, with a knife in his belt, and the rifle in one hand and my food in

the other. He stopped on the floor below, stood the rifle against the
wall, and – you remember those square tins?'

'Yes.'

'He pulled an automatic out of his pocket, and hid it down behind
one of them.'

'An automatic? You mean a pistol?'

'Well, I think they're the same. This, anyway.'

His hand reached under the sheepskin cloak, to produce a
deadly-looking gun. He paused, weighing it on his hand, and
grinning at me with the expression of a small boy caught with some
forbidden firework.

'Colin!'

'I suppose it's Alex's. Pity he didn't get time to use it first. Heavy,
isn't it?' He held it out obligingly.

'I wouldn't touch it if you paid me! Is it loaded?'

'No, I took them out, but I brought them along. See?'

'You seem to know how to handle the thing,' I said, reassured.

'Not really, but we mess around with rifles in the Cadets, and one
can guess. Not much use against a rifle, of course, but it makes you
feel sort of better to have it, doesn't it?'

'For heaven's sake!' I stared at this capable child with – it must
be confessed – a touch of exasperation. The rescue was going all
wrong. Colin, it now seemed, was escorting me to Mark. No doubt
Lambis would be detailed to see me home . . .

'As a matter of fact,' said Colin frankly, 'I'm terrified of it.' He put
it away. 'I say, haven't we climbed far enough? It's getting pretty
open here.'

We were approaching the head of the gorge. Some way farther up
I could see where the stream sprang out of the welter of rocks and
trees under the upper ridge. I thought I recognized the old, arthritic
olive-tree where Lambis had hidden the food.

'Yes, this is where we leave cover. For a start, you can let me show
myself first again, in case anyone's about.'

'Okay. But d'you mind if we have a rest first – just for a minute?
Here's a decent place to sit.'

He clambered a little way up the south side of the gully, where
there was some flattish ground, and lay down in the sun, while I sat
beside him.

'Finish your story,' I said.

'Where was I? Oh, Josef hiding the gun. Well, he picked up his
rifle and came upstairs. While I was trying to eat, he just sat there,

with the rifle across his knees, watching me. It put me off my food.'

'I can imagine.'

'I'd been trying to think up some Greek, but I don't really know any.' He grinned. 'You just about heard my full repertoire when you woke me up.'

'You did wonders. If I hadn't known, I'd just have thought you were dim, and a bit sulky. Where'd you get the fancy dress? Sofia?'

'Yes. Anyway, in the end I managed to think up a bit of classical Greek, and tried that. I remembered the word for "brother"—"*adelphós*"—and tried that on him. Apparently it's still the same word. I'd never have thought,' said Colin ingenuously, 'that Thucydides and all that jazz would ever have come in useful.'

'It worked, then?'

His mouth thinned, no longer young-looking. 'I'll say it did. He said, "*Nekrós*", and even if it hadn't been obvious what that means, he drew his hand across his throat, like this, as if he was cutting it. Then he grinned, the stinking little sod. I'm sorry.'

'What? Oh—it's all right.'

'Mark always goes down my throat with his boots on if I swear.'

'*Mark* does? Why?'

'Oh, well—' He rolled over, staring down the gully—'I mean, naturally one swears at school, but at home, in front of the girls, it's different.'

'If Charlotte's at RADA,' I said dryly, 'I'd have thought she'd have caught up with you by now.'

He laughed. 'Oh, well, I told you he was a bit of a square. But he's all right, old Mark, as brothers go.' He returned briskly to his narrative. 'After that, Josef just shut me up when I tried to speak. It was after he'd gone that I realized he'd let me see him. He'd sat there in full view, with daylight coming through the shutters. The only reason for that I could think of was that they were going to kill me anyway. I tried pretty hard to get away, that day, but I only hurt my wrists. But it wasn't Josef, that evening, after all, it was Sofia. She came very late—nearly morning, it must have been—and she untied me. I didn't realize at first that she'd done it—I couldn't move. She rubbed my legs, and put oil on my wrists, and bandaged them, then she gave me some soup. She'd brought it all the way in a jug, and it was only just warm, but it was awfully good. And some wine. I ate a bit, wondering how soon my legs would work, and if I could get away from her, then I realized she was signing me to go with her. Mind you, I was scared to, at first. I thought this might be—well, the pay-off. But there wasn't any future in staying where I was, so I followed her downstairs. She went first, and I managed to sneak the pistol from behind the tin, then went down after her. It was pretty dark, just breaking dawn. It was then I saw I'd been in a windmill. The other mills were all standing quiet, like ghosts. It was beastly cold. Oh, I forgot, she'd brought this sheepskin thing, and the stick, and I was jolly glad of them both, I may tell you; I was as shaky as a jelly for the first few minutes. She took me quite a long way, I had no idea where, through some trees and past a little cairn affair—'

'The shrine. There's a Madonna in it.'

'Oh, is there? It was too dark to see that. We went quite a way, and then it was light enough to see, more or less, and we'd got to that wide track, so she stopped. She pointed the way to me, and said something I couldn't make out. Perhaps she was telling me it was the track to the church, where they'd first found us; she'd think I'd know the way from there. Anyway, she sort of pushed me on my way and then hurried back. The sun came up with a bang, and it was light, and you know the rest.'

'So I missed her, after all. If only I'd pulled myself together, and stayed on watch! Well, then, I suppose you just decided it was safer to lie up in the gully and hide during daylight?'

'Yes. As a matter of fact, I was too tired and stiff to get far, so I thought I'd hole up out of sight and rest for a bit. I had the gun, after all; it made me feel a lot safer.' He laughed. 'I certainly never meant to go "out" like that! It must have been hours!'

'You were dead to the wide. Are you all right now? Shall we go on?'

'Sure. Man, oh man, *get* those birds! What are they?'

The shadows had moved across the uneven ground below us, swinging smoothly in wide, easy circles. I looked up.

'Oh, Colin, they *are* lammergeiers! Bearded vultures! I thought I saw one yesterday! Aren't they rather gorgeous?'

I could find time, today, to be moved and excited by this rare, huge bird, as I had been moved by the beauty of the speckled snake. I had seen the lammergeier before, at Delphi, and again yesterday, but never so close, never so low, never the two of them together.

As I stood up, they swung higher.

'It's the biggest bird of prey in the "old world",' I said. 'I believe the wing span's nearly ten feet. And they're rather handsome, too, not like the other vultures, because they haven't got that beastly bare neck, and—Colin? Is anything the matter? Aren't you well?'

He had made no move to rise when I did, and he wasn't watching the birds. He was staring, fixed, at something near the foot of the gully.

I looked. At first, I saw nothing. Then I wondered why I hadn't seen it straight away.

Near a little clump of bushes, not very far from where we sat, someone had recently been digging. The earth lay now in a shallow, barrow-shaped heap, and someone had thrown stones and dry thorns over it to obliterate the marks of recent work. But it had been a hasty job, done perhaps without the right tools, and, at the end nearest us, the crumbling stuff had already fallen in a bit, exposing an earthy shape that could have been a foot.

The shadows of the vultures crawled across it; and again, across it.

Before I could speak, Colin was on his feet, and slithering down the slope.

'Colin!' I was stumbling after him. 'Colin, don't go over there! Come back, *please*!'

He took no notice. I doubt if he heard me. He was standing over the grave. It was a foot, no doubt of that. I grabbed him by the arm.

'Colin, please come away, it's beastly, and there's no point in poking around here. It'll be that man they killed, that poor Greek, Alexandros . . . I suppose they had to bring him across here, where there was enough soil –'

'He was buried in the field by the mill.'

'What?' I said it blankly, my hand falling from his arm.

'He was buried in the field by the mill.' Colin had turned to stare at me, with that stranger's face. You'd have thought he'd never seen me before. 'I heard them digging. All the first night, I heard them digging. And then again yesterday, someone was there, tidying up. I heard him.'

'Yes. Stratos. I saw him.' I looked at him stupidly. 'Well, who can it be? It's so –so recent . . . you'd think –'

'You were lying to me, weren't you?'

'I? Lying to you? What do you mean?' Then the look in his face shocked me into understanding. I said sharply: 'It's not *Mark*, don't be silly! I wasn't lying, it was only a flesh-wound, and he was better –*better*, do you hear? And last night, even if the wound *was* bleeding again, it –couldn't have been as bad as *that*!' I found I had hold of his arm again, and was shaking it. He stood like stone. I dropped the arm, and said, more quietly: 'He'd be all right. Lambis wouldn't be far off, and he'd look after him. It *was* healing cleanly, Colin, I'll swear it was.'

'Well, then, who's this?'

'How do I know? It *must* be the man they killed.'

'I tell you, he was buried in the field. I heard them.'

'All right, you heard them. That still doesn't make it Mark. Why should it?'

'Josef shot him. That was why Josef didn't get back for me last night, when I'll swear he meant to. He was up here, burying Mark. Or else Stratos . . . What time was Stratos at that shed with you last night?'

'One o'clock, twenty past, I hardly know.'

'Stratos went back to kill him later. He knew it hadn't just been the cat. He only wanted to put you off and get you back to the hotel, so's he could—'

'Mark might have had something to say about that!' I was still trying to sound no more than reasonable. 'Give him a little credit!'

'He was hurt. And if he'd been raking round the village for hours, he'd be flaked out, you know he would. If it comes to that, the blood mayn't have been from his shoulder at all. Perhaps that was where Stratos—'

'Colin! Shut up and don't be silly!' I could hear the nerves shrilling through my voice like wires. I swallowed, and managed to add, more or less evenly: 'Stratos didn't leave the hotel again before I went back to the shed and found Mark gone. Do you think I wasn't watching? Give me some credit, too! And they'd hardly have killed him in the village and carried him up here to bury him . . . Anyway, what about Lambis? Where's he in all this?'

'Perhaps they killed him, too. Or he got away.'

'He wouldn't run away.'

'Why not? If Mark was dead, and he thought I was, too, why should he stay? If he'd any sense at all, he'd go . . . with the caique.'

His stony insistence was carrying through to me. I found I was shaking. I said, more angrily than I had meant to: 'This is all bilge! You haven't a thing to go on! It isn't Mark, I tell you it isn't! It . . . this could be anyone. Why, it mightn't even *be* anyone. Just because a bit of soil looks like a—Colin, what are you doing?'

'I have to know. Surely you see that? I've got to know.' And with a stiff, abrupt little movement, that somehow had whole chapters of horror in it, he reached out a foot, and dislodged a little of that dry dirt.

A small cascade of it trickled down with a whispering sound. It was the foot that was exposed, and the ankle, in a sock that had been grey. There was no shoe. A bit of the trouser-leg was showing. Dark grey flannel. There was a triangular tear in it that I remembered well.

There was a moment's complete stillness, then Colin made a sound, a small, animal noise, and flung himself to his knees at the other end of the mound, where the head should be. Before I had quite realized what he was about, he was tearing at the bushes and stones with his hands, flinging them aside, careless of cuts and scratches, digging like a dog into the pile of dirt. I don't know what I was doing: I believe I tried to pull him back, but neither words nor frantic hands made any impression at all. I might as well not have been there. The dust rose in a smoking cloud, and Colin coughed and scrabbled, and then, as he dug lower, the dust was caked . . .

He was lying on his face. Under the dirt now was the outline of his shoulders. Colin scooped a drift of stony earth away, and there was the head . . . Hiding it, half-buried, was a branch of withered scrub. I stooped to pull this aside, but gently, as if it could have scratched the dead flesh. Its leaves crumpled in my hands, with the smell of dried verbena. And then, sticking up in obscene tufts from the red dust, I saw the dark hair, with the dirt horribly matted over a sticky blackness . . .

I'm not clear about what happened next. I must have flinched violently back, because the branch I was grasping came dragging out from the piled earth, dislodging as it did so a fresh heap of stuff which came avalanching down from above over the half exposed head and shoulders. My own cry, and Colin's exclamation as his wrists and hands were buried deep in the falling debris, were followed, sharply, by another sound that split the still air with its own kind of terror. A shot.

I think I simply stood there, stupid and sick, with the branch in my hand, and Colin, startled into a moment's immobility, kneeling at my feet. Then he moved. Vaguely I remember him dragging his hands out of the earth, and more stuff tumbling with its choking cloud of dust, and the branch being torn from my hands and flung down where it had been . . . then I was crouching in the shelter of a thicket a little way off, with my head in my hands, sweating and sick and cold, till Colin came pelting after me, to seize me by the shoulder and shake me, not gently.

'Did you hear the shot?'

'I—yes.'

He jerked his head seawards. 'It came from over there. It'll be them. They may be after Lambis.'

I merely stared. Nothing that he said seemed to mean very much. 'Lambis?'

'I'll have to go and see. I—can come back for him later.' Another jerk of the head, this time towards the grave. 'You'd better stay out of sight. I'll be okay, I've got this.' His face still had that stunned, sleepwalker's look, but the gun in his hand was real enough.

It brought me stumbling to my feet. 'Wait. You're not going alone.'

'Look, I've got to go that way anyway, I've got to find the caique, it's all I can do. But for you—well, it's different now. You don't have to come.'

'I do. I'm not leaving you. Go on. Keep right up under the cliffs where the bushes are.'

He didn't argue further. He was already scrambling up the side of the gully, where the cover was thickest. I followed. I only asked one more question, and then I didn't quite dare make it a direct one. 'Was he—was he covered right up again?'

'Do you think I'd leave him for those stinking birds?' said Colin curtly, and swung himself up among the trees at the gully's edge.

Chapter 15

No spectre greets me—no vain Shadow this:
Come, blooming Hero . . .!
WORDSWORTH: *Laodamia*

THE RUINED CHURCH was tiny. It stood in a green hollow full of flowering weeds. It was just an empty shell, cruciform, the central cupola supporting four half-cups that clung against it like a family of limpets clinging to the parent, and waiting for the rising tide of green to swamp them. This, it threatened soon to do: a sea of weeds—mallow and vetch, spurge and thistle—had washed already half up the crumbling walls. Even the roof was splashed with green, where the broken tiles had let fern-seeds in to mantle their faded red. A wooden cross, bleached by the sea-winds, pricked bravely up from the central dome.

We paused at the lip of the hollow, peering down through the bushes. Nothing moved: the air hung still. Below us now we could see the track running past the door of the church, and then lifting its dusty length through the maquis towards the sea.

'Is that the way to the caique?' I whispered.

Colin nodded. He opened his lips as if to say something, then stopped abruptly, staring past me. As I turned to look, his hand shot out to grip my arm. 'Over there, see? I saw someone, a man. I'm sure I did. Do you see where that streak of white runs down, above the knot of pines? To the right of that . . . no, he's gone. Keep down, and watch.'

I flattened myself beside him, narrowing my eyes against the bright afternoon glare.

His hand came past me, pointing. 'There!'

'Yes, I can see him now. He's coming this way. Do you think?'

Colin said sharply: 'It's Lambis!'

He had half-risen to one knee, but I shot out a hand and pulled him down. 'You can't be sure at this distance. If it was Lambis, he'd be keeping under cover. Hang on.'

Colin subsided. The small figure came rapidly on; there must have been a path there; he made good speed along the hillside towards where the main track must lie, and he was certainly making no attempt at concealment. But now I saw him more clearly; brown trousers, dark-blue seaman's jersey and khaki jacket, the way he moved . . . Colin was right. It was Lambis.

I was going to say as much when I saw, a little way beyond Lambis and above the path he was following, another man emerging from a tangle of rocks and scrub where he must have been concealed. He began to make his way more slowly along, above Lambis' path, converging downhill upon it. He was still hidden from the advancing Lambis, but he was plain enough to me . . . the loose breeches and bloused jacket, the red Cretan cap, and the rifle.

I said hoarsely: 'Colin . . . above Lambis . . . that's Josef.'

For seven or eight paralysed seconds we watched them: Lambis, unaware of his danger, coming steadily and rapidly on; Josef, moving slowly and carefully, and, as far as I could make out, already within easy range . . . The gun nosed forward beside me, light trembling on the barrel, which was not quite steady.

'Shall I fire a shot to warn him?' breathed Colin. 'Or would Josef—'

'Wait!' My hand closed on his wrist again. I said, unbelievingly: 'Look!'

Lambis had paused, turned, and was looking around him as if expecting someone. His attitude was easy and unafraid. Then he saw Josef. He lifted a hand, and waited. The Cretan responded with a gesture, then made his way unhurriedly down to where Lambis awaited him.

The two men stood talking for a few minutes, then I saw Lambis' arm go out, as if he were indicating some path, and Josef lifted the field-glasses to his eyes, and turned them eastwards. They swept past the church, the hollow, the bushes where we lay, and passed on. He dropped them, and presently, after a little more talk, he moved off again, alone, at a slant which would by-pass the hollow, and take him straight down towards the coastal cliffs.

Lambis stood watching him for a moment, then turned towards

us, and came rapidly on his way. His course would lead him straight to the church. And–I saw it, as he came nearer–he now had Josef's rifle.

Colin and I looked at one another.

'*Lambis?*'

Neither of us said it, but the question was there, hanging between us, in the blank, frightened bewilderment of our faces. Vaguely, I remembered Lambis' evasive replies when I asked him about his birthplace. It had been Crete; was it here, perhaps? Agios Georgios? And had he used Mark and Colin as the cover for bringing his caique here, for some purpose connected with Stratos and his affairs?

But there was no time to think now. Lambis was approaching fast. I could hear his footsteps already on the rock beyond the hollow.

Beside me, Colin drew in his breath like a diver who has just surfaced, and I saw his hand close round the butt of the gun. He levelled it carefully across his wrist, aiming at the point where Lambis would appear on the track beside the church.

It never occurred to me to try to stop him. I simply found myself wondering what the range of an automatic was, and if Colin was a good enough shot to get Lambis at the foreshortened angle he would present.

Then, I came to myself. I put my lips to Colin's ear. 'For heaven's sake, hang on! We've got to talk to him! We've got to know what's happened! And if you fire that thing, you'll bring Josef back.'

He hesitated, then, to my relief, he nodded. Lambis came out into the clearing below us. He was walking easily, without even a hand on his knife–as well he might, I thought bitterly. I remembered the way he had followed Josef out of sight yesterday–to have a conference, no doubt. Another thought struck me: if Josef had been to the village, then he would have told Stratos and Sofia that I was involved. But they had not known . . . or they surely could not have behaved the way they did. So he hadn't yet been back to the village . . . and now we would do our best to see that he never got back there again.

The rights and wrongs of it never entered my head. Mark was dead, and that thought overrode all else. If Colin and I could manage it, Josef and the treacherous Lambis would die, too. But first, we had to know just what had happened.

Lambis paused at the door of the church to light a cigarette. I saw Colin fingering the gun. There was sweat on his face, and his body was rigid. But he waited.

Lambis turned, and went into the church.

There was the sound, magnified by the shell of the building, of stone against stone, as if Lambis were shifting pieces of loose masonry. He must have used this place as a cache, and he had come this way to collect something he had hidden there.

Colin was getting up. As I made to follow, he whispered fiercely: 'Stay where you are!'

'But, look—'

'I'll manage this on my own. You keep hidden. You might get hurt.'

'Colin, listen, put the gun out of sight. He doesn't know we saw him with Josef—we can go down there openly, and tell him you're found. If he thinks we don't suspect him, we can get the rifle from him. *Then* we can make him talk.'

As clearly as if the boy's face were a screen, and a different picture had flashed on to it, I saw the blind rage of grief give way to a kind of reason. It was like watching a stone mask come alive.

He pushed the gun back out of sight under his cloak, and made no objection when I stood up with him. 'Pretend you're a bit shaky on your pins,' I said, and slipped a hand under his elbow. We went down into the hollow.

As we reached level ground, Lambis must have heard us, for the slight sounds inside the church stopped abruptly. I could smell his cigarette.

I squeezed Colin's elbow. He called out, in a voice whose breathlessness (I thought) wasn't entirely faked:

'Mark? Lambis? Is that you?'

Lambis appeared in the doorway, his eyes screwed up against the sun.

He started forward. '*Colin!* How on earth—? My dear boy—you're safe! Nicola—*you* found him?'

I said: 'Have you anything to drink, Lambis? He's just about done.'

'Is Mark there?' asked Colin, faintly.

'No. Come inside out of the sun.' Lambis had Colin's other arm, and between us we steered him into the church's airy shade. 'I was just on my way down to the caique. There's water in the flask. Sit the boy down, Nicola . . . I'll get him a drink.'

Mark's haversack lay in one corner, where Lambis had dragged it from its hiding-place in a tumble of masonry. Apart from this, the place was empty as a blown egg, the stone-flagged floor swept clean

by the weather, and the clustered domes full of cross-lights and
shadows, where the ghost of a Christos Pantokrator stared down
from a single eye. The rifle stood where Lambis had set it, against
the wall by the door.

He was stooping over the haversack, rummaging for the flask. His
back was towards us. As Colin straightened, I let his arm go, and
moved to stand over the rifle. I didn't touch it; I'd as soon have
touched a snake; but I was going to see that Lambis had no chance to
grab it before Colin got control. The automatic was levelled at
Lambis' back.

He had found the thermos. He straightened and turned, with this
in his hand.

Then he saw the gun. His face changed, almost ludicrously.
'What's this? Colin, are you mad?'

'Keep your voice down,' said Colin curtly. 'We want to hear about
Mark.' He waved his gun. 'Go on. Start talking.'

Lambis stood like a stone, then his eyes turned to me. He was
looking scared, and I didn't blame him. Colin's hand wasn't all that
steady, and the gun looked as if it might go off at any moment. And
Lambis' question hadn't been quite idle: Colin did indeed look more
than a little unhinged.

'Nicola,' said the Greek sharply, 'what is this? Have they turned
his brain? Is that thing loaded?'

'Nicola,' said Colin, just as sharply, 'search him. Don't get
between him and the gun – Lambis, stand still, or I promise I'll shoot
you here and now!' This as Lambis' eyes flicked towards his rifle.
'Hurry up,' added Colin, to me. 'He hasn't a gun, but he carries a
knife.'

'I know,' I said feebly, and edged round behind Lambis.

Needless to say, I had never searched anyone before, and had
only the vaguest recollection, from films and so on, of how it was
done. If it hadn't been for the grim relics buried in the gully, and for
the look in Colin's face, the scene would have been pure farce.
Lambis' English had deserted him, and he was pouring forth a flood
of questions and invective which Colin neither heeded nor understood, and to which I didn't even listen. I found the knife straight
away, in his pocket, and dropped it into my own, feeling stupid, like
a child playing pirates. I stood back.

Lambis said furiously, in Greek: 'Tell him to put that thing down,
Nicola! What the hell are you playing at, the pair of you? He'll shoot
someone! Has he gone crazy with what they did to him? Are you

mad, too? Get hold of that bloody gun, and we'll get him down to–'

'We found the grave,' I said, in English.

He stopped in mid-tirade. 'Did you?' The anger seemed to drop from him, and his face looked strained all at once, the dark sunburn looking almost sickly in the queer cross-lights of the church. He seemed momentarily to have forgotten Colin and the gun. He said hoarsely: 'It was an accident. I would have you to understand that. You know I would not mean to kill him.'

I was standing back against the door-jamb–the unheeded Doric column–fingering in my pocket the knife I had taken from him. Under my hand I could feel the chasing of the handle, and remembered suddenly, vividly, the pattern of the blue enamelling on the copper shaft. I remembered his using this very knife to slice the corned beef for Mark . . .

'*You* did it?' I said.

'I did not want him dead.' He was repeating himself in a kind of entreaty. 'When you get back to your people in Athens, perhaps you will help me . . . if you tell them that this was an accident . . .'

Something broke inside me. Where I found the Greek words I do not know: looking back, what I spoke was probably mainly English, with bits of Greek and French thrown in. But Lambis understood, and so–he told me later–did Colin.

'*Accident?*' I forgot the need for quiet, and my voice rose sharply. 'Accident? Then I suppose it's an accident that you're running round now on the hillside with that swine who shot at Mark and wanted to murder Colin? And don't think I don't know all about you and your precious friends, because I do! You can take it from me, I know every move your filthy gang have been making–Stratos, and Tony, and Sofia, and Josef . . . and now you! And don't try to pretend you're not in it up to your neck, because we *saw* you–no, hold your damned mouth, and let me finish! Help you? You want shooting out of hand, and I shan't raise a finger to stop Colin doing it, but first of all we want to know just what you're doing in all this. Who pays you, and why? Why did you have to bring him here? And why did you kill him? Why did you have to pretend to save his life, you filthy Judas? Was it because I happened along? If I'd stayed–he was such a marvellous person–if only I'd known–I'd have murdered you myself before I'd have let you hurt him! If only I'd stayed . . .'

The tears came, then, uncontrollably, but the blurring of my vision didn't prevent me from seeing, over the speechless, half-comprehending stupefaction of Lambis' face, the flash of a different expression, as his eyes flickered from my face to something just beyond me. Behind me, and beyond, outside the door . . .

A shadow moved in the doorway. Baggy breeches and a Cretan cap. A man coming in fast, with a knife in his hand.

I shrieked: 'Colin! Look out!'

Colin whirled, and fired. Lambis shouted something at the same moment, and jumped for him. The shot thudded into the door-jamb, midway between the newcomer and me, and the noise slammed, deafeningly, round and round the walls. Then Lambis had Colin's gun-hand; his other arm was tight round the boy's body; the gun went flying to the floor. I never moved. In the same moment that I cried out, I had seen the newcomer's face.

Now, I said: 'Mark!' in a high, silly voice that made no sound at all.

The shot had stopped him just inside the doorway. Lambis let Colin go, and stooped to pick up the gun. Colin stood blinking against the light, looking dazed and stupid, as if a touch would have knocked him over.

'Colin,' Mark said.

Then Colin was in his arms, not saying a word, not making a sound, you'd have sworn not even breathing. 'What have they done to you? Hurt you?' I hadn't heard that voice from Mark before. The boy shook his head. 'You're really all right?' The boy nodded. 'That's the truth?' 'Yes.' 'Then we'll go. This is the end, thank God. We'll go straight to the caique.'

I didn't hear if there were any more. I turned and walked past them, and out of the church. Lambis said something, but I took no notice. Regardless now of who could see me, I started up the slope of the hollow, back towards Agios Georgios.

The tears still blurred my eyes, and twice made me stumble; stupid tears, that need never have been shed. I dashed them away. I had cried more over this affair than I remembered having done for years. It was time I got out of it. It was over.

Besides, it was getting late, and Frances would be wondering what had happened to me.

Chapter 16

This done, he march'd away with warlike sound,
And to his Athens turn'd.
                    DRYDEN: *Palamon and Arcite*

BEFORE I HAD gone thirty yards, I heard him behind me.

'Nicola!'

I took no notice.

'Nicola . . . please wait! I can't go at this speed.'

I faltered, then looked back. He was coming down the track with no noticeable difficulty. The only sign of his recent injury was the sling, made from the hanging fold of the Cretan head-dress, that cradled his left arm. He looked very different from the unkempt, half-bearded invalid of yesterday; he had shaved, and washed his hair, but—as with Colin—it was the relief and happiness of the moment that altered his appearance so completely. My first thought was a vague surprise that I should have recognised him so quickly; my second, that the 'heroic' costume suited him disturbingly well.

'Nicola—' he sounded breathless—'don't hurry off, please; I've got to thank you—'

'You shouldn't have bothered. It's all right.' I thrust my damp handkerchief out of sight into a pocket, gave him a smile of a sort, and turned away again. 'You and Colin had better get down to the caique, and away. You're all right now? You look a whole lot better.'

'Lord, yes, I'm fine.'

'I'm glad. Well, all the best, Mark. Good-bye.'

'Wait, please. I—'

'Look, I've got to get back. Frances will be sending out search parties, and it'll take me all of three hours to get home.'

'Nonsense!' He was standing in front of me now, squarely in the middle of the path. 'Two hours downhill, if that. Why did you run away like that? You must know –'

'Because it's all over and done with, and you don't want me mixed up in it any more. You and Lambis and Colin can go to your b-boat and sail away, and that is that.'

'But, my dear, for goodness' sake give us time to thank you! It's you who've done everything, while I was laid up there, about as useful as a pint of milk! And now everything's wonderful – mainly thanks to you. Look, don't be so upset –'

'I'm not upset at all. Don't be absurd.' I sniffed, and looked away from him at the level brilliance of the sun. To my fury, I was beginning to cry again. I rounded on him. 'We thought he'd murdered you. We found that grave, and . . . *it* . . . had your clothes on. It was quite horrible, and I was sick. If that isn't enough to upset me –'

'I know. I'm desperately sorry that you should have come across that. It's the man Colin calls Josef; you'll have guessed that. Lambis killed him, yesterday morning, when he followed him down the hill, remember? He didn't mean to; naturally what he wanted out of Josef was information about Colin, but it happened accidentally. Lambis had been stalking him, not daring to get too close, because of the rifle, when he came suddenly round a bend of that gully, and there was Josef having a drink, with the gun laid to one side. I suppose the noise of the stream had prevented his hearing Lambis coming. Well, catching him like that, Lambis jumped him. Josef hadn't time to reach the rifle, and pulled his knife, but Lambis was on top of him, so he didn't get a chance to use it. He went down, hard, with his head against the rock, and that was that.'

'I . . . see. Yesterday? When Lambis came back, and sent me away, for the food . . . he told you then?'

'Yes. He'd hidden the body behind some bushes, and come back to report.'

'You never said a word to me.'

'Of course not. But you see why we didn't dare to go down and stir up the local police? We didn't even know who the man was, or where he was from. And Lambis was worried sick, naturally. I thought it best to let ill alone, until we knew where we were.'

'If I'd known . . .' I was thinking about the spectre of Josef, which had stalked so frighteningly behind my shoulder this last twenty-four hours. 'You could have trusted me.'

'Good God, you know it wasn't that! I just thought the less

you knew about that, the better. I didn't want you involved.'

That did it. I said furiously: 'Involved? Heaven give me strength, *involved*? I suppose I hadn't been involved enough already? I'd been scared to death by Lambis, I'd spent a perfectly beastly night with you, and I'd ruined a very expensive petticoat. I'd also dressed your horrible shoulder, and cooked and slaved and—and *worried* myself silly! About Colin, I mean. And all you could think of was to get rid of me because I'm a g-girl, and girls are no use, and you were too damned bossy and stiff-necked to admit I *could* help! Well, Mr. Godalmighty Mark Langley, I *did* find Colin, and if he'd still been locked up in that filthy windmill, I'd *still* have found him! I *told* you I could go about on the mountain and in the village safely, and I can, and I have, and I've found out more than you and that horrible Lambis have in *days*. And you needn't think I'm going to tell you *any* of it, because you can just go and find it out for yourselves! *You* didn't tell me anything, so of course I thought he'd murdered you, and Colin and I were going to shoot you both, and you're jolly lucky we didn't!'

'I'll say we are. That bullet was pretty near on target as it was.'

'Stop laughing at me!' I cried furiously. 'And don't think I'm crying about *you*, or that I meant a *single word* I said about you to Lambis just now! I couldn't have cared less if it *had* been you in the g-grave!'

'I know, I know—'

'And I'm not crying, I never cry, it was only that awful body . . . and . . . and—'

'Oh, Nicola, darling, I'm sorry, truly I am. I'm not laughing. I'd give anything if the pair of you hadn't had that shock, and I'm desperately sorry you had that fright just now, over Lambis and me. But we'd been planning to go down into the village, you remember, and I thought Josef's clothes might just help me to get by, in the dark.' He grinned. 'In any case, my own were pretty well past it. Those pants were hardly decent as it was.'

'I saw the tear in them when Colin pulled the earth off, and the s-socks had a h-hole in.'

And I sat down on a stone, and wept bitterly.

He dropped down beside me, and his arm went round my shoulders, 'Oh, Nicola . . . Dear heaven, can't you see, this is just the sort of thing I was trying *not* to let you in for?' He shook me, gently. 'And they weren't my socks, darling, I did draw the line at his footgear and underthings! We took everything else he had, and buried his boots . . . All right, go on, cry, you'll feel better just now.'

'I'm not crying. I never cry.'

'Of course you don't. You're a wonderful girl, and if you hadn't come along when you did, we'd have been sunk.'

'W-would you?'

'Certainly. I might have died of Lambis' poultices, or Josef would have found me in the hut, or Colin might never have got to us safely . . . What's more, you saved me from getting shot last night, though you didn't know it. I was in that shed, along with the cat, when you stopped to have a smoke with your fierce friend in the lane.'

'I know. I went back later. There was blood on the wall.'

'You went back?' His arm moved as a muscle tightened, and I heard his voice change. 'You *knew*? So–when you tried to stop that chap coming in–?'

'He's Josef's friend.' I was crumpling my wet handkerchief into a small, tidy ball. I still hadn't looked at Mark. 'He's one of them. I told you I'd found them.'

There was a sharp silence. I heard him draw in his breath to speak, and said quickly: 'I'll tell you all about them. I–I didn't really mean it when I said I wouldn't; of course I will. But tell me about you first. When I found the blood last night I thought . . . I'm not sure what I thought. Are you really all right?'

'Yes, perfectly. I knocked my shoulder, swanning around there in the dark, and started it bleeding, but it stopped soon enough, and there seems to be no damage.'

'What happened yesterday after I'd left you?'

'Nothing, really. After Lambis had seen you down to the cultivation, he doubled back to meet me, and we buried Josef after a fashion. It took a fair time, and when we'd finished I was so knocked up that I wasn't much use for anything, but I wasn't going to waste any more time before we took a look at the village. I told you Lambis hadn't been sure which way Josef was heading when he killed him, but the odds were it was Agios Georgios . . . Anyway, we went down as far as we dared, and lay up above the village and watched till dark. I felt better after the rest, so we got down into the place and did the best kind of search we could. I thought the Cretan clothes a good idea–if anyone caught a glimpse of me skulking up a back alley, I wouldn't look so blatantly foreign, and I might just have got by with grunting "good night" in Greek. Well, we neither of us found a trace of Colin, as you know. You said he was in the windmill?'

'Yes. But go on; what happened when you got out of the shed?'

'Nothing whatever. I met Lambis as arranged, and we got up into the rocks again and holed up till morning. I was very little use to anyone by that time, and getting pretty sure we'd never find Colin . . .' A pause. 'This morning Lambis went down again, but all I could do was get up to the church to cache our stuff, then take the rifle and hide where I could watch the track where the first murder took place. I thought someone might possibly come to look for Josef, or for traces of me. If they had come, in Josef's clothes I could probably have got well within range before they saw it wasn't him. But never mind that now. Nobody came—not even you. You must have by-passed the track. Which way did you come?'

'We stayed under cover, in the little gully where the body was. Didn't you hear me singing? After I'd found Colin I tried to locate you.'

He shook his head. 'Not a thing. I wish I had. And Lambis drew blank, too. He'd gone to look at the cultivation.'

'This morning? We were there, Frances and I.'

'I know. He saw you both at one of the windmills. Was that the one?' He smiled. 'There's irony for you. He saw you go in, so he didn't bother about that one; he just hung around till you'd gone, and the Greek woman, then broke into the other mill. And found nothing, of course. Then he made his way back to me. That was all. A fine, useless effort.'

'I begin to see why this is such good guerilla country. If it hadn't been so awful it would be comic—the whole boiling of us climbing about on the mountain, with never a glimpse of each other. Was it you who fired a shot?'

'Yes, to guide Lambis to me. A shot's safer than shouting; it's a sound one takes for granted in the country. Did that frighten you, too?'

I shook my head, but said nothing. I wasn't going to explain to Mark that the shot had been the least of my worries at the time. I stuffed the handkerchief away into my pocket, rubbed the back of my hand hard over my eyes, and smiled at him.

'All right now!' he said gently.

'Of course.'

'That's my girl.' His arm came round me again in a quick, hard hug, then let me go. 'Now come back with me, and we'll have our council of war.'

Colin and Lambis were sitting by the bushes that edged the hollow. They had chosen a flat little clearing, where the small flowers grew, and the baby cypresses like thin dark fingers pointed up through the green. These smelt delicious in the hot sunshine. Below us, the bank was thick with the creamy rock-roses. The track wound down through them, to disappear among the folded ridges that marked the coast. Here and there, a gap showed a blinding wedge of sea.

As we came up, Colin was laughing at something Lambis had said. The haversack was open between them, and Colin was already rootling purposefully through what food was there. He waved my wine-bottle at Mark as we approached.

'Hurry up, Marco Polo, if you want any of this. It's nearly all gone.'

'Then I suggest you leave some for Nicola. Where'd you get it, anyway?'

'She brought it.'

'Then most certainly she ought to drink it. Hand it over. Here, Nicola, have some now.'

'It was for you,' I said.

' "My wine is dew of the wild white rose",' misquoted Mark, 'and what could be nastier, come to think of it? No, really, I'm getting almost used to water; drink it yourself.'

As I obeyed, I saw Colin grin at Lambis' puzzled look. 'Don't listen to Mark. That was just Keats. Go on, Lambis, this one's a classic, say "What are Keats?" '

Lambis grinned. It was obvious that he was used to being Colin's butt, and for the moment the two of them seemed much of an age. Lambis, like the others, looked quite different; much younger, and with the heavy, sullen set gone from his mouth. I realized that it had been put there by worry, and felt more than ever ashamed.

'Well,' he was saying placidly, 'what are they?'

Colin opened his mouth to whoop with mirth, then quickly shut it again. 'So I should think,' said his brother. 'If you did but know it, Lambis' English is a darn' sight better than yours. The Lord alone knows where you get it, things must have changed a lot since I was at that Borstal of yours myself. A Borstal—' to Lambis—'is an English school. Now, attention all, this is serious, and we haven't a lot of time. Nicola, here's a place to sit.'

As the Greek moved aside to make room for me, I smiled at him a little shyly. 'Lambis, I ought to have known. I'm sorry, I truly am. It was only because we'd had such a shock, Colin and I . . . and I honestly couldn't imagine who else *could* be buried there. And then there were the clothes. I said some awful things. Can you forgive me?'

'It does not matter. You were a little disturbed with seeing the dead body. Such things are not nice for ladies.' And on this masterly piece of understatement Lambis grinned amiably, and dismissed the matter.

'Well,' said Mark crisply, taking charge, 'we can't keep you very long, so if you could bear to start . . .'

I said: 'I've been thinking. I really think you'd better hear Colin's side of it first. One or two things he overheard, when he was actually in the lions' den, seem to provide a clue to the rest.'

So Colin told them his story, and afterwards Mark—a rather grimmer-faced Mark—detailed him to keep a look-out with the field-glasses, while he and Lambis turned back to me.

'I don't know quite where to start'—I felt suddenly shy—'because a lot of it may mean nothing. Shall I just try to tell you more or less all that's happened, and let you draw conclusions?'

'Please. Even if it's irrelevant.'

'*Oriste?*' from Lambis.

'Even if it's rot,' translated Colin, over his shoulder.

'Even if it doesn't seem to matter,' amended his brother. 'Don't take any notice of the brat, Lambis, he's above himself.'

'And that,' said Colin, 'is an idiom, meaning—'

'Belt up or I'll do you,' said Mark, coming down to Colin's level with a rush. 'Nicola?'

I told them then, as briefly as I could, all that had happened since I had left the mountain-side on the previous day. When I had finished, there was silence for perhaps a minute.

Then Mark said, slowly: 'It makes a picture, of a sort. I'll try to sum up, shall I, from the fragments we've got? I think you were right—the bits that Colin overheard provide the clue to the rest. The main thing is, that something Stratos had, and had promised to divide later, was "hot".' He glanced at Lambis. 'That's a slang expression—thieves' language, if you like. It means that they had stolen property in their possession, which the police were on the look-out for, and which could be identified if found.'

'In the plural,' I said. ' "They" were hot.'

'Yes, in the plural. Things small enough, in the plural, to be portable; small enough to come through the Customs (we'll look at that later, but we can assume they brought them from London); things small enough to hide, even in Agios Georgios.'

'Jewels?' suggested Colin, bright-eyed. I could see that, for him, this was becoming simply an adventure–something with a happy ending already settled by his brother's presence, to be stored up, and talked about next term at school. At least, I thought thankfully, he didn't seem the type to store up nightmares.

Mark saw it too. He gave Colin a fleeting grin. 'All the treasures of the East, why not? But I'm afraid it doesn't really matter terribly what it is . . . for the moment, anyway. All *we* need is a coherent story that we can present to the Consul and the police in Athens . . . something that'll tie Stratos and Co. up good and hard with Alexandros' murder. Once that's done, our end of the story'll be accepted, however many alibis are cooked up in Agios Georgios. If we can establish the fact that Josef was a criminal and a murderer, then Lambis will get away with justifiable homicide, or self-defence, or whatever they do get away with here. And that's all I'm bothered with just now. He wouldn't be in this mess, but for us, and all I care about is to see he gets clear out of it.'

Lambis glanced up, caught my eye, and grinned. He had his knife out, and was whittling away at a curly piece of wood, carving it to a shape that looked like a lizard. I watched, fascinated, as it began to take shape.

Mark went on: 'Now, it's the London end of it that'll give us the connection . . . Colin heard them say that any investigation would "get back to the London affair". This is what's valuable–we can be sure the connection between Stratos and the murdered man is originally a London one, and it sounds to me as if the London police are on the job already–or have been. The stuff was "hot", after all.' He paused. 'Let's see how much we can assume. Stratos and Tony came from London six months ago, and brought with them this "hot" stolen property. They have arranged to settle here, probably until the hue and cry has died down; then Tony will take his share, and go. They must have intended to leave England anyway, since Stratos apparently wound up his affairs, and what better cover could they have than Stratos' own home, where he'd come naturally, and where Tony might very well come to help him start up his business? You know –' looking up '– it does sound as if the loot, whatever it is, must be pretty considerable.'

'You mean because it's worth a long wait.'

'Exactly. You can't tell me your friend Tony wants to spend years of his life in Agios Georgios. Do you think for one minute that that tin-pot hotel is worth his while?'

'Oh, it's a change from the dear old Vicarage,' I said.

' "The loot," ' said Lambis. 'What is that?'

'The swag,' said Colin. 'The lolly, the pickings, the—'

Lambis put a hand to the side of his head, and pushed him over into a rosemary bush.

'The stolen property,' I said, laughing.

'Order, children,' said Mark. 'Stratos and Tony, then, are concerned in some crime in London, presumably a top-flight robbery. They blind off with the—they leave the country with the stolen property (how good you are for us, Lambis) and settle down here to wait. Stratos must be the leader, or senior partner, since he has the stuff hidden away, and Tony doesn't know where it is. Then we come to Alexandros.'

'He came looking for Stratos,' I said. 'He knew Tony, and talked English to him, and Tony took him along to meet Stratos. I'll bet Alexandros came from London, too.'

Colin rolled over eagerly. 'He was their partner in the robbery, and they did him down, and he came to claim his share, so they murdered him!'

'Could be,' said Mark, 'but Stratos did appear quite happy to cut his sister in on the deal—I mean, divide the, er—'

'Loot,' said Lambis.

'—the loot with his sister. So it doesn't seem likely that he'd murder a partner just because he claimed his share. Tony doesn't seem to think there's much risk, anyway.'

I said, hesitantly: 'Couldn't it be quite simple—that it did happen much as Colin says, but that they did quarrel, and Stratos just lost his temper? I'll swear he's that kind of man; one of those big, full-blooded toughies—*pallikaráthes*, Lambis— who can suddenly lose all their self-control, and who're strong enough to do a lot of damage when they do. And in a country where everybody carries guns as a matter of course . . . Mark, you saw the actual murder. You said they were shouting. Wasn't it done like that?'

'Well, yes, it was. They were arguing violently, then the whole thing seemed to explode . . . but don't ask me who exploded first, or how. The murder does seem likely to have its roots back in something that happened in London; this "affair", whatever it is, that they're so afraid is going to catch them up. Apparently that, let alone the Alexandros murder, is serious enough to frighten them into a dashed silly action like taking Colin along. I imagine that Stratos probably—and Tony certainly—hold British passports. It would be interesting to know if we have an extradition treaty with Greece.'

'I can tell you that,' I said. 'We have.'

'Ah,' said Mark. He glanced at his watch. 'Let's cut this short. I think we've got all we need. We can give the police a lead to Stratos and Co. long before they suspect we're even operative. It shouldn't be hard for the London end to identify a couple of Soho Greeks and a —well, Tony; they're probably marked down as "wanted" anyway, only they've just not traced them. Then, if the police here slap a watch on to them immediately, they may find the stuff . . . and there's your connection, your motive . . . *and* Lambis in the clear for attacking a potential murderer.'

'The police'll have to be quick,' I said uneasily. 'Stratos must know Colin'd go straight for help.'

'If he knows he's escaped. But if Colin was right—and I think he was—then they did mean to kill him, and Sofia knew this. She may let Stratos think Colin has been disposed of. We can't count on it, but she might keep her mouth shut for a while, for her own sake. Stratos'll worry about where Josef has got to, but I doubt if—yet—he'll take the desperate step of bolting from Agios Georgios.'

'If I were Stratos,' I said, 'I'd shift the body—Alexandros', I mean—just in case of an inquiry. It was silly to bury it on their own land.'

'If you'd tried burying someone up here in four inches of dust,' said Mark, 'you'd see their point. But I agree. He very well may. The fact that they put him there at all might mean that they didn't intend Colin to get away, after what he'd seen and heard.'

'They *were* going to kill me?'

'I don't see how else they'd be safe,' said Mark frankly. 'They could be fairly sure I was lying dead somewhere. Without Lambis, I would have been. You can be sure they were only waiting for definite news of me. Even if Sofia had persuaded Stratos to let you alone, she must have known she couldn't protect you for ever . . . not from the kind of man Josef appears to have been, anyway . . . so she decided to let you go.'

Colin looked anxious. 'Will she be all right when they do find out I've gone?'

Mark glanced at me.

I said slowly: 'I'm sure Stratos wouldn't harm her, even if he dared. I've been thinking about it, and I don't think you need worry seriously. He might hit her in a temper, but he'd never kill her. And she's used to rough treatment, poor soul. What's more, the fact that she did save you, may save *her* from quite a lot, once the police inquiries get going.' I glanced at Lambis. 'And you . . . you can be pretty sure she'll be happier and better off as a widow than she ever has been since she married that beastly waster.'

'That is good to hear,' was all Lambis said, but I thought his expression was lighter as he bent again over the little lizard.

'It's true. Look, I must go.'

'Lord, yes, you must,' said Mark. 'Sister Ann, do you see anyone coming?'

Colin put the glasses to his eyes again.

'Not a sausage.'

'Not a what?' Lambis looked up, blade suspended again over the lizard's spine.

'Not a sausage,' repeated Colin. 'You know quite well what—'

'I know quite well what not a sausage is,' retorted Lambis. '*Óchi loukánika*. But I do not know that you have an idiom where it walks about in the mountains. I like to learn.'

'Get you!' said Colin, admiringly. I reflected that by the time Lambis had spent a month in the company of the brothers Langley, his knowledge of the odder byways of the English language would be remarkable.

Mark was getting to his feet. I noticed all at once that he was looking tired. There were lines from nostrils to mouth, and a shadow round his eyes. He put a hand down to me, and pulled me to my feet. 'I wish you hadn't to go down there.'

'The way I feel now,' I said frankly, 'if it weren't for Frances, I'd go down to your caique with you now, luggage or no luggage, and hightail it straight for Athens! But that's only the way I *feel*. Cold reason tells me that none of them will even think of suspecting that I know anything about it!'

'I'm sure they won't.' But the look he gave me was doubtful. 'The only thing is . . . I don't feel we can just set off now for Athens, without making quite certain that you and your cousin really are safe.'

'Well, but why shouldn't we be?'

'No reason at all. But we've no possible way of knowing what's

been going on down there since Colin got away, and I—well, I just
don't like cutting communications altogether, without knowing
what sort of situation we're leaving behind us. You'll be pretty
isolated, if anything should happen, and you're right in Stratos'
territory.'

I realized then why he was watching me so doubtfully; he was
waiting for me to assert my independence. For once, I had not the
least desire to do so. The thought of leaving these capable males, and
walking down alone to Stratos' hotel, was about as attractive as
going out unclothed into a hail-storm.

'When are your friends calling for you?' asked Mark.

'On Monday.'

He hesitated again. 'I'm sorry, but I really think . . . I'd be
inclined not to wait until Monday.'

I smiled at him. 'I'm with you there. All else apart, I quite
definitely do *not* want to be around when the police start nosing
about. So I think we'll find a good excuse for leaving, tomorrow as
ever was. The sooner I see the bright lights of Heraklion, the
happier I shall be!'

'That's very wise.' He looked immeasurably relieved. 'Can you
invent a good reason?'

'Easily enough. Don't worry, we'll think up something that won't
alarm your birds. They'll be so glad to get rid of us, all things
considered, that they won't ask any questions.'

'True enough. Can you get in touch with the boat that was going
to pick you up?'

'No, but it's calling at Heraklion first for supplies, and to let the
party visit Cnossos and Phestos. Frances and I can have a car sent for
us tomorrow, and we'll go to the Astir Hotel and wait for them . . .'
I laughed. 'And I defy any harm to come to us there!'

'Fine,' said Mark. 'The Astir? As long as I know where you are
. . . I'll get in touch with you as soon as I can.'

We had begun, as we talked, to walk slowly back down the slope
towards the church. 'What will you do when you leave?' I said. 'Go
to Heraklion, or make for Athens straight away?'

'I'd like to get straight to Athens, to the British Authority there,
and get the London inquiries started, but I don't know. Lambis,
how long will it take us to Athens?'

'In this weather, anything from twelve to fifteen hours.'

'Fair enough. That's what we'll do. I imagine the Embassy will
rally round with flags flying, when they hear one of their ewe

lambs is a witness in the middle of a capital crime.'

'They'll be furious, more like,' I said ruefully.

'Which brings me to the last thing.' We had reached the church, and stopped there, by the door.

'Yes?'

'I said before that I don't want to leave the place tonight, without knowing you're all right.'

'I know you did, but how can you? Once I'm clear away from here, you can take it for granted.'

'I'm not taking anything about your safety for granted.'

It was odd, but this time his cool assumption of responsibility never raised a single bristle: not a stir. All I felt was a treacherous glow, somewhere in the region of the stomach. I ran a hand down the genuine Doric column, rubbing an abstracted thumb along the raw edge of the bullet-hole. 'I don't see how.'

'Well, I've been thinking how. Listen, everyone. Lambis is going with Nicola now, to see her safe down to the fields. Colin and I'll wait here for you, Lambis, in the church. I–I'll rest till you get back. Then we three are going down to the caique, and we'll put straight out from shore. It'll be dusk before long, so we'll wait for that, then move along, well out, till we get west of Agios Georgios. After dark, we'll put in nearer, and lie off for a while. The sea's like glass, and looks like staying that way, thank heaven. Lambis, d'you know anything about the coast west of the village?'

'A little only. It is much like this, small bays at the foot of rocks like these. Near the village there is shallow bays, sandy.'

'Is there anywhere where a caique could put in, if necessary?'

Lambis frowned, considering. 'I do not know. I have noticed a bay, a little way to the west–'

I said: 'I think there is. There's a bay the children called the Dolphins' Bay, past the second headland along from the village. There are rocks running right out into deep water: I saw them from a distance, a sort of low ridge running out like a pier. It must be deep alongside, because the children told me you could dive from them.'

Lambis nodded. 'I think that is the bay I saw. Past the second headland to the west of the village? Yes, I notice the place as we come by.'

'Could you put in there, if necessary?' asked Mark.

'I can use my lights, once we have the headland between us and the hotel?'

'Surely.'

Lambis nodded. 'Then in this weather it should be quite easy. Okay.'

'Fine.' Mark turned to me. 'Now, how about this? If, when you get down there this evening, you think there's the least thing wrong—any sort of suspicion, any danger . . . oh, you know what I mean . . . In other words, if you get the feeling that you and Frances ought to get out of there, and fast, without waiting for morning, then we'll be waiting at the mouth of your Dolphins' Bay till, what shall we say?—two in the morning. No, half-past: that should give you time. Have you an electric torch? Good. Well, any time between midnight and two-thirty a.m. we'll be watching for it. We'll have to fix a signal . . . say, two long flashes, then two short, then pause half a minute, and repeat. We'll answer. That do?'

I grinned at him. 'Corny.'

'Oh, sure. Can you think of anything better?'

'No.'

'What happens if the bay's full of light-fishers?' asked Colin.

'It won't be,' I said. 'There are *scháros*-pots there, and they're collected before that time. No, it's fine, Mark. I can hardly wait.'

'Man, oh man, it's terrific!' Colin still had that boys'-adventure-story glow about him.

Mark laughed. 'It's pretty silly, really, but it's the best we can do, short of putting into Agios Georgios and scaring every bird within miles.'

'It won't be necessary, anyway,' I said. 'It's just a flourish, to go with that pirate's rig of Mark's. Now I'll go. Anybody coming, Sister Ann?' This to Colin, who had mounted some sort of decaying buttress outside the church wall, and was once again raking the hillside beyond the hollow with Josef's glasses.

'*Óchi loukánika.*'

'Then I'll be off. Heavens, if I make the hotel by dinner-time it's all I can do! *What* excuse can I give for staying out till now? No, don't worry, I'll simply say I came over to see the church—Stratos suggested it to me himself, so he'll probably be pleased. Nothing succeeds like the truth.'

'You told me,' said Colin, from above us, 'that you were supposed to be collecting flowers.'

'Oh, lord, yes! Well, I'll grab a handful or two on the way down.'

'Have this for a start . . . and this . . . and this . . .' Colin had already yanked half a dozen random weeds from the overgrown stones above his head. 'And I'm sure *this* one's as rare as rare . . .' He stretched to pull down a straggling handful from a high vertical crack.

'Frances is going to be very impressed by that lot,' said Mark drily. 'And so's Stratos, come to that.'

'Why not? All these are probably howlingly rare in England.'

'Including the dandelion? Don't forget he's lived twenty years there, and Tony's English.'

'Well, Londoners.' Colin scrambled down, unabashed. 'They won't know any better. You can tell them it's a Cretan variety, only found here at two thousand feet. And look at that purple thing, dash it, I'll bet they haven't even got *that* at Kew! There, Nicola—' and he pushed the bunch of exotic weeds at me—'and don't forget this is *"dandeliona Langleyensis hirsuta"*, and fearfully rare.'

'Well, I wouldn't know any better.' I accepted them gratefully, refraining from pointing out that *dandeliona Langleyensis* was, in fact, a hawkweed. 'Thanks a lot, I'm sure Frances will love them.'

'I'll ring you up at the Astir,' said Mark, 'and let you know what's going on. Then I suppose we meet in Athens?'

'If we don't all forgather in Dolphins' Bay tonight,' I said cheerfully. ' 'Bye for now. See you both in Athens. Be good, Colin, take care of Mark. And stop worrying about me. I'll be all right.'

'Famous last words,' said Colin gaily.

'Shut up, you clot,' said Mark, quite angrily.

Chapter 17

But having done whate'er she could devise,
And emptied all her Magazine of lies
The time approach'd . . .
   DRYDEN: *The Fable of Iphis and Ianthe*

LAMBIS LEFT ME at the stepping-stones, which was just as well. Tony was waiting for me at the shrine, sitting on the rocks among the verbena, smoking.

'Hullo, dear. Had a nice day?'

'Lovely, thanks. I suppose my cousin gave up, and went back for tea?'

'She did. She seemed quite happy about you, but I was trying to make up my mind to come and look for you. These aren't the hills to be messing about on by yourself.'

'I suppose not.' I sat down beside him. 'But I stayed pretty well on the track, and anyway, if one goes high enough, one can see the sea. I couldn't really have got lost.'

'You could have turned an ankle. Cigarette? No? Then we'd have had to spend all night looking for you. Calamity!'

I laughed. 'I suppose so. But one can't spend one's whole life expecting the worst, and I did so want to get over to see the church.'

'Oh, so that's where you've been?'

'Yes. My Danish friend told me about it, and Mr. Alexiakis said it was easy to find if one kept to the track, so I went over. It's a long way, but it's well worth the trek, isn't it?'

Tony blew a smoke ring, and tilted his head gracefully to watch it widen, blur, and wisp off into the sunlight. 'Me, I wouldn't know, dear, I've never been further than this. Mountains are not, but not, my thing.'

'No? They're not Frances' thing either. At least, they used to be, but she broke her ankle once, and it's a bit gammy, so she doesn't do much scrambling now.' This was true.

'So she said. Are those for her?'

'Yes.' I allowed myself a dubious look at the flowers in my hand. Lambis and I had added what we could on the way down, but even the eye of faith could hardly have called it a selection to excite a botanist. I had intended to root out the more obvious undesirables before I got to the hotel; as it was, I could only hope that Tony hadn't noticed that most of the gems of my collection grew right down as far as the village street. 'I don't know if she'll want any of these.' I looked hopefully at him. 'Do you know anything about flowers?'

'I can tell a rose from a lily, and an orchid from either.'

'Oh, well, I don't know much about them myself. I just brought what I saw. Birds are more my line, but Frances says I don't know much about them, either.' I turned the bunch of flowers over. 'These are probably common as mud, most of them.'

'Well, that's a dandelion, for a start. Really, dear –'

'Hawkweed, quite a different thing. Variety *Langleyensis hirsuta*, and only found above two thousand feet. I do know *that* one. Frances told me where to look for it.'

'Oh? Well, you seem to have had quite a day. Did you see anyone else up there?'

'Not a soul.' I smiled. 'You said we'd come to the right place if we wanted peace and quiet. There wasn't a sign of life, unless you count the birds – and all I saw of *them* was a hoodie, and a pair of lesser kestrels, and a mob of goldfinches near the stepping-stones.'

Tony, it appeared, did not count the birds. He got up. 'Well, are you rested? Shall we go down?'

'Good heavens, did you come right up here just to meet me?'

'I wanted a walk. The lemons smell good, don't they?' We left the lemon-grove, and skirted the field where the cornmill stood. A swift glance showed me that the door was tightly shut, and that no key jutted from the lock. I looked away quickly, my mind racing. Had Tony really come up here to meet me, perhaps to find out where I had been and what I had seen; or had he come up to the mill? Did he know that Colin was no longer there? If so, did he suspect Sofia, or would he assume that Josef had taken the boy up into the hills to silence him? It was even possible that Sofia herself had confided in him; he, like her, had been opposed to the idea of further murder. I stole a glance at him. Nothing in his face or bearing betrayed that he was thinking of anything more serious than how to avoid the mule-droppings in the track. Certainly there was no hint that he was engaged in a kind of verbal chess with me.

Well, so far we had each made the move we wanted. And if I could, I would avoid letting him make another. Quickly, I tried a diversion. I pointed up into an ilex-tree. 'Look, there's a jay! Aren't they pretty things? They're so shy at home that you hardly ever see them properly.'

'Is that what it was?' He had hardly glanced at it. He made his next move; pawn advancing to queen's square: 'Don't you think these windmills are just ducky?'

'They're lovely.' I hoped the queen's hesitation wasn't showing. But whatever he knew, or didn't know, I must say and do the natural thing. I said it, with a rough-and-ready compromise. 'We took some ciné-film up here this morning – there were people working in the fields, and Frances got some lovely shots of that mill.'

'Was Sofia up here?'

'Mr. Alexiakis' sister? Yes, she was. She's very nice, isn't she? I'd never have taken her for his sister; she looks so much older.'

'That's the difference between the fleshpots of Soho and the empty fish-nets of Agios Georgios, dear. Especially if your husband's a fisherman who won't fish. Josef's idea of bringing home the bacon is to slope off into the hills armed to the teeth like a Cretan brigand. Not that there's anything to shoot in these parts. If he brings home a rock-partridge once a month he thinks he's done his bit towards the happy home.'

I laughed. 'Have I seen him yet? Does he spend his time playing backgammon at the hotel?'

'Not he. No, he's off somewhere just now on a ploy of his own. I thought you might have seen him up yonder. That's why I asked. Did Sofia let you in to the mill?'

Check to the queen. This diversion hadn't worked, either. Then I saw that my trapped feeling came only from myself, from the guilty knowledge of my own involvement. Tony could have no possible reason for suspecting I knew anything at all. The only reason he would be asking me these questions was if he really wanted to know.

Sofia, then, had told him nothing. For one frantic moment I wondered what to say. Then I saw, sharply, that Sofia would have to protect herself. It was my job to look after my own side, and that included me. It would be no help to Tony and Stratos, now, to know that Colin had gone. They couldn't get him. And Sofia would have to face them some day. Meanwhile I must look after myself, and Frances. The truth was the only armour for innocence.

I had stooped to pick an iris, and this had given me the moment I wanted. I straightened up, tucking the flower into the bunch I carried. 'Into the mill? Yes, she did. She was awfully kind, because I think she was in a hurry, but she showed us round, and Frances got some lovely shots of the interior. We were awfully lucky to run across her; I'd never have known whose mill it was, and it's usually kept locked, I suppose?'

'Yes,' said Tony. The light eyes showed nothing but mild interest. 'You saw the whole works, then? How nice. The millstones and all that?'

'Oh, yes. She showed Frances how they worked.'

'Ah,' said Tony. He dropped his cigarette on the dusty path, and ground it out with his heel. He smiled at me: Tony, to whom it didn't matter whether or not Colin had been murdered in the small hours of the morning; Tony, the passer-by on the other side; the chess-expert who was enjoying a game that made my palms sweat with the effort of being natural. 'Well, dear,' he said lightly, 'I'm glad you had a good day. Ah, there's the bridge, not far to go now. You'll just about have time to change before dinner, *and* it's octopus, which you'll adore, if you've a taste for flavoured india-rubber.'

So the game was over. Relief made me as gay as he was. 'I don't mind it, but it's not the main dish, surely? Oh, Tony, and I'm ravenous!'

'I gave you each enough lunch for two.'

'You certainly did. I ate nearly all of it, what's more, and left the rest for the birds. If you'd given me less, I'd have been down a couple of hours ago. I hope you didn't want the bottle back?'

'No. I hope you buried it out of sight? It offends the gods of the place,' said Tony, blandly, 'if undesirable objects are left unburied hereabouts.'

'Don't worry, I buried it under some stones—after pouring the correct libations with the last of the wine.'

'Correct libations?'

'One for Zeus—he was born up there, after all. And then my own private one for the moon-spinners.'

'The what?'

'The moon-spinners. Three ladies who spin the moon away every month, to bring a good dark night at the end of it. The opposite of

the hunter's moon—a night that's on the side of the hunted things
. . . like Josef's rock-partridges.'

'A night of no moon,' said Tony. 'Well, isn't that interesting?
What my dear old father used to call a night for the Earl of Hell.'

I raised my eyebrows. 'That seems an odd expression for a Vicar.'

'A what?' For one glorious moment I saw Tony disconcerted.
Then the pale eyes danced. 'Oh, yes. But then my father was such
an *odd* Vicar, dear. Ah, well, I dare say your libation will work.
There'll be no moon tonight. Black enough,' he added cheerfully, 'to
hide anything. Or anybody.'

*   *   *

Frances was sitting in the garden, but the door to the hall was
open, and as soon as Tony and I entered the hotel, she saw us, and
came hurrying in.

'My dear! Practically a search-party! Tony was sure you'd be
lying with a broken leg, surrounded by vultures, but I assured him
you'd be all right! Had a good day?'

'Wonderful! I'm sorry if I worried you, but I decided while I was
up there that I'd make for that old Byzantine ruin I told you about,
and it's positively miles! But I had a marvellous day!'

Tony had lingered to watch our meeting, but now disappeared
through the door behind the reception table. He left it ajar. I heard
Stratos' voice say something in soft Greek which I couldn't catch.

Frances' eyes were on my face, worried and questioning. I must
have looked very different from the depressed messenger she had
seen off that morning.

'Are those for me?' She was conscious, as I was, of the open door.

'Yes . . . If only you'd come a little bit farther up, I found the very
thing we were looking for! Brought it back, too, alive and undamaged.
Here, hawkweed *Langleyensis hirsuta*, as good as new.'

I detached the common little hawkweed from the bunch, and
handed it to her. I saw a spasm pass across her face, to be followed
swiftly by something like understanding. Her eyes came up to mine.
I nodded, every muscle of my face wanting to grin with triumph;
but I fought them into stillness. I saw her eyes light up. 'It should be
all right, shouldn't it?' I said, touching the yellow petals. 'It's quite
fresh and undamaged.'

'Darling,' said Frances, 'it's a treasure. I'll put it straight away. I'll
come up with you.'

I shook my head at her quickly. It might be better not to look as if we wanted to hurry off together into privacy. 'Don't bother, I'll bring the things down for you when I've changed. Here are the rest. I don't suppose there's much that matters, but there wasn't much time. Order a *tsikóuthia* for me, will you, like a lamb? I'll join you out there till dinner, and let's pray it's soon, I'm starving.'

I ran upstairs to my room, where the last of the sunlight still lingered as a rosy warmth on the walls. The shadows of the vine were blurred now, ready to fade and spread into the general darkness.

I took off my linen jacket, and dropped it on the bed, then kicked off my dusty shoes. Only now did I begin to realize how tired I was. My feet were aching, and grimed with dust that had seeped through my canvas shoes. The thin straw matting felt gratefully smooth and cool to my bare feet. I pulled off my frock and threw it after the jacket, then went over to the window, pushed it wide, and leaned on the cool stone sill, looking out.

In the distance, above their gold-rimmed bases, the cliffs towered, charcoal-black. Below them, the sea lay in indigo shadow, warmed, where the sun still touched it, to a deep shimmering violet. The flat rocks near the hotel, lying full in the lingering light, were the colour of anemones. The ice-daisies had shut, and the mats of leaves that covered the rocks looked dark, like seaweed. The wind had changed with evening, and a light breeze blew off-shore, ruffling the water. Two gulls sailed across the bay, shadows identifiable only by their long, grieving cry.

I looked out towards the open sea. A caique was setting out for the night's fishing, with its *gri-gri*, the unpronounceable little Indian file of small boats following behind it, like ducklings behind the mother duck; light-fishers being towed out to the good fishing-grounds. Presently, away out, the lights would scatter and bob on the water like points of phosphorus. I watched them, wondering if the mother-boat were the *Eros*, and looked beyond her, straining my eyes over the dimming sea for a glimpse of another caique, a stranger, slipping lightless along, far out.

Then I pulled myself up. This wouldn't do. If I was to play the innocent, I must clear my mind of any thoughts of the others. In any case, they were out of my picture. Lambis' caique would slip past in the darkness towards the Bay of Dolphins, with three people on board who had probably forgotten all about me, and had their faces and thoughts thankfully set for Athens, and the end of their adventure. And meanwhile I was tired, hungry, and dusty, and I was wasting time. If Stratos' hotel would run to a hot bath . . .

It would. I bathed fast, then, back in my room, hurried into a fresh frock, and quickly did my face and hair. The bell sounded just as I was slipping on my sandals. I seized my handbag, and ran out, almost colliding with Sofia on the landing.

I had apologized, smiled, and asked how she did, before it struck me, like a fresh shock, that this very day I had seen her husband's grave. The thought caught at my speech, and made me trail off into some stammered ineptitude, but she seemed to notice nothing wrong. She spoke with her former grave courtesy, though, now that I was looking for them, I could see the strain lines, and the smudges of sleepless terror under her eyes.

She looked past me through the open door of my room.

'I'm sorry, I should have tidied it,' I said hurriedly, 'but I've only just got in, and the bell went . . . I did clean the bathroom.'

'But you should not trouble. That is for me.' She walked into my room and stooped to pick up my shoes. 'I will take these down and brush them. They are very dirty. You went far today, after I saw you at the mill?'

'Yes, quite a long way, right across to the old church your brother told me of. Look, don't bother about those old things –'

'Yes. They must be cleaned. It is no trouble. Did you meet anybody . . . up there?'

I wondered if it was Josef she was worrying about, or Colin. I shook my head. 'Nobody at all.'

She was turning the shoes this way and that in her hands, as if studying them. They were navy canvas, much the same colour as the ones Colin had been wearing. Suddenly, I remembered the way his foot had prodded at that dreadful grave. I said, almost sharply: 'Don't bother about those, really.'

'I will do them. It is no trouble.'

She smiled at me as she said it, a gesture of the facial muscles that accentuated, rather than hid, the strain below. Her face looked like yellowed wax smeared thinly over a skull, all teeth and eye-sockets. I remembered Colin's brilliant blaze of happiness, the vivid change in Mark, and the light-hearted way the two of them had fooled with Lambis. This, we owed to Sofia. If only, if only it were true that Josef had been a brute, and could die unmourned. If only it were true that she had hated him . . . But could one ever really, honestly, hate a man with whom one had shared a bed, and to whom one had borne a child? I thought not, but then, one thinks like that at twenty-two . . .

I lingered for a moment longer, fretted by that feeling of guilt, which was surely not mine, then, on an awkward 'Thank you,' I turned and hurried down the outer stair and round the side of the hotel to where Frances awaited me with a vermouth for herself and a *tsikóuthia* for me.

'How you can drink that stuff. It's quite revolting.'

'All true Philhellenes cultivate the taste. Oh, that's *good*.' I stretched back in my chair, and let the drink trickle back over my palate and into my throat. I lifted the glass to Frances, and at last allowed the triumph of the day to reach my mouth and eyes. 'It's been a lovely day,' I said, 'a wonderful day. Here's to . . . us, and our absent friends.'

We drank. Frances regarded me smilingly. 'I'll tell you something else, you ignorant little blighter. Among that first-class bunch of weeds you brought me, you have put, by–I am sure–the merest chance, a thing that is really quite interesting.'

'Great Zeus almighty! Good for me! D'you mean Hairy Hawkweed?'

'I do not. It's this.' A few plants stood in a glass of water at her elbow. She detached one of them gently, and handed it to me. 'It was clever of you to bring the root as well. Careful, now.'

The plant had round leaves, furry with white down, and purple, trailing stems, vaguely familiar. 'What is it?'

'*Origanum dictamnus*,' said Frances.

'Oh?'

'You may well look blank. Dittany, to you, a kind of marjoram. You may even have seen it in England–not that you'd have noticed, but it's found sometimes in rock-gardens.'

'Is it rare, or something?'

'No, but it's interesting that you found it here. It's a Cretan plant–hence the name. *Dictamnus* means that it was first found in this very spot, on Dicte.'

'Dicte? The birthplace of Zeus! Frances, this is exciting!'

'And *Origanum* means "joy of the mountain". Not because it's anything much to look at, but because of its properties. The Greeks and Romans used it as a healing herb, and as a dye, and for scent. They also called it "the herb of happiness" and used it to crown their young lovers. Nice, isn't it?'

'Lovely. Have you just been looking all this up to impress me with?'

'I have, actually.' She laughed, and picked up the book that lay on the table beside her. 'It's a book on Greek wild-flowers, and it quotes some rather nice things. There's a long bit about *Origanum*, quoted from a medical book by a first-century Greek, Dioscorides. It's in a rather heavenly seventeenth-century translation. Listen.' She turned a page and found the place –

' *"Dictamnus, which some call Pulegium Sylvestre (but some Embactron, some Beluocas, some Artemidion, some Creticus, some Ephemeron, some Eldian, some Belotocos, some Dorcidium, some Elbunium, ye Romans Ustilago rustica) is a Cretian herb, sharp, smooth, like to Pulegium. But it hath leaves greater, and downy and a kind of woolly adherence, but it bears neither flower nor fruit, but it doeth all things that the Sative Pulegium, but more forcibly by a great deal, for not only being drank but also being applied and suffumigated its expells the dead Embrya. And they say also that ye goats in Crete being shot, and having fed on the herb do cast out ye arrows . . . Ye root of it doth warm such as taste it; it is also a birth hastener, and likewise ye juice of it being drank with wine helpeth ye bitten of serpents . . . But ye juice of it, being dropt into a wound, it forthwith cures."* What are you looking like that for?'

'Nothing. I was just wondering if the Cretans still used it for healing. I mean, a thing that'll do anything, "from abortion to snake-bite –" '

'Nothing more likely. They'll have lores passed down, time out of mind. Ah, well, so that's "the joy of the mountain".' She took it from me and replaced it in water. 'Well, it's nothing very great, I suppose, but it would be very interesting to see it actually growing. Do you remember where you got it?'

'Oh, my goodness, I'm not sure.' Lambis and I had, so to speak, grazed in motion, like harried deer. 'But I could probably pin it down to within a couple of square miles. Very steep,' I added kindly, 'about one in three . . . and occasionally perpendicular. Would you have liked – I mean, do you really want to go and see it?' Mark's plan for our leaving was humming in my head like a knell. Poor Frances; it seemed hard. And what danger, what possible danger could there be?

'I would, rather.' Frances was watching me with a slightly puzzled look.

'I – I'll try to remember where it was,' I said.

She watched me a moment longer, then got briskly to her feet.

'Well, let's go and eat. You look dog-tired. Tony has promised octopus, which he says is a delicacy unknown even to the better London restaurants.'

'Understandably.'

'Oh? Oh dear. Well, all experience is an arch wherethrough,' said Frances. 'Oh, give me the polythene bags, will you? It doesn't matter about the rest, but I'd like to get *Origanum* safely under hatches. I'll look at it later.'

'Oh, lord, I forgot them. I did get them from your room, but I dropped them in my jacket pocket, and then came down without it. I'll get them now.'

'Don't bother; you've done enough for one day; it can wait.'

'No, really, it'll only take a second.' As we traversed the hallway I caught a glimpse of Sofia, with my shoes in her hand, vanishing through Stratos' office door. She must have finished upstairs, so, I thought thankfully, I shouldn't run into her again. Disregarding Frances' protest, I left her at the restaurant door, and ran up to my room.

Sofia had left it very tidy: my jacket hung behind the door, the discarded dress lay neatly over the chair-back, the towels had been folded, and the coverlet taken off the bed. Frances' polythene bags weren't in the first pocket I tried—when was anything, ever?—but I found them in the other, and ran downstairs again.

Dinner was a cheerful meal, and even the octopus passed muster, as we ate it under Tony's apparently anxious surveillance. The lamb which followed it was wonderful, though I had not even now grown reconciled to eating the tender, baby joints from the suckling lambs. 'They can't afford to let them graze,' I said, when I saw that Frances was distressed. 'There just isn't enough pasture to let them grow any bigger. And if you're going to be in Greece over Easter, I'm afraid you'll have to get used to seeing the Paschal lamb going home with the family to be eaten. The children treat it as a pet, and play with it, and love it; then its throat is cut, and the family weeps for it, and finally feasts on it with rejoicing.'

'Why, that's horrible! It's like a betrayal!'

'Well, that's what it's symbolizing, after all.'

'I suppose so. But couldn't they use our sort of symbols, bread and wine?'

'Oh, they do. But the Easter sacrifice in their own homes—well, think it over. I used to think the same as you, and I still hate to see the lambs and calves going home to their deaths on Good Friday. But isn't it

a million times better than the way we do it at home, however
"humane" we try to be? Here, the lamb's petted, unsuspicious,
happy—you see it trotting along with the children like a little dog. Till
the knife's in its throat, it has no idea it's going to die. Isn't that better
than those dreadful lorries at home, packed full of animals, lumbering
on Mondays and Thursdays to the slaughterhouses, where, be as
humane as you like, they can smell the blood and the fear, and have to
wait their turn in a place just reeking of death?'

'Yes. Yes, of course.' She sighed. 'Well, I don't feel so dreadful for
having enjoyed that. The wine's rather good; what did you say it
was?'

'*King Minos.*'

'Then here's to the "herb of happiness".'

'Here's to it, and to *hawkweed Langleyensis*—oh!'

'Now what?'

'I've just remembered, where I found it, your dittany.'

'Oh? Good. I hope it's somewhere I can get at.'

I said slowly: 'I think it is. It was actually growing at the old
church; in fact, it was growing *on* it. And I'm sure there was more
where that piece came from.'

'That's fine; I'd very much like to see it growing. Did you say
there was a reasonable track the whole way?'

'There's a track, yes, but I wouldn't call it "reasonable". It's
beastly rough in places. You'd be all right though, if you watched
your step. All the same—' I smiled at her, my illogical feeling of guilt
fading—'it would be much easier, and far more fun, going by boat.
Apparently there's an old harbour not too far from the church. We
might take a caique along the coast one day, and just walk straight
into the hills from there.' I was thinking, thankfully, that now I
needn't feel so guilty about having to drag Frances away from here
in the morning. We could take a car over from Heraklion to Agia
Gallini, and hire a caique from there, and I would show her the
exact spot where Colin had pulled the dittany off the wall of the little
church.

'We'll have to fix it up,' said Frances, 'but it can wait a day or two;
you won't want to go straight to the same place tomorrow. Oh,
Tony, may we have coffee on the terrace, please? If you're ready,
Nicola . . .?'

'I think I'll get my jacket after all,' I said, as I rose. 'Give *Origanum*
to me; I'll put him out of harm's way upstairs.'

I laid the polythene bag with its precious plant carefully on my table, and lifted my jacket down from behind the door. As I put it on, something–something hard–in one of the pockets, swung against a corner of the table with a dull little thud. I put my hand in, and touched cold metal; the thin, sharp blade of a knife.

The cold shape met my palm with the tingle of a small electric shock. Then I remembered. I brought the thing out of my pocket, and looked at it. Lambis' knife, of course; the one I had taken from him during that ghastly, serio-comic skirmish up there in the ruined church. I should have remembered to return it. Well, I could still do so, when my gay 'see you in Athens' came true.

I was turning to put the thing out of sight in my case, when something occurred to me that brought me up all standing, with a little formless fear slipping over my skin like ice-water. When I had come up to get the polythene bags for Frances, surely I had felt in both pockets of the jacket? Surely I had? I frowned, thinking back. Then certainty came; I had had my hand in both pockets; I could not have missed the knife. It hadn't been there.

Sofia. It was the only explanation. Sofia must have found the knife when she hung my jacket up. She had taken it . . . why? To show to Stratos and Tony? Had she taken it with her, that time I saw her vanishing into Stratos' office, only to return it quietly while I was at dinner? *Why?*

I sat down abruptly on the edge of the bed, furious at the wave of panic which swept over me, trying to think coherently.

Lambis' knife. It didn't matter; I must remember that. It didn't matter. Nobody here would recognize it: nobody here had seen Lambis, or even knew of his existence. The knife could not possibly link me with the affair; not possibly.

Why, then, had Sofia done what she had done? Simply because, I told myself, she and her companions were, like all criminals, touchy at the least thing. It wasn't usual for the ordinary, innocent woman tourist to carry an unsheathed and very business-like knife. She had thought it worth showing to her brother; but that was, surely, as far as it would go? There was no reason why I should not have bought such a thing as a souvenir; business-like though it was, it was also rather pretty, with the copper hilt worked with blue enamel, and a sort of filigree chasing on the root of the blade. I turned it over in my hand, examining it. Yes, that was the story: if anyone asked me, I would say that I had bought the thing in Chania, partly as a toy, and partly because I knew I should want some sort of tool to dig up plants for Frances. That was why I had taken it with me today . . .

Yes, that would do . . . I had used it today . . . that would account for the used look of the thing, and the couple of chips and notches that showed in the enamel of the handle.

I stood up, relieved, and ready to dismiss my fears. That story would do, and meanwhile I would put it away, and I must certainly remember to return it to Lambis. He would have been missing it.

The thing slipped from my fingers, and fell, to quiver, point down, in the floor-boards. I was sitting on the bed again, my hands to my cheeks, my eyes shut in a vain effort to blot out the picture that my memory had conjured up . . .

Lambis, relaxed in the sunshine beside Colin, whittling away at the little wooden lizard. After we had left the church; after I had taken this knife from his pocket. He hadn't missed it at all; his own knife, his accustomed knife, had had a wooden handle . . . I remembered it now, and remembered the sheath of embossed leather that he had worn thrust into his waistband, and which lay beside him as he did his carving . . .

And this knife? This enamelled copper affair that I had taken from his pocket, and forgotten to return? This pretty, deadly bit of Turkish enamel-work?

'*He pulled his knife,*' Mark had said, '*and then went down hard, with his head on the rock, and that was that . . . We took everything else he had, and buried the boots.*'

Josef. Josef's weapon, marked and notched into unmistakability. Found in my pocket by Josef's wife. Shown to Tony; shown to Stratos. Then quietly slipped back where they had found it.

I didn't stop then to consider what they might make of it, or if I could invent some story of finding it on the hillside. I just sat there, fighting off the waves of senseless panic that bade me get away, myself and Frances, get away, straight away, that very night, to friends and lights and normal places and people and sanity.

To Mark.

After a bit, I put the knife in my suitcase, steadied myself, and went down the stairway.

Chapter 18

Thus far her Courage held, but here forsakes:
Her faint Knees knock at ev'ry Step she makes.
DRYDEN: *Cinyras and Myrrha*

'AH, MISS FERRIS,' said Stratos.

He was in the hallway, behind the table, not doing anything, just standing there, waiting for me. From behind the closed door of the office came voices, Tony's and Sofia's, the latter lifted on a high, urgent note, which stopped abruptly as Stratos spoke.

'I hope you had a pleasant day,' he said.

'Very, thank you,' I smiled, hoping he couldn't tell that my lips were stiff, and the nerves tingling in my finger-tips. 'A pretty long one, but I've enjoyed it thoroughly.'

'So you've been across to the old church, Tony tells me?' His tone was quite normal, friendly even, but something in it drove me to respond as if to an accusation.

'Oh, yes, I did.' My voice was hoarse, and I cleared my throat. 'The track was quite easy to follow and the church was well worth visiting–you were quite right about that. I was only sorry I hadn't a camera with me.'

'Ah, yes, it is Miss Scorby who is the photographer, is it not?' Still nothing in the even voice that I could put a name to. The black Greek eyes watched me. I find it hard at the best of times to read in them any but the more normal expressions: Stratos' eyes, now, might as well have been behind smoked glass.

I smiled into those blank eyes, and put another brick of truth on

the wall of innocence I was trying to build. 'We got some marvellous pictures this morning, up in the fields. I think the one of
your sister at the mill should be a winner. Did she tell you she'd
been playing film star?'

It was difficult to keep myself from glancing towards the office
door. Behind it, Sofia was talking again, on a dreadful wailing note.
Stratos' eyelids flickered, and he raised his voice. 'Sofia told me
about it, yes. She showed you over the mill, I believe.' Behind him
the sounds sank abruptly to a murmur; then I heard Tony speaking
softly and urgently. 'I hope you found it interesting,' said Stratos
politely.

'Oh, very. I only wish I could have seen it working, but I suppose
that only happens when someone wants some corn grinding?'

'Perhaps that will happen while you are here.' His voice was
non-committal, his eyes suddenly alive, intent and wary.

I saw then. He had not yet had time to think, to assess what had
happened. Tony must have told him that Colin was no longer in the
mill, and Sofia—bewildered and no doubt frightened by the discovery of Josef's knife in my pocket—had walked into the conference, to be met with angry accusations, and a startled reassess-
ment of the situation. What I was hearing now from behind the
office door must be the tail-end of quite a pretty scene. And it was
apparent that Stratos himself was considerably shaken; he was
confused, alarmed, and very ready to be dangerous, but for the
present, wariness held him back. He wasn't prepared, yet, to be
bolted into the open. He wanted time to think. And all he needed
from me, for the moment, was reassurance on two points: namely,
that nothing had happened to make me suspicious and therefore
dangerous: and—a corollary to this—that I was prepared to stay
placidly in Agios Georgios, under his eye, until my holiday came to
its natural end. The one would presuppose the other. I only hoped
that the knowledge would content him.

I said, smoothly enough: 'If it does, I hope you'll let me know.'

I smiled at him again, and turned away, but he made a slight
movement as if he would have stopped me. 'Tell me this, Miss
Ferris—'

He was interrupted. The office door opened, and Tony came out.
He didn't come far; just shut the door, very softly, behind him, and
stayed there leaning back against the jamb, loose-limbed and
graceful as ever. He was smoking, the cigarette hanging from the
corner of his mouth. He neither smiled nor greeted me, just stood

there, and when he spoke he didn't trouble to remove the cigarette.

'Were you asking Miss Ferris about the fishing?' he said.

'Fishing?' The Greek's head jerked round, and the men's eyes met. Then Stratos nodded. 'I was just going to.' He turned back to me. 'You were asking me before about the fishing.'

'Fishing?' It was my turn to sound blank.

'You said you would like to go fishing, did you not?'

'Oh. Yes, I did. Of course.'

'Would you care to come out tonight?'

'Tonight?' For a moment, both thought and speech were beyond me. My brain felt light and empty as a bubble. Then I saw what to say. Whatever he suspected, whatever he was trying to find out about me, it could do nothing but good to establish those two facts for him here and now.

I said: 'Why, I'd love it! Thank you so much! You mean light-fishing?'

'Yes.'

'But you've missed the *gri-gri*.'

'Oh, you saw them? I do not go with them. I told you I fish for pleasure, not for food. I stay near the shore. Then you will come?'

'I'd love it,' I said enthusiastically. 'What about Frances?'

'I have spoken to her. She does not wish to go.'

'Oh, I see. Then –'

'I'll come with you.' Tony had removed the cigarette at last, and was smiling at me, his eyes light and cold.

I smiled back at him. I was sure, now, that they weren't going to mention the knife, and relief made me genuinely gay. 'Will you really? That'll be fun! I didn't think boats would have been your thing, somehow.'

'Oh, they're not. But this is a trip I wouldn't miss for worlds, dear. I can crew for Stratos.'

'There's no need.' The Greek spoke roughly. His big hands moved sharply among some papers on the table in front of him, and I saw a vein beating in his temple, up near the hair-line. I wondered just what was going on; if Tony was insisting on coming along in order to keep a tight eye on his companion, or merely to help him in whatever plans he might have for me . . .

'Will you be going tomorrow night?' I asked.

'Tomorrow night?'

I moistened my lips, looking from one to the other in what I hoped was pretty apology. 'The thing is . . . if it's all the same to you . . . I think I honestly am a bit tired tonight. I've had a long day, and now that heavenly dinner's made me sleepy. *Would* you be going out tomorrow night?'

A tiny pause. 'I might.'

'Then would you—yes, I think I *would* rather leave it till then, if it's all the same to you?'

'Of course.' Of all the emotions, relief is the hardest to conceal, and I thought there was relief in the gesture with which he dismissed the plan. He was sure of me now. He smiled. 'Any time. The boat is at your service.'

I lingered, hesitating. There was no harm in making him even surer. 'There was one thing I was going to suggest, Mr. Alexiakis. You remember how you said we might make a sea-trip one day in the *Eros*? Well, I did wonder if we might hire it some day soon? I wondered if it would be possible to take a trip along the coast, that way'—I waved vaguely eastwards—'to where the ancient harbour was? The thing is, I found a plant growing on the ruins today, that's got my cousin all excited. She says it's Cretan dittany, do you know it?'

He shook his head.

'Well, she wants to see it growing, and to photograph it, but I think it would be too far and too rough for her to go the whole way over by the track. I did wonder if it wouldn't be rather fun to take the sea-trip. I thought if we could land at the old harbour, then we could simply walk inland to the church; it can't be far, I could see the sea from just above it. Then she could see the dittany growing, and get her pictures. Come to that, I'd like some pictures of the church myself, and of the harbour. Do you think we could do that? There's no hurry,' I finished, 'any day will do, when you're not wanting the caique.'

'Of course,' he said heartily, 'of course. It is a good idea. I will take you myself. You must just tell me the day before you wish to go. And, for the light-fishing . . . that is settled? Tomorrow night?'

'Yes. Thank you, I'll look forward to it.'

'So shall I,' said Stratos, smiling, 'so shall I.'

This time, he made no attempt to detain me when I went out to where Frances sat with the coffee, under the tamarisks. Their boughs were ethereal in the diffused electric light, like clouds. Behind them was the black, murmuring sea, and the black, blank sky. The night of no moon. I thought of Stratos, the *pallikarás*, with that vein beating in his temples, and a murder weighing on his mind. And of

Tony. And of myself, out in a small boat with them, alone out there somewhere in the blackness . . .

I didn't really pause to ask myself what he could be planning to do, or whether I really had won for myself a respite until tomorrow. I only knew that somewhere out in that same blackness was a lightless caique, with Mark on board, and that, come hell or high water, Frances and I were getting out of this place tonight.

*   *   *

The stone treads of the stairway were comfortingly silent under our feet. Somewhere, once, a dog barked, and then fell quiet. The sea whispered faintly under the off-shore wind; a wilderness of darkness; a huge, quiet creature breathing in the night.

'Keep to the rocks if you can,' I breathed to Frances. 'The shingle will make a noise.'

We padded, soft-shoed, along the smoothed ridges of the rock, where the mats of ice-daisies muffled our steps. The night was so dark that, even from here, the solid oblong of the hotel was hardly visible—would have been quite hidden if it had not been blocked in with whitewash. No light showed. Further down the village the darkness was thick also; only two pinpricks of light showed where someone was still awake well after midnight. The faintest ghost of a glimmer from the church hinted at lamps left burning in front of the ikons all night.

We felt our way along, each yard an agony of suspense; having to move so slowly, but longing to switch on the torch and hurry, hurry . . .

Now, perforce, we were on shingle. It sounded as loud as an avalanche under our cautious steps. After a dozen slithering paces, I put a hand on Frances' arm, and drew her to a halt.

'Wait. Listen.'

We waited, trying to hear beyond the sound of our own breathing. If we had made any noise loud enough to be heard, so, if we were being followed, would our pursuers.

Nothing; only the breathing of the sea.

'You're sure there'll be no moon?' whispered Frances.

'Sure.' The sky was black velvet, obscured by the veil of cloud drawing slowly across from the White Mountains. Later, perhaps, it would be thick with stars, but now it was black, black and comforting for the hunted. The moon-spinners had done their work.

Somewhere out beyond the black horizon, the drowned moon was waiting to unspin in stranded light towards the shore. But not tonight.

I touched Frances' arm again, and we went on.

It is only when one has been out in the night for some time that one begins to see the different densities, even the colours, of darkness. The sea, a living darkness; the shingle, a whispering, shifting, clogging darkness; the cliffs that rose now on our right, a looming lamp-black mass that altered the sound of our footsteps, and of our very breathing. Our progress here was painfully slow, with the cliffs pressing close on our right, thrusting out jagged roots of rock to trip us, and, on the other side, barely a yard away, the edge of the sea, giving a foot, taking a foot, always moving, only visible as a faintly luminous line of pale foam; the only guide we had.

I have no idea how long this part of the journey took. It seemed like hours. But at last we had traversed the full curve of the bay, and towering in front of us was the high, cathedral-like cliff that stuck out into the sea, right out into deep water that lapped hollowly round its base, creaming up among the fallen boulders of the narrow storm-beach which provided the only way round. We had clambered round the point by daylight; could it be done in the dark?

It had to, of course. But, as a form of exercise, I cannot recommend carrying a suitcase for a mile or so along sand and shingle at dead of night, and then edging one's way along a narrow path where a false step will mean plunging into a couple of fathoms of sea that, however quiet, is toothed like a shark with jagged fangs of rock.

I glanced back as I reached the point. The last pinprick of light from the village had disappeared; the bay we had traversed showed only as a gap of darkness.

Frances, behind me, said breathlessly: 'Out to sea . . . lights. All over the place.'

I turned to look, disconcerted to see the blackness alive with tiny lights. Then I realized what it was.

'It's the light-fishers,' I told her. 'They're a long way out. I saw them going. I suppose we were too low to see them from the bay. Can you manage this? We oughtn't to show the torch yet.'

'Faint yet pursuing,' she said cheerfully. 'Actually, I can see fairly well; I've got my night-sight now.'

The second bay was small, only an inlet, paved with beautifully firm, pale sand that showed up well in the gloom, and provided safe walking. We made good time, and in ten more minutes we had reached the second headland, where, too, the going was comparatively easy. A fairly obvious path had been beaten along the narrow storm-beach which lay piled against the point like the foam under a moving prow. I made my way cautiously round the cliff, then down to the hard sand of the Bay of Dolphins. I could see Frances, still on the path, as a vaguely moving shadow, feeling her way carefully down to where I waited.

'All right?'

'Yes.' She was breathing rather heavily. 'Is this the bay?'

'Yes. The spit of rock runs out from the far side of it. We'll have to get out along that, over the deep water. Now we can use the torch, thank heaven. Here –' I pressed it into her hand – 'you'd better have it. Give me your case.'

'No. I can easily –'

'Don't be daft, it isn't far, and my own weighs nothing. The going's tricky here . . . it looks as if there are rock-pools and things . . . so one of us had better be mobile, and light the way. You can take my shoulder-bag; here. I'll follow you.'

Reluctantly, she handed me her case, and took the bag and the torch. The beam of light looked brilliant after the unalleviated blackness; it threw the sand and rocks into such vivid relief that for the first few moments the sense of distance and proportion was almost annulled.

At least, that was how it seemed to me, and I must suppose that is what happened to Frances, for she had taken only three or four steps when, suddenly, with a bitten-off exclamation of pain, she seemed to lurch forward, then pitched down on to the sand as if shot. The darkness came down like a blanket as the torch flew out of her hand, to be doused on the nearest rock with the ominous, the final sound of breaking glass.

I dropped the cases and was down beside her. 'Frances! What is it? What happened?'

Such had been the havoc wrought on my nervous system during the last three days that I honestly believe that, for a mad moment, I expected to find her dead.

But she was very much alive, and swearing. 'It's my blasted ankle. Did you ever *know* such a fool, and I had the torch, too. Is the bloody thing broken?'

'I'm afraid so. But your foot –'

'Oh, it's the same old ankle. It's all right, don't worry, it's only wrenched; the usual. If I sit here a moment and swear hard enough, it'll pass off. Hell, and I'm wet! You were right about the rock-pools; the sand just seemed to shelve straight down into one, or something. I couldn't see. And now, if the torch has gone–' She broke off, aghast. 'Nicky, *the torch*!'

'Yes, I know. It can't be helped. He–he'll surely come close in to look for us, anyway, and we can hail him.'

'If we see him.'

'We'll hear, surely?'

'My dear girl, he won't use his engine, will he?'

'I don't know. He might; there are those other boats out fishing, it wouldn't be the sort of sound that people would notice. It'll be all right, Frances, don't worry.'

'It'll have to be,' she said grimly, 'because *our* boats are nicely burned. I can't see us trekking all that way back, somehow, not now.'

'If the worst comes to the worst,' I said, falsely cheerful, 'I'll stagger back with the cases and unpack, sharpish, then go and tell them we've been having a midnight swim, and will they please come out and collect you.'

'Yes,' said Frances, 'and then they'll come streaming along in force, and run into Mark and Co.'

'Then it'd be over to Mark. He'd like that.'

'Maybe. Well, it serves me right for not bringing you up better. If I'd taught you to mind your own business–'

'And pass by on the other side?'

'Yes, well, there it is. If we will be anti-social, and come to the god-forsaken corners of the earth in order to avoid our fellow-trippers, I suppose we have to take what comes. You couldn't have done anything else, even to this horror-comic episode tonight. One can't touch murder and not be terrified. We can't get out fast enough, in my opinion. *Damn* this ankle. No, don't worry, it's beginning to cool down a bit. What's the time?'

'Nearly half-past one. Have you any matches?'

'No, but there's my lighter. That might do it. I *am* sorry about the torch.'

'You couldn't help it.'

'Give me a hand now, and help me up, will you?'

'There. Manage? Good for you. I'll tell you what, I'll dump the cases here, back against the cliff, and we'll get you along the "pier" if we can–as far as we can, anyway. Then I can come back for them

. . . or maybe we'd better leave them till we see Mark coming in. Sure you can make it?'

'Yes. Don't worry about me. Look, is that the torch?'

A tiny edge of starlight on metal showed where it lay. Eagerly I picked it up and tried it. Useless. When I shook it gently, there was the rattle of broken glass.

'*Kaput?*' asked Frances.

'Very *kaput*. Never mind. The luck couldn't run all the way all the time. Press on regardless.'

It was a slow, dreadful progress across the bay, our steps less certain than ever after the brief illumination and the fall. Frances hobbled along nobly, and I tried to seem unhurried, and perfectly confident and at ease; but the night was breathing on the back of my neck, and I was flaying myself mentally for having tried this final escapade at all. Perhaps I had been stupid to panic so, over the discovery of Josef's knife. Perhaps they hadn't even seen it; it had been in my pocket all the time. Perhaps Stratos' manoeuvre to get me to himself out in the light-boat had been no more than the host's anxiety to please, and there had never been any danger except in my own imagination. I need never have subjected Frances to this ghastly trek, this schoolboy's escapade that probably wouldn't even work. If I'd kept my head and waited till tomorrow . . . Tomorrow, we could have telephoned for a car, and then walked to it, in sunlight, through the public street.

But here we were in the dark, committed. It must have been all of thirty minutes more before I had got Frances out along the ridge of rock. With my help, she shuffled, half-crawling, along it, until she had found a place to sit, a few feet above the deep water. She fetched a long sigh of relief, and I saw her bend, as if to massage her ankle.

'You were marvellous,' I told her. 'Will you give me the lighter now?'

She felt in her pocket, and passed it to me. I went a little further along the rock-ridge. Its top sharpened presently into a hog's-back, then dropped steeply to deep water, where the ridge had been broken and split by the sea. Ahead of me I could see the fangs of rock which marked the broken ridge, running straight out to sea, their bases outlined with ghostly foam, as the breeze freshened beyond the immediate shelter of the cliffs.

I found a flat place to stand, then, with the lighter ready in my hand, faced out to sea.

They should see the flame quite well. I remembered hearing how, in the blackout during the war, flyers at some considerable height could see the match that lit a cigarette. Even if I couldn't manage the pattern of flashes that we had agreed upon, surely a light, any light, from this bay at this time, would bring Mark in . . .? And once he was near enough, a soft hail would do the rest.

I cupped a hand round the lighter, and flicked it. Flicked it again. And again . . .

When my thumb was sore with trying, I allowed myself to realize what had happened. I remembered the splash with which Frances had fallen, and the way she had wrung out the skirts of her coat. The lighter had been in the pocket. The wick was wet. We had no light at all.

I stood there, biting my lips, trying to think, straining eyes and ears against the darkness.

The night was full of sound. The sea whispered and hummed like a great shell held to the ear, and the dark air around me was alive with its noise. There were more stars now, and I thought I should even be able to see if any craft bore shorewards. The great space of the sea ahead looked almost light, compared with the thick blackness of the cliffs towering round me.

Then I heard it; or thought I did. The slap of water against a hull; the rattle of metal somewhere on board.

Stupidly, I was on tiptoe, straining forward. Then, some way out, well beyond the encircling arms of the bay, a light came past the point from my right, bearing eastward. A small boat, not using an engine, moving slowly and erratically across the black void, the light making a dancing pool on the water. One of the *gri-gri*, standing in nearer the shore; that was all. I thought I could see a figure outlined against the light, crouching down in the bows. At least, I thought, he wasn't likely to spot Lambis' caique, riding lightless somewhere out in the roads; but, with the light-boat so near, I dared not risk a hail for Mark to hear.

I went back to Frances, and told her.

'Then we'll have to go back?'

'I don't know. He'll have seen the light-boat, too. He may think we daren't flash our signal because of that. He—he may stand in to the bay, just to see.' I paused, in a misery of indecision. 'I—I don't see how we *can* go back now, Frances. They may have found out—that man—'

'Look!' she said sharply. 'There!'

For a moment I thought she was just pointing at the light-boat, which, pursuing its slow course across the mouth of the bay, would soon be cut off from view by the eastern headland.

Then I saw the other boat, low down in the water; a shape, silent and black, thrown momentarily into relief as the light passed beyond it. The unlighted boat lay, apparently motionless, a little way outside the arms of the bay.

'That's it!' My voice was tight in my throat. 'That's him. He's not coming in. He's doing just what he said he would; waiting. There, the light-boat's out of sight; Mark would expect us to signal now, if we were here . . . And we can't afford to wait any longer to see if he will come in . . . It's ten past two already. Can't you do it either?'

'Afraid not.' She was working away at the lighter. 'It's had a pretty fair soaking. I'm afraid it's no use—what *are* you doing, Nicola?'

I had dropped my coat on the rock beside her, and my shoes went to join it. 'I'm going out after him.'

'My dear girl! You can't do that! Look, can't we risk shouting? He'd hear us, surely?'

'So would anyone else within miles, the way sound carries over water. I daren't. Anyway, we've no time to try: he'll be away in twenty minutes. Don't worry about me, he's well within range, and the water's like glass in the bay.'

'I know, the original mermaid. But don't for pity's sake go beyond the headland. I can see the white-caps from here.'

My frock, and the jersey I had been wearing over it, went down on the pile. 'All right. Now don't *worry*, I'll be okay. Heaven knows I'll be thankful to be doing something.' My petticoat dropped to the rock, then my socks, and I stood up in briefs and bra. 'Not just the correct dress for calling on gentlemen, but highly practical. I've always longed to swim naked, and I dare say this is as near as I'll get. Here's my watch. Thanks. See you later, love.'

'Nicky, I wish you wouldn't.'

'Damn it, we've got to! We can't go back, and we can't stay here. Needs must—which is the only excuse for heroics. Not that these are heroics; if you want the truth, nothing could keep me out. I'm sticky as all-get-out after that horrible walk. Keep working at that beastly lighter, it may yet function. *Adío, thespoints.*'

I let myself down into the water without a splash.

The first shock of it was cold to my over-heated body, but then the silky water slid over the flesh with the inevitable shiver of pure pleasure. The filmy nylon I was wearing seemed hardly to be there.

I thrust away from the rock into the smooth, deep water, shook the hair back from my eyes, and turned out to sea.

I swam steadily and strongly, making as little splash as I could. From this angle, the cliffs stood up even more massively against the night sky.

I headed straight out to sea, with the ridge of rock to my right as a guide, and soon drew level with the place where I had stood with the lighter. Beyond this spot, the ridge of rock was split and broken by the weather into a line of stacks and pinnacles. As I left the shelter of the inner bay, I could feel that the breeze had stiffened slightly: I could see foam creaming at the bases of the rock-stacks, and now and again a white-cap slapped salt across my mouth. Where I swam, fairly near the rocks, the lift and fall of the water against them was perceptible.

Another fifty yards or so, and I paused, resting on the water, stilling my breathing as best I could, and trying to see and hear.

Now more than ever I was conscious of the fresh breeze blowing out from the land. It blew steadily across the water, bringing with it, over the salt surface, the tang of verbena, and the thousand sharp, sweet scents of the maquis. I wondered if it would set up any currents that might make it hard for me to get back, if I should have to . . .

From my position, low down in the water, I could no longer see the outline of the caique—if, indeed, I had ever seen it. It might, I told myself, have drifted in-shore a little, until its black silhouette was merged in the dense blackness of the eastern headland; but this, with the off-shore breeze, was unlikely. Even to keep her from drifting seawards, they would have to use anchor or oars.

I strained across the moving, whispering darkness. As before, it was full of sounds, far fuller than when, on the ridge, I had stood insulated by the air from the subdued and roaring life of the sea. Now, the humming was loud in my ears, drowning all other sounds, except the suck and slap of water against the rock-stacks hard to my right . . .

Meanwhile, time was running out. And I had been right. Lambis was making no attempt to stand into the bay. Why should he, indeed? If I was to find the caique, I would have to leave the line of the ridge, and swim across the open bay, with the tip of the headland as a guide.

I hesitated there, treading water, strangely reluctant, all at once, to leave even the cold shelter of the stacks for the undiscovered darkness of the open bay. I suppose there is nothing quite so lonely as the sea at night. I know I hung there in the black water, suddenly frightened, doubtful, half-incredulous of the fact that I was there at all; conscious only that behind me was an alien country where I had behaved foolishly, and where folly was not tolerated; and that before me was the limitless, empty, indifferent sea.

But I was committed. I had to go. And, if they weren't there, I had to come back . . .

I took a breath, and turned away from the rock-ridge, bearing steadily seawards, towards the dim outline of the headland, the point where I thought the caique might be lying. I swam fast. It might take me ten minutes to come within distance of a soft hail. And in about ten minutes he would up anchor, and go . . .

I had travelled, I suppose, 'not more than thirty yards, when I was brought up sharply in my course by a new sound, not of the sea; the sound—unmistakable, and near—of metal on wood. A boat's sound. But this came, not from ahead of me, but from the right, further out to sea.

I stopped, treading water again, conscious now of the fast beating of my heart. A line of foam ran past me. The sea hummed. I was inside its great, roaring shell, rocked to and fro in an echoing confusion of din like the noises of a hollow cave. Under my body, fathoms down, throbbed the organ-pipes of the sea.

Another moment of deep fear, loneliness, and confusion swept over me with a cold splash like spray. But I dared not hesitate. If this were not he, I might be too late. I must try a hail now . . . But, if it were not he . . .

Then I saw it, unmistakably, and near. A boat, a dim shape, dark against darkness, the froth running white from her slowly-dipping oars. No light; no sound, save for the rattle of rowlocks that had caught my ear. She was seaward of me, standing across the bay towards the outer fangs of the rock-ridge. Lambis was coming in after all, without the signal; no doubt to reconnoitre the ridge before finally turning for the open sea, and Athens.

I put my head down, made a diving turn, and went at my fastest crawl back towards the ridge. My hand touched rock, I surfaced, clung, and turned, with my body held against the stack by the lifting water.

I had crossed the boat's course with plenty to spare; she was still slightly to seaward of me, but closing in, bearing for shore. And now she was level with me, looming between me and the stars. I shook the water out of my eyes, tightened my grip on the rock, and hailed her.

It came very breathlessly: 'Ahoy there! Sailor!'

Silence. She bore on her way. The wind must have caught my voice and eddied it away in the rush and lap of the water. She was passing, soon to be lost again in the darkness. I could feel her wash lifting me against the rock.

I let myself go with it, hauling on my hand-grip as I did so. The wash carried me back, and up, against my rock-stack; a crevice gave me another handhold, then a slippery foothold. I reared myself up out of the water, and let it hold me there, spread by it against the rock, where my body would show paler. I dared not leave the rock, for fear of being run down. I called again, not caring how loudly, and heard how this time the rock caught the cry, and echoed it uncannily across the black water.

'Ahoy! Ahoy! *Náfti!*'

The jerking clack of wood on wood, and she came up as sharply as a checked horse. Then the high prow slanted, swung, and she had veered head on to me.

I gave a little sobbing breath of relief. It was over. And of course it was Mark. I had had time, now, to realize that no other boat would have put into this bay, along this perilous ridge, in this unlighted and stealthy silence. Only a few minutes more, and Frances and I would both be safely aboard, and that would be that . . .

He was looming right over me. The faint line of frost under the bows seemed to brush my thighs. Then he swung broadside again, within feet of me, and the oars bit water. The boat halted, slid a little, backed water. I heard an exclamation, half of surprise, half of what sounded like fear.

I called softly: 'It's all right. It's me, Nicola. I was swimming out.'

There was silence. Feet away, the boat loomed.

'Mark—' I said.

Then, suddenly, a light flashed on; an enormous, blinding light; a pharos of a light. Straight above my head twin massive lamps were suspended in nothing. The beams, converging in a glaring ring, stabbed down on to the water, on to me. I was blinded, pinned down, held, dazzled and helpless to move or think, in that appalling light.

I believe I cried out, cowering back against the rock, and, at the same moment, I heard him shout. It was a rough voice, and it spoke in Greek, but there was no time for this to register with me. Fear stabbed through at a purely instinctive level, and already, before he had moved, I had dived away into the dark beyond the floodlit pool.

I heard an oar strike rock, as he thrust against it, and the nose of the boat turned with me. The light followed. I had seen, in that sharp, immediate flash of terror, what this was: it was a light-boat, too small (but the dark had hidden this) for an inter-island caique; too furtive—surely—for one of the *gri-gri*. And I thought I knew whose light-boat.

A moment later, I was proved right. Noise ripped the night open, as the motor started. No, this wasn't one of the harmless *gri-gri* that the caique had towed out to sea; this was a boat with an outboard. Like Stratos'.

Stratos' own. I heard him shout: '*You? I knew it! And Josef?*' He was standing there now, brilliantly lit beside the lanterns, and the six-pronged trident flashed as he drove it down, straight at me.

Chapter 19

It was the fatal and perfidious bark . . .
MILTON: *Lycidas*

NO TIME TO think, certainly no time to cry out through the choking swirl of water; impossible to shout to him, ask what he was doing, what danger I could be to him, now that the others were safely away . . .

The harpoon went by me with a hiss; bubbles ripped back from the blades in a sparkling comet's tail. I twisted aside, kicking my way frantically out of the merciless light.

The spear reached the bottom of its run, jerked the rope tight; then he hauled it back, as the boat swerved after me. The rope touched me as he dragged it up; the small graze, even through the rip of the water, touched the skin with terror, like a burn. I had a glimpse of him, towering beside the lanterns, hauling in the glittering coils of rope with rapid, practised hands. Momentarily, he had had to let the tiller swing, and the light swerved away. Dark water swirled in the shadow of the boat, hiding me. I jack-knifed away again, towards the deep, black water. But *Psyche* came up to the tiller with a jerk, and turned with me, as if locked to my wake by radar . . .

For a split, crazy second, I thought of diving under her; then I knew it would be a dive to certain death: if the screw didn't get me, I would be a sitter for Stratos and the light as I came up. As it was, this could only have one end, and that a quick one . . . He needn't even risk another miss with the spear; another half-minute of this dreadful, uneven hunt, and I should be done, gasping on the surface, ready to be spitted . . .

Full in the glare, I turned to face the spear, and threw an arm up towards him. I was trying, I think, to get my breath to shout; to gain a little time in which his crazy anger might be checked, reasoned with. But even as I turned, he swung his spear-arm up again. The long shaft gleamed golden, the barbed blades glittered; the light beat me down, hammered me into the water, held me there, like a moth frying on a flame. His other hand was on the tiller. If the spear missed this time, the boat, swinging on that radar-beam, would run me down, and plough me back into the sea.

I gulped air, watching for the first flash of metal as his muscles tensed for the throw. The flash came: I turned and dived for the darkness. Nothing followed, no blades, no rope; he must have missed. I held myself under as long as I could, thrusting down and away, steeply, into deep water . . .

The moment came when I had to turn upwards. I was rising towards the light . . . it was everywhere . . . the sea paled to a luminous green, to a wavering of blue and gold, barred with the ripples of the boat's passage, blocked with the formidable shadow of her keel.

The turquoise and gold thinned, lightened, fizzed with sparks as the foam ran from her screw . . .

Just before I broke surface I saw him, a shadow towering above a shadow, tall on the thwarts, huge, distorted, wavering like a pillar of cloud. He was up there, waiting, the spear still poised. I don't pretend I saw anything except the moving shadows above the light, but I knew, as surely as if the sea were clear glass, that he still had the spear. He hadn't thrown it before, it had been a feint. He would get me now, as, gasping and exhausted, I surfaced for the last time.

Then something touched me, drove at my outstretched hand, breaking my dive, and sending me sprawling untidily to the surface. The boat rocked past, her bow-wave piling. The spear drove down at the same moment, a flash among the million flashing and glittering points of light; stars, water-drops, splashing foam, the dazzle of my water-filled eyes. There was a crack, a dreadful jarring, a curse. The world swam, and flashed, and was extinguished, as the massive shape of blackness surged up between me and the light. I hadn't even known what had knocked me to the surface, but the animal in me was already clinging, gasping and sobbing for air, to solid rock. That last, long dive had taken me into the wake of one of the stacks of the rock-ridge. The spear, striking prematurely, had hit it, and the prow of Stratos' boat, following me too closely, had taken it with a jarring graze, and was even now, roughly headed off by the rock, swerving fast away.

The moment's respite, the solid rock of my own element, were enough. My mind cleared of its helpless terror as the air poured into my body, and I saw that I was safe, as long as I kept among the rocks.

Psyche turned again, wheeling for my side of the stack. I dropped back into the sea, and plunged round into the darkness at the other side.

I reached out for a handhold, to rest again until she could come around.

Something caught at me then, holding me back from the rock; something under the water . . . It was thin and whippy as a snake, and it wrapped round my legs, dragging me down like the weight roped to the feet of a man condemned to die by drowning.

I fought it, with the new strength born of instinctive terror. I had forgotten the other danger; the light and the spear were of the upper air, this horror came from the world below. This was the swimmer's nightmare, the very stuff of horror; the weed, the tentacle, the rope of a net . . . It held me fast, pulled me down, choking. And now the light was coming back.

My flailing hand met rock again; clung, with the thing dragging at my knees. I was done; I knew it. The light was coming.

Then it vanished, switched off. The sudden darkness, printed with its image still, roared and dazzled. But the roaring was real, the night suddenly shaking with a confused uproar of engines, a medley of shouting, the sharp crack of a backfiring motor—and then I saw other lights, small and dim and moving wildly across the water. The darkened light-boat hung between me and the stars, as if hesitating, then, suddenly, her motor was gunned, and the jet of white foam that shot from her stern almost dragged me off my rock. Her wake arrowed away, to be lost under the dark. In its place, came, gently, a biggish shadow, with riding-lights steady at mast and prow.

Someone said: 'Hang on, sweetheart,' and someone else said, in Greek: 'God protect us, the sea lady,' and Colin's voice said breathlessly: 'She's hurt.'

Then a boat-hook ground into the rock beside me, and the boat swung in gently. Hands reached, grabbed. The side of the caique dipped, and I managed to grab it and was dragged half inboard, to hang gasping and slack over the side until the hands gripped again and lifted me in, and whatever it was that had twined round my legs and tried to drown me, came too.

I was down in the well of the caique, hunched on the thick rope matting, gasping and shivering and sick. Vaguely I was aware of Mark's voice and hands; something dry and rough rubbed me smartly into warmth, something sharp and aromatic was forced down my throat, while the caique swung and ground against the rock, and Mark cursed steadily under his breath in a way I hadn't thought he was capable of. Then came the dry roughness of a tweed coat round my bare shoulders, and another mouthful of the heady Greek brandy, and I was sitting up, with Mark's sound arm around me, feeling the warmth of his body comforting my own, and clutching his coat to my nakedness with numbed and flaccid fingers.

'Stay quiet; it's all right, just stay quiet.' It was the voice he had used to comfort Colin.

I shook, clinging to him. 'The spear,' I said, 'the weeds.'

'I know. It's all right now. He's gone.' Reassurance seemed to flow from him in tangible waves. 'It's finished; you're quite safe. Now relax.'

'It was because of Josef's knife. I took it out of Lambis' pocket in the church, when we held him up. I forgot it. It was in my pocket. They saw it. H—he must have come after us.'

A moment or so, while he assessed this. 'I see. But it still doesn't explain why he—'

'*Mark!*' A shadow that I recognized as Colin dropped down to squat beside us.

'What?'

'This stuff that came up with her. It isn't weeds, it's rope.'

'Rope?' I shivered again, uncontrollably, and the protecting arm tightened. 'You mean a—a *net*?'

'No. It's a length of rope, with a float, and a sort of lobster-pot at the other end.'

The *scháros*-pots; of course. It seemed like a memory from another life.

I said: 'He has pots laid along there. I forgot. That was all it was, then. It felt horrible, like weed.'

'Chuck it back in,' said Mark.

'But there's something inside.' Colin sounded suddenly excited. 'Not fish. A sort of package.'

Mark let me go. 'Send a light down, Lambis.' He got down on his

knees beside Colin. The wicker pot lay between them, a dark stain
of water spreading from it. Gingerly Mark thrust his fingers in, and
brought out a package, which he laid on the boards. Colin leaned
close. Lambis, from his place beside the engine, peered in over their
shoulders. The three faces were grave, absorbed, tense with a
curiosity that was just about to break into excitement. The caique
throbbed softly, swinging away from the rocks in a long, gentle drift
seawards. We had all completely forgotten Frances.

Mark unwrapped the package. A layer of oilskin or polythene;
another; a third. Then a bag of some soft species of skin, chamois-
leather, I supposed, drawn together at the neck. Its coverings had
kept it quite dry.

Mark pulled the draw-string loose, then up-ended the bag. There
was a glitter and a coloured flash, a gasp from Colin and a grunt
from Lambis. Mark picked up a kind of chain, very heavily ornate,
and worked in gold; as he ran it through his fingers, red glowed and
burned among the gold. Colin reached out, gingerly, and picked up
something—it looked like an eardrop—with a hoar-frost glitter round
a flash of green.

'I said it was jewels,' he said breathlessly.

'This is the loot?' Lambis' voice, over my shoulders, was deep
with satisfaction.

'This is the loot, the highly identifiable loot.' Mark let the gold
and ruby necklace trickle back into the mouth of the bag. 'It begins
to make sense now, doesn't it? We wanted evidence, and oh boy!
what evidence we've got! If this isn't why Alexandros was murdered, then I'm the Queen of the May!'

' "The London job",' I quoted.

'Big deal, eh?' Colin still sounded almost awe-stricken. He was
turning the emerald drop from side to side, letting it catch the light.
'I wonder how many pots he's got?'

'That's a question that can wait for the police. Let's put these
things back. Drop that in here, will you?' Mark held out the bag for
the ear-ring, then pulled the drawstring tight, and began to tie it.

I said slowly: 'He must have thought that's what I was after. The
knife made him suspicious, but he thought we were safe under his
eye for a bit. Then he came out here to check over his pots, and
found me beside them, in the water. I'm not surprised, after all
that's happened recently, that he saw red, and went for me
regardless. I wonder if he even thought Josef might be double-
crossing him? With me, I mean. He did shout something about

him, and of course he must be wondering like mad where he is.'

'What *were* you doing in the water?'

'We broke the torch, so we couldn't signal. I was coming for you. I –*Mark!*' I put a hand to my head, which was only just beginning to clear of the sea-noises and the confused terror of the chase. 'I must have gone crazy myself! Get Lambis to put back to the rocks! There's –'

'You're hurt?' Lambis interrupted me sharply. 'That is blood, no?'

'No . . .' I must have looked at him with vague surprise. I had felt nothing, was feeling nothing even now; my flesh was still cold and damp to the touch, and too numb to feel pain. But as Mark snatched up the lantern, and swung its light round to me, I saw that there was, indeed, blood on my thigh, and a dark line of it creeping down on to the deck. 'He must have got me with the edge of the spear,' I said, faintly, because I was beginning to shake again. 'It's all right, it doesn't hurt. We'd better go back –'

But I was interrupted again, this time by Mark, who leaped –no, surged –to his feet. 'The bloody-minded *bastard*' Colin and I –crouched at his feet like famine, sword and fire at the heels of the war-god –gaped up at him, dumbly.

'By God, I'll not stand for this!' Mark towered over us, possessed, apparently, by one sudden, glorious burst of sheer, uninhibited rage. 'I'm damned if we cut and run for Athens after this! We're getting after him, if it's the last thing we do! Lambis, can you catch him?'

I saw a grin of unholy joy split the Greek's face. 'I can try.'

'Then get weaving! Colin, throw me the first-aid box!'

I began feebly: 'Mark, no –'

I might have known they would take no notice of me, and this time it was three to one. My feeble protest was drowned by the roar of the caique's engine, as she jumped forward with a jerk that set every board quivering. I heard Colin shout: 'Man, oh *man*, Lambis, cool it wild!' as he dived into the cabin. Mark dropped back to his knees beside me, saying, simply and rudely: 'Shut up. We're going back, and that's that. Hell's teeth, do you think I'd have sat there and let them do all they've done, if they hadn't had Colin to hold me to ransom with? What d'you take me for, a bloody daffodil? Now I've got you and Colin safe under hatches, I'm going to do what I'd have done in the first place, if I'd been fit, and the pair of you hadn't been a sitting target for them. And now shut up, and for a change you can sit quiet and let *me* bandage *you*! Colin! Where the –oh, thanks!' This as the first-aid box hurtled from the cabin door. Mark caught it, and pulled it open. 'And find the girl something to wear, will you? Now, keep still, and let me get that tied up.'

'But Mark, what are you going to do?' I sounded infuriatingly humble, even to myself.

'Do? Well, my heaven, what d'you think? I'm going to hand him over to the police myself, personally, and if I've got to paste the living daylights out of him to do it, well, that'll suit *me*!'

I said meekly: 'Do you have to be quite such a sadist with the Elastoplast?'

'What?' He stared at me quite blankly. He really was looking very angry indeed, and quite dangerous. I smiled at him happily, well away now (as I was aware) on what Frances would have called Stage Three. Then the black look faded, to be succeeded by a reluctant grin. 'Was I hurting? I'm very sorry.' He finished the job quite gently.

'Not so much as I hurt you, I expect. Look, do you really think this is a good idea? I know how you feel, but–'

A quick look up, where, even in the lantern-light, I could read irony. 'Darling, I admit I lost my temper, but there's more to it than a simple desire to clobber this thug. For one thing, this is the chance to connect him here and now with the jewels and Alexandros' murder–if we can catch him and identify him before he gets the chance to run home and cook up alibis with Tony. What's more, if we don't get straight back and alert the village elders, what's to stop Stratos and Tony lifting whatever other lobster-pots they've got, and being a hundred miles away, with bulk of said loot, before we even sight Piraeus?'

'I see.'

He shoved the things back in the box, and clipped the lid shut. 'Mad at me?'

'What on earth for?'

'Because when my girl gets hurt, I've got to have another reason for hitting the chap that did it?'

I laughed, without answering, and slipped painlessly into Stage Four–a stage Frances wouldn't have recognised, as it was new to me, too.

'Will these do?' Colin emerged from the cabin, clutching a thick, fisherman's-knit jersey, a cotton-mesh vest, and a pair of jeans. 'You can put them on in the cabin, it's warm there.'

'They look marvellous, thanks awfully.' I got up stiffly, Mark helping me, then Colin put the clothes into my hands, and retired modestly aft into the shadows.

The cabin was warm after the smartly-moving breeze on deck. I took off Mark's jacket. The wisps of nylon which – I suspected – had been almost non-existent as garments when wet, had now more or less dried on me, and were ready to reassume their functions as clothing. I rubbed my cold flesh again vigorously with the rough towel, then wriggled into the jeans. They must be Colin's; they would be tight on him, and were even tighter on me, but they were warm, and fitted comfortably enough over the Elastoplast. The jersey – Mark's, at a guess – was wonderfully warm and bulky, and came fairly well down over the jeans. I pushed open the cabin door, and peered out.

A rush of starry wind met me, the roar of the motor, the slap and race of water . . . We had swerved, close in, round the second headland, and were tearing across the mouth of the bay towards Agios Georgios. I could see, low down, a few dim lights, and a yellow gleam that must mark the harbour mouth. Our own riding-lights were out. Lambis, at the tiller, was hardly visible, and Mark and Colin, standing together in the well, were two shadows peering intently forward. The caique jumped and bucked like a bolting horse as the cross-wind met her round the headland.

I opened my mouth to say 'Can I do anything?' then shut it again. Common sense suggested that the question was a purely rhetorical gesture, and therefore better unasked. Besides, I knew nothing about boats, and these three were a team which, freed now of everything but a single purpose, looked a formidable proposition enough. I stayed quietly in the shelter of the cabin door.

To seaward of us, the light-boats bobbed and twinkled. Some had worked their way in-shore, and one – probably the one that had passed so close to the Bay of Dolphins – was barely fifty feet from us as we roared past.

I could see the faces of its two occupants, open-mouthed and curious, turned towards us. Lambis yelled something, and their arms shot out, pointing, not towards Agios Georgios, but at the inner curve of the bay, where the hotel lay.

Lambis called something to Mark, who nodded, and the caique heeled till she lay hard over, then drove towards the looming crescent of cliff that held the bay.

Colin turned and saw me, and flashed a torch. 'Oh, hullo! Were the things all right?'

'Fine, I'm as warm as anything now. The pants are a bit tight, that's all, I hope I don't split them.'

'They don't look it, do they, Mark?'

Mark turned, looked obediently, and said, simply: 'Boy, oh *boy*!'

Colin, laughing, vanished past me into the cabin.

'Well, well,' I said, 'something tells me you must really be feeling better.'

'Sure. Try me. Just one hundred per cent—*there he is!*'

I dived after him to the side, peering to starboard. Then I saw it, too, barely a hundred yards ahead of us, a small shape, a dark tip on an arrow of white, hurtling into the curve of the bay.

'They're right, he's making for home!'

'Nicola!' Lambis hailed me from the stern. 'What is it like? Is there a landing-place?'

'No, but there's flat rocks right to the edge of the water. It's quite deep, right up to them.'

'How deep?' This was Mark.

'I can't say, but deep enough for a caique. He takes the *Eros* in himself, and it's bigger than this. I've swum there; I'd say eight feet.'

'Good girl.' I must be far gone, I thought, when this casual accolade from an obviously preoccupied man could make me glow all through. Stage Five? Heaven alone knew—and heaven alone could care, because I didn't . . .

Next moment a more substantial warmth met my hands, from the mug which Colin thrust into them. 'Here, it'll warm you up, it's cocoa. I'd say you've just time, before we waltz in to clobber the bastards.'

This got through. Mark half-turned, but at this moment the note of the caique's engine changed, and Lambis spoke, urgently and quietly:

'Here, we go in now. See him? He will make fast in a moment. Colin, light the lamp again; he must have seen us now. When we get in, you make her fast; I will go to help Mark. Take the boat-hook; you know what to do.'

'Yes.' But the boy hesitated a moment. 'If he has a gun?'

'He won't use it,' said Mark. 'He can't know who we are, for a start.'

This was undoubtedly true, but it had already occurred to me that Stratos might be making a fairly shrewd guess. In any case, whether or not he guessed whose caique was pursuing him, he must know that its owners had rescued me from his murderous attack, and were bound on an errand, if not of violent retribution, then, at least, of angry inquiry—which would lead to the very uproar he wanted to avoid. We were, in other words, hard on the heels of a man both angry and involved to the point of desperation.

'Anyway,' Mark was saying, 'we've got one too, remember. Now, don't worry, here we go.'

I pushed the empty mug back into the cabin, and shut the door. I half expected to be told to go in after it, but nobody even noticed me. Lambis and Mark were both leaning out, watching the dim rocks of the shore rush to meet us. Colin, on the prow, held the boat-hook at the ready. The caique heeled more sharply still, then drove in.

Stratos had seen us, of course. But even at the cost of helping us, he had to have light. As the light-boat ran in to the landing, he switched on the huge lamps, and I heard Lambis give a grunt of satisfaction.

Stratos cut his engine, and the boat lost way abruptly, slipping alongside the rocks. I saw him, the figure of my nightmare, rope in one hand, boat-hook in the other, poised beside the lights. Then his boat touched, kissed stone, and jarred to a rocking halt as the boat-hook flashed out and held her. I saw him glance back, and seem to hesitate. Then the lights went out.

'Ready?' Lambis' voice was almost inaudible, but it affected me like a shout.

'Okay,' said Mark.

The three of them must, of course, have worked together at berthing the caique many times before. This time, done fast and in semi-darkness, it was a rough berthing, but still surprisingly slick.

The engine accelerated briefly, and was killed. The caique jumped forward, then skidded sideways against the moored boat, using her as a buffer. I heard poor *Psyche* grind against the rock as the caique scraped along her sides. She was empty. Stratos was already on shore: I saw him, caught momentarily in our lurching lights, bending to fling a couple of rapid loops of rope round a stanchion.

Then Mark, in a standing leap from the caique's bows, landed beside him.

As the Cretan swung to face the challenge, Mark hit him. I heard the blow connect, sickeningly, and Stratos went staggering back. Mark jumped after him, and then they were beyond the reach of our lights, a couple of plunging, swearing shadows, somewhere in the scented darkness under the tamarisks.

Lambis pushed past me, scrambling ungracefully on the thwarts to leap ashore. Colin said urgently: 'Here, *you* tie her up,' shoved a rope into my hand, and jumped after Lambis, belting across the gravel into the darkness, where the roughhouse of the century was now playing havoc with the peaceful island night. Tables hurtled over, chairs went flying, someone shouted from a near-by house, dogs barked, cocks crew, Stratos was shouting, Colin yelled something, and then a woman cried out from somewhere, shrill and frightened. Stratos' homecoming could not have been more public if he had had television cameras and a brass band.

A light flashed on in the hotel.

I could hear a babel of shouts, now, in the village street, and running footsteps, and men's voices, curious and excited. They were bringing lights . . .

I suddenly realized that the caique–with me in it–was beginning to drift away from shore. Shaking like a leaf with cold, nerves and reaction, I managed somehow to find the boat-hook, pull her in, and crawl out on to the rock. I went stiffly to my knees, and began to wind the rope round the stanchion. I remember that I wound it very carefully, as if the safety of us all depended on how neatly I curled the rope round the metal. Four, five, six careful turns . . . and I believe I was even trying solemnly to knot the thing–all the while straining to see what was happening out there under the tamarisks–when the shadowy mêlée grew dimmer still, and I realized that the light in the hotel had gone out again.

Feet came running, lightly. I heard a quick tread on the gravel, then he was coming, fast, along the rock towards me, dodging through the shadows. A glimmer of light from one of the advancing lanterns touched him. It was Tony.

I was full in his way, sitting there numbly, holding my rope. I don't even remember being afraid, but even if I had been, I doubt if I could have moved. He must have been armed, but he neither touched me nor turned aside for me–he simply jumped straight over me, so lightly that one almost expected Weber's long harp *glissandos* to pour spectrally from the wings.

'Excuse me, dear–' His voice was quick and high, and only a little breathless. Another leap landed him in the frantically-rocking *Psyche*. There was a jerk at her rope as he cut it, the engine burst raucously into life, and *Psyche* lurched away from the rock so sharply that she must have shipped water.

'. . . High time to leave.' I thought I heard the light, affected voice quite plainly. 'Such a *rough* party . . .'

Then lights everywhere, and men shouting, and the dogfight was coming my way.

Here was Mark, with a stain spreading across his shirt, reeling backwards from a blow, to trip over a chair, which, collapsing, crashed with him to the ground. Stratos aimed a kick at his head, which went wide as Lambis, charging through a tangle of metal tables, knocked him aside; and then the pair of them hurtled, furniture flying, through a crackling fog of tamarisk-boughs, to fetch up hard against a tree-trunk. A *pithos* of carnations went rolling wildly: Stratos, who must know, even in semi-darkness, the hazards of his own territory, side-stepped it, but it struck Lambis full in the legs, just as the Cretan managed, at last, to pull his knife.

Lambis, lunging for the knife-hand, trod on the rolling pot, missed, and went down, tangled with carnations, and swearing lamentably. And now Mark, on his feet again, was lurching forward through the cheval-de-frise of tables, with behind him a crowd of milling, shadowy figures responding enthusiastically –if blindly –to Lambis' shouts.

Stratos didn't wait. He must have seen Tony, heard *Psyche's* engine, and thought the boat was ready there, and waiting. He swept aside the tamarisk-branches with one powerful arm, and, knife at the ready, came racing for the edge of the sea.

He had suffered a good deal of damage; I saw that straight away, but it didn't seem to affect the speed of this final, express-train rush for freedom. Then he saw me, crouching there over the stanchion, full in his path . . . and, in the same moment, he must have seen that *Psyche* had gone . . . but the caique was there, and he hesitated only fractionally before he came on.

The knife flashed as he lifted it, whether for me or the rope I was never to know, for Colin flew yelling out of the dark like a mad terrier, and fastened on the knife-arm with –apparently –arms, legs, and teeth combined.

It hardly checked the Cretan. He stumbled, half-turned, brought his free hand round in a smashing blow which brushed the boy off like a fly from a bull's flank, then, a mad bull charging, he hurtled towards me down the last stretch of rock.

I lifted the rope I was holding, and it caught him full across the shins.

I have never seen a man go such a purler. He seemed to dive forward, full length, towards the rocks. The breath was driven out of him in a gasping cry, then, out of nowhere, Mark plummeted down on top of him in a sort of flying tackle, rolled over with him, then let his arms drop, and got rather unsteadily to his feet.

'One more to you,' he said, and grinned. Then he pitched down on top of the Cretan's unconscious body, and went out like a light.

Chapter 20

THE CABIN OF the caique was very full. There was Mark, rather white, and newly bandaged; myself looking, in Colin's pants and Mark's enormous sweater, like a beatnik after a thick night; Lambis, looking tough and collected, but still smelling exotically of carnations; Colin, with a new bruise on his cheek, silent, and rather close to Mark's side. That was the crew. With us, at the tiny cabin table, sat the headman of Agios Georgios, and three of the village elders, old men dressed in the savage splendour of Cretan heroic costume, which I suspected (from the speed with which they had arrived on the scene with every button in place) that they slept in. These were our judges—the Lord Mayor and all the Commissioners of Assize—while outside, in the well of the deck, and sitting on the engine coamings, and along the rocks, sat the whole array of jurors, the entire male population of Agios Georgios.

Four men had taken Stratos up to the hotel, there to watch over—and watch—him. Tony had, in the general confusion, got clear away. Although by this time most of the light-boats—attracted by the bedlam of noise and lights at the hotel—were converging on us across the bay, none of those near enough had had an engine, so Tony had dodged his way to freedom with the utmost ease and—it was reported—all the loose cash from the hotel, together with a sizeable number of his own portable possessions. But it should be simple, they said, to pick him up . . .

Myself, I rather doubted this. The cool-headed Tony, with his genius for dissociating himself from trouble, at large in the Aegean

with a good boat, and the coasts of Europe, Africa, and Asia Minor
to choose from? But I said nothing. We ourselves had need of all the
sympathetic attention we could command.

It had not taken long for the four of us to tell our story. We had
omitted nothing, down to the smallest detail of Josef's death. Over
this, there were grave looks, and some head-shaking, but I could see
that the main climate of opinion was on our side. It seemed obvious
that the actual acts of violence which Stratos had committed meant
little, in themselves, to these men, and it might have gone differently
with us if we had killed Stratos himself, whatever he had done in the
course of his own private quarrel. But the death of Josef the Turk –
and a Turk from Chania, at that – was (one gathered) quite a different
thing. And in the matter of poor Sofia Alexiaki, who would have
enough to bear when her brother's story came to light, it could be
seen as the mercy of heaven that now, at last, as a widow, she could once
more be a free woman, and a Christian. She could even – Christ be
praised – make her Communion this very Easter Sunday . . .

The rest was to be as easy. When Stratos later recoverd consciousness, to be confronted with the discovery of the jewels in his
fishing-grounds, the body of Alexandros (which was in fact found
buried in the field by the mill), the guilty defection of Tony, and,
finally, the death of Josef, he took the easiest way out for himself,
and told a story which, in essentials, seemed to be an approximation
of the truth.

He and Alexandros were not (as Colin's theory had had it) thieves,
but had for some years been partners as 'fences', or receivers of
stolen goods, with Tony as a kind of assistant and liaison officer.
Stratos, running an honestly profitable little restaurant in Frith
Street, had provided unimpeachable 'cover', and he and Alexandros
had apparently had no connection other than a friendship between
compatriots. Even this friendship had a perfectly natural explanation, for Alexandros was a Cretan, too, a native of Anoghia, the
village which lay in the heights beyond the ruined Byzantine
church. So things had gone on prosperously for a time, until the
affair of the big Camford House robbery.

But Stratos had the good business man's instinct for getting out of
the deal at the right moment, and, well before the robbery at
Camford House, he had set about realizing his assets at leisure, and
in good order, ostensibly to retire with his 'pile' to his native village.
Alexandros – who could see only that a highly lucrative partnership
was packing up in the moment of its greatest prosperity – bitterly

opposed Stratos' move. Argument after argument supervened, culminating in a violent quarrel on the very eve of Stratos' departure, when Alexandros was driven to utter threats which he almost certainly had no intention of carrying out. The inevitable happened; tempers snapped, and knives were drawn—and Alexandros was left for dead in a back alley at least two miles from Frith Street, while Stratos and Tony innocently embarked that same night on the flight for Athens, for which their bookings had been made at least six weeks previously.

Recovering slowly in a London hospital, Alexandros held his tongue. Possibly he realized now—in the hue and cry over the disappearance of the Camford jewels—that Stratos' withdrawal had been opportune. The only thing was, Stratos had taken the lot . . .

As soon as he was fit, and sure that the police had not yet connected the obscure stabbing affair in Lambeth with the Camford robbery, Alexandros in his turn retired—armed—to his native land.

If it could ever be said that stupidity rated a punishment as final as murder, it would seem that Alexandros asked for what he got. Stratos and Tony received him—understandably—with a certain wariness, but soon, somehow, the affair was patched up, and there followed a scene of reconciliation and apology, made more plausible by the presence of Sofia and Josef. Stratos would, in good time, divide the spoils, and the three men would go their separate ways, but meanwhile it was only reasonable for all three to lie low for a period, until the jewels could, in some form or other, find their way gradually on to the market. This agreed, the family party (well wined and dined, Soho-fashion, by Tony) set out to escort Alexandros over to his own village, but on the way an argument had arisen, over the disposal of the jewels, which had sprung almost immediately into a quarrel. And then, Alexandros had laid a hand to his gun . . .

It is probable, even, that Alexandros was not quite so stupid or credulous as the story made him. Stratos swore, and continued to swear, that he himself had never intended murder. It was Josef who had killed Alexandros, Josef who had shot at Mark, and who had gone, on his own initiative and without orders from Stratos, to make sure of Mark's death. As for Colin, who had been dragged off in a moment of panic-stricken and drunken confusion, Stratos swore that it was he himself who had given the order for Colin's release, and here (he said, and nobody doubted him) his sister would bear him out.

And, finally, the attack on me . . . Well, what did anyone expect? He had gone to make a routine check of his spoils, and had found a girl whom he suspected of some connection with Josef's mysterious absence, diving after his pots. He had only done what any man would have done in his place—and here, it was obvious, the meeting rather agreed with him—and in any case he had only been trying to frighten, not kill me.

But all this was for morning. Now, the first explanations over, our story pieced together, weighed, and at last accepted, someone came across from the hotel with coffee for everyone, and glasses of spring water. By the time dawn broke, Agios Georgios had settled happily down to the greatest sensation since the Souda Bay landing.

I sat, weary, drowsy, and warm, with the cut in my thigh throbbing painfully, and my body relaxed into the curve of Mark's arm. The air of the cabin was slate-grey with smoke and the walls vibrated with the noise of talking, and the clash of glasses as emphatic fists struck the little table. I had long since stopped trying to follow the thick, rapid Greek. Leave it to Mark, I thought sleepily; leave it all to Mark. My part in it was over; let him cope with the rest, then, soon, we could all sail away, free at last to salvage what remained of our respective holidays . . .

A memory cut through the smoky cabin like a knife-blade of cold air. I sat up abruptly, out of the circle of Mark's arm.

'*Mark! Mark*, wake up! There's Frances!'

He blinked. 'Do you mean to tell me—dear heaven, of course, I'd clean forgotten! She must be back there in the bay!'

'Well, of course she is! She's sitting on a rock with a twisted ankle. Frances, I mean, not the rock. Oh dear, how could we? That's twice I've remembered—at least forgotten, but—'

'Pull yourself together,' said Mark kindly. 'Look, sweetie, don't start another panic; she'll be all right. Believe it or not, it's barely an hour and a half since we picked you up. If we go straight back there now—'

'It's not that! She'll be wondering what happened! She must be half out of her mind!'

'Not she,' he said cheerfully. 'She'd see us haul you in. She was yelling for help while you were in the water, with Stratos after you. It was the noise she made that brought us in—that, and the odd way his light was behaving, so near our rendezvous. Then, once we got near enough, there was too much to do, and I clean forgot her. Oh, and she threw a rock at Stratos.'

'*Did* she? Good for her! Did she hit him?'

'Did you ever know a female hit anything? That she aimed at, I mean? She hit me,' said Mark. He got to his feet, and addressed the concourse in Greek. This was to the effect that there was another English lady to be rescued, some way westwards along the coast, and that they would have to trust him and his party not to run away, but we must immediately go and fetch her.

Instantly every man present was on his feet. I am not quite sure what happened, amid the passionate babel of Cretan Greek, but in a very few minutes, as the caique swung away from the shore, she was as well attended as a Cunarder edging her way out into Southampton Water. Not a man in Agios Georgios but would have died on the spot sooner than stay behind. Those light-boats that possessed engines had now caught up with us, lights blazing. Those that had not, bobbed valiantly in our wake. Astern of us loomed the bigger mother-shapes of the *Agia Barbara*, and the innocent *Eros*. It was a noble procession.

To Frances, sitting nursing her sore ankle on her lonely rock, we must have been a brave sight, a pack of lighted boats swinging round the headland, our lamps yellow against the growing dawn.

Our caique drew ahead of the rest, and slid alongside the rock-ridge. Colin shot out the boat-hook, and held us fast. Mark hailed her, cheerfully.

'Ahoy, there, Andromeda! Perseus here, with apologies, but there was a little matter of a dragon.'

I ran to the side. 'Frances! Are you all right? I'm most dreadfully sorry –'

'Well,' said Frances, 'I can see you're all right, which is all that matters, though I did have information to that effect. How nice to be rescued in style! I'm glad to see you, Perseus. You're a little late for the other dragon but, as you see, he did me no harm.'

Mark's brows knitted. 'The other dragon?'

I put my hand to my mouth. 'Tony? You mean Tony? *Here?*'

'As ever was.'

'What happened?'

'He came to collect the remainder of the jewels. The Camford House robbery, I understand.' Frances was bland. 'How well I remember the fuss when it happened.'

'But he didn't know where they were,' I said blankly. 'I *know* he didn't. Colin said –'

'Yes, he did.' Mark's voice was grim. 'Fool that I am, I heard

Stratos tell him tonight. He shouted out something about the *scháros*-pots, when we were crashing around in the hotel garden like demented buffaloes. I don't know whether he was just cursing me, or whether he was letting Tony know, so that he could pick them up. But Tony heard, and it seems he didn't waste any time.' He looked at Frances. 'Do you mean to tell me that while we've been sitting jabbering like monkeys in Agios Georgios, he's just calmly walked away with the rest of the jewels?'

'Not all of them; only one potful. I don't know how many there are, and neither did he. He didn't even know where the pots were laid, and of course, even with the lights, it wasn't easy to find them. He hauled up four in turn, and only one of them had what he was looking for. The rest were fish-pots, quite genuine. He was quite–er–picturesque about them. Then we heard the flotilla coming, and he cut his losses, and went. He said he'd got quite enough to make the whole thing worth while.'

' "He said"? You mean he saw you?'

'He could hardly avoid it, could he? At least one of the pots was almost at my feet. Don't look so horrified, my dear, he was very polite, and quite amusing. He simply kept nicely out of range–not that I could even have begun to try to stop him–and he told me all about it. He really did seem pleased that Colin had got safe away.'

'Small thanks to him,' I said tartly.

'So I told him. But I gather you've quite a lot to thank Sofia for. Apparently she refused from first to last to take anything from Stratos, because she thought it was all the proceeds of crime. She wouldn't have given him away, but it seems she did threaten to turn the lot of them in, Josef and herself included, if they hurt Colin. Master Tony passed that on to me, so that I could put in a word for her. And he sent you his love, Nicola; he was sorry to have to pass out of your life, but you'll get a picture postcard from the Kara Bugaz.'

'From the what? Where on earth's that?'

'I doubt if it need worry you. I've a strong feeling that we'll never hear of Little Lord Fauntleroy again, from the Kara Bugaz or anywhere else. Oh yes, and I was to tell you how much he approves of your trousers.'

'Well,' said Mark, 'that's one thing over which he and I see eye to eye. Aren't you coming off your rock? I know we're pretty crowded, but I can guarantee Lambis to get you back without foundering, and Colin makes a smashing cup of cocoa.'

Frances smiled at the three of them. 'So that's Lambis . . . and this is Colin. I can hardly believe we've never met till now, I seem to know you so well.' She put out a hand, and Mark jumped to the ridge, and helped her to her feet. 'Thank you, Perseus. Well, Nicola, so this is your Mark?'

'Why, yes,' I said.

This Rough Magic

For
JOHN ATTENBOROUGH

Author's Note

Among the many debts I have incurred while writing this book, two are outstanding. I should like to thank especially Mr. Michael Halikiopoulos, Director of the Corfu Tourist Services, 5 Arseniou Street, Corfu, for all his kindness, and for the help he gave me. My other debt is to Mr. Antony Alpers, whose enchanting *Book of Dolphins* (John Murray, 1960) provided not only the inspiration, but also a great deal of information for this book.

M.S.

Chapter 1

. . . A relation for a breakfast.
The Tempest. Act V. Scene 1.

'AND IF IT'S a boy,' said Phyllida cheerfully, 'we'll call him Prospero.'

I laughed. 'Poor little chap, why on earth? Oh, of course . . . Has someone been telling you that Corfu was Shakespeare's magic island for *The Tempest*?'

'As a matter of fact, yes, the other day, but for goodness' sake don't ask me about it now. Whatever you may be used to, I draw the line at Shakespeare for breakfast.' My sister yawned, stretched out a foot into the sunshine at the edge of the terrace, and admired the expensive beach sandal on it. 'I didn't mean that, anyway, I only meant that we've already got a Miranda here, and a Spiro, which may not be short for Prospero, but sounds very like it.'

'Oh? It sounds highly romantic. Who are they?'

'A local boy and girl: they're twins.'

'Good heavens. Papa must be a literary gent?'

Phyllida smiled. 'You could say so.'

Something in her expression roused my curiosity, just as something else told me she had meant to; so I—who can be every bit as provoking as Phyllida when I try—said merely: 'Well, in that case hadn't you better have a change? How about Caliban for your unborn young? It fits like a glove.'

'Why?' she demanded indignantly.

' "This blue-eyed hag was hither brought with child," ' I quoted. 'Is there some more coffee?'

'Of course. Here. Oh, my goodness, it's nice to have you here,

Lucy! I suppose I oughtn't to call it luck that you were free to come just now, but I'm awfully glad you could. This is heaven after Rome.'

'And paradise after London. I feel different already. When I think where I was this time yesterday . . . and when I *think* about the rain. . .'

I shuddered, and drank my coffee, leaning back in my chair to gaze out across pine tops furry with gold towards the sparkling sea, and surrendering myself to the dreamlike feeling that marks the start of a holiday in a place like this when one is tired, and has been transported overnight from the April chill of England to the sunlight of a magic island in the Ionian Sea.

Perhaps I should explain (for those who are not so lucky as I) that Corfu is an island off the west coast of Greece. It is long and sickle-shaped, and lies along the curve of the coast; at its nearest, in the north, it is barely two miles off the Albanian mainland, but from the town of Corfu, which is about half-way down the curve of the sickle, the coast of Greece is about seven or eight miles distant. At its northern end the island is broad and mountainous, trailing off through rich valleys and ever-decreasing hills into the long, flat scorpion's tail of the south from which some think that Corfu, or Kerkyra, gets its name.

My sister's house lies some twelve miles north of Corfu town, where the coast begins its curve towards the mainland, and where the foothills of Mount Pantokrator provide shelter for the rich little pocket of land which has been part of her husband's family property for a good many years.

My sister Phyllida is three years older than I, and when she was twenty she married a Roman banker, Leonardo Forli. His family had settled in Corfu during the Venetian occupation of that island, and had managed somehow to survive the various subsequent 'occupations' with their small estate more or less intact, and had even, like the Vicar of Bray, contrived to prosper. It was under the British Protectorate that Leo's great-grandfather had built the pretentious and romantic Castello dei Fiori in the woods above the little bay where the estate ran down to the sea. He had planted vineyards, and orange orchards, including a small plantation (if that is the word) of the Japanese miniature oranges called *koùm koyàt* for which the Forli estate became famous. He even cleared space in the woods for a garden, and built—beyond the southern arm of the bay and just out of sight of the Castello—a jetty and a vast boat-house which (according to Phyllida) would almost have housed the Sixth Fleet, and had indeed housed the complicated flock of vessels in which his guests used to visit him. In his day, I gathered, the Castello had been the scene of one large and continuous house-party: in summer they sailed and fished, and in the fall there were hunting-parties, when thirty or so guests would invade the Greek and Albanian mainlands to harry the birds and ibexes.

But those days had vanished with the first war, and the family moved to Rome, though without selling the Castello, which remained, through the twenties and thirties, their summer home. The shifting fortunes of the Second World War almost destroyed the estate, but the Forlis emerged in post-war Rome with the family fortunes mysteriously repaired, and the then Forli Senior—Leo's father—turned his attention once more to the Corfu property. He had done something to restore the place, but after his death three years ago his son had decided that the Castello's rubbed and faded splendours were no longer for him, and had built a pair of smallish modern villas—in reality twin bungalows—on the two headlands enclosing the bay of which the Castello overlooked the centre. He and Phyllida themselves used the Villa Forli, as they called the house on the northern headland; its twin, the Villa Rotha, stood to the south of the bay above the creek where the boat-house was. The Villa Rotha had been rented by an Englishman, a Mr. Manning, who had been there since the previous autumn working on a book ('You know the kind,' said my sister, 'all photographs, with a thin trickle of text in large type, but they're *good*.') The three houses were connected with the road by the main drive to the Castello, and with each other by various paths through the woods and down into the bay.

This year the hot spring in Rome, with worse promised, had driven the Forlis early to Corfu. Phyllida, who was pregnant, had been feeling the heat badly, so had been persuaded to leave the two older children (whose school term was still running) with their grandmother, and Leo had brought her over a few days before I arrived, but had had to go back to his business in Rome, with the promise to fly over when he could at week-ends, and to bring the children for Easter. So Phyllida, hearing that I was currently at a loose end, had written begging me to join her in Corfu and keep her company.

The invitation couldn't have been better timed. The play I was in had just folded after the merest face-saver of a run, and I was out of a

job. That the job had been my first in London–my 'big
chance'–accounted partly for my present depression. There was
nothing more on the cards: the agencies were polite, but evasive; and
besides, we had had a dreadful winter, and I was tired, dispirited,
and seriously wondering, at twenty-five, if I had made a fool of
myself in insisting against all advice on the stage as a career. But–as
everyone knows who has anything to do with it–the stage is not a
profession, but a virus, and I had it. So I had worked and scraped
my way through the usual beginnings until last year, when I had
finally decided, after three years of juvenile leads in provincial rep.,
that it was time to try my luck in London. And luck had seemed at
last to be with me. After ten months or so of television walk-ons and
the odd commercial, I had landed a promising part, only to have the
play fold under me like a dying camel, after a two-months' run.

But at least I could count myself luckier than the other few
thousand still fighting their way towards the bottom rung of the
ladder: while they were sitting in the agents' stuffy offices here was I
on the terrace of the Villa Forli, with as many weeks in front of me
as I cared to take in the dazzling sunshine of Corfu.

The terrace was a wide, tiled platform perched at the end of the
promontory where wooded cliffs fell steeply to the sea. Below the
balustrade hung cloud on cloud of pines, already smelling warm and
spicy in the morning sun. Behind the house and to either side sloped
the cool woods where small birds flashed and twittered. The bay
itself was hidden by trees, but the view ahead was glorious–a stretch
of the calm, shimmering Gulf that lies in the curved arm of Corfu.
Away northward, across the dark blue strait, loomed, insubstantial
as mist, the ghostly snows of Albania.

It was a scene of the most profound and enchanted peace. No
sound but the birds; nothing in sight but trees and sky and
sun-reflecting sea.

I sighed. 'Well, if it isn't Prospero's magic island it ought to
be . . . Who are these romantic twins of yours, anyway?'

'Spiro and Miranda? Oh, they belong to the woman who works
for us here, Maria. She has that cottage at the main Castello
gate–you'd see it last night on your way in from the airport.'

'I remember a light there . . . A tiny place, wasn't it? So they're
Corfu people– what's the word? Corfusians?'

She laughed. 'Idiot. Corfiotes. Yes, they're Corfiote peasants.
The brother works for Godfrey Manning over at the Villa Rotha.
Miranda helps her mother here.'

'Peasants?' Mildly intrigued, I gave her the lead I thought she wanted. 'It does seem a bit odd to find those names here. Who was this well-read father of theirs, then? Leo?'

'Leo,' said his loving wife, 'has to my certain knowledge read nothing but the Roman *Financial Times* for the last eight years. He'd think "Prospero and Miranda" was the name of an Investment Trust. No, it's even odder than you think, my love . . .' She gave her small cat-and-canary smile, the one I recognised as preceding the more far-fetched flights of gossip that she calls 'interesting facts that I feel you ought to know' . . . 'Actually, Spiro's officially called after the island saint—every second boy's called Spiridion in Corfu—but since our distinguished tenant at the Castello was responsible for the christening—and for the twins as well, one gathers—I'll bet he's down as Prospero in the parish register, or whatever they have here.'

'Your "distinguished tenant"?' This was obviously the *bonne bouche* she had been saving for me, but I looked at her in some surprise, remembering the vivid description she had once given me of the Castello dei Fiori: 'tatty beyond words, sort of Wagnerian Gothic, like a set for a musical version of *Dracula*'. I wondered who could have been persuaded to pay for these operatic splendours. 'Someone's rented Valhalla, then? Aren't you lucky. Who?'

'Julian Gale.'

'*Julian Gale?*' I sat up abruptly, staring at her. 'You can't mean—*do* you mean Julian Gale? The actor?'

'As ever was.' My sister looked pleased with the effect she had produced. I was wide awake now, as I had certainly not been during the long recital of our family affairs earlier. Sir Julian Gale was not only 'an actor', he had been one of the more brilliant lights of the English theatre for more years than I could well remember. And, more recently, one of its mysteries.

'Well!' I said. 'So this is where he went.'

'I thought you'd be interested,' said Phyl, rather smugly.

'I'll say I am! Everyone's still wondering, on and off, why he packed it in like that two years ago. Of course I knew he'd been ill after that ghastly accident, but to give it up and then just quietly vanish . . . You should have heard the rumours.'

'I can imagine. We've our own brand here. But don't go all shiny-eyed and imagine you'll get anywhere near him, my child. He's here for privacy, and I mean for privacy. He doesn't go out at all—socially, that is—except to the houses of a couple of friends, and they've got *Trespassers Will Be Shot* plastered at intervals of one yard all over the grounds, and the gardener throws all callers over the cliff into the sea.'

'I shan't worry him. I think too darned much of him for that. I suppose you must have met him. How is he?'

'Oh, I—he seems all right. Just doesn't get around, that's all. I've only met him a couple of times. Actually it was he who told me that Corfu was supposed to be the setting of *The Tempest*.' She glanced at me sideways. 'I—er—I suppose you'd allow him to be "a literary gent"?'

But this time I ignored the lead. '*The Tempest* was his swan-song,' I said. 'I saw it at Stratford, the last performance, and cried my eyes out over the "this rough magic I here abjure" bit. Is that what made him choose Corfu to retire to?'

She laughed. 'I doubt it. Didn't you know he was practically a native? He was here during the war, and apparently stayed on for a bit after it was over, and then I'm told he used to bring his family back almost every year for holidays when the children were young. They had a house near Ipsos, and kept it on till quite recently, but it was sold after his wife and daughter were killed. However, I suppose he still had . . . connections . . . here, so when he thought of retiring he remembered the Castello. We hadn't meant to let the place, it wasn't really fit, but he was so anxious to find somewhere quite isolated and quiet, and it really did seem a godsend that the Castello was empty, with Maria and her family just next door; so Leo let it go. Maria and the twins turned to and fixed up a few of the rooms, and there's a couple who live at the far side of the orange orchards; they look after the place, and their grandson does the Castello garden and helps around, so for anyone who really only wants peace and privacy I suppose it's a pretty fair bargain . . . Well, that's our little colony. I won't say it's just another St. Trop. in the height of the season, but there's plenty of what you want, if it's only peace and sunshine and bathing.'

'Suits me,' I said dreamily. 'Oh, how it suits me.'

'D'you want to go down this morning?'

'I'd love to. Where?'

'Well, the bay, of course. It's down that way.' She pointed vaguely through the trees.

'I thought you said there were notices warning trespassers off?'

'Oh, goodness, not literally, and not from the beach, anyway, only the grounds. We'd never let anyone else have the bay, that's what we come here for! Actually it's quite nice straight down from here on the north side of the headland where our own little jetty is, but there's sand in the bay, and it's heaven for lying about, and quite private . . . Well, you do as you like. I might go down later, but if you want to swim this morning, I'll get Miranda to show you the way.'

'She's here now?'

'Darling,' said my sister, 'you're in the lap of vulgar luxury now, remember? Did you think I made the coffee myself?'

'Get you, Contessa,' I said, crudely. 'I can remember the day –'

I broke off as a girl came out on to the terrace with a tray, to clear away the breakfast things. She eyed me curiously, with that unabashed stare of the Greeks which one learns to get used to, as it is virtually impossible to stare it down in return, and smiled at me, the smile broadening into a grin as I tried a 'Good morning' in Greek – a phrase which was, as yet, my whole vocabulary. She was short and stockily built, with a thick neck and round face, and heavy brows almost meeting over her nose. Her bright dark eyes and warm skin were attractive with the simple, animal attraction of youth and health. The dress of faded red suited her, giving her a sort of dark, gentle glow that was very different from the electric sparkle of the urban expatriate Greeks I had met. She looked about seventeen.

My attempt to greet her undammed a flood of delighted Greek which my sister, laughing, managed at length to stem.

'She doesn't understand, Miranda, she only knows two words. Speak English. Will you show her the way down to the beach when you've cleared away, please?'

'Of course! I shall be pleased! '

She looked more than pleased, she looked so delighted that I smiled to myself, presuming cynically that it was probably only pleasure at having an outing in the middle of a working morning. As it happened, I was wrong. Coming so recently from the grey depressions of London and the backstage bad tempers of failure, I wasn't able as yet to grasp the Greek's simple delight in doing anyone a service.

She began to pile the breakfast dishes on her tray with clattering vigour. 'I shall not be long. A minute, only a minute . . .'

'And that means half an hour,' said my sister placidly, as the girl bustled out. 'Anyway, what's the hurry? You've all the time in the world.'

'So I have,' I said, in deep contentment.

*   *   *

The way to the beach was a shady path quilted with pine needles.
It twisted through the trees, to lead out suddenly into a small
clearing where a stream, trickling down to the sea, was trapped in a
sunny pool under a bank of honeysuckle.

Here the path forked, one track going uphill, deeper into the
woods, the other turning down steeply through pines and golden
oaks towards the sea.

Miranda paused and pointed downhill. 'That is the way you go.
The other is to the Castello, and it is private. Nobody goes that way,
it is only to the house, you understand.'

'Whereabouts is the other villa, Mr. Manning's?'

'On the other side of the bay, at the top of the cliff. You cannot see
it from the beach because the trees are in the way, but there is a path
going like this'—she sketched a steep zigzag—'from the boat-house up
the cliff. My brother works there, my brother Spiro. It is a fine
house, very beautiful, like the Signora's, though of course not so
wonderful as the Castello. *That* is like a palace.'

'So I believe. Does your father work on the estate, too?'

The query was no more than idle; I had completely forgotten
Phyllida's nonsense, and hadn't believed it anyway, but to my
intense embarrassment the girl hesitated, and I wondered for one
horrified second if Phyllida had been right. I did not know, then,
that the Greek takes the most intensely personal questions serenely
for granted, just as he asks them himself, and I had begun to
stammer something, but Miranda was already answering:

'Many years ago my father left us. He went over there.'

'Over there' was at the moment a wall of trees laced with shrubs of
myrtle, but I knew what lay beyond them; the grim, shut land of
Communist Albania.

'You mean as a prisoner?' I asked, horrified.

She shook her head. 'No. He was a Communist. We lived then in
Argyrathes, in the south of Corfu, and in that part of the island there
are many such.' She hesitated. 'I do not know why this is. It is
different in the north, where my mother comes from.' She spoke as
if the island were four hundred miles long instead of forty, but I
believed her. Where two Greeks are gathered together, there will be
at least three political parties represented, and possibly more.

'You've never heard from him?'

'Never. In the old days my mother still hoped, but now, of

course, the frontiers are shut to all, and no one can pass in or out. If he is still alive, he must stay there. But we do not know this either.'

'D'you mean that no one can travel to Albania?'

'No one.' The black eyes suddenly glittered to life, as if something had sparked behind their placid orbs. 'Except those who break the law.'

'Not a law I'd care to break myself.' Those alien snows had looked high and cold and cruel. I said awkwardly: 'I'm sorry, Miranda. It must be an unhappy business for your mother.'

She shrugged. 'It is a long time ago. Fourteen years. I do not even know if I remember him. And we have Spiro to look after us.' The sparkle again. 'He works for Mr. Manning, I told you this—with the boat, and with the car, a wonderful car, very expensive—and also with the photographs that Mr. Manning is taking for a book. He has said that when the book is finished—a real book that is sold in the shops—he will put Spiro's name in it, in print. Imagine! Oh, there is nothing that Spiro cannot do! He is my twin, you understand.'

'Is he like you?'

She looked surprised. 'Like me? Why, no, he is a man, and have I not just told you that he is clever? Me, I am not clever, but then I am a woman, and there is no need. With men it is different. Yes?'

'So the men say.' I laughed. 'Well, thanks very much for showing me the way. Will you tell my sister that I'll be back in good time for lunch?'

I turned down the steep path under the pines. As I reached the first bend something made me glance back towards the clearing.

Miranda had gone. But I thought I saw a whisk of faded scarlet, not from the direction of the Villa Forli, but higher up in the woods, on the forbidden path to the Castello.

Chapter 2

Sir, I am vex'd.
IV. 1.

THE BAY WAS small and sheltered, a sickle of pure white sand holding back the aquamarine sea, and held in its turn by the towering backdrop of cliff and pine and golden-green trees. My path led me steeply down past a knot of young oaks, straight on to the sand. I changed quickly in a sheltered corner, and walked out into the white blaze of the sun.

The bay was deserted and very quiet. To either side of it the wooded promontories thrust out into the calm, glittering water. Beyond them the sea deepened through peacock shades to a rich, dark blue, where the mountains of Epirus floated in the clear distance, less substantial than a bank of mist. The far snows of Albania seemed to drift like cloud.

After the heat of the sand, the water felt cool and silky. I let myself down into the milky calm, and began to swim idly along parallel to the shore, towards the southern arm of the bay. There was the faintest breeze blowing off the land, its heady mixture of orange-blossom and pine, sweet and sharp, coming in warm puffs through the salt smell of the sea. Soon I was nearing the promontory, where white rocks came down to the water, and a grove of pines hung out, shadowing a deep, green pool. I stayed in the sun, turning lazily on my back to float, eyes shut against the brilliance of the sky.

The pines breathed and whispered; the tranquil water made no sound at all . . .

A ripple rocked me, nearly turning me over. As I floundered, trying to right myself, another came, a wash like that of a small boat passing, rolling me in its wake. But I had heard neither oars nor engine; could hear nothing now except the slap of the exhausted ripples against the rock.

Treading water, I looked around me, puzzled and a little alarmed. Nothing. The sea shimmered, empty and calm, to the turquoise and blue of its horizon. I felt downwards with my feet, to find that I had drifted a little further out from the shore, and could barely touch bottom with the tips of my toes. I turned back towards the shallows.

This time the wash lifted me clear off my feet, and as I plunged clumsily forward another followed it, tumbling me over, so that I struggled helplessly for a minute, swallowing water, before striking out, thoroughly alarmed now, for shore.

Beside me, suddenly, the water swirled and hissed. Something touched me—a cold, momentary graze along the thigh—as a body drove past me under water . . .

I gave a gasp of sheer fright, and the only reason I didn't scream was because I gasped myself full of water, and went under. Fighting back, terrified, to the surface, I shook the salt out of my eyes, and looked wildly round—to see the bay as empty as before, but with its surface marked now by the arrowing ripples of whatever sea-creature had brushed by me. The arrow's point was moving fast away, its wake as clear as a vapour-trail across the flat water of the bay. It tore on its way, straight for the open sea . . . then curved in a long arc, heading back . . .

I didn't wait to see what it was. My ignorant mind, panic-stricken, screamed 'Sharks!' and I struck out madly for the rocks of the promontory.

It was coming fast. Thirty yards off, the surface of the water bulged, swelled, and broke to the curved thrust of a huge, silver-black back. The water parted, and poured off its sides like liquid glass. There was a gasping puff of breath; I caught the glimpse of a dark bright eye, and a dorsal fin cusped like a crescent moon, then the creature submerged again, its wash lifting me a couple of yards forward towards my rock. I found a handhold, clung, and scrambled out, gasping, and thoroughly scared.

It surely wasn't a shark. Hundreds of adventure stories had told me that one knew a shark by the great triangular fin, and I had seen pictures of the terrible jaws and tiny, brutal eye. This creature had breathed air, and the eye had been big and dark, like a dog's—like a seal's, perhaps? But there were no seals in these warm waters, and besides, seals didn't have dorsal fins. A porpoise, then? Too big . . .

Then I had the answer, and with it a rush of relief and delight. This was the darling of the Aegean, 'the lad who lives before the wind', Apollo's beloved, 'desire of the sea', the dolphin . . . the lovely names went rippling by with him, as I drew myself up on to the warm rock in the shade of the pines, clasped my knees, and settled down to watch.

Here he came again, in a great curve, smooth and glistening, dark-backed and light-bellied, and as graceful as a racing yacht. This time he came right out, to lie on the surface watching me.

He was large, as dolphins go, something over eight feet long. He lay rocking gently, with the powerful shoulders waiting curved for the plunge below, and the tail—crescent-shaped, and quite unlike a fish's upright rudder—hugging the water flatly, holding the big body level. The dark-ringed eye watched me steadily, with what I could have sworn was a friendly and interested light. The smooth muzzle was curved into the perpetual dolphin-smile.

Excitement and pleasure made me light-headed. 'Oh, you darling!' I said foolishly, and put out a hand, rather as one puts it out to the pigeons in Trafalgar Square.

The dolphin, naturally, ignored it, but lay there placidly smiling, rocking a little closer and watching me, entirely unafraid.

So they were true, those stories . . . I knew of the legends, of course—ancient literature was studded with stories of dolphins who had befriended man; and while one couldn't quite accept all the miraculous dolphins of legend, there were also many more recent tales, sworn to with every kind of modern proof. There was the dolphin called Pelorus Jack, fifty years ago in New Zealand, who saw the ships through Cook Strait for twenty years; the Opononi dolphin of the fifties, who entertained the holiday-makers in the bay; the one more recently in Italy, who played with the children near the shore, attracting such large crowds that eventually a little group of business-men from a near-by resort, whose custom was being drawn away, lay in wait for the dolphin, and shot her dead as she came in to play. These, and others, gave the old legends rather more than the benefit of the doubt.

And here, indeed, was the living proof. Here was I, Lucy Waring, being asked into the water for a game. The dolphin couldn't have made it clearer if he'd been carrying a placard on that lovely moon's-horn fin of his. He rocked himself, watching me, then half-turned, rolled, and came up again, nearer still . . .

A stray breeze moved the pines, and I heard a bee go past my cheek, travelling like a bullet. The dolphin arched suddenly away in a deep dive. The sea sucked, swirled, and settled, rocking, back to emptiness.

So that was that. With a disappointment so sharp that it felt like a bereavement, I turned my head to watch for him moving out to sea, when suddenly, not far from my rock, the sea burst apart as if it had been shelled, and the dolphin shot upwards on a steep slant that took him out of the water in a yard-high leap, and down again with a smack of the tail as loud as a cannon-shot. He tore by like a torpedo, to fetch up all standing twenty yards out from my rock, and fix me once again with that bright, humorous eye.

It was an enchanting piece of show-off, and it did the trick. 'All right,' I said softly, 'I'll come in. But if you knock me over again, I'll drown you, my lad, see if I don't!'

I lowered my legs into the water, ready to slide down off the rock. Another bee shot past above me, seawards, with a curious, high humming. Something—some small fish, I supposed—splashed a white jet of water just beyond the dolphin. Even as I wondered, vaguely, what it was, the humming came again, nearer . . . and then another white spurt of water, and a curious thin, curving whine, like singing wire.

I understood then. I'd heard that sound before. These were neither bees nor fish. They were bullets, presumably from a silenced rifle, and one of them had ricocheted off the surface of the sea. Someone was shooting at the dolphin from the woods above the bay.

That I was in some danger from the ricochets myself didn't at first enter my head. I was merely furious, and concerned to do something quickly. There lay the dolphin, smiling at me on the water, while some murderous 'sportsman' was no doubt taking aim yet again . . .

Presumably he hadn't yet seen me in the shadow of the pines. I shouted at the top of my voice: 'Stop that shooting! Stop it at once!' and thrust myself forward into the water.

Nobody, surely, would fire at the beast when there was the chance of hitting me? I plunged straight out into the sunlight, clumsily breasting the water, hoping that my rough approach would scare the dolphin away from the danger.

It did. He allowed me to come within a few feet, but as I lunged further, with a hand out as if to touch him, he rolled gently away from me, submerged, and vanished.

I stood breast-deep, watching the sea. Nothing. It stretched silent and empty towards the tranquil, floating hills of the mainland. The ripple ran back to the shore, and flattened, whispering. The dolphin had gone. And the magic had gone with him. This was only a small—and lonely—bathing-place, above which waited an unpleasant and frustrated character with a gun.

I turned to look up at the enclosing cliffs.

The first thing I saw, high up above the bay's centre, was what must be the upper storeys of the Castello dei Fiori, rearing their incongruously embattled turrets against a background of holm-oak and cedar and Mediterranean cypress. The house was set well back, so that I could not see the ground-floor windows, but a wide balcony, or terrace, edged with a stone balustrade, jutted forward right to the cliff's edge over the bay. From the beach directly below nothing of this would be visible through the tangle of flowering shrubs that curtained the steep, broken cliff, but from where I stood I could see the full length of the balustrade with its moss-grown statues at the corners, a stone jar or two full of flowers showing bright against the dark background of cypress, and, a little way back from the balustrade, a table and chairs set in the shadow of a stone-pine.

And a man standing, half invisible in the shade of the pine, watching me.

A moment's study convinced me that it could not be Sir Julian Gale. This man was too dark, and even from this distance looked quite unfamiliar—too casual in his bearing, perhaps, and certainly too young. The gardener, probably; the one who threw the tres-passers over the cliff. Well, if Sir Julian's gardener had the habit of amusing himself with a bit of shooting-practice, it was high time he was stopped.

I was out of the water before even the dolphin could have dived twice, had snatched up shoes and wrap, and was making for a dilapidated flight of steps near the cliff which, I assumed, led up to the terrace.

From above I heard a shout, and looked up. He had come forward to the balustrade, and was leaning over. I could barely see him through the thick screen of hibiscus and bramble, but he didn't look like a Greek, and as I paused, he shouted in English, 'That way, please!' and his arm went out in a gesture towards the southern end of the bay.

I ignored it. Whoever he was—some guest of Julian Gale's

presumably—I was going to have this out with him here and now,
while I was hot with temper; not wait until I had to meet him at
some polite bun-fight of Phyllida's . . . 'But you really mustn't shoot
at dolphins, Mr. Whosit, they do no harm . . .' The same old polite
spiel, gone through a thousand times with stupid, trigger-happy
men who shot or trapped badgers, otters, kestrels—harmless creatures, killed because some man wanted a walk out with his dog on a
fine day. No, this time I was white-hot, and brave with it, and I was
going to say my piece.

I went up those steps like a rocket leaving the launching-pad.

They were steep and crooked, and wound up through the thickest
of the wood. They skirted the roots of the cliff, flicked up and round
thickets of myrtle and summer jasmine, and emerged into a sloping
glade full of dappled sunlight.

He was there, looking annoyed, having apparently come down
from the terrace to intercept me. I only realised, when I stopped to
face him, how very much at a disadvantage I was. He had come
down some fifty feet; I had hurtled up a hundred or so. He
presumably had a right to be where he was; I had not. He was also
minding his own business, which was emphatically none of mine.
Moreover he was fully dressed, and I was in swimming costume,
with a wet wrap flying loose round me. I clutched it to me, and
fought for breath, feeling angrier than ever, but now this didn't help
at all, as I couldn't get a word out.

He said, not aggressively but not politely: 'This is private ground,
you know. Perhaps you'd be good enough to leave by the way you
came? This only takes you up to the terrace, and then more or less
through the house.'

I got enough breath to speak, and wasted neither time nor words.
'Why were you shooting at that dolphin?'

He looked as blank as if I had suddenly slapped his face. 'Why
was I what?'

'That was you just now, wasn't it, shooting at the dolphin down
in the bay?'

'My dear g–' He checked himself, and said, like someone dealing
with a lunatic, 'Just what are you talking about?'

'Don't pretend you don't know! It must have been you! If you're
such death on trespassers, who else would be there?' I was panting
hard, and my hands were shaking as I clutched the wrap to me
clumsily. 'Someone took a couple of pot-shots at it, just a few
minutes ago. I was down there, and I saw you on the terrace.'

'I certainly saw a dolphin there. I didn't see you, until you shouted and came jumping out from under the trees. But you must be mistaken. There was no shooting. I'd have been bound to hear it if there was.'

'It was silenced, of course,' I said impatiently. 'I tell you, I was down there when the shots came! D'you think I'd have come running up here for the fun of the thing? They were bullets all right! I know a ricochet when I hear it.'

His brows snapped down at that, and he stared at me frowningly, as if seeing me for the first time as a person, and not just a nuisance to be thrown down the cliff as quickly as possible.

'Then why did you jump into the water near the dolphin?'

'Well, obviously! I wanted to drive it away before it got hurt!'

'But you might have been badly hurt yourself. Don't you know that a bullet ricochets off water the way it does off rock?'

'Of course I do! But I had to do something, hadn't I?'

'Brave girl.' There was a dryness in his voice that brought my cooling temper fizzing to the boil again. I said hotly:

'You don't believe me, do you? I tell you it's true! They *were* shots, and *of course* I jumped in to stop you! I knew you'd have to stop if someone was there.'

'You know,' he said, 'you can't have it both ways. Either I did the shooting, or I don't believe there was any shooting. Not both. You can take your pick. If I were you, I'd choose the second; I mean, it's simply not credible, is it? Even supposing someone wanted to shoot a dolphin, why use a silencer?'

'*I'm* asking *you*,' I said.

For a moment I thought I had gone too far. His lips compressed, and his eyes looked angry. There was a short silence, while he stared at me frowningly, and we measured one another.

I saw a strongly built man of about thirty, carelessly dressed in slacks and a sleeveless Sea Island shirt which exposed a chest and arms that might have belonged to any of the Greek navvies I was to see building the roads with their bare hands and very little more. Like theirs, too, his hair and eyes were very dark. But something at once sensual and sensitive about the mouth contradicted the impression of a purely physical personality; here, one felt, was a man of aggressive impulses, but one who paid for them in his own private coinage.

What impression he was getting of me I hated to think—damp

hair, flushed face, half-embarrassed fury, and a damned wrap that kept slipping – but of one thing I could feel pretty sure: at this very moment he was having one of those aggressive impulses of his. Fortunately it wasn't physical . . . yet.

'Well,' he said shortly, 'I'm afraid you'll have to take my word for it. I did not shoot at the beast, with a rifle or a catapult or anything else. Will that do? And now if you'll excuse me, I'll be obliged if you would –'

'Go out by the way I came in? All right. I get the message. I'm sorry, perhaps I was wrong. But I certainly wasn't wrong about the shooting. I don't see any more than you do why anyone should do it, but the fact remains that they did.' I hesitated, faltering now under his indifferent eye. 'Look, I don't want to be any more of a nuisance, but I can't just leave it at that . . . It might happen again . . . Since it wasn't you, have you any idea who it could have been?'

'No.'

'Not the gardener?'

'No.'

'Or the tenant at the Villa Rotha?'

'Manning? On the contrary, if you want help in your protection campaign I suggest you go to the Villa Rotha straight away. Manning's been photographing that beast for weeks. It was he who tamed it in the first place, he and the Greek boy who works for him.'

'Tamed it? Oh . . . I see. Well, then,' I added, lamely, 'it wouldn't be him, obviously.'

He said nothing, waiting, it seemed, with a kind of neutral patience for me to go. I bit my lip, hesitating miserably, feeling a fool. (Why did one always feel such a fool when it was a matter of kindness – what the more sophisticated saw as sentimentality?) I found that I was shivering. Anger and energy had drained out of me together. The glade was cool with shadows.

I said: 'Well, I imagine I'll see Mr. Manning some time soon, and if he can't help, I'm sure my brother-in-law will. I mean, if this is all private land, and the shore as well, then we ought to be able to stop that kind of trespasser, oughtn't we?'

He said quickly: 'We?'

'The people who own the place. I'm Lucy Waring, Phyllida Forli's sister. I take it you're staying with Sir Julian?'

'I'm his son. So you're Miss Waring? I hadn't realised you were here already.' He appeared to be hesitating on the brink of some apology, but asked instead: 'Is Forli at home now?'

'No,' I said shortly, and turned to go. There was a trail of bramble across my shoe, and I bent to disengage it.

'I'm sorry if I was a little abrupt.' His voice had not noticeably softened, but that might have been due to awkwardness. 'We've had rather a lot of bother with people coming around lately, and my father . . . he's been ill, and came here to convalesce, so you can imagine that he prefers to be left to himself.'

'Did I look like an autograph hunter?'

For the first time there was a twitch of amusement. 'Well, no. But your dolphin has been more of an attraction even than my father: the word got round somehow that it was being photographed here-abouts, and then of course the rumour started that a film was being made, so we got a few boat-loads of sightseers coming round into the bay, not to mention stray parties in the woods. It's all been a bit trying. I wouldn't mind, personally, if people wanted to use the beach, if it weren't that they always come armed with transistor radios, and that I cannot stand. I'm a professional musician, and I'm here to work.' He added, dryly: 'And if you're thinking that this gives me the best of reasons for wanting to get rid of the dolphin, I can only assure you again that it didn't occur to me.'

'Well,' I said, 'it seems there's no more to be said, doesn't it? I'm sorry if I interrupted your work. I'll go now and let you get back to it. Good-bye, Mr. Gale.'

My exit from the clearing was ruined by the fact that my wrap caught on the brambles, and came clean off me. It took me some three horrible minutes to disentangle it and go.

But I needn't have worried about the threat to my dignity. He had already gone. From somewhere above, and alarmingly near, I heard voices, question and answer, so brief and idle as to be in themselves an insult. Then music, as a wireless or gramophone let loose a flood of weird atonal chords on the still air.

I could be sure I was already forgotten.

Chapter 3

This gallant which thou seest
Was in the wrack: and but he's something stain'd
With grief (that's beauty's canker) thou might'st call him
A goodly person.

I. 2.

BY THE TIME I had showered and dressed I felt calmer, and very ready to tell Phyllida all about it, and possibly to hear her barbed comments on the unaccommodating Mr. Gale. But when I looked on the terrace she was not to be seen, only the table half-laid for lunch, with the silver thrown down, as if hastily, in the middle of the cloth. There was no sign of Miranda or her mother.

Then I heard the door from the kitchen premises swing open and shut, and the quick tap of my sister's steps crossing the hall, to enter the big living-room she called the *salotto*.

'Lucy? Was that you I heard?'

'I'm out here.' I made for the french windows as I spoke, but she had already hurried out to meet me, and one look at her face drove all thoughts of my morning's adventure from my head.

'Phyl! What's the matter? You look ghastly. Is it Caliban?'

She shook her head. 'Nothing so simple. There's been bad news, an awful thing. Poor Maria's boy's been drowned. Spiro, the boy I told you about at breakfast.'

'*Phyl!* Oh, my dear, how frightful! But—how? When?'

'Last night. He was out with Godfrey in the boat—Godfrey Manning, that is—and there was an accident. Godfrey's just come over with the news, and I've been breaking it to Maria and Miranda. I—I've sent them home.' She put a hand to her head. 'Lucy, it was so awful! I simply can't tell you. If Maria had even *said* anything, but she didn't, not one single word . . . Oh well, come on in. Godfrey's still here, you'd better come and meet him.'

I drew back. 'No, no, don't you bother about me: I'll go to my room, or something. Mr. Manning won't want to have to do the polite. Poor Phyl; I'm sorry . . . Look, would you like me to take myself right away for the rest of the day? I'll go and get lunch somewhere, and then –'

'No, please, I'd rather you stayed.' She dropped her voice for a moment. 'He's taking it pretty hard, and quite honestly I think it might do him good to talk about it. Come on in . . . God! I could do with a drink! Caliban'll have to lump it, for once.' She smiled a bit thinly, and led the way in through the long window.

The *salotto* was a long, cool room, with three big windows opening on the terrace with its dazzling view. The sun was tempered by the wistaria that roofed the terrace, and the room was cool and airy, its duck-egg blue walls and white paint setting off to perfection the gilt of the Italian mirrors and the pale-gold polished wood of the floor. A calm room, with the kind of graceful simplicity that money and good taste can produce. Phyllida had always had excellent taste. It was a good thing, I sometimes reflected, that she, and not I, had married the rich man. My own taste – since I had outgrown the gingham-and-Chianti-bottle stage – had been heavily conditioned by the fact that I had lived for so long in a perpetual welter of junk-shop props picked up cheaply and licked into stage-worthiness for the current show. At best, the effect was a kind of poor man's Cecil Beaton; at worst, a cross between sets designed by Emmett and Ronald Searle for a stage version of Samuel Becket's *Watt*. That I enjoyed my kind of life didn't stop me from admiring my sister's undoubted talent for elegance.

There was a table at the far end of the room, laden with bottles. A man stood with his back to us, splashing soda into a glass. He turned as we came in.

My first quick impression was of a mask of rather chilly control held hard down over some strong emotion. Then the impression faded, and I saw that I was wrong; the control was not a mask; it was part of the man, and was created by the emotion itself, as a Westinghouse brake is slammed on automatically by the head of steam. Here was something very different from Mr. Gale. I looked at him with interest, and some compassion.

He was tall, and toughly built, with brown hair bleached by the sun, a narrow, clever face, and grey eyes which looked tired and dragged down at the corners, as if he had had no sleep. I put his age somewhere in the middle thirties.

Phyllida introduced us, and he acknowledged me civilly, but all his attention was on my sister. 'You've told them? Was it very bad?'

'Worse than bad. Get me a drink, for heaven's sake, will you?' She sank into a chair. 'What? Oh, Scotch, please. What about you, Lucy?'

'If that's fruit juice in the jug, may I have that, please? Is there ice?'

'Of course.' He handed the drinks. 'Look, Phyl, ought I to go and talk to them now? There'll be things they'll want to ask.'

She drank, sighed, and seemed to relax a little. 'I'd leave it for now, if I were you. I told them they could go home, and they didn't say a word, just picked up their things. I suppose the police'll be there to see them . . . Later on they'll want to hear every last detail from you, but just at the moment I doubt if Maria's fit to take anything in at all, except that he's dead. As a matter of fact, I don't think she even took *that* in, I don't think she believes it, yet.' She looked up at him. 'Godfrey, I suppose . . . I suppose there couldn't be any doubt?'

He hesitated, swirling the whisky in his glass, frowning down at it. The lines of fatigue were deep in his face, and made me wonder if he were older than I had thought.

'Well, yes. That's rather the hell of it, don't you see? That's why I didn't come over till now . . . I've been phoning around all over the place, trying to find out if he could possibly have got ashore either here or on the mainland, or if he'd been . . . well, found. If his body had been washed ashore, that is.' He looked up from the drink. 'But I'm morally certain there's no chance. I mean, I saw him go.'

'And how far out were you?'

He grimaced. 'About dead centre.'

'From here?'

'Further north, out from Kouloura, right in the strait. But that's still a mile each way.'

I said: 'What happened?'

They both started as if they had forgotten my presence completely. Godfrey Manning straightened his shoulders, and smoothed back his hair in a gesture I was to know well.

'Do you know, I'm still hardly sure. Does that sound incredibly stupid? It's no more than the truth. I've been over it so many times in my mind since it happened that I'm beginning to wonder now how much I really do remember. And, of course, a night without sleep doesn't help.' He crossed to the table to pour himself another drink, saying over his shoulder: 'The worst of it is, I can't get rid of the feeling that there must have been something I could have done to prevent it.'

Phyllida cried out at that, and I said quickly: 'I'm sure that's not true! I'm sorry, I shouldn't have asked. You won't want to talk about it any more.'

'It's all right.' He came back to a chair, but didn't sit in it, just perched rather restlessly on the arm. 'I've already been through it with the police, and given Phyl a sketch of a sort. You might say the worst part is over . . . except, God help me, that I'll have to talk to the boy's mother. She'll want to know rather more than the police were concerned with . . . As a matter of fact, it would be quite a relief to talk it out.' He took a pull at the whisky as if he needed it, and looked at me straight for the first time. 'You hadn't met Spiro?'

'I only came last night.'

His mouth turned down at the corners. 'What a start to your visit. Well, he was Miranda's twin–I take it you'll have met her and her mother?–and he works, or rather worked, for me.'

'Phyl told me.'

'I was lucky to have him. He was a clever mechanic, and that's something not so easy to find in these parts. In most of the villages the only "machines" are donkeys and mules, and there's no work for a mechanically-minded boy. They move to the towns. But of course Spiro wanted work near home; his father's dead, and he wanted to live with his mother and sister. I came here last year, and he's worked for me all that time. What he didn't know about boats wasn't worth knowing, and when I tell you that I even let him loose on my car, you'll realise he was pretty good.' He nodded towards the window, where a big portfolio lay on a table. 'I don't know if Phyl told you, but I'm working on a book, mainly photographs, and even with that Spiro was invaluable. He not only picked up enough to help me technically–with the processing and so on–but I actually got him to model for a few of them.'

'They're marvellous, too,' Phyllida told me warmly.

He smiled, a tight, meaningless little smile. 'They are good, aren't they? Well, that was Spiro. Not a world-beater, whatever poor Miranda says about him. What brains he had were in his hands, and he was slow, and as stubborn as a blind mule–but he was tough, and you could trust him. And he had that one extra, priceless quality which was worth the earth to me – he photographed like a dream. He was a "natural" for the camera – you simply couldn't miss.' He swallowed the last of his whisky, and stooped to set the glass down. The click of glass on wood sounded oddly final, like the full stop after the valediction. 'Which brings me to last night.'

There was a little pause. The tired grey eyes came back to me.

'I've been doing some experiments in night photography – fishing-boats at night, moonscapes, that kind of thing . . . and I wanted to try my hand at the sunrise over the mainland, while there's still snow on the mountains. Spiro and I took my boat out last night. There was a stiffish breeze, but it was nothing to worry about. We went up the coast. You'll know, perhaps, that Mount Pantokrator lies north of here? Well, the coast curves right out, running almost due east under the shelter of the mountain. It's only when you come to the end of this, and turn north through the open strait, that you get the weather. We got there within half an hour or so of dawn, and turned up about opposite Kouloura – that's the narrowest bit between here and the mainland. The sea was choppy, but nothing a sailor would call rough, though the wind was still rising from the north . . . Well, I was in the cabin, busy with my camera, and Spiro was aft, when the engine suddenly stopped. I called to ask what was wrong, and he shouted that he thought something was fouling the screw, and he'd have it clear in a minute. So I went on with my job, only then I found he'd let the boat's head fall away, and she'd turned across the wind, and was rolling rather too much for comfort. So I went out to see what was going on.'

He lifted one hand in a slight, but oddly final gesture. 'Then it happened. I saw Spiro in the stern, leaning over. The boat was heeling pretty steeply, and I think – I can't be sure – that I yelled to him to take care. Then a gust or a wave or something got her on the beam, and she kicked over like a mule. He'd had hold of the toe-rail, but it was slippery, and he lost it. I saw him grab again as he went over, but he missed. He just disappeared. By the time I got to the stern I couldn't even see him.'

'He couldn't swim?'

'Oh, yes, but it was very dark, and the boat was drifting fast, with a fair sea on by that time. The wind must have got up more than I'd realised while I was working in the cabin, and we must have been driven yards apart in as many seconds. Even if he'd stayed afloat it would have been hard to find him . . . and I don't think he can have done, or he'd have shouted, and I'd surely have heard something. I yelled myself hoarse, as it was, and there was no answer . . .'

He got up again, restlessly, and prowled over to the window. 'Well, that's all. I threw a lifebelt out, but we were being blown away at a fair speed, and by the time I'd got the engine started, and gone back to where I thought he'd gone overboard, there wasn't a sign. I must have been somewhere near the right place, because I found the lifebelt. I cruised about for a couple of hours—rather stupidly, I suppose, but then one can't somehow give up and go. A fishing-boat came within hail, and helped, but it was no use.'

There was a pause. He stood with his back to us, looking out.

Phyllida said drearily: 'It's a horrible thing to happen. Horrible.'

'And was the propeller fouled after all?' I asked.

He turned. 'What? No, it wasn't. At least, I saw nothing there. It was a choked jet. It only took a few seconds to put right. If he'd looked there first . . .' He lifted his shoulders, letting the sentence hang.

'Well,' said Phyl, with an attempt at briskness. 'I honestly don't see why you should reproach yourself at all. What could you have done more?'

'Oh, it's not that I blame myself for what happened, I know that's absurd. It's my failure to find him that I find so hard to live with. Casting round for two hours in that black windy sea, and knowing all the time that at any minute it would be too late . . . Don't misunderstand me, but it would be a lot easier if I'd had to bring the boy's body home.'

'Because his mother can't believe he's gone?'

He nodded. 'As it is, she'll probably hope against hope, and sit waiting for him to turn up. And then when—if—his body is washed ashore, this will all be to go through again.'

Phyllida said: 'Then all we can do is hope the body will turn up soon.'

'I doubt if it will. The wind and tide were setting the other way. And if he went ashore on the Albanian coast, we may never hear about it. She may wait for years.'

'The way she did for his father,' I said.

He stared at me, as if for some seconds he hardly saw me. 'His father? Oh, God, yes, I forgot that.'

Phyllida stirred. 'Then go on forgetting it, for heaven's sake, Godfrey! You're not to flay yourself over this any more! The situation's horrible enough without your trying to blame yourself for something you couldn't help, and couldn't have prevented!'

'As long as his mother and sister understand that.'

'Of course they will! Once the shock's over, and you can talk to them, you'll have to tell them the whole story, just as you've told us. You'll find they'll accept it, without even thinking of praise or blame—just as they'd accept anything fate chose to hand out to them. These people do. They're as strong as their own rocks, and so's their faith.'

He was looking at her in some surprise. People who only see the everyday side of Phyllida—the volatile, pretty-butterfly side—are always surprised when they come up against her core of solid, maternal warmth. He also looked grateful, and relieved, as if she had somehow excused him from blame, and this mattered.

She smiled at him. 'Your trouble is, you've not only had a rotten experience and a bad shock, but now you're dreading having to face Maria, and stand a scene; and I don't blame you one bit.' Her frankness was as comfortable as it was devastating. 'But you needn't worry. There'll be no scenes, and it won't even occur to them to ask you questions.'

'You don't quite understand. Spiro wasn't to have gone with me last night—he had a date of some sort in the town. I persuaded him to break it. His mother didn't even know till the last minute.'

'So what? No doubt you were paying him overtime of a sort, the way you always did? I thought as much . . . oh, yes, I knew all about it, Maria told me. Believe me, they were terribly grateful for the work you gave him, *and* for the way you paid, always so generous. Spiro thought the world of you, and so does Maria. Good heavens, *you* to worry what they'll say to you?'

'Could I offer them anything, do you think?'

'Money?' She knitted her brows. 'I don't know. I'll have to think. I don't know quite what they'll do now . . . But don't let's worry about that yet. I'll ask a tactful question or two, and let you know, shall I? But I'll tell you one thing, you'd better take those pictures home with you when you go. I've not looked at them properly, but it'd be a pity if Maria saw them just now.'

'Oh. Yes, of course. I'll take them.'

He picked up the portfolio, and stood holding it irresolutely, as if he didn't quite know what to do next. One habit my profession has taught me is to watch faces and listen to voices; and if the people concerned are under some kind of stress, so much the better. As an

actress I shall never be in the top class, but I am fairly good at
reading people, and I felt here, in Godfrey Manning's hesitation and
hunger for reassurance, something not quite in character: the
contrast between the man as one felt he should be, and what shock
had made of him, was obscurely disquieting, like watching an actor
badly miscast. It made me say hastily, and not very tactfully –almost
as if any diversion were better than none:

'Are those the photographs for your book?'

'Some of them, prints I brought the other day for Phyl to look at.
Would you care to see them?'

He came quickly across the room, and laid the portfolio on a low
table beside my chair. I wasn't sure that I wanted, at this moment,
to look at the prints, among which were presumably some of the
dead boy, but Phyl made no protest, and to Godfrey Manning, quite
obviously, it was some kind of a relief. So I said nothing as he pulled
the big prints from between the guard sheets and began to spread
them out.

The first ones he showed me were mainly of scenery; bold pieces
of cliff and brilliant sea, with the bright tangled flowers splashing
down over sunlit rock, and pictures of peasant women with their
goats and donkeys passing between hedgerows of apple blossom and
purple broom, or stooping over a stone cistern with their piles of
coloured washing. And the sea; this was in most of the pictures;
sometimes just the corner of a pool laced with seaweed, or the inside
of a curling wave, or the pattern of withdrawing foam over damp
sand; and one marvellous one of a rocky inlet where, smiling and
with bright intelligent eye, the dolphin lay watching the camera.

'Oh, look, the dolphin!' I cried, for the first time remembering my
morning's adventure. Godfrey Manning looked curiously at me, but
before I could say anything further Phyllida had lifted the print
aside, and I found myself staring down at a picture of the dead boy.

He was very like his sister; there was the round face and wide
smile, the sunburned skin, the thick black hair as springy as heather.
I saw at once what Godfrey had meant when he called the boy a
'natural model'; the sturdy body and thick neck which gave Miranda
her heavy, peasant look, were translated in the boy into a kind of
classical strength, the familiar, deliberately thickened lines of
sculpture. He fitted into the background of rock and sea as
inevitably as the pillars of the temple at Sunium.

Just as I was wondering how to break the silence, my sister broke
it quite easily.

'You know, Godfrey, I'm quite sure that later on, when things ease off a bit, Maria would love to have one of these. Why don't you do one for her?'

'If you think she would . . . It might be an idea. Yes, and I could frame it for her.' He began to put the prints back into the portfolio. 'Some time, perhaps, you'd help me choose the one you think she'd like?'

'Oh, there's no question,' said Phyllida, and pulled one out of the pile. 'This. It's the best I've seen in years, and exactly like him.'

He gave it a brief glance. 'Oh, yes. It was a lucky one.' His voice was quite colourless.

I said nothing, but stared and stared.

There was the dolphin, arching gently out of a turquoise sea, its back streaming silver drops. Standing thigh-deep beside the animal, laughing, with one hand stretched out to touch it, was the boy, bronzed and naked, his arrow-straight body cutting the arc made by the silver dolphin at the exact point known to painters as golden section. It was one of those miracles of photography–skill and chance combining to throw colour, light and mass into a flawless moment caught and held for ever.

I said: 'It's marvellous! There's no other word for it! It's a myth come true! If I hadn't seen the dolphin myself, I'd have thought it was faked!'

He had been looking down at the picture without expression. Now he smiled. 'Oh, it's genuine enough. Spiro tamed the beast for me, and it would come right in to play when he went swimming. It was a most co-operative creature, with a lot of personal charm. Did you say you'd seen it?'

'Yes. I've just been down for a swim, and it came to take a look at me. What's more, I may tell you, you nearly lost your dolphin for good and all this morning.'

'Lost the dolphin?' said Phyl. 'What on earth d'you mean?'

'Someone was shooting at it,' I said crisply. 'I came panting up here to tell you about it, but then your news knocked it clean out of my head till now.' I glanced up at Godfrey. 'When I was down in the bay, there was somebody up in the woods above, with a rifle, taking pot-shots. If I hadn't been there, and shooed the dolphin away, he'd probably have got it.'

'But . . . this is incredible!' This, at least, had broken through his preoccupation with Spiro's death. He stared at me frowningly. 'Someone up in these woods, shooting? Are you sure?'

'Quite sure. And, which makes it worse, the rifle was silenced – so it wasn't just some sportsman out after hares or something, amusing himself by sniping at the dolphin. It was a deliberate attempt to kill it. I was sitting up under the trees, and I suppose he hadn't seen me. But when I yelled and jumped in beside the dolphin, the shooting stopped.'

'But, Lucy!' Phyllida was horrified. 'You might have been hurt!'

'I didn't think,' I confessed. 'I was just so blazing mad, I had to stop him somehow.'

'You never do think! One of these days you *will* get hurt!' She turned, with a gesture half of exasperation, half of amusement, to Godfrey. 'She's always been the same. It's the only thing I've ever seen her really fly off the handle about – animals. She even rescues drowning wasps, and spiders out of the bath, and worms that come out when it rains and get caught crossing the road. The funny thing is, they see her coming. She once put her hand down on an adder, and it didn't even bite her.'

'It was probably knocked cold,' I said curtly, as embarrassed under Godfrey's amused look as if I was being accused of some odd perversion. I added, defiantly: 'I can't stand seeing anything hurt, that's all. So from now on I'll keep my eye on it if I have to bathe there every day. That dolphin of yours has got itself a one girl guard, Mr. Manning.'

'I'm delighted to hear it.'

Phyl said: 'I still can't believe it. Who in the world could it have been, up in those woods with a gun?'

I thought for a moment that he was going to answer, but he turned back to his task of stowing away the photographs, shutting the portfolio on the last of them with a snap. 'I can't imagine.' Then, to me: 'I suppose you didn't see anyone?'

'Oh, yes.'

This produced a gratifying amount of sensation. Phyllida gave a little squeak, and clapped a hand to where, roughly, one imagined Caliban to be. Godfrey Manning said quickly: 'You did? Where? I suppose you didn't get near enough to see who it was?'

'I did indeed, in the wood below the Castello terrace, and he was utterly beastly!' I said warmly. 'He said he was Julian Gale's son, and –'

'Max Gale!' This from Phyllida, incredulously. 'Lucy, you're not trying to tell me that Max Gale was running round in the woods with a rifle, loosing it off at all and sundry? Don't be silly!'

'Well, he did say it wasn't him,' I admitted, 'and he'd got rid of the gun, so I couldn't prove it was, but I didn't believe him. He *looked* as if he'd be capable of anything, and anyway, he was quite foully rude, and it wasn't a bit necessary!'

'You were trespassing,' said Godfrey dryly.

'Even so, it couldn't have been him!' said my sister positively.

'Probably not,' said Godfrey.

She looked at him sharply. 'What is it?'

'Nothing.'

But she had obviously understood whatever it was he hadn't said. Her eyes widened. 'But why in the world—?' She caught her breath, and I thought she changed colour. 'Oh, my God, I suppose it could be . . .! But Godfrey, that's frightful! If he got his hands on a gun—!'

'Quite. And if he did, naturally Gale would cover up.'

'Well, but what can we do? I mean, if there's any danger—'

'There won't be, now,' he said calmly. 'Look, Phyl, it'll be all right. If Max Gale didn't know before, he does now, and he'll have the sense to keep anything like that out of the old man's hands.'

'How?' she demanded. 'Just tell me how? Have you ever been in that ghastly museum of a place?'

'No. Why? Is there a gun-room or something?'

'Gun-room!' said Phyllida. 'Give me strength! Gun-room! The Castello walls are just about papered with the things! Guns, daggers, spears, assegais, the lot. I'll swear there's everything there from carbines to knuckle-dusters. There's even a cannon at the front door! Good heaven's, Leo's grandfather *collected* the things! Nobody's going to know if a dozen rifles or so go missing!'

'Now isn't that nice?' said Godfrey.

'Look,' I said forcibly, 'one minute more of this, and I shall scream. What's all the mystery? Are you two talking about Julian Gale? Because if you are I never heard anything so silly in my life. Why in the world should *he* go round getting savage with a rifle? He might pick off a few theatre critics—I can think of one who's been asking for it for years—but not that dolphin! It's just not possible.'

'D'you know him?' Godfrey Manning's tone was abrupt and surprised.

'I've never met him, he's way out of my star. But I've known stacks of people who've worked with him, and they all adored him. I tell you, it's not in character. And if you ask how I know that, let me tell you I've seen every play he's been in for the last ten years, and if there's one kind of person who can't hide what sort of man he is under everything he has to do and say, it's an actor. That's a paradox, I suppose, but it's true. And that Julian Gale could kill a living creature straight out of a Greek myth—no, it simply isn't on. Unless he was drunk, or went raving mad—'

I stopped. The look that had flashed between them would have wrecked a geiger-counter. There was a silence that could be felt.

'Well?' I said.

Godfrey cleared his throat awkwardly. He seemed uncertain of how to begin.

'Oh, for goodness' sake, if she's going to be here for a few weeks she'd better know,' said my sister. 'She's almost certain to meet him sooner or later. I know he only goes to the Karithis' place, and to play chess with someone in Corfu, and they never leave him alone the rest of the time, but I met him myself at the Karithis', and she may come across him any day in the grounds.'

'I suppose so.'

She turned to me. 'You said this morning that you wondered why he disappeared like that after he'd retired. You knew about the car smash three or four years ago, when his wife and daughter were killed?'

'Oh, lord, yes. It happened just the week before he opened in *Tiger Tiger*. I saw it after it had been running about a month. Lucky for him it was a part to tear a cat in, so he was better than ever, if possible, but he'd lost a couple of stones' weight. I know he was ill after he left the cast, and rumours started going round then that he was planning to retire, but of course nobody really believed them, and he seemed quite all right for the Stratford season; then they suddenly announced *The Tempest* as his last appearance. What happened, then? Was he ill again after that came off?'

'In a way. He finished up in a nursing home with a nervous breakdown, and he was there over a year.'

I stared at her, deeply shocked. 'I never knew that.'

'Nobody knew,' said my sister. 'It's not the sort of thing one advertises, especially if one's a public person like Julian Gale. I only knew myself because Max Gale said something to Leo when they rented the house, and then a friend of mine told me the rest. He's supposed to be better, and he does go out sometimes to visit friends, but there's always someone with him.'

I said flatly: 'You mean he has to be watched? You're trying to tell me that Julian Gale is—' I paused. Why were all the words so awful?

If they didn't conjure up grotesque images of Bedlam, they were even worse, genteel synonyms for the most tragic sickness of all, '–Unbalanced?' I finished.

'I don't know!' Phyllida looked distressed. 'Heaven knows one doesn't want to make too much of it, and the very fact that he was discharged–if that's the word–from the home must mean that he's all right, surely?'

'But he *must* be all right! Anyway, you said you'd met him. How did he seem then?'

'Perfectly normal. In fact, I fell for him like a ton of bricks. He's very charming.' She looked worriedly across at Godfrey. 'But I suppose these things can recur? I never thought . . . the idea wasn't even raised . . . but if I'd thought, with the children coming here for their holidays and everything–'

'Look,' said Godfrey briskly, 'you're making altogether too much of this, you know. The very mention of a gun seems to have blown everything up right out of proportion. The man's not a homicidal maniac or anything like it–and never has been, or he wouldn't be here at all.'

'Yes, I suppose you're right. Silly of me to panic.' She gave a sigh, and subsided in her chair. 'In any case Lucy probably dreamed it! If she never even saw a gun, and never heard it, either . . .! Oh, well, let's forget it, shall we?'

I didn't trouble to insist. It no longer mattered. What I had just learned was too fresh and too distressing. I said miserably: 'I wish I'd been a bit nicer to Mr. Gale, that's all. He must have had a foul time. It's bad enough for other people, but for his son–'

'Oh, honey, don't look so stricken!' Phyl, her worry apparently gone, was back in the role of comforter. 'We're all probably quite wrong, and there's nothing the matter at all, except that the old man needs a bit of peace and quiet to recuperate in, and Max is seeing he gets it! If it comes to that, I wouldn't be surprised if it's Max who insists on the quarantine for his own sake; he's writing the score for some film or other, so the story goes, and he never appears at all. Hence all the "trespassers will be shot" stuff, and young Adonis playing bodyguard.'

'Young *who?*'

'Adonis. The gardener.'

'Good heavens! Can anyone get away with a name like that, even in Greece?'

She laughed. 'Oh, he does, believe you me!'

She turned to Godfrey then, saying something about Adonis, who had apparently been a close friend of Spiro's. I caught Miranda's name again, and something about a dowry, and difficulties now that the brother was dead; but I wasn't really listening. I was still caught up unhappily in the news I had just heard. We do not take easily to the displacing of our idols. It was like making a long and difficult journey to see Michelangelo's David, and finding nothing there but a broken pedestal.

I found I was re-living, as clearly as if it had been yesterday, that 'last appearance' in *The Tempest*; the gentle, disciplined verses resigning Prospero's dark powers, and with them, if this story were true, so much more:

> '. . . *This rough magic*
> *I here abjure: and when I have requir'd*
> *Some heavenly music (which even now I do)*
> *To work mine end upon their senses, that*
> *This airy charm is for, I'll break my staff,*
> *Bury it certain fathoms in the earth,*
> *And deeper than did ever plummet sound*
> *I'll drown my book . . .*'

I stirred in my chair, pushed my own distress aside with an effort of will, and came back to the *salotto*, where Godfrey Manning was taking his leave.

'I'd better go. I meant to ask you, Phyl, when's Leo coming over?'

'He may manage this next weekend, I'm not sure. But definitely for Easter, with the children. D'you have to go? Stay to lunch, if you like. Maria's done the vegetables, thank goodness—how I hate potatoes in the raw!—and the rest's cold. Won't you stay?'

'I'd like to, but I want to get back to the telephone. There may be news.'

'Oh, yes, of course. You'll phone me straight away if you hear anything, won't you?'

'Certainly.' He picked up the portfolio. 'Let me know as soon as you think Maria would like to see me.'

He said his good-byes, and went. We sat in silence till the engine of his car faded among the trees.

'Well,' said my sister, 'I suppose we'd better find something to eat. Poor Godfrey, he's taking it hard. A bit surprising, really, I never thought he'd be knocked endways quite like that. He must have been fonder of Spiro than he cares to admit.'

'Phyl,' I said abruptly.

'Mm?'

'Was that true, or was it just another of your stories, when you said Julian Gale was probably Miranda's father?'

She looked at me sideways. 'Well . . . Oh, damn it, Lucy, you don't have to take everything quite so literally! Heaven knows–but there's something in it, only I don't know what. He christened the girl "Miranda", and can you imagine any Corfiote hatching up a name like that? And then Maria's husband deserted them. What's more, I'll swear Julian Gale's been supporting the family. Maria's never said a word, but Miranda's let things drop once or twice, and I'm sure he does. And why, tell me that? Not just because he happened to know the husband during the war!'

'Then if Miranda and Spiro were twins, he's Spiro's father, too?'

'The facts of life being what they are, you might even be right. Oh!' She went rigid in her chair, and turned large eyes on me. 'You mean–you mean someone ought to go and break the news to him?' All at once she looked very uncertain and flustered. 'But, Lucy, it's only a rumour, and one could hardly assume it, could one? I mean, think if one went over there, and –'

'I didn't mean that,' I said. 'In any case, it's not our job to tell him, Maria'll tell him herself. He'll hear soon enough. Forget it. Where's this lunch you were talking about? I'm starving.'

As I followed her out to the kitchen, I was reflecting that Julian Gale had almost certainly had the news already. From my chair facing the *salotto* windows, I had seen Maria and her daughter leave the house together. And not by the drive that would take them back to their own cottage. They had taken the little path that Miranda had showed me that morning, the path that led only to the empty bay, or to the Castello dei Fiori.

Chapter 4

He is drown'd
Whom thus we stray to find, and the sea mocks
Our frustrate search on land: well, let him go.

III. 3.

DAYS WENT BY, peaceful, lovely days. I kept my word, and went down daily to the bay. Sometimes the dolphin came, though never near enough for me to touch him, and, although I knew that for the animal's own sake I ought to try to frighten him and drive him away, his friendly presence delighted me so much that I couldn't bring myself to what would seem an act of betrayal.

I did keep a wary eye on the Castello terrace, but there was no further shooting incident, nor had there been any rumour that a local man might have been trespassing with a rifle. But I swam every day, and watched, and never left the bay until the dolphin had finally submerged and headed for the open sea.

There had been no news of Spiro. Maria and her daughter had come back to the Villa Forli the morning after the boy's death, and had gone stoically on with their work. Miranda had lost the plump brightness that characterised her; she looked as if she cried a lot, and her voice and movements were subdued. I saw little of Maria, who kept mostly to the kitchen, going silently about her work with the black head-kerchief pulled across her face.

The weather was brilliant, and hot even in the shade. Phyllida was rather listless. Once or twice she went with me on my sight-seeing trips, or into the town of Corfu, and one evening Godfrey Manning took us both to dine at the Corfu Palace Hotel, but on the whole the week slipped quietly by, while I bathed, and

sat on the terrace with Phyllida, or took the little car and drove
myself out in the afternoons to explore.

Leo, Phyllida's husband, hadn't managed to get away for the
weekend, and Palm Sunday came without a visit from him. Phyllida
had advised me to go into the town that morning to watch the Palm
Sunday procession, which is one of the four occasions in the year
when the island Saint, Spiridion, is brought out of the church where
he lies the year round in a dim shrine all smoky with taper-light, and
is carried through the streets in his golden palanquin. It is not an
image of the Saint, but his actual mummified body which is carried
in the procession, and this, somehow, makes him a very personal
and homely kind of patron saint to have; the islanders believe that he
had Corfu and all its people in his personal and always benevolent
care, and has nothing to do but concern himself deeply in all their
affairs, however trivial–which may explain why, on the procession
days, just about the whole population of the island crowds into the
town to greet him.

'What's more,' said my sister, 'it's a pretty procession, not just a
gaggle of top brass. And St. Spiro's golden chair is beautiful; you
can see his face quite clearly through the glass. You'd think it would
be creepy, but it's not, not a bit. He's so tiny, and so . . . well, he's a
sort of *cosy* saint!' She laughed. 'If you stay long in Corfu you'll begin
to get the feeling you know him personally. He's pretty well in
charge of the island, you know, looks after the fishing, raises the
wind, watches the weather for the crops, brings your boys safe
home from sea . . .' She stopped, then sighed. 'Poor Maria. I
wonder if she'll go today? She doesn't usually miss it.'

'What about you?' I asked. 'Are you sure you won't come with
me?'

She shook her head. 'I'll stay at home. You have to stand about for
rather a long time while the procession goes past, and there'll be a bit
of a crush. Caliban and I take up too much room. Home for lunch?
Good. Well, enjoy yourself.'

The little town of Corfu was packed with a holiday crowd, and
the air was loud with bells. Caught up in the river of people which
flowed through the narrow streets, I wandered happily along under
the sound of the bells, which competed with the subdued roar of
voices, and the occasional bursts of raucous brass from some upper
window, where a village band was struggling with some last-minute
practice. Shops were open, selling food and sweets and toys, their
windows crammed with scarlet eggs ready for Easter, cockerels,

dolls, baskets of tiny crystallised oranges, or enormous rabbits laden with Easter eggs. Someone tried to sell me a sponge the size of a football, and someone else to convince me that I must need a string of onions and a red plush donkey, but I managed to stay unburdened, and presently found my way to the Esplanade, which is Corfu's main square. Here the pavements were already packed, but when I tried to take my place at the back, the peasants—who must have come into town in the early morning, and waited hours for their places—made way for me with insistent gestures, almost forcing me forward into the place of honour.

Presently, from somewhere, a big bell struck, and there came the distant sound of the bands starting up. The vast crowd fell almost silent, all eyes turned to watch the narrow mouth of Nikephoros Street, where the first banners glinted, slowly moving up into the sunlight of the square. The procession had begun.

I am not sure what I had expected—a spectacle at once quaint and interesting, because 'foreign'—something to take photographs of, and then forget, till you got them out to look at, some evening at home. In fact, I found it very moving.

The bands—there were four of them, all gorgeously uniformed —played solemnly and rather badly, each a different tune. The village banners with their pious legends were crudely painted, enormous, and cruelly heavy, so that the men carrying them sweated and trembled under the weight, and the faces of the boys helping them wore expressions of fierce and dedicated gravity. There were variations in the uniforms of the school-children that were distinctly unconventional, but the standard of personal beauty was so high that one hardly noticed the shabby coats of the boys, or the cheap shoes the girls wore; and the young servicemen in their reach-me-down uniforms, with their noticeable absence of pipeclay and their ragged timing, had still about them, visibly, the glamour of two Thermopylaes.

And there was never a moment's doubt that all this was done in honour of the Saint. Crowded along the pavements in the heat, the people watched in silence, neither moving nor pushing. There were no police, as there would have had to be in Athens: this was their own Spiridion, their island's patron, come out into the sunlight to bless them.

And here he came. The Archbishop, a white-bearded ninety-two, walked ahead, followed by Church dignitaries, whose robes of saffron and white and rose shone splendidly in the sun, until, as they passed nearer, you saw the rubbed and faded patches, and the darns. Then came the forest of tall white candles, each with its gilt crown and wreath of flowers, and each one fluttering its long ribbons of white and lilac and scarlet. Then finally, flanked by the four great gilded lanterns, and shaded by its canopy, the gold palanquin approached, with the Saint himself inside it, sitting up for all to see; a tiny, withered mummy, his head sagging on to his left shoulder, the dead features flattened and formless, a pattern of shadows behind the gleaming glass.

All around me, the women crossed themselves, and their lips moved. The Saint and his party paused for prayer, and the music stopped. A gun boomed once in salute from the Old Fort, and as the echo died a flight of pigeons went over, their wings whistling in the silence.

I stood watching the coloured ribbons glinting in the sun, the wreaths of flowers fading already, and hanging crookedly from the crowned candles; the old, upraised hand of the Archbishop, and the faces of the peasant-women near me, rapt and shining under the snowy coifs. To my own surprise I felt my throat tighten, as if with tears.

A woman sobbed, in sudden, uncontrollable distress. The sound was loud in the silence, and I had glanced round before I could prevent myself. Then I saw it was Miranda. She was standing some yards from me, back among the crowd, staring with fiercely intent eyes at the palanquin, her lips moving as she crossed herself repeatedly. There was passion and grief in her face, as if she were reproaching the Saint for his negligence. There was nothing irreverent in such a thought; the Greek's religion is based on such simplicities. I suppose the old Church knew how great an emotional satisfaction there is in being able to lay the blame squarely and personally where it belongs.

The procession had passed; the crowd was breaking up. I saw Miranda duck back through it, as if ashamed of her tears, and walk quickly away. The crowds began to filter back again down the narrow main streets of the town, and I drifted with the tide, back down Nikephoros Street, towards the open space near the harbour where I had left the car.

Half-way down, the street opens into a little square. It chanced that, as I passed this, I saw Miranda again. She was standing under a plane tree, with her back to me, and her hands up to her face. I thought she was weeping.

I hesitated, but a man who had been hovering near, watching her, now walked across and spoke. She neither moved, nor gave any sign that she had heard him, but stood still with her back turned to him, and her head bowed. I couldn't see his face, but he was young, with a strong and graceful build that the cheap navy blue of his Sunday best suit could not disguise.

He moved up closer behind the girl, speaking softly and, it seemed, with a sort of urgent persuasion. It appeared to me from his gestures that he was pressing her to go with him up one of the side streets away from the crowd: but at this she shook her head, and I saw her reach quickly for the corner of her kerchief, and pull it across to hide her face. Her attitude was one of shy, even shrinking, dejection.

I went quickly across to them.

'Miranda? It's Miss Lucy. I have the car here, and I'm going back now. Would you like me to take you home?'

She did turn then. Above the kerchief her eyes were swollen with tears. She nodded without speaking.

I hadn't looked at the youth, assuming that he would now give up his importunities and vanish into the crowd. But he, too, swung round, exclaiming as though in relief:

'Oh, thank you! That's very kind! She ought not to have come, of course—and now there's no bus for an hour! Of course she must go home!'

I found myself staring, not at his easy assumption of responsibility for the girl, or even at the near-perfect English he spoke, but simply because of his looks.

In a country where beauty among the young is a commonplace, he was still striking. He had the fine Byzantine features, with the clear skin and huge, long-lashed eyes that one sees staring down from the walls of every church in Greece; the type which El Greco himself immortalised, and which still, recognisably, walks the streets. Not that this young man conformed in anything but the brilliant eyes and the hauntingly perfect structure of the face: there was nothing to be seen here of the melancholy and weakness which (understandably) tends to afflict the saintly persons who spend their days gazing down from the plaster on the church walls—the small-lipped mouths, the meekly slanted heads, the air of resignation and surprise with which the Byzantine saint properly faces the sinful world. This youth had, indeed, the air of one who had faced the sinful world for some years now, but had obviously liked it enormously, and had cheerfully sampled a good deal of what it had to offer. No church-plaster saint, this one. And not, I judged, a day over nineteen.

The beautiful eyes were taking me in with the frank appraisal of the Greek. 'You must be Miss Waring?'

'Why, yes,' I said, in surprise; then suddenly saw who, inevitably, this must be. 'And you're – Adonis?'

I couldn't for the life of me help bringing out the name with the kind of embarrassment one would feel in labelling one's own compatriot 'Venus' or 'Cupid'. That in Greece one could meet any day a Pericles, an Aspasia, an Electra, or even an Alcibiades, didn't help at all. It was the looks that did it.

He grinned. He had very white teeth, and eyelashes at least an inch long. 'It's a bit much, isn't it? In Greek we say "Àdoni".' (He pronounced it À-thoni.) 'Perhaps you'd find that easier to say? Not quite so cissy?'

'You know too much by half!' I said, involuntarily, and quite naturally, and he laughed, then sobered abruptly.

'Where is your car, Miss Waring?'

'It's down near the harbour.' I looked dubiously at the crowded street, then at the girl's bent head. 'It's not far, but there's a dreadful crowd.'

'We can go by a back way.' He indicated a narrow opening at the corner of the square, where steps led up into the shadow between two tall houses.

I glanced again at the silent girl, who waited passively. 'She will come,' said Adoni, and spoke to her in Greek, briefly, then turned to me, and began to usher me across the square and up the steps. Miranda followed, keeping a pace or so behind us.

He said in my ear: 'It was a mistake for her to come, but she is very religious. She should have waited. It is barely a week since he died.'

'You knew him well, didn't you?'

'He was my friend.' His face shut, as if everything had been said. As, I suppose, it had.

'I'm sorry,' I said.

We walked for a while in silence. The alleys were deserted, save for the thin cats, and the singing-birds in cages on the walls. Here and there, where a gap in the houses laid a blazing wedge of sunlight across the stones, dusty kittens baked themselves in patches of marigolds, or very old women peered from the black doorways. The

smell of charcoal-cooking hung in the warm air. Our steps echoed up
the walls, while from the main streets the sound of talk and laughter
surged back to us, muted like the roar of a river in a distant gorge.
Eventually our way opened into a broader lane, and a long flight of
shallow steps, which dropped down past a church wall straight to
the harbour square where I had left Phyl's little Fiat.

There were crowds here, too, but these were broken knots of
people, moving purposefully in search of transport home, or the
midday meal. Nobody paid any attention to us.

Adoni, who apparently knew the car, shouldered his way purposefully through the groups of people, and held out a hand to me
for the keys.

Almost as meekly as Miranda (who hadn't yet spoken a word) I
handed them over, and our escort unlocked the doors and ushered
her into the back seat. She got in with bent head, and sat well back
in a corner. I wondered, with some amusement, if this masterful
young man intended to drive us both home—and whether Phyl
would mind—but he made no such attempt. He shut the driver's
door on me and then got in beside me.

'You are used to our traffic now?'

'Oh, yes.' If he meant was I used to driving on the right-hand
side, I was. As for traffic, there was none in Corfu worth mentioning; if I met one lorry and half a dozen donkeys on an average
afternoon's excursion it was the most I had had to contend with. But
today there was the packed and teeming harbour boulevard, and
possibly because of this, Adoni said nothing more as we weaved our
way through the people and out on to the road north. We climbed a
steep, badly cambered turn, and then the road was clear between
high hedges of judas trees and asphodel. The surface was in places
badly pitted by the winter's rain, so I had to drive slowly, and the
third gear was noisy. Under cover of its noise I said quietly to
Adoni:

'Will Miranda and her mother be able to keep themselves, now
that Spiro has gone?'

'They will be cared for.' It was said flatly, and with complete
confidence.

I was surprised, and also curious. If Godfrey Manning had made
an offer, he would surely have told Phyllida so; and besides,
whatever he chose to give Maria now, he would hardly feel that he
owed this kind of conscience-money. But if it was Julian Gale who
was providing for the family, as Phyllida had alleged, it might mean

that her story of the twins' parentage was true. I would have been
less than human if I hadn't madly wanted to know.

I put out a cautious feeler. 'I'm glad to hear that. I didn't realise
there was some other relative.'

'Well,' said Adoni, 'there is Sir Gale, in a way, but I didn't mean
him or Max. I meant that I would look after them myself.'

'You?'

He nodded, and I saw him throw a half-glance over his shoulder
at Miranda. I could see her in the driving-mirror; she was taking no
notice of our soft conversation in English, which in any case may
have been too rapid for her to follow, but was staring dully out of the
window, obviously miles away. Adoni leaned forward and put a
finger on the radio button, a gadget without which no Greek or
Italian car ever seems to take the road. 'You permit?'

'Of course.'

Some pop singer from Athens Radio mooed from under the dash.
Adoni said quietly: 'I shall marry her. There is no dowry, but that's
no matter, Spiro was my friend, and one has obligations. He had
saved to provide for her, but now that he is dead her mother must
keep it; I can't take it.'

I knew that in the old Greek marriage-contract, the girl brought
goods and land, the boy nothing but his virility, and this was
considered good exchange; but families with a crop of daughters to
marry off had been beggared before now, and Miranda, cir-
cumstanced as she was, would hardly have had a hope of marriage.
Now here was this handsome boy calmly offering her a contract
which any family would have been glad to accept, and one in which,
moreover, he was providing all the capital; of the virility there could
certainly be no doubt, and besides, he had a good job in a country
where jobs are scarce, and, if I was any judge of character, he would
keep it. The handsome Adoni would have been a bargain at any
reckoning. He knew this, of course, he'd have been a fool not to; but
it seemed that he felt a duty to his dead friend, and from what I had
seen of him, he would fulfil it completely, efficiently, and to
everyone's satisfaction – not least Miranda's. And besides (I thought,
prosaically), Leo would probably come through with a handsome
wedding present.

'Of course,' added Adoni, 'Sir Gale may give her a dowry, I don't
know. But it would make no difference; I shall take her. I haven't
told her so yet, but later, when it's more fitting, I shall tell Sir Gale,
and he will arrange it.'

'I—yes, of course. I hope you'll both be very happy.'

'Thank you.'

I said: 'Sir Julian is . . . he makes himself responsible for them, then?'

'He was godfather to the twins.' He glanced at me. 'I think you have this in England, don't you, but it is not quite the same? Here in Greece the godfather, the *koumpàros*, is very important in the child's life, often as important as the real father, and it is he who arranges the marriage contract.'

'I see.' As simple as that. 'I did know Sir Julian had known the family for years, and had christened the twins, but I didn't know he—well, had a responsibility. The accident must have been a dreadful shock to him, too.' I added, awkwardly: 'How is he?'

'He is well. Have you met him yet, Miss Waring?'

'No. I understood he didn't see anyone.'

'He doesn't go out much, it's true, but since the summer he has had visitors. You've met Max, though, haven't you?'

'Yes.' There had been nothing in Adoni's voice to show what he knew about that meeting, but since he called him 'Max', without prefix, one might assume a relationship informal enough for Max to have told him just what had passed. Anyway, this was the faithful watch-dog who threw the callers over the cliff. No doubt he had heard all about it—and might even have had orders regarding further encroachments by Miss Lucy Waring . . .

I added, woodenly: 'I understood he didn't see anyone, either.'

'Well, it depends,' said Adoni cheerfully. He pulled a duster out from somewhere under the dashboard, and began to polish the inside of the screen. 'Not that this helps much, it's all the insects that get squashed on the outside. We're nearly there, or you could stop and I'd do it for you.'

'It doesn't matter, thanks.'

So that was as far as I'd get. In any case, Miranda seemed to be coming back to life. The back seat creaked as she moved, and in the mirror I could see that she had put back her kerchief, and was watching the back of Adoni's head. Something in her expression, still blurred though it was with tears, indicated that I had been right about the probable success of the marriage.

I said, in the brisk tone of one who changes the subject to neutral ground: 'Do you ever go out shooting, Adoni?'

He laughed, undeceived. 'Are you still looking for your criminal? I think you must be mistaken—there's no Greek would shoot a dolphin. I am a sailor, too—all Corfiotes are sailors—and the dolphin is the beast of fair weather. We even call it "dolphin weather"—the summer time, when the dolphins go with the boats. No, me, I only shoot people.'

'*People?*'

'That was a joke,' explained Adoni. 'Here we are. Thank you very much for bringing us. I'll take Miranda to her mother now, then I've promised to go back to the Castello. Max wants to go out this afternoon. Perhaps I shall see you there soon?'

'Thank you, but I—no, I doubt if you will.'

'That would be a pity. While you are here, you should see the orange orchards; they are something quite special. You have heard of the *koùm koyàts*—the miniature trees? They are very attractive.' That quick, enchanting smile. 'I should like to show them to you.'

'Perhaps some time.'

'I hope so. Come, Miranda.'

As I put the car into gear, I saw him usher the silent girl through her mother's door as if he already owned the place. Suppressing a sharp—and surely primitive—envy for a woman who could have her problems simply taken out of her hands and solved for her, willy-nilly, I put down my own independent and emancipated foot, and sent the little Fiat bucketing over the ruts of the drive, and down the turning to the Villa Forli.

At least, if Max Gale was to be out, I could have my afternoon swim in peace.

* * *

I went down after tea, when the heat was slackening off, and the cliff cast a crescent of shade at the edge of the sand.

Afterwards I dressed, picked up my towel, and began slowly to climb the path back to the villa.

When I reached the little clearing where the pool lay, I paused to get my breath. The trickle of the falling stream was cool and lovely, and light spangled down golden through the young oak-leaves. A bird sang somewhere, but only one. The woods were silent, stretching away dim-shadowed in the heat of the late afternoon. Bee-orchises swarmed by the water, over a bank of daisies. A blue tit flew across the clearing, obviously in a great hurry, its beak stuffed with insects for the waiting family.

A moment later the shriek came, a bird's cry of terror, then the rapid, machine-gun swearing of the parent tit. Some other small birds joined the clamour. The shrieks of terror jagged through the peaceful wood. I dropped my towel on the grass, and ran towards the noise.

The blue tits met me, the two parent birds, fluttering and shrieking, their wings almost brushing me as I ran up a twisting path, and out into the open stretch of thin grass and irises where the tragedy was taking place.

This couldn't have been easier to locate. The first thing I saw as I burst from the bushes was a magnificent white Persian cat, crouched picturesquely to spring, tail jerking to and fro in the scanty grass. Two yards from his nose, crying wildly, and unable to move an inch, was the baby blue tit. The parents, with anguished cries, darted repeatedly and ineffectually at the cat, which took not the slightest notice.

I did the only possible thing. I dived on the cat in a flying tackle, took him gently by the body, and held him fast. The tits swept past me, their wings brushing my hands. The little one sat corpse-still now, not even squeaking.

I suppose I could have been badly scratched, but the white cat had strong nerves, and excellent manners. He spat furiously, which was only to be expected, and wriggled to be free, but he neither scratched nor bit. I held him down, talking soothingly till he was quiet, then lifted him and turned away, while behind me the parent birds swooped down to chivvy their baby out of sight.

I hurried my captive out of the clearing before he got a chance to see where the birds were making for, and away at random through the bushes. Far from objecting to this, the cat seemed now rather pleased at the attention than otherwise; having had to surrender to *force majeure* he managed—in the way of his species—to let me know that he did in fact prefer to be carried . . . And when, presently, I found myself toiling up a ferny bank which grew steeper, and steeper yet, he even began to purr.

This was too much. I stopped.

'I'll tell you something,' I said to him, 'you weigh a ton. You can darned well walk, Butch, as from now! And I hope you know your way home from here, because I'm not letting you go back to those birds!'

I put him down. Still purring, he stropped himself against me a couple of times, then strolled ahead of me up the bank, tail high, to where at the top the bushes thinned to show bright sunlight. There he paused, glancing back and down at me, before stalking forward out of view.

He knew his way, no doubt of that. Hoping there was a path there that would take me back clear of the tangled bushes, I clambered up in his wake, to find myself in a big clearing, full of sunshine, the hum of bees, and a blaze of flowers that pulled me up short, gaping.

After the dappled dimness of the wood, it took some moments before one could more than blink at the dazzle of colour. Straight ahead of me an arras of wistaria hung fully fifteen feet, and below it there were roses. Somewhere to one side was a thicket of purple judas-trees, and apple blossom glinting with the wings of working bees. Arum lilies grew in a damp corner, and some other lily with petals like gold parchment, transparent in the light. And everywhere, roses. Great bushes of them rampaged up the trees; a blue spruce was half smothered with sprays of vivid Persian pink, and one dense bush of frilled white roses must have been ten feet high. There were moss roses, musk roses, damask roses, roses pied and streaked, and one old pink rose straight from a mediæval manuscript, hemispherical, as if a knife had sliced it across, its hundred petals as tightly whorled and packed as the layers of an onion. There must have been twenty or thirty varieties there, all in full bloom; old roses, planted years ago and left to run wild, as if in some secret garden whose key is lost. The place seemed hardly real.

I must have stood stock still for some minutes, looking about me, dizzied with the scent and the sunlight. I had forgotten roses could smell like that. A spray of speckled carmine brushed my hand, and I broke it off and held it to my face. Deep among the leaves, in the gap I had made, I saw the edge of an old metal label, and reached gingerly for it among the thorns. It was thick with lichen, but the stamped name showed clearly: Belle de Crécy.

I knew where I was now. Roses: they had been another hobby of Leo's grandfather's. Phyl had some of his books up at the Villa, and I had turned them over idly the other night, enjoying the plates and the old names which evoked, like poetry, the old gardens of France, of Persia, of Provence . . . Belle de Crécy, Belle Isis, Deuil du Roi de Rome, Rosamunde, Camäieux, Ispahan . . .

The names were all there, hidden deep in the rampant leaves, where some predecessor of Adoni's had lovingly attached them a century ago. The white cat, posing in front of an elegant background of dark fern, watched benevolently as I hunted for them, my hands filling with plundered roses. The scent was heavy as a drug. The air

zoomed with bees. The general effect was of having strayed out of
the dark wood into some fairy-tale. One almost expected the cat to
speak.

When the voice did come, suddenly, from somewhere above, it
nearly startled me out of my wits. It was a beautiful voice, and it
enhanced, rather than broke, the spell. It spoke, moreover, in
poetry, as deliberately elegant as the white cat:

> *'Most sure, the goddess*
> *On whom these airs attend: vouchsafe my prayer*
> *May know if you remain upon this Island?'*

I peered upwards, at first seeing no one. Then a man's head
appeared at the top of the wistaria—and only then did I realise that
the curtain of blossom hung in fact down some kind of high retaining
wall, which it had hidden. I saw, between the thick trusses of
flowers, sections of the stone balustrading. The terrace of the
Castello. The rose garden had been planted right up beside it.

I wanted to turn and run, but the voice held me. Needless to say it
was not Max Gale's; this was a voice I had heard many times before,
spinning just such a toil of grace as this in the stuffy darkness of
London theatres.

'*My prime request*,' added Sir Julian Gale, '*Which I do last pronounce,*
and which in fact you may think impertinent, *Is, O you wonder, If you
be maid, or no?*'

I suppose if I had met him normally, on our common ground of
the theatre, I might have been too overawed to do more than stutter.
But here at least the answer was laid down in the text, and had,
besides, the advantage of being the truth. I narrowed my eyes
against the sun, and smiled up at the head.

> '*No wonder, sir,*
> *But certainly a maid.*'

'*My language! Heavens!*' The actor abruptly abandoned the Bard,
and looked delighted. 'I was right! You're Max's trespasser!'

I felt myself flushing. 'I'm afraid I am, and I seem to be
trespassing again. I'm terribly sorry, I didn't realise the terrace was
quite so near. I wouldn't have dreamed of coming so far up, but I
was rescuing a bird from Butch there.'

'From whom?'

'The cat. Is he yours? I suppose he's called something terribly aristocratic, like Florizel, or Cosimo dei Fiori?'

'As a matter of fact,' said Julian Gale, 'I call him Nit. I'm sorry, but it's short for Nitwit, and when you get to know him, you'll see why. He's a gentleman, but he has very little brain. Now you're here, won't you come up?'

'Oh, no!' I spoke hastily, backing a little. 'Thanks all the same, but I've got to get back.'

'I can't believe there's all that hurry. Won't you please take pity on me and break the deadly Sabbath peace up a little? Ah!' He leaned further over. 'Not only trespass, I see, but theft as well! You've been stealing my roses!'

This statement, uttered in the voice whose least whisper was clearly audible in the back row of the gallery, had all the force of an accusation made before the High Praesidium. I started guiltily, glanced down at the forgotten blooms in my hands, and stammered:

'Well, yes, I–I have. Oh, murder . . . I never thought . . . I mean, I took it they were sort of wild. You know, planted ages ago and just left . . .' My voice faltered, as I looked round me and saw what I hadn't noticed before, that the bushes, in spite of their riotous appearance, were well shaped, and that the edges of the mossed paths were tidily clipped. 'I–I suppose this is your garden now, or something? I'm most terribly sorry!'

' "Or something?" By heaven, she picks an armful of my beloved Gallicas, and then thinks they come out of my garden "or something"! That settles it, young woman! By all the rules, you have to pay a forfeit. If Beauty strays into the Beast's garden, literally loaded with his roses, she's asking for trouble, isn't she? Come along, now, and no arguments!There are the steps. Nit'll bring you up. Nitwit! Show the lady the way!'

The white cat rose, blinked at me, then swarmed in an elaborately careless manner up the wistaria, straight into Julian Gale's arms. The latter straightened, smiling.

'Did I say he hadn't much brain? I traduced him. Do you think you could manage something similar?'

His charm, the charm that had made Phyllida fall for him 'like a ton of bricks', was having its effect. I believe I had completely forgotten what else she had told me about him.

I laughed. 'In my own plodding way, I might.'

'Then come along.'

The way up was a flight of shallow steps, half hidden by a bush of

York and Lancaster. It curved round the base of some moss-green statue, and brought me out between two enormous cypresses, on to the terrace.

Julian Gale had set the cat down, and now advanced on me.

'Come in, Miss Lucy Waring. You see, I've heard all about you. And here's my son. But, of course, you've already met . . . '

Chapter 5

You do look, my son, in a mov'd sort,
As if you were dismay'd: be cheerful, sir.

IV. I.

MAX GALE WAS sitting there under the stone-pine, at a big table covered with papers. As he got to his feet, I stopped in my tracks.

'But I thought you weren't here!' I hadn't thought I could have blurted out anything quite so naïve. I finished the performance by blushing furiously and adding, in confusion: 'Adoni said . . . I thought . . . I'm sure he said you'd be out!'

'I was, but only till tea-time. How do you do?' His eyes, indifferent rather than hostile, touched mine briefly, and dropped to the roses in my hands. It was possibly only to fill the sizzling pause of embarrassment that he asked: 'Was Adoni down in the garden?'

I saw Sir Julian's glance flick from one to the other of us. 'He was not, or he might have stopped her pillaging the place! She's made a good selection, hasn't she? I thought she should be made to pay a forfeit, *à la* Beauty and the Beast. We'll let her off the kiss on such short acquaintance, but she'll have to stay and have a drink with us, at least!'

I thought I saw the younger man hesitate, and his glance went down to the littered table as if looking there for a quick excuse. There wasn't far to look; the table was spread with scribbled manuscript scores, notebooks, and papers galore, and on a chair beside it stood a tape-recorder with a long flex that trailed over the flags and in through an open french window.

I said quickly: 'Thank you, but I really can't—'

'You're in no position to refuse, young lady!' Sir Julian's eyes held a gleam of amusement, whether at my reluctance or his son's it was impossible to guess. 'Come now, half an hour spent entertaining a recluse is a small price to pay for your loot. Have we some sherry, Max?'

'Yes, of course.' The colourlessness of his voice might after all only be in comparison with his father's. 'I'm afraid we've no choice, Miss Waring. Do you like it dry?'

'Well . . .' I hesitated. I would have to stay now. I could hardly snub Sir Julian, who was after all my host, and besides, I had no wish to pass up the chance to talk to a man who was at the head of my own profession, and whom I had admired and loved for as long as I could remember. 'Actually, if there is one, I'd love a long drink, long and cold . . .? I've just been swimming, and I'm genuinely thirsty. Would there be any orange juice, or something like that?'

'You ask that here? Of course.' Max Gale smiled at me suddenly, and with unexpected charm, and went into the house.

As at the Villa Forli, there were long windows opening from the terrace into some big room, all of them shuttered against the sun except the one through which Max Gale had vanished. Through this dark opening I thought I could make out the shapes of a grand piano, what looked like a huge gramophone, and a revolving bookcase. The tops of the two last were stacked with books and records.

'Sun or shade?' asked Sir Julian, pulling up a gaudy camp chair for me. I chose sun, and he settled himself beside me, the sombre wall of cypresses beyond the balustrade making as effective a backcloth for him as the ferns had for the white cat. The latter, purring, jumped up on to the actor's knee, turned carefully round twice, and settled down, paws going.

The pair of them made a striking picture. Sir Julian was not–had never been–handsome, but he was a big man, of the physical type to which the years can add a sort of heavy splendour. (One remembered his Mark Antony, and how after it all other attempts at the part seemed to be variations of his; attempts, in fact, to play *him*.) He had the powerful breadth of chest and shoulder that runs to weight in middle age, and his head was what is commonly called leonine–thick grey hair, a brow and nose in the grand manner, and fine grey eyes–but with some hint of weakness about the jaw from which the charm of the wide mouth distracted you. His eyes looked pouchy and a little strained, and there were sagging lines in his face which naturally I had never seen across the footlights, lines which might be those of petulance or dissipation, or merely a result of his illness and consequent loss of weight. It was difficult to tell just where his undeniable attractiveness lay; it would, indeed, be hard to give any definite description of him: his face was too familiar for that, melting as one watched him into one character after another that he had made his own, as if the man only existed as one saw him on the stage – king, madman, insurance salesman, soldier, fop . . . as if in leaving that lighted frame, he ceased to exist. It was a disquieting idea when one remembered that he had, in fact, left his frame. If he could not be himself now, he was nothing.

He glanced up from the cat, caught me staring, and smiled. He must be very used to it. What he cannot have realised is that I was trying to find in his face and movements some evidence of nervous strain that might justify Phyllida's fears. But he seemed quite self-contained and relaxed, his hands (those betrayers) lying motionless and elegantly disposed – perhaps just a bit too elegantly disposed? – over the cat's fur.

'I'm sorry,' I said, 'was I staring? I've never been so close to you before. It's usually the upper circle.'

'With me tastefully disguised behind several pounds of false beard, and robed and crowned at that? Well, here you see the man himself, poor bare forked creature that he is. I won't ask you what you think of him, but you must at least give me your opinion of his setting. What do you think of our crumbling splendours?'

'The Castello? Well, since you ask . . . I'd have said it wasn't quite *you*. It would make a marvellous background for a Gothic thriller – *Frankenstein*, or *The Mysteries of Udolpho*, or something.'

'It would, wouldn't it? One feels it ought to be permanently shrouded in mist, with vampires crawling down the walls – not surrounded by flowers and the peace and sunshine of this enchanted island. However, I suppose it's highly appropriate for a decayed actor to retire to, and it's certainly a haven of peace, now that Max has clamped down on the sightseers.'

'I heard you'd been ill. I'm sorry. We – we miss you terribly in London.'

'Do you, my dear? That's nice of you. Ah, Max, here you are. Miss Waring thinks the house is a perfect setting for Frankenstein and his monster.'

'I did not! I never said – I certainly didn't put it like that!'

Max Gale laughed. 'I heard what you said. You could hardly insult this kind of crazy baroque anyway. Loco rococo. This is fresh orange, is that all right for you?'

'Lovely, thank you.'

He had brought the same for himself, and for his father. I noticed that the latter's hand, as he put it out for the glass, shook badly, and his son quickly lifted a small iron table within reach, set the glass down on that, and poured the iced juice in. Sir Julian dropped his hands back into the cat's fur, where they once more lay statue-still. I had been right about the self-consciousness of that pose. But it hadn't been vanity, unless it is vanity that conceals a weakness of which one is ashamed.

As Max Gale poured my drink, I made to lay the roses on the table, but he set the jug down and put out a hand.

'Give them to me. I'll put them in water for you till you go.'

'So I'm to be allowed to keep them, after I've paid the forfeit?'

'My dear child,' said Sir Julian, 'you're welcome to the lot! I hope you don't take my teasing seriously, it was only an excuse to make you come up. I'm only glad you liked them so much.'

'I love them. They look like the roses in old pictures – you know, real roses in old story-books. *The Secret Garden*, and Andrew Lang's *Sleeping Beauty*, and the *Arabian Nights*.'

'That's just what they are. That one was found growing on a pavilion in Persia, where Haroun al Raschid may have seen it. This is the one out of the Romance of the Rose. And this was found growing in Fair Rosamund's garden at Woodstock. And this, they say, is the oldest rose in the world.' His hands were almost steady as he touched the flowers one by one. 'You must come back for more when these die. I'd leave them in the music-room, Max, it's reasonably cool . . . Now, pay up, Miss Lucy Waring. I'm told you're in the business, and one of the reasons I lured you up here was to hear all you can give me of the latest gossip. The facts I can get from the periodicals, but the gossip is usually a great deal more entertaining – and quite often twice as true. Tell me . . .'

I forget now just what he asked me, or how much I was able to tell him, but though I moved in very different theatrical circles from him, I did know a good deal of what was going on in Town; and I remember that in my turn I found it exciting to hear him using, casually and in passing, names which were as far above my touch as the clouds on Mount Pantokrator. He certainly gave me the impression that he found me good value as an entertainer, but how far this was due to his own charm I can't guess, even today. I know that when, finally, he turned the conversation to my affairs, you'd have thought this was the big moment towards which all the star-spangled conversation had been leading.

'And now tell me about yourself. What are you doing, and where? And why have we never met before?'

'Oh, heavens, I'm not anywhere near your league! I'd only just got to the West End, as it was!'

I stopped. The last phrase had been a dead giveaway, not only of the facts, but of feelings which I had not discussed, even with Phyllida. I had my vanities, too.

'Play folded?' Where a layman's sympathy would have jarred, his matter-of-fact tone was marvellously comforting. 'What was it?'

I told him, and he nodded.

'Yes, that was McAndrew's pet pigeon, wasn't it? Not a very wise venture on Mac's part, I thought. I read the play. Who were you? What's-her-name, the girl who has those unlikely hysterics all over Act Two?'

'Shirley. Yes. I was rotten.'

'There was nothing there to get hold of. That sort of fantasy masquerading as working-class realism needs rigid selection and perfect timing—not merely uncontrolled verbal vomit, if you'll forgive the phrase. And he never can do women, haven't you noticed?'

'Maggie in *The Single End*?'

'Do you call her a woman?'

'Well . . . I suppose you're right.'

'I'm right in telling you not to blame yourself over Shirley. What comes next?'

I hesitated.

'Like that, is it?' he said. 'Well, it happens. How wise of you to cut and run for Corfu while you could! I remember . . .' And he turned neatly off into a couple of malicious and very funny stories involving a well-known agent of the thirties, and a brash young actor whom I had no difficulty in identifying as Sir Julian Gale himself. When he had finished, and we had done laughing, I found myself countering with some of my own experiences which I had certainly never expected to find funny—or even to tell anybody about. Now, for some reason, to talk about them was a kind of release, even a pleasure, while the crenellated shadow of the Castello advanced unheeded across the weedy flags, and Sir Julian Gale listened, and commented, and asked questions, as if he had 'lured' me to his terrace for no other reason than to hear the life story of a mediocre young actress who would never play anything but seconds in her life.

A slight sound stopped me, and brought me sharply round. I had forgotten all about Max Gale. I hadn't heard him come out of the house again, but he was there, sitting on the balustrade well within hearing. How long he had been there I had no idea.

It was only then that I realised how the light had faded. My forfeit was paid, and it was time to be gone, but I could hardly take my leave within seconds, as it were, of acknowledging Max Gale's presence. I had to make some motion of civility towards him first.

I looked across at him. 'Did you go to watch the procession this morning, Mr. Gale?'

'I? Yes, I was there. I saw you in the town. Did you get a good place?'

'I was on the Esplanade, at the corner by the Palace.'

'It's rather . . . appealing, don't you think?'

'Very.' I smiled. 'Being a musician, you'd appreciate the bands.'

He laughed, and all at once I saw his father in him. 'Very much. And when all four play at the same time, it really is something.'

'The leitmotif for your *Tempest*, Max,' said his father, stroking the white cat. ' "*The isle is full of noises.*" '

Max grinned. 'Perhaps. Though even I might fight shy of reproducing some of them.'

Sir Julian turned to me. 'My son is writing a score for a film version of *The Tempest*.'

'Is that what it's to be? How exciting! I gather you've come to the right place to do it, too. Is that why you chose Corfu after you'd drowned your book at Stratford, Sir Julian?'

'Not really; the thing's fortuitous. I've known the island on and off for thirty years, and I've friends here. But it's a pleasant chance that brought this work to Max when we happened to be marooned here.'

'Do you really think this is Prospero's island?'

'Why not?' asked Julian Gale, and Max said, 'That's torn it,' and laughed.

I looked at him in surprise. 'What have I said?'

'Nothing. Nothing at all. But if you will invite a man to explain a theory he's been brooding over for weeks, you must be prepared for a lecture, and by the gleam in my father's eye, nothing can save you now.'

'But I'd love to hear it! Besides, your father could make the Telephone Directory sound like *War and Peace* if he tried, so his private theory about *The Tempest* ought to be *something*! Don't take any notice of him, Sir Julian! Why do you think this might be Prospero's island?'

'You are a delightful young lady,' said Sir Julian, 'and if you wish to dig my roses out by the roots and carry them away, I shall send Adoni to help you. No, on second thoughts, Max can do it. It would be good for him to do a little real work, instead of floating around in that lunatic fringe where musicians seem to live . . . Who was it who said that the really wise man isn't the man who wants a thing proved before he'll believe in it, but the man who is prepared to believe anything until it's shown to be false?'

'I don't know, but it sounds to me like somebody's definition of a visionary or a genius.'

'*All* the roses,' said Sir Julian warmly. 'Did you hear that, Max? My theories about *The Tempest* are those of a visionary and a genius.'

'Oh, sure,' said his son.

He was still sitting on the balustrade, leaning back against the stone urn that stood at the corner. I had been watching his face covertly for some resemblance to his father, but, except for his build, and an occasional chance expression, could see none. His eyes were dark, and more deeply set, the mouth straighter, the whole face less mobile. I thought the hint of the neurotic was there, too, in the faint lines between the brows, and somewhere in the set of the mouth. The careful under-emphasis in all he said and did might well be a deliberate attempt to control this, or merely to avoid profiting by his father's charm. Where Sir Julian seemed automatically, as it were, to make the most of his lines, Max threw his away. It seemed to me that he was even concerned not to be liked, where his father, consciously or not, had the actor's need to be loved.

'There is no evidence of any kind,' Sir Julian was saying, 'to connect this island with the island of the play, any more than we can prove it was the "Scheria" of Odysseus and Nausicaa; but in both cases tradition is strong, and when traditions persist hard enough, it seems only sensible to conclude that there may be something in them worth investigating.'

'Schliemann and Troy,' murmured Max.

'Exactly,' said Sir Julian. He gave me that sudden smile that was so like his son's. 'So, being like Schliemann a genius and a visionary, and being determined to believe that Corfu *is* Prospero's island, I've been looking for evidence to prove it.'

'And is there any?'

'Perhaps not "evidence". That's a strong word. But once you start looking, you can find all sorts of fascinating parallels. Start with the easiest, the description of the natural details of the island, if you can remember them.'

'I think I can, fairly well. There's rather more physical description of the setting than you usually find in Shakespeare, isn't there?'

'I'd say more than anywhere, except *Venus and Adonis*. And what description one gleans from the play fits this island well enough; the pines, tilled lands, the fertility (not so many of the Mediterranean islands are really fertile, you know), the beaches and coves, the lime groves outside Prospero's cave . . .' He lifted a hand to point where a group of trees stood golden-green beside the pines on the southern promontory. 'There are young limes growing all down the cliff beyond Manning's villa, and the whole coast is honeycombed with caves. You might say these things are found on any island, but one thing isn't—the brine-pits that Caliban talks about, remember?'

'And there are some here?'

'Yes, down at Korissia, in the south. They've been there for centuries.'

'What about the pignuts and filberts he promised to dig up? Do they grow here?'

'Filberts certainly, and pignuts, too, if he means the English sort. And if he means truffles—as I believe—yes, those too.'

'And the marmosets?' I asked it diffidently, as one who puts a question in doubtful taste.

Sir Julian waved the marmosets aside. 'A momentary confusion with the still-vex'd Bermoothes. No doubt Ariel had been shooting a nice line in travel-tales, and the poor monster was muddled.'

Max said: 'You can't argue with a man with an obsession. Humour him, Miss Waring.'

'I'll do no such thing! If a theory's worth holding, it's worth fighting over! What about the *story*, then, Sir Julian? Take the start of it, the shipwreck. If the ship was on its way from Tunis to Naples, you'd think Corfu was just a little too far off course—'

'Ah, yes, you run up against the same thing in the Odysseus story, where they're supposed to have rowed—rowed, mark you—from Scheria to Euboea in a single night. But to my mind that does nothing to discount Corfu's claim to be Scheria. It's poetic truth, the kind of telescoping that you find in the seven days of Creation—one assumes that the gods helped them. The same with the Neapolitan ship in *The Tempest*. The storm was a tremendous one, an historic tempest. The ship was blown right off her course, and could have been driven blindly along for days before fetching up on these coastal rocks. Can't you see that what makes the story plausible is its very unlikelihood?'

'Have a heart,' said his son, 'of course she can't.'

'It's very simple. The fact that the ship did end up here, so fantastically off course, made it necessary later on to explain the storm as being magical, or somehow supernatural.'

'Just a minute,' I said quickly. ' "The fact?" Are you trying to say that the business of the shipwreck is *true*?'

'Only that like all legends it could be founded on the truth, just as there really was a Cretan labyrinth, and a Troy that burned. It's my guess—strictly as a visionary—that there was in fact some spectacular wreck here, that became the basis of a legend.'

'No more than a guess? You haven't found any actual Corfiote story, or any real record?'

'No.'

'Then why here? Why Corfu? Your geographical details don't prove a thing. They might confirm, but they're hardly a start.'

Sir Julian nodded, smoothing the cat's head with a gentle finger. 'I started at the wrong end. I should have begun, not with the "facts", but with the play—the play's king-pin, Prospero. To my mind, the conception of his character is the most remarkable thing about the play; his use as a sort of summing-up of Shakespeare's essay on human power. Look at the way he's presented: a father-figure, a magician in control of natural forces like the winds and the sea, a sort of benevolent and supernatural Machiavelli who controls the island and all who are in it.'

He finished on a faint note of inquiry, and looked at me with raised eyebrows, waiting for my reply.

'Saint Spiridion?'

'Saint Spiridion. Exactly!' He glanced up at Max, as if showing off the cleverness of a favourite pupil. I saw Max smile faintly. 'Even the name . . . you'll notice the similarity; and its abbreviation, Spiro, makes it even closer.' The shadow which touched his face was gone immediately. 'Saint Spiridion—his body, that is—was brought here in 1489, and in no time at all he had the reputation for all sorts of magic, miracles if you like, especially weather-magic. There was another saint, a female, brought with him. Her mummy is also in a church in the town, but she didn't catch the public imagination, so she doesn't get the outings. In fact, I can't even remember her name.'

'I've never even heard she existed,' I said.

He smiled. 'It's a man's country. But she may well be the origin of the *idea* of Miranda, the magician's daughter. She would hardly survive into legend merely as a female companion, or even as a wife. Magicians don't have them, for reasons which I suppose it would be fascinating to explore, but which you might disagree with, Miss Lucy Waring.'

'I know, Delilah and Co. All right, I don't resent it, it's a man's world. If it comes to that, witches don't have husbands, not the real old fairy-story witches, anyway.'

'Fair enough.' Sir Julian leaned back in his chair. 'Well, there you have your starting point, the fabulously fertile island of Corfu, guarded by a saint who is believed to control the weather. Now we postulate a tempest, some historic humdinger of a storm, when some important ship–perhaps even with a few Italian V.I.P.'s on board–was driven far off course and wrecked here, but with her passengers saved from drowning by some apparent miracle that would be imputed to the Saint. So, a legend starts to grow. Later the Germanic elements of fairy-tale are added to it–the "magic", the beautiful daughter, the fairy characters.' He paused, with a mischievous gleam at me. 'It would be nice if one could somehow equate the elementals with the facts of the island's history, wouldn't it? I've tried my hardest to see the "foul witch Sycorax" from "Argier", as a sort of personification of the Moslem rulers who penned the heavenly power–Ariel–in a cloven pine till the Saint-magician released him . . . But I'm afraid I can't quite make that one stick.'

'What a pity!' I said it quite without irony: I was enjoying myself vastly. 'And Caliban? Paganism or something?'

'If you like. There's the brutality, the sexuality, and the superbly sensitive poetry. And he was certainly a Greek.'

'How d'you work that out?' I asked, startled.

He chuckled. 'He welcomed Prospero to the island with "water with berries in it". Haven't you come across the Greek custom of giving you berried jam in a glass of water?'

'No, I haven't. But really, you can't have that! It could even be coffee! What would that make him? French?'

'All right,' he said amiably, 'we'll leave poor Caliban as an

"infernal" seeking for grace. Well, that's all.' Here the white cat
stretched, flexed its claws, and yawned, very loudly. Sir Julian
laughed. 'You shouldn't have encouraged me. Nitwit has heard it all
before, and so, I'm afraid, has poor Max.'

'Well, I hadn't, and it's fascinating. One could have endless fun. I
must read it again and look for all these things. I wish I thought my
sister had a copy here.'

'Take mine,' he said immediately. 'It should be somewhere on top
of the bookcase, I think, Max . . . Thanks very much.' This as his
son went to get it.

I said quickly: 'But if you're working on it –'

'Working?' The word, lightly spoken as it was, sounded somehow
out of tune. 'You've just heard how seriously. In any case I use a
Penguin for working, one I can mark and cut up . . . Ah, thank you,
Max; and here are your roses, too. That's my own copy; it's a bit
ancient, and I'm afraid it's been scribbled in, but perhaps you can
ignore that.'

I had already seen the pencilled notes. Holding the book as if it
were the original Blackfriars prompt copy, with the author's jottings
in the margin, I got to my feet. Sir Julian rose with me, and the
white cat, displaced, jumped down and stalked with offended
dignity off the terrace and down the steps to the rose garden.

'I'll really have to go,' I said. 'Thank you for the book, I'll take
great care of it. I–I know I've stayed far too long, but I've really
loved it.'

'My dear child, you've done us both a kindness. I've enjoyed your
visit enormously, and I hope you'll come back soon. As you see,
there's a limit to the amount of my conversation that Max and the cat
will stand, and it's pleasant to have a good-mannered and captive
audience again. Well, if you must . . . '

The woods were dark already with the quickly falling twilight.
Mr. Gale, accompanying me politely to the edge of the rose garden,
pointed out the path which led down to the clearing where the pool
lay. The beautiful Nitwit was there, dreamily regarding a large
moth which hovered near some honeysuckle. Max Gale picked him
up, said good-bye to me, and went quickly back. A very few
minutes later I heard the sound of the piano. He had lost no time in
getting back to work. Then the woods closed in and I was out of
hearing.

The woods were always quiet, but now, with the darkness

muffling their boughs, they seemed to hold a hushed and heavy stillness that might be the herald of storm. The scent of flowers hung like musk on the air.

As I picked my way carefully down the path I was thinking of the recent interview; not of the 'theory' with which Sir Julian had been beguiling his exile, but of Sir Julian himself, and what Phyl and Godfrey had said about him.

That there had been—still was—something badly wrong seemed obvious: not only was there the physical evidence that even I could see, there was also that attitude of watchful tension in the younger man. But against this could be set the recent conversation, not the normal—and even gay—tone of it, but the use of certain phrases that had struck me. Would a man who had recently emerged from a mental home talk so casually and cheerfully about the 'lunatic fringe' inhabited by his son? A son had, after all, a big stake in his father's sanity. And would the son, in his turn, speak of his father's 'obsession', and the need to 'humour' him? Perhaps if the need were serious, this was Mr. Gale's way of passing off a potentially tricky situation? Perhaps that edgy, watchful air of his was on my behalf as much as his father's?

Here I gave up. But as for the idea of Sir Julian's roaming the countryside with a rifle to the danger of all and sundry, I could believe it no more than formerly. I would as soon suspect Phyllida, or Godfrey Manning himself.

And (I thought) I would suspect Max Gale a darned sight sooner than any.

I could hear the trickle of water now, and ahead of me was the break in the trees where the pool lay. At the same moment I became conscious of a strange noise, new to me, like nothing more or less than the clucking and chattering of a collection of hens. It seemed to come from the clearing.

Then I realised what it was; the evening chorus at the pool—the croaking of the innumerable frogs who must live there. I had stopped at the edge of the clearing to pick up my towel, and some of them must have seen me, for the croaking stopped, and then I heard the rhythmic plopping of small bodies diving into the water. Intrigued, I drew back behind the bushes, then made a silent way round the outer edge of the clearing towards the far side of the pool, where there was cover. Now I was above the bank. I gently pressed the branches aside, and peered down.

At first, in the dusk I could see nothing but the dark gleam of the water where the sky's reflection struck it between the upper boughs, and the matt circles of the small lily leaves and some floating weed. Then I saw a frog, a big one, sitting on a lily-pad, his throat distended and pulsing with his queer little song. His body was fat and freckled, like a laurel leaf by moonlight, and the light struck back from eyes bright as blackberry-pips. Close by him sang another, and then another . . .

Amused and interested, I stood very still. Growing every moment in volume, the chorus gobbled happily on.

Silence, as sudden as if a switch had been pressed. Then my frog dived. All around the lily-pads the surface ringed and plopped as the whole choir took to the water. Someone was coming up the path from the bay.

For a moment I wondered if Phyllida had been down to the beach to find me; then I realised that the new-comer was a man. His steps were heavy, and his breathing, and then I heard him clear his throat softly, and spit. It was a cautious sound, as if he were anxious not to make too much noise. The heavy steps were cautious, too, and the rough, hurried breathing, which he was obviously trying to control, sounded oddly disquieting in the now silent woods. I let the bushes slip back into place, and stood still where I was, to wait for him to pass.

The dimming light showed him as he emerged into the clearing; Greek, someone I hadn't seen before, a young man, thick-set and broad-chested, in dark trousers and a high-necked fisherman's sweater. He carried an old jacket of some lighter colour over one arm.

He paused at the other side of the pool, but only to reach into a pocket for a cigarette, which he put between his lips. But in the very act of striking the match, he checked himself, then shrugged, and put it away again, shoving the cigarette behind his ear. He could not have indicated his need for secrecy more plainly if he had spoken.

As he turned to go on his way, I saw his face fairly clearly. There was a furtive, sweating excitement there that was disturbing, so that when he glanced round as if he had heard some noise, I found myself shrinking back behind my screen of leaves, conscious of my own quickened heart-beats.

He saw nothing. He drew the back of a hand over his forehead, shifted his coat to the other arm, and trod with the same hasty caution up the steep path towards the Castello.

Above me a sudden gust of wind ran through the treetops, and chilly air blew through the trunks with the fresh, sharp smell of coming rain.

But I kept quite still until the sound of the Greek's footsteps had died away, and beside me the frog had climbed out again on to his lily-pad, and swelled his little throat for song.

Chapter 6

Methinks he hath no drowning mark upon him.
I. I.

FOR SOME REASON that I never paused to examine, I didn't tell my sister about my visit to the Gales, not even when next morning she decided that for once she would go down to the bay with me, and, as we passed the pool, pointed out the path that led up to the Castello.

The clearing looked very different this morning with the high clear light pouring into it. There had been a sudden little snap of storm during the night, with a strong wind that died with the dawn, and this had cleared the air and freshened the woods. Down in the bay the sand was dazzling in the morning sun, and the wake of the wind had left a ripple at the sea's edge.

I spread a rug in the shade of the pines that overhung the sand, and dumped our things on it.

'You are coming in, aren't you?'

'Sure thing. Now I'm down here, nothing will stop me from wallowing in the shallow bit, even if I do look like a mother elephant expecting twins. That's a smashing swimsuit, Lucy, where'd you get it?'

'Marks and Spencers.'

'Good heavens.'

'Well, I didn't marry a rich man,' I said cheerfully, pulling up the shoulder-straps.

'And a fat lot of good it does me in my condition.' She looked sadly down at her figure, sighed, and dropped her smart beach coat down beside the hold-all containing all the sun-lotions, magazines,

Elizabeth Arden cosmetics and other paraphernalia without which she would never dream of committing herself to the beach. 'It isn't fair. Just look at me, and these things come from Fabiani.'

'You poor thing,' I said derisively. 'Will they go in the water? And for Pete's sake, are you going to bathe with that Koh-i-noor thing on?'

'Heavens, no!' She slipped the enormous marquise diamond off her finger, dropped it into the plastic bag that held her cosmetics, and zipped the bag shut. 'Well, let's go in. I only hope your friend doesn't mistake me for the dolphin, and let fly. Much the same general shape, wouldn't you say?'

'You'll be all right. He doesn't wear yellow.'

'Seriously, there *isn't* anyone watching, is there, Lucy? I'd just as soon not have an audience.'

'If you keep near inshore they can't see you anyway, unless they come to the front of the terrace. I'll go and look.'

The water in the shade of the pines was a deep, deep green, lighting to a dazzling pale blue where a bar of sand ran out into the bay. I walked out along this, thigh-deep, until I was about fifty yards from the shore, then turned and looked up towards the terrace of the Castello. There was no one visible, so I waved to Phyllida to follow me in. As we swam and splashed, I kept an eye open to seaward for the dolphin, but, though I thought once that I could see a gleaming wheel turning a long way out, the creature did not approach the bay. After a time we waded back to the beach, where we lay sunning ourselves and talking idly, until Phyl's remarks, which had been getting briefer and briefer, and more and more sleepy, ceased altogether.

I left her sleeping, and went back into the water.

Though I had kept a wary eye on the woods and the terrace every time I bathed, I had never seen anyone since the first day, so it was with a slight feeling of surprise that I now saw someone sitting there, at the table under the stone-pine. Grey hair. Sir Julian Gale. He lifted a hand to me, and I waved back, feeling absurdly pleased that he should have bothered. He turned away immediately, his head bent over a book. I caught the flutter of its pages.

There was no one with him on the terrace, but as I turned to let myself down into the deep water beyond the bar, something else caught my eye.

In one of the upper windows, which stood open, something had flashed. And behind the flash I saw movement, as whoever stood watching there lifted the binoculars again to focus them on the bay. . .

There is something particularly infuriating about being watched in this way. I should have dearly loved to return rudeness for rudeness by pulling a very nasty face straight at the Castello windows, but Sir Julian might have seen it, and thought it was meant for him, so I merely splashed back to the sand-bar, where I stood up, and, without another glance, stalked expressively (Drama School exercise; Outraged Bather driven from water) towards the rocks at the southern edge of the bay. I would finish my swim from the rocks beyond the point, out of range of the Castello.

I hadn't reckoned on its being quite so difficult to stalk with dignity through three feet of water. By the time I reached the end of the sand-bar and the deep pool near the rocks, I was furiously angry with Max Gale, and wishing I had gone straight out on to the beach. But I was damned if I would be driven back now. I plunged across the deep water, and was soon scrambling out under the pines.

A path ran through the tumble of rocks at the cliff's foot, leading, I supposed, to Godfrey Manning's villa, but its surface looked stony, so I stayed on the rocks below. These, scoured white by the sea and seamed with rock pools, stretched out from the cliff in stacks and ridges, with their roots in the calm, creaming water.

I began to pick my way along between the pools. The rocks were hot, and smooth to the feet. There were crevices filled with flowering bushes, running right down to the water's edge where the green swell lifted and sank, and here and there a jut of the living cliff thrust out into the water, with the path above it, and bushes at its rim hanging right out over the sea.

At the point I paused. Here the rocks were more broken, as if the tide was driven hard that way when there was a wind, and under the cliff was a pile of broken rock and sea-wrack, some of which looked fresh enough to have come up in last night's squall. Further round, beyond the next curve of the cliff, I could see where a cove or inlet ran in, deep and narrow and surrounded by thick trees which stretched right up the slopes of the cliff; there were pines and oaks and hollies, and among them the limes of which Sir Julian had spoken. Through the boughs of a young thicket at the cliff's foot I caught a glimpse of red tiling which must be the roof of Godfrey's boat-house.

There was nobody about. I decided to finish my bathe in the deep water off the point and then return by the path.

I made my way carefully through the piled rocks and the sea-wrack. Here and there a shallow pool barred the way, and I paddled across with caution, wondering uneasily about sea-urchins, which in these waters (I had read) can drive poisonous spines into your feet. *Like hedgehogs, which Lie tumbling in my barefoot way, and mount Their pricks at my foot-fall* . . . Poor Caliban. Was Julian Gale right, I wondered? I had read *The Tempest* late into the night, following up the fascinating game he had suggested, and I had even had a few ideas myself, things I must ask him when I went to the Castello again . . . If I ever went to the Castello again . . . But of course I would have to return the Shakespeare . . . If I could find out from Miranda or Adoni or someone when Max Gale was likely to be out . . .

I had come to the edge of a deep inlet, a miniature cove running back through the rocks. This would be as good a place as any. I paused, peering down into it, to see what the bottom was like.

The water was the colour of Imperial jade. Tiny, shrimp-like creatures scudded here and there among the olive and scarlet bladders, and shoals of small fish darted and nibbled. The shadows cast by the sun looked blue-black, and were alive with the movements of crabs which shuffled through the brown weed that clothed the bottom. The weed itself moved all the time, faintly and continuously, like rags in the swell. A cuttlefish bone showed white and bare. *Of his bones are coral made. These are pearls* . . .

The body was lying half in, half out, of the largest patch of shadow. The sun, shining straight into my eyes, had hidden it till now, the hump of flesh and clothes not holding any kind of human shape, just a lump of rags rolled over and over by the swell and dumped there, jammed somehow under an overhang at the base of the pool.

Even now, with the sun directly in my eyes, I could hardly be sure. Sick and shaken, I hesitated: but of course I would have to look. I sank to my knees at the edge of the pool, and shaded my eyes to peer downwards . . .

The rags moved in the faint swell like weed. Surely it was only weed . . .? But then I saw the head, the face, a shape blurred and bleached under dark hair. Some sea-creatures had already been at it. The tiny fish flicked to and fro, busily, in the green water.

Spiro, I thought, *Spiro* . . . And his mother would have to see this. Surely it would be better to say nothing, to let the tide carry it away again; let the busy sea-creatures purge and clean it to its sea-change, like the cuttlefish bone showing white beside the dark hair . . .?

Then reason threw its ice-water on my confusion. She would have to be told. It would be more cruel not to tell her. And there was no tide here. Without another storm, the thing could be held down here for days, for anyone to find.

Some freak current thrust a tentacle of movement through the pool. The water swayed, and the dead man moved his head. With the movement, I knew him. It wasn't specifically the face that I recognised; that would have been impossible: but somehow everything came together in the same moment to enforce recognition – the shape of face and head, the colours, better seen now, of the sodden lumps of rag that had been navy trousers and sweater and light grey jacket . . .

It wasn't Spiro, after all; not, that is, unless it had been Spiro in the woods last night, still alive, and making his way up towards the Castello.

There could be no doubt about it, no possible doubt. This was the man I had seen last night in the clearing. I found that I was sitting back on my heels, slumped to one side, with a hand out to the hot face of a boulder beside me. It was one thing to find a dead man; but to recognise him, and to know where he had been shortly before he had met his death . . .

I had my eyes shut, as tightly as the fingers that gripped the hot stone. The sunlight boiled and fizzed against the closed lids. I bit my lips, and breathed slowly and hard, and concentrated on not being sick. Phyllida; the thought was as bracing as sal volatile; Phyllida mustn't see this, or even be allowed to suspect the horror that lay just round the point from her. I must steady myself decently, then go back to Phyllida, and somehow persuade her to leave the beach soon. Then get quietly to the telephone, and get in touch with the police.

I opened my eyes, with a silly hope that somehow I had been wrong, and there was no dead man there in the water. But he still lay in his splash of inky shadow, grotesque and faintly moving and familiar. I got to my feet, held myself steady by the boulder for another full minute, then, without looking back, made my way through the tumble of rock towards the thicket that edged the cliff path. It was only when I had reached the bushes, and was wondering if I could pull myself up the eight feet or so to the path, that some sound, vaguely heard a few moments ago, and now repeated, made me pause and glance to my left, towards the boat-house. Someone had slammed a door. Something appeared to be wrong with the catch, because I heard, clearly now, an exclamation of irritation, and the slam was repeated. This time the door shut firmly, and a moment later I heard footsteps, and Godfrey Manning came briskly into view along the path.

I wasn't sure if he was coming my way, or if the path branched off above the trees somewhere for the Villa Rotha. I opened my mouth to call him, hoping that this wouldn't also bring Phyllida, but at the same moment Godfrey glanced up and saw me below him on the rocks. He lifted a hand in greeting, but before he could call out I put a finger to my lips, then beckoned urgently.

Not surprisingly, he looked startled, but his expression deepened sharply into concern as he approached and paused on the path above me.

'Lucy? Is something wrong? Are you feeling ill? The sun?' Then his voice changed. 'It's not that damned lunatic again with the rifle?'

I shook my head. Infuriatingly, after I had so far controlled myself, I found I couldn't speak. I pointed.

He glanced over towards the pool, but at that distance nothing was visible. Then he swung himself lightly down through the bushes to where I stood, and his arm went round me, gently.

'You'd better sit down . . . There. Better? All right, don't try to talk any more. Something scared you, over there in the big pool? Relax a minute now; I'll go and take a look, but don't you move. Just sit there quietly, and don't worry. I won't be long.'

I sat with my hands jammed tightly together between my knees, and watched my feet. I heard Godfrey's steps, quick and confident, cross the rocks towards the pool. Then there was silence, prolonged. The sea murmured, and some cliff-building swallows twittered shrilly as they cut in and out above the path.

I looked up. He was standing stock-still where I had stood, staring down. He was in profile to me, and I could see that he looked considerably shaken. It was only then that it occurred to me that he, too, must in the first moment of shock have expected it to be Spiro. If I had been capable of reasoned thought or speech, I should have known this, and spared him.

I cleared my throat. 'It's not. . . Spiro, is it?'

'No.'

'Do you know who it is?'

I thought he hesitated, then he nodded. 'His name's Yanni Zoulas.'

'Oh? You *do* know him?' Somehow this shook me, too, though it was reasonable to assume that the man had been drowned locally. 'Is he from near here, then?'

'Yes, from the village.'

'What–what do you suppose happened?'

'God knows. Some accident at sea, that's obvious. He was a fisherman, and usually went out alone . . . You must have seen his boat; it was always plying to and fro along this bit of shore–the rather pretty blue boat, with the dark brown sail. But in last night's sea . . . I wouldn't have thought . . .'

His voice trailed away as he stared frowningly down at the pool. Then he turned and made his way back across the rock to where I sat.

'Two in a week?' I said. It came out as a query, asked quite as if Godfrey could supply the answer. I hadn't meant even to say it aloud, and could have bitten my tongue with vexation as soon as it was out.

'Two in a week?' He spoke so blankly that it was evident my meaning hadn't registered. 'Oh, I see.'

'I'm sorry. It was stupid of me. I was thinking aloud. I shouldn't have reminded you. It's just one of those ghastly coincidences.'

'Normally,' he said, 'I'd have said I didn't believe in coincidence. In fact, if I hadn't seen with my own eyes what happened to Spiro, I'd certainly be starting to wonder what was going on around here.' He paused, and his eyes went back to the pool. 'As it is, all that has happened is that two young men from the same district have died this week by drowning, and in a community that lives largely by the sea, that's hardly surprising. Only . . .' He stopped.

'Only what?'

He looked at me with troubled eyes. 'One doesn't expect an epidemic of it in summer weather, that's all.'

'Godfrey, what is it? You look as if you thought–' I, too, checked myself, biting my lip. He watched me bleakly, saying nothing. I finished, rather hoarsely: 'Are you trying to tell me that this wasn't an accident?'

'Good God, no! Just that it poses problems. But none that you need worry about. In any case, they may never arise.'

None that you need worry about . . . Heaven knew what he'd have said if he had had even the slightest inkling of the problem it had set me . . . Why I still said nothing about last night I am not quite sure. I think now that this last incident took its place in a context of violence, felt rather than apprehended, that made it unsurprising, and that forced me, through some instinct of fear, to hold my tongue. It was as if the first shot from that silenced rifle had been the signal for danger and fear to crowd in; as if by my silence I could still detach myself from them, and stay inside my own bubble of security, keep my own enchanted island free of invaders from the violent world I had come here to escape.

So I said instead: 'Has he any people?'

'A wife. They live with his parents. You probably know the house, it's that pink one at the crossroads.'

'Yes, I do. It's very pretty. I remember thinking that the folk in it must be well off.'

'They were. They're going to miss him.'

I looked at him, startled, not by the words, which were trite, but by the quite undue dryness of his tone.

'You *are* getting at something. You *know* something about this, don't you? Why won't you tell me?'

He hesitated, then smiled suddenly. 'I don't really know why not. It hardly concerns me, and it certainly won't touch you. It's only that when the police move in on this something might crop up that could be awkward.'

'Such as?'

He lifted his shoulders. 'No plain and simple fisherman lived as well as Yanni and his family. Rumour has it that he was a smuggler, with a regular "milk run" into Albania, and that he made a good bit on the side.'

'Well, but surely . . . I'd have imagined that an awful lot of men played around with that sort of thing hereabouts? And Corfu's very well placed, just next door to the Iron Curtain. I suppose any sort of "luxury goods" would go well there. But how could anyone like Yanni Zoulas get supplies of things like that?'

'How do I know? He'd have his contacts; someone in Corfu town, perhaps, who has connexions with Athens or Italy . . . But I'm sure that Yanni Zoulas wouldn't be in it on his own account. He wasn't exactly a master mind. He probably did it for a salary.'

I licked my lips. 'Even so . . . You wouldn't suggest that there could be any connection—that he was *killed* because of this? Is that what you're getting at? That—that would make it murder, Godfrey.'

'No, no. For goodness' sake, I wasn't suggesting anything like that! Good God, no! Don't upset yourself. Why, you're as white as a sheet! Look, the idea's pure nonsense . . . I doubt if poor Yanni would ever be important enough to get himself murdered! You can forget that. But it did occur to me to wonder if he could have run into trouble on the other side—coastguard trouble: I believe they're hot stuff over there, searchlights, machine-guns, the lot. If he did, and was wounded, and then ran for home, that might account for an accident happening on a night that wasn't particularly rough. He might have fainted and gone overboard.'

'I see. But even if the police do find out something about it, his family won't be in trouble, will they?'

'I doubt it. It isn't that.'

'Then what's worrying *you*?'

'It might bring them closer to young Spiro than would be quite pleasant,' said Godfrey frankly. 'I've a strong suspicion that he'd been out with Yanni more than once. It didn't worry me, and I asked no questions; the boy had a mother and sister to keep, and how he did it was his own affair. But I don't want them to find out about it now. It would serve no purpose, and might distress his mother. According to her, Spiro was *sans peur et sans reproche*, and a good Christian into the bargain. I'm sure she'd label smuggling as immoral, however lightly you or I might regard it.'

'I didn't say I regarded it lightly. I think that if you live under a country's protection you should obey its laws. I just wasn't surprised. But, you know, even if the police do find out something discreditable about Spiro, I'm sure they'd never tell Maria. Police are human, when all's said and done, and the boy's dead.'

'You're probably right. Ah, well . . .' He stretched, and sighed. 'Hell, what a wretched business. We'd better go and get it over. Do you feel as if you'd like to move now?'

'Oh, yes, I'm fine.'

He took my arm, and helped me up the rough bank to the path.

'I'm going to take you up to my house now, to telephone,' he said. 'It's nearer, and there's no need to alarm your sister till you're feeling a bit more the thing yourself. The police will want to see you, and you can see them at my place, if you like, then I'll take you home by road, in the car . . . Now, did you have some clothes with you, or some sort of wrap and shoes? If you wait here a moment, I'll get them.'

'They're back in the bay, but I'm afraid Phyl's there, too. I left her asleep on the beach. She's probably awake by now, and wondering where I am.'

'Oh.' He looked uncertain. 'Well, that alters things, doesn't it?

We'll have to tell her. I don't know much about these things, but will
it—well, upset her, or anything?'

'I think she'll be okay as long as she doesn't see the body. She'll
have to know soon enough . . . Wait a minute, someone's coming.
That'll be her.'

A second later she appeared on the path, round the point of the
cliff. She must have been awake for some time, for all traces of the
sea had been removed; she was freshly made up, her hair was
shining and immaculate, she had clipped a pretty beach skirt on over
her bathing costume, and she wore her gay beach coat. As usual, the
sight of her brought my own shortcomings immediately to mind. I
was conscious for the first time of what I must look like, with the salt
dried on my skin, my hair damp, and my face—I imagined—still
sallow with shock.

She said gaily: 'I thought I heard voices! Hullo, Godfrey! Were
you on your way over to us, or did you just come down to swim?'

'Neither. I was down at the boat-house giving the boat a
once-over, when I saw Lucy.'

I said: 'Are those my shoes you've brought? Thanks very much.
How did you guess I'd be wanting them?'

'Well, dearie, knowing you,' said Phyllida, 'when I woke up and
found you'd vanished, I knew you'd be straying along here poking
around in the rock-pools, and heaven knew how far you'd get.' She
laughed up at Godfrey. 'It wouldn't surprise me in the least to find
her with a jam-jar full of assorted shrimps and things to take home. I
remember once—' She stopped. There was a pause, in which she
looked from one to the other of us. Then her voice sharpened.
'Lucy. Godfrey. Something's wrong. What is it?'

He hesitated just that second too long. 'Your sister was feeling the
heat a bit, and I offered to take her up to my house and give her a
drink. She told me you were on the beach, so I was just coming
across for you. I hope you'll come up too?'

His tone was perfect, easy and natural, but my sister was never
anybody's fool. She had seen all she needed to see in my face, and in
the fact that Godfrey's hand still supported my arm.

She said, more sharply still: 'Something *is* wrong. Lucy, you look
awful . . . And it's not the heat, either; don't give me that; you never
felt the heat in your life. What's happened? Have you hurt yourself,
or something?'

'No, no. There's nothing the matter with me, honestly.' I
disengaged myself gently, and looked up at Godfrey. It struck me

suddenly, irrelevantly, that he was better-looking than I had thought. The sunlight showed up the deep tan of his skin, and the crisp hair bleached fair at the front. Against the tan his eyes looked a very clear grey.

I said: 'You may as well tell her straight away.'

'Very well. Phyl, I'm afraid a beastly thing's happened. One of the local fishermen's been drowned, and washed ashore over there, and Lucy found the body.'

'Oh, my God, how ghastly! Lucy, my dear . . . you poor kid! I suppose it looked –' Then her eyes widened, and a hand went up to her face. 'Did you *see*? Could you tell? I mean . . . after a week . . .'

'It's not Spiro.' Godfrey spoke quickly, almost harshly.

'*It's not?*' The hand dropped, and she let out a long breath of relief. 'Oh, I was so sure . . . But does that mean *two*, in just a few days? Have you any idea who it is?'

'It's a local man called Yanni Zoulas. I doubt if you know him. Look, we were just going up to telephone. Will you come with us? If I just go back now to the bay for the rest of –'

He stopped abruptly, and turned. A shadow fell across me where I sat pulling on my sandals. Max Gale's voice said, just behind me: 'Is anything the matter?'

I know I jumped as if he had hit me. The other two were caught gaping, as if in some guilty act. He must be stones heavier than Phyllida, but we had none of us heard a sound. I thought: he must move like a cat.

For seconds, nobody replied. It was a queer, hair-pricking little pause, during which the men eyed each other like unfriendly dogs circling one another, and I sat with a sandal half on, watching them.

'The matter?' said Godfrey.

I knew then that he didn't want to tell Gale what had happened. The knowledge, somehow not surprising, came like a cold breath along my skin. Mr. Gale glanced from Godfrey to Phyl, then down at me, and I bent my head quickly, pulled the sandal on, and began to fasten the strap.

He said impatiently: 'It's obvious there's something. I was watching the bay with glasses, and I thought I saw something odd – some debris or other floating, away out; I couldn't make it out. Then Miss Waring came this way, and I saw her on the rocks that run out from the point. She stopped and looked into one of the pools, and her reactions made it pretty obvious that there was something very wrong indeed. Then you went over and made it rather plainer. What is it? Or shall I go and see for myself?'

It was Phyllida who answered him. She must not have felt the overtones that had chilled me – but then she didn't know what I knew. She said, in a sort of rush: 'It's a dead body. Drowned. In that pool, there. We were just going up to phone the police.'

There was a moment in which I seemed to hear the cliff-swallows, very loud and shrill, just overhead. Then Max Gale said: 'Who is it? Do you know?'

Godfrey still said nothing. He had not taken his eyes off the other man's face. It was Phyllida who answered.

'I forget the name. Godfrey says he's from the village. Yanni something.'

'Yanni Zoulas,' I said.

He looked down at me as if he was aware fully for the first time that I was there. I got the strong impression that he wasn't seeing me even now. He didn't speak.

'Did you know him?' I asked.

The dark eyes focused on me for a moment, then he looked away again, over towards the pool. 'Why, yes, slightly.'

Godfrey said: 'You say you were watching something floating, some debris. You couldn't say what sort of thing? Could it have been flotsam from a sunk boat?'

'Eh? Well, I told you I couldn't see at that distance, but it could have been . . . My God, yes, I suppose it could!' All of a sudden Gale was fully with us; his gaze sharpened, and he spoke abruptly. 'I wonder what time he went out last night? I thought I heard a boat soon after midnight, bearing north-east.' He looked at Godfrey. 'Did you hear it?'

'No.'

'Last night?' said Phyllida. 'Did it happen as recently as that? Could you tell, Godfrey?'

'I'm not an expert. I don't know. I don't think he's been there long. However, it shouldn't be hard to find out when he was last seen.'

I had been watching Max Gale's face. He was looking thoughtful now, grave – anything but the way I knew he ought to be looking. 'It must have happened within the last forty-eight hours. I saw his boat myself on Saturday. It went past the bay at about three in the afternoon.'

If I hadn't known what I did, I'd never have known that he was lying – or rather, implying a lie. For a moment I even wondered if

perhaps Yanni had not been on his way to the Castello last night,
then I remembered that Mr. Gale had, in the last few minutes, given
me another reason for doubting his good faith. He looked down
suddenly, and caught me watching him. I bent my head again, and
fiddled with the second sandal.

'Well,' said Godfrey, 'it'll be easy enough to check with his
family, and the sooner we let the experts get on with the job, the
better. Shall we go? One thing, nobody need stay with the body.
There's no tide to shift it. . . . Where are you going?'

Max Gale didn't trouble to answer; he was already swinging
himself down to the rocks below us. Godfrey made a quick,
involuntary movement as if to stop him, then he shrugged, said
softly to us: 'Do you mind? We won't be long,' and slithered in his
turn down through the bushes.

Gale was bending over the pool. Like Godfrey, he stood looking
down at the body for some time in silence, then he did what neither
Godfrey nor I had done: he lay flat at the edge of the rock, and
reached down through the water as if to touch the dead man. I saw
Godfrey make another of those sharp involuntary movements, but
he must have decided that what evidence there was could hardly be
damaged further by a touch, for he said nothing, merely stooping
down himself to watch with close attention.

'What in the world are they doing?' asked Phyl, rather petulantly.

I was clasping my knees, hugging myself together closely. In spite
of the sun, I had begun to feel cold. 'I don't know and I don't care. I
hope they hurry, that's all. I want to get some clothes on and get the
police over and done with.'

'You poor lamb, are you cold? Here, have my coat.' She took it off
and dropped it over my shoulders, and I hugged it gratefully round
me.

'Thanks a lot. That's marvellous.' I laughed a little. 'At least it
puts me in competition again! I wish you didn't always look as if
you'd just got back from Elizabeth Arden, when I feel like a bit of
Mr. Gale's debris. It was probably me he saw floating. If, that is, he
saw anything.'

She looked quickly down at me. 'What does that mean? It sounds
loaded.'

'Not really.'

She sat down beside me. 'You don't often make remarks for
nothing. What *did* you mean?'

'I'm not happy about this affair, that's all.'

'Well, heavens, who is? But is it an "affair"?'

'I don't know. There's a feeling . . . a feeling that there's something going on. I can't put it better than that, and I'm probably wrong, but I think—*I think*—Godfrey feels it, too. Why don't he and Mr. Gale like one another?'

'I didn't know they didn't. They were a bit wary today, weren't they? I suppose Godfrey's more upset than he lets on . . . after all, it's rather soon after the Spiro business . . . And Max Gale doesn't just put himself out to be charming, does he?'

'He has things on his mind,' I said.

The remark was intended merely as an evasion, to imply only that his personal worries—over his father—made him difficult to know or like, but she took it to refer specifically to what had just happened. She nodded.

'I thought so, to . . . Oh, nothing special, just that he seemed to be thinking about something else. But what did you mean?' She shot me another look. 'Something's really worrying you, isn't it?'

I hesitated. 'Did it strike you as odd, the way Mr. Gale took the news?'

'Well, no, it didn't. Perhaps because I know him better than you. He's never very forthcoming. What sort of "odd" did you mean?'

I hesitated again, then decided not to specify. 'As if he wasn't surprised that a body should·roll up here.'

'I don't suppose he was. He'd be expecting it to be Spiro.'

'Oh, of course,' I said. 'Look, they seem to be coming back.'

Mr. Gale had finished whatever grisly examination he had been conducting, and had withdrawn his hand. He rinsed it in the salt water, then stood up, drying it on a handkerchief. As far as I could make out, the two men still hadn't spoken a word. Now Godfrey said something, with a gesture towards Phyl and myself, and they turned together and started over to us.

'Thank goodness,' I said.

'You'll feel better when you've had a drink, old dear,' said my sister.

'Coffee,' I said, 'as hot as love and as sweet as hell.'

'Godfrey might even run to that, you never know.'

The men scrambled up to the path beside us.

'Well?' said Phyl and I, together.

They exchanged a glance, which might even be said to hold complicity. Then Gale said: 'It should be interesting to hear what the doctor has to say. He seems to have been knocked about the head a bit. I was wondering if the neck was broken, but I don't think so.'

Godfrey's eyes met mine. I stood up. 'Well, when the boat's found, there may be something there to show how it happened.'

'For all we know,' said Godfrey, 'that's been done, and the hue and cry's on already. Let's go, shall we?'

'Thank goodness!' I said. 'But I still want to get dressed. My things—'

'Good God, I was forgetting. Well, hang on another minute or two, I won't be long.'

Max Gale said, in that abrupt, rather aggressive way of his: 'You three start up the path. I'll go and pick your stuff up and bring it along.'

He had so plainly not been invited to go with us, and just as plainly fully intended to hear all that was said to the police, that I thought Godfrey was going to demur. But Phyllida got eagerly to her feet.

'Yes, let's get away from here! It's giving me the grue. Mr. Gale, if you *would* be an angel . . . I've left some things, too, they're under the pine trees.'

'I saw where they were. I won't be long. Don't wait for me; I'll catch you up.'

He went quickly. Godfrey looked after him, the grey eyes curiously cold. Then he caught me watching him, and smiled. 'Well, this way.'

The path followed the cliff as far as the boat-house, then turned up a steep zigzag through the trees. We toiled up it, grateful for the shade. Godfrey walked between us, in a sort of awkwardly divided solicitude that might at any other time have been amusing; but just now all I could think of was a bit of solitude in his bathroom, then a comfortable chair, and—failing the coffee—a long, cool drink. I hoped Max Gale would hurry with the clothes. I thought he probably would: he wouldn't want to miss what was said to the police. It had surprised me that he had risked this by offering to go back.

Godfrey had paused to help Phyl negotiate a dry gully which the winter's rain had gouged across the path. I was a few paces ahead of them when I came to a corner where a sudden gap in the trees gave a view of the point below.

I might have known there would be a good reason for Max Gale's offer. He was back at the rock pool, lying flat as before, reaching down into the water. I could just see his head and shoulders. Just as

I caught the glimpse of him he withdrew his arm and got quickly to his feet. As he turned, I drew back into the shade of the trees, and just in time, for he glanced up briefly before he vaulted up to the path, and out of sight.

'Tired?' asked Godfrey, just behind me.

I started. 'No, not a bit. Just getting my breath. But I'll be glad when it's all over.'

'So shall we all. I seem to have spent the whole week with the police as it is.' He added, rather bitterly: 'At least they know their way here, and most of the questions to ask.'

Phyllida touched his arm gently. 'Poor Godfrey. But we're terribly grateful. And at least this time it doesn't touch you . . . except as a rather ghastly sort of coincidence.'

His eyes met mine. They held the bleak expression I was beginning to know.

'I don't believe in coincidence,' he said.

Chapter 7

What have we here, a man, or a fish? dead or alive?

II. 2.

EITHER SHE HAD been more distressed than she had allowed us to
see, or else the trip down to the beach in the heat, with the bathe and
the climb to the Villa Rotha, had been too much for Phyllida.
Though we spent the rest of the day quietly, and she lay down after
lunch for a couple of hours, by evening she was tired, fidgety, and
more than somewhat out of temper, and very ready to be persuaded
to go to bed early.

Maria and Miranda had gone as soon as dinner was over. By ten
o'clock the house was very quiet. Even the pines on the hill behind it
were still, and once I had shut the windows I could hear no sound
from the sea.

I felt tired myself, but restless, with sleep still a long way off, so I
went along to the scrubbed and empty kitchen, made myself more
coffee, then took it through to the *salotto*, put my feet on a chair,
some Mozart on the gramophone, and settled myself for a quiet
evening.

But things didn't quite work out that way. The calm, beautiful
room, even the music, did not manage to keep at bay the thoughts
that had been knocking for admission since that morning. In spite of
myself, my mind went persistently back to the morning's incidents;
the discovery in the pool, the two men's raw antagonism, and the
long, wearying aftermath of interrogation, with the fresh problems
it had brought to light.

The police from Corfu had been civil, thorough, and kind. They
had arrived fairly soon after we had reached Godfrey's house, and

had gone straight down with the two men to see the body. Shortly
after that a boat had arrived from somewhere, and presently
departed with its burden. Another came soon afterwards, and
cruised off out to sea – searching, one assumed, for the 'debris' which
Mr. Gale insisted that he had seen. From the terrace of the Villa
Rotha Phyl and I had watched it tacking to and fro some way out
from land, but with what success it had been impossible – failing Mr.
Gale's binoculars – to guess.

Then the men came back. The questions had been searching, but
easy enough for my part to answer, because of course nobody
imagined that I had ever seen Yanni before in my life, so the only
questions I was asked were those touching on my finding of the body.

And when Max Gale reiterated to the police that he had not laid
eyes on Yanni Zoulas since a possible glimpse of his boat on
Saturday afternoon, I had not said a word.

It was this that bore on me now, heavily, as I sat there alone in the
salotto, with darkness thickening outside the windows, and moths
thumping against the lighted glass. And if I was beginning to get too
clear an idea why, I didn't want to face that, either. I pushed that
line of thought to one side, and concentrated firmly on the facts.

These were, in their own way, comforting. Godfrey had rung up
in the late afternoon to give us the latest reports. It appeared that
Yanni's boat had been found drifting, and on the boom were traces
of hairs and blood where, as the boat heeled in a sudden squall, it
must have struck him and sent him overboard. An almost empty
bottle of ouzo, which had rolled away behind a pile of rope and
tackle, seemed to provide a clue to the young fisherman's carelessness. The doctor had given it as his opinion (said Godfrey) that
Yanni had been dead when he went into the water. The police did
not seem inclined to press the matter further. Of the debris reported
by Mr. Gale no trace had been found.

Finally – Godfrey was a little cryptic over this part of the message,
as the telephone was on a party line – finally, no mention had been
made of any illegal activities of the dead man. Presumably his boat
had been searched, and nothing had come to light, so the police (who
preferred to turn a blind eye to small offences unless action was
forced on them) were satisfied that the fatal voyage had been a
routine fishing trip, and that Yanni's death had been accidental. It
was obvious that they had no intention of opening any further line of
inquiry.

So much for Godfrey's anxiety. My own went a little further.

It had transpired, from police inquiries, that the last time Yanni's family had seen him alive was on Sunday: he had spent the day with them, they said, going with them to watch the procession, and returning home in the late afternoon. Yes, he had seemed in good spirits. Yes, he had been drinking a fair amount. He had had a meal, and then had gone out. No, he had not said where he was going, why should he? They had assumed he was going fishing, as usual. He had gone down to the boat. Yes, alone; he usually went alone. That was the last time they had seen him.

It was the last time anyone had seen him, according to the police report. And I had said nothing to make them alter it. Where Godfrey had been worrying about the inquiry's leading back to Spiro, I was worrying about its involving Julian Gale. That Max Gale was somehow implicated seemed obvious, but I had my own theories about that, and they hardly justified turning the police searchlight on Yanni's activities, and so wrecking Sir Julian's precarious peace. With Yanni's death an accident—and I saw no reason to doubt this—it didn't matter if he had indeed paid a furtive visit to the Castello before going out last night. So if Max Gale chose to say nothing about it, then it was none of my business. I could stay in my enchanted bubble and keep quiet. It didn't matter one way or the other . . .

But I knew quite well that it did, and it was this knowledge that kept me sleepless in my chair, while one record followed another, unheeded, and the clock crawled on towards midnight. For one thing, I had had information forced on me that I would rather not have owned. For another—

The record stopped. With its slow, deliberate series of robot clicks, the auto-changer dropped another on the turntable, moved a gentle arm down on it, and loosed Gervase de Peyer's clarinet into the room in a brilliant shower of gold.

I switched my own thoughts back into the groove of facts. One thing at a time. The best way of forgetting how you think you feel is to concentrate on what you know you know . . .

Godfrey had been sure that Yanni was a smuggler, and that he must have some 'contact' who was probably his boss. I was pretty sure now that the contact was Max Gale. It all tied up: it would explain that furtive visit just before Yanni's voyage, and Gale's silence on the subject. It would also account for the thing that had so much worried me this morning—Gale's reaction to the news of Yanni's death. He had not been surprised at the news that a body was on the rocks, and this was not, as Phyl had assumed, because he thought it was Spiro. To me it was obvious that Spiro had never entered his head. His first question had been 'Who is it? Do you know?' though the obvious assumption would have been the one the rest of us had made, that this must be the body of the drowned boy.

If my guess about him was correct, then his actions were perfectly consistent. He had known Yanni was to make a trip the night before; he must know there was some risk involved. He would obviously not have expected Yanni to meet his death, but, once faced with a drowned body, he had had no doubts as to who it would be. His story of floating debris was nonsense, of that I was sure: what had happened was that he had seen me, and then Godfrey, at the rock-pool, had jumped to conclusions, and had made an excuse to come down to see for himself. There had been that sharp 'Who is it?' and then the next, immediate, reaction—to examine the body as closely as he dared, presumably for any evidence of violence. No doubt if such evidence had been there, he would have had to come out with the truth, or part of it. As it was, he held his tongue, and no doubt shared Godfrey's relief that the matter need not be brought into the open.

Yes, it all tied up, even Gale's surreptitious return to the pool, presumably to examine the body more closely than he had dared with Godfrey there, and to remove anything Yanni might have been carrying which might link him with his 'contact'. And it was Gale's luck that the boat had proved innocent: either poor Yanni had been on his way home when the accident happened, or last night's trip had, in fact, merely been a routine one to the fishing-grounds. Even the attack on the dolphin took its place with the rest. I was certain, now, that Gale had shot at the creature because he was afraid it would attract the tourist crowds, and destroy his badly-needed privacy. But the anger that this action had roused in me didn't give me the right, I decided, to open up a field of inquiry that would probably hurt Spiro's people, and would certainly hurt Yanni's. The two bereaved families had already quite enough to bear. No, I would hold my tongue, and be thankful that I had been allowed to stay inside my enchanted bubble with a quiet conscience. And as for Max Gale—

The Clarinet Concerto came to an end, the bright pomp ascending jubilant into a triumph of golden chords. The player switched itself off. In the silence that followed I heard sounds from Phyllida's room. She was up and busy.

I glanced at the clock. Twenty past twelve. She should have been asleep long ago. I went across the hallway to her door.

'Phyllida?'

'Oh, come in, come in!'

She sounded thoroughly edgy and upset. I went in, to find her out of bed and rummaging through a drawer, dragging the contents out anyhow and strewing them on the floor. She was looking enchantingly pretty in some voluminous affair of yellow nylon, with her hair down, and her eyes wide and dark-shadowed. She also looked as if she were on the verge of tears.

'What's up? Are you looking for something?'

'Oh, God!' She jerked open another drawer and rummaged in it, and slammed it shut again. 'Not that it'll be *there* . . . I would do a damn fool thing like that, wouldn't I?'

I looked at her in some alarm. Phyllida hardly ever swears. 'Like what? Lost something?'

'My ring. The diamond. The god-damned Forli blasted diamond. When we were down at the bay. I've only just this moment remembered it, what with everything. I had it on, didn't I? *Didn't I?*'

'Oh, my heaven, yes, you did! But don't you remember, you took it off before we went in the water? Look, stop fussing, Phyl, it's not lost. You put it in your make-up bag, that little zip thing covered with roses. I saw you.'

She was at the wardrobe now, feeling in the pockets of the beach coat. 'Did I or did I not put it on again after I'd left the water?'

'I don't think so. I don't remember . . . No, I'm sure you didn't. I'd have noticed it on your hand. You didn't have it on when we were having coffee up at Godfrey's. But honey, it'll be in the little bag. I know you put it there.'

She shoved the coat back, and slammed the wardrobe shut. 'That's the whole blasted point! The beastly bag's still down on the beach!'

'Oh, no!'

'It must be! I tell you, it's not here, I've looked everywhere.' The bathroom was ajar, and on the floor her beach bag lay in a heap with slippers and towel. She picked up the bag for what was obviously the umpteenth time, turned it upside down, shook it, and let it fall. She kicked over the towel with her foot, then turned to face me, eyes tragic, hands spread like a mourning angel invoking a blessing. 'You see? I bloody *left* the thing, on the bloody *beach*!'

'Yes, but listen a minute . . .' I thought back rapidly. 'Perhaps you did put it back on. After all, you used the zip bag when you did your face. Did you put the ring on then, and take it off again when you washed at Godfrey's? Perhaps you left it in his bathroom.'

'I'm sure I didn't. I can't remember a thing about it, and I know that if I *had* the thing on when I washed at Godfrey's, I'd have known it. You can't help knowing,' she said ingenuously, 'when you're flashing a thing like that about on your hand. Oh, what a *fool* I am! I didn't mean to bring it here at all, but I forgot to put it in the bank, and it's safer on my hand than off it . . . Or so I thought! Oh hell, hell, *hell*!'

'Well, look,' I said soothingly, 'don't start to worry yet. If you didn't put it back on, it's still in the little bag. Where was that when you last saw it?'

'Just where we were sitting. It must have got pushed to one side under the trees or something, and when Max Gale went back for our things he just wouldn't see it. He'd just grab the things and chase after us.'

'Probably. He'd be in a hurry.'

'That's what I mean.' She noticed nothing in my tone, but spoke quite simply, staring at me with those wide, scared eyes. 'The wretched thing's just *sitting* there on the sand, and—'

'Well, for heaven's sake don't look like that! It'll be as safe as a house! Nobody'll be there, and if they were, who'd pick up a scruffy plastic bag with make-up in?'

'It's not scruffy, and Leo gave it to me.' She began to cry. 'If it comes to that, he gave me the beastly ring, and it belongs to his beastly family, and if I lose it—'

'You haven't lost it.'

'The tide'll wash it away.'

'There's no tide.'

'Your foul dolphin'll eat it. *Something*'ll happen to it, I know it will.' She had cast reason to the winds now, and was crying quite hard. 'Leo had no business to give me anything like that and expect me to watch it all the time! Diamonds are hell, anyway—if they're not in the bank you feel as miserable as sin, and if they *are* in the bank you're all frustrated, so you simply can't win, they're not worth having, and that ring cost thousands and thousands, and it's worse in lire, *millions* of lire,' wept Phyl unreasonably, 'and there'll be his mother to face, not to mention that ghastly collection of aunts, and did I tell you his uncle's probably going to be a C-Cardinal—'

'Well, honey, this won't exactly wreck his chances, so take a pull at yourself, will you, and—hey! Just what do you think you're doing?'

She had yanked the wardrobe door open again, and was pulling out a coat. 'If you think I'll get a wink, a *single wink* of sleep, while that ring's lying out there—'

'Oh, no, you don't!' I said with great firmness, taking the coat from her and putting it back. 'Now, don't be a nit! Of course you're worried stiff, who wouldn't be, but you're certainly not going down there tonight!'

'But I've got to!' Her voice thinned and rose, and she grabbed for the coat again. She was very near to real hysteria.

I said quickly: 'You have not. I'll go myself.'

'You can't! You can't go alone. It's after midnight!'

I laughed. 'So what? It's a nice night, and I'd a darned sight rather take a walk out than see you work yourself into a fit of the screaming abdabs. I don't blame you, I'd be climbing the walls myself! Serve you right for flashing that kind of ice around, my girl!'

'But, Lucy—'

'I mean it. I'll go straight away and get the wretched thing, so for sweet Pete's sake dry your eyes or you'll be fretting yourself into a miscarriage or something, and then Leo *will* have something to say, not to mention his mother and the aunts.'

'I'll come with you.'

'You'll do no such thing. Don't argue. Get back into bed. Go on . . . I know exactly where we were sitting, and I'll take a torch. Now mop up, and I'll make you some Ovaltine or something, and then go. Hurry up now, get in!'

I don't often get tough with Phyllida, but she is surprisingly meek when I do. She got in, and smiled shakily.

'You're an angel, you really are. I feel so ashamed of myself, but it's no use, I shan't rest till I've got it . . . Look, I've had an idea, couldn't we just ring Godfrey, and ask him to go? Oh, no, he said he was going to be out late, didn't he? Well, what about Max Gale? It's his fault, in a way, for not seeing the thing . . . We could ring him up to ask if he'd noticed it, and then he'd have to offer to go down—'

'I'm not asking favours of Max Gale.'

This time she did notice my tone. I added, hastily: 'I'd rather go myself. I honestly don't mind.'

'You won't be scared?'

'What's there to be scared of? I don't believe in ghosts. Anyway, it's not so dark as it looks from in here; the sky's thick with stars. I suppose you've got a torch?'

'There's one in the kitchen, on the shelf beside the door. Oh, Lucy, you are a saint! I shouldn't have slept a wink without that beastly thing safe in its box!'

I laughed at her. 'You should be like me, and get your jewellery you-know-where. Then you could lose the lot down on the beach, and not worry about Leo's beating you.'

'If that was all I thought would happen,' said Phyllida, with a spice of her usual self, 'I'd probably enjoy it. But it's his mother.'

'I know. And the aunts. And the Cardinal. Don't come that one over me, my girl, I know darned well they all spoil you to death. Now, stop worrying. I'll bring you the Ovaltine, and you shall have the Grand Cham's diamond safe under your pillow "or ere your pulse twice beat." See you.'

*   *   *

The woods were still and silent, the clearing full of starlight. The frogs had dived at my approach; the only sound now from the pool was the lap and stir of the lily-pads as the rings of water shimmered through them and set them rocking.

I paused for a moment. I had told Phyllida that I didn't believe in ghosts, and I knew I had no reason to be afraid, but for the life of me I couldn't help glancing towards the place where Yanni had appeared last night, while just for a moment I felt my skin prickle and brush up like a cat's fur.

Next moment, very faintly, I heard the piano. I tilted my head to listen to the thin, falling melodic line that crept down through the trees. I recognised phrases that I had heard last night. It was this, no doubt, that had unconsciously given me pause, and called up poor Yanni for me.

The ghost had gone. The pathway to the beach was just a pathway. But I didn't follow it yet: slowly, rather as if I were breasting water instead of air, I climbed the path to the Castello.

I paused at the edge of the rose garden, hanging back in shadow. The roses smelt heavy and sweet. The music was clear now, but muted, so that I guessed it came from the house rather than the terrace. I recognised another passage, a simple, almost lyrical line that suddenly broke and stumbled in the middle, like a step missed in the dark. I found it disquieting. After a while the pianist stopped, started again, played for another half-minute before he broke off to go back a few bars; then the same long phrase was played over several times before being allowed to flow on unchecked.

The next time he stopped I heard the murmur of voices. Julian Gale's tones carried beautifully; Max replied indistinguishably. Then the piano began again.

He was there, and working. They were both there. As if I had had something proved to me—whatever it was I had come for—I turned away and, with the help of the torch, followed the Castello's own path downhill, through the clearing where I had met Max Gale, and on down the broken steps to the bay.

After the heavy shade of the path, the open beach seemed as light as day. The white crescent of sand was firm and easy walking. As I left the wood I switched off the torch, and went rapidly across the bay to where we had been sitting that morning. The pines, overhanging, made a black pool of shadow, so black that for a moment it looked as if something was lying there. Another body.

But this time I didn't pause. I knew it for a trick of the shadows, no more; just another ghost to fur the skin with gooseflesh; an image painted on the memory, not of the living Yanni this time, but of the dead.

The music sounded faintly from above. I kept the torch switched off in case the flash attracted the Gales' attention, and approached the trees.

Something *was* lying there. Not shadows; it was solid, a long dark bundle-shape, like the thing in the rock-pool. And it was real.

This time the shock really did hit me. I still remember the kick over the heart, the sharp, frightening pain that knocked all the blood in my body into hammering motion, the way a kick starts a motor-cycle engine. The blood slammed in heavy, painful strokes in my head, my fingers, my throat. My hand tightened so convulsively on the torch that the switch went down and the light came on, pinpointing whatever it was that lay there under the pines.

It wasn't a body. It was a long, smoothly-wrapped bundle of something, longer than a man. It was lying just where we had been sitting that morning.

I had my free hand clamped tightly against my ribs, under the left breast. It is a theatrical gesture, but, like all the theatre's clichés, it is based soundly on truth. I believe I felt I must hold my terrified heart from battering its way out of the rib-cage. I must have stood there for several minutes, rigid, unable either to move forward or to run away.

The thing didn't move. There was no sound, other than the distant notes of the piano, and the soft hushing of the sea.

My terror slowly faded. Body or no body, it obviously wasn't going to hurt me, and, I thought grimly, I'd be better facing a dozen bodies than going back to Phyllida without the Forli diamond.

I pointed the torchlight straight at the thing under the trees, and approached it bravely.

The bundle stirred. As my breath whistled sharply in, I saw, in the torchlight, the gleam of a living eye. But then in the split half-second that prevented me from screaming, I saw what—not who—this was. It was the dolphin.

Apollo's child. Amphitryte's darling. The sea-magician. High and dry.

The eye moved, watching me. The tail stirred again, as if trying to beat movement out of the hard earth as it would from water. It struck the edge of the crisping ripples with a splash that seemed to echo right up the rocks.

I tiptoed closer, under the blackness of the pines. 'Darling?' I said softly. 'What's the matter? Are you hurt?'

The creature lay still, unblinking, the eye liquid and watchful. It was silly to look, as I did, for recognition, but at least I could see no fear of me. I shone the torch carefully over the big body. There seemed to be no wound, or mark of any kind. I examined the sand round about. There was no blood, only a wide, dragged wake where the animal had been hauled or thrown out of the water. Near a pine-root the torchlight caught the pale gleam of Phyllida's make-up bag. I snatched this up; I didn't even look inside, but rammed it into my pocket and then forgot it. Presumably the diamond was safe inside it, but more important now than any diamond was the dolphin, stranded and helpless, a prey for anyone who wanted to hurt him. And that someone did want to hurt him, I very well knew . . . Moreover, unless he could be got back into the water, he would die as soon as the sun got up and dried his body out.

I straightened up, trying to force my thoughts into order, and to recall everything I had ever read or known about dolphins. It was little enough. I knew that, like whales, they sometimes stranded themselves for no obvious reason, but that if they were unhurt and could be re-floated fairly soon, they would suffer no ill effects. I knew, too, they they must be kept wet, or the skin cracked and went septic, and that they breathed through an air-hole on the top of the head, and that this must be kept clear.

I shone the torch again. Yes, there was the air-hole, a crescent-shaped, glistening nostril on top of the head. It was open, but half clotted with sand thrown up as the creature had ploughed ashore. I fixed the torch as best I could in the crotch of a pine bough, dipped my hands in the sea, and gently wiped the sand from the hole.

The dolphin's breath was warm on my hands, and this was somehow surprising; the creature was all at once less alien, his friendliness and intelligence at the same time less magical and more touching. It was unthinkable that I might have to watch him die.

I ran my hands over his skin, noticing with fear how rough this was; the breeze was drying it out. I tried to judge the distance I would have to drag him. Now and again a ripple, driven by that same breeze, washed right up to the dolphin's tail, but this was the thinnest film of water licking up from the shallows four yards away. Another few feet out, as I knew, the sand shelved sharply to deeper water beside the rocks. Once get him even half floating, and I should be able easily to manage his weight.

I switched off the torch, then put my arms round the dolphin as far as I could, and tried to pull him. But I could't get hold of him; my hands slipped over the faultless streamlining of his body. Nor could I grasp the dorsal fin, and when I tried tugging at his flippers he fidgeted for the first time, and I thought he was going to struggle, and work himself farther up the shore. Finally, kneeling, I got my shoulder right against his, and tried to thrust him backwards with all the strength I could muster. But he never moved an inch.

I stood back at length, panting, sweating, and almost in tears. 'I can't do it. Sweetie, I can't even budge you!' The bright liquid eye watched me silently. Behind him, four yards away, the sea heaved and whispered under the tail of the wind. Four yards; life or death.

I reached the torch down from the tree. 'I'll go and get a rope. If I tie it round you, I could pull you. Get a leverage round a tree—anything!' I stopped to caress his shoulder, whispering: 'I'll hurry, love, I'll run all the way.'

But the feel of the dolphin's skin, dry and roughening, made me hesitate. It might take some time to find a rope, or get help. No good going for Godfrey; if he was still out, it would be time lost. And I couldn't go to the Castello. I would have to go all the way home. I had better throw some sea-water over the animal's skin before I left him, to keep him safe while I was away.

I kicked off my sandals and ran into the shallows. But the spray I splashed up barely reached beyond his tail, and (so shallow was the water here) came up full of sand and grit that would dry on him even more disastrously than before.

Then I remembered the plastic bag, stupidly small, but better than nothing. I ran out of the water, dragged the bag from my pocket, shone the torch down, and tipped Phyllida's make-up out on the sand. The Forli diamond fell into the torchlight with a flash and a shimmer. I snatched it up and pushed it on my finger, and dropped the rest of the things back into my pocket, along with the torch. Then I ran back to the sea's edge, and scooped up my pathetic pint of water to throw over the dolphin.

It seemed to take an age. Stooping, straightening, running, tipping, stooping, running, tipping . . . When I reached the beast's shoulders I put a hand over the air-hole and poured the water carefully round it: unbelievably, dolphins could drown, and under the circumstances one couldn't expect the right reflexes to be working. When I poured water over his face the first time he blinked, which startled me a little, but after that he watched me steadily, the nearer eye swivelling as I moved to and fro.

At last he seemed wet enough to be safe. I dropped the dripping bag, wiped my hands on my coat, which was probably already ruined beyond repair, pulled on my sandals, and patted the damp shoulder again.

'I'll be back, sweetie, don't worry. I'll be as quick as I can. Keep breathing. And let's pray no one comes.'

This was the nearest I had got to admitting, even to myself, why I had been whispering, and why, as soon as I no longer needed the light, I had snapped the torch out.

I ran back across the sand. The piano had stopped, but I could still see the faint glow of light from the open terrace window. Nothing moved on the terrace itself. Then I was in the shadow of the wood, where the path to the Villa Forli went up steeply. Using the torch once more, I clambered breathlessly. The breeze, steady now, had filled the wood with a rustling that drowned my steps.

And now the starlit clearing. The frogs plopped into the pool. The stream glittered in the flying edge of my torchlight. I switched off as I emerged from the trees, and crossed the open space quietly, pausing at the far side of it to get my breath, leaning up against a young oak that stood where the path tunnelled afresh into the black burrow of the woods.

As I came out from under the oak, something moved on the path.

I checked, fingers fumbling clumsily with the torch. It flashed on, catching the edge of a side-stepping figure. A man, only a yard or so away. I would have run straight into him.

The bushes rustled just beside me. Someone jumped. The torch was struck out of my hand. I whipped round, and I think I would have screamed to wake the dead, only he grabbed me, pulled me to him brutally, and his hand came down hard over my mouth.

Chapter 8

Pray you tread softly, that the blind mole may not
Hear a foot fall: we now are near his Cell.

IV. i.

HE WAS VERY strong. I struggled and fought, necessarily in silence, but I couldn't do a thing. I must have hurt him, though, in clawing at his hand, for he flinched, and I heard his breath go in sharply. He took the hand away with a hissed *'Keep quiet, will you?'* in English, and then made it certain by jamming my head hard into the front of his jacket, so that I was not only dumb, but blinded, too. His coat was damp, and smelt of the sea. I got the swift impression of other movement near by, but heard nothing above my own and my assailant's breathing, and the thudding of my heart. The pressure of his hand on the back of my head was hurting me, and a button scored my cheek. My ribs, held in the hard embrace of his other arm, felt as if they were cracking.

I stopped fighting and went slack, and straight away the cruel grip eased, but he still held me pressed to him, both arms caught now and firmly pinioned. As his hold relaxed I pulled my head free. If I screamed, they would hear me from the Castello terrace . . . they could be down here in a few seconds . . . surely, even Max Gale—

'Where have you been?' demanded my captor.

I gaped at him. As soon as he saw I had no intention of screaming, he let me go. *'You?'* I said.

'Where have you been?'

I had my hands to my face, rubbing the sore cheeks. 'What's that got to do with you?' I asked furiously. 'You go a bit far, don't you, Mr. Gale?'

'Have you been up at the Castello?'

'I have not! And if I had–'

'Then you've been to the beach. Why?'

'Is there any reason–?' I began, then stopped. Fright and fury, together, had let me forget for a moment what else had happened that day. Max Gale might have no business to demand an account of my movements, but he might well have the best of reasons for wanting to know them.

Nothing was to be gained by refusing to tell him. I said, rather sulkily: 'I went down to get Phyl's ring. She left it on the beach this morning. You needn't look as if you don't believe me; it was in a little bag, and you missed it. There, see?' I flashed the diamond at him, then pushed the hand deep into my coat pocket, almost as if I expected him to grab it from me, and glared up at him. 'And now perhaps you'll tell me what *you're* playing at? This game of yours is way beyond a joke, let me tell you! It'll be mantraps next, I suppose. You hurt me.'

'I'm sorry. I didn't mean to. I thought you were going to scream.'

'Good heavens, of course I was! But why should you have minded if I had?'

'Well, I–' He hesitated. 'Anyone might have heard . . . My father . . . It might have startled him.'

'Thoughtful of you!' I said tartly. 'It didn't matter, did it, if you scared *me* half out of my wits? What a model son you are, aren't you? I'm surprised you could bring yourself to go out so late and leave your father alone! If it comes to that, where've *you* been, that you don't want anyone to know about?'

'Fishing.'

'Oh?' The heavily ironic retort that jumped to my lips withered there and died. I said slowly: 'But you were up there at the Castello half an hour ago.'

'What do you mean? I thought you said you hadn't been near the Castello.'

'The noise you make with that piano,' I said nastily, 'you could hear it from the mainland. I heard you from the beach.'

'That's impossible.' He spoke abruptly, but with a note of puzzlement.

'I tell you I did! You were playing the piano, and then talking to your father. I know your voices. It *was* you.'

He was silent for a moment. Then he said slowly: 'It sounds to me as if you heard a working session on tape being played through, comments and all. But I still don't see how that could be. My father isn't there. He's away staying the night at a friend's house.'

'How far away?'

'If it's anything to do with you, Corfu.'

'You must think I've a scream like a steam whistle,' I said dryly.

'What? Oh, I . . .' he had the grace to stammer slightly . . . 'I'm afraid I did rather say the first thing that came into my head. But it's true that he's not at home.'

'And neither were you?' I said. 'Well, whoever was playing the tape, it certainly made a wonderful alibi.'

'Don't be silly.' His laugh was excellently done. He must have some of his father's talent, after all. Possibly only someone as experienced with actors' voices as I could have told that the easy amusement was assumed over some urgent preoccupation. 'Your imagination's working overtime, Miss Waring! Please don't go making a mystery out of this. All that'll have happened is that my father's decided for some reason to come home, and he was amusing himself with the tape-recorder. As for myself, I've been out fishing with Adoni . . . And if it's any satisfaction to you, *you* frightened *me* half out of my wits. I'm afraid my reactions were a bit rough. I'm sorry for that. But if someone suddenly breaks out of the dark and runs straight into you, you—well, you act according.'

'According to what? Jungle law?' I was still smarting. 'I wouldn't have said those reactions were exactly normal, unless you were expecting . . . Just what *were* you expecting, Mr. Gale?'

'I'm not sure.' This, at any rate, sounded like the truth. 'I thought I heard someone coming up from the beach, fast, and trying not to be heard, but the breeze was covering most of the sounds, and I couldn't be certain. Then the sounds stopped, as if whoever it was was hiding and waiting. Naturally that made me begin to wonder what they might be up to, so I waited, too.'

'I only stopped to get my breath. Your imagination's working overtime, Mr. Gale.'

'Very probably.' I wasn't sure if he had even noticed the gibe. His head was bent, and he seemed to be studying one of his hands, turning it this way and that. 'Well, just as I decided I'd been mistaken, you erupted from the trees like a deer on the run. I grabbed you. Pure reflex.'

'I see. And I suppose it was pure reflex that you knocked the torch out of my hand before I could see anything?'

'Of course,' he said woodenly.

'And that even when you saw who it was, you acted like a—a *Gestapo*?' No reply to that. I can only suppose that excitement and the moment's fright had pumped too much adrenalin into my bloodstream; I think I was a bit 'high' with it. I remember feeling vaguely surprised that I was not in the least afraid of him. At some level, I suppose, I was reasoning that the man (in spite of his dubious bit of adventuring in what Godfrey had called the 'milk run') was hardly a dangerous criminal, and that he obviously intended me no harm: on the conscious level I was damned if I went tamely home now without finding exactly what was going on around here. It had already touched me far too closely to be ignored. The enchanted bubble had never really existed. I was beginning to suspect that there was no such thing.

So I asked, as if it were a matter of purely academic interest: 'I still want to know why it should have mattered to you where I'd been? Or that I might recognise you? Or was it the others I wasn't supposed to see?'

I thought for a moment that he wasn't going to answer. From somewhere farther up in the wood, an owl called breathily once, and then again. In the pool, a frog tried his voice tentatively for a moment, lost his nerve, and dived again. Max Gale said, quietly: 'Others?'

'The men who went past while you were holding me.'

'You're mistaken.'

'Oh, no, I'm not. There was somebody else there. I saw him beside the path, just as you jumped on me.'

'Then you probably recognised him as well. That was Adoni, our gardener. You've met him, I believe?'

You wouldn't have thought he was admitting another lie, or even conceding a slight point. The tone was that of a cool, social brush-off. I felt the adrenalin soaring dangerously again as he added, calmly: 'He usually comes with me when I go fishing. What's the matter? Don't you believe me?'

I managed to say, quite pleasantly: 'I was just wondering why you didn't beach the boat in your own bay. This seems a funny way to come—if you've just been fishing.'

'The wind was getting up, and it was easier to come in the other side of the point. And now, if you'll excuse me—'

'You mean,' I said, 'that you left your boat on *our* side of the

point? Tied to our jetty, even? Now, isn't that too bad? I think
you'd better go straight down again and move it, Mr. Gale. We don't
like trespassers at the Villa Forli.'

There was a short, sharp pause. Then, unexpectedly, he laughed.
'All right. One to you. But not tonight. It's late, and I've got things
to do.'

'I suppose you ought to be helping Adoni to carry home the fish?
Or would it be more correct to call it "the catch"?'

That got through. You'd have thought I'd hit him. He made a
sudden movement, not towards me, but I felt my muscles tighten,
and I think I even backed a pace. I wondered why I had ever thought
him a subdued edition of his father. And, quite suddenly, I was
scared.

I spoke quickly: 'You needn't worry. I don't mean to give you
away! Why should I? It's nothing to me, but you must see it's awful
to be in the middle of something and not know just what's going on!
Oh, yes, I know about it, it was obvious enough. But I'll not say
anything—I think too much of Miranda and her mother, and, if it
comes to that, of your father, to drag the police back here with a lot
more questions. Why should I care what you've got yourself into?
But I *do* care about Adoni . . . Did you know he's going to marry
Miranda? Why did you have to involve him in this? Hasn't there
been enough trouble?'

After that first, uncontrollable start, he had listened without
movement or comment, but I could see his eyes on me, narrow and
intent in the dim light. Now he said, very quietly: 'Just what are you
talking about?'

'You know quite well. I suppose poor Yanni never got the job
done last night, so you've been across there tonight, to the Albanian
coast, to do it yourself. Am I right?'

'Where did you get this . . . fantasy?'

'Fantasy, nothing,' I said roundly. 'Godfrey Manning told me this
morning.'

'*What?*' If I had got through before, this was straight between the
joints of the harness. The word alone sent me back another pace,
and this time he followed. I felt my back come up against a tree, and
turned aside blindly—I think to run away—but his hand shot out and
took my wrist, not hard, but in a grip I couldn't have broken without
struggling, and probably not even then. 'Manning? *He* told you?'

'Let me go!'

'No, wait a minute. I'm not going to hurt you, don't be scared . . .
But you've got to tell me. What did Manning say to you?'

'Let me go, please!'

He dropped the wrist immediately. I rubbed it, though it was not
in the least hurt. But I was shaking now. Something had happened
that had changed the whole pitch of the scene; in place of the slightly
pleasurable bitchiness of the previous exchange, there was now
something urgent, hard, and yes, threatening. And it was Godfrey's
name that had done it.

Gale repeated: 'What did he tell you?'

'About Yanni? That he was a smuggler, and that he would
probably have a "contact" or whatever you call it, who'd get his
supplies for him, and that he hoped the police wouldn't tumble to it,
because Spiro had been in it too, and it would hurt Maria if it came
out.'

'That was all?'

'Yes.'

'When did he tell you all this?'

'This morning, at the point, before you came down.'

'Ah.' I heard his breath go out. 'Then you weren't up at
Manning's house just now?'

'Of course I wasn't! Have you any idea what time it is?'

'I–of course. I'm sorry. I didn't think. I wasn't trying to be
offensive. Did Manning tell you that I was Yanni's "contact"?'

'No. I worked that out for myself.'

'You did? How?'

I hesitated. The feeling of fear had gone, and common sense had
come back to tell me that I was in no danger. Smuggler or not, he
would hardly murder me for this. I said: 'I saw Yanni coming up to
the Castello last night.'

'I . . . see.' I could almost feel the amazement, the rapid reassess-
ment of the situation. 'But you said nothing to the police.'

'No.'

'Why not?'

I said carefully: 'I'm not quite sure. To begin with, I kept quiet
because I thought I might be mistaken, and Yanni possibly hadn't
been going up to the Castello at all. If I'd thought you'd had
anything to do with his death, I'd have told straight away. Then
later I realised that there *was* some connection between you and
Yanni, and that you'd known he was going out last night.'

'How?'

'Because you weren't surprised when you heard he'd been drowned –'

'You noticed that, did you? My mistake. Go on.'

'But you *were* shocked. I saw that.'

'You see a darned sight too much.' He sounded grim. 'Was that what made you decide I hadn't killed him?'

'Good heavens, no! It wouldn't have occurred to me that you'd killed him! If I'd thought it was anything but an accident, I'd have told the whole thing straight away! It–it wasn't, was it?'

'Not that I'm aware of. Go on. What else did you see?'

'I saw you go back to the body, and have another look at it.'

'Did you, by God? From the path? Careless of me, I thought I was out of view. Who else saw that?'

'Nobody.'

'You're sure of that?'

'Pretty well.'

'And you said nothing about that, either? Well, well. So it was entirely your own idea that I was smuggling, along with Yanni?'

'Yes.'

'And now you've found out for certain. Do you still propose to say nothing?'

I said, without challenge, but out of simple curiosity: 'How would you make sure of it?'

He said, equally simply: 'My dear, I couldn't begin to try. I can only tell you that it's urgent that nobody should know I've been out tonight, nobody at all, and beg you to keep quiet.'

'Then don't worry. I will.'

There was a short pause. 'As easy as that?' he said, in an odd tone.

'I told you–for your father's sake,' I said, perhaps a little too quickly, 'and for Maria's. The only thing is–'

'Yes?'

'Things go in threes, they say, and if anything should happen to Adoni–'

He laughed. 'Nothing shall, I promise you! I couldn't take the responsibility for damaging a work of art like Adoni! We-ll . . .' There was a whole world of relief in the long-drawn syllable. Then his voice changed; it was brisk, easy, normal. 'I mustn't keep you any more. Heaven knows what the time is, and you must get home with that treasure trove of yours. I'm sorry I missed it this morning, and gave your sister a bad half-hour . . . And I'm sorry I frightened you just now. To say that I'm grateful is the understatement of the year. You'll let me see you home?'

'There's no need, really, thank you. In any case, hadn't you better get up there to help Adoni?'

'He's all right. Didn't you hear the signal?'

'Signal? But there hasn't been–' I stopped as I saw him smile. 'Not the owls? No, really, how corny can you get! Was that really Adoni?'

He laughed. 'It was. The robber's mate is home and dry, complete with "catch". So come along now, I'll take you home.'

'No, really, I–'

'Please. After all, these woods are pretty dark, and you were nervous, weren't you?'

'Nervous? No, of course not!'

He looked down in surprise. 'Then what in the world were you racing back like that for?'

'Because I–' I stopped dead. The dolphin. I had forgotten the dolphin. The breeze, riffling the treetops, breathed gooseflesh along my skin. I thought of the dolphin, drying in it, back there on the beach. I said quickly: 'It was so late, and Phyl was worrying. Don't bother, please, I'll go alone. Good night.'

But as I reached the tunnel of trees, he caught me up. 'I'd sooner see you safely home. Besides, you were quite right about shifting the boat; I'd rather have her nearer to hand in the morning. I'll take her across into the lee of the pines.'

For the life of me, I couldn't suppress a jerk of apprehension. He felt it, and stopped.

'Just a minute.'

His hand was on my arm. I turned. It was very dark under the trees.

He said: 'You've found out more about me than is quite comfortable. It's time you were a little bit honest about yourself, I think. Did you meet anyone down in the bay?'

'No.'

'See anyone?'

'N-no.'

'Quite sure? This is important.'

'Yes.'

'Then why don't you want me to go down there?'

I said nothing. My throat was stiff and dry as cardboard. Tears of strain, fear and exhaustion were not very far away.

'Look,' he said, urgently and not unkindly, 'I have to know. Some day I'll tell you why. Damn it, I've got to trust *you*; what about your trusting me for a change? Something did happen down there to scare you, didn't it? It sent you running up here like a hare in front of a gun. Now, what was it? Either you tell me what it was, or I go down, and look for myself. Well?'

I threw in my cards. I said shakily: 'It was the dolphin.'

'The dolphin?' he echoed, blankly.

'It's in the bay.'

There was a pause, then he said, with a sharpness that was part exasperation, part relief: 'And am I supposed to be going down there to shoot it in the middle of the night? I told you before that I'd never touched the beast!' He added, more kindly: 'Look, you've had a grim sort of day, and you're frightened and upset. Nobody's going to hurt your dolphin, so dry your eyes, and I'll take you back hom ⌐ now. He can look after himself, you know.'

'He can't. He's on the beach.'

'He's what?'

'He's stranded. He can't get away.'

'Well, my God, you don't *still* think I'd do him any harm –?' He stopped, and seemed for the first time to take in what I had been telling him. '*Stranded?* You mean the creature's actually beached?'

'Yes. High and dry. He'll die. I've been trying and trying to move him, and I can't. I was running just now to get a rope, that's why I was hurrying. If he's out of water too long the wind'll dry him, and he'll die. And all this time we've been wasting –'

'Where is he?'

'The other side, under the pines. What are you–oh!' This was an involuntary cry as his hand tightened on my arm and swung me round. 'What are you doing?'

'Don't worry, this isn't another assault. Now listen, there's a rope in my boat. I'll go down and get it, and I'll be with you as soon as I can. Get away back to your dolphin now, and wait for me. Can you keep him going another twenty minutes? Good. We'll manage him between us, don't worry. But'–a slight pause–'be very quiet, do you mind?'

Before I could reply, he was gone, and I heard him making a swift but still stealthy way back the way he had come.

Chapter 9

To the elements
Be free, and fare thou well.
V. 1.

THERE WAS NO time for doubt or questioning. That could come later. I obeyed him, flying back down the path to the beach, back across the pale sand to where the big bulk still lay motionless.

The dark eye watched. He was alive. I whispered: 'It's all right now, he's coming,' and went straight back to my scooping and tipping of sea-water. If I noticed that I hadn't bothered, even in my thoughts, to specify the 'he', that was another question that could wait till later.

He came, sooner than I had expected. A small motor-boat came nosing round the bay, without her engine, just with a dip and splash of oars as she was poled gently along. The breeze and the lapping of the sea on the rocks covered all sound until the boat was a rocking shadow within yards of me. I saw him stand up then, and lever it nearer the shore. Timber grated gently on rock, and he stepped out, making fast to a young pine, and then he was beside me on the sand, with a coil of rope over his arm.

'Good God. How did he get out here?'

'They do,' I said, 'I've read about it. Sometimes a storm blows them in, but sometimes they get their radar-beams fogged up, or something, and they come in at a fast lick and before they know where they are, they're high and dry. We're lucky there's only a foot or so of tide, or the water might have been miles away from him by now. Can you move him, d'you think?'

'I can try.' He stooped over the animal. 'Trouble is, you can't really get a hold. Didn't you have a torch?'

'I dropped it when you savaged me up in the wood.'

'So you did. There's one in the boat—no, perhaps not, we'll do without. Now, can you get to his other side?'

Together we fought to grasp and lift the dolphin, and with some success, for we did drag and shove him a foot or so downshore. But the dolphin himself defeated us; frightened, possibly, of the man's presence, or hurt by our tugging and by the friction of sand and pebbles, he began to struggle, spasmodically but violently; and at the end of the first strenuous minutes we had gained only a foot. I was exhausted, and Max Gale was breathing very hard.

'No good.' He stood back. 'He weighs a ton, and it's like trying to get hold of an outsize greased bomb. It'll have to be the rope. Won't it hurt him?'

'I don't know, but we'll have to try it. He'll die if he stays here.'

'True enough. All right, help me get it round the narrow bit above the tail.'

The dolphin lay like a log, his eye turning slowly back to watch us as we bent to tackle the tail-rope. Without the torch it was impossible to tell, but I had begun to imagine that the eye wasn't so bright or watchful now. The tail felt heavy and cold, like something already dead. He never flickered a muscle as we fought to lift and put a loop round it.

'He's dying,' I said, on a sort of gulp. 'That fight must have finished him.' I dashed the back of my hand over my eyes, and bent to the job. The rope was damp, and horrible to handle, and the dolphin's tail was covered with coarse sand.

'You do tear yourself up rather, don't you?'

I looked up at him as he worked over the loop. His tone was not ungentle, but I got the impression from it that half his mind was elsewhere: he cared nothing for the dolphin, but wanted merely to get this over, and get back himself to whatever his own queer and shady night's work had been.

Well, fair enough. It was good of him to have come at all. But some old instinct of defensiveness made me say a little bitterly:

'It seems to me you can be awfully happy in this life if you stand aside and watch and mind your own business, and let other people do as they like about damaging themselves and each other. You go on kidding yourself that you're impartial and tolerant and all that, then all of a sudden you realise you're dead, and you've never been alive at all. Being alive hurts.'

'So you have to break your heart over an animal who wouldn't even know you, and who doesn't even recognise you?'

'Someone has to bother,' I said feebly. 'Besides, he does recognise me, he knows me perfectly well.'

He let that one pass, straightening up from the rope. 'Well, there it is, that's the best we can do, and I'm hoping to heaven we can get it off again before he takes off at sixty knots or so . . . Well, here goes. Ready?'

I dropped my coat on the sand, kicked off my sandals, and splashed into the shallows beside him. We took the strain of the rope together. It didn't even strike me as odd that we should be there, hands touching, working together as naturally as if we had done it every day of our lives. But I was very conscious of the touch of his hand against mine on the rope.

The dolphin moved an inch or two; another inch; slid smoothly for a foot; stuck fast. This way, he seemed even heavier to haul, a dead weight on a rope that bit our hands and must surely be hurting him abominably, perhaps even cutting the skin . . .

'Easy, now,' said Max Gale in my ear.

We relaxed. I let go the rope, and splashed shorewards. 'I'll go and take a look at him. I'm so afraid he's –'

'Blast!' This from Gale, as the dolphin heaved forward suddenly, beating with his tail, slapping up water and sand. I heard the rope creak through Gale's hands, and another sharp curse from him as he plunged to keep his footing.

I ran back. 'I'm sorry . . . Oh! What is it?' He had twisted the rope round his right hand and wrist, and I saw how he held his left arm up, taut, the fingers half clenched as if it hurt him. I remembered how he had examined it, up in the glade. This must be why he had made such heavy weather of fixing the rope, and had been unable to shift the dolphin.

'Your hand?' I said sharply. 'Is it hurt?'

'No. Sorry, but I nearly went in then. Well, at least the beast's still alive. Come on, we'll have another go before he really does take fright.'

He laid hold once more, and we tried again. This time the dolphin lay still, dead weight again, moving slowly, slowly, till the lost ground was regained; but then he stuck once more, apparently immovable.

'There must be a ridge or something, he sticks every time.' Gale paused to brush the sweat out of his eyes. I saw him drop his left hand from the rope and let it hang.

'Look,' I said tentatively, 'this'll take all night. Couldn't we possibly—I mean, could the *boat* tow him out . . . with the engine?'

He was silent for so long that I lost my nerve, and said hurriedly: 'It's all right, I do understand. I—I just thought, if Adoni really had got safe in, it wouldn't matter. Forget it. It was marvellous of you to bother at all, with your hand and everything. Perhaps . . . if I just stay here all night and keep him damp, and if you could . . . *do* you think you could ring Phyl for me and tell her? You could say you saw me from the terrace, and came down? And if you could come back in the morning, when it doesn't matter, with the boat, or with Adoni . . .' He had turned and was looking down at me. I couldn't see him except as a shadow against the stars. 'If you wouldn't mind?' I finished.

'We'll use the boat now,' he said, abruptly. 'What do we do—make the rope fast to the bows, and then back her out slowly?'

I nodded eagerly. 'I'll stay beside him till he's floated. I'll probably have to hold him upright in the water till he recovers. If he rolls, he'll drown. The air-hole gets covered, and they have to breathe terribly often.'

'You'll be soaked.'

'I'm soaked now.'

'Well, you'd better have my knife. Here. If you have to cut the rope, cut it as near his tail as you can.'

I stuck the knife in my belt, pirate-wise, then splashed back to where the dolphin lay. It wasn't my imagination, the lovely dark eye was duller, and the skin felt harsh and dry again. I put a hand on him and bent down.

'Only a minute now, sweetheart. Don't be frightened. Only a minute.'

'Okay?' called Max softly, from the boat, which was bobbing a few yards from shore. He had fixed the rope; it trailed through the water from the dolphin's tail to a ring on the bows.

'Okay,' I said.

The engine started with a splutter and then a throbbing that seemed to fill the night. My hand was on the dolphin's body still . . . Not even a tremor; boats' engines held no terrors for him. Then the motor steadied down to a mutter, and the boat began to back quietly out from shore.

The rope lifted, vibrated, with the water flying from it in shining spray; then it tightened. The engine's note quickened; the rope stretched, the starlight running and dripping along it. The loop, fastened just where the great bow of the tail springs out horizontally from the spine, seemed to bite into the beast's flesh. It was very tight; the skin was straining; it must be hurting vilely.

The dolphin made a convulsive movement, and my hand clenched on the knife, but I kept still. My lip bled where I was biting it, and I was sweating, as if I was being hurt myself. The boat's engine beat gently, steadily; the starlight ran and dripped along the rope. . .

The dolphin moved. Softly, smoothly, the huge body began to slide backwards down the sand towards the water. With my hand still on the loop of the tail-rope, I went with it.

'It's working!' I said breathlessly. 'Can you keep it very slow?'

'Right. That okay? Sing out as soon as he's afloat, and I'll cast off here.'

The dolphin slithered slowly backwards, like a vessel beginning its run down the launching-ramp. The grating of sand and broken shells under his body sounded as loud to me as the throbbing engine a few yards out to sea. Now, at last, he touched water . . . was drawn through the crisping ripples . . . was slowly, slowly, gaining the sea. I followed him as he slid deeper. The ripples washed over my feet, my ankles, my knees; the hand that I kept on the loop of rope was under water to the wrist.

And now we had reached the place where the bottom shelved more steeply. All in a moment I found myself standing nearly breast-deep, gasping as the water rose round me in the night chill. The dolphin, moving with me, rocked as the water began to take his weight. Another few seconds, and he would be afloat. He only moved once, a convulsive, flapping heave that twanged the rope like a bow-string and hurt my hand abominably, so that I cried out, and the engine shut to a murmur as Max said sharply:

'Are you hurt?'

'No. Go on. It held him.'

'How far now?'

'Nearly deep enough. He's quiet now, I think he's . . . Oh, God, I think he's dead! Oh, Max . . .'

'Steady, my dear, I'll come. Hold him, we'll float him first. Say when.'

'Nearly . . . *Right! Stop!*'

The engine shut off, as suddenly as if a soundproof door had slammed. The dolphin's body floated past me, bumping and wallowing. I braced myself to hold him. Max had paid out the rope, and was swiftly poling the boat back to her mooring under the pines. I heard the rattle of a chain as he made fast, and in another few moments he was beside me in the water, with the slack of the rope looped over his arm.

'How goes it? Is he dead?'

'I don't know. I don't know. I'll hold him up while you get the rope off.'

'Turn his head to seaward first, just in case . . . Come along, old chap, round you come . . . There. Fine. Now hang on, my dear, I'll be as quick as I can.'

The dolphin lay motionless in my arms, the air-hole flaccid and wide open, just out of water, his body rolling heavily, like a leaky boat about to founder. 'You're all right now,' I told him, in an agonised whisper that he certainly couldn't hear, 'you're in the sea . . . the *sea*. You can't die now . . . you can't. . .'

'Stop worrying.' Max's voice came, cheerfully brisk, from the other end of the dolphin. 'St. Spiridion looks after his own. He is a bit sub., poor beast, isn't he? However, heaven keep him so till I've got this damned rope off him. Are you cold?'

'Not very,' I said, teeth chattering.

As he bent over the rope again, I thought I felt the dolphin stir against me. Next moment I was sure. The muscles flexed under the skin, a slow ripple of strength ran along the powerful back, a flipper stirred, feeling the water, using it, taking his weight . . .

'He's moving!' I said excitedly. 'He's all right! Oh, Max— quick—if he takes off now—'

'If he takes off now, we'll go with him. The rope's wet, I can't do a thing, I'll have to cut it. Knife, please.'

As he slid the blade in under the rope and started to saw at it, the dolphin came to life. The huge muscles flexed smoothly once, twice, against me, then I saw the big shoulders ripple and bunch. The air-hole closed.

I said urgently: 'Quick! He's going!'

The dolphin pulled out of my arms. There was a sudden surge of cold water that soaked me to the breast, as the great body went by in a splendid diving roll, heading straight out to sea. I heard Max swear sharply, and there was a nearer, secondary splash and swell, as he disappeared in his turn, completely under the water. The double wash swept over me, so that I staggered, almost losing my footing, and for one ghastly moment I thought that Max, hanging grimly on to the rope, had been towed straight out to sea in the dolphin's wake, like a minnow on a line. But as I regained my own balance, staggering back towards shallower water, he surfaced beside me, waist-deep and dripping, with the cut loop in his hand, and the rope trailing.

I gripped his arm, almost crying with relief and excitement. 'Oh, Max!' I staggered again, and his soaking arm came round me. I hardly noticed. I was watching the dark, starry sea where, far out, a trail of sea-fire burned and burst in long, joyous leaps and curves, and vanished into the blackness . . .

'Oh, Max . . . Look, there he goes, d'you see the light? There . . . he's gone. He's gone. Oh, wasn't it *marvellous*?'

For the second time that night I felt myself gripped, and roughly silenced, but this time by his mouth. It was cold, and tasted of salt, and the kiss seemed to last for ever. We were both soaked to the skin, and chilled, but where our bodies met and clung I could feel the quick heat of his skin and the blood beating warm against mine. We might as well have been naked.

He let me go, and we stood there staring at one another.

I pulled myself together with an effort. 'What was that, the forfeit for the roses?'

'Hardly. Call it the climax of a hell of a night.' He pushed the soaking hair back off his forehead, and I saw him grin. 'The recreation of the warrior, Miss Waring. Do you mind?'

'You're welcome.' *Take it lightly, I thought, take it lightly.* 'You and Adoni must have had yourselves quite a time out fishing.'

'Quite a time.' He was not trying to take it any way at all; he merely sounded cheerful, and decidedly pleased with himself. 'As a matter of fact, that was the pent-up feelings of a hell of a week. Didn't you see it coming? My father did.'

'Your father? After that first meeting? I don't believe you. You looked as if you'd have liked to lynch me.'

'My feelings,' he said carefully, 'could best be described as mixed. And damn it, if you will persist in being half naked every time you come near me—'

'Max Gale!'

He laughed at me. 'Didn't they ever tell you that men were only human, Lucy Waring? And some a bit more human than others?'

'If you call it human. You flatter yourself.'

'All right, darling, we'll call it the forfeit for the roses. You took a fair number, didn't you? Splendid. Come here.'

'Max, you're impossible . . . Of all the complacent—this is ridiculous! What a time to *choose* . . .'

'Well, my love, since you spark like a cat every time I come near you, what can I do but duck you first?'

'Shows what a lot you know about electricity.'

'Uh-huh. No, keep still a minute. You pack a pretty lethal charge, don't you?'

'You could blow a few fuses yourself, if it comes to that . . . For pity's sake, we must be mad.' I pushed him away. 'Come on out. I'd love to die with you and be buried in one grave, but not of pneumonia, it's not romantic . . . *No*, Max! I admit I owe you anything you like, but let's reckon it up on dry land! Come on out, for goodness' sake.'

He laughed, and let me go. 'All right. Come on. Oh, God, I've dropped the rope . . . no, here it is. And that's to pay for, too, let me tell you; a brand new sisal rope, sixty feet of it—'

'You're not the only one. This frock cost five guineas, and the sandals were three pounds ten, and I don't suppose they'll ever be quite the same again.'

'I'm perfectly willing to pay for them,' said Max cheerfully, stopping in eighteen inches of water.

'I'm sure you are, but it's not your bill. Oh, darling, don't be crazy, come *out*!'

'Pity. Who do you suppose settles the dolphin's accounts? Apollo, or the Saint? I think I'd opt for Apollo if I were you. Of course, if you've lost your sister's diamond it'll step the bill up quite a lot.'

'Murder! Oh, no, here it is.' The great marquise flashed blue in the starlight. 'Oh, Max, seriously, thank you most awfully—you were so wonderful . . . I've been such a fool! As if you could ever—'

His hand tightened warningly on my arm, and in the same moment I saw a light, a small dancing light, like that of an electric torch, coming round the point along the path from the Villa Rotha. It skipped along the rocks, paused on the moored boat, so that for the first time I saw her name, *Ariel*; then it glanced over the water, and caught us, dripping and bedraggled, splashing out of the shallows. We were also, by the time it caught us, at least four feet apart.

'Great God in heaven!' said Godfrey's voice. 'What goes on? Gale—Lucy . . . you're soaked, both of you! Is this another accident, for heaven's sake?'

'No,' said Max. 'What brought you down?'

His tone was about as informative, and as welcoming, as a blank wall with broken glass on the top. But Godfrey seemed not to have noticed. He had already jumped lightly down from the rocks to the sand beneath the pines. I saw the torchlight pause again, then rake the place where the dolphin had lain, and the wide, gouged track where he had been dragged down to the sea. My coat lay there in a huddle, with the sandals kicked off anyhow.

'For pity's sake, what gives?' Godfrey sounded distinctly alarmed, and very curious. 'Lucy, you haven't had trouble, have you? Did you get the diamond?'

'How did you know that?' I asked blankly.

'Good God, Phyl rang up, of course. She said you'd come down hours ago, and she was worried. I said I'd come and look for you. I'd only just got in.' The torchlight fingered us both again, and rested on Max. 'What's happened?'

'Don't flash that thing in my face,' said Max irritably. 'Nothing's happened, at least not in the sense you mean. That dolphin of yours got itself stranded. Miss Waring was trying to heave it back into the water, and couldn't manage, so I brought the boat along and towed the beast out to sea. We got drenched in the process.'

'You mean to tell me'—Godfrey sounded frankly incredulous—'that you brought your boat out at this time of night to rescue *a dolphin* ?'

'Wasn't it good of him?' I put in eagerly.

'Very,' said Godfrey. He hadn't taken his eyes off Max. 'I could have sworn I heard you go out some time ago.'

'I thought you were out yourself?' said Max. 'And had only just come in?'

Here we were again, I thought, the stiff-backed dogs warily circling. But it might be that Max's tone was repressive only because he was talking through clenched teeth—owing to cold, rather than emotion—because he added, civilly enough: 'I said "along", not "out". We went out, as it happened, some time after ten. We got in a few minutes ago. Adoni had just gone up when Miss Waring came running. I was still in the boat.'

Godfrey laughed. 'I'm sorry. I didn't mean to belittle the good deed! What a piece of luck for Lucy and the dolphin!'

'Yes, wasn't it?' I said. 'I was just wondering what on earth to do, when I heard Mr. Gale. I'd have come for you, but Phyl had said you wouldn't be there.'

'I wasn't.' I thought he was going to say something further, but he changed it to: 'I went out about ten-thirty, and I'd only just got into the house when the telephone rang. Did you find the ring?'

'Yes, thank you. Oh, it's been quite a saga, you've no idea!'

'I'm sorry I missed it,' he said. 'I'd have enjoyed the party.'

'I enjoyed it myself,' said Max. 'Now, look, to hell with the civilities, you'll have to hear it all some other time. If we're not to die of pneumonia, we've got to go. Where are your shoes, Miss Waring? Oh, thanks.' This as Godfrey's torch picked them out, and he handed them to me. 'Get them on quickly, will you?'

'What's this?' Godfrey's voice altered sharply.

'My coat.' I paid very little attention to his tone; I was shivering freely now, and engaged in the very unpleasant struggle to get my sandals on over wet and sandy feet. 'Oh, and there's Phyl's bag. Mr. Gale, would you mind – ?'

'That's blood!' said Godfrey. He was holding the coat up, and his torch shone, powerful as a headlamp, on the sleeve. I looked up, startled.

It was indeed blood. One sleeve of the coat was streaked with it.

I felt, rather than saw, Max stiffen beside me. The torch beam started its swing towards him. I said, sharply, '*Please* put the torch out, Godfrey! I don't feel decent in this sopping dress. Give me the coat, please. Yes, it's blood . . . The dolphin had got a cut from a stone or something; it bled all over me before I saw it. I'll be lucky if I ever get the stain out.'

'Hurry up,' said Max brusquely, 'you're shivering. Put this round you. Come on, we'll have to go.'

He slung the coat round my shoulders. My teeth were chattering now like a typewriter; the coat was no comfort at all over the soaked and clinging dress. 'Y-yes,' I said, 'I'm coming. I'll tell you about it when I see you, Godfrey. Th-thanks for coming down.'

'Good night,' said Godfrey. 'I'll come over tomorrow and see how you are.'

He turned back into the shadow of the pines. I saw the torchlight move slowly over the ground where the dolphin had lain, before it dodged once again up on to the rocks.

Max and I went briskly across the sand. The wind blew cold on our wet clothing.

'The coat cost nine pounds fifteen,' I said, 'and *that* bill's yours. That dolphin wasn't bleeding. What have you done to your hand?'

'Nothing that won't mend. Here, this way.'

We were at the foot of the Castello steps and I would have gone past, but he put out a hand and checked me.

'You can't go all the way home in those things. Come on up.'

'Oh, no, I think I'd better –'

'Don't be silly, why not? Manning'll telephone your sister. So can you, if it comes to that. And I'm going to escort you all the way over there and then tramp back myself in these. What's more, these blasted boots are full of water.'

'You might have drowned.'

'So I might. And how much would that have been to Apollo's account?'

'You know how much,' I said, not lightly at all, but not for him to hear.

Chapter 10

He is drunk now; where had he wine?
V. 1.

THE TERRACE WAS empty, but one of the long windows stood open, and Max led the way in through this.

The room was lit only by one small shaded lamp on a low table, and looked enormous and mysterious, a cave full of shadows. The piano showed its teeth vaguely near a darkened window, and the unlit stove and the huge gramophone loomed like sarcophagi in some dim museum.

Sir Julian sat in an arm-chair beside the lamp, which cast an almost melodramatic slant of light on the silver hair and emphatic brow. The white cat on his knee, and the elegant hand that stroked it, completed the picture. The effect was stagey in the extreme. Poe's *Raven*, I thought appreciatively; all it needs is the purple drapes, and the croaking from the shadows over the door . . .

In the same moment I became aware of other, even less comfortable stage effects than these. On the table at his elbow, under the lamp, stood a bottle of Turkish gin, two-thirds empty, a jug of water, and two glasses. And Sir Julian was talking to himself. He was reciting from *The Tempest*, the speech where Prospero drowns his book; he was saying it softly, an old magician talking half to himself, half to the heavenly powers from whose kingdom he was abdicating. I had never heard him do it better. And if anyone had wanted to know how much sheer technique – as opposed to nightly sweat and blood in front of the lights – was worth, here was the answer. It was doubtful if Sir Julian Gale even knew what he was saying. He was very drunk indeed.

Max had stopped dead just inside the window, with me close behind him, and I heard him make some sort of sound under his breath. Then I saw that Sir Julian was not alone. Adoni detached himself from the thicker darkness beyond the lamp, and cáme forward. He was dressed, like Max, in a fisherman's sweater and boots, rough clothing which only served to emphasise his startling good looks. But his face was sharp with anxiety.

'Max –' he began, then stopped abruptly as he saw me, and the state we were both in. 'It was *you*? What's happened?'

'Nothing that matters,' said Max shortly.

This wasn't the time to choose words, or, certainly, to resent them. So much was made more than ever obvious as he advanced into the light, and I saw him clearly for the first time that night. Whatever aggressive high spirits had prompted the little interlude there in the sea had vanished abruptly; he looked not only worried now, but angry and ashamed, and also very tired indeed. His left hand was thrust deep into his trouser-pocket, and there was some rag – a handkerchief, perhaps – twisted round the wrist, and blotched with blood.

Sir Julian had turned his head at the same time.

'Ah, Max . . .' Then he, too, saw me, and the hand which had been stroking the cat lifted in a graceful, practised gesture that looked as natural as breathing. '*Most sure, the goddess, On whom* –no, we had that before, didn't we? But how delightful to see you again, Miss Lucy . . . Forgive me for not getting up; the cat, as you see . . .' His voice trailed away uncertainly. It seemed he was dimly realising that there was need of more excuse than the cat would provide. A smile, loose enough to be disturbing, slackened his mouth. 'I was having some music. If you'd care to listen . . .'

The hand moved, not very steadily, to the switch of the tape-recorder which stood on a chair beside him, but Adoni stooped quickly and laid a hand over it, with a gentle phrase in Greek. Sir Julian gave up the attempt, and sank back in his chair, nodding and smiling. I saw with horrified compassion that the nod had changed to a tremor which it cost him an effort to check.

'Who's been here, father?' asked Max.

The actor glanced up at him, then away, with a look that might, in a less distinguished face, have been called shifty. 'Been here? Who should have been here?'

'Do you know, Adoni?'

The young man lifted his shoulders. 'No. He was like this when I got in. I didn't know there was any in the house.'

'There wasn't. I suppose he was alone when you got in? You'd hardly have given me the "all clear" otherwise.' He glanced down at his father, who was taking not the slightest notice of the conversation, but had retreated once more into some private world of his own, some gin-fumed distance apparently lit by strong ambers and swimming in a haze of poetry. 'Why did he come back, I wonder? He hasn't told you that?'

'He said something about Michael Andiakis being taken ill, but I haven't had time to get anything more out of him. He's not been talking sense . . . he keeps trying to switch that thing on again. It was going when I got up to the house. I got a fright; I thought someone was here with him.'

'Someone certainly has been.' Max's voice was tight and grim. 'He didn't say how he got back from town?'

Adoni shook his head. 'I did think of telephoning Andiakis' house to ask, but at this time of night . . .'

'No, you can't do that.' He bent over his father's chair and spoke gently and clearly. 'Father. Who's been here?'

Sir Julian, starting out of his dream, glanced up, focused, and said, with dignity: 'There were matters to discuss.'

His enunciation was as faultless as ever; the only thing was, you could hear him working to keep it so. His hands lay motionless now on the cat's fur, and there, again, you could see the controls being switched on. The same with Max, who had himself well in hand now, but I could hear the effort that the patient tone was costing him. Watching them, I felt myself so shaken with compassion and love that it seemed it was that, and not my wet clothes, which made me shiver.

'Naturally,' said Sir Julian clearly, 'I had to ask him in when he had driven me home. It was very good of him.'

Max and Adoni exchanged glances. 'Who had?'

No reply. Adoni said: 'He won't answer anything straight. It's no use.'

'It's got to be. We've got to know who this was and what he's told him.'

'I doubt if he told him much. He wouldn't say anything to me, only tried to turn the tape on, and talked on and on about the story you are writing the music for, you know, the old story of the island that he was telling Miranda and Spiro.'

Max pushed the damp hair off his brow with a gesture almost of desperation. 'We've got to find out—now, before he passes out. He knew perfectly well where we were going. He agreed to stay out of the way. My God, I was sure he could be trusted now. I thought he'd be safe with Michael. Why the *hell* did he come home?'

'Home is where the heart is,' said Sir Julian. 'When my wife died, the house was empty as a lord's great kitchen without a fire in it. Lucy knows, don't you, my dear?'

'Yes,' I said. 'Shall I go, Max?'

'No, please . . . if you don't mind. If you'll please stay. Look, father, it's all right now. There's only me and Adoni and Lucy. You can tell us about it. Why didn't you stay at Michael's?'

'Poor Michael was playing a very interesting game, Steinitz gambit, and I lost a rook in the first few minutes. Do you play chess, my dear?'

'I know the moves,' I said.

'Five moves would have done it. White to play, and mate in five moves. A foregone conclusion. But then he had the attack.'

'What sort of attack?' asked Max.

'I had no idea that his heart wasn't all it should be, for all he never drinks. I am quite aware that this is one reason why you like me to visit Michael, but a drink occasionally, for purely social reasons, never does the least harm. My heart is as strong as a bell. As strong as a bell. One's heart,' added Sir Julian, with the air of one dismissing the subject, 'is where the home is. Good night.'

'Just a minute. You mean Michael Andiakis has died of a heart attack? I *see*. I'm sorry, father. No wonder you felt you needed—'

'No, *no*! Who said he had died? Of course he didn't, I was there. I helped him. It was a good thing I was with him, the doctor said so, a very good thing. But then if I hadn't been there, I doubt if Michael would have had the attack at all. He always did get too excitable over our little game. Poor Michael.'

'You called the doctor?'

'I told you,' said his father impatiently. 'Why can't you listen? I think I'd like to go to bed.'

'What happened when the doctor came?'

'He put Michael to bed, and I helped him.' It was the first direct answer he had given, and he seemed to feel obscurely that something was wrong, for he gave that sidelong look at his son before going on: 'It's as well that I'm as sound as a bell myself, though I have never understood why bells should be particularly–particularly sound. Sweet bells jangled, out of tune and harsh. Then I went to get the doctor.' He paused. 'I mean the daughter. Yes, the daughter.'

Adoni said: 'There's a married daughter who lives in Capodistrias Street. She has three children. If she had to bring them with her, there would be no room for Sir Gale to stay.'

'I see. How did you get the lift back, father?'

'Well, I went to Karamanlis' garage, of course.' Sir Julian suddenly sounded sober, and very irritable. 'Really, Max, I don't know why you talk as if I'm incapable of looking after myself! Please try to remember that I lived here before you were born! I thought Leander might oblige me, but he was away. There was only one boy on duty, but he offered to get his brother to take me. We had a very interesting chat, very interesting indeed. I knew his uncle, Manoulis was the name. I remember once, when I was at Avra–'

'Was it Manoulis who brought you home?'

Sir Julian focused. 'Home?'

'Back here?' amended Max quickly.

The older man hesitated. 'The thing was, I had to ask him in. When he came in for petrol and saw me there, you might say he had to offer the lift, but all the same, one has to be civil. I'm sorry, Max.'

'It's all right, I understand. Of course one must. He brought you home, and you felt you'd have to ask him in, so you bought the gin?'

'Gin?' Sir Julian was drifting again. I thought I could see something struggling in his face, some intelligence half drowned with gin and sleep, holding on by a gleam of cunning. 'That's Turkish gin, too, terrible stuff, God knows what they put in it. It was what he said he liked . . . We stopped at that taverna–Constantinos' it used to be, but I forget the name now–two miles out of Ipsos. I think he must have guessed there wouldn't be any in the house.'

Max was silent. I couldn't see his face.

Adoni broke the pause. 'Max, look.' I had seen him stoop to pick something up, and now he held out a hand, with some small object on the palm; a cigarette stub. 'It was down there, by the stove. It's not one of yours, is it?'

'No.' Max picked the thing up, and held it closer to the light.

Adoni said: 'It is, isn't it?'

'Obviously.' Their eyes met again, over the old man's head. There was a silence, in which the cat suddenly purred. ' *"Things to discuss."* ' Max quoted it softly, but with a new note in his voice that I found frightening. 'What the sweet hell can *he* have wanted to discuss with my father?'

'This meeting,' said Adoni, 'could it be accidental?'

'It must have been. He was driving by, and picked my father up. Pure chance. Who could have foreseen that? Damn and damn and damn.'

'And getting him . . . like this?'

'Letting him get like this. There's a difference. That can't have been deliberate. Nobody knew he was like this except us, and Michael and the Karithis'.'

Adoni said: 'Maybe he's been talking this sort of nonsense all evening. Maybe *he* couldn't get any sense out of him, either.'

'He couldn't get any sense out of me,' said Sir Julian, with intense satisfaction.

'Oh, my God,' said Max, 'let's hope he's right.' He flicked the cigarette butt back towards the stove, and straightened his shoulders. 'Well, I'll get him to bed. Be a good chap and look after Miss Lucy, will you? Show her the bathroom—the one my father uses is the least repulsive, I think. Find her a towel and show her a spare bedroom—the one Michael sleeps in. There's an electric fire there.'

'All right, but what about your hand? Haven't you seen to it at all?'

'Not yet, but I will in a moment . . . Go on, man, don't fuss. Believe me, I'd fuss plenty if I thought it was serious; I'm a pianist of a sort, don't forget! Lucy, I'm sorry about this. Will you go with him now?'

'Of course.'

'This way,' said Adoni.

The massive door swung shut behind us, and our steps rattled across the chequer-board marble of the hall floor.

It would have taken Dali and Ronald Searle, working overtime on alternate jags of mescal and Benzedrine, to design the interior of the Castello dei Fiori. At one end of a hall was a massive curved staircase, with a wrought-iron banister and bare stone treads. The walls were panelled in the darkest possible oak, and what small rugs lay islanded on the marble sea were (as far as I could judge in the gloom) done in uniform shades of drab and olive-green. A colossal open fireplace, built for roasting oxen whole by men who had never roasted, and would never roast, an ox whole in their lives, half-filled one wall. The hearth of this bristled with spits and dogs and tongs and cauldrons and a hundred other mediæval kitchen gadgets whose functions I couldn't even guess at; they looked like–and probably were–instruments of torture. For the rest, the hall was cluttered like a bargain basement: the Gales must have thrown most of the furniture out of their big living-room to clear the acoustics–or perhaps merely in the interests of sane living–and as a result the hall was crammed full of enormous, over-stuffed furniture in various shades of mud, with innumerable extras in the way of bamboo tables, Chinese screens, and whatnots in spindly and very shiny wood. I thought I glimpsed a harmonium, but might have been wrong, because there was a full-sized organ, pipes and all, in the darkness beyond a fretwork dresser and a coat-rack made of stags' antlers. There was certainly a harp, and a small forest of pampas grass stuck in what I am sure was the severed foot of an elephant. These riches were lit with a merciful dimness by a single weak bulb in a torch held by a fully armed Javanese warrior who looked a bit like a gila monster in rut.

Adoni ran gracefully up the wide stairs in front of me. I followed more slowly, hampered by my icily clinging clothes, my sandals leaving horrible wet marks on the treads. He paused to wait for me, eyeing me curiously.

'What happened to you and Max?'

'The dolphin–Spiro's dolphin–was stranded on the beach, and he helped me to float it again. It pulled us both in.'

'No, did it really?' He laughed. 'I'd like to have seen that!'

'I'm sure you would.' At least his spirits didn't seem to have been damped by the recent scene in the music-room. I wondered if he were used to it.

'When you ran into Max, then, you were coming for help? I see! But why were you out on the beach in the dark?'

'Now don't *you* start!' I said warmly. 'I had plenty of that from Max! I was down there picking up a ring–this ring–that my sister had left this morning.'

His eyes and mouth rounded at the sight of the diamond. '*Po po po!* That must be worth a few drachs, that one! No wonder you didn't mind making a journey in the dark!'

'Worth more than your journey?' I asked innocently.

The beautiful eyes danced. 'I wouldn't say that.'

'No?' I regarded him uneasily. What on earth–what in heaven–could they have been up to? Drugs? Surely not! Arms? Ridiculous! But then, what did I know about Max, after all? And his worry in case his father might have 'talked' hadn't just been worry; it had been fear. As for Adoni—I had few illusions as to what my young Byzantine saint would be capable of . . .

He asked: 'When you first went out through the wood, you saw nobody?'

'Max asked me that. I heard Sir Julian playing the tape-recorder, but I've no idea if his visitor was still there. I gather you know who it was?'

'I think so. It's a guess, but I think so. Sir Gale may tell Max when they are alone, I don't know.'

'Max doesn't normally have drink in the house at all?'

'None that his—none that can be found.'

'I see.'

I did indeed see. I saw how the rumours had arisen, and just how false Phyl's picture of the situation had been. Except in so far as this sort of periodic 'bender' was a symptom of mental strain, Sir Julian Gale was sane enough. And now that I thought even further back, there had been whispers in the theatre world, possibly strong ones among those who knew him, but on my level the merest breath . . . rumours scotched once and for all by Sir Julian's faultless performances right up to the moment of retirement. Well, I had had a personal demonstration tonight of how it had been done.

'We thought he was better,' said Adoni. 'He has not done this for, oh, a long time. This will make Max very . . .' He searched for a word and came up with one that was, I felt, not quite adequate . . . 'unhappy.'

'I'm sorry. But he does seem to have been pushed into it this time.'

'Pushed in? Oh, yes, I understand. That is true. Well, Max will deal with it.' He gave a little laugh. 'Poor Max, he gets everything to deal with. Look, we had better hurry, or you will get cold, and then Max will deal with *me*!'

'Could he?'

'Easily. He pays my wages.'

He paused, and pressed a switch in the panelling, invisible except to its intimates. Another dim light faltered into life, this time held aloft by a startling figure in flesh-pink marble, carved by some robust Victorian with a mind above fig-leaves. A wide corridor now stretched ahead of us, lined on one side by massive, iron-studded doors, and on the other by what would, in daylight, be stained-glass windows of a peculiarly repulsive design.

'This way.'

He led the way quickly along the corridor. To either side the light glimmered yellow on the pathetic heads of deer and ibexes, and case after case where stuffed birds stood enthroned and moth-eaten. Every other available foot of wall-space was filled with weapons—axes, swords, daggers, and ancient firearms which I (who had furnished a few period plays in my time) identified as flintlocks and muskets, probably dating from the Greek War of Independence. It was to be hoped that Sir Julian and his son were as blind to the murderous décor as Adoni appeared to be.

'Your bathroom is along there.' He pointed ahead to a vast door, opposite which hung a tasteful design in crossed whips and spurs. 'I'll just show you where everything is, then I must go and dress his wrist.'

'How badly is he hurt? He wouldn't say.'

'Not badly at all. I think it's only a graze, for all it bled a lot. Don't worry, Max is sensible, he'll take all the care he should.'

'And you?' I said.

He looked surprised. 'I?'

'Will you take care of yourself as well? Oh, I know it's nothing to do with me, Adoni, but . . . well, be careful. For Miranda's sake, if not for your own.'

He laughed at me, and touched a thin silver chain at his neck which must have held a cross or some sort of medal. 'Don't you worry about me, either, Miss Lucy. The Saint looks after his own.' A vivid look. 'Believe me, he does.'

'I take it you did well tonight?' I said, a little dryly.

'I think so. Here we are.' He shoved the door wide, and found another switch. I glimpsed the splendours of marble and mahogany beyond him. 'The bedroom is the next one, through there. I'll find you a towel, and later I shall make you something hot to drink. You can find the way down?'

'Yes, thank you.'

He rummaged in a cupboard the size of a small garage, and emerged with a couple of towels. 'Here you are. You have everything now?'

'I think so. The only thing is—do I have to touch that thing?'

'That thing' was a fearsome contraption which, apparently, heated the water. It looked like a stranded mine, and sat on a panel of dials and switches that might have come straight off the flight deck of an air-liner designed by Emmett.

'You are as bad as Sir Gale,' said Adoni indulgently. 'He calls it Lolita, and refuses to touch it. It's perfectly safe, Spiro made it.'

'Oh.'

'It did go on fire once, but it's all right now. We re-wired it only last month, Spiro and I.'

Another dazzling smile, and the door shut gently. I was alone with Lolita.

You had to climb three steps to the bath, which was about the size of a swimming-pool, and fairly bristling with gadgets in blackened brass. But I forgave the Castello everything when I turned the tap marked C, and the water rushed out in a boiling cloud of steam. I hoped poor Max wouldn't be long before he achieved a similar state of bliss—it was to be assumed there was another bathroom, and another Lolita as efficient as mine—but just at the moment I spared Max no more than the most passing of thoughts, and none whatever for the rest of the night's adventures. All I wanted was to be out of those dreadful, sodden clothes, and into that glorious bath . . .

By the time I was languidly drying a body broiled all over to a glowing pink, my underclothing, which was mostly nylon, was dry. The dress and coat were still wet, so I left them spread over the hot pipes, put on the dressing-gown which hung behind the door, then padded through into the bedroom to attend to my face and hair.

I had what I had salvaged of Phyl's makeup, which included a comb, so I did the best I could with the inevitable dim light, and a cheval-glass, swinging between two mahogany pillars, that seemed designed to hang perpetually facing the carpet, until I found on the floor and replaced the wedge of newspaper that had held it in position since, apparently, July 20th, 1917.

In the greenish glass my reflection swam like something that might well have startled the Lady of Shalott out of her few wits. The dressing-gown was obviously one of Sir Julian's stagier efforts; it was long, of thick, dark red silk, and made one think of Coward comedies. With Phyl's lipstick, and my short, damply curling hair, and the enormous diamond on my hand, it made a pretty high camp effect.

Well, it was no odder than the other guises he had seen me in up to now. I wondered if this, too, would qualify as 'half-naked'. Not that it mattered, just now he would have other things very much on his mind.

I grimaced briefly at the image in the glass, then went out, back along Murder Alley, and down the stairs.

Chapter 11

The very instant that I saw you, did
My heart fly to your service, there resides
To make me slave to it.

III. 1.

THE MUSIC-ROOM door was standing open, but, though the lamp still burned, there was no one there. The gin had vanished, too, and in its place was something that looked like the remains of a stiff Alka-Seltzer, and a cup that had probably contained coffee.

As I hesitated in the doorway, I heard a quick step, and the service door under the stairway opened with a swish of chilly air.

'Lucy? Ah, I thought I heard you. You're all right? Warm now?'

'Lovely, thank you.' He himself looked a different person. I noticed that there was a fresh white bandage on his wrist, and that his dry clothes—another thick sweater and dark trousers—made him look as tough as before, but younger, rather nearer Adoni's league. So did the look in his face; he looked tired still, but with a tautness that now seemed to have some sort of affinity with Adoni's dark glow of excitement. A worthwhile trip, indeed . . .

I said quickly: 'Your clothes . . . You're surely not planning to go out again?'

'Only to drive you home, don't worry. Come along to the kitchen, will you? It's warm there, and there's coffee. Adoni and I have been having something to eat.'

'I'd adore some coffee. But I don't know if I ought to stay—my sister really will have the wind up by now.'

'I rang her up and told her what had happened . . . more or less.' He grinned, a boy's grin. 'Actually, Godfrey Manning had already called up and told her about the dolphin, and that her ring was safe, so she's quite happy, and says she'll expect you when she sees you. So come along.'

I followed him through the service door and down a bare, echoing passage. It seemed that the Castello servants could not be allowed to share the glories which fell to their betters, for 'below stairs' the Castello was unadorned by dead animals and lethal weapons. Personally I'd have traded the whole building, organ pipes and all, for the kitchen, a wonderful, huge cavern of a place, with a smaller cave for fireplace, where big logs burned merrily in their iron basket, adding their sweet, pungent smells to the smells of food and coffee, and lighting the big room with a living, beating glow. Hanging from the rafters, among the high, flickering shadows, bunches of dried herbs and strings of onions stirred and glimmered in the updraught of warm air.

In the centre of the kitchen was about an acre of scrubbed wooden table, and in a corner of the room Adoni was frying something on an electric cooker which had probably been built, or at any rate wired, by himself and Spiro. There was a wonderful smell of bacon and coffee.

'You can eat some bacon and eggs, surely?' asked Max.

'She will have to,' said Adoni briefly, over his shoulder. 'I have done them already.'

'Well . . .' I said, and Max pulled out a chair for me at the end of the table nearest to the fire, where a rather peculiar assortment of plates and cutlery were set in a space comprising about a fiftieth of the table's total area. Adoni put a plate down in front of me, and I realised that I was suddenly, marvellously hungry. 'Have you had yours?' I asked.

'Adoni has, and I've just reached the coffee stage,' said Max. 'Shall I pour some for you straight away?'

'Yes, please.' I wondered whether it would be tactful to ask after Sir Julian, and this made me remember my borrowed finery. 'My things were still wet, so I borrowed your father's dressing-gown. Will he mind, do you think? It's a terribly grand one.'

'*Present Laughter*,' said Max. 'Of course he won't. He'd be delighted. Sugar?'

'Yes, please.'

'There. If you can get outside that lot I doubt if the pneumonia bugs will stand a chance. Adoni's a good cook, when pushed to it.'

'It's marvellous,' I said, with my mouth full, and Adoni gave me that heart-shaking smile of his, said, 'It's a pleasure', and then, to

Max, something that I recognised (from a week's painful study of a phrase book) as, 'Does she speak Greek?'

Max jerked his head in that curious gesture–like a refractory camel snorting–that the Greeks use for 'No', and the boy plunged forthwith into a long and earnest speech of which I caught no intelligible word at all. It was, I guessed, urgent and excited rather than apprehensive. Max listened, frowning, and without comment, except that twice he interrupted with a Greek phrase–the same one each time–that checked the flow and sent Adoni back to speak more slowly and clearly. I ate placidly through my bacon and eggs, trying not to notice the deepening frown on Max's face, or the steadily heightened excitement of Adoni's narrative.

At length the latter straightened up, glancing at my empty plate. 'Would you like some more? Or cheese, perhaps?'

'Oh, no, thank you. That was wonderful.'

'Some more coffee, then?'

'Is there some?'

'Of course.' Max poured it, and pushed the sugar nearer. 'Cigarette?'

'No, thanks.'

He was returning the pack to his pocket when Adoni, who had been removing my plate, said something quickly and softly in Greek, and Max held the pack out to him. Adoni took three cigarettes, with the glimmer of a smile at me when he saw that I was watching, then he said something else in Greek to Max, added 'Good night, Miss Lucy', and went out through a door I hadn't noticed before, in a far corner of the kitchen.

Max said easily: 'Forgive the mystery. We've been putting my father to bed.'

'Is he all right?'

'He will be.' He threw me a look. 'I suppose you knew about his–difficulty?'

'No, how could I? I'd no idea.'

'But if you're in the business . . . I thought it must surely have got round.'

'It didn't get to me,' I said. 'I suppose there must have been rumours, but all I ever knew was that he wasn't well. I thought it was heart or something. And honestly, nobody knew here– at least, Phyl didn't, and if there'd been any talk you can bet she'd be the first to hear it. She just knew what you told Leo, that he'd been ill, and in a nursing home. Does it happen often?'

THIS ROUGH MAGIC 599

'If you'd asked me that yesterday,' he said, a little bitterly, 'I'd
have said it probably wouldn't happen again.'

'Did he talk when you took him upstairs?'

'A little.'

'Tell you who it was?'

'Yes.'

'And what they'd talked about?'

'Not really, no. He just kept repeating that "he hadn't got
anything out of him". That, with variations. He seemed rather more
pleased and amused than anything else. Then he went to sleep.'

I said: 'You know, I think you can stop worrying. I'd be willing to
bet that your father's said nothing whatever.'

He looked at me with surprise. I hadn't realised before how dark
his eyes were. 'What makes you so sure?'

'Well . . .' I hesitated. 'You were a bit upset, in there, but I had
nothing to do but notice things. I'll tell you how it struck me. He
was certainly drunk, but I think he was hanging on to something he
knew . . . he'd forgotten *why*, but just knew he had to. He knew he
hadn't to say anything about–about whatever you and Adoni were
doing. He was so fuddled that he couldn't sort out who was safe and
who wasn't, but he wasn't parting with anything; he even kept
stalling you and Adoni because I was there, and even about things
that didn't matter, like what happened at Mr. Andiakis'.' I smiled.
'And then the way he was reciting, and fiddling with the tape-
recorder . . . you can't tell me he normally gives private renderings
of Shakespeare in his own drawing-room? Actors don't. They may
go on acting their heads off off-stage, but they aren't usually bores.
It struck me–look, I'm sorry, am I speaking out of turn? Perhaps
you'd rather I didn't–'

'God, no. Go on.'

'It struck me that he was reciting because he knew that once he'd
got himself–or the tape–safely switched into a groove, he could just
go on and on without any danger of being jumped into saying the
wrong thing. When I heard it, he was probably playing the tape to
his visitor.'

His mouth twitched in momentary amusement. 'Serve him right.
What's more, I'm certain that the meeting at the garage was an
accident. If Adoni and I had been suspected, we'd have been
watched, and perhaps followed . . . or intercepted on our way
home.'

'Well, there you are; and it stands to reason that if your father had told him anything, or even dropped a hint where you both were, there's been masses of time to have the police along, or . . . or anything.'

'Of course.' The look he gave me was not quite easy, for all that.

I hesitated. 'Worrying about your father, though—that's a different thing. I don't know about these things. Do you think it may have, well, started him drinking again?'

'One can't tell. He's not an alcoholic, you know; it wasn't chronic, or approaching it. It's just that he started to go on these periodic drunks to get out of his jags of depression. We can only wait and see.'

I said no more, but turned my chair away from the table to face the fire, and drank my coffee. The logs purred and hissed, and the resin came bubbling out of one of them, in little opal globes that popped and swelled against the charring bark. The big airy room was filled with the companionable noises of the night; the bubbling of the resin, the spurt and flutter of flames, the creak of some ancient wooden floor settling for the night, the clang of the old hot-water system. As I stretched Sir Julian's bedroom slippers nearer the fire a cricket chirped, suddenly and clearly, about a yard away. I jumped, then, looking up, caught Max watching me, and we smiled at one another. Neither of us moved or spoke, but a kind of wordless conversation seemed to take place, and I was filled with a sudden, heart-swelling elation and happiness, as if the sun had come out on my birthday morning, and I had been given the world.

Then he had turned away, and was looking into the fire again. He said, as if he was simply going on from where we had left off:

'It started just over four years ago. Father was rehearsing at the time for that rather spectacular thing that Blair wrote for him, *Tiger Tiger*. You'll remember it; it ran for ever. Just eight days before the play was due to open, my mother and sister were both killed together in a motor accident. My sister was driving the car when it happened; it wasn't her fault, but that was no comfort. My mother was killed instantly; my sister regained consciousness and lived for a day—long enough to guess what had happened, though they tried to keep it from her. I was away at the time in the States, and, as bad luck would have it, was in hospital there with appendicitis, and couldn't get home. Well, I told you, it was only eight days before *Tiger Tiger* was due to open, and it did open. I don't have to tell you what a situation like that would do to someone like my father . . . It would damage anybody, and it half killed him.'

'I can imagine.' I was also imagining Max himself, chained to his alien hospital bed, getting it all by telephone, by cable, through the mail . . .

'That was when he started drinking. It was nearly two months before I got home, and a lot of the damage had been done. Of course, I had realised how it would hit him, but it took the shock of actually coming home to make me realise . . .' He paused. 'You can imagine that, too; the house empty, and looking lost, almost as if it hadn't even been dusted for weeks, though that was silly, of course it had. But it felt deserted—echoing, almost. Sally—my sister—had always been a bit of a live-wire. And there was Father, as thin as a telegraph post, with his hair three shades whiter, drifting about that damned great place like a dead leaf in a draughty barn. Not sleeping, of course, and drinking.' He shifted in his chair. 'What was that he said about the house being like a lord's kitchen without a fire?'

'It's from a play, Tourneur's *Revenger's Tragedy*. "Hell would look like a lord's great kitchen without fire in't." '

' "Hell"?' he quoted. 'Yes, I see.'

I said quickly: 'It wasn't even relevant. It only occurred to him as a sort of image.'

'Of emptiness?' He smiled suddenly. 'Sweet of you, but don't worry, things pass.' He paused. 'That was the start. It got better, of course; shock wears off, and with me at home he didn't drink so much, but now and again, when he was tired or over-strained, or just in one of those damned abysmal depressions that his sort of person suffers—they're as real as the measles, I don't have to tell you that—he would drink himself blind, "just this once". Unhappily, it takes remarkably little to do it. Well, if you remember, the play ran for a long time, and he stayed in it eighteen months. In all that time I only got him away for three weeks, then back he'd go to London, and after a while the house would get him down, and "just this once", he'd go on another drunk.'

'You couldn't get him to sell the house and move?'

'No. He'd been born there, and his father. It was something he wouldn't even begin to think about. Well, a couple of years of that, and he was going downhill like something on the Cresta Run. Then the "breakdowns" started, still, thanks to his friends, attributed publicly to strain and overwork. He had the sense to know what was happening to him, and the integrity and pride to get out while he could still do it with his legend intact. He did what he could . . . went into a "home" and was "cured". Then I got him to come away

here, to make quite sure he was all right, and to rest. Now he's
breaking his heart to get back, but I know he won't do it while
there's any danger of its starting again.' He gave a quick sigh. 'I
thought he was through with it, but now I don't know. It isn't just a
question of will-power, you know. Don't despise him.'

'I know that. And how could I despise him? I love him.'

'Lucy Waring's speciality. Given away regardless and for no
known reason. No, I'm not laughing at you, heaven forbid . . . Will
you tell me something?'

'What?'

'Did you mean what you said down there on the beach?'

The abrupt, almost casual question threw me for a moment. 'On
the beach? When? What did I say?'

'I realise I wasn't meant to hear it. We were just starting up the
steps.'

There was a pause. A log fell in with a soft crash and a jet of
hissing light.

I said, with some difficulty: 'You don't ask much, do you?'

'I'm sorry, that was stupid of me. Skip it. My God, I choose my
moments, as you say.'

He leaned down, picked a poker up from the hearthstone, and
busied himself with rearranging the pieces of burning wood. I stared
at his averted face, while a straitjacket of shyness gripped me, and
with it a sort of anger at his obtuseness in asking this. I couldn't have
spoken if I'd tried.

A jet of flame, stirred by the poker, leaped up and caught the
other log. It lit his face, briefly highlighting the traces of the night's
excitement and pain and tension, the frowning brows so like his
father's, the hard, exciting line of his cheek; his mouth. And the
same brief flash lit something else for me. I was the one who was
stupid. If one asks a question, it is because one wants to know the
answer. Why should he have to wait and wrap it up some other way
when the 'moment' suited me?

I said it quite easily after all. 'If you'd asked me a thing like that
three hours ago, I think I'd have said I didn't even like you, and I
. . . I think I'd have believed it . . . I think . . . And now there you
sit looking at me, and all you do is look—like that—and my damned
bones turn to water, and it isn't fair, it's never happened to me
before, and I'd do anything in the world for you, and you know it,
or if you don't you ought to—No, look, I—I didn't mean . . . you
asked me . . .'

It was a better kiss this time, no less breathless, but at least we were dry and warm, and had known each other nearly two hours longer . . .

From somewhere in the shadows came a sharp click, and a whirring sound. Instantly, we were a yard apart.

A small, fluting voice said: '*Cuckoo, cuckoo, cuckoo, cuckoo,*' and clicked back into silence.

'That damned clock!' said Max explosively, then began to laugh. 'It always frightens me out of my wits. It sounds like someone sneaking in with a tommy-gun. I'm sorry, did I drop you too hard?'

'Right down to earth,' I said shakily. 'Four o'clock, I'll have to go.'

'Wait just a little longer, can't you? No, listen, there's something you've got to know. I'll try not to take too long, if you'll just sit down again . . . ? Don't take any notice of that clock, it's always fast.' He cocked an eyebrow. 'What are you looking at me like that for?'

'For a start,' I said, 'men don't usually jump sky-high when they hear a noise like a tommy-gun. Unless they could be expecting one, that is. Were you?'

'Could be,' he said cheerfully.

'Goodness me! Then I'll certainly stay to hear all about it!' I sat down, folding my silk skirts demurely about me. 'Go on.'

'A moment, I'll put another log on the fire. Are you warm enough?'

'Yes, thank you.'

'You won't smoke? You never do? Wise girl. Well . . .'

He leaned his elbows on his knees, and stared once more at the fire.

'. . . I'm not quite sure where to start, but I'll try to make it short. You can have the details later, those you can't fill in for yourself. I want to tell you what's happened tonight, and especially what's going to happen tomorrow—today, I mean—because I want you to help me, if you will. But to make it clear I'll have to go back to the start of the story. I suppose you could say that it starts with Yanni Zoulas; at any rate that's where I'll begin.'

'It was true, then? He was a smuggler?'

'Yes, indeed. Yanni carried stuff regularly—all kinds of goods in short supply—over to the Albanian coast. Your guess was right about the "contacts": he had his "contact" on the other side, a man called Milo, and he had people over here who supplied the stuff and paid him. But not me. Your guess was wrong there. Now, how much d'you know about Albania?'

'Hardly a thing. I did try to read it up before I came here, but there's so little to read. I know it's Communist, of course, and at daggers drawn with Tito's Yugoslavia, *and* with Greece on the other border. I gather that it's a poor country, without much workable land and no industries, just peasant villages perched on the edge of starvation, like some of the Greek ones. I don't know any of the towns except Durres on the coast, and Tirana, the capital, but I gathered that they were still pretty Stone Age at the end of the war, but trying hard, and looking round for help. That was when the U.S.S.R. stepped in, wasn't it?'

'Yes. She supplied Albania with tools and tractors and seeds and so forth, all it needed to get its agriculture going again after the war. But it wasn't all plain sailing. I won't go into it now – in fact I'm not at all sure that I've got it straight myself – but a few years ago Albania quarrelled with Russia, and broke with the Comintern, but, because it still badly needed help (and possible support against Russia) it applied to Communist China; and China, which was then at loggerheads with Russia, jumped happily in to play fairy god-mother to Albania as Russia had done before – and presumably to get one foot wedged in Europe's back door. The situation's still roughly that, and now Albania's closed its frontiers completely, except to China. You can't get in, and by heaven, you certainly can't get out.'

'Like Spiro's father?'

'I suspect he didn't want to. But you might say he brings us to the next point in the story, which is Spiro. I suppose you've heard about our connexion with Maria and her family?'

'In a way. Adoni told me.'

'My father was here in Corfu during the war, and he was working in with Spiro's father for a time – a wild type, I gather, but rather picturesque and appealing. He appealed to the romantic in my father, anyway.' Max grinned. 'One gathers they had some pretty tearing times together. When the twins were born, father stood godfather to them. You won't know this, but over here it's a relationship that's taken very seriously. The godfather really does take responsibility – he has as much say in the kids' future as their father does, sometimes more.'

'I gathered that from Adoni. It was obvious he had a say in the christening, anyway!'

He laughed. 'It certainly was. The isle of Corfu went to his head even in those days. Thank God I was born in London, or I've a feeling nothing could have saved me from Ferdinand. Would you have minded?'

'Terribly. Ferdinand makes me think of a rather pansy kind of bull. What is your name, anyway? Maximilian?'

'Praise heaven, no. Maxwell. It was my mother's name.'

'I take it you had a godfather with no obsessions.'

He grinned. 'Too right. In the correct English manner, he gave me a silver teaspoon, then vanished from my life. But you can't do that in Corfu. When Spiro's own father did actually vanish, the godfather was almost literally left holding the babies.'

'He was still over here when that happened?'

'Yes. He was here for a bit after the European war finished, and during that time he felt himself more or less responsible for the family. He would have been if he'd been a Greek, since Maria had no relatives, and they were as poor as mice, so he took the family on, and even after he'd gone home sent money to them every month.'

'Good heavens! But surely, with children of his own—'

'He managed.' Max's voice was suddenly grave. 'We're not rich, heaven knows . . . and an actor's life's a darned uncertain one at best . . . but it's rather frightening how little a Greek family can manage on quite cheerfully. He kept them completely till Maria went out to work, and even after that he more or less kept them until the children could work, too.' He stretched out a foot and shoved the log deeper on its bed of burning ash. 'We came over here for holidays most years; that's where I learned my Greek and the kids their English. We had a whale of a time, and father always loved it. I was thankful I had somewhere like this to bring him when the crash came . . . it was like having another family ready-made. It's helped him more than anything else could have done. Being wanted does.'

'Good heavens, the thousands that want him! But I know it's different. So he came back here for peace to recover in, and then Spiro was killed. It must have hit him terribly.'

'The trouble was,' said Max, 'that Maria wouldn't believe the boy could be dead. She never stopped begging and praying my father to find out what really happened to him, and to bring him back. Apparently she'd made a special petition to St. Spiridion for him, so she simply wouldn't believe he could have drowned. She got some sort of idea that he'd gone after his father, and must be brought home.'

The second cigarette stub went after the first. It hit a bar of the fire, and fell back on the hearthstone. He got up, picked it up and dropped it on the fire, then stayed on his feet with a shoulder propped against the high mantel.

'I know it wasn't reasonable, not after Manning had told her what had happened, but mothers don't always listen to reason, and there was always the faint chance that the boy *had* survived. My father didn't feel equal to handling it, and I knew that neither he nor Maria would have any peace of mind till they found what had become of his body, so I took it on. I've been having inquiries made wherever I could, here and on the mainland, to find out in the first place if he'd been washed ashore, dead or alive. I've also had someone in Athens trying to get information from the Albanian side. Where Spiro went in, the current sets dead towards the Albanian coast. Well, I did manage to get through in the end, but with no results. He hadn't been seen, either on the Greek coast or the Albanian.'

I said: 'And I read you a lesson on helping other people. I'm sorry.'

'You couldn't know it was any concern of mine.'

'Well, no, it did rather seem to be Godfrey's.'

'I suppose so; but the local Greeks at any rate assumed that it was my father's job–or mine–to do it. So the police kept in touch with us, and we knew we'd get any information that was going. And when Yanni Zoulas went across on his routine smuggling trip on Saturday night, and did actually get some news of Spiro through his Albanian "contact", he came straight to us. Or rather, as straight as he could. You saw him on his way up to see us, on Sunday evening.'

I was bolt upright in my chair. '*News of Spiro?* Good news?'

I knew the answer before he spoke. The gleam in his eyes reminded me suddenly, vividly, of the way Adoni had looked at me on the staircase, glowing.

'Oh, yes. He came to tell us Spiro was alive.'

'*Max!*'

'Yes, I know. You can guess how we felt. He'd been washed ashore on the Albanian side, with a broken leg, and in the last stages of exhaustion, but he'd survived. The people who found him were simple coast folk, shepherds, who didn't see any reason to report things to the People's Police, or whatever it's called over there. Most people know about the smuggling that goes on, and I gather that these folk assumed that Spiro was mixed up in something of the sort, so they kept quiet about him. What's more, they informed the local smuggler, who–naturally–knew Milo, Yanni's "contact", who in turn passed the news along to Yanni on Saturday.'

'Oh, Max, this is marvellous! It really is! Did Yanni actually see him?'

'No. It all came at rather third hand. Milo hasn't much Greek, so all that Yanni got from him were the bare facts, and an urgent message that Spiro somehow managed to convey that no one, no one at all—not even Maria—had to be told that he was still alive, except myself, my father, and Adoni . . . the people who'd presumably get him out somehow.' He paused, briefly. 'Well, obviously we couldn't go to the police and get him out by normal channels, or the people who'd rescued him would be in trouble, not to mention Yanni and Milo. So Yanni fixed up a rendezvous to bring the boy off by night.'

'And he went back last night after he'd seen you, and ran into the coastguards and got hurt?'

But he was shaking his head. 'He couldn't have gone back alone; getting that boy off wasn't one man's job—don't forget he was strapped to a stretcher. No, when Yanni came up on Sunday night, he came to ask me to go across with him. The rendezvous was fixed for tonight; Milo and his friend were to have Spiro there and Yanni and I were to take him off. So you see—'

I didn't hear what he was going to say. It had all come together at last, and I could only wonder at my slowness in not seeing it all before. My eyes flew to his bandaged wrist, as the events of the night came rushing back: the secrecy of his journey through the woods, the impression I had had of more than one man passing me there, the owl's call, Adoni's vivid face . . .

I was on my feet. 'The catch! Adoni and the catch! You took Adoni, and went over there yourself tonight! You mean it's *done?* You've actually *brought Spiro home?*'

His eyes were dancing. 'We have indeed. He's here at this moment, a bit tired, but alive and well. I told you our night's work had been worth while.'

I sat down again, rather heavily. 'I can hardly take it in. This is . . . wonderful. Oh, Maria will be able to light herself a lovely candle this Easter! Think of it, Maria, Miranda, Sir Julian, Godfrey, Phyl . . . how happy everyone's going to be! I can hardly wait till daylight, to see the news go round!'

The glow faded abruptly from his face. It must have been only imagination, but the gay firelight seemed dimmer, too.

He said sombrely: 'I'm afraid it mustn't go round yet, not any further.'

'But—' I stared, bewildered—'not to his mother or sister? Why on earth not, if he's safely home? Surely, once he's out of Albania he has nothing to fear? And Milo needn't be involved at all—no one need even know Spiro was ever on Albanian soil. We could invent some story—'

'I'd thought of that. The story will be that he was thrown ashore on one of the islands in the strait, the Peristeroi Islands, and that he managed to attract our attention when we were out fishing. It won't fool the Greek police, or the doctor, but it'll do for general release, as it were. But that's not the point.'

'Then what is?'

He hesitated, then said, slowly: 'Spiro may still be in danger . . . Not from the other side, but here. What touched him, touched Yanni, too. And Yanni died.'

Something in his face—his very reluctance to speak—frightened me. I found myself protesting violently, too violently, as if by protesting I could push the unwanted knowledge farther away. 'But we *know* what happened to Spiro! He went overboard from Godfrey's boat! How can he be in any danger now? And Yanni's death was an accident! You said so!'

I stopped. The silence was so intense that you could hear the crazy ticking of the cuckoo clock, and the scrape of silk on flesh as my hands gripped together in my lap.

I said quietly: 'Go on. Say it straight out, you may as well. You're insinuating that Godfrey Manning—'

'I'm insinuating nothing.' His voice was curt, even to rudeness. 'I'm telling you. Here it is. Godfrey Manning threw Spiro overboard, and left him to drown.'

Silence again, a different kind of silence.

'Max, I—I can't accept that. I'm sorry, but it isn't possible.'

'It's fact, no more nor less. Spiro says so. Yes, I thought you were forgetting that I've talked to him. He says so, and I believe him. He has no reason to lie.'

Seconds were out with a vengeance. Now that he had decided he must tell me, he hurled his facts like stones. And they hit like stones.

'But—*why*?'

'I don't know. Neither does the boy. Which, when you come to think about it, makes it the more likely that he's telling the truth. It's something he'd have no reason to invent. He's as stunned by it as you are.' He added, more gently: 'I'm sorry, Lucy, but I'm afraid it's true.'

I sat in silence for a minute or two, not thinking, but looking down at my hands, twisting and turning the great diamond, and watching the firelight break and dazzle among its facets. Slowly, the stunned feeling faded, and I began to think . . .

'Did you suspect Godfrey before?'

'No,' he said, 'why should I? But when I got that message from Yanni, I did wonder why Godfrey hadn't to be told. After all, it seemed reasonable to keep the news from Spiro's mother and sister, because they'd be so elated that they might give everything away before Yanni had done the job; but Godfrey was a different matter. He would presumably be worrying about Spiro, and he has by far the best boat. What's more, he's an experienced seaman, and I'm not. I'd have expected him to be asked in on the rescue, rather than me and Adoni . . . It wasn't much, but it did make me wonder. Then when Yanni was found dead next day, on top of Spiro's odd warning, I wondered still more.'

I said: 'You're not suggesting now—you *can't* be suggesting that Godfrey killed Yanni Zoulas? Max—'

'What I've told you about Spiro is fact: what happened to Yanni is guesswork. But to my mind the one murder follows the other as the night the day.'

'*Murder* . . .' I don't think I said it aloud, but he nodded as if I had.

'I'm pretty sure of it. Same method, too. He'd been hit hard on the head and thrown into the sea. The bottle of ouzo was a nice touch, I thought.'

'He was hit by the boom. The police said there were hairs—'

'He could also have been hit *with* the boom. Anyone can crack an unconscious man's head on a handy chunk of wood like that, hard enough to kill him before you throw him overboard—and hard enough to hide the crack you knocked him out with. I'm not bringing this out as a theory: I'm only saying it could have been done.'

'Why did you go back to the body after we'd left?'

'After Yanni left us on Sunday night I heard his boat go out, and I did wonder if he'd been stupid enough to go back on his own, and had run into trouble with the coastguards. From all that we'd been able to see he might have had a bullet hole in him somewhere, or some other evidence that would start a serious investigation. I was pretty anxious in case they started patrolling local waters before I'd got Spiro safely home.'

'I see. And your own wrist—was that the coastguards?'

'Yes, a stray bullet, and a spent one at that. It's honestly only a

graze; I'll get it looked at when I get Spiro's leg seen to. They must
have heard something, and fired blind. We were just about out of
range, and well beyond their lights.'

I said, rather wearily: 'I suppose you do know what you're saying,
but it all seems so . . . so impossible to me. And I don't understand
even the start of it.'

'My God, who does? But I told you, it's all guesswork about
Yanni, and there's no future in discussing that now. The first thing
is to talk to Spiro again. I've only had time to get the barest
statement from him, and I want to hear the rest before I decide
what's best to do. He should be fit enough by now to tell us exactly
what happened and, whether he knows it or not, he may have some
clue as to why Manning tried to kill him. If he has, it may be a
pointer to Yanni's death. And whatever it is that makes two murders
necessary . . .' He straightened abruptly, his shoulder coming away
from the mantel. 'Well, you can see that we have to get the boy
safely into the hands of the authorities with his story, before
Godfrey Manning has even a suspicion that he's not as dead as
Yanni. Will you come with me now and see him?'

I looked up in surprise. 'Me? You want me to?'

'If you will. I told you I wanted you to help me, and—if you'll
agree—you'd better know as much as we do about it.'

'Of course, whatever I can.'

'Darling. Come here. Now, stop looking like that, and stop
worrying. It's all impossible, as you say, but then this sort of
situation is bound to be, when one gets mixed up in it oneself. All
we can do is play for safety, and that means, for the moment,
believing Spiro. All right?'

I nodded, as best I could with my head comfortably against his
shoulder.

'Then listen. What I've got to do, as I see it, is get the boy straight
off to Athens in the morning, to the hospital, then to the police.
Once he's told his story there, he'll be safe to come home.' He loosed
me. 'Well, shall we go?'

'Where is he?'

He laughed. 'Right below our feet, in a very Gothic but reasonably safe dungeon, with Adoni standing guard over him with the
one efficient rifle in this damned great arsenal of Leo's. Come along,
then. Straight under the cuckoo clock, and fork right for the
dungeons!'

Chapter 12

My cellar is in a rock by th' sea-side,
where my wine is hid.

II. 2.

A WIDE FLIGHT of stone steps led downwards from just beyond the
door. Max touched a switch, and a weak yellow light came on to
show us the way. He shut the ponderous door, and I heard a key
grate in the lock behind us.

'I'll go first, shall I?'

I followed him, curiously looking about me. The rest of the
building had led me to expect goodness knew what horrors down
here: it would hardly have come as a surprise to have found
mouldering skeletons dangling in chains from the walls. But the
underground corridor into which the stairs led us was innocent of
anything except racks of wine – largely empty – which lined the wide
passage-way. The floor was clean, and the walls surprisingly free of
the dust and webs which would have accumulated in a similar place
in England. The air smelt fresh, and slightly damp.

I said as much to Max, who nodded. 'You'll see why in a minute.
This is the official wine-cellar, but it leads off into a natural cave
farther along. I don't know where the opening is – it's probably no
bigger than a chimney – but the air's always fresh, and you can smell
the sea. There are more wine racks down there. In the last century,
when one drank one's four bottles a day, rather a lot of room was
needed. Anyway, it must have seemed natural to use the caves in the
cliff when they built the Castello.'

'It's rather exciting. I suppose these are the caves your father was
talking about.'

'Yes. Most of the cliffs along this coast have caves in them, but, as
you can imagine, he'd love to think the Castello cave was the original
Prospero's cell. When I point out that it doesn't look as if it had ever
been open to the outside air, he says that doesn't matter. I gather it's
more "poetic truth", like the marmosets.'

'Well, it's a lovely romantic theory, and I'm all for it! After all,
what are facts? We get those every day . . . Whereabouts are we
now, in relation to "outside"?'

'At present we're still moving along under the foundations of the
house. The cave itself is in the southern headland, fairly deep down.
We go down more steps in a moment, and then there's a natural
passage through to the cave. Wait, here we are.'

He had stopped two-thirds of the way along the corridor, and put
a hand up to the empty racks. I watched him, puzzled. He laid hold
of what looked like part of the wall of racks, and pulled. Pon-
derously, and by no means silently, a narrow section swung out into
the corridor. Beyond where it had been was a gap in the wall,
opening on blackness.

'Goodness me!' I exclaimed, and Max laughed.

'Marvellous, isn't it? I tell you, the Castello's got everything! As a
matter of fact, I have a suspicion that old Forli kept the better
vintages down here, out of the butler's reach . . . Careful, now,
there's no light from here on. I've brought a torch–here, take it for a
moment, will you, while I shut this behind us. Don't look so scared!'

'It won't stay shut and trap us here for ever, till our bones bleach?'

'Not even till morning, I'm sorry to say. There. The torch,
please. I'll go ahead.'

The second flight sloped more steeply down, and, instead of
being made of smooth slabs, seemed to be hacked out of solid rock.
At the foot of the flight a rock-hewn passage curved away into
darkness, still descending. Max went ahead, shining the beam for
me. Here and there the walls showed a glint of damp, and the fresh
smell was stronger, and perceptibly salty, while the hollow rock
seemed–perhaps only in imagination–to hold a faint, echoing hum
like the shushing of the sea through the curves of a shell. A moment
I thought I heard it, then it was gone, and there was only the still,
cold air, and the sound of our footsteps on the rock.

The yellow torchlight flung sharp lights and shadows on Max's
face as he turned to guide me, sketching in, momentarily, the face of
a stranger. His shadow moved, distorted and huge on the rough
walls.

'Is it much further?' My voice sounded unfamiliar, like a whisper in an echo-chamber.

'Round this corner,' said Max, 'and down five, no, six steps–and there's the watch-dog.'

A flash of the torch showed the pale blur of a face upturned, and a gun barrel gleaming blue.

'Adoni? It's Max, and I've brought Miss Lucy along. Is he all right?'

'He's fine now. He's awake.'

Behind Adoni hung a rough curtain of some material like sacking, from beyond which came a dim, warm glow. Adoni drew the curtain aside for me and stood back. Max put the torch out and motioned me past him. I went into the cave.

This was large, with a great arched roof lost in shadows where stalactites hung like icicles; but the walls had been whitewashed to a height of six feet or so, and were lined with wine racks and crates and the comfortable, bulging shapes of barrels. On one of these, up-turned to make a table, stood an old-fashioned lantern, a coach-lamp of about 1850 vintage, probably borrowed from the museum upstairs, which dispensed a soft orange light and the cheerful twinkle of brass. The air was warmed by a paraffin stove which stood in the middle of the floor, with a pan of coffee on it. Somewhere in the shadows a drip of water fell regularly–some stalactite dripping fresh water into a pocket of rock; the sound was as homely as a dripping tap. The unexpected effect of cosiness was enhanced by the smell of cigarettes and coffee and the faint fumes of the paraffin stove.

The injured boy lay at the far side of the cave, on a bed pushed up against a row of crates. The bed was a makeshift affair which nevertheless looked extremely comfortable–a couple of spring mattresses laid one above the other, with blankets galore, and feather pillows, and a vast eiderdown. Some sort of cage had been rigged up under the bedclothes to keep their weight off the injured leg.

Spiro, lying there in what looked like a pair of Sir Julian's pyjamas (pale blue silk with crimson piping), looked comfortable enough, and not at the moment particularly ill. He was propped up on his pillows, drinking coffee.

He looked up across the cup, a little startled at the sight of me, and threw a quick question at Max, who answered in English:

'It's Kyria Forli's sister. She's my friend, and yours. She's going to help us, and I want her to hear your story.'

Spiro regarded me steadily, without noticeable welcome, the round dark eyes, so like his sister's, wary and appraising. I could recognise the boy in the photographs, but only just; there was the thick, springing hair and the stocky body, with obvious strength in the shoulders and thick neck; but the bloom of health and sun-light—and happiness—was gone. He looked pale, and—in the pyjamas—young and unprotected-looking.

Max pulled a box forward for me to sit on. 'How do you feel?' he asked the boy. 'Is it hurting?'

'No,' said Spiro. That this was a lie was quite obvious, but it was not said with any sort of bravado. It was simply that one did not admit to weakness, and pain was weakness.

'He has slept,' said Adoni.

'Good.' Max perched himself half sitting against the cask which held the lantern. His shadow, thrown hugely up the wall, arched brooding and gigantic across the cave. He studied the younger boy for a minute or two, then said, briskly:

'If you're feeling better, I want you to tell us exactly what happened to you. All the details this time, please.'

'All the what?'

'Everything you can remember,' said Max, and Adoni, from the head of the bed, added a soft gloss in Greek.

'All right.' Spiro drained the coffee-cup and handed it up, without looking, to Adoni. The latter took it, set it quietly aside, then crossed back to the bed and sat down, curling up gracefully, naturally, like a cat, near the head of the bed away from the injured leg. He reached into a pocket for two of the cigarettes he had got from Max, stuck them in his mouth, lit them both, and handed one to Spiro. Spiro took it without word or glance, but there was no suggestion, as there had been with me, of anything withdrawn or unfriendly. It was obvious that these two young men knew each other almost too well to need words. They sat there side by side against the pillows, Adoni relaxed and graceful, Spiro square and watchful and smoking jerkily, with his hand cupped working-class fashion round the cigarette.

He sent one more wary glance at me, then took no more notice of me: all his attention was on Max, almost as if the latter were judging him—at once judge and saviour and final court of appeal. Max listened without moving, the huge, curved shadow thrown right up the wall and over half the ceiling of the cave.

The boy spoke slowly, with the signs of fatigue deepening in his face. I have no recollection now of what language he spoke; whether his English was good, or whether Max and Adoni eked it out with translation; the latter, I suspect; but whatever the case, the story came over vividly and sharply in that darkened cellar-cave, with the lantern light, and the smell of the cigarettes, and the two boys curled in the welter of bedclothes, and the faint tangy scent from the silk of Julian Gale's dressing-gown.

I suppose that the strange, secret surroundings, the time of night, my own weariness and recent emotional encounter with Max, had edged the scene somehow; but it seemed real now only as a dream is real. In the dream I found I had already accepted Godfrey's guilt; I only waited to hear how he had done it. Perhaps in the light of morning things would take a different dimension; but now it seemed as if any tale could be true, even the old man's romantic theory that this was Prospero's cave, and that here on this rough floor the Neapolitan lords had waited to hear the story from the long-drowned Duke, as I now waited to hear Spiro's.

*　　*　　*

There had been nothing, he said, that had struck him as unusual about the trip that night. The only thing that had surprised him was that the sky was none too clear, and from what the wireless had said, it might well be stormy at dawn. He had pointed this out to Godfrey, but Godfrey had said, a little abruptly, that it would clear. They had got the boat out, and gone shortly before midnight. As Spiro had anticipated, the night was black and thick, but he had said nothing more to Godfrey, who had stayed in the cabin, allegedly busying himself with his camera and equipment.

'He seemed much as usual?' asked Max.

Spiro frowned, considering this. 'I cannot say,' he said at length. 'He was quiet, and perhaps a bit sharp with me when I protested about the weather, but all day he had been the same. I thought he was still angry with me because I had gone into the boat-house that morning on my own to service the engine, so I said nothing, and thought nothing. He pays me, and that is that.'

'All the same, that might be interesting,' said Max slowly. 'But go on now. You were out in the strait, and the night was black.'

Spiro took a quick drag on the cigarette, and reached awkwardly, hampered by the leg, to tap the ash on to the floor. Adoni slipped the saucer from under the empty coffee-cup, and slid it within his reach.

'I reckoned we were about half-way over,' said Spiro, 'in the strait between Kouloura and the mainland. We had gone close to the Peristeroi Islands; there was enough of a sea running to see the white foam quite distinctly. I asked Mr. Manning if we should lie up a little in the lee of them, and wait for the cloud to clear; there were gaps under the wind, where you could see stars; but he said no, we would go farther across. We went on for a time, till I reckoned we were about two miles out. He came out of the cabin then, and sent me in to make some coffee.' The boy glanced up under his thick brows at Max. 'The camera was there, on the table, but I did not think he could have been looking at it, because he had had no light on, only a storm lantern hardly lit. At the time I did not think of these things; while we took pictures at night, we always—naturally—ran without lights. But afterwards, when I had all that time lying in bed, and nothing to do but think, and wonder . . . then I remembered all the things that seemed strange. It was strange that we were going at all on that dark night to take pictures; it was strange that he lied to me about the camera; and the next thing that happened was more strange still.'

Adoni grinned. 'I know, the engine failed. And what was so strange about that, when you'd been taking it to bits that morning, my little genius?'

Spiro smiled for the first time, and said something in Greek which nobody bothered to translate for me. 'If that had happened,' he added, with fine simplicity, 'it would indeed have been strange. But it did not.'

'But you told us before—'

'I told you the engine stopped. I did not say that it failed. There was nothing wrong with the engine.'

Max stirred. 'You're sure, naturally.'

The boy nodded. 'And it didn't need a genius with engines to know there was nothing wrong. Even you'—a glint at Adoni—'even you would have known, my pretty one.' He ducked aside from Adoni's feint, and laughed. 'Go on, hit me, no doubt you could do it now.'

'I'll wait,' said Adoni.

Spiro turned back to Max. 'No, the engine was all right. Listen. I heard it stop, then Mr. Manning called me. I put my head out of the door and shouted that I would take a look—the engine hatch is under the cabin steps, you understand. But he said, "I don't think it's there, Spiro, I think something's fouled the screw and stalled it. Can you take a look?" I went to the stern. He was standing there, at the tiller. He said, "Steady as you go, boy, she's pitching a bit. Here, I'll hold the torch for you." I gave him the torch, and then I leaned over to see if the shaft was fouled. The boat was pitching, and the toe-rail was wet, but I was holding on tightly. I should have been quite safe.'

He paused, and stirred in the bed, as if the leg was hurting him. Adoni slipped to the floor and padded across to where a bottle stood on a box beside two empty glasses. He slopped some of the wine—it looked like the dark, sweet stuff they called *demèstica*—into one of the glasses and took it to the other boy, then glanced inquiringly at Max, who shook his head. Adoni set the bottle down, and returned to his place on the bed, adjusting his body, cat-like, to the new position of the injured boy.

'It all happened very fast. The boat gave a lurch, very sharp, as if Mr. Manning had turned her across the wind too quickly. I was thrown against the rail, but still safe enough, because I had a good grip, but then something hit me from behind, on the head. It does not stun me, but I think I try to turn and put an arm up, then the boat pitches again, and before I know what has happened, I am falling. I try to grip the rail, but it slips from me. Something hits me across the hand—here—and I let go. Then I am in the water. When I come up, the boat is still near, and I see Mr. Manning in the stern, peering out for me in the darkness. I shout—not loudly, you understand, because I am full of water, and too cold, gasping for air. But he must have heard me.'

He shot a look up at Max, all of a sudden vivid, alive with pure hatred.

'And if he did not hear me, then he saw me. He put the torch on, and shone it on me in the sea.'

'Yes?' said Max. His voice was expressionless, but I got the impression of a cold wind stirring in the cellar. Adoni felt it, too. He glanced fleetingly up at Max before his eyes went back to Spiro.

'I was not afraid, you understand,' said Spiro. 'not of him. It did not occur to me that it was he who had hit me, I thought it had been some accident. No, I was not afraid. I am a good swimmer, and though he had no engine, the boat was drifting down towards me, and he could see me. In a moment he could pick me up again. I called out again, and swam towards him. I saw he had the starting-handle in his hand, but I still did not imagine what this was for. Then as I came within reach, he leaned down and hit me again. But the boat was pitching and he had to hold the rail, so he could not

point the torch properly. The blow touched me, but this time I saw
it coming, and I ducked away, and he hit my arm and not my head. I
think he felt the blow, but did not see, because the torch went out,
and a big wave swept me away from the boat's stern and out of his
sight. You can imagine that this time I let it take me. I saw the light
go on again, but I made no sound, and let myself be carried away
into the dark. Then I heard the engine start.' He drained the glass,
and looked up at Max. 'He looked for me for a little while, but the
current took me away fast, and the waves hid me. Then he turned
the boat away, and left me there in the sea.'

There was silence. Nobody moved. For me, the dreamlike feeling
persisted. The cave seemed darker, echoing with the sounds of the
sea, the mutter of the receding boat, the empty hissing of waves
running under the night wind.

'But the Saint was with you,' said Adoni, and the deep human
satisfaction in his voice sent the shadows scurrying. The cave was
warm again, and full of the soft light from the English Victorian
lantern.

Spiro handed the empty glass to Adoni, pulled the bedclothes
more comfortably round him, and nodded. 'Yes, he was with me.
Do you want the rest, Kyrie Max? You know what happened.'

'I want Miss Lucy to hear it. Go on, but make it short. You're
tired, and it's very late.'

The rest of the story was pure classic, made predictable and
credible by half a hundred stories from Odysseus to St. Paul.

It was the murderer's bad luck that the wind that night had set a
fast current in to the Albanian coast. Spiro was a fair swimmer, and
the Ionian Sea is very salt, but even so he would have been hard put
to it to survive if he had not gone overboard into the stream of the
current. Between that, the buoyancy of the water, and his own
stubborn efforts, he managed to keep afloat long enough for the
sea-race to throw him ashore some time just before dawn.

By the time he neared the shore he was almost exhausted, all his
energy taken by the mere effort of keeping afloat, and at the mercy
of the tide. He was not even aware that he had come to shore, but
when a driving swell flung him against the cruel coastal rocks, he
found just enough strength to cling there, resisting the backward
drag once, twice, three times, before he could pull himself clear of it
and crawl further up the slimy rock.

And here the luck turned. St. Spiridion, having seen him ashore,
and out of his own territory, abandoned him abruptly. Spiro

slipped, fell back across a jut of sharp rock with a broken leg twisted under him, and at last fainted.

He had no recollection of being found – by an old shepherd who had clambered down a section of cliff after a crag-fast ewe. When Spiro woke he was bedded down, roughly but dry and warm, in the shepherd's cottage, and it appeared that the shepherd had some rough surgical skill, for the leg had been set and strapped up. The old woman produced a drink that sent him to sleep again, and when he woke for the second time, the pain was a good deal easier, and he was able to remember, and think . . .

'And the rest you know.' He yawned suddenly, tremendously, like an animal, and lay back among the blankets.

'Yes, the rest we know.' Max got to his feet, stretching. 'Well, you'd better get some sleep. In the morning – my God, in about three hours! – I'm going to get you out of here, don't ask me how, but I'll do it somehow, with Mr. Manning none the wiser. I want to get that leg of yours properly seen to, and then you've got to tell your story to the right authorities.'

The boy glanced up, weariness and puzzlement lending his face a sullen, heavy look. 'Authorities? Police? You mean you are going to accuse Kyrios Manning of trying to drown me? On my word alone? They will laugh at you.'

'It's not just a question of accusing Mr. Manning of throwing you overboard. What I want to know is why? There's something here that must be investigated, Spiro. You'll have to trust me. Now, just for a few minutes longer, I want you to think back. You must have thought about it a lot yourself, while you were lying in bed . . . Why do you think he did it? Have you any idea at all? You surely don't imagine it was because he was irritated with you for over-hauling the engine without being told?'

'Of course not.'

'There was nothing else – nothing had happened at any other time?'

'No. I have thought. Of course I have thought. No.'

'Then we come back to the morning of the trip. When one has nothing to go on, one looks for anything, however slight, that's out of pattern – out of the ordinary. Did you usually overhaul that boat by yourself?'

'No, but I have done so before.' Spiro stirred, as if his leg hurt him. 'And I have been alone on it before.'

'You have always asked him first?'

'Of course.'

'But this time you didn't . . . Why did you go to work on the boat this time without asking him?'

'Because he had told me that he meant to go out, and he wanted the engine serviced. I was to go that morning after breakfast, and work on it. But I had got up very early, to swim, and when I had done, I thought I would go straight along and start work. I knew where he kept the extra key, so I let myself in, and made some coffee in the galley, then opened the big doors for the light and started work. It was a good morning, with the summer coming, and I felt good. I worked well. When Mr. Manning had finished his breakfast and came down, I was half finished already. I thought he would be pleased, but he was very angry and asked how I got in, and then I didn't like to tell him that I had seen where he hid the key, so I said the door was not locked properly, and he believed this, because the catch is stiff sometimes. But he was still very angry, and said he would have the lock changed, and then I was angry also, and asked if he thought I was a thief, and if he thought so he had better count the money in his wallet which he had left in the galley. As if I would touch it! I was very angry!' Spiro remembered this with some satisfaction. 'I told him also that I would mend his lock for him myself, and that I would never come to his house again. After that he was pleasant, and said he was sorry, and it was all right.'

Max was frowning. 'It was then that he asked you to go out that night?'

'I think . . . Yes, it must have been. He had said, before, that he did not want me with him, but he changed his mind . . . I thought because he was sorry he had spoken to me like that.' He added, naïvely: 'It was a way to give me extra money without offence.'

'Then it looks as if that was when he decided to take you and get rid of you. You can see that it only makes sense if he thought you'd seen something you shouldn't have seen . . . And that means in the boat, or the boat-house. Now, think hard, Spiro. Was there anything unusual about the boat? Or the boat-house? Or about anything that Mr. Manning said, or did . . . or carried with him?'

'No.' The boy repeated himself with a kind of weary emphasis. 'I have thought. Nothing.'

'The wallet. You say he'd left his wallet lying. Where did you find it?'

'Down beside the stove in the galley. It had slipped there and he had not noticed. I put it on the cabin table.'

'Were there papers in it? Money?'

'How should I know?' Spiro ruffled up again, like a young turkey-cock, then subsided under Max's look with a grin. 'Well, I did take a look, a very small one. There was money, but I don't know how much, I only saw the corners. It wasn't Greek money, anyway, so what use did he think it would have been to me? But if it had been a million drachmas, I would not have taken it! You know that, Kyrie Max!'

'Of course I know it. Did he leave you alone in the boat after this?'

'No. When I had finished there, he asked me to go up to the house and help him with some photographs. I worked there all day. He telephoned to the Forli house to tell my mother that I was to go with him that night.'

'In fact, he made sure that you saw nobody all that day . . . Did you ever have any suspicion that he did anything illegal on these expeditions?'

'No—and why should it matter? I would not have told the police.' Spiro's eyes glinted up at him. 'He would not be the only one.'

Max declined the gambit, merely nodding. 'All right, Spiro, I'll not bother you any more now. Adoni, I'm going to lock the pair of you in while I take Miss Lucy home. I'll be back within the half-hour. You have the gun.'

'Yes.'

'And this.' Spiro searched under his pillow and produced, with as much drama as if it had been a handkerchief, a Commando knife sharpened to a murderous glitter.

'That's the stuff,' said Max cheerfully. 'Now, you go to sleep, and very soon I'll get you away.' He stooped, and dropped a hand for a moment on the boy's shoulder. 'All will be well, *Spiro mou*.'

Adoni followed us to the door.

'And Sir Gale?' he asked softly.

'I'll look in on him,' promised Max. 'He'll sleep soundly enough, you can be sure of that. He's in no danger, so stop worrying, and get some sleep yourself. When I get back I'll spend the rest of the night in the kitchen. If you need me, you've only to come to the upper door and call me. Good night.'

'Good night, Adoni,' I said.

'Good night.' Adoni gave me that smile again, perhaps a little frayed at the edges, then let the curtain fall into place across the cave entrance, lopping off the warm glow and shutting Max and me out into the darkness of the rocky passage.

He switched on the torch, and we started up the steps. The rough walls, the curving passage-way, the hewn flight of stairs, swam past in a sort of dream of fatigue, but a corner of my brain still felt awake and restless, alert to what he was saying.

'You can see now why I'm hiding that boy away till I can smuggle him out to Athens? It's not so much that he's in actual danger still—though he may well be—as simply that we stand a far better chance of finding out what Manning's up to if he has no idea that we suspect him. It's something big—that seems obvious . . . And I'm pretty sure in my own mind where to start looking for it.'

'The boat?'

'Either that or the boat-house. He's up to something involving that boat, and the damned good "cover" that his photography gives him. If you accept Spiro's story, which I do, his little quarrel with Manning that morning provides the only faint clue . . . the only deviation from pattern that I can see . . . and it could tie in with Yanni's death as well. I've been thinking about that. When Yanni brought Spiro's message here on Sunday night we discussed it pretty freely, and I let it be seen that I thought it very odd that Manning hadn't to be told. Yanni then said that he'd seen Manning's boat out at odd times and in odd places, and that he'd thought for some time he was up to no good, and when I mentioned the photographs, he just shrugged and looked cynical. Well, that's nothing to go by—a man like Yanni would think that photography was a pretty queer occupation for anyone; but he could have very well been suspicious and curious enough after our conversation to go down that night and snoop around the boat-house, or somewhere else he had no right to be, and so got himself murdered. It's my guess he was taken by surprise and knocked out from behind, then bundled into his own boat, with Manning's dinghy attached, taken out to sea, had his head smashed on the boom, and was dumped overboard. Manning then set the boom loose, emptied a bottle of ouzo around, turned the boat adrift, and rowed himself silently home. Oh, yes, it could have been done. He couldn't take him a great distance, since he'd have to row himself home, and then there was the squall which washed the body straight back—but it worked; he got away with it. An impulsive chap, our Godfrey . . . and with one hell of a lot at stake, that's for sure. Yes, I could bear to know just what it is.'

I said in quick apprehension: 'You've got to promise me something.'

'What's that?'

'You're not going there tonight? You wouldn't be so silly!'

He laughed. 'You're dead right I would not, my love! I've got to see Spiro safe where he belongs before I go arguing with anyone with Manning's peculiar ideas on life and death. He must have shot at the dolphin, you'd realised that?' He nodded at my exclamation. 'Who else? There's only one plausible reason, the one you imputed to me, that the word had gone round, and people were beginning to come to this piece of coast to see the creature. When Manning first saw you there in the bay, he may have thought you were one of them—a stranger, getting too close to whatever he was trying to keep secret. As Spiro and Yanni did.'

'But . . . those beautiful pictures! They really are beautiful, Max! He *couldn't* destroy it when he'd worked with it like that! He must have been fond of it!'

His smile was crooked. 'And of Spiro, too?' I was silent. 'Well, here we are. A moment while I push the racks back.'

'What do you want me to do?'

'Something I know will be safe, and I hope will be easy. Cover my trip back from Athens with Spiro.'

'Of course, if I can. How?'

'By keeping Manning away from Corfu harbour tomorrow at the time when I'm likely to be there. It would be quicker to go by plane, but I can't take the boy that way without the whole island knowing, so I'll have to take him in my car, hidden under a rug or something, across by the *Igoumenitsa.*'

'The what?'

'The ferry to the mainland. I'll drive to Jannina and get the Athens plane from there. It means we can't get there and back in the one day, but I'll try to get home tomorrow, and I'll ring up this evening to let you know which ferry we'll get. The late one doesn't get in till a quarter to eleven; it's pitch dark then, and I doubt if he'd be around. But I'd like to get the earlier one if I can, and that gets in at five-fifteen . . . So if you could bear to be having tea with him or something, till after six, to give me time to drive home. . .?'

'Just at the moment I feel it would choke me, but I'll do my best,' I said.

We were back in the kitchen. Its light and warmth and comfortable food-smells closed round us like memories from a real, but distant world, something safe and bright beyond the tossing straits of the night's dream. He pulled the great door shut behind us, and I heard the key drive the lock shut with a grating snap.

'There. Now you must go home. Come upstairs and get your things, and I'll look along to see if my father's safely asleep.'

'Let's hope Phyl is, too, or heaven knows what story I'll have to cook up! Anything but the truth, I suppose!' I stared up at him. 'I can't believe it. You realise that, don't you? I know it's true, but I can't believe it. And in the morning in daylight, it'll be quite impossible.'

'I know. Don't think about it now. You've had yourself quite an evening, as they say; but you'll feel different when you've had some sleep.'

'My watch has stopped. Oh hell, I suppose I got water in it. What's the time, Max?'

He glanced at his wrist. 'So has mine. Blast. That little sea-bathe doesn't seem to have done either of us much good, does it?'

I laughed. 'Things that might have been better expressed, Mr. Gale?'

He reached out, and pulled me to him. 'Things that might have been better done,' he said, and did them.

Chapter 13

While you here do snoring lie,
Open-ey'd Conspiracy
His time doth take.

II. 1.

I SLEPT VERY late that day. The first thing I remember is the sound
of shutters being folded back, and then the sudden hot blaze of
sunlight striking across the pillow into my eyes.

Phyllida's voice said: 'And high time, too, Rip Van Winkle!'

As I murmured something, dragging myself up out of the depths
of sleep, she added: 'Godfrey rang you up.'

'Oh?' I blinked into the sunlight. 'Rang *me* up? What did he
want—did you say *Godfrey*?' The jerk of recollection brought me
awake and up off the pillow so sharply that I saw her look of
surprise, and it helped me to pull myself together.

'I was dreaming,' I said, rubbing my eyes. 'What on earth's the
time?'

'High noon, my child.'

'Goodness! What was he ringing about?'

'To know if you'd got safely home with the ring, of course.'

'Did he expect Mr. Gale to steal it *en route*?'

Too late, I heard the tartness in my voice, and my sister looked at
me curiously, but all she said was: 'I woke you up too suddenly.
Never mind, I brought some coffee. Here.'

'Angel . . . Thank you. Heavens, I must have slept like the dead
. . . Your ring's over there on the dressing-table. Oh, you've got it.'

'You bet your sweet life I have. I came in a couple of hours ago
and took it, but I couldn't bear to wake you, you were flat out, you
poor kid.' She turned her hand in the sunlight, and the diamond
flashed. 'Thank heaven for that! Bless you, Lucy, I'm really terribly

grateful! I'd have gone stark ravers if I'd had to sit there all night,
wondering if someone had wandered by and picked it up. And I
wouldn't have dared go down myself! What on earth time did you
get in?'

'I hardly know,' I said truthfully. 'My watch stopped. I thought
I'd got water in it, but I'd only forgotten to wind it up. Some ghastly
hour of the morning.' I laughed. 'There were complications, actually. Didn't Godfrey tell you about them?'

'I didn't quite get that bit. Something about the dolphin being up
on the beach, and you and Max Gale wrestling about with it in the
water. I must say it all sounded highly unlikely. What did happen?'

'More or less that.' I gave her a rapid—and suitably expur-
gated—version of the dolphin's rescue, finishing with Godfrey's
arrival on the beach. 'And you'll find the wreck of your precious
plastic bag in the bathroom, I'm afraid. I'm fearfully sorry, but I had
to use something.'

'Good heavens, that old thing! It couldn't matter less!'

'I'm relieved. The way you were talking last night I thought it was
practically a holy relic.'

She shot me a look as she disappeared through the bathroom door.
'I was not myself last night, and you know it.'

'Well, no.' I reached for the coffee-pot which she had put down
beside the bed, and poured myself more coffee.

She emerged from the bathroom, holding the bag between thumb
and forefinger. ' "Wreck" was the word, wasn't it? I suppose you
don't even know what happened to my Lizzie Arden lipstick?'

'Lord, I suppose that was a holy relic, too?'

'Well, it was gold.'

I drank coffee. 'You'll find it in Sir Julian Gale's dressing-gown
pocket. I forgot it. I'm sorry again. You might say I was not myself
last night either.'

'Julian Gale's dressing-gown? This gets better and better! What
happened?' She sat down on the edge of the bed. 'I tried like mad to
stay awake till you got in, but those beastly pills put me right out,
once Godfrey'd phoned and I stopped worrying. Go on. I want to
know what I've missed.'

'Oh, nothing, really. We were both soaked, so I had to go up to
the Castello to get dry, and they gave me coffee, and I had a bath
. . . Phyl, the bathroom! You'd hardly *believe* the ghastly—oh, sorry!
I forgot, it's the Forli ancestral palace. Well, then, you'll know the
bathroom.'

'There are two,' said Phyl. 'Don't forget there are twenty bedrooms. One must have one's comforts. I'll say I know the bathrooms. Was it the one with the alabaster bath, or the porphyry?'

'You make it sound like the New Jerusalem. I don't know, I don't live at those levels. It was a rather nasty dark red with white spots, exactly like stale salami.'

'Porphyry,' said my sister. 'Was the water hot?'

'Boiling.'

'*Was* it? They must have done something, then. It never used to get more than warm, and in fact I seem to remember a tap for sea-water, which was pumped up in some weird way from the caves. There are caves under the Castello.'

'Are there?'

'They used to use them to keep the wine in.'

'Really. How exciting.'

'Only, shrimps and things kept coming in, which was discouraging, and once a baby squid.'

'It must have been.'

'So Leo stopped it. It was supposed to be terribly health-giving, but there are limits.'

'I'm sure there are,' I said. 'Shrimps in the wine would be one of them.'

'Shrimps in the *wine*? What on earth are you talking about?'

I put down my empty cup. 'I'm not quite sure. I thought it was the wine-cellars.'

'The sea-water baths, idiot! Leo stopped them. Oh, I see, you're laughing at me . . . Well, go on, anyway. You had a bath. But I still don't see how you got hot water; they *can't* have got the furnaces to work. They used to burn about a ton of coal a day, and it practically needed three slaves to stoke all round the clock.'

'Adoni and Spiro invented a geyser.'

'Dear God,' said Phyl devoutly, 'does it work?'

'Yes, I told you, the water was marvellous. What's more, there were hot pipes to dry my things on, *and* an electric fire in the bedroom next door. Well, while my things dried I wore Sir Julian's dressing-gown—which is why I left all your make-up in the pockets—and had coffee and bacon and eggs in the kitchen. Then Max Gale brought me home with the diamond, and that's the end of the saga.' I leaned back and grinned at her. 'As a matter of fact, it was rather fun.'

'It sounds it! Was Max Gale civil?'

'Oh, yes. Very.'

'I must say I'm surprised he helped you. I thought he was supposed to be trying to get rid of the dolphin.'

'It can't have been him, after all. He helped me as soon as I asked him. And it wasn't his father, either, I'm certain of that. I think it must just have been some beastly local lad out for a bit of fun.' I sat up and pushed back the coverlet. 'I'd better get up.'

My sister glanced at her wrist, and stood up with an exclamation. 'Heavens, yes, I'll have to run if I'm to be ready.'

'Where are you going?'

'To get my hair done, and I've got some shopping to do, so I thought I'd have lunch in town. I ought to have waked you before to ask if you'd like to come, but you looked so tired . . . there's cold meat and a fruit flan if you stay home, but you're welcome to come if you like. Can you make it? I'll have to leave in about twenty minutes.'

I hesitated. 'Did Godfrey expect me to ring him back or anything?'

'Oh heavens, yes, I'd forgotten. He's pining to hear all about last night at first hand, I gather. I told him I'd be out to lunch, or I'd have asked him over, but I think he was going to ask you to lunch with him.' She paused, a hand on the door. 'There's the phone now, that'll be him. What shall I tell him?'

I reached for my stockings, and sat down to pull them on. The action covered some rapid thinking.

Godfrey would obviously be very curious to know what had passed at the Castello last night—what Sir Julian had told us, and what Max's reactions had been. If I could put him off till tomorrow, I might use this curiosity to keep him out of Max's way.

I said: 'Say I'm in the bathroom or something, and can't come to the phone now, and tell him I'm going out with you, and I don't know when I'll be in, but I'll ring him . . . No, he can ring me. Some time tonight.'

Phyl raised an eyebrow. 'Hard to get, huh? All right. Then you are coming with me?'

'No, I'll never make it, thanks all the same. I'll laze around and go down to the beach later.'

'Okay,' said my sister amiably, and went to silence the telephone.

I had no intention of going down to the beach, as it happened, it being more than likely that Godfrey would see me there and come down. But I did want to go over to the Castello to find out if Max and Spiro had got safely away. I hesitated to use the party telephone, and in any case I doubted if Sir Julian would want to talk to me this morning, but I had hopes of finding Adoni about in the garden, and of seeing him alone.

So I ate my cold luncheon early, and rather hurriedly, then, telling Miranda that I was going down to the beach for the afternoon, went to my room for my things.

But she was waiting for me in the hall as I came out, with a small package in her hand.

'For me?' I said. 'What is it?'

'Adoni just brought it. It's some things you left there last night.'

I took it from her. Through the paper I could feel the small hard shapes of Phyl's lipstick and powder-box. 'Oh, that's good of him. I was thinking I'd have to go across to collect them. Is he still here?'

'No, miss, he wouldn't stay. But I was to say to you that all was well.'

There was just the faintest lift of curiosity in her voice. I noticed then how bright her eyes were, and that the flush was back in her cheeks, and for a moment I wondered if Adoni had given her some hint of the truth.

'I'm glad of that. Did he tell you about the adventure we had last night?'

'The dolphin? Yes, he told me. It must have been strange.' The strangest thing to her Greek mind was, I could see, that anyone should have gone to that amount of trouble. 'But your coat, Miss Lucy! I don't know if it will ever come right!'

I laughed. 'It did get rather a beating, didn't it? I thought you'd be wondering what I'd been doing.'

'I knew you must have fallen in the sea, because of your dress and coat . . . and the bathroom, *po po po*. I have washed the dress, but the coat must go to a proper cleaner.'

'Oh, goodness, yes, you mustn't bother with it. Thanks very much for doing the dress, Miranda. Well, when you see Adoni, will you thank him for bringing these things? And for the message. That was all, that all was well?'

'Yes.'

'That's fine,' I said heartily. 'I did wonder. Sir Julian wasn't feeling well last night, and I was worried.'

She nodded. 'He will be all right this morning.'

I stared for a moment, then realised that she knew exactly what my careful meiosis meant, and was untroubled by it. The Greek mind again; if a man chose to get drunk now and again, what did it matter except to himself? His women would accept it as they accepted all else. Life here had its shining simplicities.

'I'm very glad,' I said, and went out towards the pine woods.

As soon as I was out of sight of the house I left the path, and climbed higher through the woods, where the trees thinned, and a few scattered pines stood on top of the promontory. I spread my rug in the shade, and lay down. The ground was felted with pine needles, and here and there grew furry leaves of ground ivy, and the pretty, dull-pink orchids, and lilac irises flecked with white. The Castello was hidden from view by its trees, but from this height I could just see, on the southern headland, the roof of the Villa Rotha. The Forli house was visible below me. In the distance, beyond the sparkling sea, lay the mountains of Epirus. The snow had almost gone, but further north the Albanian peaks still gleamed white. There, beneath them, would be the rocks where Spiro had gone ashore, and where Max had brought him off under the coastguards' guns. And there, a coloured cluster under the violet hills of Epirus, was Igoumenitsa, where the ferry ran . . .

I had brought a book but couldn't read, and it was not long before I saw what I had been expecting: Godfrey, coming with an air of purpose along the path round the headland. He didn't descend into the bay; just stood there, as if looking for someone who might have been on the beach or in the sea. He waited a little while, and I thought at one point that he was going to cross the sand and climb to the Forli house, but he didn't. He hung around for a few minutes more, then turned and went back.

Some time later my eye was caught by a glimpse of moving white, a glint beyond the treetops that rimmed the sea; and presently a boat stole out under sail from beyond the further headland, cutting a curved path of white through the glittering blue.

I lay, chin on hand, watching her.

She was not unlike a boat that Leo had owned some years back, and on which I had spent a holiday one summer, the year I had left school. She was a powered sloop, perhaps thirty feet overall, Bermuda rigged, with—as far as I could make out—a mast that could be lowered. That this was so seemed probable, since from something Godfrey had said I assumed she was Dutch built, so might presumably be adapted for canal cruising, and negotiating low bridges. In any case I had gathered last night that she was customarily moored not in the bay, but in the boat-house; and even if this was built on the same lavish scale as the Castello, and designed to house several craft, it would have to be a vast place indeed to take the sloop's forty-odd-foot mast. Her hull was sea-grey, with a white line at the bows. She was a lovely craft, and at any other time I would have lain dreamily admiring her sleek lines and the beauty of her canvas, but today I merely wondered about her speed – seven or eight knots, I supposed – and narrowed my eyes to watch the small black figure at the tiller, which was Godfrey.

The sea raced glittering along the grey hull (grey for camouflage?); the white wake creamed; she turned, beautiful, between me and the sun, and I could see no more of her except as a winged shape heading in a long tack out to sea, and then south, towards Corfu town.

* * *

'Lucy?' said the telephone.

'Yes. Hullo. You're very faint.'

'Did you get the message from Adoni?'

'Yes. Just that all was well, so I assumed you'd got away safely. I hope it still is?'

'So far, a bit discouraging, but I'm still hoping. What about you?'

'I'm fine, thank you, and all's well here. Calm and normal, as far as I can see. Don't worry about this end.'

'Ah.' A slight pause. Though I knew there was no one else in the house, I found myself glancing quickly around me. Max's voice said, distant in my ear: 'You know this libretto I came over here to discuss with that friend of mine? We've been talking over the story all afternoon now, and he's not very keen on it. Says it's not plausible. I'm not sure if I'm going to be able to persuade him to do much about it.'

'I get it,' I said, 'but look, this line's all right. My sister's out, and so is the other party on the line; I saw his boat go out, with him in it, quite a bit ago, and it's not back yet. I've been watching till now. You can say what you like.'

'Well, I'm not sure how good their English is at the Corfu exchange,' said Max, 'but you'll have gathered it's not very good news in any language. We've been with the police all afternoon, and they've listened civilly enough, but they're not inclined to take it all that seriously – certainly not to take action against our friend without some solid proof.'

'If he were to be watched –?

'They're inclined to think it's not worth it. The general idea is that it's only another spot of illegal trading, and no one's prepared to take it seriously enough to spend money on investigating.'

'Don't they believe the boy's story, then?'

He hesitated. 'I can't quite make that out. I don't think they do. They think he may be mistaken, and they're favouring the idea of an accident.'

'A nice, trouble-free verdict,' I said dryly. 'And was Y.'s death an accident, too?'

'They're inclined to stick to the first verdict there as well. The trouble is, you see, they're furious with me over last night's little effort, which I've had to tell them about, and which might have started some trouble. The Greek-Albanian frontier's always like a train of dynamite with a slow fuse crawling up to it. Oh, they did admit in the end that I could hardly have called the police in on a rendezvous with Milo and his pal, but I did also withhold evidence in the inquiry on Y.Z. after they'd been so helpful to Father and myself over Spiro . . . I must say I rather see their point, but my name's mud for the moment, and they're simply not prepared to take action on my say-so, especially if it means coming in over the heads of the local coppers. You see, there's no possible motive.'

'But if it was . . . "illegal trading"?'

'That would hardly have led to murder. As we know, it's barely even taken seriously from this side of the border.'

'I see.'

'So they look like accepting accident on both counts. And, of course, damn it, we can't prove a thing. I simply don't know what's going to happen.'

'Can you bring him back – the boy?'

'I don't know that either. As far as the hospital's concerned it's all right, but as to whether it's safe for him . . . If only one could find even some shred of an idea why it happened, let alone proof that it did . . . If I didn't know the boy so well, and if it weren't for Y.'s death, I'd take the same attitude as the police, I can tell you that. You were right last night when you said it was incredible. In the cold light of day the idea's fantastic – but still my bones tell me it's true . . . Ah, well. I'm going to talk to them again later tonight, and there's still tomorrow. We may get something done yet.'

'When will you come back?'

'Tomorrow. I'll try to manage the earlier time I gave you.'

'All right. I'm fairly sure I can have that under control. You won't be met.'

'Well, that's one load off my mind.' I heard him laugh. 'We managed fine on the way out, but the hospital's fitted a wonderful new cast that won't go in the boot, so it's the back seat and a rug—and a damned awkward situation if anyone were hanging about. Will it be hard to arrange?'

'Dead easy—I think. I'm not sure which is the spider and which is the fly, but I don't think I'll even have to try.'

'Well, for pity's sake watch your step.'

'Don't worry, he'll get nothing out of me. I may be a darned bad actress on the stage, but off it I'm terrific.'

He laughed again. 'Who's telling whom? But that's not what I meant.'

'I know. It's all right, I'll be careful.'

I heard him take a long breath. 'I feel better now. I'll go and tackle this bunch of very nice but all too sensible policemen again. I must go. Bless you. Take care of yourself.'

'And you,' I said.

The receiver at the other end was cradled, and through the wire washed the crackling hiss of the miles of sea and air that lay between us. As I put my own receiver down gently, I found that I was staring out of the long glass pane of the door that led to the terrace. It framed an oblong of the empty evening sky, dusk, with one burning planet among a trail of dusty stars. I sat for a few minutes without moving, one hand still on the receiver, not thinking of anything, just watching that bright planet, and feeling in me all tensions stilled at once, as if someone had laid a finger across a thrumming string.

When the telephone rang again, right under my hand, I hardly even jumped. I sat back in the chair and put the receiver to my ear.

'Yes?' I said. 'Oh, hullo, Godfrey. Yes, it's Lucy. In Corfu, are you? No, I've been home a little while. I was wondering when you'd ring . . .'

Chapter 14

He's safe for these three hours.
III. 1.

HE CALLED FOR me next day immediately after lunch. He had
suggested that I lunch with him, and certainly he had sounded
flatteringly anxious for my company, but since I didn't imagine he
really wanted anything from me but information, and I had no idea
how long I could hold him, I pleaded an engagement for lunch, but
allowed myself to be suitably eager for a drive in the afternoon.

I even managed to suggest the route. Not that there was much
choice in the matter; the road north was barely navigable by a car
one cared about, so I could hardly suggest that Godfrey took it. We
would have to go south on the road by which Max and Spiro would
eventually be driving home, but there was, happily, a road leading
off this to Palaiokastritsa, a famous beauty-spot on the western coast
which I could be legitimately anxious to visit. It was in fact true that
I had looked the place up on the map, but had put off going there
because the road seemed mountainous and I had been slightly
nervous of tackling it in Phyl's little car. With me driving (I told
Godfrey) it would be nerve-racking, and with Phyl driving it would
be suicide . . . But if Godfrey would drive me, and if he had a car
that would manage the gradients . . .

He had laughed, sounding pleased, and had professed himself
delighted to brave any gradients I wished, and yes, he had a car that
would manage it quite easily . . .

He certainly had. It was a black XK 150, blunt-nosed, powerful,
and about as accommodating on the narrow roads as a bull seal on

his own bit of beach. It nosed its way impatiently along the drive, humming like a hive of killer bees, bucked on to the rutted sweep of the Castello's private road, and turned to swoop down to the gate where Maria's cottage stood.

Maria was outside, bending over a rusty tin with a stick, stirring what seemed to be hen food. When she heard the car she straightened up with the tin clutched to her breast, and the hens clucking and chattering round her feet. Godfrey, slowing down for the turn into the main road, raised a hand and called out a greeting, to which she returned a look of pleasure mingled with respect, as warm a look as I had seen on her face in the last week or so. I had noticed the same look, shy but pleased, in Miranda's face, as she had showed him into the *salotto* earlier, as if the two women were grateful to Spiro's employer for his continued kindness to them in their bereavement.

I stole a look at him as the car swerved – rather too fast, and with a blare of its twin horns that sent Maria's hens up in a squawking cloud – on to the main road. I don't know quite what I had expected to see this afternoon – some smooth-skinned monster, perhaps, with hoofs, horns and tail all visible to the eye of knowledge – but he was just the same, an undeniably attractive man, who handled his exciting car with skill and obvious enjoyment.

And this man, I thought, was supposed to have brushed the boy – the beloved son and brother – off the stern of his boat as if he were a jellyfish, and then sailed on, leaving him to drown . . .

He must have felt me watching him, for he flicked me a glance, and smiled, and I found myself smiling back spontaneously, and quite without guile. In spite of myself, in spite of Max, and Spiro's story, I could not believe it. The thing was, as I had said to Max, impossible in daylight.

Which was just as well. If I was to spend the next few hours with him, I would have to shut my mind to all that I had learned, to blot out the scene in the cellar, drop Spiro out of existence as if he were indeed dead. And, harder than all, drop Max. There was a curiously strong and secret pleasure, I had found, in speaking of him as 'Mr. Gale' in the off-hand tones that Godfrey and Phyllida commonly used, as one might of a stranger to whom one is under an obligation, but whom one hardly considers enough to like or dislike. Once, as I had mentioned his name in passing, my eye, downcast, caught the faint mark of a bruise on my arm. The secret thrill of pleasure that ran up my spine startled me a little; I slipped my other hand over the mark to hide it, and found it cupping the flesh as if it were his, and not my own. I looked away, out of the car, and made some random remark about the scenery.

It was a very pretty road. To our left was the sea, blue and smooth, broken only by a tiny white crescent of sail thin as a nail-paring and almost lost in the heat haze. On the right was a high hedge of apple blossom and judas-trees, their feet deep in a vivid bank of meadow flowers, yellow and purple and white. Two little girls, in patched and faded dresses of scarlet, stood barefoot in the dust to watch us go by, one of them holding a bough of oranges as an English child might hold a stick of balloons, the fruit bulging and glowing among the green leaves.

The road straightened, and the XK 150 surged forward with a smooth burst of speed. My spirits lifted. This was going to be easy; in fact there was no reason why I shouldn't simply relax and enjoy it too. I sat back and chatted on – I hoped naturally – about nothings; the view, the people Phyl had met yesterday in Corfu, the prospect of Leo's coming with the children for Easter . . .

We flashed by a fork in the road.

I sat up sharply. 'That was the turning, wasn't it? I'm sure the signpost said Palaiokastritsa!'

'Oh, yes, it was. I'm sorry, I wasn't thinking; I meant to have told you, I'm not taking you there today. It's a long way, and we've hardly time. We'll go another day, if you like, when we don't have to be back early.'

'*Do* we have to be back early?'

The question slipped out before I thought, ingenuous in its dismay. I saw the faint shadow of gratified surprise in his face, and reflected that after my evasions over the telephone he had every right to find provocation in it.

'I'm afraid so. I'm going out tonight. I don't say we couldn't do it, but it's a shame to go all the way for a short time; it's a lovely place, and there's a lot to see. Besides which, it's a damned waste to go there and not have lunch; there's a restaurant right on the beach where they keep crayfish alive in pots in the sea, and you choose your own and they take them out fresh to cook.' A sideways look at me and a teasing smile. 'I suppose you disapprove, but I can tell you, they're wonderful. I'll take you there soon, if you promise not to stand me up for lunch next time.'

'I didn't – that would be lovely.'

We flicked through a tiny village, one narrow street of houses and a baked white church with a red roof. The snarl of the engine echoed back in a quick blast from the hot walls, and we were through, nose down through a scatter of goats, children, a scraggy puppy, and a donkey trailing a frayed end of rope. The children stared after us, admiring and unresentful.

'One thing,' said Godfrey cheerfully, 'one doesn't have to plan one's outings here according to the weather. The sun's always on call in this blessed isle, and one day's as good as another.'

That's what you think, I said savagely to myself. My hands were tight together in my lap now, as much because of his driving as in a panic-stricken attempt to think of the map. How to get him off this road, head him away from Corfu?

I said aloud: 'I'll hold you to that one day, *and* I'll eat the crayfish! I can't feel strongly about fish, I'm afraid! Where are we going then, Pellekas?' For Pellekas one turned off just at the north end of Corfu—the only other turning before the town.

'No, the Achilleion.'

'Oh? That's a wonderful idea!'

It was a bloody awful idea, as well I knew. To get there one went right through Corfu—not quite to the harbour, but near enough—and, of course, the whole way home we would be using the same road as Max. Well, I'd just have to see that we didn't head for home around five-thirty, and I could only hope there was plenty of scope for sightseeing to the south of Corfu town. I reached for my handbag and fished in it for the guide I had brought, adding with great enthusiasm: 'I'd planned to visit it one day, but there was the same objection—Phyl told me it was on top of a hill with the most ghastly zigzag going up to it! Yes, here it is . . . "The villa of Achilleion, erected for the Empress Elizabeth of Austria . . . The villa, which is in Italian Renaissance style, was purchased in 1907 by the German Emperor. The gardens are open to visitors (admission one drachma, applied to charitable purposes)." '

'What? What on earth's that?'

'An ancient Baedeker I found on Phyl's shelves. It was my grandfather's—date 1909. It's really rather sweet. Listen to the bit at the beginning about the history of the island . . . he says "it came into the possession of" the Romans, then "fell to the share of" the Venetians, then "was occupied by" the French: then "was under Turkish, then Russian sway", but—notice the *but*—from 1815 to 1863 it "came under the protection of" the British. Rule, Britannia. Those were the days.'

'They certainly were.' He laughed. 'Well, you can see the whole palace as well, today, and it will cost a damned sight more than a drachma, and I imagine the gate money'll go straight to the Greek Government. As usual, charity begins at home . . . I wish there'd been some classical relics to take you to–Phyl told me you were interested–but I don't know any, apart from some temple or other inside the Mon Repos park, which is private. However, you might say Achilles is the patron saint of the Achilleion, so perhaps it'll do! There's some talk of turning it into a casino, so this may be the last chance of seeing it more or less in the original state. And the drive up there is very pretty, you'll enjoy it.'

'You're very kind,' I said. It was all I could do not to stare. He spoke so easily and charmingly, sitting there relaxed and handsome at the wheel, the sun throwing up fair highlights in his hair, and a dusting of freckles along the bare brown arms. He was wearing an open-necked shirt, with a yellow silk scarf tucked in at the neck–Top People summer uniform–which suited him very well. He looked calm and contented, and perfectly normal.

Well, why not? When a felon's not engaged in his employment, he has to look as ordinary as possible for his own skin's sake. I supposed it was perfectly possible for a man to drown two young men one week, and enjoy a pleasant day out with a girl the next, take a lot of trouble to plan an outing for her, and even enjoy the view himself. . .

'And there's a marvellous view,' he said. 'The palace is set on a steep wooded hill over the sea. From the belvedere you can see practically the whole way from Vutrinto in Albania, to Perdika along the Greek coast. On a clear day the harbour at Igoumenitsa's quite plain.'

'How splendid.'

'And now supposing you tell me exactly what happened last night at the Castello?'

It took every scrap of discipline and technique I had not to jump like a shot rabbit. 'What happened? Well . . . nothing much–what should? I got home with the diamond, you know that.'

'Oh, to hell with the diamond, you know quite well what I mean.' He sent me another sideways, amused look. 'Did you see Julian Gale?'

'Oh. Yes, I did. Adoni was with him when we got up there.'

'Ah, yes, the faithful watch-pup. He would be. How was Sir Julian?'

'He went to bed pretty soon,' I said cautiously. I kept my eyes on
the road, and in the windscreen I saw Godfrey glance at me again.
'He was–tired,' I said.

'Say what you mean,' said Godfrey. 'He was stoned.'

'How do you know?' The question came out flatly and even
accusingly, but since he himself had hit the ball into the open with
the last phrase there was no reason why I shouldn't keep it there.

'Come off it, they knew who'd been with him, didn't they?'

'We-ll, it was mentioned.' I leaned back in my seat and let a spice
of mischievous amusement creep into my voice. It sounded so like
Phyl as to be startling. 'Mr. Gale wasn't awfully pleased with you,
Godfrey.'

'Damn it all, what's it got to do with me if he wants to get
plastered? By the time I saw which way the land lay, he was
half-way there. Do they imagine it was up to me to stop him?'

'I wouldn't know. But I'd watch out for Mr. Gale, if I were you.'

'So?' His mouth curved. 'Pistols for two and coffee for one, or just
a horsewhip? Well, maybe he does owe it me, after all.'

I knew then. I'm not sure what it was, something in his voice, or
the infinitesimal degree of satisfaction at the corners of his mouth;
something at once cruel and gay and quite terrifying. All the
daylight doubts fled, once and for ever. Of course he was a
murderer. The man was a natural destroyer. *Evil be thou my Good*
. . . and the instinct that had allowed him to create those pictures
wasn't even incongruous: no doubt it had given him much the same
pleasure to destroy Spiro as it had to photograph him. Destroying
Sir Julian would hardly have cost him a moment's thought.

I dragged my eyes and thoughts away from the evil sitting beside
me in the car, and concentrated on the idyll of silver olive and black
cypress through which the XK 150 slashed its way in a train of dust.

'What a lovely road.'

'I wish they'd do something about these pot-holes, that's all. Don't
side-track, Lucy. Was it really horsewhips?'

'I wouldn't be surprised. I mean, Mr. Gale had had a trying
evening. I'd had hysterics all over him and dragged him out to help
with the dolphin, and he fell slap in the sea, and then on top of it all
when we got up to the house we found his father drunk . . . in front
of me, too. You can't blame him if he's out for your blood.'

'I suppose not.' He didn't sound as if it worried him vastly.
'Where is he today?'

'I believe he said he was going to Athens. It was just some remark to Adoni–I didn't take much notice. But you're probably safe for today.'

He laughed. 'I breathe again. Just look at the colour of that girl's frock, the one picking up olives over there, that dusty red against the rather acid green.'

'Don't *you* side-track. I want to know what happened.'

He raised his brows. 'Heavens, nothing, really. I saw the old man at the garage on the harbour, and he was looking for a lift, so I took him home. I was rather pleased to have the chance to talk to him, as it happened–you can never get near him alone, and it was too good a chance to miss.'

'What on earth did you want to get him alone for? Don't tell me you're looking for a walk-on in the next Gale play!'

He grinned. 'That'll be the day–always providing there is one. No, there were things I wanted to know, and I thought he'd be the softest touch. Max Gale and I aren't just the best of friends, and the watch-pup dislikes me. I can't think why.'

'Godfrey! Are you telling me you got him drunk on purpose?'

'Good God, no. Why should I? I wasn't trying to get State secrets out of him. But by the time he'd had a couple there was no stopping him, and it wasn't my business to stop him, was it? I admit I didn't try.' That fleeting smile again, gone in an instant; a flash of satisfaction, no more. 'It was quite entertaining up to a point.'

'What on earth *were* you wanting to get out of him?'

'Only what the police were up to.'

'Police?'

He glanced at me with a lifted eyebrow. 'Don't sound so startled. What have you been doing? No, it's only that on this island everything gets to the Gales' ears and to no one else's. I had a hell of a job finding anything out about the Spiro affair–nobody seemed to think it was my business, but I'm damned sure they tell the Gales everything that turns up.'

'Well, I gather there's some sort of family connection.'

'So I'm told. But I don't see why that gives them an "exclusive" on a police inquiry that involved me as closely as Spiro's death did.'

'I do so agree,' I said sympathetically. 'It must have been a terribly nerve-racking time for you.'

'It still is.' Certainly if I hadn't known what I knew, I'd have heard nothing in the grave rejoinder but what should properly be there. But, keyed as I was, the two brief syllables hid a whole world of secret amusement. I found that the hand in my lap was clenched tightly, and deliberately relaxed it.

'Did Sir Julian have any news? What has turned up about Spiro?'

'Search me. He wouldn't say a word. We had a couple of drinks at the *taverna*, and I thought his manner was a bit odd; I thought at first he was being cagey, and there was something he didn't want to tell me, but after a bit I realised that he was merely feeling his corn, and trying to hide it. It's my guess the poor old chap hasn't had anything stronger than half a mild sherry for a year.' His mouth twitched. 'Well, after that I'm afraid I did rather give the party a push along the right lines . . . I wanted to lay in a few bottles for myself—I was out of ouzo, for one thing, and there was a new *koùm koyàt* liqueur I was wanting to try, so I bought them, but when I suggested we should go along to my place the old man wouldn't have it. He was mellowing a bit by that time, and insisted on taking me to the Castello, and buying a bottle of gin to treat me to. It didn't take much of that stuff to get him good and lit, but I'm afraid it finished any hope I'd had of getting sense out of him. He'd got it fixed in his head that the only reason I'd gone to the Castello was to hear the recording of their blasted film music.' He gave a short laugh where the exasperation still lingered. 'Believe you me, I got the lot, words and all.'

'Oh, I believe you! Hunks of *The Tempest*?'

'Did he do that for you, too?'

I laughed. 'He was reciting when Mr. Gale and I got up to the house. As a matter of fact I enjoyed it. He did it marvellously, gin or no gin.'

'He's had plenty of practice.'

The cruel words were lightly spoken, but I think it was at that moment that I began to hate Godfrey Manning. I remembered Max's face, strained and tired; Sir Julian's, blurred and drowning, holding on to heaven knew what straw of integrity; the two boys curled close together on the makeshift bed; Maria's grateful humility. Until this moment I had been content to think that I was helping Max: this had franked a piece of deception whose end I had not let myself explore. But now I explored it, and with relish. If Godfrey Manning was to be proved a murderer, then presumably he was going to be punished for it; and I was going to help with everything I had. Something settled in me, cold and hard. I sat down in the saddle and prepared to ride him down.

I felt him glance at me, and got my face into order.

'What actually happened when you got to the house?' he asked.

'What did he tell them, Max and the model-boy?'

'Nothing, while I was there. No, honestly, Godfrey!' I was pleased to hear how very honest I sounded. 'They only guessed it was you who'd been with him because you'd thrown a Sobranie butt into the stove.'

He gave a crack of laughter. 'Detectives Unlimited! You did have an exciting night, didn't you? Did they let anything drop in front of you—about Spiro, I mean?'

'Not a thing.'

'Nor Yanni Zoulas?'

I turned wide, surprised eyes on him. 'Yanni—oh, the fisherman who was drowned. No, why?'

'I wondered. Pure curiosity.'

I said nothing, letting the silence hang. Now we were getting somewhere . . . It was obvious that he was still uncertain whether the police really had accepted 'accident' as the verdict on Spiro and Yanni; and I thought it was obvious, too, that he badly wanted to know. And since he wasn't the man to sweat about what he had done, it must be what he still had to do that was occupying him: he needed a clear field, and no watchers. His efforts with Sir Julian, and now with me, showed that he had no suspicion that he was being watched, just that he badly needed a green light, and soon.

Well, I thought cheerfully, leaning back in my seat, let him sweat a bit longer. He'd get no green light from me.

The road was climbing now, zigzagging steeply up a wooded hill clothed with vineyards and olive-groves, and the fields of green corn with their shifting grapebloom shadows.

He said suddenly: 'Didn't you see him go back to the body after we'd left it?'

'What? See who?'

'Gale, of course.'

'Oh, yes . . . sorry, I was looking at the view. Yes, I did. Why?'

'Didn't you wonder why he did that?'

'I can't say I did. I suppose he just wanted another look.' I gave a little shiver. 'Better him than me. Why, did you think he saw something we didn't?'

He shrugged. 'Nothing was said to you?'

'Nothing at all. Anyway, I hardly know the Gales; they wouldn't tell me things any more than you. You aren't beginning to think there was more in Yanni's death than met the eye?'

'Oh, no. Let's just say it's curiosity, and a little natural human resentment at having things taken out of my hands. The man was drowned on my doorstep – as Spiro was from my boat – and I think I should have been kept in the picture. That's all.'

'Well,' I said, 'if anything had turned up about Spiro, Maria would know, and she'd tell my sister and me straight away. If there is anything, I'll let you know. I realise how you must be feeling.'

'I'm sure you do. And here we are. Shall we see if they'll let us in for one drachma?'

*　　*　　*

The gates were open, rusting on their seedy pillars. Huge trees, heavy already with summer, hung over the walls. A sleepy janitor relieved us of twenty drachmas or so and nodded us through.

The house was very near the gate, set among thick trees. The doors were open. I had vaguely expected a museum of some kind, a carefully kept relic of the past, but this was merely an empty house, a summer residence from which the owners had moved out, leaving doors and windows unlocked so that dead leaves and insects had drifted year by year into the deserted rooms, floorboards had rotted, paintwork had decayed, metal had rusted . . . The place was a derelict, set in the derelict remains of formal gardens and terraces, and beyond the garden boundaries crowded the trees and bushes of a park run wild.

I remember very little now of my tour of the Achilleion. I am sure Godfrey was a good guide; I recollect that he talked charmingly and informatively all the time, and I must have made the right responses; but I was obsessed with my new hatred of him, which I felt must be bound to show as plainly as a stain; in consequence I was possibly even a little too charming back again. I know that as the afternoon went on his manner warmed perceptibly. It was a relief to escape at length from the dusty rooms on to the terrace.

Here at least the air was fresh, and it wasn't quite as hard to linger admiringly as it had been in the dusty rooms of the palace, with their unkempt and shabby grandeurs. The terrace was floored with horrible liver-coloured tiles, and the crowding trees below it obscured any view there might have been, but I did my best with the hideous metal statues at the corners and the row of dim-looking marble 'Muses' posing sadly along a loggia. I was a model sightseer. I stopped at every one. You'd have thought they were

Michelangelos. Three-fifteen . . . three-twenty . . . even at three
minutes per Muse it would only keep us there till three-forty-
seven . . .

There remained the garden. We went in detail round it; arum
lilies deep in the weeds at the foot of palm-trees; a few unhappy
paeonies struggling up in the dank shade; a dreadful statue of
Achilles triumphant (six minutes) and a worse one of Achilles dying
(four); some Teutonic warriors mercifully cutting one another's
throats in a riot of brambles (one and a half). I would even have
braved the thorny tangle of the wood to admire a statue of Heine
sitting in a chair, if the gate hadn't been secured with barbed wire,
and if I hadn't been afraid that I would wear out even Godfrey's
patience.

I needn't have worried. It was unassailable. He had to put the
time in somehow, and I am certain that it never once crossed his
mind that a day out with him could be anything but a thrill for me
from first to last.

Which, to be fair, it certainly was. The thrill that I got, quite
literally, when he took me by the elbow to lead me gently back
towards the gate and the waiting Jaguar went through my bone-
marrow as if the bones had been electrically wired. It was only
twenty past four. If we left for home now, and if Godfrey, as
seemed likely, suggested tea in Corfu, we should just be in nice time
to meet the ferry.

There was one more statue near the gate, a small one of a
fisher-boy sitting on the fragment of a boat, bare-legged, chubby,
smiling down at something, and wearing a dreadful hat. It was on
about the same level of genius as the Muses, but, of course, I
stopped in front of it, rapt, with Baedeker at the ready and my eyes
madly searching the tiny print to see if there were any other 'sights'
between here and Corfu which I could use to delay my blessedly
complacent guide.

'Do you like it?' Godfrey's tone was amused and indulgent. He
laid the back of a finger against the childish cheek. 'Do you notice? If
this had been done seven years ago instead of seventy it might have
been Spiro. One wonders if the model wasn't a grandfather or
something. It's very like, don't you think?'

'I never knew Spiro.'

'Of course not, I forgot. Well, Miranda, then.'

'Yes, perhaps I do see it. I was just thinking it was charming.'

'The face is warm,' said Godfrey, running a light hand down the

line of the cheek. I turned away quickly, feeling my face too naked.
Half past four.

He dropped his hand. 'You keep looking at your watch. I suppose
you're like Phyl, always gasping for tea at this time? Shall we go and
look for some in Corfu?'

'What's the other way? The coast looked so lovely from the
belvedere.'

'Nothing much, the usual pretty road, and a fishing village called
Benitses.'

'There'll be a *kafenèion* there, surely? That would be more fun for
a change. Wouldn't there be tea there?'

He laughed. 'The usual wide choice, Nescafé or lemonade. There
might even be some of those slices of bread, cut thick and dried in
the oven. I've never yet discovered who eats them or even how. I
can't even break them. Well, on your head be it. Jump in.'

We got tea after all at Benitses, at a plain, clean little hotel set right
on the sea. It couldn't have been better placed – for me, that is.
There were tables outside, and I chose one right on the dusty shore,
under a pepper-tree, and sat down facing the sea. Just beside us a
whole stable of coloured boats dozed at their moorings, vermilion
and turquoise and peacock, their masts swaying gently with the
breathing of the sea; but beyond them I saw nothing but one red sail
dancing alone on the empty and glittering acres.

Godfrey glanced over his shoulder. 'What's going on there that's
so interesting?'

'Nothing, really, but I could watch the sea by the hour, couldn't
you? Those boats are so pretty. Your own is a real beauty.'

'When did you see her?'

'Yesterday afternoon. I saw you go out.'

'Oh? Where were you? I'd been looking for you down on the
beach.'

'What a pity! No, I didn't go down after all, I stayed up in the
woods and slept.' I laughed. 'I rather needed the sleep.'

'You'd certainly had a strenuous time. I wish I'd seen your rescue
act with the dolphin. Some pictures by flash would have been
interesting.' He stirred the pale tea, squashing the lemon slice
against the side of the cup. 'I read somewhere – I think it was
Norman Douglas – that while dolphins are dying they change colour. I believe it can be a remarkable display. Fascinating if one could
get that, don't you think?'

'Marvellous. Did you say you were going out tonight?'

'Yes.'

'I suppose you couldn't do with a crew? I'd adore to come.'

'Brave of you, under the circumstances. You'd not be afraid to crew for me?'

'Not in the least, I'd love it. You mean I may? What time are you going?'

If he had accepted the offer I'm not sure what I'd have done; broken an ankle at least, I expect. But he said:

'Of course you may, some day soon, but you've got me wrong, I didn't mean I was going out with the boat tonight. Actually, I'm going by car to visit friends.'

'Oh, I'm sorry, I must have got hold of the wrong end of the stick. A pity, I was getting all excited.'

He smiled. 'I tell you what; I'll take you sailing soon—Friday, perhaps? or Saturday? We'll go round to Lake Kalikiopoulos and look for the place—one of the places, I should say—where Odysseus is supposed to have stepped ashore into the arms of Nausicaa. Would that be classical enough for you?'

'It would be marvellous.'

'Then I'll look forward to it . . . Look, there's the ferry.'

'Ferry?' It came out in a startled croak, and I cleared my throat. 'What ferry?'

'The mainland boat. She crosses to Igoumenitsa and back. There, see? It's not easy to see her against the glitter. She'll be in in about twenty minutes.' He looked at his watch, and pushed back his chair. 'Hm, she's late. Well, shall we go?'

'I'd like to go upstairs, please, if they have one.'

The owner of the hotel, who was at Godfrey's elbow with the check, interpreted this remark with no difficulty, and led me up an outside stair and along a scrubbed corridor to an enormous room which had been made into a bathroom. It was spotlessly clean, and furnished, apart from the usual offices, with a whole gallery of devotional pictures. Perhaps others before me had fled to this sanctuary to think . . .

But it was Baedeker I had come to study. I whipped it open and ran a finger down the page. The print was hideously small, and danced under my eyes. *One drachma a day for the dragoman is ample . . . valets-de-place, 5 dr. per day, may be dispensed with . . .*

Ah, here was something that might be expected to appeal to an avid classicist like myself. *The tomb of Menecrates, dating from the 6th or 7th Century B.C. . . .* And bang on the way home, at that. Now, if only I could persuade Godfrey that my day would be blighted if I didn't visit this tomb, whatever it was . . .

I could; and it was a winner, for the simple reason that nobody knew where it was. We asked everybody we met, and were directed in turn, with the utmost eagerness and goodwill, to a prison, a football ground, the site of a Venetian fort, and a pond; and I could have felt sorry for Godfrey if I hadn't seen quite clearly that he thought that I was trying desperately to spin out my afternoon with him. The man's armour was complete. In his vocabulary, God was short for Godfrey.

I was paid out when we did finally run Menecrates to earth in the garden of the police station, and the custodian, welcoming us as if the last tourist to visit it had been Herr Karl Baedeker himself in 1909, pressed on me a faded document to read, and thereafter solemnly walked me round the thing three times, while Godfrey sat on the wall and smoked, and the lovely dusk fell, and the hands of my watch slid imperceptibly round, and into the clear . . .

'After six o'clock,' said Godfrey, rising. 'Well, I hope you've time to have a drink with me before I take you home? The Astir has a very nice terrace overlooking the harbour.'

'That would be wonderful,' I said.

Chapter 15

I prithee now lead the way without any more talking.
                                                    II. 2.

IT WAS QUITE dark when Godfrey finally drove me back to the Villa
Forli. I said good-bye at the front door, waited till the car had
vanished among the trees, then turned and hurried indoors.

A light from the kitchen showed that either Miranda or her
mother was there; but the *salotto* was empty in its cool, grey dusk,
and no light showed from Phyl's bedroom door. In a moment I knew
why: I had made straight for the telephone, and just before I lifted
the receiver I saw the pale oblong of a note left on the table beside it.
I switched on the table-lamp, to find a note from Phyl.

> 'Lucy dear (it ran), *Got a wire this afternoon to say that Leo and the kids
> are coming on Saturday, and he can stay two whole weeks. Calloo, callay!
> Anyway, I've gone into Corfu to lay in a few things. Don't wait for me if
> you're hungry. There's plenty for G. too, if he wants to stay. Love, Phyl.'*

As I finished reading this, Miranda came into the hall.

'Oh, it's you, Miss Lucy! I thought I heard a car. Did you see the
letter from the Signora?'

'Yes, thank you. Look, Miranda, there's no need for you to stay.
Mr. Manning's gone home, and my sister may be late, so if there's
something cold I can get –'

'I came to tell you. She telephoned just a few minutes ago. She has
met friends in Corfu – Italian friends who are spending one night
only – and is having dinner with them. She said if you wanted to go,
to get a taxi and join them at the Corfu Palace, but' – a dimple

showed – 'none of them speaks any English, so she thinks you would rather stay here, yes?'

I laughed. 'But definitely yes. Well, in that case, I'll have a bath, and then have supper as soon as you like. But I can easily look after myself, you know. If you'll tell me what there is, you can go home if you want to.'

'No, no, I shall stay. There is a cold lobster, and salad, but I am making soup.' She gave her wide, flashing smile. 'I make good soup, Miss Lucy. You will like it.'

'I'm sure I shall. Thank you.'

She didn't go, but lingered at the edge of the light thrown by the little lamp, her hands busily, almost nervously, pleating the skirt of the red dress. I realised, then, suddenly, what my preoccupation hadn't let me notice till now; this was not the subdued and tear-bleached Miranda of the last week. Some of the gloss was back on her, and there was a sort of eagerness in her face, as if she was on the edge of speech.

But all she said was: 'Of course I will stay. I had a day off this afternoon. A day off? Is that what the Signora calls it?'

'Yes, that's right. The afternoon off. What do you do when you get an afternoon off?'

She hesitated again, and I saw her skin darken and glow. 'Sometimes also Adoni has the afternoon off.'

'I see.' I couldn't quite keep the uneasiness out of my voice. So she had spent the afternoon with Adoni. It might be that fact alone which had set her shining again, but I wondered if anyone as young as Adoni could possibly be trusted not to have told her about Spiro. Even for myself, the temptation to break the news to the girl and her mother had been very strong, while for the nineteen-year-old Adoni, longing, like anyone of his age, to boast of his own share in last night's exploits, the urge must have been overwhelming. I added: 'No, don't go for a moment, Miranda; I want to make a phone call in rather a hurry, and I don't know how to ask for the number. The Castello, please; Mr. Max.'

'But he is not there, he is away.'

'I know, but he was to be back before six.'

She shook her head. 'He will not be here till late, Adoni told me so. Mr. Max rang up at five o'clock. He said he would be home tonight, but late, and not to expect him to dinner.'

'Oh.' I found that I had sat down rather heavily in the chair beside the telephone, as if the news was in actual physical fact a let-down. I

did not think then of the effort that had been wasted, but simply of
the empty spaces of the evening that stretched ahead, without news
. . . and without him. 'Did he say anything else?'

'Only that "nothing had changed".' She gave the words inverted
commas, and there was something puzzled and inquiring in her look
that told me what I had wanted to know. Adoni had after all kept his
word: the girl had no idea that there was anything afoot.

Meanwhile I must make do with what crumbs I had. 'Nothing
had changed.' We could presumably expect him on the late ferry,
but if nothing had changed, it didn't sound as if a police escort was
likely, so he might not bring Spiro back with him, either. More I
could not guess, but my part in the affair was decidedly over for the
day; I couldn't have kept Godfrey any longer, and it didn't seem
now as if it was going to matter.

'Where was Mr. Max speaking from?'

'I don't know. From Athens, I suppose.'

'From *Athens*? At five o'clock? But if he was planning to come
back tonight –'

'I forgot. It couldn't have been Athens, could it? Adoni didn't say,
just that it was the mainland.' She waved a hand largely. 'Somewhere over there, that's all.' And, her tone implied, it didn't matter
much one way or the other. Outside Corfu, all places were the same,
and not worth visiting anyway.

I laughed, and she laughed with me, the first spontaneous sound
of pleasure that I had heard from her since the news of her brother's
loss. I said: 'What is it, Miranda? You seem excited tonight. Has
something nice happened?'

She was opening her lips to answer, when some sound from the
kitchen made her whisk round. 'The soup! I must go! Excuse me!'
And she vanished towards the kitchen door.

I went to have my bath, then made my way to the dining-room,
where Miranda was just setting the contents of a large tray out in
lonely state at one end of the table. She showed no desire to leave
me, but hovered anxiously as I tasted the soup, and glowed again at
my praise. We talked cooking all through the soup, and while I
helped myself to the lobster salad, I asked no more questions, but
ate, and listened, and wondered again what magic the 'afternoon off'
with young Adoni had done for her. (I should here that
Miranda's English, unlike Adoni's, was not nearly as good as I have
reported it; but it was rapid enough, and perfectly understandable,
so for the sake of clarity I have translated it fairly freely.)

'This is a dressing from the Signora's book,' she told me, handing a dish. 'She does not like the Greek dressing, so I have tried it from the French book. Is it good? You had a nice day, Miss Lucy?'

'Lovely, thanks. We went to the Achilleion.'

'I have been there once. It is very wonderful, is it not?'

'Very. Then we had tea at Benitses.'

'Benitses? Why did you go there? There is nothing at Benitses! In Corfu it is better.'

'I wanted to see it, and to drive back along the sea. Besides, I was longing for some tea, and Corfu was too far, and I wanted to look at some antiquities on the way home.'

She knitted her brows. 'Antiquities? Oh, you mean statues, like the ones on the Esplanade, the fine English ones.'

'In a way, though those aren't old enough. It really means things many hundreds of years old, like the things in the Museum in Corfu.'

'Are they valuable, these antiquities?'

'Very. I don't know if you could say what they were worth in terms of money, but I'd say they're beyond price. Have you seen them?'

She shook her head. She said nothing, but that was because she was biting her lips together as if forcibly to prevent speech. Her eyes were brilliant.

I stopped with my glass half-way to my mouth. 'Miranda, what is it? Something *has* happened – you can't pretend – you look as if you'd been given a present. Can't you tell me?'

She took in her breath with something of a gulp. Her fingers were once again pleating and unpleating a fold of her skirt. 'It is something . . . something Adoni has found.'

I put down the glass. It clattered against the table. I waited.

A silence, then she said, with a rush: 'Adoni and I, we found it together, this afternoon. When I got the afternoon off, I went over to the Castello . . .' She sent me a sideways glance. 'Sometimes, you see, Adoni works in the garden while Sir Gale sleeps, and then we talk. But today, Mr. Karithis was visiting with Sir Gale, and they told me Adoni had gone to swim. So I went down to the bay.'

'Yes?' She had my attention now, every scrap of it.

'I could not find him, so after a bit I walked along the path, round the rocks towards the Villa Rotha. Then I saw him. He was up the cliff, coming out of a bush.'

'Coming out of a *bush*?'

'It was really a cave,' explained Miranda. 'Everybody knows that
there are caves in the rock under the Castello, they used to use them
for wine; and Adoni told me that he had seen down through a crack,
and heard water, so he knew that there must be more caves below.
This island is full of caves. Why, over near Ermones –'

'Adoni had found a new cave?'

She nodded. 'He had not been on that part of the cliff before. I did
not know he was interested in – I don't know the word – exploring?
Thank you. But today he said he wanted to find out where the water
was that lay under the Castello, and he knew that Mr. Manning was
away with you, so it was all right. I think' – here she dimpled – 'that
he was not very pleased to see me. I think he had heard me, and
thought it was Mr. Manning come back. He looked quite
frightened.'

And well he might, I thought. My heart was bumping a bit. 'Go
on, what had he found?'

Her face went all at once solemn, and lighted. 'He had found
proof.'

I jumped. *'Proof?'*

'That is what he said. Myself, I do not think that proof is needed,
but that is what he said.'

'Miranda!' I heard my voice rise sharply on the word, and
controlled it. 'Please explain. I have no idea what you're talking
about. What proof had Adoni found?'

'Proof of St. Spiridion and his miracles.'

I sat back in my chair. She stared at me solemnly, and as the
silence drew out I felt my heart-beats slowing down to normal. I had
a near-hysterical desire to laugh, but managed to stop myself. After
a while I said gently: 'Well, go on. Tell me . . . no, don't hover
there, I've finished, thank you. Look, would you like to bring the
coffee, and then sit down here and have some with me and tell me all
about it?'

She hurried out, but when she came back with the coffee, she
refused to take any with me, or to sit down, but stood gripping a
chair-back, obviously bursting to get on with her story.

I poured coffee. 'Go on. What's this about the Saint?'

'You were at the procession on Palm Sunday.'

'Yes.'

'Then perhaps you know about the Saint, the patron of this
island?'

'Yes, I know about him. I read a lot about the island before I came here. He was Bishop of Cyprus, wasn't he, who was tortured by the Romans, and after he died his body was embalmed, and carried from place to place until it came to Corfu. We have a Saint like that in England, too, called Cuthbert. There are lots of stories about him, and about the miracles his body did.'

'In England also?' It was plain that she had never credited that cold and misty land with anything as heart-warming as a real Saint. 'Then you understand that we of Corfu are taught all about our Saint as children, and many stories of the miracles and marvels. And they are true. I know this.'

'Of course.'

She swallowed. 'But there are other stories – stories that Sir Gale has told me of the Saint, that I have never heard before. He – my *koumbàros* – told us many tales when we were children, Spiro and me. He is a very learned man, as learned as the *papàs* (the priest), and he knows very many stories about Greece, the stories of our history that we learn in school, Pericles and Alexander and Odysseus and Agamemnon, and also stories of our Saint, things that happened long, long ago, in this very place, things that the *papàs* never told us, and that I have not heard before.'

She paused. I said: 'Yes?' but I knew what was coming now.

'He has told us how the Saint lived here, in a cave, and had his daughter with him, a princess she was, very beautiful. He had angels and devils to do his bidding, and worked much magic, raising storms and stilling them and saving the shipwrecked sailors.'

She paused doubtfully. 'I do not believe, me, about the daughter. The Saint was a bishop, and they do not have daughters. Perhaps she was a holy nun . . . It is possible that Sir Gale has got the story a little bit wrong?'

'Very possible,' I said. 'Was the daughter called Miranda?'

'Yes! It was after this holy woman, a Corfiote, that I was called! Then you know this story too?'

'In a way.' I was wondering, in some apprehension, what rich and strange confusion Sir Julian's Shakespearian theories might have created. 'In the English story we call him Prospero, and he was a magician – but he wasn't a bishop; he was a Duke, and he came from Milan, in Italy. So you see, it's only a –'

'He lived in a cave behind the grove of lime-trees along the cliff.' She waved northwards, and I recognised Sir Julian's cheerfully arbitrary placing of the scene of *The Tempest*. 'And there he did all his magic, but when he became old he turned to God, and drowned his books and his magic staff.'

'But, Miranda . . .' I began, then stopped. This wasn't the time to try to point out the discrepancies between this story and that of the Bishop of Cyprus, who (for one thing) had already been with God for some thousand years when his body arrived at the island. I hoped there was some way of explaining how legends grew round some central figure like alum crystals round a thread. 'Yes?' I said again.

She leaned forward over the chair-back. 'Well, Adoni says that Mr. Max is making a play out of this story, like . . . like . . .' She searched her mind, and then, being a Greek, came up with the best there is . . . 'like *Oedipus* (that is a play of the old gods; they do it in Athens). I asked Sir Gale about this play, and when he told me the story I said that the priests should know of this, because I had not heard it, and the *papàs* in my village has not heard it either, and he must be told, so that he can ask the Bishop. Why do you smile, Miss Lucy?'

'Nothing.' I was thinking that I need hardly have worried. The Greeks invented cynicism, after all; and every Greek is born with an inquiring mind, just as every foxhound is born with a nose. 'Go on; what did Sir Julian say?'

'He laughed, and said that his story – of the magic and the books – is not true, or perhaps it is only a little true, and changed with time, and that the poet who wrote the story added things from other stories and from his own mind, to make it more beautiful.' She looked earnestly at me. 'This happens. My *koumbàros* said it was like the story of Odysseus – that is another story of this island that we have in our schools, but you will not know it.'

'I do know the story.'

She stared. 'You know this, too? Are all English so learned, Miss Lucy?'

I laughed. 'It's a very famous story. We have it in our schools, too.'

She gaped. This was fame indeed.

'We learn all your Greek stories,' I said. 'Well, Sir Julian's story of the magician may have some tiny fragment of truth in it, like the legends about Odysseus, but I honestly think not much more. I'm sure he didn't mean you to believe it word for word. The story he told you, that Mr. Max is making a film play out of, is just

something that a poet invented, and probably nothing to do with the
real St. Spiridion at all. And you must see for yourself that the bit
about the cave and the princess can't possibly be true –'

'But it is!'

'But look, Miranda, when the Saint was brought here in 1489, he
was already –'

'Dead many years, I know that! But there is *something* that is true
in Sir Gale's story, and the priests must be told of it. We can prove
it, Adoni and I! I told you, we found the proof today!'

'Proof that *The Tempest* is true?' It was my turn to stare blankly.
Somehow, after the mounting excitement of Miranda's narrative,
this came as a climax of the most stunning irrelevance.

'I don't know about any tempest, but today we found them, in the
cave behind the lime-trees. There's a passage, and a cave, very deep
in the cliff, with water, and that is where he drowned his books.'
She leaned forward over the chair-back. 'That is what Adoni found
today, and he took me in and showed me. They are there in the
water, plain to see, in the very same place where Sir Gale told
us – the magic books of the Saint!'

Her voice rose to a dramatic stop that Edith Evans might have
envied. Her face was shining, lighted and full of awe. For a full
half-minute all I could do was sit there, gazing blankly back at her,
framing kind little sentences which might explain and question
without too cruel a disillusionment. Adoni had been with her, I
thought impatiently; what in the world had Adoni been thinking
about to allow this fantasy to go on breeding? Certainly he would
not share her beliefs, and she would have accepted an explanation
from him, whereas from me, now . . .

Adoni. The name stabbed through the haze in my mind like a
spearpoint going through butter-muslin. What Adoni did, he
usually had a good reason for. I sat up, demanding sharply: 'Adoni
found these – things – in a cave in the cliff? Where's the entrance?'

'Round the point, half-way up the cliff, above the boat-house.'

'Ah. Could it be seen from the bay – our bay?'

She shook her head. 'You go half-way up the path to the Villa
Rotha. Then it is above the path, in the rocks, behind bushes.'

'I see.' My heart was bumping again. 'Now, when Adoni saw it
was you, what did he say? Try to remember exactly.'

'I told you, he was angry at first, and would have hurried me
away, because we should not have been there. Then he stopped and
thought, and said no, I must come into the cave, and see what he had

found. He took me in; it was a steep passage, and long, going right down, but he had a torch, and it was dry. At the bottom was a big cave, full of water, very deep, but clear. Under a ledge, hidden with pebbles, we saw the books.'

'A moment. What made you think they were books?'

'They looked like books,' said Miranda reasonably. 'Old, old books, coloured. The corners showed from under the pebbles. You could see the writing on them.'

'*Writing?*'

She nodded. 'Yes, in a foreign tongue, and pictures and magical signs.'

'But, my dear girl, books? In sea-water? They'd be pulp in a couple of hours!'

She said simply: 'You forget. They are holy books. They would not perish.'

I let that one pass. 'Didn't Adoni try to get at them?'

'It was too deep, and very cold, and besides, there was an eel.' She shivered. 'And he said they must not be disturbed; he would tell Sir Gale, he said, and Mr. Max, and they would come. He said that I was his witness that he had found them there, and that I was to tell nobody about them, except you, Miss Lucy.'

I put my hands flat on the table and held them there, hard. I could feel the blood pumping in the finger-tips.

'He told you to tell me?'

'Yes.'

'Miranda. You told me earlier that Adoni had said these books were "proof". Did he say proof of what?'

She knitted her brows. 'What could he have meant, but proof of the story?'

'I see,' I said. 'Well, that's marvellous, and thank you for telling me. I can hardly wait to see them, but you won't tell anyone else, will you, anyone at all, even your mother? If – if it turns out to be a mistake, it would be dreadful to have raised people's hopes.'

'I won't tell. I promised Adoni. It is our secret, his and mine.'

'Of course. But I'd love to ask him about it. I think I'll go over to the Castello now. D'you think you could get him on the phone for me?'

She glanced at the clock. 'There will be nobody there now. Sir Gale was going back to Corfu with Mr. Karithis for dinner, and Adoni went with them.'

'But Max has the car. Adoni didn't have to drive them, surely?'

'No, Mr. Karithis brought his car. But Adoni wanted to go into Corfu, so he went with them, and he said he would come back with Mr. Max later.'

Of course he would. Whatever he had found in the cave by the Villa Rotha, whatever 'proof' he had now got, Adoni would get it to Max at the first possible moment, and if he was right about his discovery—and I had no doubt he was—then tonight the hounds would close in, and the end I had wanted this afternoon to hasten, would come.

I glanced at my watch. If the ferry docked at ten-forty-five . . . give Max an hour at most to hear Adoni's story and possibly collect police help in Corfu . . . half an hour more for the drive . . . at the outside that made it a quarter past midnight. Even if Godfrey had got back from his date, whatever it was, he might be in bed by that time, not where he would hear or see explorers probing the secrets of the cliff . . .

My hands moved of their own accord to the edge of the table, and gripped it. My thoughts, till now formlessly spinning, settled and stood.

Godfrey had said he was going out tonight; and there was the impression I had had of urgent business to be done and a clear field needed to do it in. Was it not conceivable that the objects so mysteriously hidden under his house were part of this same night's business? That in fact by the time Max and the police were led to the cave in the small hours, the 'proof' would have gone? And even with Adoni's word and that of his witness there would be nothing to show what had been there, or where it had gone? We would be back where we were, possibly with Godfrey's business finished, and himself in the clear . . .

Reluctantly, I worked it out. Reluctantly, I reached the obvious, the only conclusion. I stood up.

'Will you show me this cave and the books? Now?'

She had started to stack the supper things back on the tray. She paused, startled. 'Now, Miss?'

'Yes, now. It may be important. I'd like to see them myself.'

'But—it's so dark. You wouldn't want to go along there in the dark. In the morning, when Adoni's back—'

'Don't ask me to explain, Miranda, but I must go now, it might be important. If you'll just show me the cave, the entrance, that's all.'

'Well, of course, Miss.' But the words dragged doubtfully. 'What would happen if Mr. Manning came down?'

'He won't. He's out, away somewhere in his car, he told me so, so he's not likely to be using the cliff path. But we'll make sure he's out, we'll ring up the house . . . I can pretend I left something in the car. Will you get me the number, please?'

Somewhere in Godfrey's empty house the telephone bell shrilled on and on, while I waited, and Miranda hung over me, uneasy, but obviously flattered by my interest in her story.

At length I put the receiver back. 'That's that. He's out, so it's all right.' I looked at her. 'Will you, Miranda? Please? Just show me where the cave is, and you can come straight back.'

'Well, of course, if you really want to . . . If Kyrios Manning is away I don't mind at all. Shall I get the torch, Miss Lucy?'

'Yes, please. Give me five minutes to get a coat, and some other shoes,' I said, 'and have you got a coat here, or something extra to put on?' I didn't bother to ask if it was something dark; by the Saint's mercy the Corfiote peasants never wore anything else.

Three minutes later I was dressed in light rubber-soled shoes and a dark coat, and was rummaging through Leo's dressing-table drawer for the gun I knew he kept there.

Chapter 16

This is the mouth o' th' Cell: no noise, and enter.

IV. 1.

THE BAY WAS dark and silent: no sound, no point of light. It was easy enough to see our way across the pale sand without using the torch we had brought; and once we had scrambled up under the shadow of the pines where the dolphin had lain, and gained the rocky path along the foot of the southern headland, we found that we could again make our way without a betraying light.

We turned off the track into the bushes some way before reaching the zigzag path that led up towards the Villa Rotha. Miranda led the way, plunging steeply uphill, apparently straight into the thickest tangle of bushes that masked the cliff. Above us the limes leaned out, densely black and silent. Not a leaf stirred. You could hardly hear the sea. Even after we had switched the torch on to help us, our stealthy progress through the bushes sounded like the charge of a couple of healthy buffaloes.

Fortunately it wasn't far. Miranda stopped where a clump of evergreens—junipers, by the scent—lay back apparently right against the cliff.

'Here,' she whispered, and pulled the bushes back. I shone the torchlight through.

It showed a narrow gap, scarcely more than a fissure, giving on a passage that sloped sharply downwards for perhaps four yards, to be apparently blocked by a wall of rock. The floor of the passage looked smooth, and the walls were dry.

I hesitated. A puff of breeze brought a murmur from the trees, and the bushes rustled. I could feel the same breeze—or was it the same?—run cold along my skin.

'The passage goes to the left there'–Miranda's whisper betrayed nothing but pleased excitement–'and then down again, quite a long way, but it is easy. Will you go first, or shall I?

I had originally intended merely to stay hidden where I could watch the cave's entrance until Adoni brought the men down, and to send Miranda home out of harm's way. But now it occurred to me that if Godfrey did come to remove the 'books' before Max arrived, I, too, should need a witness. This was to put it at its highest. To put it at its lowest, I wanted company. And even if Godfrey found us (which seemed unlikely in this tangle of darkness), there was no risk of our meeting with Yanni's fate. I was prepared, and there was the gun–the gun, and the simple fact th it two people were more than twice as hard to dispose of as one.

But still I hesitated. Now that we were here, in the quiet dark, with the sounds and gentle airs of the night so normal around us, I wanted nothing so much as to see for myself what it was Adoni had found. If Godfrey did come tonight to remove it, if I should be unable to get a look at it, or to follow him, then we were back at the post, and no better off than before . . .

Three parts bravado, three parts revenge for these people I had come so quickly to love and admire, and three parts sheer blazing human curiosity–it was no very creditable mixture of emotions that made me say with a briskness that might pass for bravery in the dark: 'Is there anywhere to hide once you get inside the cave?'

I saw the glint of her eyes, but she answered simply: 'Yes, a lot of places, other caves, with fallen rocks, and passages–'

'Fair enough. Let's go. You lead the way.'

Behind us, the juniper rustled back into its place across the gap.

The passage led steadily downwards, as sharply right-angled as a maze; I guessed that the mass of rock had weathered into great rectangular blocks, and that the passage led down the cracks between them. Here and there side-cracks led off, but the main route was as unmistakable as a highway running through a labyrinth of country lanes.

Miranda led the way without faltering; left, then right, then straight on for thirty feet or so, then right again, and along . . . well into the heart of the promontory, I supposed. At the end of the last stretch it looked as if the floor of the passage dropped sheer away into black depths.

She paused, pointing. 'The cave is down there. You can climb down quite easily, it is like steps.'

A few moments later we were at the edge of the drop, with before us a sort of subterranean Giants' Staircase – a vast natural stairway of weathered rock leading down block by block on to a ledge that ran the length of a long, lozenge-shaped cave floored with black water. The ledge was some four feet above the level of the water, overhanging the smooth, scooped-out sides of the pool.

We clambered down the stairway, and I shone the light forward into the cave.

This was large, but not awesomely so. At the end where we stood the roof was not so very high – perhaps twenty feet; but as the torchlight travelled further, it was lost in the shadows where the roof arched upwards into darkness. There, I suppose, would be the funnelled cracks or chimneys which carried the fresh air into the upper caves, and through which Adoni had first detected the existence of the one where we now stood. Further along the ledge there were recesses and tunnels leading off the main cave, which promised a good choice of bolt-hole should the need arise. The walls were of pale limestone, scoured and damp, so that I guessed that with the wind on shore the sea must find its way in through more of the cracks and crevices. Now the deep vat of sea-water at our feet lay still and dead, and the place smelt of salt and wet stone.

Miranda gripped my arm. 'Down there! Shine the light. Down there!'

I turned the torch downwards. At first I could see nothing but the rich dazzle as the water threw back the beam, then the light seemed to soak down through the water like a stain through silk, and I saw the bottom, a jumble of smooth, round pebbles, their colours all drained by the torchlight to bone-white and washed green and pearl. Something moved across them, a whip of shadow flicking out of sight into a crevice.

'See?' Miranda crouched, pointing. 'In under the ledge, where the stones have been moved. There!'

I saw it then, a corner like the corner of a big book, or box, jutting out from among the pebbles. It looked as if the object, whatever it was, had been thrust well under the ledge where we stood, and the stones piled roughly over it.

I kneeled beside Miranda, peering intently down. Some stray movement of the sea outside had communicated itself to the pool, and the water shifted, shadows and reflections breaking and coalescing through the rocking torch-beam. The thing was coloured, I thought, and smooth-surfaced; a simple mind conditioned by Sir

Julian's stories might well have thought it was a book: myself, I took it for the corner of a box with some sort of a label. Vaguely, I could see what might be lettering.

'You see?' Miranda's whisper echoed in the cave.

'Yes, I see.' Any thoughts I might have had of braving the eel and the icy water to get at the object died a natural and unregretted death. Even if I could have dived for the thing, and lifted it, I couldn't have climbed the four smooth feet of overhang out of the pool without a rope.

'It is a book, yes?'

'It could be. But if it is, I don't think you'll find it's a very old one. The only way it could be kept down there is if it was wrapped in polythene or something, and that means –'

I broke off. Something had made a noise, some new noise that wasn't part of the cave's echo, or the faint whispers of the night that reached us through the invisible fissures in the cliff. I switched the light out, and the darkness came down like a candle-snuffer, thick as black wool. I put a hand on the girl's arm.

'Keep very still. I heard something. Listen.'

Through the drip of water on limestone it came again; the sound of a careful footstep somewhere in the passage above.

Here he came. Dear God, here he came.

Miranda stirred. 'Someone coming. It must be Adoni back already. Perhaps –'

I stopped her with a touch, my lips at her ear. 'That won't be Adoni. We mustn't be found here, we've got to hide. Quickly . . .'

I took her arm, pulling her deeper into the cave. She came without question. We kept close to the wall, feeling our way inch by inch till we came to a corner, and rounded it safely.

'Wait.' I dared a single brief flash of the torch, and breathed relief. We were in a deep recess or blocked tunnel, low-roofed, and filled with long-since-fallen debris, that burrowed its way back into the cliff above the water-level.

I put the light out. Slowly, carefully, and almost without a sound, we slithered our way into cover, deep into a crevice under a wedged block of limestone, flattening ourselves back into it like starfish hiding from the pronged hooks of the bait-fishers.

Not a moment too soon. Light spread, and warmed the cave. I was too deeply tucked back into the cleft to be able to see more than a curved section of the roof and far side of the main cave, but of course I could hear very clearly, as the cave and the water magnified

every sound; the tread of boots on rock; the chink as the powerful
torch was put down somewhere and the light steadied; the man's
breathing. Then the splash as something–whether his body or
something else I couldn't tell–was let down into the pool.

A pause, while the water lapped and sucked, and the breathing
sounded loud and urgent with some sort of effort. Then a different
splashing noise, a sucking and slapping of water, as if something had
been withdrawn from the pool. Another pause, filled now with the
sounds of dripping, streaming water. Then at last the light moved,
the slow footsteps retreated, and the sea-sounds of the disturbed
pool, slowly diminishing, held the cave.

I felt Miranda stir beside me.

'He has taken the book. Could it not be Adoni, Miss Lucy?
Perhaps he has come back to get the book for Sir Gale? Who else
would know? Shall I go–?'

'No!' My whisper was as urgent as I could make it. 'It's not Adoni,
I'm sure of that. This is something else, Miranda . . . I can't tell you
now, but trust me, please. Stay here. Don't move. I'm going to take
a look.'

I slid out of the cleft and switched on the torch, but kept a hand
over the glass, so that the light came in dimmed slits between my
fingers. I caught the gleam of her eyes watching me, but she neither
moved again nor spoke. I inched my cautious way forward to the
main cave, to pause at the corner of the ledge, switch off the torch,
and listen yet again. There was no sound but the steady drip of
water, and the faint residual murmur from the pool.

Flashing the light full on, I knelt at the edge, and looked down.

As I expected, the pile of stones had been rudely disturbed, and,
as far as I could judge, had dwindled in height. But there must have
been more than one of the rectangular objects there, for I could see
another corner jutting from the cobbles at a different angle from the
one that had been visible before. And there on the ledge leaning
against the wall as if waiting for him to come back, was an iron
grapple, a long hooked shaft which dripped sluggishly on to the
limestone.

I stood up, thinking furiously. So much for that. Adoni had been
right; here was the key we were wanting, the clue to Godfrey's
murderous business. And it was surely simple enough to see what I
ought to do next. I had no means of telling what proportion of his
cache Godfrey had taken, or if he would come back tonight for the
rest; but in either case, nothing would be gained by taking the

appalling risk of following him now. If he came back, we might meet in the passage. If he didn't—well, the rest of the 'proof' would still be safely there for Max when he arrived at last.

And so, let's face it, would I . . .

I was hardly back in my niche before we heard him coming back, the light growing and brightening before him up the limestone walls. The performance was repeated almost exactly; the plunge of the grapple, the grating haul through the pebbles, the withdrawal, the pause while the water drained . . . then once more the light retreated, and we were left in blackness, with the hollow sucking of the troubled pool.

'Wait,' I whispered again.

As soon as I got to the main cave I saw that the grapple had gone. I crouched once more on the streaming rock and peered down. As I expected, the pile of pebbles had settled lower, spreading level as what it had hidden had been dragged away. The pool was empty of its treasure.

No need, this time, to stop and think. The decision was, unhappily, as clear as before. I would have to follow him now. And I had better hurry.

In a matter of seconds I was back beside Miranda. 'You can come out now. Quick!'

She materialised beside me. Her breathing was fast and shallow, and she was shivering, She was still taut and bright-eyed, but the quality of her excitement had changed. She looked scared.

'What is it, Miss? What is it?'

I tried to sound calm and sure. 'The "books" have gone, and it was Mr. Manning who took them, I'm sure it was. I have to see where he puts them, but he mustn't see us. D'you understand, *he mustn't see us* . . . I'll explain it all later, but we'll have to hurry now. Come on.'

We heaved ourselves up the last of the Giants' Staircase, and crept from angle to angle of the passage, lighting the way warily, and stopping at each corner to listen ahead. But nothing disturbed us, and soon we were at the mouth of the cleft, cautiously parting the junipers. The air smelt warm and sweet after the cave, full of flower-scents and the tang of bruised herbs; and a breeze had got up and was moving the bushes, ready to mask what sounds we made.

We edged down, feeling our way, through the tangle of bushes and young trees. Although no moon was visible, the sky was alight with stars, and we went quickly enough. I dared not make for the path, but pushed a cautious way, bent double, above one arm of the zigzag from which I thought we should be able to see the boat-house, and at length we came to the end of the ridge where honeysuckle and (less happily) brambles made thick cover between the young limes.

We were just above the boat-house. Its roof was silhouetted like a black wedge against the paler sea beyond. I thought, but could not quite make out, that the landward door stood open.

Next moment it shut, softly, but with the definite *chunk* of a spring-locking door. A shadow moved along the boat-house wall, and then he came quietly up the path. We lay mouse-still, hardly breathing. He rounded the corner below us, and came on up, with a quick, stealthy stride whose grace I recognised, and next moment, as he passed within feet of us, I saw him clearly. He had changed from the light clothes of the afternoon, and now wore dark trousers, and a heavy dark jersey. He carried nothing in his hands. He went straight on past us, and his light tread was lost in the movements of the breeze.

In the heavy shadow where we lay I couldn't see Miranda, but I felt her turn to look at me, and presently she put out a hand and touched my arm. The hand was trembling.

'Miss—Miss, what *is* it?'

I put a hand over hers, and held it. 'You're quite right, it's not just a case of being caught trespassing; it's something much more serious, and it might be dangerous. I'm sorry you're in it, too, but I want your help.'

She said nothing. I took a breath, and tightened my hand over hers.

'Listen. I can't tell you it all now, but there have been . . . things have been happening, and we think . . . Mr. Max and I . . . that they have something to do with your brother's accident. Adoni thinks so, too. We want to find out. Will you just trust me and do as I say?'

There was a pause. Still she didn't speak, but this time the air between us was so charged that I felt it vibrate like a bow-string after the shaft has gone.

'Yes.'

'You saw who it was?'

'Of course. It was Mr. Manning.'

'Good. You may be asked . . . what is it?'

'Look there.' She had moved sharply, pointing past me up the cliff to where, above the black trees, a light had just flashed on. The Villa Rotha.

I felt my breath go out. 'Then he's safe there for a bit, thank God. I wish I knew the time.'

'We dare not shine the torch?'

'No. I should have looked before. Never mind. It looks as if he's put those things in the boat-house; I wish to heaven I dared go down and take a look at them . . . he did say he was going out tonight, and *not* with the boat, but he might only have been putting me off so that he'd be able to go to the cave. He may hang around here all night . . . or he may have been lying, and he'll come down again and take the boat, and that will be that.' I stirred restlessly, watching that steady square of light with hatred. 'In any case, the damned thing's locked. Even if . . .'

'I know where the key is.'

I jerked round to peer at her. '*You do?*'

'Spiro told me. There was an extra key which was kept underneath the floor, where the house reaches the water. I know the place; he showed me.'

I swallowed. 'It's probably not there now, and in any case . . .'

I stopped abruptly. The light had gone out.

Minutes later, we heard the car. That it was Godfrey's car there could be no manner of doubt; he switched on her lights, and they swept round in a wide curve, lancing through the trees and out into space, to move on and vanish in the blackness over the headland as the engine's note receded through the woods. There was a brief, distant thrumming as he accelerated, then the sound died, and there was darkness.

'He's gone,' said Miranda, unnecessarily.

I sat up. I was furious to find that my teeth were chattering, and clenched them hard, pushing a hand down into the pocket where Leo's gun hung heavy and awkward against my thigh. Two things were quite certain; I did not want to go anywhere near Godfrey Manning's boat-house; and if I didn't, I should despise myself for a coward as long as I lived. I had a gun. There was probably a key. I had at least to try it.

'Come on, then,' I said, and pushed my way out of cover and dropped to the path, Miranda behind me. As we ran downhill I gasped out instructions. 'You must get straight back to the house. Can you get into the Castello?'

'Yes.'

'Then go there. That way, you'll see them as soon as they get home. But try to telephone Adoni first . . . Do you know where he might be?'

'Sometimes he eats at Chrisomalis', or the Corfu Bar.'

'Then try them. If he's not there, some of his friends may know where he'll be. He may have gone down to the harbour to wait, or even to the police . . . Try, anyway.'

We had reached the boat-house. I stopped at the door, trying it . . . futilely, of course: it was fast locked. Miranda thrust past me, and I heard her fumbling in the shadows round the side of the building, then she was beside me, pushing the cold shape of a Yale key into my hand.

'Here. What shall I tell Adoni?'

'Don't tell him what's happened. Mr. Manning may get back to the house, and pick the phone up, you never know. Just say he must come straight back here, it's urgent, Miss Lucy says so . . . He'll understand. If he doesn't, tell him anything you like—tell him I'm ill, and you have to have help—anything to get him back here. He's not to tell Sir Julian. Then you wait for him . . . Don't leave the Castello, and don't open the door to anyone else except Max or the police . . . or me. If I'm not back by the time he comes, tell him everything that's happened, and that I'm down here. Okay?'

'Yes.' She was an ally in a million. Confused and frightened though she must have been, she obeyed as unquestioningly as before. I heard her say, 'The Saint be with you, Miss,' and then she was gone, running at a fair speed along the shore path to the Castello's bay.

With one more glance up at the lightless headland, and a prayer on my own account, I prodded around the lock with a shamefully shaky key, until at last I got it home.

The catch gave, stiffly, and I slipped inside.

Chapter 17

No tongue: all eyes: be silent.
IV. 1.

THE BOAT-HOUSE was a vast structure with a high roof lost in shadows, where the sea-sounds echoed hollowly, as in a cave. Running round the three walls was a narrow platform of planks set above the water, and along the near side of this lay the sloop. The rapidly dimming light of my torch showed me the lovely, powerful lines, and the name painted along the bows: *Aleister.* It also showed me, propped against the wall by the door, the grapple from the cave.

There was no hiding-place in the boat-house other than the boat itself. I clicked the lock shut behind me, then stepped in over the cockpit coaming, to try the cabin door.

It was unlocked, but I didn't go straight in. There was a window in the back of the boat-house, facing the cliff, which showed a section of the path, then the black looming mass of cliff and tree, and—at the top—a paler section of sky where stars burned. With eyes now adjusted to the darkness, I could just make out the sharp angle of some part of the Villa Rotha's roof. So far, excellent. If Godfrey did come back too soon, I should have the warning of the car or house lights.

Inside the cabin, I let the torchlight move round once, twice . . .

The layout was much as I remembered in Leo's boat. Big, curtained windows to either side, under which were settee berths with cushions in bright chintz; between these a fixed drop-leaf table above which swung a lamp. A curtain was drawn over the doorway in the forward bulkhead, but no doubt beyond it I would find another berth, the W.C., and the usual sail bags, ropes, and spare anchor stowed in the bows. Immediately to my right, just inside the door, was the galley, and opposite this the quarter berth—a space-saving berth with half its length in the cabin, and the other half burrowing, as it were, into the space beyond the after bulkhead, under the port cockpit seat. The quarter berth was heaped with blankets, and was separated from the settee berth by a small table with a cupboard underneath.

And everywhere, lockers and cupboards . . .

I started, methodically, along the starboard side.

Nothing in the galley; the oven empty, the cupboards stocked with cooking equipment so compact as to leave no hiding-place. In the lockers, crockery, photographic stuff, tins of food, cardboard boxes full of an innocent miscellany of gear. In the wardrobe cupboards, coats, oilskins, sweaters and a shelf holding sea-boots, and shoes neatly racked, all as well polished and slick as Godfrey himself . . .

It was the same everywhere; everything was open to the searcher, all the contents normal and innocent—clothing, spare blankets, photographic equipment, tools. The only place not open to the prying eye was the cupboard at the end of the quarter berth, which was locked. But—from its shallow shape, and my memory of Leo's boat—I imagined that this was only because it held the liquor; there was none elsewhere, and it was hardly big enough to store the packages I was looking for. I left it, and went on, even prodding the mattresses and feeling under the piled blankets, but all that came to light was a paperbacked copy of *Tropic of Cancer*, which I pushed back, rearranging the blankets as they had been before. Then I started on the floor.

Here there would be, I knew, a couple of 'traps', or sections of the flooring which were made to lift out and give access to the bilges. Sure enough, under the table, and set in the boards, my eye caught the gleam of a sunken ring which, when pulled, lifted an eighteen-inch square of the planking, like a small trap-door. But there was no treasure cave below, only the gleam of bilge-water shifting between the frames with the boat's motion, and a faint smell of gas. And the same with the trap in the fo'c'sle.

The engine hatchway under the cabin steps was hardly a likely place for a cache; all the same, I looked there, and even lifted the inspection cover off the fresh-water tank, to see nothing but the ghostly reflection of the torchlight and my own shadow shivering on the surface of the full forty-gallon complement of water. Not here . . .

I screwed the cover down with hands that sweated now, and shook, then I put the torch out and fled up the steps and on to the deck.

The window first . . . No lights showed outside, but I had to make sure. I ran aft, ducked under the boom, and climbed on the stern seat to peer anxiously out.

All was dark and still. I could—I must—allow myself a little longer.

I started over the cockpit, using the torch again, but keeping a wary eye on the boat-house window. Here, too, all seemed innocent. Under the starboard seat was the space occupied by the Calor gas cylinders, and nothing else. Under the stern seat was nothing but folded tarpaulins and skin-diving equipment. The port seat merely hid the end of the quarter berth. Nothing. Nor were there any strange objects fastened overside, or trailing under the *Aleister* in the sea; that bright idea was disposed of in a very few seconds. I straightened up finally from my inspection, and stood there, hovering, miserably undecided, and trying hard to think through the tension that gripped me.

He must have brought the packages here. He had not had time to take them up to his house, and he would hardly have cached them somewhere outside when he had the *Aleister* handy, and, moreover, no idea that he was even suspected. He might, of course, have handed them to some accomplice there and then, and merely have been returning the grapple to the boat-house, but the accomplice would have had to have some means of transport, which meant either a donkey or a boat; if a donkey, Miranda and I must surely have heard it; we might not have heard a rowing-boat, but why should Godfrey use one, when the *Aleister* and her dinghy lay ready to his own hand? No, it was obvious that there could be no innocent explanation of his use of the hidden cave.

But I had looked everywhere. They were not in the boat, or tied under the boat; they were not on the platform, or on the single shelf above it. Where in the world could he, in this scoured-out space, have hidden those bulky and dripping objects so quickly and effectively?

An answer came then—so obvious as to be insulting. In the water. He had moved them merely from the bottom of the cave to the bottom of the bay. They must be under the *Aleister*, right under, and if I could only see them, there was the grapple ready to hand, with the water still dripping off it to make a pool on the boards.

I was actually up on the cockpit coaming, making for the grapple, when I saw the real answer, the obvious, easy answer which I should have seen straight away; which would have saved me all those precious minutes, and how much more besides; the trail of drops leading in through the boat-house door and along the platform; the trail left by the dripping packages, as obvious to the intelligent eye as footprints in fresh snow. I had no excuse, except fear and haste, and (I thought bitterly) Nemesis armed with a nice, heavy gun had no business to be afraid at all.

And the trail was already drying. I was calling myself names that I hadn't even known I knew, as I shone the yellow and flickering torchlight over the boards of the platform.

Yes, there they were, the footprints in the snow; the two faint, irregular trails, interweaving like the track of bicycle wheels, leading in through the door, along the platform, over the edge . . .

But not into the water after all. They went in over the side of the *Aleister* and across her deck and straight in through the cabin door.

I was in after them in a flash. Down the steps, to the table . . . I had never even glanced at the bare table top, but now I saw on the Formica surface the still damp square where he had laid the packages down.

And there the trail stopped. But this time there was only one answer. The trail had stopped simply because all Godfrey had had to do from there was to open the trap-door under the table, and lift the things straight down.

I had the trap open again in seconds. I laid it aside. The square hole gaped.

I ran back to the steps and peered up at the window. No light showed. I dropped on my knees beside the trap, clicked on the torch and sent the small yellow eye which was all it had left skidding over the greasy water in the *Aleister's* bilges.

Nothing. No sign. But now I knew they had to be there . . .

And they were there. I had gone flat down on the floor, and was hanging half inside the trap-door before I saw them, but they were there; not in the bottom, but tucked, as neatly as could be, right up under the floorboards, in what were obviously racks made specially to carry them. They were clear of the water, and well back from the edges of the hatch, so that you would have had—like me—to be half in the bilges yourself before you saw them.

I ducked back, checked on the window again, then dived once more into the bilges.

Two sweating minutes, and I had it, a big, heavy square package wrapped in polythene. I heaved it out on deck, spreading the skirts of my coat for it so that I in my turn would leave no trail, then turned the light on it.

The torch was shaking now in my hand. The yellow glow-worm crawled and prodded over the surface of the package, but the glossy wrapping almost defeated the miserable light, and all I got, in the three seconds' look I allowed myself, was the impression of a jumble of faint colours, something looking like a picture, a badge, even (Miranda had been right) a couple of words . . . LEKE, I read, and in front of this something that could be—but surely wasn't—NJEMIJE.

Somewhere something slammed, nearly frightening me out of what wits I still had. The torch dropped with a rattle, rolling in a wide semicircle that missed the trap by millimetres. I grappled it back again, and whirled to look. There was nothing there. Only darkness.

Which was just as well, I thought, recovering my senses rather wryly. Even if I had reacted properly, and grabbed for the gun instead of the torch, I couldn't have got it. Prospero's damned book, or whatever the package was, was sitting right on top of it, on the skirts of my coat. I had a long way to go, I reflected bitterly, before I got into the James Bond class.

The wind must be rising fast. The big seaward doors shook again, as if someone was pulling at the padlock, and the other door bumped and rattled. The water ran hissing and lapping along the walls, and shadows, thrown by some faint reflection of starlight, shivered up into the rafters.

The window was still dark, but I had had my warning, and enough was enough. The trap-door went snugly back into place, my torch dropped into my other pocket, and, clasping the package to me with both hands, I clambered carefully out of the *Aleister*.

At the same instant as I gained the platform, I saw the movement on the path outside the window. Only a shadow, but as before there was no mistaking the way he moved. No light, no nothing, but here he was, just above the boat-house, and coming fast.

And here was I, stuck with my arms full of his precious package for which he had almost certainly tried to do double murder. And I couldn't get out of the place if I tried.

*   *   *

The first thing was to get rid of the package.

I crouched and let the thing slide down between the platform and the boat. The boat was moored close, and for a panic-stricken moment I thought there wasn't enough room there; the package was tangled in my coat, then it jammed in the gap, and I couldn't move it either way, and when I tried to grab it back I couldn't; it was slippery and I couldn't get a grip on it again . . .

I flung myself down, got a shoulder to the *Aleister*, and shoved. She moved the inch or so I needed, and with a brief, sharp struggle I managed to ram the package through and down.

It vanished with a faint splash. And then, like an echo, came the fainter but quite final splash of Leo's gun slipping from the pocket of my coat, to vanish in its turn under the water.

For one wild, crazy moment of fear I thought of swinging myself down to follow gun and package and hide under the platform, but I couldn't get down here, and there was no time to run the length of the boat. In any case he would have heard me. He was at the door. His key scraped the lock.

There was only one place big enough to hide, and that was right bang in the target area. The boat itself. It did cross my mind that I could stand still and try to bluff it out, but even had the *Aleister* been innocent, and Godfrey found me here at this hour, inside a locked door, no bluff would have worked. With the boat literally loaded, I hadn't a hope. It was the cabin or nothing.

I was already over the side, and letting myself as quietly as a ghost into the cabin, as his key went home in the lock and turned with a click. I didn't hear the door open. I was already, like a hunted mouse, holed up in the covered end of the quarter berth, with the pile of blankets pulled up as best I could to hide me.

The blankets smelt of dust, and carbolic soap. They covered me with a thick, stuffy darkness that at least felt a bit like security. The trouble was that they deprived me of my hearing, the only sense that was left to tell what Godfrey was up to. Strain as I might through the thudding of my own heart-beats, I could only get the vaguest impression of where he was and what he was doing. All I could do was lie still and pray he wouldn't come into the cabin.

The boat rocked sharply, and for a moment I thought he was already in her, but again it was only the wind. This seemed to be rising still, in sharper gusts which sent little waves slapping hard along the hull, and sucking up and down the piles on which the platform stood. I could feel the jerking motion as the *Aleister* tugged at her rope, then she bucked, sharply and unmistakably; Godfrey had jumped into her.

Minutes passed, filled with the muffled night-noises, but I could feel, rather than hear, his weight moving about the boat, and strained my senses, trying to judge where he was and what he was doing. The boat was steadier now, swaying gently to the small ripples passing under her keel. A draught moved through the cabin, smelling freshly of the sea-wind, so that I guessed he must have left the boat-house door open, and this might mean he didn't mean to stay long . . .

The wind must be quite strong now. The boat swayed under me, and a hissing wave ran right along beside my head. The *Aleister* lifted to it with a creak of timber, and I heard the unmistakable sound of straining rope and the rattle of metal.

Then I knew what had happened. There was no mistaking it, rope and metal and timber active and moving—the boat was alive, and out in the living sea. He must have swung the big doors open without my hearing him, then poled her gently out, and now she was alive, under sail, slipping silently along shore, away from the bay.

I couldn't move. I simply lay there, shivering under my load of blankets, every muscle knotted and tense with the effort of keeping my head, and trying to think . . .

Max would surely be back by now; and even if he was still in Corfu, Adoni was probably already on his way home . . . and he would have left Miranda's message for Max, so Max wouldn't linger in Corfu, but would come straight here, and probably bring the police. When they got down to the boat-house and found the boat gone, and me with it, they would guess what had happened. There wasn't—I knew this—much hope of their finding the *Aleister* in the darkness, but at least I might have a card or two I could play if Godfrey found me. Under the circumstances he could hardly expect to get away with my disappearance as well.

Or so I hoped. I knew that if he discovered about the missing package he would probably search the sloop, and find me. But since there was nothing I could do about that, my only course was to stay hidden here, and pray for a choppy sea that would keep him on deck looking after the *Aleister*. Why, he might not even come below at all . . .

Just three minutes later, he opened the cabin door.

Chapter 18

What shall I do? say what? what shall I do?
                                                    I. 2.

I HEARD THE click, and felt the sudden swirl of fresh air, cut off as
the door shut again.

There was the rasp of a match; the sharp tang of it pierced right
up into my hidden corner, and with it the first smoke of a
newly-lighted cigarette. He must have come in out of the wind for
this, and now he would go . . .

But he didn't. No movement followed. He must be very near me;
I could feel, like an animal in the presence of danger, the hair
brushing up along my skin. Now I was thankful for the chop and
hiss of water, and for the hundred creaking, straining noises of the
Aleister scudding on her way through the darkness. Without them, I
thought he would have heard my heart-beats.

He can only have stood there for a few seconds, though for me it
was a pause prolonged almost to screaming-point. But it seemed he
had only waited to get his cigarette properly alight: he struck
another match, dropped it and the box after it on the table, and then
went out and shut the door behind him.

Relief left me weak and sweating. The closed end of the berth
seemed like an oven, so I pushed the blanket folds back a little, to let
the air in, and cautiously peered over them, out into the cabin.

A weapon; that was the first thing . . . I had the torch, but it was
not a heavy one, and would hardly count as adequate armament
against a murderer. Not that it was easy in the circumstances to
think of anything (short of Leo's gun) that would have been
'adequate', though I would have settled for a good, loaded bottle, if
only the damned cupboard had been open. But bottles there were

none. I cast my mind furiously back over the cabin's contents . . .
The galley? Surely the galley must be packed with implements?
Pans were too clumsy; it must be something I could conceal . . . a
knife? I hadn't opened the shallow drawers during my search, but
one of them was bound to hold a knife. Or there was the starting
handle for the engine, if I could get the engine hatch opened silently,
and then station myself on the galley side, behind the door, and wait
for him . . .

Cautiously, one eye on the door, I reached down to push the
blanket aside, ready to slide out of the quarter berth.

Then froze, staring with horror at the foot of the berth.

Even in the almost-darkness I could see it, and Godfrey, in the
matchlight, must have seen it quite clearly – my toe, clad in a light
yellow canvas shoe, protruding from the huddle of blankets. I was
about as well hidden as an ostrich beak deep in sand.

Now I knew what had happened. He had come in quickly out of
the wind to light his cigarette, had seen what he thought was a foot,
had struck another match to make sure – and, having made sure, had
done what?

I was answered immediately. The boat had levelled and steadied,
as if she were losing way. Now, seemingly just beside me, the
engine fired with a jerk and a brief, coughing roar that nearly sent
me straight through the bulkhead; then it was throttled quickly back
to a murmur, the merest throb and quiver of the boards, as the
Aleister moved sedately forward on an even keel. He had merely
turned the boat head to wind without taking in the mainsail, and
started the engine, so that she would hold herself steady without
attention. I didn't have to guess why. His quick step was already at
the cabin door.

I whisked off the berth, dropped my wet coat, and straightened
my dress. There wasn't even time to dive across the cabin and open
the knife-drawer. As Godfrey opened the door I was heading for the
table and the box of matches, apparently intent on nothing more
deadly than lighting the lamp.

I threw a gay greeting at him over my shoulder.

'Hullo, there. I hope you don't mind a stowaway?'

The wick caught and the light spread. I got the globe fitted back at
the third try, but perhaps he hadn't noticed my shaking hands. He
had moved to draw the curtains.

'Naturally, I'm delighted. How did you know I'd decided to come
out after all?'

'Oh, I didn't, but I was hoping!' I added, with what I'm sure was a ghastly archness: 'You saw me, didn't you? You were coming in to unmask me. What's the penalty for stowing away in these seas?'

'We'll arrange that later,' said Godfrey.

His voice and manner were pleasant as ever, but after that first bright glance I didn't dare let him see my eyes; not yet. There was a mirror set in a cupboard door: I turned to this and made the gestures of tidying my hair.

'What brought you down?' he asked.

'Well, I wanted a walk after supper, and—have you a comb, Godfrey? I look like a mouse's nest!'

Without a word he took one from a pocket and handed it to me. I began, rather elaborately, to fuss with my hair.

'I went down to the beach; I had a sort of vague idea the dolphin might come back—they do, I believe. Anyway, I went to look, but it wasn't there. I walked along the path a bit, listening to the sea, and wishing you *had* been going out. Then I heard you—I knew it must be you—over at the boat-house, so I hurried . . . You know, just hoping.'

He had moved so that he was directly behind me. He stood very close, watching my face in the glass. I smiled at him, but got no response; the light eyes were like stones.

'You heard me at the boat-house?'

'Yes. I heard the door.'

'When was this?'

'Oh, goodness knows, half an hour ago? Less? I'm no good over times. I'd have called out, but you seemed to be in a hurry, so—'

'You saw me?'

His breath on the back of my neck brought panic, just a flash of it, like a heart-spasm. I turned away quickly, handed him his comb, and sat down on the settee berth, curling my legs up under me with an assumption of ease.

'I did. You were just coming out of the boat-house, and you went rushing off up the path to the house.'

I saw the slightest relaxation as he registered that I hadn't seen him coming down from the cave with the packages. He drew on his cigarette, blowing out a long jet of grey smoke into a haze round the lamp. 'And then?'

I smiled up at him—I hoped provocatively. 'Oh, I was going to call after you, but then I saw you had a sweater and things on, so you probably *were* going out after all. I thought if I just stuck around you'd be back, and I could ask you.'

'Why didn't you?'

'Why didn't I what?'

'Ask me.'

I looked embarrassed and fidgeted with a bit of blanket. 'Well, I'm sorry, I know I should have, but you were quite a time, and I got bored and tried the door, and it was open, so –'

'The door was open?'

'Yes.'

'That's not possible. I locked it.'

I nodded. 'I know. I heard you. But it hadn't quite caught, or something, you know how those spring locks are. I'd only tried it for something to do – you know how one fidgets about – and when it opened I was quite surprised.'

There was no way of knowing whether he believed me or not, but according to Spiro the catch had been stiff, and Godfrey had no idea I could have known that. I didn't think he could have changed the lock as he had threatened, for I had heard him myself wrestling with it on Monday; but that was a chance I had to take.

He tapped ash into a bowl on the liquor cupboard, and waited. He looked very tall; the slightly swaying lamp was on a level with his eyes. I toyed with the idea of giving it a sudden shove that would knock his head in, but doubted if I could get there quickly enough. Later, perhaps. Now I smiled at him instead, letting a touch of uncertainty, even of distress, appear.

'I – I'm sorry. I suppose it was awful of me, and I should have waited, but I was *sure* you wouldn't mind me looking at the boat –'

'Then why did you hide when I came down?'

'I don't know!' The note of exasperated honesty came out exactly right. 'I honestly don't know! But I was *in* the boat, you see, in here, actually, poking about in the cupboards and the ga – kitchen and everything –'

'What for?'

'What *for* ?' Every bit of technique I'd ever had went into it. 'Well, what does a woman usually poke around in other people's houses for? And a boat's so much more fun than a house; I wanted to see how it was fitted, and the cooking arrangements, and – well, every-thing!' I laughed, wooing him back to good temper with all I had, playing the ignorant; it might be as well not to let him know how much I knew about the sloop's lay-out. 'And it really is smashing, Godfrey! I'd no idea!' I faltered then, biting my lip. 'You're annoyed with me. You *do* mind. I–I suppose it *was* the hell of a nerve . . . In fact, I knew it was, and I suppose that's why I hid when I heard you at the door . . . I suddenly thought how it must look, and you might be furious, so I got in a panic and hid. I had a vague idea that if you weren't going sailing after all I could slip out after you had gone. That's all.'

I sat back, wondering if tears at this point would be too much, and deciding that they probably would. Instead, I looked at him meltingly through my lashes – at least, that's what I tried to do, but I shall never believe the romantic novelists again; it's a physical impossibility. Godfrey, at any rate, remained unmelted, so I abandoned the attempt, and made do with a quivering little smile, and a hand, genuinely none too steady, brushing my eyes. 'I'm sorry,' I said, 'I truly am. Please don't be angry.'

'I'm not angry.' For the first time he took his eyes off me. He mounted a step to pull the door open, and looked out into the blackness. What he saw appeared to satisfy him, but when he turned back he didn't shut the door.

'Well, now you are here you might as well enjoy it. I can't leave the tiller much longer, so come along out. That's not a very thick coat, is it? Try this.' And he pulled open the cupboard and produced a heavy navy duffel coat, which he held for me.

'Don't bother, mine will do.' I stood up and reached for my own coat, with the torch in the pocket, then remembered how wet it was. For the life of me, I couldn't think offhand of any reason for the soaked skirt where I had knelt in the puddles of water. I dropped the coat back on the bunk. 'Well, thanks awfully, yours'll be warmer, I suppose. It sounds like quite a windy night now.'

As he held it for me to put on, I smiled up at him over my shoulder. 'Have you forgiven me? It was a silly thing to do, and you've a right to be furious.'

'I wasn't furious,' said Godfrey, and smiled. Then he turned me round and kissed me.

Well, I had asked for it, and now I was getting it. I shut my eyes. If I pretended it was Max . . . no, that wasn't possible. Well, then, someone who didn't matter – for instance, that rather nice boy I'd once had an abortive affair with but hadn't cared about when it came to the push . . . But that wouldn't work either. Whatever Godfrey was or wasn't, he didn't kiss like a rather nice boy . . .

I opened my eyes and watched, over his shoulder, the lovely, heavy lamp swinging about a foot away from his head. If I could

manoeuvre him into its orbit . . . I supposed there were circumstances in which it was correct, even praiseworthy, for a girl to
bash a man's head in with a lamp while he was kissing her . . .

The *Aleister* gave a sudden lurch, and yawed sharply. Godfrey
dropped me as if I had bitten him.

'Put the lamp out, will you?'

'Of course.'

He ran up the steps. I blew the lamp out, and had the glass back in
a matter of seconds, but already the *Aleister* was steady again, and
Godfrey paused in the doorway without leaving the cabin, and
turned back to hold a hand down to me.

'Come out and see the stars.'

'Just a moment.'

His voice sharpened a fraction. He wasn't as calm as he made out.
'What is it?'

'My hankie. It's in my own coat pocket.' I was fumbling in the
dimness of the quarter berth among the folds of coat and blanket.
The torch dropped sweetly into the pocket of the duffel coat; I
snatched the handkerchief, then ran up the steps and put a hand into
his.

Outside was a lovely windswept night, stars and spray, and black
sea glinting as it rushed up to burst in great fans of spindrift. Dimly
on our left I could see the coast outlined black against the sky, a mass
of high land blocking out the stars. Low down there were lights,
small and few, and seemingly not too far away.

'Where are we?'

'About half a mile out from Glyfa.'

'Where's that?'

'You know how the coast curves eastwards here along the foot of
Mount Pantokrator, towards the mainland? We're about halfway
along the curve . . .'

'So we're running east?'

'For the moment. Off Kouloura we turn up into the strait.'

(*'I reckoned we were about half-way over,'* Spiro had said, 'in the strait
between Kouloura and the mainland.')

'You'll feel the wind a bit more when we get out of the lee of
Pantokrator,' said Godfrey. 'It's rising quite strongly now.' He
slipped an arm round me, friendly, inexorable. 'Come and sit by me.
She won't look after herself for ever. Do you know anything about
sailing?'

'Not a thing.' As he urged me towards the stern seat, my eyes

were busily searching the dimly seen cockpit. Only too well did I
know there was no handy weapon lying about, even if that lover-like
arm would have allowed me to reach for it. But I looked all the same.
It had occurred to me that he probably carried a gun, and I had
already found out that there was nothing in the pocket nearest me,
the left; if he got amorous again it might be possible to find out if it
was in the other pocket . . . As he drew me down beside him on the
stern seat I pulled the duffel coat round me for protection against his
hands, at the same time relaxing right into the curve of his shoulder.
I was thinking that if he wore a shoulder holster he would hardly
have cuddled me so blithely to his left side, and I was right. There
was no gun there. I leaned cosily back, and set myself to show him
how little I knew about sailing. 'How fast will it go?'

'About eight knots.'

'Oh?' I let it be heard that I had no idea what a knot was, but
didn't want to expose my ignorance. He didn't enlighten me. He
settled the arm round me, threw his cigarette overside, and added:
'Under sail, that is. Six or seven under power.'

'Oh?' I had another shot at the same intonation, and was
apparently successful, because he laughed indulgently as he turned
to kiss me again.

The *Aleister* tilted and swung up to a cross-sea, and the boom
came over above us with the mainsail cracking like a rifle shot. It
supplied me with an excuse for the instinctive recoil I gave as his
mouth fastened on mine, but next moment I had hold of myself, and
responded with a sort of guarded enthusiasm while my open eyes
watched the boom's pendulum movements above our heads, and I
tried to detach my mind from Godfrey, and think.

What he was doing was obvious enough: not being sure yet of my
innocence, he hadn't wanted to risk leaving me unguarded while he
got the mainsail in and took the *Aleister* along under power. All he
could do was hold her as she was, head to the wind, the engine
ticking over, the idle mainsail weathercocking her along, until he
had decided what to do with me. It was just my luck, I thought
sourly, stroking his cheek with a caressing hand, that the wind was
more or less in the direction he wanted. If he was aiming (as I
supposed he was) for the same place as on the night he had tried to
drown Spiro, then he must still be pretty well on course.

A sudden gust on the beam sent the *Aleister's* bows rearing up at an
angle that brought the boom back again overhead with a creak and a
thud, and Godfrey released me abruptly, his right hand going to the

tiller. And as he moved, leaning forward momentarily, I saw my weapon.

Just beyond him, hanging on its hooks behind the stern cockpit seat, was the sloop's lifebelt, and attached to this by a length of rope was the smoke flare . . . a metal tube about a foot long, with a drum-shaped float of hollow metal about two-thirds of the way up its length. It was heavy enough, and deadly enough in shape, to make a formidable weapon if I could only manage to reach it down from the hook a foot to my side of the lifebelt. The rope attaching it was coiled lightly over the hook, and would be some ten or fifteen feet long–ample play for such a weapon. It only remained to get hold of it. I could hardly reach past him for it, and would certainly get no chance to use it if I did. If I could only get him to his feet for a moment, away from me . . .

'Why do you leave the sail up?' I asked. 'I'd have thought it ought to come down if the engine was going.'

'Not necessarily. I'll want to take her in under sail soon, and in the meantime she'll take care of herself this way.'

'I see.' It was all I could do, this time, to sound as if I didn't. I saw, all right. He would take her in under sail for the same reason that he had taken her out: for silence. And it was pretty obvious where we were heading. We were making for the Albanian coast with our cargo; and 'in the meantime' I, no doubt, would be shed as Spiro had been shed. After I had gone he could spare both hands for the *Aleister*.

I took a deep breath of the salt air, and leaned my head confidingly against his shoulder. 'Heavenly, isn't it? I'm so glad I stowed away, and that you're not really angry with me about it. Look at those stars . . . that's a thing one misses terribly in London now; no night sky; only that horrible dirty glare from five million sodium lamps. Oughtn't you to have a light, Godfrey?'

'I ought, but I don't. As long as I don't meet anyone else breaking the law, *we* see *them*, so there's no harm done.'

'Breaking the law?'

I thought he was smiling. 'Running without lights.'

'Oh. You're taking photographs, then? Of the dawn?' I giggled. 'What'll Phyl say *this* time, I wonder, when I land home with the milk?'

'Where is she tonight? Did she know you'd come out?'

'She's out with friends at the Corfu Palace. I got a note from her when I got in, and it was too late to join them, so I just stayed home.

I . . . felt kind of blue. We'd had such a lovely day, you and I. I just couldn't stay in the house, somehow.'

'Poor Lucy. And then I was foul to you. I'm so sorry. Anybody know where you are?'

The question was casual, almost caressing, and it went off like a fire alarm. I hesitated perhaps a second too long. 'Miranda was in the house. I told her I was coming out.'

'To the boat-house?'

'Well, no. I didn't know that myself, did I?'

He did not reply. I had no way of knowing whether my wretched bluff had worked. The cool uncommitted tone–pleasant enough–and the cold sensuality of his love-making, gave no clue at all to what he felt, or planned to do. It was a personality from which normal human guesses simply glanced off. But whether or not he had accepted my innocence, I had reckoned that nothing I could say would make any difference to my fate. The only weapon I held so far against him was the knowledge I possessed: that Spiro was alive, that Godfrey might be accused of Yanni's murder, that Adoni and Miranda had seen the packages, and that Miranda had watched him carrying them to the boat-house, and must know where I was now. And finally, that Godfrey on his return would certainly be met by Max, Adoni and (by now) the police, who this time would not be prepared to accept easily any story he might dream up. In plain words, whether he killed me or not, his game was up.

The trouble was, it worked both ways. If it made no difference what he did with me, then obviously his best course would be to kill me, and make his getaway (surely already planned for) without going back at all into the waiting hands of Max and the Greek police.

So silence was the only course. It was faintly possible that, if he believed me innocent, he might abandon his mission and take me home, or that I might be able to persuade him to relax his watch on me for long enough to let me get hold of the more tangible weapon that hung beyond his right shoulder . . .

I said quickly: 'Listen. What's the matter with the engine? Did you hear that?'

He turned his head. 'What? It sounds all right to me.'

'I don't know . . . I thought it made a queer noise, a sort of knocking.'

He listened for a moment, while the engine purred smoothly on, then shook his head. 'You must be hearing that other boat–there's one over there, see, north-east of us, out from Kentroma. You can hear it in the gusts of the wind.' His arm tightened as I twisted to look, pulling away as if to get to my feet. 'It's nothing. Some clapped-out old scow from Kentroma with a pre-war engine. Sit still.'

I strained my eyes over the black and tossing water to where the light, dim and rocking, appeared and disappeared with the heaving sea. Up-wind of us, I was thinking; they'd never hear anything: and if they did, they'd never catch the *Aleister* with her lovely lines and silken engine.

Suddenly, only a short way from us, a flash caught my eye, a curve and splash of light where some big fish cut a phosphorescent track like a line of green fire.

'Godfrey! Look!'

He glanced across sharply. 'What?'

I was half out of my seat. 'Light, lovely green light, just there in the sea! Honestly, it was just *there* . . .'

'A school of fish or some such thing.' His tone was barely patient, and I realised with a jerk of fear that his mind was moving towards some goal of its own. 'You often see phosphorescence at night hereabouts.'

'There it is again! Could it be photographed? Oh, look! Let me go a moment, Godfrey, please, I –'

'No. Stay here.' The arm was like an iron bar. 'I want to ask you something.'

'What?'

'I've had the answer to one question already. But that leaves me with another. Why did you come?'

'I told you –'

'I know what you told me. Do you expect me to believe you?'

'I don't understand what you –'

'I've kissed women before. Don't ask me to believe you came along because you wanted to be with me.'

'Well,' I said, 'I admit I wasn't expecting it to be quite like that.'

'Like what?'

'You know quite well.'

'I believe I do. But if you follow a man round and hide in his bed and play Cleopatra wrapped in a rug you can hardly expect him to say it with lace-edged Valentines.'

It was like acid spilling over a polished surface, to show the stripped wood, coarse and ugly. There had been splashes of the same corrosive this afternoon. If there had been light enough to see by, he would have caught me staring.

'Do you have to be so offensive? I know you were annoyed, but I thought you'd got over that, and if you want the truth I can't see why you should mind so damned much if someone *does* have a look at your boat. I've told you exactly what happened, and if you don't believe me, or if you think I should fall straight into bed with you here and now, you can just think again. It's not a habit of mine.'

'Then why did you behave as if it were?'

'Now, look –!' I broke off, and then laughed. At all costs I mustn't let him force a showdown on me yet. I would have to let anger go, and try a bit more sweet apology. 'Look, Godfrey, forget it! I'm sorry, it's silly to blame you, I did ask for it . . . and I *was* putting on a bit of an act in the cabin, I admit it. That was silly, too. But when a woman gets in a jam, and finds herself faced with an angry male, it's an instinct to use her sex to get her out of it. I haven't shown up a bit well tonight, have I? But I never thought you would be quite so furious, or quite so . . . well, quick off the mark.'

'Sexually? How little you know.'

'Well, you've had your revenge. I haven't felt so idiotic and miserable since I remember. And you needn't worry that I'll follow you around again . . . I'll never face you by daylight again as long as I live!'

He did not answer, but to my stretching senses it was as if he had laughed aloud. I could feel the irony of my words ring and bite in the windy air. A little way to starboard the trail of green fire curved and flashed again, and was gone. I said: 'Well, after that, I suppose I must ask you to ruin your trip finally and completely, and take me home.'

'No use, my dear.' The words were brisk, the tone quite different. I felt a quiver run through me. 'Here you are, and here you stay. You're coming the whole way.'

'But you can't want me –'

'I don't. You came because you wanted to – or so you say – and now you'll stay because I say you have to. I've no time to take you back, even if I wished to. You've wasted too much of my time as it is. I'm on an urgent trip tonight and I'm running to schedule –'

'Godfrey –'

'– taking a load of forged currency across to the Albanian coast. It's under the cabin floor. Seven hundred thousand leks, slightly used, in small denominations; and damned good ones too. If I'm caught, I'll be shot. Get it?'

'I . . . I don't believe you, you're ribbing me.'

'Far from it. Want to see them?'

'*No*. No. I'll believe you, if you like, but I don't understand. Why? What would you do a thing like that for?'

Kentroma was abeam of us now, about the same distance away. I thought I saw the faint outline of ghostly foam very near, and the loom of land, and my heart leapt; but it vanished. A small rocky islet at most, lightless, and scoured by the wind. As we ran clear of it I felt the sudden freshening kick of the wind, no longer steady from the east but veering and gusting as the mountains to either side of the strait caught and volleyed the currents of air.

And there, not so far off now, were the lights of Kouloura, where the land ended and the strait began . . .

I dragged my mind back to what he was saying.

'. . . And at the moment the situation in Albania is that anything could happen, and it's to certain interests – I'm sure you follow me? – to see that it does. The Balkan pot can always be made to boil, if you apply heat in the right place. You've got Yugoslavia, and Greece, and Bulgaria, all at daggers drawn, all sitting round on the Albanian frontier, prepared for trouble, but none of them daring to make it.'

'Or wanting to,' I said sharply. 'Don't give me that! The last thing Greece wants is any sort of frontier trouble that she can be blamed for . . . oh!'

'Yes, I thought you might see it. Dead easy, isn't it? A lovely set-up. Communist China sitting pretty in Albania, with a nice little base in Europe, the sort of foothold that Big Brother over there'd give his eye teeth to have. And if the present pro-Chinese Government fell, and the fall was attributed to Greece, there'd be a nice almighty Balkan blow-up, and the Chinese would be out and Russia in. And maybe into Greece as well. Get it now?'

'Oh, God, yes. It's an old dodge, Hitler tried it in the last war. Flood a country with forged currency and down goes the Government like a house of cards. How long has this been going on?'

'Ferrying the currency? For some time now. This is the last load. D-Day is Good Friday; it's to filter as from then, and believe you me, after that the bang comes in a matter of days.' He laughed. 'They'll see the mushroom cloud right from Washington.'

'And you? Where will you see it from?'

'Oh, I'll have a ringside seat, don't worry – but it won't be the Villa Rotha. "G. Manning, Esq." will be vanishing almost immedi-

ately . . . You wouldn't have got your trip out with me on Saturday
after all, my dear. A pity, I thought so at the time. I enjoyed our day
out; we've a lot in common.'
'Do you have to be so insulting?'
It didn't even register. He was staring into the darkness to the
north. 'The thing I really regret is that I'll never be able to use the
photographs. Poor Spiro won't even get that memorial. We'll soon
be reaching the place where I threw him in.'
There had been no change of tone. He was still holding me, his
arm about as personal as a steel fetter; which was just as well; the
touch of his body jammed against mine was making my skin crawl.
The cracking of the sail as the boom moved overhead made me jump
as if he had laid a whip to me.
'Nervy, aren't you?' said Godfrey, and laughed.
'Who's paying you?'
'Shall we just leave it that it isn't Greece?'
'I hardly supposed that it was. Who is it?'
'What would you say if I told you I was being paid twice?'
'I'd say it was a pity you couldn't be shot twice.'
'Sweet girl.' The smooth voice mocked. 'That's the least of what
the Greeks would do to me if they caught me!'
'Where's the currency made? I can't believe anyone in Corfu . . .'
'Oh, God, no. There's a clever little chap who lives out near
Ciampino . . . I've been getting my photographic supplies from him
for a long time now. He used to work in the local branch of Leo's
Bank. It was through him I was brought in on this . . . and, of
course, because I knew Leo.'
I must have gone white: I felt the blood leave my face, and the
skin round my mouth was cold and rigid. 'Leo? I will not believe that
Leo even *begins to know* about this!'
He hesitated fractionally. I could almost feel the cruel impulse to
lie; then he must have decided it would be more amusing after all to
keep the credit. 'No, no. Pure as the driven snow, our Leo. I only
meant because I had an "in" with him to get the house, a perfect
situation for this job, and of course with that boathouse, which is
ideal. And then there's my own cover, being next door to the Forlis
themselves . . . If anything had gone wrong and inquiries had been
made, where do you suppose the official eye would have gone first?
Where but the Villa Forli, where the Director of the Bank lived?
And by the time they got round to the Villa Rotha, it would be
empty of evidence, and possibly – if things were really bad – of me.'

'And when the "mushroom cloud" goes up? I take it that part of the plan is to have the currency traceable to Greece?'

'Of course. Eventually, as far back as Corfu, but with luck, no farther.'

'I see. I suppose Spiro had found out?'

He lifted his shoulders. 'I doubt it. But there was a chance he'd seen a sample I was carrying in my wallet.'

'So you murdered him on the off-chance.' I drew in my breath. 'And you don't even care, do you? It's almost funny to think what a fuss I made about the dolphin . . . You must have shot at him for sheer jolly fun, since you were leaving in a few days anyway.' I peered at him in the darkness. 'How do people *get* like you? You simply don't care who or what you wreck, do you? You're a traitor to your own country, and the one you're a guest in, and not only that, you wreck God knows how many people into the bargain. I don't only mean Spiro, I mean Phyl and Leo and the children. You know what it will do to them.'

'Don't be sentimental. There's no room for that sort of talk in a man's world.'

'Funny, isn't it, how often that so-called "man's world" works out as a sort of juvenile delinquents' playground? Bombs and lies and cloak-and-dagger nonsense and uniforms and loud voices. All right, have it your own way, but remember I'm an actress, and I'm interested in how people work, even sawn-off morons like you. Just tell me *why?*'

I felt it at last, the movement of anger through his body. His arm had slackened.

'Do you do it for the money?' My voice nagged sharply at him. 'But surely you've got money. And you've got a talent of a sort with a camera, so it can't be frustration – unless that turn-of-the-century technique of yours can't get you any sex that's willing. And you can't be committed politically, since you bragged you were working for two sides. Why, then? I'd love to know, just for the record, what makes a horror-comic like you tick over.'

'You've got a poisonous tongue, haven't you?'

'It's the company I keep. Well? Just a wrecker, is that it? You do it for kicks?'

I heard his breath go in, then he laughed, an ugly little sound. I suppose he could afford to. He must have found, back there in the cabin, that I had no weapon on me, and he knew I couldn't escape him now. His hold was loose on me, but he could still have grabbed me if I had moved. I sat still.

'Just exactly that,' he said.

'I thought as much. It measures up. Is that why you called your boat *Aleister*?'

'What a well-read little girl it is, to be sure! Of course. His motto was the same as mine, *"Fais ce que veult"*.'

' "Do what thou wilt"?' I said. 'Well, Rabelais had it first. I doubt if you'll ever be anything but third-hand, Godfrey. Throwing people overboard hardly gets you into the master class.'

He made no reply. The lights of Kouloura were coming abeam of us. The wind backed in a sudden squall, leaping the black waves from the north. His hand moved on the tiller, and the *Aleister* bucked and rose to meet it. The stars swung behind the mast, tilted. The wind sang in the ropes. The deck heeled steeply as the starboard rail lifted against the rush of stars. The boom crashed over.

'Is that what you're going to do with me?' I asked. 'Throw me overboard?'

The *Aleister* came back head to wind, and steadied sweetly. Godfrey's hand left the tiller.

'By the time I do, by God,' he said, 'you'll be glad to go.'

Then he was out of his seat, and swinging round on me, his hands reaching for my throat.

I flinched back as far as I could from the brutal hands, dragging the torch from my pocket as I went. My back came up hard against the port coaming. Then he was on me. The boat lurched; the boom thudded to starboard with the sail cracking like a whip; a glistening fan of water burst over the rail so that his foot slipped and the wet hands slithered, missing their grip on my throat.

The *Aleister* was turning into the seas; the boom was coming back. His hands had found their hold, the thumbs digging in. I braced my back against the coaming, wrenched my left hand free and smashed a blow with the torch at his face.

It wasn't much of a blow. He didn't let go, but he jerked back from me instinctively, straightening his body, dragging me with him . . .

I kicked upwards with my right foot past his body, jammed the foot against the tiller with all my strength, and shoved it hard over.

The *Aleister*, already starting the swing, came round like a boomerang, heeling so steeply into the starboard tack that the rail went under.

And the boom slammed over with the force of a ramjet, straight at Godfrey's head.

Chapter 19

Swum ashore, man, like a duck: I can swim like a duck I'll be sworn.

II. 2.

IF I HAD been able to take him completely by surprise, it would have ended the business then and there. But he had felt my foot go lashing past his body, and the sudden heeling of the *Aleister* gave him a split second's warning of what must happen. His yachtsman's instinct did the rest.

He ducked forward over me, one arm flying up to protect his head – but I was in his way, hitting at his face, struggling to thrust him back and up into the path of the boom as it came over with a whistle and a crash that could have felled a bull.

It struck him with appalling force, but a glancing blow, the upflung arm taking the force of the smash. He was flung sprawling right across me, a dead weight bearing me back helplessly against the seat.

I had no idea if he were still conscious, or even alive. The seat was wet and slippery; my hands scrabbled for a hold to drag myself free, but before I could do this the *Aleister*, caught now with the wind on her beam, swung hard into the other tack. Godfrey's body was flung back off mine. He went to the deck all anyhow, and I with him, helplessly tangled in the loose folds of the duffel coat. The two of us slithered together across the streaming boards, to fetch up hard against the starboard side of the cockpit.

The *Aleister* kicked her way upwards, shuddered, hung poised for the next perilous swing. I tore myself free of the tangling coat and managed somehow to claw my way to my feet, bent double to avoid the murderous boom, staggering and sprawling as the deck went up like a lift, and the boom came back again to port with a force that threatened to take the whole mast overside. I threw myself at the wildly swinging tiller, grabbed it somehow and clung there, fighting to steady the sloop and trying, through the bursting fans of spray, to see.

At first I thought he was dead. His body sprawled in a slack heap where it had been thrown back to the port side by the last violent tack. His head rolled, and I could see the blur of his face, not the pale oval that had been visible before, but half an oval . . . half his face must be black with blood. Then the *Aleister* shipped another wave, and the cold salt must have brought him sharply to his senses, for the head moved, lifting this time from the deck, and a hand went with terrifying precision to the edge of the cockpit seat, groping for a hold to pull his body up . . .

I thrust the tiller hard to starboard again and laid the sloop right over. His hand slipped, and he was thrown violently back across the deck. It was now or never. I let go the tiller and tore the smoke flare down from its hook behind me. I could only pray that its rope was long enough to let me reach Godfrey where he lay against the side, his left hand now strongly grasping the seat, his right dragging at something in his pocket.

I lifted the metal flare and lurched forward.

Too late: the gun was in his hand. He was shouting something: words that were lost in the noise of wind and cracking spars and the hammering of the boom. But the message was unmistakable. I dropped the smoke flare, and leapt back for the stern seat.

The pale half-face turned with me. The gun's eye lifted.

I yanked wildly at the lifebelt hanging there on its hooks. It came free suddenly, and I went staggering against the side with it clutched to me like a shield. As I gripped the coaming and hauled myself up, the engine controls were just beside my feet. I kicked the throttle full open, and jumped for the rail.

The *Aleister* surged forward with a roar. I saw Godfrey let go his hold, dash the blood from his eyes with his free hand, jerk the muzzle of the gun after me, and fire.

I heard no shot. I saw the tiny jet of smoke spurt and vanish in the wind. I put a hand to my stomach, doubled up and pitched headlong into the sea.

*   *   *

I was coughing, swallowing salt water, gasping with lungs that hurt vilely, fighting the black weight of the sea with a wild instinct that brought me at last to the surface. My eyes opened wide, stinging, on pitch blackness. My arms flailed the water; my legs kicked like those of a hanging man; then I went out of control, lurching forward again and down, down . . .

The cold water closing over me for the second time struck me back to full consciousness. Godfrey. The shot which—fired at a dim target on a wildly bucking boat—had missed me completely. The lifebelt which had been torn from me as I fell, its rope pulled tight on the hooks by my own hasty action with the smoke flare. The *Aleister*, which I had sent swerving away fast at full throttle from the place where I went in, but whose master would have her under control again, searching for me to make sure . . .

I fought my panic down, as I had fought the sea. I surfaced easily enough, and this time the thick blackness was reassuring. I felt a shoe go, and even this little load lightened me. I trod water, retching and gasping, and tried to look about me.

Darkness. Nothing but darkness, and the noises of wind and sea. Then I heard the engine, I couldn't judge how far from me, but in the pauses of the wind it seemed to be coming nearer. He would come back to look for me; of course he would. I hoped he would think I had been hit and couldn't possibly survive, but he could hardly take the risk. He would stay here, beating the sea between me and the land, until he found me.

A mounting hill of a wave caught and lifted me. As I reached its crest I saw him; he had a light on, and the *Aleister*, now bare of canvas, was slipping along at half-throttle, searching the waves. She was still a good way off, and moving away from me at a slant, but she would be back . . .

What was more, she was between me and the land. I saw this now, dimly, a black mass studded with faint points of light. It seemed a lot further away than it had from the deck of the *Aleister*.

Half a mile, he had said. I could never swim half a mile; not in this sea. The water was very buoyant, and I was lightly clad, but I wasn't in Spiro's class as a swimmer, and could hardly hope for his luck. I dared do no other than swim straight towards the nearest land, and if Godfrey hunted about long enough he would be bound to see me.

He had turned, and was beating back on a long tack, still between me and the shore. All around me the crests of the seas were creaming

and blowing. I was carried up climbing slopes of glass, their tops
streaming off against the black sky till the whole night seemed a
windy race of wet stars. Foam blew into my eyes, my mouth. My
body was no longer mine, but a thing of unfamiliar action, cold and
buoyant. I could do little more than stay afloat, try to swim in the
right direction, and let the seas take me.

As I swam up the next mounting wave I caught, clearly, the reek
of petrol in the wind, and saw a light not two hundred yards away.
The engine was throttled back to the merest throb, and the boat
circled slowly round the beam, which was directed downwards into
the water. I even thought I saw him stooping over the side, reaching
for something – my shoe, perhaps, kept floating by its rubber sole.
He might take it as evidence that I was drowned; on the other hand,
he might beat in widening circles round the place until he found
me . . .

Then not far away I saw another light, dimmer than the *Aleister's*,
and riding high. The *Aleister's* light went out. I heard the beat of
another engine, and the second light bobbed closer. Faintly, a hail
sounded. The clapped-out old scow from Kentroma was coming to
take a look at the odd light on her fishing pitch . . .

The *Aleister's* throttle opened with a roar, and I heard it dwindling
away until the wind took all sound.

Then I shouted.

The sound came out as little more than a gasping cry, a feeble yell
that was picked up by the wind and thrown away like the cry of a
gull. The Kentroma boat may have attempted to go in the track of
the *Aleister*, I do not know, but I had lost sight of her yellow light,
and the sound of her engine, long before I gave up from sheer
exhaustion, and concentrated on swimming rather than merely
keeping afloat.

It was then that I realised that the sea was dropping. I was well
into the lee of the great curve of Corfu, where Pantokrator broke the
winds and held the Gulf quiet. And the lights of Kouloura were a
long way to my right. I had been drifting westwards, far faster than
I could have swum.

The discovery was like a shot of Benzedrine. My brain cleared. Of
course. We had been still some distance from the east-bound current
that had carried Spiro to the Albanian coast. And tonight it was an
east wind. Where I had gone in the drift must be strongly to the
south-west. He had thrown Yanni's body in in the Gulf, and Yanni's
body had fetched up at the Villa Rotha. I doubted if St. Spiridion

would take me quite so neatly home, but at least, if I could stay afloat, and make some progress, I might hope to stay alive.

So I swam, and prayed, and if St. Spiridion got muddled up in my wordless prayers with Poseidon and Prospero, and even Max, no doubt it would come to the right ears in the end.

Twenty minutes later, in a sea that was little more than choppy, and with the roar of the rocky shore barely a hundred yards ahead, I knew I couldn't make it. What had been chance for Spiro was none at all for me. Under the lee of the cliff, some freak current was setting hard off shore, probably only the backwash of the main stream that had brought me here, striking the coast at an angle and being volleyed back to the open water, but where I had till now been able to keep afloat and even angle my course slightly north across the current, I no longer had strength to fight any sea that wasn't going my way: my arms felt like cotton-wool, my body like lead; I gulped and floundered as the cross-waves met me, and every little slapping crest threatened to submerge me.

Eventually, one did. I swallowed more water, and in my panic began to struggle again. I burst free of the water, my eyes wide and sore, arms flapping feebly now, failing to drive me on or even to keep me above water. The roar of the breakers came to me oddly muffled, as if they were far away, or as if their noise came only through the water that was filling my ears . . . I was being carried back, down, down, like a sackful of lead, like a body already drowned, to be tumbled with the other sea-wrack on the rocks in the bright morning . . .

It was bright morning now. It was silly to struggle and fight my way up into darkness, when I could just let myself drift down like this, when in a moment or two if I put my feet down I would find sand, golden sand, and sweet air, sweet airs that give delight and hurt not . . . no, that was music, and this was a dream . . . how silly of me to panic so about a dream . . . I had had a thousand dreams like this, floating and flying away in darkness. In a few moments I would wake, and the sun would be out, and Max would be here . . .

He was here now. He was lifting me. He thrust and shoved at me, up, up, out of the nightmare of choking blackness, into the air.

I could breathe. I was at the surface, thrown there by a strength I hadn't believed a man could command outside his own element. As I floundered forward, spewing the sea from burning lungs, his body turned beside me in a rolling dive that half-lifted, half-threw me across the current; then before the sea could lay hold on me again to whirl me back and away, I was struck and butted forward, brutally, right into the white surge and confusion of the breakers, rolling over slack and jointless as a rag in the wind.

A huge wave lifted me forward, tumbled me over helpless in its breaking foam, then dropped me hard in its wake. I went down like a stone, hit something, and went flat on the bottom . . . pancaked on the sand of a sloping beach, with the sea recoiling past me, my hands already driven into the land, like hooks to hold me there against the drag and suck of the retreating wave. The sea tore and pulled and streamed back past me. Sobbing and retching, I crawled and humped myself up the slope, while wave after wave, diminishing, broke over me and then drew back, combing the sand where I clung. And then I was crawling through the creaming shallows, on to the firm dry beach.

I have a half memory, just as I collapsed, of looking back for my rescuer and of seeing him rear up from the waves as if to see me safe home, his body gleaming black through the phosphorescence, the witches' oils of his track burning green and white on the water. The starlight caught the cusp of the dorsal fin, glittered there briefly, then he was gone, with a triumphant smack of the tail that echoed right up the rocks.

Then I went out flat on the sand, barely a foot above the edge of the sea.

Chapter 20

Though the seas threaten they are merciful.
I have curs'd them without cause.

V.i.

THERE WAS A light, hanging seemingly in the sky far above me.

When this resolved itself into a lamp set in a cottage window, high up near the head of the cliffs, it still seemed as remote as the moon. I cannot even remember now what it cost me to drag myself in my dripping, icy clothes up the path that clung to the rock face, but I suppose I was lucky that there was a path at all. Eventually I made it, stopping to lean – collapse – against the trunk of an ancient olive that stood where a stream cut through the path to fall sharply seawards under a rough bridge.

Here a shallow valley ran back through a gap in the cliff. Dimly I could see the stretches of smoothed ground between the olive trees, painfully cultivated with beans and corn. Here and there among the trees were the scattered lights of the cottages, each with its own grove and its grazing for goats and sheep. The groves were old; the immense heads of the trees stirred and whispered even in that sheltered spot, and the small hard fruit pattered to the ground like rain. The twisted boughs stood out black against the light from the nearest window.

I forced my shivering, lead-weight limbs to move. Under my feet the rubbery olives rolled and squashed. The stems of camomile caught between my bare toes, and I stubbed my foot on a stone and cried out. Immediately there was a volley of barking, and a dog – one of the vicious, half-wild dogs that are a hazard of the Greek countryside – hurled itself towards me through the trees. I took no notice of it, except to speak as I limped forward, and the dog, every hair on end, circled behind me, growling. I felt the touch of his nose, cold on the cold flesh of my leg, but he didn't snap. Next moment the cottage door opened, loosing a shaft of light across the grass. A man, in thickset silhouette, peered out.

I stumbled into the light. 'Please,' I said breathlessly, in English, 'please . . . can you help me?'

There was a startled moment of silence, while he stared at me, coming ghostlike out of the night, soaked and filthy with sand and dust, with the dog circling at my heels. Then he shouted something at the dog which sent it swerving away, and fired some sharp question at me. I didn't know what it was; didn't even recognise the language, but in any case I doubt if I could have spoken again. I just went forward blindly towards the light and the human warmth of the house, my hands stretched out like those of the traditional suppliant, and came heavily to my knees over the threshold, right at his feet.

The blackout cannot have lasted more than a couple of seconds. I heard him call out, then there came a woman's voice, questioning shrilly, and hands were on me, half-lifting, half-dragging me in to the light and warmth of a room where the embers of a wood fire still burned red. The man said something rough and urgent to his wife, and then went quickly out, slamming the door. For a dazed, frightened moment I wondered where he had gone, then as the woman, chattering in some undistinguishable gutturals, began to fumble with my soaked and clinging clothes, I realised that her husband had merely left the cottage's single room while I undressed.

I struggled out of the sopping clothes. I suppose the old woman was asking questions, but I couldn't understand, and in fact hardly heard. My brain was as numb as my body with the dreadful cold and shivering of exhaustion and shock. But presently I was stripped and dried – on a fine linen towel so stiff and yellowed that I imagine it must have been part of the woman's dowry, never used till now – and then a rough blanket was wrapped round me, I was pushed gently into a wooden chair near the fire, logs were thrown on, a pot shoved down into the leaping flames, and only when my discarded clothes were carefully hung up above the fireplace – with much interested fingering of the nylon – did the old woman go to the door and call her man back.

He came in, an elderly, villainous-looking peasant, with a ferocious moustache, and a dirty home-made cigarette drooping from his lips. He was followed, inevitably, by two others, shortish, tough-bodied men out of the same mould, with dark, fierce faces. They came into the light, staring at me. My host asked a question. I shook my head, but the thing that mattered most to me at that moment was easy enough. I put an arm out of my blanket to make a gesture embracing my surroundings. 'Kerkyra?' I asked. 'This–Kerkyra?'

The storm of nods and assenting 'ne's' that this provoked broke over me with a physical sense of relief. To open human communications, to know where one was on the map . . . of such is sanity.

Heaven knows what I had expected the answer to be; I suppose that shreds of nightmare still clung to me, and it needed the spoken assurance to bring me finally out of the bad dream–the isolated near-death of the sea, the prison of the *Aleister* with Godfrey, the unknown black cliff I had been climbing. This was Corfu, and these were Greeks. I was safe.

I said: 'I'm English. Do you speak English?'

This time heads were shaken, but I heard the word go round, '*Anglìtha*', so they had understood.

I tried again. 'Villa Forli? Castello dei Fiori?'

Again they understood. Another fire of talk where I caught a word I knew, '*thàlassa*', which means the sea.

I nodded, with another gesture. 'Me,' I said, indicating my swaddled person, '*thàlassa* . . . boat . . .' A pantomime, rather hampered by the blanket . . . 'swim . . . drown.'

Exclamations, while the woman thrust a bowl into my hands, with the words of invitation and sympathy. It was soup of some kind–beans, I think–and rather thick and tasteless, but it was hot and filling, and under the circumstances delicious. The men looked the other way politely while I ate, talking in quickfire undertones among themselves.

As I finished, and gave the bowl back to the woman, one of them–not my host–came forward a pace, clearing his throat. He spoke in very bad German.

'You are from the Castello dei Fiori?'

'*Ja*.' My German was very little better than his, but even a smattering might see us through. I said slowly, picking the words: 'To go to Castello, how far?'

More muttering. 'Ten.' He held up his fingers. '*Ja*, ten.'

'Ten kilometres?'

'*Ja*.'

'Is-a road?'

Ja, ja.

'Is-a car?'

'No.' He was too polite to say so, but the impression that the single syllable gave was that of course there was no car. There never had been a car. What would they want with a car? They had the donkeys and the women.

I swallowed. So I wasn't yet free of the nightmare; I still had the long frustrations of the impossible journey ahead of me. I tried, not very coherently, to think what Godfrey would do.

He was bound to discover at his rendezvous that the package was missing, and would know that I must have taken it, and where I must have hidden it. But I hoped he would decide that as yet no one else could have reason to suspect him: he might well reckon that if there had been any suspicion of him, his journey would have been intercepted. No, it was to be hoped that he would think I had made a chance discovery—possibly that I had seen him carrying the packages, had hunted for them out of curiosity, and having seen them, had realised that something big was afoot, and had been frightened into hiding and carrying out the elaborate pantomime of innocence on the *Aleister* to save my skin. I was sure that he wouldn't even give Miranda a thought.

Well, he had got rid of me. My disappearance would provoke a hue and cry which he might well find embarrassing after what had happened to Spiro and Yanni, and this might decide him to cut his losses here and now, but the sudden absence of 'G. Manning, Esq.' would naturally focus official attention on his house, and the boat-house, so (since it was unlikely that any official alarm had been raised for me yet) I felt sure that he would have to risk going back tonight to find and remove the last package of forged currency.

And this was where I had to come in. Even if Max were there to receive him, it would take evidence to hold him—hard evidence, not just the hearsay of Adoni and Miranda or even Spiro, which I was sure Godfrey could cut his way through without much trouble. Once they had taken their hands off him for five minutes, 'G. Manning, Esq.', with his prepared getaway, could vanish without trace, for good and all.

I looked up at the ring of men.

'Is-a telephone?' I asked it without much hope, but they all brightened. Yes, of course there was a telephone, up in the village, further up the hill, where the road started. (This came in Greek from everybody at once, with gestures, and was surprisingly easy to understand.) Did I want the telephone now? They would take me there . . .

I nodded and smiled and thanked them, and then, indicating my clothes, turned an inquiring look on the woman. In a moment the men had melted from the room, and she began to take my things off the line. The nylon was dry, but the cotton dress was still damp and unpleasant. I threw the blanket off thankfully – it smelt of what I tried charitably to imagine was goat – and began to dress. But when I tried to put on my frock the old woman restrained me.

'No, no, no, *this* . . . it is an honour for me. You are welcome . . .' The words couldn't have been plainer if she had said them in English. '*This*' was a blouse of white lawn, beautifully embroidered in scarlet and green and gold, and with it a full black skirt, gay with the same colours at the hem – the Corfiote national dress, worn for high days and holidays. Either this also had been part of her trousseau as a young bride, or else it was her daughter's. It fitted, too . . . I put it on. The skirt was of thick, handwoven stuff, and there was a warm jacket to go over the blouse. She hovered round me, delighted, stroking and praising, and then called the men in to see.

They were all waiting outside, not three now, but – I counted – sixteen. On an impulse I stooped and kissed the wrinkled cheek of the old woman, and she caught my hand in both of hers. There were tears in her eyes.

'You are welcome,' she said. 'English. You are welcome.'

Then I was outside, swept up by the band of men and escorted royally up the stony track through the groves to the tiny village, to knock up the sleeping owner of the shop where stood the telephone.

* * *

No reply from the Castello. I hesitated, then tried the Villa Forli.

The bell had hardly sounded before Phyl was on the line, alert and anxious.

'*Lucy!* Where in the world – ?'

'It's all right, Phyl, don't worry. I'm sorry I couldn't ring you up before, but I'm quite okay.'

'Where *are* you? I tried Godfrey, but – '

'When?'

'An hour ago – three-quarters, perhaps. He wasn't in, so I thought you might be out with him. Are you?'

'No. Listen, Phyl, will you do something for me?'

'What? What *is* all this?'

'I'll tell you when I see you, but there's no time now. Just don't ask any questions, but will you ring up Godfrey's house again now? If he answers, tell him I'm not home yet, and ask if I'm still with him – just as you would if you hadn't heard from me, and were worried. It's terribly important not to let him know I rang up. Will you do that? It's *terribly* important, Phyl.'

'Yes, but –'

'Then please do it, there's an angel. I promise you I'll be home soon and tell you all about it. But I must know if he's got home. As soon as you've rung him, ring me back here.' I gave her the number.

'How in the world did you get *there*? Did you go out with him again? I know you were in to supper, because it wasn't washed up; Miranda seems to have just walked out and left everything.'

'That was my fault. I sent her on a message.'

'You did? Look, just what *is* going on? What with all the supper things just left lying, and you half-way up Pantokrator in the middle of the night –'

'You might say Godfrey ditched me. You know, the long walk home.'

'*Lucy!* You mean he tried something on?'

'You might say so,' I said. 'I don't like your Godfrey, Phyl, but just in case he's home by now, I'll ring off and wait to hear from you. But please do just as I say, it's important.'

'My God, I will. Let him worry,' said Phyl, viciously. 'Okay, sweetie, hang on, I'll ring you back. D'you want me to come for you?'

'I might at that.'

'Stinking twerp,' said my sister, but presumably not to me, and rang off.

*　　*　　*

There were twenty-three men now in the village shop, and something had happened. There were smiles all round. As I put down the receiver, my German-speaking friend was at my elbow.

'*Fräulein*, come and see.' He gestured proudly to the door of the shop. 'For you, at your service.'

Outside in the starlight stood a motor-cycle, a magnificent, almost new two-stroke affair, straddled proudly but shyly by a youth of about twenty. Round this now crowded the men, delighted that they had been able to help.

'He comes from Spartylas,' said my friend, pointing behind the shop up the towering side of Pantokrator where, a few miles away, I could see a couple of vague lights which must mark another village. 'He has been visiting in Kouloura, at the house of his uncle, and we heard him coming, and stopped him. See? It is a very good machine, as good as a car. You cannot stay here, this village is not good enough for a foreigner. But he will take you home.'

I felt the tears of emotion, brought on by anxiety and sheer exhaustion, sting my eyes. 'You are too good. You are too good. Thank you, thank you all.'

It was all I could say, and it seemed to be all they could desire. The kindness and goodwill that surrounded me were as palpable as light and fire; it warmed the night.

Someone was bringing a cushion; it looked like the best one his house could offer. Someone else strapped it on. A third man thrust the bundle containing my damp frock into a carrier behind the saddle. The youth stood smiling, eyeing me sideways curiously.

The telephone rang once briefly, and I ran back.

'Yes?'

'Lucy. I got the Villa Rotha, but he's not there.'

'No reply?'

'Well, of course not. Look, can't you tell me what all this is about?'

'Darling, I can't, not just now . . . I'll be home soon. Don't worry. But don't tell anyone I rang you up. *Anyone*. Not even Max.'

'Not *even* Max? Since when did – ?'

'And don't bother to come for me, I've got transport. Be seeing you.'

The shopkeeper refused to take money for the telephone. It was a pleasure, I gathered, a pleasure to be roused from his bed in the middle of the night by a half-drowned, incoherent stranger. And the men who had helped me would not even take my thanks; it was a privilege to help me, indeed it was. They sat me on the pillion, showed me where to put my feet and how to hang on to the young man's waist, wished me God-speed, and stood back as my new friend kicked the engine into an unsilenced roar that slashed through the village like Pandemonium itself. It must have woken every sleeper within miles. No doubt they would count this, also, as a privilege . . .

We roared off with a jerk and a cloud of smoke. The road was rutted, surfaced with loose gravel, and twisted like a snake through the olive-groves that skirted the steep cliffs, some three hundred feet above the sea. Not a fast road, one would have said – but we took it fast, heeling over on the bends as the *Aleister* had heeled to the seas, with gravel spurting out under our front wheel like a bow wave, and behind us a wake of dust half a mile long. I didn't care. The feel of the wind in my hair, and the bouncing, roaring speed between my thighs was at once exciting and satisfying after the terrors and frustrations of the night. And I couldn't be afraid. This was – quite literally – the 'god in the machine' who had come to the rescue, and he couldn't fail me. I clung grimly to his leather-clad back as we roared along, the shadowy groves flicking past us in a blur of speed, and down – way down – on our left the hollow darkness of the sea.

The god turned his curly head and shouted something cheerfully. We shot round a bend, through a small stream, up something remarkably like a rough flight of steps, and met the blessed smooth camber of a metalled road.

Not that this was really an improvement; it swooped clean down the side of Pantokrator in a series of tight-packed hairpin bends which I suppose were steep and dangerous, but which we took at a speed that carried us each time to the very verge, where a tuft or so of daisies or a small stone would catch us and cannon us back on to the metal. The tyres screeched, the god shouted gaily, the smell of burning rubber filled the night, and down we went, in a series of bird-like swoops which carried us at last to the foot of the mountain and the level of the sea.

The road straightened. I saw the god's hand move hopefully to the throttle.

'Okay?' he yelled over his shoulder.

'Okay!' I screamed, clinging like a monkey in a hurricane.

The hand moved. The night, the flying trees, the hedgerows ghostly with apple blossom, accelerated past us into a streaming blur . . .

All at once we were running through a village I knew, and he was slowing down. We ran gently between walls of black cypress, past the cottage in the lemon-grove, past the little tea-garden with its deserted tables under the pine, and up to the Castello gate, to stop almost between the pillars.

The youth put his feet down and turned inquiringly, jerking a thumb towards the drive, but I shook my head. It was a long walk up through the grounds of the Castello, but until I knew what was going on I certainly wasn't going to advertise my homecoming by roaring right up to the front door.

So I loosed my limpet-clutch from the leather jacket, and got rather stiffly off my perch, shaking out the pretty embroidered skirt, and pulling my own bedraggled cotton dress from the carrier.

When I tried to thank my rescuer, he smiled and shook his head, wheeling the machine back to face the way we had come, and shouting something which, of course, must mean: 'It was a pleasure.'

As his hand moved on the controls I put mine out quickly to touch it.

'Your name?' I knew the Greek for that. 'Your name, please?'

I saw him grin and bob his head. 'Spiridion,' he said. 'God with you.'

Next second he was nothing but a receding roar in the darkness, and a cloud of dust swirling to settle in the road.

Chapter 21

*Thou dost here usurp
The name thou ow'st not, and hast put thyself
Upon this Island, as a spy . . .*

I. 2.

THERE WAS NO light in the Castello. The house loomed huge in the starlight, turreted and embattled and almost as romantic-looking as its builder had intended. I walked round it to the terrace, treading softly on the mossed tiles. No light there either, no movement, nothing. The long windows were blank and curtained, and – when I tried them – locked.

Keeping to the deepest shadows, I skirted the terrace till I reached the balustrade overhanging the cliff and the bay. The invisible sea whispered, and all round me was the dark, peppery smell of the cypresses. I could smell the roses, too, and there were bats about, cutting the silence with their thin, knife-edge cries. A movement caught my eye and made me turn quickly – a small slither of pale colour vanishing like ectoplasm through the stone balustrade, and drifting downhill. The white cat, out on his wild lone.

Then I caught a glimpse of light. This came from somewhere beyond the trees to the right, where the Villa Rotha must lie. As softly as the white cat, and almost as silently as the ghost from the sea that I was, I crept off the terrace and padded down through the woods towards the light.

I nearly fell over the XK 150, parked among the trees. He must simply have driven her away from the house, so that a chance caller would assume he was out with the car, and look no further.

A few minutes later I was edging my way through the thicket of myrtle that overhung the bungalow.

This was, as I have said before, the twin of the Forli house. The main door, facing the woods, had a cleared sweep of driveway in front of it, and from this a paved path led round the house to the wide terrace overlooking the sea. A light burned over the door. I parted the leaves and peered through.

Two cars stood on the sweep, Max's big, shabby black Buick, and a small car I didn't know.

So he was back, and it was battle-stations. I wondered if the other car was the police.

My borrowed rope soles made no sound as I crept round towards the terrace, hugging the house wall.

The terrace, too, was the twin of Phyllida's, except that the pergola was covered with a vine instead of wistaria, and there was no dining-table, only a couple of large chairs and a low table which held a tray with bottles and glasses. I by-passed these quietly, making for the french windows.

All three were shut and curtained, but the centre one showed a gap between the curtains some three inches wide through which I could see the room; and as I reached it I realised that I would be able to hear as well . . . In the glass beside the window-catch gaped a big, starred hole where someone had smashed a way in . . .

The first person I saw was Godfrey, near the window and to one side of it, sitting very much at his ease in a chair beside the big elm-wood desk, with a glass of whisky in his hand. He was still dressed in the jersey and dark trousers, and over the back of his chair hung the navy duffel coat which I had torn free of before I went into the sea. I was delighted to see that one side of his face bore a really classic bruise, smeared liberally with dried blood, and that the good-looking mouth appeared to hurt him when he drank. He was dabbing at a swollen lip with his handkerchief.

The room had seemed at that first glance full of people, but the crowd now resolved itself into a fairly simple pattern. A couple of yards from Godfrey, in the middle of the floor and half turned away from me, stood Max. I couldn't see his face. Adoni was over beside the door, facing towards the windows, but with his attention also riveted on Godfrey. Near me and just to one side of my window was Spiro, sitting rather on the edge of a low chair, with the injured leg in its new white cast thrust out awkwardly in front of him, and Miranda crouched on the floor beside his chair, hugging its arm against her breast as (it seemed) she would have liked to hug Spiro's. The two faces were amazingly alike, even allowing for the difference of male from female; and at the moment the likeness was made more striking still by the expression that both faces shared; a pure, uncomplicated hatred, directed unwinkingly at Godfrey. On the floor beside the boy's chair lay a rifle, and from the way his hand hung near it, twitching from time to time, I guessed that only a forcible order from the police had made him lay it down.

For the police were here. Across the width of the room from Godfrey, and near the door, sat a man I recognised as the Inspector (I didn't know the Greek equivalent) from Corfu who had been in charge of the inquiry into Yanni's death. This was a stoutish, grey-haired man with a thick moustache and black, intelligent eyes. His clothes were untidy, and had obviously been hastily put on, and in spite of the deadpan face and calm, steady stare I sensed that he was not quite sure of his ground, even ill at ease.

Godfrey was speaking in that light, cool voice that I knew so well, so very well.

'As you wish, Mr. Papadopoulos. But I warn you that I'm not prepared to overlook what happened down in my boat-house, or the fact that these two men have apparently broken into my house. As for the girl, I'm not quite sure what it is that I'm supposed to have done with her, but I have given you a complete account of our movements this afternoon, and I'm sure you can find any number of people who will bear me out.'

'It's your movements tonight that we're interested in.' Max's voice was rough, and only precariously controlled. 'For a start, what happened to your face?'

'An accident with the main-boom,' said Godfrey shortly.

'Another? Rather too common, these accidents, wouldn't you say? How did it happen?'

'Are you a yachtsman?'

'No.'

'Then don't ask stupid questions.' Godfrey gave him a brief, cold look. 'You've had your turn, damn you. Back down. You've no more right to question me than you had to manhandle me or break in here to ransack the place. If you hadn't telephoned for the police, you can be very sure I'd have done so myself. We'll talk about your methods later.'

Papadopoulos said heavily: 'If you please, Max. Now, Mr. Manning, you have told us that you have not seen Miss Lucy

Waring since shortly after seven this last evening, when you took her home?'

'That is so.' To the Inspector his tone was one of tired but patient courtesy. He was playing his part to perfection. All his dislike of Max was there, patent through tonight's more immediate outrage, with weariness and puzzlement and a nice touch of worry about me. 'I took her home before dinner. I myself had to go out again.'

'And you have not seen her since?'

'How often must I–? I'm sorry, Inspector, I'm a little tired. No, I have not seen her since.'

'You have given us an account of your movements after you took Miss Waring home. Now, when you finally went down to take out your boat you found the boat-house still locked, and as far as you are aware there was nobody there?'

'That is so.'

'There was nothing to indicate that anyone–Miss Waring or anyone else–had been there, and gone again?'

I thought Godfrey hesitated, but it was barely perceptible. He must be very sure that he had sunk me without trace. 'No.'

'You heard what this girl had to say?'

'Miranda?' Godfrey's tone was not even contemptuous, merely lightly dismissive. 'She'd say anything. She's got some bee in her bonnet over her brother, and she'd invent any tale to see me in trouble. Heaven knows why, or where the boy's got this incredible idea of his from. I've never been happier about anything in my life than I was to see him here tonight.'

Spiro said something in Greek, one short, vicious-sounding phrase whose import there was no mistaking, and which drew a shocked glance from his sister. He made it clear. 'I spit,' he said, and did so.

'Spiro!' said Max sharply, and Godfrey raised an eyebrow–a very civilised eyebrow–at the Inspector, and laughed.

'Satan rebuking sin? Always an amusing sight, don't you think?'

'I'm sorry,' said Papadopoulos. 'You will control yourself, Spiro, or you will go. Let us go back, Mr. Manning. You must excuse me, my English is not so very good; I do not follow this about Satan, and bees, was it? Bees in the bonnet?' He glanced up at Max, who hesitated, and Adoni snapped out some phrase in Greek. 'I see.' The stout man sat back. 'You were saying?' to Godfrey.

'I was saying that whatever Miranda accuses me of, the fact remains that she did not see Lucy Waring enter my boat-house or go near my boat. There is nothing to show that she did either.'

'No. Well, Mr. Manning, we'll leave that for the moment . . . Yes, Max, I know, but there is nothing more we can do until Petros gets up here from the boat-house and reports on his search there. He will be here before long. Meanwhile, Mr. Manning, with your permission, there are a few other questions I want to ask you.'

'Well?'

'Forgetting about Miss Waring's movements for the moment, I should like to hear about yours . . . after you went down to your boat-house. When Mr. Gale met you on your return, and accused you –'

'Attacked me, you mean.'

'As you wish. When he asked you where you had been, you told him this was a "normal trip". What do you mean by a "normal trip", Mr. Manning? Fishing, perhaps?'

Adoni said, without expression: 'His cameras were in the cabin.'

'So you were out taking photographs, Mr. Manning? May one know where?'

There was a short silence. Godfrey took a sip of whisky, then sat for a moment staring down at the glass, swirling the spirit round gently. Then he looked up, meeting the policeman's eye, and gave a faint smile that had the effect of a shrug.

'I can see that I'll have to make a clean breast of it. I never thought you'd get on to me. If it hadn't been for this misunderstanding about the girl, I doubt if you would have . . . Or were you tipped off?'

There was no change in the Inspector's expression, but I saw Max stiffen, and Adoni was staring. Capitulation, when they hadn't even brought up a gun?

'If you please,' said Papadopoulos courteously, 'I do not understand. If you would use simpler English –'

'More idioms,' said Adoni. 'He means that he knows you've been told about him, so he's going to confess.'

'I meant no such thing. Keep your pretty mouth shut, if you can. This is between men.' Godfrey flung it at him without even a glance, indifferently, as one might swat a midge. Adoni's eyes went back to him, and his expression did not change, but I thought, with a queer jump of the heart: Your mistake, Godfrey . . .

'Please,' said Papadopoulos. 'Let us not waste time. Well, Mr. Manning?'

Godfrey leaned back in his chair, regarding him coolly. You'd have thought there was nobody else in the room. 'With your man down there searching my boat it's not much use pretending I have been taking photographs, is it? You have only to look at the cameras . . . No, as a matter of cold truth, I had business over the other side.' If the room had been still before, it was stiller now. I thought dazedly: He can't confess like that . . . Why? Why? Then I saw. Miranda had told the police what she knew, and Godfrey realised now that she had been with me on the shore. I did not think that the cave or the packages had been mentioned yet in front of him, but he could guess that she had seen as much as I, and must have told the police about the packages. Moreover, a police constable was now searching the *Aleister*, and, if he was even half good at his job, he would find the cache under the cabin floor. I guessed that Godfrey was intent on getting some relatively harmless explanation in before the inevitable discovery was made.

'Whereabouts on the other side?' asked Papadopoulos.

'Albania.'

'And the business?'

'Shall we call it "importing"?'

'What you call it does not matter. This, I understand perfectly.' The Greek regarded him for a moment in silence. 'So you admit this?'

Godfrey moved impatiently. 'I have admitted it. Surely you aren't going to pretend you didn't know that this went on? I know you've shut your eyes to the way Yanni Zoulas was killed, but between ourselves –'

'Yanni Zoulas?' I saw Papadopoulos flash a glance at Max. Godfrey was taking the wind out of this sail, too, before it had even been hoisted.

'Ah,' said Godfrey, 'I see you understand me. I thought you would.'

'You know something about Zoulas' death that you didn't tell the police?'

'Not a thing. I'm only guessing, from my own experiences with the coastguard system the other side. It's quite remarkably efficient.'

'So you think he ran into trouble there?'

'I think nothing. I was only guessing. But guesses aren't evidence, are they' The grey eyes touched Max's briefly. 'I only mean that if one runs the gauntlet of those coasts often enough, it's not surprising if one gets hurt. What was surprising was that the police made so little of it. You must have known what he was doing.'

'What was Zoulas' connection with you?'

'With me? None at all. I didn't know the man.'

'Then how do you know this about him?'

Godfrey smiled. 'In the trade, word goes round.'

'He was not connected with you?'

'I've answered that. Not in any way.'

Papadopoulos said: 'It has been suggested that Spiro here, and after him Yanni Zoulas, discovered something about your business . . .'

I missed the rest. From somewhere behind me, below the terrace, came the moving flicker of a torch, and the sound of footsteps. This would be the constable coming up from his search of the boat-house. I drew away from the lighted window, wondering if I should approach him now and tell him about the package I had sunk in the boat-house; then I remembered that he probably spoke no English. He passed below the end of the terrace, and trod gently round the house.

I tiptoed back to the window. It was just possible that the man had found the package, and if so, I might as well wait a little longer, and hear what Godfrey's defence would be, before I went in to blow it apart.

He had changed his ground, and was now giving a fine rendering of an angry man who has got himself in hand, but only just. He said, with controlled violence: 'And perhaps you will tell me what in hell's name I could be doing that would drive me to wholesale murder?'

'I cannot,' said Papadopoulos regretfully. 'From what you are telling me of the type of goods you "trade in", I cannot. Radio parts, tobacco, antibiotics? And so on and so on . . . The usual list, Mr. Manning. One wonders merely why it should have paid you . . . The rent of this house, your boat, the trouble to make the contacts, the risks . . . You are not a poor man. Why do you do it?'

'Christ,' said Godfrey, 'is it so hard to understand? I was stuck here working on my damned book, and I was bored. Of course I don't need the money. But I was bored, and there was the boat, and the promise of a bit of fun with her . . .' He broke off, turning up a hand. 'But do you really want all that tonight? Say I do it for kicks, and leave it at that. Apollo will translate.'

Adoni said gently: 'He means that he likes risks and violence for their own sakes. It is a phrase that irresponsible criminals use, and adolescents.'

Max laughed. Godfrey's hand whitened on his glass. 'Why, you little –'

'Markos!' Max broke across it, swinging round on the Greek. I saw his face for the first time. 'None of this matters just now! I'm sorry, I realise that if this man's smuggling across the border it's very much your affair, but all that really matters here and now is the girl. If he insists that –'

'A moment,' said Papadopoulos, and turned his head. Adoni put a hand to the door beside him and pulled it open, and the constable came into the room.

He had obviously not found the package, and apparently nothing else either, for when his superior barked a question at him he spread empty hands and shrugged, answering with a swift spate of Greek. Max asked another question in Greek, and the man turned to him, speaking volubly and with many gestures. But I no longer paid him any heed. As I had craned forward to see if the package was in his hands, I must have made some movement that caught Adoni's attention. I found myself meeting his eyes, clear across the room.

Nobody was looking at him; all eyes were for the newcomer, except Spiro's, whose flick-knife gaze never left Godfrey. Nobody seemed to notice as Adoni slipped quietly out through the open door, pulling it shut behind him.

I backed quickly away from the window, out of the fringe of light, and soft-footed my way back round the corner of the house.

A light step beside me in the darkness, and a whisper: '*Miss Lucy!* Miss Lucy! I thought – I could not be sure – in those clothes . . . But it is you! We thought you must be dead!' Somehow his arms were round me, quite unselfconsciously hugging me to him. It was amazingly comforting. 'Oh, Miss Lucy, we thought you had gone with that devil in his boat, and been killed!'

I found myself clinging to him. 'I did. I did go with him . . . and he did try to kill me, but I got away. I went overboard, like Spiro, and he left me to drown, but – *Adoni!* You mustn't say things like that! Where *did* you learn them? No, hush, they'll hear you . . .'

'We've got to get him now. We've got to make sure of him.'

'We will, I promise you we will. I know all about it now, Adoni. It's not just Spiro and Yanni and me – he's a traitor and a paid spy, and I can prove it.'

'So?' He let me go. 'Come in now, Miss Lucy, there's no need to be afraid of him. Come in straight away. Max is half crazy, I thought he would kill him.'

'Not for a minute . . . No, wait, I *must* know what's happened. Can you tell me, very quickly? Those are the Corfu police, aren't they? Didn't anyone come from Athens?'

'No. The Athens people said that Max must bring Spiro home, and go to the Corfu police in the morning. They said they would look into it, but I don't think they were much interested—they had their hands full after that Communist demonstration on Tuesday, and this is the affair of the Corfu people, anyway. So Max and Spiro came back alone, and I met the ferry. I told Max about the cave and the boxes that were hidden there, and he was afraid to waste more time by going to the police then—it was eleven o'clock, and only the night man on duty—so he decided to drive home quickly and go to the cave himself.'

'Then you hadn't had any message from Miranda?'

'No. She telephoned the Corfu Bar, but I hadn't been in there. I'd gone to Dionysios' house, a friend of mine, and had supper there, and then we went to the Mimosa on the harbour, to wait for the ferry. They sent a boy running to look for me from the Corfu Bar, but he didn't find me. When we got to the Castello, Miranda was waiting for us, and after a time she remembered, and told us about you.'

'After a time?'

I heard the smile even through the whisper. 'There was Spiro.'

'Oh, lord, yes, of course! She'd forget everything else. Well, I don't blame her . . . Go on. She told you about me.'

'Yes. I have never seen Max like that before. We ran down to the boat-house, he and I, but the boat was gone, and you. We searched there, and along the shore, and then went up to the Villa Rotha. It was locked, so Max broke the window, and we looked for you, but found nothing. So he got to the telephone, and got Mr. Papadopoulos at his home, and told him everything very quickly, and told him to bring Spiro and Miranda from the Castello as he came. Then Max and I went back to the boat-house to wait for Mr. Manning.'

'Yes?'

'We waited for some time. Then we saw him coming, no engine, just the sail, very quiet. We stood in the shadow, just inside the doors, waiting. He did not come in through the doors, but just to the end of the jetty, and he berthed the boat facing the sea, then got out very quietly and tied her up, so we knew he meant to leave again soon. Then he came back along the jetty and into the boat-house.'

He stirred. 'We took him, Max and I. He fought, but we had him. Then Max sent me to look in the boat for you, and when I got back

Mr. Manning was pretending to be surprised and very angry, but Max just said, "Where is she? Where's my girl?" and had him by the throat, and I thought he was going to kill him, and when Mr. Manning said he knew nothing Max said to me, "Hurry up, Adoni, before the police get here. They won't like it." '

'Won't like what?'

'What we would have done to make him talk,' said Adoni simply. 'But the police came then. Mr. Manning was very angry, and complained, and one could see that Mr. Papadopoulos was uncomfortable. We had to come up to the house. The other man stayed to search the boat. You saw him come back just now? He hasn't found anything, only the place under the deck where Mr. Manning had hidden the boxes . . . But you heard all that, didn't you?'

'Guessed it. It was in Greek.'

'Of course. I forgot. Well, that was all. Wait a moment . . .' He vanished round the house wall, and in a few seconds materialised again beside me. A glass was pushed into my hand. 'Drink this. There was some whisky on the terrace. You're cold?'

'No. Excited. But thanks all the same.' I drank the spirit, and handed back the glass. I saw him stoop to put it down somewhere, then he straightened, and his hand closed over my arm. 'What now, Miss Lucy? You said we could get him. Is this true?'

'Quite true. There's not time enough to tell you it all now, but I must tell you some of it—enough—just in case anything happens to me . . . Listen.' In a few brief sentences I gave him the gist of what Godfrey had told me. 'So that's it. Athens can follow up his contacts, I suppose, and it should be possible to work out roughly where he'd go ashore, in the time it took him. They'll have to get on to Tirana straight away and find some way of stopping the stuff circulating. But that's not our concern. What we have to do now is to get the police to hold him, and hold him good and hard.'

'What's your proof you said you had? Enough to make them listen?'

'Yes, I've got one of the boxes of currency. Yes, really. I dumped it off the platform in the boat-house about half-way along the left side. I want you to go down and get it.'

'Of course. But I'll go in with you first.'

'There's no need. I'd rather you got the box safe. He knows I took it—he must know—and he'll have a good idea where I hid it. He's a dangerous man, Adoni, and if this should go wrong . . . I don't want to run any risks at all of his getting down there somehow and getting away, or of his having another shot at killing me, if he thinks I'm the only one who knows where the box is. So we'd better not both be exposed to him at once. You must go and get it straight away.'

'All right. Be careful of yourself.'

'I'll do that. The swine had a gun. I suppose you took it?'

'Yes. And the police took it from us.'

'Well, here we go.' I took a shaky little breath. 'Oh, Adoni . . .'

'You are afraid?'

'Afraid?' I said. 'It'll be the entrance of my life. Come on.'

*   *   *

The scene was unchanged except that the constable now stood in Adoni's place by the door. Godfrey had lit a cigarette, and looked once more at his ease, but still ruffled and irritated, like a man who has been caught out in some misdemeanour for which he will now have to pay a stiff fine. They had apparently got to the cave and the packages which were, according to Godfrey, radio sets. He was explaining, wearily yet civilly, how the 'sets' had been packed and stored.

I put a cautious hand in through the broken pane, and began to ease the window-catch open. It moved stiffly, but without noise.

. . . 'But surely this can wait till morning? I've admitted to an offence, and I'm perfectly willing to tell you more, but not now –and certainly not in front of a bunch of amateurs and children who seem to be trying to pin a mass murder on me.' He paused, adding in a reasonable voice: 'Look, Inspector, if you insist, I'll come in to Corfu with you now, but if Miss Waring is genuinely missing, I really do think you should concentrate on her, and leave my small sins till morning.'

The Inspector and Max started to speak together, the former stolidly, the latter with passion and anger, but Miranda cried out suddenly for the first time, on a piercing note that drowned them both.

'He knows where she is! He has killed her! Do not listen to him! He has killed her! I know she went to the boat! He took her and killed her, as he tried to kill Spiro my brother!'

'It is true,' said Spiro violently. 'As God watches me now, it is true.'

'Oh, for God's sake,' said Godfrey. He got abruptly to his feet, a man whose patience has suddenly given way. 'I think this has gone on long enough. I've answered your questions civilly, Papadopoulos, but it's time this scene came to an end! This is my house, and I'll put up with you and your man if I have to, but I'm damned if I sit here any longer being yapped at by the local peasants. I suggest you clear them out of here, now, please, this minute, and Gale with them.'

The catch was off. As the window yielded softly to my hand, I heard Max say, in a voice I hardly knew was his:

'Markos, I beg of you. The girl . . . there's no time. Give me five minutes alone with him. Just five minutes. You'll not regret it.'

Papadopoulos' reply was cut off by a crash as Godfrey slammed the flat of his hand down on the desk, and exploded.

'This is beyond anything! It's more, it's a criminal conspiracy! By God, Inspector, you'll have to answer for this! What the hell are you trying to do, the lot of you? Papadopoulos, you'll clear these people out of my house immediately, do you hear me? I've told you all I'm going to tell you tonight, and as for Lucy Waring, how often do I have to repeat that I took the damned girl home at seven, and I haven't seen her since? That's the truth, I swear to God!'

No actress ever had a better cue. I pulled the window open, and went in.

Chapter 22

Let us not burthen our remembrances, with
A heaviness that's gone.

V. i.

FOR A MOMENT no one moved. I was watching Godfrey, and
Godfrey alone, so I was only conscious of the moment's desperate
stillness, then of exclamations and confused movement as Max
started forward, and Papadopoulos jerked out a restraining hand and
gripped his sleeve.

I said: 'I suppose you weren't expecting me, Godfrey?'

He didn't speak. His face had drained, visibly, of colour, and he
took a step backwards, his hand seeking the edge of the desk. Down
beside me I caught the flutter of a hand as Miranda crossed herself.

'Lucy,' said Max hoarsely, 'Lucy – my dear –'

The Inspector had recovered from his surprise. He sat back. 'It is
Miss Waring, is it not? I did not know you for the moment. We
have been wondering where you were.' I noticed suddenly that
Petros, the constable, had a gun in his hand.

I said: 'I know. I'm afraid I've been listening, but I wanted to hear
what Mr. Manning had to say; and I wanted to know what had
happened since I left him an hour or so ago.'

'By God,' said Max, 'we were right. Markos –'

'An hour ago, Miss Waring? He was out in his boat an hour ago.'

'Oh, yes. I was with him. I must have gone overboard some way
to the east of Kouloura, beyond the island.'

'Ah . . .' said Spiro, his face blazing with excitement and
satisfaction. There were exclamations, and I saw Petros move
forward from the door, gun in hand. Godfrey hadn't spoken or
moved. He was leaning on the desk now as if for support. He was

very pale, and the bruised side of his face stood out blacker as the blood ebbed from the rest.

'Are we to understand –?' began Papadopoulos.

Max said: 'Look at his face. He tried to kill you?'

I nodded.

'*Max!*' cried Papadopoulos warningly. 'Petros? Ah . . . Now, Miss Waring, your story, please, and quickly.'

'Yes, of course, but there's something–something urgent–that I've got to tell you first.'

'Well?' demanded the Inspector.

I opened my mouth to answer, but what I had to say was drowned by the sudden, strident ringing of the telephone. The sound seemed to rip the quiet room. I know I jumped, and I suppose everyone's attention flicked to the instrument for a split second. The constable, who held the gun, made an automatic move towards it as if to answer it.

It was enough. I hardly even saw Godfrey move, but in one lightning movement the hand that leaned on the edge of the desk had flashed an inch lower, flicked open a drawer, jerked a gun up, and fired, all in one movement as swift and fluid as the rake of a cat's paw. Like an echo, Petros' gun answered, but fractionally too late. His bullet smacked into the wall behind the desk, and then his gun spun smoking to the floor and skidded, scoring the polish, out of sight under the desk. Petros made some sound, clapped a hand to his right arm, and reeled back a pace, right into Max's path as the latter jumped forward.

Simultaneously with the crack of the gun Godfrey had leaped for the open window where I stood, two paces from him. I felt my arm seized and twisted up behind my back in a brutal grip, as he dragged my body back against him as a shield. And a hostage. The gun was digging into my side.

'*Keep back!*'

Max, who was half-way across the room, stopped dead. Papadopoulos froze in the act of rising, his hands clamped to the arms of his chair. The constable leaned against the wall where Max's thrust had sent him, blood oozing between his fingers. The twins never moved, but I heard a little sobbing moan from Miranda.

I felt myself sway as my knees loosened, and the gun jabbed cruelly. 'Keep on your feet, bitch-eyes,' said Godfrey, 'or I'll shoot you here and now. The rest of you listen. I'm going now, and the girl with me. If I'm followed, I don't have to tell you what'll happen to her. You've shown me how little I've got to lose . . . Oh, no, I'm not taking her with me . . . She's a damned uncomfortable companion on a boat. You can come down for her as soon as you hear me leave – not before. Understand? Do it before, and . . .' A movement with the gun completed the sentence, so that I cried out, and Max moved uncontrollably. 'Keep your distance!' snapped Godfrey.

He had been slowly pulling me backwards towards the window as he spoke. I didn't dare fight, but I tried to hang against him like a dead weight.

Max said hoarsely: 'He won't leave her alive, Markos. He'll kill her.'

'It won't help him.' I managed to gasp it somehow. 'I told . . . everything . . . to Adoni. Adoni knows . . .'

'Shut your God-damned mouth,' said Godfrey.

'You heard that?' said Max. 'Let her go, blast your soul. You don't imagine you can get away with this, do you? Let her go!'

Papadopoulos said quickly: 'If you do not hurt the girl, perhaps we will –'

'It will give me great pleasure,' said Godfrey, 'to hurt her very much.' He jerked hard on my arm, and took a step towards the window. 'Come along, you. Where's the pretty-boy, eh? Where did he go?'

He stopped. We were full in the window. For a moment I felt his body grow still and rigid against mine, then he pulled me out of the shaft of light, backing up sharply against the window frame, with me swung round to cover him, and the gun thrust forward now beside my waist, and nosing round in a half circle. Behind us, out on the dark terrace, something had moved.

Adoni . . . It was Adoni with the package, delivering it and himself neatly into the muzzle of Godfrey's gun.

The next second I knew I was wrong. There was the tinkle of glass, the splashing of liquid, and the sound of someone humming a tune. 'Come where the booze is cheaper,' sang Sir Julian happily, helping himself to Godfrey's whisky. Then he saw us. The slurred and beautiful voice said, cheerfully: 'Hullo, Manning. Hope you don't mind my coming over? Saw the light . . . thought Max might be here. Why, Lucy, m'dear . . .'

I think I must have been half fainting. I have only the haziest recollection of the next minute or so. Sir Julian came forward blinking amiably, with a slopping glass in one hand, and the bottle still grasped in the other. His face had the gentle, foolish smile of someone already very drunk, and he waved the bottle at Godfrey.

'Helped myself, my dear Manning. Hope you don't mind?'

'You're welcome,' said Godfrey shortly, and jerked his head. 'Into the room.'

Sir Julian seemed to have noticed nothing amiss. I tried to speak and couldn't. Dimly, I wondered why Max had made no sound. Then his father saw him. 'Why, Max . . .' He paused, as if a vague sense of something wrong was filtering through the fog of alcohol. His eyes came uncertainly back to Godfrey, peering through the shaft of light thrown by the window. 'There's the telephone. Someone's ringing up.' He frowned. 'Can't be me. I thought of it, but came instead.'

'Inside, you drunken old fool,' said Godfrey, and dragged at my arm to pull me out past him.

Sir Julian merely smiled stupidly, raised the bottle in a wavering salute, and then hurled it straight at the light.

It missed, but only just. It caught the flex, and the light careened wildly up to the ceiling and swung down again, sending wild shadows lurching and flying up the walls so that the ensuing maelstrom of action seemed like something from an old film, flickering drunkenly, and far too fast . . .

Something white scraped along the floor . . . Spiro's cast, thrust hard against Godfrey's legs. Godfrey staggered, recovered as his shoulder met the window frame, and with an obscene little grunt in my ear, fired down at the boy. I felt the jerk of the gun against my waist and smelt the acrid tang of singeing cloth. He may have been aiming at Spiro, but the light still reeled as if in an earthquake, and, off balance as I was, I spoiled his aim. The bullet hit the cast, which shattered. It must have been like a blow right across the broken leg. The boy screamed, rolling aside, with Miranda shrieking something as she threw herself down beside him.

I don't know whether I tore myself away, or whether Godfrey flung me aside, but suddenly I was free, my arm dropping, half broken, to my side. As I fell he fired again, and then something hit me, hurling me down and to the floor. Max, going past me in a silent, murderous dive for Godfrey's gun hand.

I went down heavily into the wreckage of the plaster cast. The place stank of whisky and cordite. The telephone still screeched. I was deafened, blinded, sobbing with pain. The two men hurtled backwards out on to the terrace, locked together in a struggle of grunting breaths and stamping feet. One of them trod on my hand as he passed. Papadopoulos thudded past, and out, and Petros was on his knees near by, cursing and groping under the desk for his gun.

Then someone's arms came round me, and held me tightly. Sir Julian reeked of whisky, but his voice was quite sober. 'Are you all right, dear child?'

I nodded. I couldn't speak. I clung to him, flinching and shaking as the sound of the fight crashed round the terrace. It was impossible, in that diffused and rocking light, to see which man was which. I saw Papadopoulos standing near me, legs apart, the gun in his hand moving irresolutely as the locked bodies stamped and wrestled past him. Godfrey's gun spat again, and the metal table whanged. Papadopoulos yelled something, and the injured constable lurched to his feet and ran to the windows, dragging the curtains wide, so that the light poured out.

But already they were beyond the reach of it, hurtling back against the balustrade that edged the steep and tree-hung cliff. I saw them, dimly silhouetted against the sky. One of them had the other rammed back across the stone. There was a crack, a sound of pain. Sir Julian's breath whistled in my ear and he said *'Christ Almighty'*, and I saw that the man over the stone was Max.

Beside us was a scraping sound and a harshly-drawn breath. Spiro's voice said urgently: *'Koumpàre . . .'* and a hand thrust Sir Julian aside. The boy had dragged himself through the welter of broken plaster to the window, and lay on his belly, with the levelled rifle hugged to his cheek. I cried out, and Sir Julian shot a hand down and thrust the barrel lower. *'No! Wait!'*

From the locked and straining bodies over the balustrade came a curse, a sudden flurry of movement, a grunt. Max kicked up savagely, twisted with surprising force, and tore sideways and free. He lost his grip of Godfrey's gun-hand, but before the latter could collect himself to use it Max smashed a blow at the bad side of his face, a cruel blow which sent Godfrey spinning back, to lose his balance and fall in his turn violently against the stone.

For two long seconds the men were feet apart. Beside me, Spiro jerked the rifle up, and fired. I heard the bullet chip stone. Max, flinching back, checked for a vital instant, and in that instant Godfrey had rolled over the wide stone parapet in a sideways, kicking vault, and had dropped down into the bushes out of sight.

By all the laws he should have broken his back, or at least a leg, but he must have been unhurt. There was a series of slithering crashes as he hurled himself downhill, and then a thud as he jumped to the track.

I don't even remember moving, but I beat Papadopoulos and Miranda to Max's side as he hung, gasping, over the parapet.

'Are you hurt?'

'No.' It was hardly a word. He had already thrust himself upright and was making for the shallow steps that led down from the terrace to the zigzag path.

Godfrey was visible below, a shadow racing from patch to patch of starlight downhill between the trees. Papadopoulos levelled his pistol across the parapet, then put it up again with an exclamation. For a moment I couldn't see why, then I realised that Adoni was on the branch of the zigzag path below Godfrey, and more or less in line with him. Godfrey hadn't seen him for the bushes in between.

But the boy must have heard the shots and the fracas up above, and now the thudding of Godfrey's racing steps must have warned him what was happening. He stopped. One moment he was there in the path, standing rigid, head up, listening, then the next he had melted into the shadow of the trees. Godfrey, unaware or uncaring, ran on and down.

Beside me, Miranda caught her breath. Papadopoulos was craning to see. Max had stopped dead at the head of the steps.

Godfrey turned the corner and ran down past the place where Adoni stood waiting.

Ran down . . . and past . . . and was lost to sight beyond the lower thicket of lime trees.

Miranda cried out shrilly, and Papadopoulos said, incredulously: 'He let him go . . .'

I said quickly: 'He has the evidence I sent him for. He had to keep it safely.'

'He is a coward!' cried Miranda passionately, and ran for the steps.

Next moment Adoni emerged from the trees. I couldn't see if he had the package, but he was coming fast uphill. Max had started down the steps in what was now obviously a futile attempt to catch the fugitive, but Miranda flew past him, shrieking, and met Adoni head on, her fists beating furiously against his chest.

'Coward! Coward! Coward! To be afraid of that Bulgar swine! After what he did to your brother, to let him go? Coward! Woman! I spit on you, I spit! If I were a man I would eat his heart out!'

She tried with the last words to tear away and past him, but he caught and held her with one arm, whirling her aside with an almost absent-minded ease as he stepped full into Max's way and thrust the other arm across his chest, barring his path. As I ran down the steps and came up to them I heard, through Miranda's breathless and sobbing abuse, Adoni saying, quick and low: 'No. No, Max. Wait. Wait and see.'

Where there had been pandemonium before, now quite suddenly there was stillness. Max, at the boy's words, had stopped dead. The three of them looked like some group of statuary, the two men still, staring into each other's eyes. Adoni full in Max's path, looking in the starlight like Michael barring the gates of Paradise; the girl collapsed now and weeping against his side. At some time the telephone must have stopped ringing. Papadopoulos had run back to it and could be heard shouting urgently into it. Sir Julian must have gone to Spiro. The constable was starting down the steps, but slowly, because of his wound, and because it was so obviously too late . . .

The last of the wind had died, and the air was still with the hush before dawn. We heard it all quite clearly, the slam of the boat-house door, and the quick thud of running feet along the wooden platform. The pause, as he reached the *Aleister* and tore her loose from her rope. He would be thrusting her hard away from the jetty . . .

The sudden stutter of her motor was as loud as gun-fire. There was a brief, racing crescendo as the *Aleister* leaped towards the open sea and freedom.

Then the sound was swallowed, shattered, blanked out in the great sheeted roar of flame as the sloop exploded. The blast hit us where we stood. The flames licked and flared over the water, and were gone. The echo of the blast ran up the cliff and beat from rock to rock, humming, before it died into the rustle of the trees.

Sir Julian was saying: 'What happened? What happened?' and I heard a flood of breathless Greek from Spiro. Papadopoulos had dropped the telephone, and ran forward above us to the parapet.

'Max? What in hell's name happened?'

Max tore his eyes from Adoni. He cleared his throat, hesitating. I said shakenly: 'I think I know. When I was on board I smelled gas . . . It's a terribly easy thing to do . . . leave a gas tap on by mistake in the galley, and then the gas leaks down and builds up under the deck boards. You don't notice it, but as soon as the engine fires, up she goes. I—I once saw it happen on the Norfolk Broads.'

'Spiro was saying something about gas.' He mopped his face. 'My

God, what a night. My God. I suppose it must have been . . . Had
he been using the galley?'

'Not on the way out. It stands to reason, anyway, he'd have
noticed the smell when he took the boxes out from under the deck, if
it had been really bad. No, he must have used it on the way home.
When I took a box out myself the smell was pretty faint. Did you get
the box, Adoni?'

'Yes.'

'You got a box?' The Inspector's attention sharpened, diverted for
a moment. 'This is what you were going to tell us, eh? Is it a radio
set?'

'It is not. It's a batch of forged currency, Inspector Papadopoulos,
part of a cargo of seven hundred thousand Albanian leks that he took
across tonight. I managed to steal one package, and hide it in the
boat-house before he – he took me. That's where Adoni's been; I sent
him to collect it.' I added: 'I think that you may find that
this – accident – has saved everybody a lot of trouble. I mean, if the
Greeks had had to shoot him . . .'

I let the sentence hang. Beside me, Max and Adoni stood very
still. The Inspector surveyed us for a moment, then he nodded.

'You may be right. Well, Miss Waring, I'll be with you again in a
minute or two, and I'll be very glad to listen to you then. You have
the box safe, young Adoni? Good. Bring it up, will you? Now we'd
better get down there and see if there's anything to pick up. Are you
still on your feet, Petros?'

The two police vanished down the track. There was another
silence. Everyone turned, as if impelled, and looked at Adoni. He
met our eyes levelly, and smiled. He looked very beautiful. Miranda
said, on a long, whispered note: 'It was you. It was you . . .' and
sank down to the ground beside him, with his hand to her cheek and
a face of shining worship lifted to his.

He looked down at her, and said something in Greek, a sentence
spoken very tenderly. I heard Max take in a sharp little breath, and
then he came to me and took me in his arms and kissed me.

*   *   *

Sir Julian was waiting for us on the terrace. We need not have
been afraid that he would comment on what had just passed between
his son and me. He was basking in a warm bath of self-
congratulation.

'The performance of my life,' he said complacently.

'It certainly was. It fooled me. Did you know he wasn't drunk?' I asked Max.

'Yes. I wasn't quite sure what he'd try on, but I thought it might break the situation our way. Which it did – but only just. You're a lousy shot, father.'

'It was the waste of good whisky. It put me off my stroke,' said his father. 'However, there was enough left in the glass to put Spiro under; I've got the poor child strapped up again, and flat out on the sofa in there. That'll be another trip to hospital as soon as it's light, I'm afraid. Oh, and I telephoned your sister, Lucy. I reassured her quite successfully. It's been quite a night, as they say.'

'And not over yet by a damned long way,' said Max, a little grimly. 'I shan't get any rest till I've heard Lucy's story . . . No, it's all right, darling, we'll leave it till Markos gets back. You won't want to go through it all again for him. You must be exhausted.'

'I think I've gone beyond that. I feel more or less all right . . . floating a bit, that's all.' I went slowly to the parapet, and leaned there, gazing out over the dark sea. The dawn was coming; the faintest glimmer touched the far Albanian snows. 'Do you suppose there'll be – anything – for them to find?'

'I'm sure there won't.' He came to my side and slipped an arm round me. 'Forget it. Don't let it haunt you. It was better this way.'

'I know.'

Sir Julian, at my other side, quoted:

'*Let us not burthen our remembrances, with*
A heaviness that's gone . . .'

And I may say, Max, that I have come to the conclusion that Prospero is not for me. A waste of talent. I shall set my sights at Stephano for this film of ours. I shall write and tell Sandy so today.'

'Then you're coming back to us?' I said.

'I shall hate it,' said Sir Julian, 'but I shall do it. Who wants to leave an enchanted island for the icy, damp, and glorious lights of London? I think I might try, don't you?'

Max said nothing, but I felt his arm tighten. Adoni and Miranda came softly up the terrace steps, heads bent, whispering, and vanished in through the french windows.

'Beatrice and Benedick,' said Sir Julian softly. 'I never thought to hear that magnificently Shakespearian outburst actually in the flesh, as it were. *"O God, that I were a man! I would eat his heart in the market-place."* Did you catch it, Lucy?'

'I didn't understand the Greek. Was that it? What did she actually say?' When he told me, I asked: 'And Adoni? What was it he said when she was kissing his hand?'

'I didn't hear that.'

Max glanced down at me, hesitated, and then quoted, rather dryly:

' "You wanted to eat his heart, little sister. I have cooked it for you." '

'Dear Heaven,' I said.

Sir Julian smiled. 'You've seen the other face of the enchanted isle tonight, haven't you, my poor child? It's a rough sort of magic for such as we are—a mere musician, and a couple of players . . .'

'Much as I adore being bracketed with you,' I said, 'it's putting me too high.'

'Then could you bear to be bracketed with me instead?' asked Max.

'Well, that is rather going to the other end of the scale,' said his father, 'but I'd be delighted if she'd give the matter some thought. Do you think, my dear, that you could ever consider dwindling as far as a musician's wife?'

I laughed. 'I'm not at all sure who this proposal's coming from,' I said, 'but to either, or to both of you, yes.'

Far out in the bay a curve of blue fire melted, rolled in a silver wheel, and was lost under the light of day.